PENGUIN BOOKS

Congo Dawn

Katherine Scholes was born in Tanzania, the daughter of a missionary doctor and an artist. She has fond memories of going on safaris to remote areas where her father operated a clinic from his Land Rover. When she was ten the family left Tanzania, going first to England, then migrating to Australia. She now lives in Tasmania but makes regular trips back to Africa where many of her books are set.

She is the author of international bestsellers including *Make Me An Idol*, *The Rain Queen*, *The Stone Angel*, *The Hunter's Wife*, *The Lioness* and *The Perfect Wife*. She is particularly popular in Europe, where she has sold over two million books.

katherinescholes.com

T0359442

The Hunter's Wife

'*Out of Africa* meets *White Mischief* . . . A bittersweet, entertaining mix of Hollywood, obsessive love and the unbearable longing for what is not possible.' *Australian Women's Weekly* Book of the Month

'Beautifully written.' *Herald Sun*

The Stone Angel

'Full of passion, fine writing and interesting observations about the way potent events that help shape one generation have an impact on the next. Wonderful stuff.' *Australian Women's Weekly* Book of the Month

'A beautifully descriptive read and a soul-searching take on human relationships.' *New Idea*

'Scholes crafts her fiction with such care and subtlety.' *Weekend Australian*

'Scholes has masterfully captured those fateful moments that can change the course of many lives. *The Stone Angel* touches the senses with its rich descriptions of coastal Tasmania and emerges as a lovingly crafted account of a home we can never run away from.' *Good Reading*

' A truly absorbing book filled with secrets and conflicts.' *Woman's Day*

'Scholes shows a rare ability to understand people in their specific geographical context and find within them the great surging passions of humanity.' *Sunday Tasmanian*

Make Me An Idol

'A superb novel.' *Cote Femme* (France)

The Perfect Wife

'*The Perfect Wife* takes readers on an exotic journey, exploring the struggle between duty, desire, jealousy and freedom in another era … hard to put down.' *Weekly Times*

Katherine
Scholes

Congo Dawn

PENGUIN BOOKS

This is a work of fiction. Names, characters, companies, places and events are either products of the author's imagination or used in a fictitious manner.

PENGUIN BOOKS

UK | USA | Canada | Ireland | Australia
India | New Zealand | South Africa | China

Penguin Books is part of the Penguin Random House group of companies whose addresses can be found at global.penguinrandomhouse.com.

Penguin
Random House
Australia

First published by Penguin Random House Australia Pty Ltd 2017
This edition published by Penguin Random House Australia Pty Ltd 2018

1 3 5 7 9 10 8 6 4 2

Text copyright © Katherine Scholes 2017

The moral right of the author has been asserted.

Cover design by Nikki Townsend Design
Cover design adaptation by Penguin Random House Australia Pty Ltd
Cover photographs: Figure in canoe: Karsten Wrobel/Getty Images; Hills: Visuals Unlimited, Inc./Adam Jones/Getty Images; green texture: hudiemm/Getty Images.
Typeset in Fairfield by Samantha Jayaweera © Penguin Random House Australia Pty Ltd
Colour separation by Splitting Image Colour Studio, Clayton, Victoria
Printed and bound in Australia by Griffin Press, an accredited ISO AS/NZS 14001 Environmental Management Systems printer.

A catalogue record for this book is available from the National Library of Australia

ISBN 978 0 14379 027 3

penguin.com.au

For my parents,
Robin and Elizabeth,
with love

ONE

1964
Melbourne, Australia

Anna switched off her electric typewriter and slipped her diary into the top drawer of her desk. As she patted the morning's paperwork into a neat pile, she did a mental check of what she'd completed: there were six letters to be signed by Mr Williams, an expense report for him to review, and the itinerary for his trip to New York.

Picking up her handbag, she took out her kid gloves and pulled them on, smoothing the soft leather over her fingers. As she stood up, she glanced automatically towards Mr Williams' door, even though she knew he'd left nearly an hour ago for an early lunch appointment. She could have stopped work then too, but at that stage the itinerary hadn't been finalised – and she was not the kind of secretary who let the morning's tasks carry over into the afternoon.

Collecting her coat, she headed for the lobby. There was a lunchroom for the office staff, but she preferred to have some fresh air. She liked to eat her sandwiches in the little square near the library, sitting on one of the park benches with pigeons pecking crumbs around her feet. At this time of the year the sun was still warm, with only a hint of the chill to come.

Outside the building, Anna paused in front of the plate-glass window, gold-tinged and overlaid with the words *Williams, Gordon*

& *Sons*. She took in her reflection, turning a little from side to side, admiring the cut of her new pink coat. It was daringly short – a new style by Mary Quant, fresh from London. Pure wool and silk-lined, it had cost her half a month's pay, but was worth every penny. Even seeing it hanging in her wardrobe made her feel like someone else: the kind of woman who was brave enough to stand out from the pack. She tightened her belt, showing off her waist. It was then that she noticed a man standing nearby. He was watching her, as men do – his gaze travelling over her body, up and down. She let her eyes slide past his as she turned and walked away.

Reaching the street corner, she waited in a crowd of pedestrians for the lights to change. Car fumes mingled with an overpowering waft of Chanel No 5. Anna glanced behind her to see who could be wearing such strong perfume during the daytime. Before she had the chance to find out, she found herself looking straight at the man from outside the office. She recognised his blue jacket and dark curly hair. As her gaze met his, he looked quickly away, studying the passing cars. There was tension in his face, as if he were focused on a crucial task. Anna eyed him uneasily and when there was a break in the traffic she hurried on.

Turning down the street that led to the library, she stopped and pretended to search in her handbag. The man strolled past her – but before long he paused, looking around as if he'd lost his way. Then he bent to re-tie his shoelace. Anna walked on. When she glanced back he was shadowing her again. She quickened her step. Not far away was an Italian bistro where the secretaries sometimes met for a drink after work. When she reached the open doorway, she ducked inside.

'*Bella signorina!*' An Italian waiter in a full-length white apron approached with a welcoming smile, ushering her to a table.

He hovered over her, offering water. She felt safe here. Half of the staff looked as if they could have been in a gangster film – broad-shouldered, dark-haired, eagle-eyed. They wouldn't put up with anyone bothering a customer.

Anna sank back in a leather-cushioned chair, removed her gloves, and lit a cigarette. Drawing in deeply and then exhaling slowly, she let the hum of lunchtime conversation flow over her. Soon her anxiety about the stranger began to seem ridiculous. She stretched out her hands, idly checking her manicure. Her nails were as long as was practical, allowing for accurate typing. She was wearing a new shade of lacquer: Satin Summer Rose. As she eyed the colour approvingly her gaze settled on her left hand, where a thin band of tender white skin still marked the place where her engagement ring had been. Three months had passed since she'd slid the ring off for the last time. At first, she'd missed the weight of the two-carat diamond. Her whole hand had seemed too light. But she was used to it now.

The aroma of tomato and herbs drifted from the kitchen. It made Anna feel hungry, but she waved away the menu, ordering only coffee. The expense of the coat had eroded her holiday savings; she had no money to spare for luxuries. Wondering if she could get away with eating her sandwiches in here, she glanced around to see who was nearby. Then she froze. There was the man in the blue jacket, striding towards her.

'Please excuse me.' Without waiting for a response he pulled out a chair and sat down. Anna spun round, seeking eye contact with one of the waiters. 'It's okay. I just want to talk to you.' He held up both hands like someone calming a flighty horse.

'You've been following me,' Anna said coldly. Now that she was safe, she felt annoyed rather than alarmed. If the man liked the look of her and wanted to introduce himself, he was going about it the wrong way. One thing was for sure: they'd never met before. Remembering faces was one of her skills. She never confused a client with a salesman, or someone's wife with his girlfriend.

'I'm Jarrod Murphy.' He extended his right hand.

Anna let it hover in the air while she put down her cigarette. Then she shook hands briefly. She noticed the blue jacket was of average quality. The man's hair needed a trim. But there was an expensive watch on his wrist. She wasn't sure what to make of him.

'I'm a private detective from Sydney,' he said, as if reading her mind. Opening a worn leather wallet, he showed her a card with the words *Peace of Mind Security Services* above a photograph of a man dimly recognisable as a younger, smarter version of himself. 'I've been looking for you, on behalf of my client.'

For a moment Anna was too taken aback to respond. Then she shook her head. 'You must be confusing me with someone else.'

Murphy pulled a notebook from his pocket and turned to a page covered in untidy handwriting. 'Anna Caroline Emerson. Born 5th February 1939, now twenty-five years old. Lives alone at 2/145 Rathdowne Street, Carlton.' He glanced up. 'I have your phone number but I wanted to talk to you face-to-face.'

Anna stared at him. It made no sense. Why would anyone be looking for her? She didn't owe money. She hadn't slept with anyone's husband, like plenty of other secretaries had. She'd done nothing that could have caused any trouble. The idea that someone had tracked her down was so ludicrous it was almost funny – except that the detective had that intense, fixed look on his face again. It came to Anna then that it must be something to do with her job. Mr Williams had some very sensitive accounts. He had warned her against disclosing confidential details to the other partners or their secretaries.

'I don't think I want to talk to you.' Anna stood up to leave.

'It's all right. My client is no threat to you.' Murphy laid his hand on her coat sleeve. 'He's on the other side of the world. In Africa.'

In spite of herself, Anna sat down. She felt anxiety rising inside her, backed by a sharp thread of excitement. 'Who?' she whispered. 'Who is this person?'

Murphy didn't answer straight away. In the dense quiet between them the lunchtime chatter seemed loud. Something dropped with a bang out in the kitchen. 'Your father.'

Anna caught her breath. Her heart leapt in her chest as his words sank in.

Your father.

The two simple words were so foreign she could barely attach meaning to them. Her mother only ever referred to her ex-husband as Karl Emerson, using his first and second names as if to suggest he was someone she and Anna barely knew.

He *was* someone they barely knew.

'He's still living in the Congo,' Murphy said. 'He wants to see you.'

Anna's lips parted but she found nothing to say.

'I know, it's been a long time. He told me that. But he is now seriously ill.' The detective fixed Anna with hooded grey eyes. 'He has cancer. He's going to die.'

Anna lit another cigarette, using the familiar movements to cover the turmoil inside her. 'Why would he want to see me? I was only seven when Mum and I came to Australia. I can hardly remember him.'

'He has no other family. You are all he's got.'

Anna looked at him in surprise. When she was younger she sometimes used to wonder about Karl Emerson's life – whether he still lived in the big house on the plantation. If he drove the silver Rolls Royce that she knew her mother had once owned. What he looked like. She had no facts to draw on; there had been no contact since her parents' divorce. She came up with various scenarios, but her thoughts always led her, eventually, down the same path. She pictured her father happily remarried and with a beautiful daughter he adored. This time around, the story would have a fairytale ending.

Anna stared at the detective as she absorbed the meaning of what he'd just said: either there had been no second family, or for some reason they, too, were now gone.

'I've had other cases like this one,' Murphy commented. 'People reach the end of the road and they want to be reminded that some part of them lives on in the next generation.' He searched Anna's face. 'Also, they can't bear to face death alone.'

Anger flared suddenly, warming Anna's cheeks. 'He should have thought of that years ago. He could have written. Or sent money. Mum had to give me everything. He didn't help at all. He didn't care about us.' She could hear the whine in her voice. She felt like a little child again.

'Look, Miss Emerson, I know it's a shock. But the situation is urgent. He hasn't got much time.' Murphy reached inside his jacket and produced an envelope, which he slid across the table. 'I am to give you this.'

Anna didn't move. Whatever might be in the envelope – a letter, or a photograph, perhaps – she knew it would be best left alone. But after only a few moments she found herself tearing open the flap.

Red-and-white lettering jumped out at her: *Qantas*. Anna

recognised the ticket folder straight away. She'd often arranged flights for Mr Williams. There was something else in the envelope. Pulling it out, she saw a second air ticket. This one bore the image of a fierce-looking leopard caught in the midst of leaping on its prey. Words floated above, as if keeping their distance from the wild animal: *Air Congo*.

'The Qantas ticket covers the route from Melbourne to Brussels, via London,' Murphy said. 'Then it's Air Congo from Brussels to Léopoldville, the capital of the Congo. A smaller plane flies on from there to Albertville, on the shores of Lake Tanganyika. That's where he is.'

Anna shook her head as if to keep his words at bay. 'This is crazy.' She flipped open the Qantas ticket and found the dates amid the dense red text. Only three weeks away. She tried to laugh, but the sound caught in her throat.

'You have a passport,' Murphy stated. 'It's current, but you've never used it. My contact in Immigration looked into it for me.'

Anna refused to signal agreement even though he was right. Mr Williams had asked her to get one the previous year in case he needed her to travel with him on business. She'd been so excited. As a child she'd flown in a plane, coming to Australia from Africa, but all she could remember was an unpleasant feeling that her ears were blocked and her voice trapped inside her head. None of her secretary friends had been in the air. Like Anna, they just watched their bosses come and go. The closest they got to the experience was reading the exotic labels on the men's luggage.

When Anna had told her mother about Mr Williams' request, Marilyn had been less than enthusiastic. Anna guessed she was probably jealous, since her own travelling days were over. Only reluctantly had she produced the required birth certificate.

'Don't lose it,' she'd warned. 'You'll have no hope of getting a replacement now the Congolese are in charge. The country is in ruins.'

Anna had studied the yellowing document, taking in the old-fashioned typing, the signatures in blue ink, the blurry purple marks of rubber stamps. It was titled *Certificate of Live Birth*. Marilyn was described as the 'married woman wife of Karl Edward Emerson, Plantation Owner'. In the section noting the place of birth was typed *Lutheran Mission Hospital, Banya, Kivu Province, Belgian Congo.*

Now, as Anna sat looking at the airline tickets, she could feel Murphy's eyes fixed on her.

'Of course, the Congo is a long way away,' he said. 'And you haven't been there since you were little. But you don't need to worry – you'll be looked after at every step. There will be no problems with money or travel arrangements. It's all in hand.' He was starting to remind Anna of the way Mr Williams dealt with business negotiations. Sometimes he called her into a meeting to take down in shorthand everything that was said. He would just keep the conversation going, any way he could, while gradually beginning to speak as if his desired outcome had been accepted. His target barely noticed when the ground began to shift, until suddenly they found themselves in a new position.

'I don't know whether you are aware,' Murphy continued, 'but there have been some problems in the Congo since Independence.' He made the statement a question, raising his voice at the end.

Anna gave an equivocal nod. She knew it was Marilyn's opinion that in just a few years the Congolese had shown quite clearly that they weren't up to the task of running their own country. It was only due to the Europeans still living there, she claimed, that the economy was still going at all.

'There's been an uprising of some sort,' the detective continued.

Anna frowned. 'You mean a rebellion?'

'Something like that. But the point is, the United Nations have sent troops in and put an end to it. So it's all settled down now. And you'll be flying the whole way; no road travel. You will be quite safe.' He smiled, leaning forward. 'You'll like Albertville, from what I hear. It's a resort town right on the lake. People take holidays there.'

Anna smoked in silence, her eyes lowered. Her thoughts were a tangled web of half-formed questions about Karl Emerson, about the Congo, about this man sitting in front of her. She felt she was standing on the brink; she could step forward into the unknown, or retreat while she still had time. She slid the tickets back across the table.

'I'm not interested, Mr Murphy. You should tell him . . . your client . . . that.'

'I understand this might be upsetting for you . . .'

'No, you don't understand. Karl Emerson pushed us out of his life a long time ago. He found another woman and didn't want my mother any more. He just sent us away.' Anna's voice cracked. 'It's too late to change things now.'

Murphy gave her a sympathetic smile. Anna took a deep breath, struggling to calm herself. She tried pretending she was in the office. Miss Elliot at secretarial school had taught the girls the vital skill of controlling emotions. A secretary has to be bright and cheerful, no matter what. But when Anna finally spoke to Murphy, she found her voice was still taut with anger.

'I'd like you to give your client a message from me,' she said. 'Tell him I wouldn't cross the road to see him, let alone travel to the Congo. I'm sorry he's all alone, but that's his own fault.'

'Give yourself some time to think,' Murphy said. 'Remember,

this is not a choice you will ever get the chance to make again.'

Anna extinguished her cigarette and stood up. As she reached for her handbag, Murphy's hand shot out to grab it first. He dropped something inside. 'I've written the phone number of my hotel on the back of my business card. Contact me if you change your mind.'

'I won't.'

'You sound very sure.' Murphy gave her a meaningful look. Anna sensed he was about to raise the stakes somehow. She took her bag from him, ready to walk away. 'Most people in your position would have a question in their mind. They'd be wondering what they might gain from this.'

'I don't know what you mean.'

'I'm talking about the estate. If there's a reunion, there could be an inheritance. I don't know the details, but your father owns some kind of plantation. He mentioned a big house. Leopard Hall.'

Leopard Hall. The name conjured a vision of a grand mansion, like something from a fairytale, set on lawns that stretched away to the edge of a dark forest. Anna didn't know if the image was from her memory, or if she'd put it together from glimpses of photographs her mother had brought with them from the Congo. Perhaps it was a bit of both. Not that it mattered. The place meant nothing to her.

'I don't want his money.' Anna snapped shut the clasp on her bag. 'Goodbye, Mr Murphy.'

The kitchen tap was dripping, a dull steady beat that seemed to slow down time. Anna knew she should get up from the couch and turn it off, but she felt too exhausted to move. She hadn't even taken off her shoes. Reaching for the glass on the coffee table, she took a swig of whisky. She'd brought home the bottle she kept in the office in case Mr Williams should ever run out. It shared space in the bottom drawer of her desk with bandaids, aspirin and some all-purpose greeting cards. There was an emergency white shirt in there, too, in Mr Williams' size – brand-new, still wrapped in cellophane.

Anna returned the glass to the table and sank back down. She looked across at the record player where her new Beatles single lay on the turntable. She tried running through the lyrics of 'Love Me Do' in her mind, even humming the tune. But no matter how she tried to distract herself, putting the bizarre meeting with the detective out of her mind, snatches of the exchange kept returning to her. She couldn't help thinking about how her mother would react if she knew that Karl Emerson had made contact. Marilyn would be outraged – and devastated. Imagining her distress made Anna feel guilty. Luckily, Marilyn would never need to know anything about it.

Anna sighed and rolled over. She found herself replaying the torturous afternoon she'd endured at the office. It had been impossible to concentrate. For the first time Anna could remember she'd sent out letters that Miss Elliot would have tagged 'acceptable' rather than 'perfect'. Her mind had wandered while Mr Williams gave her dictation. She'd even had to ask him to repeat himself.

'Are you unwell?' he'd asked, looking concerned.

'I'm fine, thank you.' She'd forced a smile. 'Please go on.'

At the end of the day it had been a relief to slip the typewriter cover over the machine and catch the tram home. Opening the front door, Anna had paused on the threshold, feeling a sense of relief as she absorbed the familiar setting. Everything was clean and tidy. She lived alone, so there was no one to ruck up the rugs or push the chairs out of line. When Anna had first moved in here the flat looked dated and run-down. But she'd added new furnishings: an orange couch, green lampshades, brown-and-cream curtains. The place now had a fresh, modern feel, as different to her mother's home as it was possible to be. Anna never tired of the pleasure it gave her.

Today, though, the ambience of her home failed to soothe her. Giving up any hope of resting, Anna forced herself to stand up, swinging her feet from the couch to the floor. There was really nothing to think about, or even to avoid thinking about. She'd made her decision, back at the bistro. Picking up her handbag she felt inside for Murphy's business card. She wanted to get rid of it, bringing the whole episode to an end.

She was halfway across to the fireplace, a box of matches in hand, before she glanced down at the card she was holding. She stopped mid-step. A man gazed up at her, unsmiling, in shades of grey and black. She was looking at a small photograph; the kind used in passports. For a moment its appearance seemed inexplicable – magical – but then Anna realised Murphy must have slipped the picture into her handbag along with his business card.

She strode to the window to find brighter light. Her eyes raked the image, taking in the deep lines on the face, the hair thinning on top, the direct gaze. The man's strong, even features would suit a politician or an actor. He wore a light shirt and a silk cravat. Turning the picture over, Anna found *Karl Emerson* scrawled in the same handwriting she remembered from Murphy's notebook.

She studied the photograph again. She saw nothing there that was familiar. Not even a dim spark fired in her memory. The man might have been a total stranger to her. It was hardly surprising that she didn't recognise him after all these years. Marilyn's photographs had done nothing to keep Karl Emerson's memory alive.

Most of the pictures on display in the sitting room, or tucked away in an album, were of her and Anna. Others were of her favourite thoroughbred, her shiny car, her friends. In photographs where Marilyn's husband had once appeared, his presence was now represented by a jagged hole.

Anna had very few memories of her life in Africa that she knew truly belonged to her. And the ones she did have were mostly triggered by taste, smell, touch . . . Sometimes a whiff of kerosene, charcoal, or the rank smell of an unwashed dog carried her back. Or the touch of soft cloth draped over her shoulders. The sound of someone singing in the dark. But the sensations, though vivid, were just fragments, cut off from anything whole.

It was the same with Karl Emerson. When Anna tried to remember him, she had only a vague impression of someone silent and tall with loud footsteps. Marilyn said he didn't like children. He hadn't wanted to be a father. So maybe Anna had never been very familiar with his touch, his smell. But his voice, the shape of his body, his posture, the details of his face – these she must have known. Forgetting them was not like losing the memory of what she used to eat for breakfast, where they went shopping, or the look of her bedroom. He must have been important to her. So had she wanted to wipe him from her mind? Had she lost the pictures of him purely by growing up? Or perhaps they were still there inside her, just deeply buried.

She dropped the picture into an ashtray, walking purposefully away. This was the man who had ruined her mother's life. He meant nothing to Anna. Yet she could not stop thinking about him. She found herself drawn back to the fireplace, this time to peer into the mirror that hung above the mantelpiece. Retrieving the photograph, she looked from her face to the picture and back, hunting for some feature that was common to them both. Even with the image of Karl being in black and white, it was clear their colouring was different. Karl was fair, probably blond, with touches of grey. Anna's hair was dark brown. Her lips were slightly thin; she'd had to learn how to use lipstick to make the most of them. His were sensuous, curved, yet not feminine. The nose, she couldn't see. But the shape of the eyes, the high forehead? Was something replicated there, or was it just her imagination?

'Your father . . . He wants to see you.'

As she recalled Murphy's words, Anna clutched the photograph to her chest. A memory came to her from only a few weeks ago. She was walking up the aisle of a church, her long silk bridesmaid's dress swishing at her ankles. The air was laced with the smell of incense, flowers and candle wax. The sound of the organ, rich and layered, rolled out over the packed pews. In her hands she held the end of the bride's satin train. Glancing to left and right, keeping her step measured, Anna took in the checkerboard pattern of guests. All the men were in plain suits, while the women wore bright colours. It was as if two tribes had mingled, one austere and sober, the other vibrant and alive. Anna wondered if the women were whispering about her to one another, or perhaps just speculating in silence. Anna Emerson, the bridesmaid, should have been looking forward to her own wedding. What had gone wrong? Why had the young man ended the engagement? Surely it hadn't been the girl's choice. She'd done so well for herself.

Suddenly she was too close to the bride. Sally and her father had slowed their step. As Anna watched, Mr Jacobs leaned close to his daughter's ear and said something. Sally turned to look at him, her gloved hand squeezing his arm. You could almost see the current of love running between them. Anna felt a stab of envy, which evaporated into a feeling of aching loss. Tears pricked her eyes. It was not just that she knew she'd never walk up the aisle with a loving father at her side like this. Her pain was deeper, older than this. She was the little girl at the school concert with no Daddy to clap and cheer. She was the one who had to ask her friend's father to help fix her bike. She was the teenager who came to the door alone to meet her boyfriends, no stern man behind her, wanting to make sure she would be safe.

When they reached the altar, Sally turned to Anna, handing over her bouquet. Anna managed a smile but the truth was she could barely breathe. Only moments ago she had been like a doll that was hollow inside – a pretty doll, her hair lacquered into an Audrey Hepburn style; her wrist graced with a new silver bracelet, the traditional gift of the best man; her pale-green dress a perfect fit. But now, instead of feeling comfortably empty, she was bursting, choking. It was all she could do not to break down and cry.

At the reception she'd stared down at the tablecloth when it was time for the father-and-daughter waltz. At the edge of her vision, Sally and Mr Jacobs were just a blur of graceful movement.

'I know this must be hard for you, dear.'

Anna looked up, meeting the sympathetic gaze of the mother-of-the-bride. For a moment Anna thought Mrs Jacobs could read her thoughts. She forced her gaze to the dance floor. Sally's groom had taken over from her father.

'Don't they look lovely together?' Anna said.

'Yes, they do.' Mrs Jacobs patted her hand. 'Don't worry. You'll meet Mr Right some day.'

Over a month had passed since the wedding. The bridesmaid's dress had been dry-cleaned and was hanging in the bedroom cupboard. But now, the emotions she'd experienced that day returned to her, fresh and sharp. Anna walked in slow circles around the room. She looked at the passport photograph again. She chewed at the side of her finger, chipping off a section of pink lacquer. She refilled her glass and took another drink of whisky.

Finally she returned to her handbag and felt inside for Murphy's business card. She was not making a decision, she told herself. She was just going to seek more information. But as she crossed to the phone, her legs felt weak. When she dialled the number of the detective's hotel, her heart was pounding. The first step, she knew, would lead to another. And there was no way of knowing where she would end up.

TWO

1964
Dar es Salaam, Tanzania

Dan sat at the edge of the patio, as close as possible to the beach. The sand was patterned with footprints, and small pink-and-white cowrie shells dotted the tide line. Behind him patrons of the outdoor bar chatted and laughed, almost drowning out the tinny sound of the record player. A woman's shrill voice rose above it all as she called out for a drink, using pidgin Swahili with an American accent.

Lounging in his chair, Dan flipped through a salt-damp copy of the *East African Standard*. He only got the chance to read a newspaper now and then, so lots of the stories didn't make much sense to him. They were following issues and events he knew nothing about. He was skim reading, barely taking anything in, when his eye was caught by a headline: CONFLICT SPREADS IN THE CONGO.

His hand hovered over the paper. He told himself to turn to the next page, right now. He'd left the Congo nearly twenty years ago. The place had nothing to do with him any more. But as he hesitated, two words jumped out at him: Kivu Province. The next moment he was bent over the paper, reading intently.

He came upon the names of towns he knew: Bukavu. Uvira. Goma. According to the paper, these places weren't caught up in the conflict as yet, but were at risk of falling into rebel hands if government forces continued to lose ground. He kept reading. The place that meant most to him was not mentioned – but then, it was in the far south of the province, well away from the front line. And anyway, it was little more than a large village that had grown up around the tin mine. The main landmark was the Lutheran mission with its hospital. Besides that there was one hotel, a post office, a couple of government buildings and the line of shops. Dan took another drink, wiping the froth from his mouth with the back of his hand. Before he could rein them in, his thoughts were leading him out of the village, along the main road, towards the plantations . . .

He threw the newspaper onto the table. He stared at it, his stomach twisted into a knot. Then he forced himself to breathe out, slowly. Cradling his glass in his hand, he looked out to sea, where dhows with red sails moved slowly towards the horizon. Seabirds flew overhead, white shapes making a shifting pattern against the pastel sky. He let the peaceful sight soothe him, pushing thoughts of the Congo away to a safe distance. As he watched the last of the sun wash the sea with pink, a waiter appeared at his shoulder, immaculately dressed in a white apron.

'Another Tusker, Bwana?' The young man held one arm behind him as he pointed towards the empty beer bottle on the table. The waiter had served Dan a couple of evenings ago. It had been his very first shift and he was keen to impress. Then, as now, every move he made was careful and correct.

Dan shook his head. 'I'm leaving soon.'

'Yes, Bwana.' The waiter picked up the bottle and marched away.

Reaching into his pocket for some coins to leave as a tip, Dan stared back over the water, through feathery palm fronds. The fishermen were beginning to light their lamps, forming pinpricks of gold on the darkening sea. He reminded himself he should make the most of being on the coast. Soon enough it would be time for him to leave. His musings were interrupted by the sound of breaking glass.

'Stupid bloody idiot! Look what you've done.'

Dan looked round to a nearby table where a heavily built man with a bald head was shouting at the young waiter. There were shards of glass on the ground nearby and a spreading pool of red wine.

'I am sorry, but it was your elbow, sir,' the waiter explained.

'How dare you answer back! Who do you think you are, you filthy *kaffir*?'

Dan recognised the clipped vowels of a South African accent. It made the insult sound even harsher than it might have done. Other waiters gathered; they looked shocked by the guest's rudeness but unwilling to intervene. Dan didn't blame them. Times had changed in this country. Three years ago Tanganyika had gained Independence. Recently it had joined with Zanzibar to form the Socialist Republic of Tanzania. The colonial era had ended. But old habits die hard. Most Africans were still not used to challenging a white man.

'Now clean it up.'

'Yes, Bwana.'

The waiter crouched on his haunches, collecting the fragments of glass. Dan noticed a middle-aged woman sitting at the bar eyeing the scene with a look of cool interest. Realising that Dan was watching her, she flicked back the mane of tawny hair that fell to her bare shoulders.

'And bring me another drink,' the South African ordered. The waiter froze, clearly unsure whether to finish collecting up the glass or hurry to the bar. The man at the table raised his hand threateningly. 'I said, get me another drink. Now!'

Dan stood up. 'Hey, that's enough, man! Calm down.'

The bald man rose to his feet. 'What's it got to do with you?'

'Well,' Dan said, 'I'm here, and I'm watching you. You can't treat the staff like that.'

'Is that right?'

Dan took a breath. 'Yes, it is. This is Tanzania, not South Africa.'

The bald man laughed, but his eyes, sunken into his face, were cold. 'If I were you, I'd stop right there. I wouldn't say another word. Old man.'

He looked Dan up and down as he emphasised the word 'old'. Dan was in his mid-fifties; the South African was probably still in his thirties – but only some of the younger man's weight was muscle.

A voice inside Dan warned him to sit down, not get involved. But the words that came out of his mouth were set on a different tack. 'Well, you're not me. I know how to behave.'

The South African moved quickly for someone so big. Within seconds he'd crossed the patio and grabbed Dan by the front of his shirt.

'Take your hands off me,' Dan said calmly.

The man just laughed, breathing beer and garlic into Dan's face, then he twisted the khaki fabric in his hand. A button fell, clinking on the stone paving. As if the sound were the crack of a starter's gun, Dan's hand whipped up, seizing the bald man's wrist, digging his fingers deep into the tendons, until the hand let go of his shirt. Then he shoved the man in the chest, pushing him towards his own table.

Dan was just smoothing down his shirt when the man lunged back at him, aiming a fist at the side of his face. It missed the mark, but a second punch slammed into Dan's shoulder. Then another connected with his temple. Dan barely flinched, but inside him, anger exploded, a white blaze filling his head. He grabbed the hand that had hit him. His own hands were strong, every muscle honed by years spent practising his hobby of woodcarving. He tightened his grip on the man's thumb, then wrenched it backwards until he heard a snap. The man shouted in agony, but fury overcame pain as he raised his fist and flung another punch at Dan's head.

Dan ducked, then caught hold of the arm. His body was ringing with adrenalin, cut off from his thoughts, running its own race. He swung his opponent's body round, using its weight as a pivot to hurl him to the ground. The man fell heavily. There was a sound that might have been another bone breaking.

Somewhere nearby a phone began to ring, but no one moved to answer it.

Dan stepped away from the inert figure. He used the tail of his shirt to wipe at the blood that dripped down his cheek. The bald man's chest was rising and falling; he was breathing. Then he started groaning. Within a few seconds he was cursing, issuing threats.

Dan looked over to the bar, wondering when the manager would arrive, and whether Dan would get a chance to explain the situation before he was asked to leave. He caught the eye of the long-haired woman perched on her stool. She raised her glass with a faintly mocking smile. She was attractive and there was an offer in her eyes, but Dan just nodded and turned away. He was heading home, where the houseboy had prepared a meal for him. After dinner he planned to read another chapter of a novel left behind by one of his clients.

In the soft evening shadows, insects hummed and frogs croaked. Dan walked up the path towards the road. A monkey jumped from one tree to another, crashing through foliage, screeching as it landed on a branch that bent low under its weight. When the animal fell quiet, Dan froze for an instant, then spun round. Someone was following him. Instinctively he measured his options for escape, then tested his stance, tightening his fists. He was not afraid that the injured man had come after him. He was not afraid of anything. He was just acting out of habit.

Round a curve in the track, a figure appeared. It was the waiter. He held out one hand. In the pink palm, lit by the rising moon, lay the button from Dan's shirt.

'Thank you,' Dan said. He was glad to have it back. He had no use for a shirt with a missing or mismatched button; a hunter's gear must be in top condition, from his gun to his shaving kit.

'Your wife can sew it back on,' the young man suggested.

'I don't have one,' Dan said. 'I'll do it myself.' He waved goodnight.

'There is another thing,' the waiter said. 'I want to thank you for protecting me.' He smiled shyly, looking even younger than before.

'I was glad to help.' Dan rubbed his hand over his face where a bruise on his cheekbone was beginning to swell. 'Goodnight.'

'Goodnight, Bwana.'

Dan slipped the button into his pocket and walked off into the deepening darkness.

The keys rattled as Dan unlocked the door, then shouldered it open. The smell of roast meat came from the kitchen, where the houseboy could be heard singing as he worked. Dan walked into a large, open room. The table was laid ready for the evening meal – one set of cutlery, one plate, one glass. There was a white napkin furled inside a wooden ring with a carved buffalo on top. Dan picked it up. Last night there had been a leopard guarding the napkin, with burned marks for spots. There was a whole set of wildlife in the sideboard drawer. Dan admired the craftsmanship. The carvings were made for tourists and sold cheaply, but the work was very skilled.

Daudi appeared, a wooden spoon in his hand. '*Karibu*,' he said in Swahili. Welcome. Then he stared at the side of Dan's face. 'What has happened?'

'Don't worry,' Dan said. 'Just bring me some ice.'

He crossed to a mirror mounted on the wall. The bleeding had stopped but his cheek was smeared with red. He scanned his face – the brown eyes set against tanned skin, the short dark hair touched with grey. By the next morning he'd look very different, as the bruising set in.

He sat down on the sofa, sinking into the foam cushions. His head was starting to throb. He gazed blankly at the line of photographs on the mantelpiece. There were formal portraits of babies and children, a couple of wedding photos and some casual family snaps. As well as people there were dogs and kittens, favourite cars too, a small plane and a racehorse. Scenes from generations of busy family life.

The pictures had nothing to do with him. This was the holiday house of some friends from Arusha; they'd offered it to Dan for as long as he wanted, insisting that he needed a proper break. It was strange, being in a family home – all the cupboards full of clothes and shoes, the porch cluttered with sunhats on hooks, rows of sandals on the floor and buckets full of beach treasures. When he'd first arrived, Dan had glanced into the children's room by mistake. In the few seconds that he'd stood there, a vision had imprinted itself on his mind. A shelf of colourful books. A white teddy bear laid out in a doll's cradle. Scribble on the wall, purple crayon. A stray shoe under the bed. A little dress with lace at the hem, torn at the front, hanging down.

Hurrying on to the spare room, Dan had emptied his canvas kitbag onto the window seat. The cupboards and drawers had been left empty, so that guests could unpack their suitcases and make themselves at home. But Dan had only a few sets of clothes to lay out, along with a wash bag, some books, his woodworking knives and a red-and-black plaid Maasai blanket that he always put over the bed, wherever he slept. This was the extent of his possessions, aside from a trunk containing items he'd inherited from his parents, which was stored in a friend's house in Arusha. In a couple of years he would be sixty. Nearly all his peers were weighed down with debts and responsibilities, built up over the years like clay on the soles of a pair of boots. But Dan was still free.

He picked up the novel he was reading, turning to the page with the bent corner. Elgar, a Texan oil man, had handed it to Dan one evening at the camp fire.

'It's unreadable,' he'd said. 'You might be able to use it for toilet paper, though.' A grim smile thinned his mouth. 'A birthday gift from my son. What did I expect? Can't see why I brought it along.'

Dan had dipped into the novel late one night when he couldn't sleep. The title, *On the Road*, suggested it might be apt for a reader who led a life of sleeping in tents and following dusty tracks. But as Dan discovered, America was a world away from Africa. He read about people and places he could barely imagine. He began to hope he might get there one day, but knew it was unlikely. He wasn't in the habit of travelling around for no reason.

This holiday in Dar es Salaam was the first proper break he'd taken in years – normally he went from one safari to another, with just a few days off to regroup. The interlude was nearly over. Soon he'd be back in the heat and chaos of Arusha, hard at work. Lists and schedules began to form in his mind. There were supplies to be ordered, vehicles to be serviced, tents to be checked for wear. He'd need an extra cook for this trip, and maybe a second tracker as well.

In less than a week he'd be meeting up with a new party of hunters. Dan would dine with the men at their hotel, play snooker, drink until late. Before they headed into the bush he had to build a bond of friendship with the group of complete strangers. Everyone's safety depended upon it. Dan had to play the part of tour guide, camp host, medical adviser and personal psychologist as well as professional hunter. It was a strange job for someone who preferred silence to small talk and liked to spend time on his own.

Fortunately, the month-long trips rarely involved women. Dan was happy to enjoy their company between safaris, but in the bush they were a distraction – or worse. They demanded the comforts of home, and were constantly anxious about insects, animals, diseases . . . All too often, their main goal in going on safari seemed to be seducing the white hunter whom their husband or father had hired. Dan never understood quite what that was all about. It was tempting to give in, sometimes, to the charms of beautiful American heiresses. But he refused to be made a trophy.

The men were easier to manage. Occasionally they were opinionated and demanding; some had to be taught how to treat the local people, the game – Africa herself – with respect. When this happened Dan was glad to deliver his clients back to the airport. But more often he enjoyed the intimacy of the safari. It was born of the shared quiet around the camp fire, as much as the thrill of pursuit and a successful kill. For a time, he felt part of a group, a family. And then, just when he'd had enough of the demands that went with this status, it would all be over. He'd be on his own again. In many ways it was a perfect life.

Dan frowned, putting aside his novel and resting his head in his hands. He was arguing with himself, he realised. The fact was, he really didn't want to return to work. He reminded himself that he needed the money. And that the upcoming safari would take him deep into the Mara, to country that he loved. He pictured the water holes, the open plains, the rocky hills. He recalled the sound of lions roaring in the night. The buzz of insects. The eerie call of the hyena prowling the camp at dusk. It was all a part of feeling at home.

But still, he didn't want to face making friends with another group of clients. He didn't want to help them shoot their prey and then supervise the salting of trophy heads, feet, pelts. But nor did he want to stay on here at the coast. These last few days he'd felt as if he were lost in a grey cloud. Everything he thought about was fuzzy and remote. This was why he didn't take holidays, he reminded himself. It wasn't good for him to be idle. The reason he'd taken up wood carving years ago was to keep himself busy when he had to sit still. But it only occupied his hands, not his head.

Daudi appeared with an ice bucket and an old tea towel. After handing them to Dan he produced an envelope from his apron pocket. Holding it respectfully in two hands, he placed it on the table.

'Something has arrived.'

The letter had an English stamp – a rosy silhouette of Queen Elizabeth's head. The address had been changed twice. The letter had gone first to the home of Dan's friend in Arusha who provided him with a permanent address as well as storing his trunk. Ellis had forwarded it to East African Safaris, the company for whom Dan worked. The manager there, Bill Hartford, had in turn posted it on to the house in Dar es Salaam. It was a miracle it had arrived here in time for Dan to receive it.

Turning over the envelope, Dan read the sender's name and address. It meant nothing to him. He tore the flap open. Inside was a roneoed form letter with Dan's name added at the top in handwriting. He ran his eyes down the page with its unevenly inked typing, to the signature at the bottom. The name was just a scribble, and didn't appear to match the one on the back of the envelope.

I request that you contact me by phone on UK 9877 3166 reverse charges at your earliest convenience. I am not able to say any more in writing. I await your call.

There was a further note scrawled by hand underneath.

I have heard of your contribution in Gondar. I want a man like you.

Dan stared at the letter, speculation whirling through his head. How had this man – whoever he was – heard of Dan's action in Abyssinia? It had been in the Second World War, twenty years ago. He'd been a young man, only just signed up with the King's African Rifles.

Gondar. The name brought up a blur of memories. Dan stared at the letter, his hand gripping the paper. He heard gunfire exploding all around him; officers shouting instructions, one shrill voice countermanding another. The air was full of dust. Men were yelling in panic or screaming with agony. But in the midst of the chaos Dan's head was clear. His body felt light as air, strong as steel.

He was leaping up onto a tank, wrenching open the turret, shooting inside. One, two, three, four. Then he was yelling at the driver – in English, but making his meaning clear. The Italian was to drive the tank to cover. Dan held a gun at the man's head, his own hand shaking. The driver hesitated only a second, then there was the rumble of the tracks turning. It was hot in the tank. Dan could hear the heaving breath of the driver. And the stillness of the four figures slumped around him.

Fear was like blood pumping through his body, rich with oxygen. He was wide-awake. Alive.

Nothing was grey.

'Is it a good letter, Bwana?' Daudi sounded both interested and concerned.

Dan shrugged. 'I have no idea.' For a few moments he sat still, turning the letter over in his hands. Then he stood up, shoving it into his pocket.

'Shall I bring dinner?' Daudi asked.

'No, thanks. Just leave it in the kitchen for me. I'm going out for a while.'

'But you are injured!'

'I need to use the phone at the club.' Dan knew he would not sleep tonight until he knew more about this strange letter that had somehow found its way to him.

Daudi shook his head. 'You should rest.'

'I'll do that later on.' Dan grabbed another ice cube and pressed it to his bruise as he walked away. Within seconds it was melting, water running down his cheek and dropping from his chin onto his shirt. It left dark patches there that looked like fallen tears.

THREE

Anna pushed open the front door, pocketing her key as she looked along the dim hallway. Light leaked from the crack beneath the closed sitting-room door. Marilyn would be in there, Anna knew, installed in her favourite armchair, gin and tonic in hand, a tray of *hors d'oeuvres* at her side. The seven o'clock news was just beginning. Anna decided to wait for the headlines to be over – interrupting one of the key rituals of her mother's day would not be the best way to announce her surprise arrival.

There was a sick feeling in Anna's stomach. She'd left this confrontation until the last moment; she was departing for the Congo in under a week. Alongside all the discussions she'd had with Murphy, and later with Mr Williams, she had tried to decide what to say to her mother, and how to say it – but had come up with no answers.

The measured tones of the newsreader droned on. Anna could only make out snatches of what he was saying. Something about the USSR and nuclear tests. And military advisers in Vietnam. She was not knowledgeable about either topic. She didn't watch the news herself. If anything really important happened in the world, she knew she'd hear about it from Mr Williams.

Anna fixed her eyes on the row of china ornaments on the sideboard. They'd been there as long as she could remember. When she was in grade three she'd knocked the shepherd to the floor by swinging her schoolbag. She'd tearfully carried his severed arm to her mother. Anna still remembered what Marilyn had said as she'd glued the piece back on. Her mother had not been angry, only sad.

'Once things are broken, they're broken, Anna. You can put them back together, but their value is gone.'

Even at that young age, Anna had realised Marilyn was not talking about the shepherd. She was talking about herself – her broken, wasted life. And Anna had understood who had done the irreparable damage.

Karl Emerson.

The arm had been set crooked, giving the smiling shepherd an oddly menacing look.

Anna tuned in to the newsreader's voice again. Now he was talking about Jacqueline Kennedy making a brave public appearance. This was a story that did have meaning for Anna. Like everyone, she was fascinated by the beautiful, grieving widow. Months had passed since the world had been shocked by the news of the American President's assassination, but his death still felt unreal. It seemed impossible that the most important man in the world could, in one instant, just cease to exist.

As soon as the full news reports began, Anna headed for the sitting room. If she didn't go in soon, she feared she might just turn around and go home.

'Hello, Mum!' she called out before entering. She wanted to ease the shock of her being here. She visited often, but never without warning.

When she walked in, Marilyn was already on her feet. She had her drink in one hand and a cracker topped with a smoked oyster in the other. In spite of her upright posture she looked much older than her fifty-seven years: deep frown lines marked her forehead and the corners of her lips turned down. There was a look of faded elegance about her: her coiffed hair was slightly messy, her gown glamorous but dated. The smell of stale French perfume floated on the air.

'It's Wednesday,' Marilyn said. 'What are you doing here? What's wrong?'

'Nothing.' Anna forced a smile. 'I just wanted to see you.'

Marilyn eyed her daughter uncertainly, as though trying to assess the meaning of this impromptu visit. 'You look pale,' she said eventually. 'You haven't been seeing that man again, have you?'

'Gregory?' Anna said, referring to her ex-fiancé. 'No.'

'Well, that's something.'

Marilyn sounded relieved. Contrary to popular opinion, it had been Anna who had broken off the engagement, and her mother had welcomed the decision. She'd found faults in Gregory's character and claimed she was concerned about how these would affect his behaviour as a husband. Anna suspected the underlying issue was Marilyn's fear that the young executive would take her daughter away to London, where his business had its head office. She let her mother think she'd taken her advice, even though the real reason Anna was now single had more to do with her own character than Gregory's. At least, that was what he had told her when she'd tried to explain how afraid she felt about making a commitment that would last forever. His words still haunted her.

You can't trust your own heart. You will never be happy.

'Would you like a drink, darling?' Marilyn asked. She gestured towards the ice bucket and a dish of lemon slices, set beside the Tanqueray and a bottle of Indian tonic.

'No, thank you.' Anna stood still, in the middle of the room, struggling to find a way to begin. She could see Marilyn assessing her new coat. Anna's mother prided herself on knowing about fashion – after all, she used to dress in Givenchy and Yves Saint Laurent. She boasted that she'd been the first woman in the Congo to be seen wearing Dior's New Look, after the end of the Second World War.

'Rather short,' Marilyn commented.

'It's from London,' Anna said. 'Mary Quant. Georges is stocking her clothes now.' She seized on the topic. Perhaps if they could talk normally, she could lead in more easily to what she had to say. But Marilyn's attention was drifting back to the television.

Crossing the room, Anna turned it off. The newsreader's voice died mid-syllable; the picture diminished to a spot, then disappeared. 'Sit down, please. I've got something important to discuss with you.'

In the sudden quiet Marilyn's eyes widened in alarm. 'What on earth is the matter?'

When Anna didn't reply, Marilyn returned to the armchair, her brows drawn together in a frown. Then a look of horror crossed her face.

'Oh, no, Anna!'

'It's nothing like that.' Anna knew what her mother was thinking. One of the girls who'd been to school with Anna had become pregnant, a disaster she'd compounded by refusing to put the baby up for adoption. 'She'll end up alone, forever, like me,' Marilyn had warned, 'raising a child without a father.' She'd made it sound as if death would be a better option.

Anna took a deep breath. 'I'm planning to take a trip.'

'You said you were saving to go to Queensland – that's no surprise. You've lost Sally, now she's married. You're going with one of those secretaries, I suppose?' There was an aggrieved note in Marilyn's voice, as though Anna choosing to spend time with someone other than her automatically robbed her of something to which she was entitled.

'I'm going on my own. To Africa.'

Marilyn's mouth opened, but no sound came out. She gave a shaky laugh. 'You're joking!'

'No.' Anna's hands balled into tense fists at her sides. 'I'm going to the Congo.'

Marilyn gasped.

'I'll explain.' Anna tried to remain calm as she described the encounter with Murphy and the proposal that had been made. At the mention of Karl Emerson's name, Marilyn's face paled. Her fingers gripped the armrests on her chair.

When Anna said that her father was dying of cancer, and all alone, Marilyn looked shocked. Then her mouth twisted. 'I wonder what happened to the Englishwoman,' she said bitterly. 'I suppose he got tired of her, too.'

Anna was quiet for a few seconds, gathering the courage to keep on. 'It doesn't sound like they had any children,' she said carefully. With a rush of warmth she remembered what Murphy had said about Karl Emerson wanting to know that some part of him would live on in the next generation. He was talking about Anna – his only descendant.

'So now he's old and sick and lonely.' Marilyn spat out the words. 'It serves him right.'

Anna kept her voice steady as she went on to outline the recent developments. There had been further meetings with Murphy, appointments with a travel agent, and a visit to the Hospital for Infectious Diseases to get some vaccinations.

Marilyn began shaking her head. 'You don't mean this. It's not really going to happen.'

'It is, Mum. I am going.'

'No, no,' she moaned. 'You can't . . .'

As Anna watched waves of shock and distress crossing her mother's face, the anxiety she'd felt about Marilyn's reaction turned to dismay. It hurt her to upset Marilyn like this. She was her life-long companion.

Abandoned by Karl Emerson, mother and daughter had had to make their own way in the world, weathering gossip about Marilyn being a divorcée, and Anna coming from a broken home. They'd had to get by on the small income Marilyn made teaching piano and French. With her relatives living in distant parts of the country, they always spent Christmas and holidays alone. They made a point of taking pleasure in the tiny unit that was their family. They didn't need other people. They were a team. It was true that Marilyn was demanding and sometimes almost cruel to her daughter. But Anna understood her. She could see how Marilyn had been damaged by the way life had treated her. And she appreciated the sacrifices Marilyn had made. If Marilyn hadn't had a child to think of, she might well have remarried. She could have been happy and secure.

'Enough!' Marilyn stood up. 'This is nonsense. Don't you see, Anna? That man is just using you, now that he's dying.'

Marilyn's refined accent became more pronounced, as it always did when she was trying to control her emotions. She'd adopted her style of speech from the English in East Africa and had carefully preserved it since her return to Australia. As a child, Anna had taken on the accent of her friends, keen to try and blend in. But since she'd become a secretary she'd cultivated the English style as well. It seemed to fit with the task of booking international phone calls and welcoming clients from around the world.

'This is typical of Karl Emerson,' Marilyn continued. 'He never cared about you. Ever. He doesn't care about you now. He just wants something from you.'

'You're probably right,' Anna said. 'I'm not naïve. I'm not saying there's going to be a happy reunion. I'm not even sure if that's what I want. I know he's selfish, dishonest, lazy, an adulterer – all the things you've told me. But he's still my father. I know what to expect. I'll accept the disappointment.'

Even as she spoke, Anna could feel, deep inside, a warm thread of hope that all these things were no longer true. That Karl Emerson might have changed.

'Please, Anna, listen to me.' Marilyn stepped forward. 'You can't go. You can't!'

Anna looked into her mother's blue-grey eyes. 'I have to.'

A tremor passed over Marilyn's face. Then she composed herself. 'I suppose you've considered the fact there's a civil war going on in the Congo. Just because it's not in the newspapers here doesn't mean the problems are over.' Her gaze was cold. Anna knew she was angry that she had to resort to such an argument in order to discourage her child from this act of betrayal. 'There are savages in charge,' Marilyn continued. 'There will be more bloodshed. And you could find yourself in the middle of it.'

'Mr Murphy has a contact in the Department of Foreign Affairs and he says it's fine to travel there. Apparently there was an uprising in some part of the country, but the United Nations stepped in. It's over now.'

'What about Mr Williams? He'll have to replace you, you know,' Marilyn warned, taking a new tack. 'You're always saying how much he relies on you. You'll have no job when you get back. You love your job.'

She emphasised 'job', implying that perhaps Anna didn't love her mother.

'Mr Williams has offered to give me leave,' Anna said. 'He thinks I should go.'

Anna had announced her plan, with great trepidation, at the end of dictation one morning. She'd asked for leave but had made it clear she wouldn't blame her boss if he asked her to resign. Mr Williams had surprised her by offering his full support. He'd even asked to speak to Mr Murphy to satisfy himself that everything was going to be properly planned; that Anna would be safe.

'You can't miss this chance,' he'd stated. 'My father died when I was a baby. I never knew him, but I've missed him all my life.'

Marilyn sniffed, as if on the brink of tears. Her eyes were watery. 'Clearly I am the last person whose opinion matters. Everything has been discussed and planned without involving me. Can you imagine how that hurts me?'

Anna bit her lip. 'I knew you'd try to stop me. I wanted everything to be in place before I told you. I'm leaving in a week.'

'Anna,' Marilyn said firmly, as if her daughter were still young. 'I do not want you to go.'

'This is my choice. It's not up to you.'

'How can you do this to me?'

'I'm sorry, Mum. I really am. I'll come back and say goodbye before I go.'

She started walking towards the door. Marilyn leapt to her feet, lunging after Anna, clutching at her coat with white-knuckled hands. 'Don't see him. You mustn't talk to him. He'll turn you against me. He'll tell you terrible lies.'

Anna stood still. There was a new edge in Marilyn's voice, a strange look in her eyes. It took a few moments to work out what emotion was driving this reaction. Not just more anger, pain or shock. It was fear. 'What do you mean? What will he tell me?'

'You don't know what you might find.'

Marilyn would not say any more. She just stared at Anna. Her gaze was a dark curtain behind which her daughter could almost see the shape of secrets hidden.

Anna kept walking. It was like swimming against the current, with a lifetime of love and obedience pulling her back. Confusion formed eddies around her. *You don't know what you might find.* What did Marilyn mean? And why was she so afraid?

Reaching into her pocket, Anna felt the smooth edges and pointy corners of the photograph. She pictured the strong, handsome face, the steady eyes. If there were secrets, she wanted to know what they were, no matter how it might affect her. Now, more than ever, she couldn't wait to see Karl Emerson – to sit at his side and hear what he had to say to her, after all these silent years.

FOUR

The room had small windows, high up, as if to allow for secrecy. Worn carpet covered the floor and framed prints of English landscapes hung at intervals along the smoke-stained walls. The closed-in air smelled of boot polish and sweat, with a faint undercurrent of Old Spice shaving cream.

Dan glanced around the makeshift recruitment office. There must have been more than twenty men sitting along both sides of the room. Some were sprawled back in the metal folding chairs, legs outstretched, hands on thighs, taking up as much space as possible. Others were hunched over, looking at the floor. A few sat up dead straight, betraying a military background. A man near the door had one leg crossed over the other. His face was fine-featured, almost effeminate, but his sleeveless shirt showed off well-toned muscles. Most were younger than Dan – too young for the Second World War, or Korea. He wondered where they'd learned how to fight.

Lots of the men were dressed in mismatched pieces of military uniform – camouflage trousers, combat jackets, khaki shirts. Only one wore a complete outfit, though Dan could not identify its origin. It reminded him of the formal blue-grey suits of the French Foreign Legionnaires. The famous white *kepi* was missing – but then, he figured, you probably didn't get to leave the Legion without handing it in.

Dan guessed most of the men had chosen their outfits for today carefully. They wanted to look practical and organised – enough like conventional soldiers to impress Major Blair. At the same time they wanted to cut an impressive figure with the other applicants. This would explain the belt covered with old army badges worn by a swarthy man sitting near the corner of the room. Or the ragged neck scarf sported by a fair-skinned redhead. The sleeves of a bush shirt rolled up to reveal bruise-blue tattoos. And the well-worn fatigues that suggested history in the battlefield. Several of the men had unkempt beards; one wore a ponytail and had a long straggly moustache.

For his part, Dan had made no changes to his appearance for this interview. He wore his usual bush gear, clean and pressed; his hair was cropped, his face closely shaven as it was every day of the year, whether he was in town or the far reaches of the bush.

Now and then another prospective soldier came in and sat down. Some of the men acknowledged one another with a nod or a grunt, but no conversation ensued. The silence seemed dense, as if each person's untold story was an aura that took up space around him. Dan recognised the tension of too many fighting men cooped up in too small a space with nothing to do. In a contest without word or movement, egos were on parade. The air felt taut. A wrong word or look, and the place could erupt – into violence or humour. It could go either way.

Dan watched from the corner of his eye as the man beside him took out a wallet, removing a photograph and a piece of folded paper. Dan glimpsed a pretty young brunette with a seductive smile before she was slipped out of sight. The man spread out a newspaper cutting, resting it on his knee. The paper was fraying at the folds, the print smudged from sweat. Dan scanned the words:

> Wanted: fit young men interested in employment with a difference. Earn a salary of over £100 a month. Telephone 836521 during business hours. Initial contract offered for six months. Immediate start.

The advertisement had been published in the Public Notices section of the *Johannesburg Star*. Dan had seen it by chance this morning while leafing through a week-old newspaper that had been left behind in the lobby of his hotel. He wondered how many of the men who now sat with him in this room had been drawn here by the advertisement – and how many had, like him, been personally invited.

When Dan had phoned Major Blair, after receiving the letter in Dar es Salaam, he'd learned that his name had been put forward by the Commanding Officer under whom he'd served in Abyssinia. The Brigadier was now in his nineties and living in a nursing home. The once brutally strong body had been weakened by age, according to Blair, but his mind was still sharp as a bayonet.

Curiosity had been Dan's main emotion when he'd made that first phone call. But he soon felt a growing connection with the man on the other end of the line. The two had checked each other's credentials, as old soldiers do. The Major had fought in Alamein and Burma. He'd even been briefly in Abyssinia. They discovered friends in common. Blair had the upper-class English accent Dan associated with high-ranking officers. Dan slipped straight back into the old army lingo. Holding the phone in his hand, he found himself standing at attention.

It was not long before Blair turned to the reason behind his letter. 'The President of the Congo has asked me to form a Commando unit.'

Dan froze. He barely heard the word 'Commando'; he didn't get past 'the Congo'. For a mad moment he had the sense that this phone call was somehow linked with him having read the newspaper article at the bar. By letting himself think about the Congo, he'd opened up a portal into the past. But that was ridiculous.

'Yes, sir,' he said, his voice giving nothing away.

'I don't know if you're up to date on the situation there?' Blair asked.

'I work in the bush,' Dan answered guardedly. 'I'm never up to date on anything.'

'Lucky you.' Blair laughed. 'But you've heard of the Simba Rebellion?'

'A bit.' Dan guessed this was the conflict threatening Kivu Province.

'I can't go into the details now. Let's just say the Congo is facing a serious crisis. If the rebellion isn't put down, it will be an absolute disaster. The Chinese are involved with the Simbas. So are the Soviets. The Cubans are supporting them too. It's not just the Congo at risk. We're talking about a Communist takeover of Africa.'

He paused to let Dan absorb the magnitude of what was being said.

'No one would want to see that,' Dan responded. The word 'Communism' conjured in his head bleak images of a government-controlled existence. Dull conformity. The spark of individuality stamped out. Brutal prison camps in Siberia for anyone who fell foul of the system.

'The Simbas simply have to be stopped.' Blair sounded like a headmaster confronting bad behaviour. 'The Congolese National Army is losing the battle. In fact, they are barely putting up a fight. That's why I've been asked to step in and form a Commando force.'

Dan gave no response. Blair was not a Congolese, so what he was talking about was a mercenary outfit. Dan Miller was a man with a solid military record, not a ruffian for hire. But then, there was nothing disreputable about Blair.

'They call us soldiers of fortune,' Blair continued, as if reading Dan's mind. 'Fair enough, we get paid to fight. But just now and then, we get to do the right thing as well. And this is one of those times.' There was a short pause. Dan heard the sound of a cigarette being lit, a deep breath being drawn in, blown out. 'That's the reason I want you to join my Commando unit, Sergeant Miller. To help save the free world. It will be the most important thing you will do in your life.'

There was no hint of cynicism or humour in the Major's voice; he was deadly serious. Dan was taken aback. If the Major were canvassing volunteers for a Commando force, he'd have to outline the cause. Few men – even mercenaries – fight purely for money. But Dan hadn't expected Blair to be this vehement. Or the stakes to be this high.

The call ended, with Dan agreeing to get back in touch when he'd had a chance to think about the proposal.

He left the club, stepping from fan-cooled air into the humid night air of Dar es Salaam. His head was aching. He felt hungry and thirsty. But he hardly noticed his discomfort. Major Blair's words rang in his ears.

Help save the free world . . . The most important thing you will do in your life . . .

It was a call to arms that seemed impossible to deny.

Then he discounted it. He was a professional hunter with book-ings on his schedule. World politics was not his responsibility. The crisis in the Congo was not like the Second World War, when everyone was involved. The Simbas were not the Nazis. Dan was no longer the young man who had signed up for the King's African Rifles, desperate for money, with a wife and baby to support. And he did not want to go back to the Congo. He'd left that part of his life behind.

As he walked on, passing through shadows cast by the light of a near full moon, he planned to throw away Blair's letter, but with each step along the street, he began thinking more and more criti-cally about the life he was leading.

Helping rich men shoot animals for trophies was not wrong, in his view. The licence fees were a vital source of funds for the Game Department. The safaris gave jobs to Africans who would otherwise be unemployed. And there was certainly no shortage of wildlife. Working as a hunter earned him good money: clients were keen to have Dan Miller. If he died tomorrow, though, they would just use someone else. And Dan had always known, deep down, that the camaraderie he felt with them out on the trail was an insipid version of the real thing: the bond men share when they fight side by side, their lives on the line.

He began reliving memories of the war. The days and nights of being on high alert. The feeling of adrenalin coursing in his veins. Pain, discomfort, fear – it meant nothing. In the face of death, he'd never felt more alive.

He stopped suddenly, standing perfectly still, in the middle of the street. It was late now; the traffic and street hawkers all gone. He could hear the rustle of palm leaves and the mewing of a stray cat.

He knew how to think without letting his thoughts take over, leading him into places he did not want to go. Over the years he'd taught himself to control his mind, as well as his body. He let himself look back now, his focus safely narrowed.

He thought of that one time in his life when he'd wanted with all his heart to fight for something more precious to him than the whole world. But he had not fought. He had surrendered. There had been no choice. Any other path would have been wrong.

Now the tables were turned. He could fight for something else that mattered. Not to him, so much, but to the whole world, if Blair was right. Dan Miller was the ideal person to help out, because he didn't care what price he paid.

This time he would not walk away.

So here he was, in Johannesburg, South Africa. Sitting in an uncomfortable chair in a temporary recruitment office set up in some vacant office space. He stretched out his legs, stifling a yawn. He'd woken early this morning after his usual sleepless night.

The door at the end of the room opened. Every eye watched as a young man in khakis and a dark-red beret came out, consulting his clipboard.

'Sergeant Miller.' He scanned the room, waiting for someone to move.

Dan stood up, raising himself to his full height. He could feel the effect of the word 'Sergeant' spreading around the room. It would only make the men look at him more critically, he knew. His rank put him well above any ordinary volunteer in the pecking order, but as yet he was unknown and unproven.

Stepping into the interview room, Dan scanned the place quickly, from habit. In seconds he took in a map of Central and

East Africa taped onto the fading wallpaper. He noticed a waste-paper bin containing a whisky bottle. An ashtray overflowing with squashed butts – mostly from roll-your-owns and filterless ciga-rettes. The ambience was as bleak and unappealing as that of the space outside the door.

In line with army regulations, Dan approached to within two steps of a large desk and saluted the officer sitting behind it.

'Stand easy,' the Major said. 'And have a seat.'

Dan took his place on a hard chair. The scarred wooden desktop stretched away from him, bare but for a pile of manila folders and a clipboard holding a thick notepad.

Blair smiled briefly, showing even teeth faintly stained with tobacco. 'Let me say straight away, I want you in my Commando unit. But you know that.'

'Thank you, sir,' Dan said.

'I just have a few boxes to tick,' Blair continued. He shuffled through some papers from one of the folders.

Dan took the moment to inspect the Major. The man's appear-ance matched his manner on the phone. Smart. Formal. Personable. He wore a freshly laundered uniform, the single crown insignia on his shoulders showing his rank. His hair was brown, with streaks of grey, and receding at the temples. He had a neatly trimmed moustache. His eyes, deep blue, were piercing – a telltale clue to what lay behind his refined English manners. Dan estimated he and the Major were about the same age. Blair's face – burned by sun and wind, like Dan's – showed his years. But Dan could see that the man was as fit and healthy as he was himself.

Dan had never lost the habit of physical training. Hunting kept him fit – he had a gun-bearer for his heavier pieces, but always carried a rifle himself; he could walk day and night if needed, on the trail of an elephant or lion, though the pace of the American tourists could hardly be called a march. To keep in top form Dan did push-ups in his tent each night, and pull-ups on the branches of trees. The African camp staff laughed at him, but he was not deterred. He didn't even know why it was so important to him to stay strong. It was as if he had some long-term plan that required it. Though he was only too well aware that the truth was he had no future goals. He sometimes wondered if the exercise was an end in itself. The only end he could come up with.

'Ah, here we are.' The Major turned to a new page of his notepad and removed the top of his fountain pen. 'Nationality?'

'British.'

Dan wanted to say Tanzanian, or African, at least. He'd been born in this part of the world and spent his whole life here. But his passport said he was an Englishman. His odd status had been brought home to him very starkly since his arrival in South Africa. Everywhere he looked, it seemed, he found signs saying *Coloured* or *White*. Hotel bars, parks, public restrooms, swimming pools. Even a drinking fountain in the main street. As a white African, he felt uneasily that whatever option he chose he would always be in the wrong place. Reading about apartheid was one thing; seeing the policy in action was shocking – especially now, in the 1960s, when many other African countries were at last being run, for better or worse, by Africans. Dan understood for the first time why his South African clients found it so hard to accept that in his safari camps the tents of the local staff were right alongside those of the guests.

'Date of birth.'

'First of July, 1908.'

Blair's questionnaire covered the bare facts of Dan's life – where he went to school, the jobs he had held. When Blair learned that

Dan had lived and worked in the Congo for many years, his eyes widened. 'The Brigadier didn't tell me that!' He leaned forwards, keenly interested. 'So the place was home to you once?'

'Yes, but that's not why I'm here,' Dan said firmly. He pressed his lips together to show that he didn't want to say any more.

'Fair enough.' Blair moved easily to the next topic, as if accustomed to having to skirt around subjects that were too painful, or shameful, to be examined.

'Right- or left-handed?' Blair queried. 'It has to be noted on your contract. You'd get more compensation, obviously, if you lost your right arm. Unless you were a leftie.'

'I am – a leftie,' Dan said.

Blair made a note on his pad. 'Marital status?'

'Divorced.'

Blair glanced up. Dan gave him a steady look, again warding off further probing. 'A long time ago.'

'Children?'

Dan gave no answer.

Blair rephrased his question. 'Young children, I mean. Dependants.'

Dan shook his head.

'A free man – lucky you!' Blair joked. 'I've got two boys at home. Three and five.'

For a few seconds Dan stared at him. Blair must have married late in life, or had a second wife. But it was not his age that caused the surprise. Dan could not imagine why a man would voluntarily risk his life to fight someone else's war – no matter how high the stakes were – if he had a young family at home. Dan had been told that Blair had headed up another Commando force, just a couple of years ago. Why was he pushing his luck again? The Major had made it clear he believed in the cause of stemming the spread of Communism. But Dan wondered if that could be the sole motivation. Perhaps Blair was one of those men who could not settle back into civilian life after being on the front line. Dan had met plenty of soldiers who'd been caught in that dilemma, after the Second World War ended. They spent their time searching for conflict, with hotel brawls and street fights often standing in for military combat. Sometimes Dan had found himself sharing their downward slide, using his fists to let go of his anger. Though in his case it was not his war service that had left him feeling cut off from normal life. It was something much worse.

'I can't offer you the contract yet, I'm afraid,' Blair continued. 'We're still working out some details. I'll take your word that you're committed.'

He waited for Dan to respond.

'Yes, sir.' Dan almost smiled as a wave of excitement washed over him. Something new was about to begin. He had more or less made his decision back in Dar es Salaam, but only now did it seem real.

'The next step is transport by air to the training base in the Congo. It's at a place called Lemba, in the south.' Blair closed his notebook. 'I hope to send the first group off within days.'

'Yes, sir.'

'Well, that's about it.'

There was a long moment of quiet. Then Blair flung down his pen. It rolled across the desk and fell onto the carpet. Blair stared at it there, while Dan wondered if he was supposed to pick it up. Then the Major sighed deeply, leaning back in his chair.

'What a rabble,' he said, shaking his head. 'I don't know if I can make anything of them. There's the usual collection of misfits, drunks, drug addicts, bleeding hearts and men having a mid-life crisis. I've got some adventurers, thank God. Some military types. The odd idealist – but they usually haven't got hold of the right facts. There's a surprising number of homosexuals.' He paused to see if Dan would betray any strong reaction. When Dan said nothing, he continued. 'I've had some good men who were homosexuals. I judge them by the rest of their story.'

'I'd have liked more Brits,' he went on. 'But advertising in the UK papers might not have gone down too well with Her Majesty's government. The upshot is, we've got far too many South Africans. They're good fighters, most of them. You know the types. Boer stock. Big blokes; strong. They've all done national service, too. But even so . . .'

Dan nodded. Blair didn't need to continue. Anyone could see it wasn't a good look for the newly independent Republic of the Congo to be hiring white men from a country ruled by apartheid to fight on its behalf, alongside the national army.

'Sometimes I wish I'd never agreed to the President's request,' Blair mused. He seemed about to say more, but then his face suddenly changed. He looked remote and cool. Dan understood why. In an unguarded moment of frustration, the Major had confided in him – Blair was no doubt regretting the lapse already. A good operational commander had to get to know his men, finding out their fears and frustrations, weaknesses and strengths. Not the other way around.

Blair picked up a phone and spoke into the receiver. 'Show the Sergeant out.'

The young soldier appeared, cradling his clipboard.

Dan saluted the Major again, spun on his heels, and marched away.

Out in the waiting room, he paused. Now that he was actually part of Blair's Commando unit, he looked at the volunteers with new interest. Which of them would be joining him? The one with the tattooed face, over in the corner? The one with the gangster's belt? Or the man with the boyish face and the physique of a boxer? Perhaps all of them. Or none.

He would soon find out.

FIVE

Anna rested her forehead against the window of the aeroplane, gazing down at the deep blue water of Lake Tanganyika. It was like a vast inland sea edged with white surf and a band of ochre-yellow beach. Bordering the lake was a carpet of dense green forest, stretching as far as the eye could see. There was no sign that anyone lived here – or ever had. It was hard to imagine that a modern town would soon come into view.

In the next seat an old nun snored lightly in her sleep. Her wrinkled face was relaxed and peaceful. Anna was glad that she was resting. When they'd been talking earlier Anna could tell the woman was exhausted, even though she'd been so warm and friendly.

Sister Emilia had taken the young Australian under her wing from the moment the two had met, when they first took their seats for the flight from Léopoldville to Albertville. This was the last leg of Anna's journey. Somewhere between Melbourne and Brussels she'd overcome her fear about being in the air. She'd given up gripping the armrest every time there was any turbulence. She'd also stopped feeling airsick, and had begun to enjoy the meals the hostesses served – at least three courses set out in little containers, with a miniature salt and pepper shaker; everything marked with the emblem of the airline. It was so neat and tidy. With a glass of wine, music and magazines to read, she understood why everyone thought air travel was so appealing.

But this last aircraft was much smaller and flew at a lower altitude. It was harder to avoid the realisation that you were up in the air in a capsule made of metal. After take-off Anna had found herself staring anxiously at the propellers through the window.

Sister Emilia had reached across and taken her hand, patting it reassuringly. Normally such a gesture from a stranger would have made Anna feel uncomfortable. But she welcomed the touch of the papery old skin, and the smile that went with it.

'Do not be afraid,' the Sister had said in halting English. 'God will keep us safe.'

It had taken the pair some time to find the best way to communicate. Sister Emilia didn't speak very much English. Her first language was Flemish, she explained, and Swahili had become her second; but she knew French as well – it was the official language of the Congo, even now, after Independence.

She was delighted to find that Anna spoke this last language almost perfectly – the fruit of years of personal tuition from Marilyn, who was determined her daughter would be a good advertisement for the lessons she offered other people's children.

Sister Emilia told Anna she was on her way back to the Congo after taking leave. She had visited her order's Mother House in Brussels and then travelled to her home village in the Flanders hills. As she spoke, the animation in her face was at odds with her severe clothing. White cloth framed her face, covering her forehead, wrapping under her chin and around her neck. She had a wide white collar that draped her shoulders, then there was a black veil and matching full-length gown with long sleeves. The outfit didn't look at all suitable for the tropics.

'How long have you spent in Africa?' Anna asked.

'I have lived in the Congo since I was a young woman, like you are now. I love the Congo. I love the Congolese.' Sister Emilia spoke with passion in her eyes. She shook her head sadly. 'It breaks my heart to see what is happening to this beautiful country. There was the trouble when Independence came. Then the uprising in Katanga. And now the Simbas . . .'

Anna stared at her. 'What do you mean?' She thought of Murphy's firm voice, insisting there were no longer any problems in the Congo. That the United Nations soldiers had put everything in order. For the first time, it occurred to her how much trust she had put in him – a complete stranger. She'd wanted to believe everything he said, and so she had. On the other hand, Mr Williams had spoken to the detective too. Surely he would have been able to tell if the man had been misrepresenting the facts, just to make sure his client got what he wanted?

The nun patted her hand again. 'I do not mean to cause you any alarm, my dear. These troubles are between different groups of Congolese. Europeans are not involved. There is nothing to worry about.' She adjusted her veil, settling back in her seat.

Anna glanced around at the other passengers. There was a middle-aged man in a safari suit doing a crossword, and a young mother with a sleeping baby, her long blonde hair falling forward over the little bundle in her lap. Nearby, an African woman wearing a colourful turban and matching dress was absorbed in a novel. None of them looked the faintest bit uneasy. And the hostesses, marching up and down in their immaculate outfits, caps perched on their perfect hairdos, seemed only concerned with handing out meal trays, drinks and extra pillows.

'Now, you must tell me why you are going to Albertville,' Sister

Emilia said. 'Are you a missionary?' She looked doubtfully at Anna's knees, exposed below the hem of her skirt.

Anna shook her head. 'I am going to visit my father.' As she said the words, a smile came to her lips. It was such a simple sentence, yet so extraordinary. 'He is ill. He asked me to come.'

'You are a good daughter. How long since you last saw one another?'

In the short silence, Anna's smiled faded. 'I last saw him when I was a little girl.' She went on to tell Sister Emilia how she barely even remembered Karl Emerson. Then she found herself going further: explaining how she'd been brought up to despise – even hate – this man who was her father. It was easier, she found, to tell her story in a foreign language. The process of translation brought clarity.

She told Sister Emilia about the contact from the detective and all that had followed. She shared her fear that she would arrive in the Congo too late. The last report Murphy had received from the hospital in Albertville indicated that Monsieur Emerson's condition was deteriorating. His daughter should hurry to his side.

Sister Emilia gave a comforting smile. 'We must pray that God will sustain him.'

Anna was quiet for a few moments, then she shook her head helplessly. 'I don't even know if I should have agreed to come. My mother is very upset. I've hurt her so much.'

Sister Emilia nodded. 'Naturally, she feels betrayed. She has been angry with this man for a long time. But it is always a good thing to forgive those who have hurt us.' She looked into Anna's eyes. When she spoke next she sounded like a seer or fortune teller. 'Something good will come from all this. I'm sure of it.'

Now, as Anna replayed the words in her mind, a shiver ran up her spine. It was excitement, but felt more like fear. She brought her hand to her mouth, about to start chewing at her fingernail, but then remembered that it wouldn't do to arrive in Albertville with ruined nail polish. Karl Emerson was a wealthy plantation owner. His friends were no doubt sophisticated and well presented. She needed to make a good impression.

Before leaving Melbourne she'd spent a whole day shopping for suitable clothes to pack. Murphy had given her a thick wad of bank notes to cover her expenses. Before choosing what to buy, Anna had devoted some time to looking at old posters for films set in East Africa. *Hatari. The African Queen. Mogambo.* The actresses seemed to wear a lot of linen and khaki; plain clothes offset by glamorous make-up. Strangely, some of them also wore leopard-print scarves or hatbands – something Marilyn despised. Anna didn't know what to make of that; perhaps people who actually lived in Africa had their own rules that were unknown to the visitors, however fashionable they might be. Anna certainly wasn't going to take a chance with any kind of animal print.

She had visited Morrison's Outfitters, a traditional shop that sold quality clothes to farmers. There she'd selected some bush skirts and shirts, an oilskin jacket and an Akubra hat for protection from the sun. She knew from the glimpses she had of Marilyn's life in the Congo that everyone dressed up for the evening, whether they were going out or staying at home, so she'd also picked out a couple of full-length gowns at Georges. She purchased some summer dresses as well, including one from Mary Quant. It would probably be quite unsuitable – too modern – but on the other hand, if Marilyn had been a fashion leader, perhaps that was what Karl Emerson would expect of his daughter.

Thinking about what she'd chosen to pack, and what she'd left out at the last minute, made Anna feel uneasy. The truth was, she had no idea what to expect in Albertville – what she would be doing; what kind of image she should aim for. She distracted herself by reading a newspaper she'd found in her seat pocket. It was the same old news – Russia was an ever-increasing threat, and events in Vietnam a growing source of concern. Somehow the two seemed to be linked. Meanwhile, President Johnson was shoring up his position as successor to Kennedy. Anna wondered idly which of these news stories would have interested Mr Williams – which ones he would have mentioned to her when she took in his morning cup of tea.

A change in the engine sound made Anna turn back to the window. Sister Emilia stirred, rousing from her sleep. The plane was descending. Fishing boats could be seen sailing on the lake. The featureless expanse of the forest was now patterned with the green bumps of tree canopies. As Anna watched, small clearings began to appear. There were farm plots with little houses and clusters of cattle. Before long, the scattered buildings condensed into villages, stretching in a line along a red-earth road. Then sprawling suburbs with proper roads came into view. It was a big town, Anna realised; almost a city. Yet it looked vulnerable, squeezed as it was between water and forest – barely able to hold its own. But as they flew on, multistorey concrete buildings passed below her. There were tree-lined boulevards, and parks and gardens with white monuments and fountains. Everything looked orderly and clean. There was a sense of authority about the structures that firmly claimed the space. Anna turned to the nun with a smile.

'It's beautiful.'

Sister Emilia smiled in reply. 'Welcome to Albertville.'

*

A blast of hot damp air met Anna as she neared the open doorway of the plane. About half of the passengers had already disembarked via a set of metal stairs that had been wheeled into place. Anna paused to let Sister Emilia go before her. As the old lady began her slow progress towards the tarmac, gripping both of the handrails, Anna looked out at the runway, squinting into the glare of mid-day sun. Not far away were two aircraft parked one behind the other – long sleek machines painted in camouflage colours with jet engines instead of propellers. They both had *U.S. Air Force* written on their sides. But there were no soldiers to be seen milling around them, no army jeeps or even stacks of cargo. The planes might have been parked there and forgotten, like toys left behind in a sandpit.

As Anna descended the stairs she looked down at a crowd of people assembled behind a barrier, waiting to greet the arrivals. Most of them were fair-skinned and blond. The women wore crisp cotton dresses, gloves, hats and sunglasses. Their children had neat ankle socks and shoes with shorts or skirts. The men were in smart jackets and long trousers. But the best-dressed of all were the Africans dotted among them. The women wore full-length gowns and matching turbans. The men's shirts were the whitest, their suits the darkest. They looked prosperous and sophisticated.

Anna felt self-conscious. She knew she was travel-worn, her clothes crumpled, hair limp. She'd broken her journey by stopping overnight in Brussels. After a good sleep and a long bath, she'd emerged refreshed from the luxury hotel Murphy had booked for her – but that felt like days ago.

Mopping sweat from her forehead, she searched the faces below, hoping to be able to identify Monsieur and Madame Rousseau, who were to collect her and take her to their home. She had no idea of their age or their appearance, but thought she might be able to identify a couple that seemed to be looking out for a stranger.

No one caught her eye. She followed Sister Emilia into a low concrete building, where the air felt even hotter, stirred by a bank of slow ceiling fans. The passengers filed past a desk where their passports were stamped.

'You are from Australia?' The Congolese officer addressed Anna in heavily accented English, his hand hovering over the ink pad. Anna nodded. 'But you were born here.'

She tried to read his expression, but found no clues to his thoughts. 'Yes.'

'You are entering the Republic of the Congo. Europeans must follow our rules now.' He looked at her with malice, as if she had committed a crime against him and his country.

'I'm not a European,' Anna said. 'I'm Australian.'

The official waved one hand. 'Americans. Australians. In Africa, you are Europeans. You are all the same.'

Anna was unsure what response was expected of her. As soon as she had her passport in her hand she hurried away.

In the arrival hall the passengers blended with the crowd from behind the barrier. The sight of so many people being greeted by friends made Anna feel lost and abandoned. Only one other passenger stood alone – a soldier. He looked distant and aloof. Anna guessed he was an officer from his smart uniform and all the coloured ribbons on his chest. He was the tallest, thinnest, fairest man she had ever seen.

On the other side of the room Sister Emilia was exchanging hugs with a group of nuns. Most of them wore black habits like hers, but one was dressed all in white. As Anna watched, this last nun turned around. Anna stared, transfixed by the young woman's beauty. She had deer-like eyes and dark winged brows. Her pale skin was like porcelain; her full lips a natural red. Catching Anna's eye she gave a small smile. Anna smiled back. She thought of going across to the group, but she and Sister Emilia had made their fare-wells before leaving their seats. She shouldn't interrupt the nuns' reunion. After all, she didn't need any help. She just had to wait here for the Rousseaus who were probably running late.

A luggage trailer was wheeled in, towed by two African men in blue uniforms. A swarm of porters materialised. Anna was soon surrounded by a whole gang of them, each one demanding he be assigned to collect her luggage.

'I have only one case,' she explained. She tried both French and English, but the porters didn't seem to understand. Before long she was being swept towards the exit, with at least three men helping carry her suitcase.

As she stepped out onto the forecourt, Anna stiffened in shock. Her gaze jumped from left to right and back. There were armed soldiers everywhere – Africans dressed for battle in green uni-forms and red berets. It took a moment for her to notice that their behaviour didn't match their daunting appearance. Many of them were talking and laughing. They seemed completely relaxed. The rifles slung casually over their shoulders seemed of little interest to anyone – they might have been hockey sticks or golf clubs.

Interspersed with the soldiers were ordinary people – African women with children in tow, selling bananas and peanuts; travel-lers climbing into taxis with their luggage. Anna watched two blond children who must have come from a fancy-dress party – one was a pirate with a black-patch eye, the other a fairy with wings tied to her back. The pair chased one another, weaving through the crowd. No one seemed worried about them. No one seemed wor-ried about anything. Anna breathed out, letting go of her shock at seeing so many uniformed men, so many guns. As Sister Emilia had promised, life really was going on as usual in Albertville, in spite of all the soldiers – or perhaps because of them.

Now the porters were holding out their hands, demanding to be paid. Anna took out her wallet, keeping it close to her chest. Shuffling through the stack of notes, she pulled out fifty dollars. It was the smallest denomination she had. She didn't know what to do. As the porters crowded in, Anna saw a flutter of black from the corner of her eye. The next moment a small white hand closed over her wallet.

'Put that away!'

Sister Emilia handed a coin to the nearest porter and shooed them all off. They protested as they left, glowering at Anna over their shoulders.

'Do not let anyone see that you have so much money,' the nun admonished. 'Where are your father's friends? Why aren't they looking after you?'

Anna swallowed. She felt overwhelmed; on the edge of tears. 'They have not come.'

'Oh, you poor child. Do you have an address? A telephone number?'

Anna took out the folder of information Murphy had given her and read out the names of Karl Emerson's friends. There was no other information about them.

'Monsieur and Madame Rousseau . . .' Sister Emilia shook her head. 'I do not know them.'

Anna felt a twinge of panic. She'd only just stepped onto Congo soil and already Murphy's plan was unravelling. Sister Emilia beckoned over a taxi driver, calling him by name. When he came near he shook hands with all the nuns, then with Anna.

'Let me help you, my sisters,' he said.

After an interchange in what Anna took to be Swahili, Sister Emilia got out some more money and handed it to the driver.

'He knows them. He will take you to their home. I have paid the fare. If there is any problem when you arrive, he will bring you to us.'

Anna smiled with relief. Now that the porters had dispersed, she reached again for her wallet. She didn't want Sister Emilia to be out of pocket. Marilyn had taught her daughter to avoid taking or giving favours, especially where money was involved. She liked to quote from Shakespeare: 'Neither a borrower nor a lender be'.

Sister Emilia waved Anna's offer aside. 'When you have some Congolese francs, make a donation to someone in need.' She took Anna's hand and said a second goodbye. As the other nuns smiled and nodded, Anna couldn't help looking again at the beautiful young woman in white – wondering where she came from and why she'd chosen the life of a nun.

The driver picked up Anna's suitcase and shepherded her towards his taxi. As she reached the rear passenger door, Anna looked over her shoulder. Part of her wanted to run back and join the nuns. She felt safe with Sister Emilia. But she had to find the Rousseaus. They were her link with Karl Emerson. And she needed to go to the hospital as soon as possible – to meet her father before it was too late.

SIX

Anna opened the window of the taxi, letting the moving air cool her sweaty face. She could feel the dust gathering on her skin. No doubt it was settling in her hair as well, making it stiff and dull, but there was nothing she could do about that. It was much too hot in the car with the windows up.

The road from the airport cut through scrubby woodland with stunted trees and bushes. It had the untidy look of forest that had been cleared and was now creeping back, sending its toughest species ahead to breach the frontier. Lurking in the distance was thick, dark green jungle.

They soon came to small farms with vegetable plots and banana plantations. Half-naked children played outside the mud houses, chickens pecking around their feet. As they neared the edge of Albertville, huts and little stalls bordered the road. It was the same scene that Anna had viewed from the air, but now she saw all the details. A woman with a baby tied to her back, crouched next to a blackened charcoal brazier. Yellow corn on the cob heaped in a basket. A rooster with torn feathers hanging down. A child alone, too close to the road.

Anna's gaze jumped from one image to another, grasping snippets of information that were no sooner interpreted than gone. It was so colourful and chaotic – so full of contrast. Elegant tropical flowers that would have graced the finest dining table grew alongside open drains and piles of burning rubbish. This was Africa, Anna told herself. This was where she was born. It felt so strange, so unimaginably different to what she now knew as home.

'*C'est notre usine Coca-Cola.*' The taxi driver's words broke into her thoughts. He was pointing ahead to where a factory loomed, sporting the familiar red-and-white logo of the soft drink.

Anna murmured her approval, realising that the driver viewed the place as a significant landmark. As she eyed a large cement model of a bottle standing in the forecourt, she realised how thirsty she was. She'd have given a lot, right then, to gulp down a cold fizzy drink.

At last they were entering the town centre, driving along a wide road lined with palm trees. There were rows of modern buildings several storeys high. Many had the long deep verandahs that were common in Australia, but instead of being made of wood, everything was cast in concrete.

They passed a place with *Hôtel Albertville* written across the facade. Anna glimpsed a couple sitting on the patio, cane chairs drawn up to a wrought-iron table. The woman wore a bright summer dress and white hat and gloves. The man was in a linen suit. Between them stood a bottle in a silver ice bucket. Anna imagined them sipping cool white wine, tendrils of cigarette smoke rising in the air between them. The sight was comforting. Ordinary people doing ordinary things.

Suddenly the driver leaned forward, hands tensing on the steering wheel. The taxi slowed down. Anna saw that the road was blocked by a roughly painted wooden pole resting between two 44-gallon drums. As the car came to a halt, a Congolese soldier – wearing the same uniform as the troops at the airport – strode over to it. He rested one hand on the roof and leaned in through the open window. Anna flinched.

'*Passeport!*' he demanded.

He studied her as she rifled in her handbag. She could feel his eyes on her, like hands trawling her bare skin. The taxi driver produced an identity card. The soldier barely glanced at it, but when he took possession of Anna's passport he carefully studied each page. He looked from the black-and-white photograph to Anna sitting in front of him, then back at the passport. He grinned and said something to the driver. Anna could see the driver's face in the rear-vision mirror – his quick eager-to-please smirk directed at the soldier, then the embarrassment in his eyes.

Anna looked down, studying her hands. She could imagine Marilyn's outrage if she were here. The insolence, the ingratitude of the Africans! Anna had heard the spiel enough times. White people had made this country, built roads, railways, ports . . . They'd brought medicine, education, employment. And now they were unwanted. It only showed, Marilyn claimed, how primitive the Africans were. They didn't know when they were well off.

But Marilyn's opinions were of no help here. Anna forced herself to lift her gaze and give the soldier a warm smile. For a moment, it had no effect. Then an answering smile spread over the man's face. Now it was Anna's turn to stare. His teeth were so white, so perfect. In the afternoon sun his skin shone like burnished bronze. As he straightened up, she noticed his fine stature. She felt small and untidy, crouched there in the back of the car.

The soldier returned the passport and waved the taxi on.

Soon they were out of the town centre, driving along residential roads. Each property had a high fence with double gates closed across a driveway. As the taxi neared a particularly impressive set of iron gates, topped with savage spikes, the driver slowed down and pressed his hand on the horn. A small boy, bare stomach protruding from a buttonless shirt, skipped out of the way as the taxi turned sharply into the driveway. A man in a brown uniform emerged from a sentry box, straightening his cap. He opened the gates, one by one – moving slowly as if to underline the importance of the task. Then he stood back to let the taxi come inside.

A gravel driveway stretched ahead, edged with white painted stones and shaded by the branches of large old trees. A well-tended lawn spread out to either side, with islands of flowering shrubs and rose beds spotted with pink and white blooms. Anna gazed around her, amazed. She was suddenly in another world. Africa seemed far away. But then, as they rounded a corner a stark pattern of black-and-white stripes caught her eye.

'A zebra!' she exclaimed.

'In Swahili we call it *punda milia*,' the driver said. 'The donkey with stripes.'

The animal grazed placidly on the mown grass, flicking its tail from side to side, swishing away flies. Anna had barely enough time to take in the unexpected sight, when they rounded another tree-lined corner and a huge house came into view.

It was unlike any other building Anna had seen during the drive through Albertville. Instead of concrete it was made from brick, with tiled gable roofs. Decorative woodwork formed dark geometric patterns on the wide facade. Lower down, creepers almost covered the walls, the vines clipped away to expose banks of six-pane windows. A shiny white Jaguar was parked near a set of stone steps that led up to a brass-bound door. Anna was reminded of photos of English country homes she'd seen in magazines. The style was called 'mock Tudor', even though the term didn't seem intended as an insult. She glanced back at the zebra, which was now nibbling delicately at one of the shrubs. The animal was the only clue that Anna had not arrived in a little corner of England.

As the taxi drew to a halt beside the steps an African man in a white uniform, a red fez on his head, came out of the front door.

'Good afternoon, Mademoiselle,' he said gravely as he opened the passenger door.

'Hello. My name is Anna Emerson. I'm from Australia. The Rousseaus are expecting me.'

A flicker of emotion crossed the man's face, then he nodded. 'Do you have luggage?'

'One case,' Anna answered.

A teenage boy appeared, seemingly from nowhere, and hurried round to the boot of the taxi.

'Please come with me.' The man gestured towards the house.

Anna waved to the driver, then turned to smile at the teenager who now had the suitcase resting on his head. It looked impossibly heavy but he seemed to manage the load with ease. The older servant led the way up the steps and pushed open the door.

Anna followed him inside, squinting in the sudden dimness. She was in a hallway panelled with timber and hung with paintings in gilt frames. Fans whirred overhead and the air was cooler, tinged with the smell of furniture polish. The teenager headed towards a staircase with her luggage, while the other servant ushered her into a formal sitting room.

Velvet drapes were drawn halfway across the windows, screening the sunshine. A huge Persian carpet filled most of the floor, its rich red and orange hues almost glowing in the soft light. The sofa and armchairs were upholstered in striped satin; the mantelpiece bore a clock under a glass dome and a pair of antique silver candlesticks. Like the garden and the exterior of the house, the room could have come straight from the pages of *English Style*.

'Please, wait here.'

Gesturing for Anna to take a seat on the sofa, the servant disappeared. Anna stood up as soon as he was gone and crossed to a mirror mounted on the wall. She ran her hands over her hair and pressed her lips together to even out her lipstick. She decided against taking out her powder compact or comb. It would be awful to be caught tidying herself up, and in this low light she didn't actually look too bad.

Instead she wandered over to a glass case containing a collection of china ornaments. She recognised the blue-and-white tones of Wedgwood pottery and the milky sheen of fine Dutch porcelain. There was a greyhound on the run, a cupid resting on a pedestal, a milkmaid, a shepherd and other old-fashioned figures. Anna didn't bother to look closely, checking for telltale hair lines – nothing in this home, she felt sure, would ever have been broken and repaired.

Anna imagined Madame Rousseau wearing a chiffon day dress and pearls, as elegant and gracious as her home. Monsieur Rousseau would be quite formal, she thought, perhaps even intimidating, in a smart suit and tie. She sent silent thanks to Marilyn for teaching her how to behave properly – even though it was something she had not always appreciated. As an older child, Anna had grown to despise her mother's insistence on cloth napkins at the family dinner table, different cutlery for each course, and all the little niceties that came under the heading 'manners' (like not asking for what you want, just waiting for it to be passed to you; like making introductions twice, while school friends giggled – 'Sally, this is Lucy', 'Lucy, this is Sally'). The formal way of life was out of place in suburban Melbourne. So was Marilyn's haughty manner with shopkeepers, waiters and tram conductors. She seemed to be constantly trying to convey the impression that she – and her daughter – belonged somewhere else. They were citizens of a more sophisticated, glamorous world. (A world from which they'd been forever expelled, Anna understood, by the heartless actions of Karl Emerson.) There was a humbler part of Marilyn's life in Africa that was never mentioned – she'd originally moved there to take up a position as a governess with a wealthy family in Kenya. As Anna reached adolescence she was increasingly critical of Marilyn's dishonesty about this, and intolerant of her grand airs. However, the formal manners of the household had turned out to be an advantage in Anna's role as an executive secretary. And now, she realised, they would be useful here as well.

Anna tensed at the sound of footsteps out in the hall. She hurried back to sit on the couch, then stood up, smoothing her skirt, straightening her shoulders.

A woman wandered in, long red hair draping her shoulders, a silky yellow gown flowing out behind her. She smiled a little vaguely in Anna's direction. 'Hi, there. You'll have to excuse me, I've just woken up.'

Anna tried not to stare. The woman was not young – she must have been at least forty – but she was as beautiful, in her way, as the nun at the airport. Her hair was thick and glossy, her eyes a light blue, her lips rosy-red. She spoke with an American accent. Anna felt even more confused. Now there was another nationality to fit into the same picture as the English house, and the French surname of its owners.

The woman yawned, making no attempt to cover her mouth. Anna was reminded of a kitten – the tongue was curled and pink.

Heavy bangles made of gold, ivory and ebony clinked together as she raised her arm, holding a cigarette to her lips. She blew out smoke, studying Anna through half-closed eyes.

'Who are you? Magadi just told me, but I wasn't listening.'

'I'm Miss Emerson.' Anna tried to sound confident and unruffled. 'You must be Madame Rousseau?'

'God, no, I'm Eliza.' The woman laughed lightly, tipping back her head. Her teeth were perfect, small; like pearls. 'Would you like a drink?' Without waiting for an answer she picked up a little hand bell and shook it.

'The Rousseaus are expecting me,' Anna said firmly. She couldn't think who this woman might be. 'I looked out for them at the airport but they didn't come.'

Eliza shook her head. 'They left for Brussels three days ago. There was a family emergency, something to do with their daughter.'

Anna stared, struggling to take in her words. 'But I'm meant to be staying with them. It was all arranged . . .' Anna tried to keep the panic out of her voice, but she could hear it seeping through. 'They are friends of my father. He's here in Albertville, and I've come to see him. Didn't they tell you I'd be arriving?'

Eliza waved one arm dismissively. 'They left in a hurry. But it doesn't matter. You can still stay here.'

'Are you sure?' Anna asked doubtfully.

Eliza gave her a small smile. 'This house belongs to me.'

Anna frowned in surprise. The woman's casual manners, along with her attire, didn't seem to fit with such a claim.

Eliza offered Anna a cigarette. They both smoked in silence for a short while. Then there was the sound of footsteps in the hall. Eliza turned expectantly towards the door as the servant appeared.

'Drinks, please, Magadi.' She raised her eyebrows at Anna. 'Gin and tonic? With ice?'

Anna fought an urge to look at her watch. Marilyn never drank before six. 'Thank you.'

'Doubles, of course,' Eliza said to Magadi. She glanced back to Anna. 'Are you hungry?' Anna just looked at her. She couldn't tell if she was hungry or not – her stomach felt knotted into a tight ball and empty at the same time. 'And food,' Eliza added.

Magadi bowed his head and retreated.

Eliza strolled over to a chaise longue and lay down, her loose gown draping the carpet. It was not a style of garment Anna had ever seen before. With wide sleeves and embroidery on the front and hem, it looked exotic and foreign.

'So, who's your father?' Eliza asked. 'I might know him. Albertville's a small place, really.' Before Anna had the chance to respond, Eliza's eyes widened. Suddenly she was fully alert. 'Oh my God. You said you were Miss Emerson. You're talking about Karl!'

'Yes,' Anna said. 'That's him!'

Eliza was silent for a moment, then she seemed to gather herself. 'I'm sorry . . . I know he's very ill. You must be upset.'

'Yes, I am,' Anna responded. The invitation to be reunited with her father was bittersweet: he was soon going to die. But that meant whatever time they had together was only going to be more precious. 'I'm excited as well. I haven't seen him since I was a child.'

'Ah,' Eliza said. 'I see.'

Anna couldn't read her expression. 'So . . . how do you know him?'

'I met him here at the house. He's been staying with the Rousseaus on and off for months, since he started needing the cancer treatment. There's no proper hospital where he lives.'

Anna leaned forward. 'What is he like?'

Eliza studied her cigarette for a few seconds. 'He's . . . very interesting. He collects African art.'

Anna stared at her, wanting more.

'That's all I can say,' Eliza said bluntly. 'I hardly know him. I haven't spent much time in Albertville lately.'

Anna picked up an evasive tone in Eliza's voice. The silence felt tense. Anna was still trying to decide what she should say next when Magadi arrived bearing a silver tray. Anna accepted a tumbler filled to the brim and clinking with ice. She drank gratefully, forgetting everything else for a moment. She was so thirsty.

Magadi placed a plate of sandwiches on a side table. They were made from white bread, the crusts removed. Slivers of green comprised the filling. The sight of food confirmed for Anna that she was in fact very hungry. She looked down at her hands. They'd been clean when she left the plane, but she'd been touching her luggage since then, the door of the taxi, and her passport, which had been in the sweaty hands of the soldier. She imagined the array of germs that must be swarming over her skin.

'I need to wash,' she said.

Magadi led the way to a guest bathroom right near the front door. There was a dressing table and an armchair along with the toilet and hand basin. As Anna scrubbed her hands, she wondered if anyone ever sat down in the chair, or if it was just for show.

Back in the sitting room, she crossed straight to the sandwich plate. She made herself pause and count to ten, to show that she was not – as Marilyn would have put it – a starving orphan. But then she consumed three sandwiches before she could stop.

She offered the plate to Eliza, but the woman shook her head.

'I can't understand why anyone would eat cucumber in a sandwich.' She smiled indulgently. 'Magadi insists on producing them.

My mother taught him how to prepare an English afternoon tea when he was just the kitchen *toto*. He's been making them ever since.'

'Your mother is English?'

'Was.'

'I'm sorry.'

'Don't be. She was ready to go when she did.' Eliza glanced around the room, her gaze softening. 'This was her very favourite house. I haven't let anyone change a thing.'

'Are you a friend of the Rousseaus?' Anna asked, still trying to make sense of how Eliza, the house, her mother, the French couple, all fitted together.

'They're my caretakers. I'm away a lot so I rely on them to look after things here. I'm lucky to have them. So many Europeans have left the country. I've got Indians in the Stanleyville place.' Eliza grinned. 'The whole house smells of curry. My father would have had a fit.' She took a long swallow of her drink, setting her bangles moving again. Then she rested the glass on her stomach.

Watching her closer up, Anna realised that the gown was made of fine silk, the rich embroidery dotted with what looked like real pearls. She studied the hands that cradled the glass. Eliza wore at least four rings, each with an impressive stone. But the finger that could have been graced by a wedding ring, Anna noticed, was bare.

Eliza sat up, shaking back her hair. 'You must be desperate to have a bath and get changed. Do you plan to go to the hospital today? Or are you too tired?'

'I'd like to go as soon as possible. My father's condition has been deteriorating these last weeks. But I don't know when visiting hours are.'

'Who cares?' Eliza stood up, rearranging a long necklace of

African beads that hung around her neck. 'They can't turn you away.'

Anna recognised the utter confidence in the woman's voice. She was reminded of Mrs Williams, with her careless charm. The wife of Anna's boss had been born wealthy – her father owned an oil company. She knew she'd always get what she wanted. Eliza, it seemed, was in the same boat. She had evidently inherited at least two properties that were run by caretakers – possibly more. She must be one of the rich Congo set, which had once included Marilyn.

'I'll drive you there if you like. I have to go into town to see someone myself.'

'Thank you,' Anna said gratefully. 'I've come all this way. It would be terrible if . . .' She couldn't bring herself to finish the sentence.

Eliza drained her glass. 'Let's get ready, then.' She picked up a sandwich and extracted the slices of cucumber, dropping them onto the plate. One missed, landing on the carpet. Anna only just managed to stop herself retrieving it. A secretary's instinct was to immediately fix anything that went wrong – but here, she reminded herself, it was the servant's job.

Eliza walked out of the room, eating her empty sandwich. She seemed full of energy now, striding along the hallway and on up the flight of stairs. Anna followed, matching her step for step. When they reached the landing Anna kept her eyes on the yellow silk gown, as it flicked around a corner. She feared that if she didn't keep up, Eliza might just disappear, and she'd be left wandering alone in this huge quiet house, trying to find where the young man had put her suitcase.

As they passed closed doors, one after another, she began to feel almost panicky. She wanted to be reunited with the things she'd brought with her. There were all the carefully chosen clothes and shoes, and her toilet bag packed with medicine. Then, there was the little stuffed toy she'd hidden in a zipped compartment. She'd had the koala for as long as she could remember; Marilyn said it had been a christening present sent out to the Congo by an Australian relative. The kangaroo fur from which it had been made was worn bare in places and one eye had been lost. Anna used to take the koala on holidays with her, or to school camps. And she'd brought it with her now, as a kind of talisman. A link with her childhood – and the world she had once shared with her father.'

At last Eliza pushed open a door, letting sunshine in onto the hall carpet. Dust danced in the shaft of light. She stood back, letting Anna walk past her.

'Downstairs in an hour,' she said, and was gone.

SEVEN

Eliza steered the Jaguar with one hand, the other resting on the gear stick. Anna sat in the passenger's seat, her handbag on her knee. A fan blew air into her face, drying beads of sweat as they formed. The motor made a soft fluttering sound, as if an insect might be caught in the blades.

As they drove, Anna kept stealing sideways glances, struggling to take in the transformation in Eliza's appearance. When they'd met in the hallway, as agreed, Anna had barely recognised her hostess. The woman in the loose gown had been replaced by someone who would not have looked out of place on a catwalk. Eliza's red hair was piled high on top of her head. She wore a double-strand pearl necklace wound close around her neck. Her dress was orange, tight at the waist, the skirt only just reaching the knee. Her eyeliner, mascara and lipstick were all perfect. She looked sophisticated and rich, with an edge of daring. She seemed much younger than she had before. Anna wondered what kind of person Eliza was going to visit. She had gone to a lot of effort, considering she wasn't even going out for dinner – she'd said she would return to the hospital to collect Anna after two hours.

Anna had deliberated over her own outfit. What do you wear, she'd asked her reflection in the bedroom mirror, when you are going to meet your father for what feels like the very first time? And what do you wear when visiting someone who is very ill? Something cheerful, or sombre? Eye-catching or demure? In the end, she'd opted for a linen shirt and skirt – one of the Hollywood actress outfits – dressed up with high heels. She'd decided she wanted to look smart and practical rather than glamorous. But now, looking at Eliza, she felt she might have made the wrong choice.

'We're in the Avenue of Storms.' Eliza gestured at the wide, palm-lined street Anna recognised from the taxi ride. 'It gets the name from the storms that form over the lake. They're caused by air crossing a large body of fresh water. Sometimes you can barely stand up in the winds that blow.'

Anna gazed out at the street. There was no sign of bad weather now. In the late afternoon sun, leaves hung limp and dusty. A flag drooped from a pole – royal blue with bits of yellow that looked like fragments of stars. Anna guessed it was the new flag of the Congo, only a few years old.

The car glided along, the suspension absorbing all the bumps that had caused the taxi to lurch and jolt. Eliza named the various landmarks along their way: the railway station, post office, several statues and monuments. As they reached the crest of a hill, she slowed down, pointing back across the city towards the lake.

For several moments the two looked at the watery vista in silence. From this vantage point the lake was even more impressive than it had been from the air. The sandy beaches were hidden by buildings and trees. The point of contact between settlement and water was the long wharf that jutted out into the bay. Several tall cranes stood along it, their angled shapes thrusting like elbows into the sky. There were three ships tied up there, and nearby a whole fleet of smaller boats were at anchor. The presence of these man-made objects was reassuring, somehow; as if humans had put a taming handprint on the vastness of the lake.

'When I was a child I thought this was the sea,' Eliza commented, breaking the quiet. 'Once we went to Hawaii for a holiday and I was so shocked to find the water was salty. I refused to swim in it.'

'You lived here as a child?' Anna asked.

'Between here and New York. My father had business interests in various parts of the Congo. He liked to keep an eye on things. And my mother loved being in Africa.' She smiled. 'Mom's idea of Africa was rather English, though – as you see from the house.'

Before long, they reached the place where the Avenue was blocked by the checkpoint. Four soldiers who had been sitting near one of the 44-gallon drums jumped to their feet. Anna braced herself for another tense encounter, but as the car came to a halt, Eliza wound down the window and shook hands with each of the men. Then she offered cigarettes all round, before giving them the near-full packet to keep. All the while she was talking in what Anna guessed was Swahili. The men laughed as if she were making clever jokes. Then Eliza reached into the glove box and pulled out a small white-and-pink bundle. She handed it to one of the soldiers, who proceeded to unroll a set of baby clothes.

'He's just had a daughter,' Eliza explained. 'His first child.'

The man showed the gift around. One by one, the tough-looking soldiers, rifles slung over their shoulders, examined a tiny crocheted matinee jacket, a pair of booties, some vests and a pink nightdress with an embroidered yoke.

'*Vizuri sana!*' the new father said, grinning broadly.

Anna smiled, guessing the meaning of the words. She glanced over to see Eliza's reaction, but found her companion deep in conversation with one of the other soldiers. From the look on his face, Anna could tell the topic was serious. The conversation went on for some time. Then everyone shook hands again, the painted pole was lifted out of the way and the Jaguar was waved on.

They drove without speaking. There was a frown on Eliza's face. She lit a cigarette and drew in deeply, as if calming herself. Anna waited uneasily for her to say something. In the end she broke the silence herself. 'How do you know these men?'

'They've been checking my identity for weeks,' Eliza said. 'Now we always have a chat.'

'Were you discussing the uprisings?' Anna asked, remembering what Sister Emilia had said. 'You looked concerned.'

'He was telling me his brother's unit is being sent to the north of Kivu Province. They've got a whole lot of new equipment – guns and ammunition, vehicles. But the men don't want to go up there. They know they'll be on the front line, fighting the Simbas.'

'They're the rebels?' Anna queried.

Eliza nodded. 'Their name means "lion" in Swahili. The government soldiers are terrified of them because they have magic powers.'

Anna eyed her in confusion. She understood Eliza was only reporting what the men had said, but there was no mocking tone in her voice, and her face was serious. It was as if she believed in magic powers herself.

'Kivu Province is where your father has his plantation,' Eliza said. Anna got the impression she was keen to change the subject. 'It's away from the fighting, though, down in the south.'

'I was born there,' Anna said. 'Not on the plantation. In a mission hospital somewhere.'

'How old were you when you left?'

'I was seven. But I don't remember much about it. Melbourne

is so different. I guess it pushed out the other memories.'

'They might come back to you,' Eliza suggested, 'now that you're here.'

'I hope so.'

Anna smiled to herself. Very soon, now, she would be face to face with her father. She would be able to ask him, at last, all the questions about her life here in the Congo she'd stored up over the years – the ones Marilyn refused even to listen to. Who were my friends? What pets did we have? How did I get the scar on my leg? Then, there were the questions Anna's mother could not have answered even if she'd wanted to. What had Karl Emerson been doing all the years since they left? Was he happy? Did he miss Marilyn? Or Anna? Did he ever regret sending them away?

Eliza swung the car off the main road, skirting a clock monument set in a tower of stone, before steering the car up a long sweeping driveway. She came to a halt in front of what looked like a hotel or a club – except that it had a sign that read *Hôpital Européen*.

'You'll find reception just inside the entrance,' Eliza said. 'And you don't need to worry, all the nurses speak English.'

'I'm fluent in French,' Anna responded.

Eliza raised her eyebrows, looking impressed. She glanced at her watch. 'I'll be back in two hours, then. If you're not ready to leave, I can wait.' She scanned Anna's face with eyes that looked even more strikingly blue now that they were surrounded by black eyeliner. 'Are you all right? I have to meet someone important, otherwise I'd offer to come with you.'

'I'm fine, thank you.' Anna was touched by Eliza's concern. 'I'd really rather be on my own.' She meant what she said; she usually found that involving other people only added complications. It had been one of her fears about marrying Gregory, though it was not something she'd even tried to explain.

'I'd feel the same in your shoes,' Eliza said. 'But remember, if there's any nonsense about visiting hours, just mention my name. Tell the Matron I said I was sure you could go any time.'

Anna looked back at her companion, realising she knew almost nothing about her – not even her surname.

'Lindenbaum.' As she dropped the name, Eliza was already peering into the rear-vision mirror, preparing to drive on.

Anna's mouth fell open. Lindenbaum was as familiar to her as Rockefeller, Guggenheim and Getty. Mr Williams spoke of the tycoons in hushed tones, describing them as the men who ran America. Anna noticed Eliza's fingers tapping on the steering wheel. She was obviously keen to get going. Opening her door, Anna eased herself out of the soft leather seat and waved goodbye.

Within seconds the Jaguar was speeding away, a cloud of white gravel dust rising in its wake.

Anna walked into a reception area where two fair-haired nurses in white caps and uniforms stood behind a polished wooden counter, examining some paperwork. A fluorescent tube suspended above their heads bathed them in a harsh glare.

As she approached the counter, Anna repeated Eliza's family name in her head like a charm. At the sound of high heels clicking over the terrazzo floor, both of the nurses looked up. One was middle-aged, with a timid face and portly figure. The other was younger. She had sharp features and an upright posture. A shiny badge that read *Matron* was pinned on her chest. She scanned Anna from head to toe and back.

'You are Mademoiselle Emerson,' she stated.

Anna stared at her. How could the Matron possibly know who she was? There must be lots of visitors coming and going from the hospital. In the brief quiet, a clock ticked somewhere. A baby wailed. Anna swallowed, her mouth feeling dry. Both of the nurses were now examining her. Avoiding meeting their gaze, Anna looked past their shoulders at the wall behind them. Her eyes settled on a polished wooden plaque with gold lettering. The name *Lindenbaum* jumped out at her. Just seeing it there seemed to boost her confidence. Lifting her chin, she gave a cool smile.

'Yes, I am Anna Emerson,' she said. 'I'm here to see my father.'

'Thank goodness for that,' said the Matron tartly. 'Every time someone goes into his room he asks where you are.'

'I only just found out he was ill.' Anna felt a wave of guilt even though she knew it was unfounded. 'I came as soon as I could.' Sudden anxiety took over. 'How is he? I know his condition has deteriorated this last week.'

The Matron raised her eyebrows. 'I wouldn't say that. He keeps surprising us.'

Anna bit her lip. Murphy had been quite clear about the growing urgency for her to depart for the Congo. He'd even booked an earlier flight with the travel agent.

'Unfortunately it's not possible for you to see him tonight. It is well past visiting hours. You must return in the morning.'

Anna shook her head. She was right here in the same building as her father, and this woman expected her to walk away! 'I need to see him now.'

'Your father is resting.'

'Please just let me stand by his bed,' Anna pleaded. 'I won't disturb him.'

There was another moment of quiet. Anna was about to mention she was a guest of Eliza Lindenbaum when the Matron nodded.

'Very well, for a few minutes, but he must not be woken. We have other patients to look after.'

'Thank you, Matron.' Anna knew it was advisable, where possible, to mention a person's title. By showing respect for someone's status, you enhanced your own.

The woman gestured towards her colleague. 'Nurse Jansen will accompany you.'

The room was dimly lit. A single bed shrouded in a green mosquito net stood in the middle of the space. Anna could only see the vague outline of a figure lying there. She glanced back at the nurse, hovering in the doorway. She was going to remain here, Anna realised, and make sure the patient was not disturbed.

Anna crept closer to the bed. She could hear the sound of steady breathing. Slowly she lifted the net.

There he lay. Karl Emerson. Her first impression was that he was too small to be responsible for all the anger and pain his name had evoked over so many years. He was lying on his back, his head tilted up by a fat pillow. The light from the hallway cast ghoulish shadows over his face. He was gaunt and wasted, his cheeks sunk into his skull. His hair was white and wispy. A green hospital sheet was drawn up to his waist. Above it, silk pyjamas with a blue and gold paisley pattern lay slick against his bony frame, revealing the outline of his ribs.

For a few seconds Anna wondered if she had been brought to the wrong room. But then, as she looked back up at the face, peering more intently, she found vestiges of the man she knew from the passport photograph. She found she could see past the ravages of his illness, glimpsing the striking, handsome person he had once been.

A drip containing clear liquid hung from a stand near the head of the bed, a transparent plastic tube running down to the back of his hand, just below the wrist, then disappearing under a piece of elastoplast. The hand was surprisingly small and finely boned, the slender fingers slightly curled. It looked fragile and vulnerable, like a bird resting there.

Anna longed to reach out and take his hand in hers. The man looked so lonely in the quiet room. Abandoned.

I've come, she wanted to say. *I'm here.*

She looked for a chair to carry to the bedside. Glancing around the ward, she saw a cabinet with a flask of water and a glass set out on a paper mat. Against the wall was a chest of drawers on which stood a vase of roses, glowing red in the dingy light. There was a card with *Bon Rétablissement* written on the front. Speedy recovery. The rest of the space was taken up with a collection of framed photographs. Anna crossed to look at them.

As she came close, her step faltered. She stared at a picture of a little girl in a party frock, about to blow out four candles on a birthday cake. A stab of jealousy shot through her. Who was this child? But then she realised. It was her.

Beside it was another image. Anna was a bit older in this one, dressed in a smart riding habit, a pair of reins in her gloved hands. Then came a Christmas photo of her: with one arm she was hugging a toy reindeer draped in tinsel; with the other she held onto the already balding koala. Next, she was crouching with a dead gazelle, holding a shotgun, pretending to be the hunter.

Anna's gaze jumped from one picture to another. They were images she'd not seen before, yet they felt familiar. Fragments of memories rose from her subconscious. The velvet nose of the horse, nudging her shoulder. Someone – a woman – singing 'Happy Birthday' in a lilting African accent. The smell of blood drying under a fierce sun.

There was one last photograph, set at the far end of the chest of drawers. The frame was more ornate, the print larger. As Anna stepped towards it, she froze. This one was not just of the child. There was another figure standing with her. A man.

Anna grabbed the picture, heading for the doorway where the light was stronger. Ignoring the curious look of the nurse, she bent her head over the image, studying every detail.

It had been taken on the front steps of a grand building that she knew must be Leopard Hall – there was a large stone leopard crouching at each side of the door. The little girl stood right next to the man, holding his hand. Anna searched his face. He was much younger than the person in the passport photograph but she could tell it was her father. She stared at the picture – the two of them, in the same frame! Karl was gazing straight into the camera. Did he look proud, standing with his daughter? Or rather stiff, almost uneasy? There was a sense of bridled energy in his posture. Was he eager to lead the girl on an adventure, or impatient for the picture to be taken so he could drop her hand and be gone? Anna examined the way their hands were clasped together, trying to glean any clue as to how close the touch had been, how intimate. The child's face was quite blank. Did she look uncomfortable? Perhaps she'd reached the age where she didn't like having her picture taken.

Anna turned away from the photograph, staring instead along the dim hallway. She could feel Marilyn's eyes behind her own, Marilyn's voice inside her mind, searching for every hint of darkness and ill intent. Anna shook her head, banishing her mother from her thoughts. Marilyn could poison this for her, she realised. She could turn all her hopes to dust.

'See? Your face is exactly the same, especially your eyes . . .' It was the nurse, whispering over her shoulder.

It was true. In this picture, you could see quite clearly the woman Anna would one day become. No wonder the Matron had been able to identify her so easily. Anna smiled. She was glad she hadn't changed, like some people did as they grew up. Tomorrow when she came back here, and her father was awake, he too would recognise her straight away. He'd know that his little girl – the one whose pictures he had kept all these years – was right here by his side, at last.

The Jaguar was parked outside the entrance to the hospital, not far from a prominent sign declaring the area was reserved for ambulances. Anna hurried round to the passenger's side. As she opened the door she was met by the strong fragrance of cigar smoke. She barely had time to sit down before the car drove off. When they were out on the main road, Eliza glanced sideways, her eyebrows raised. 'You saw him?'

Anna smiled, nodding. 'He was asleep. I just sat by his bed. But it was . . .' She hunted for the right words. 'Well, it was him! He was there!'

'It must have been quite a moment,' Eliza said. 'Seeing him after so long.'

'Yes, it was.' Anna swallowed, overwhelmed by emotion. 'You know, there were framed photographs of me, all set out on the dresser. Six or seven of them. One had him – my father – in it too.

But there were none of anyone else.' She could hear the childish pride in her voice.

'That's nice,' Eliza said. 'He must be very fond of you.' She lit a cigarette, tossing the used match out of the window. Anna eyed her uncertainly, detecting a note of sarcasm. Anna remembered how Eliza had reacted when she'd first learned that Karl Emerson was Anna's father. She'd said she barely knew him, but her manner had been abrupt, almost cagey. A shocking thought suddenly came to Anna. Maybe there was some animosity between the two. Perhaps Eliza didn't like Karl Emerson for some reason. Part of Anna wanted to ask her if this was the case, but another part didn't want to know the answer.

As she turned to look out of the side window, Anna was aware of an unfamiliar emotion hatching inside her. It took her a little time to work out what it was. Then she knew. She felt protective of Karl Emerson. The experience of seeing him in his hospital bed looking so vulnerable had awoken something deep inside her. It had been sleeping so long she hadn't known it was there, but now she could feel it, warm and throbbing with life – the part of a girl's heart that belongs to her father.

They drove on for a while, with neither of them speaking. Then Eliza pointed towards the rear of the car. 'We have to make a quick stop on the way home. A man left his hat.'

Turning round, Anna saw a military cap – khaki cloth with a leather visor – resting on the seat. Pinned on the front was a gold badge bearing the emblem of an eagle with outstretched wings. Beside it, on the red leather upholstery, was a solid clump of ash. It still held the shape of the cigar from which it had fallen. Anna knew from Mr Williams – who entertained important clients with port and Havanas – that this was the sign of a top quality cigar. It meant the tobacco had been well packed. Anna pictured the owner of the cap with its smooth contours and shiny badge – a man with high status and expensive tastes – making himself at home in the back seat of Eliza Lindenbaum's car.

Before long, they were back in the Avenue of Storms, passing between the two lines of palm trees. They neared the Hôtel Albertville where Anna had seen the couple sharing a bottle of wine on her way from the airport. It had been only a few hours ago, but it felt like days.

'Good. He's outside – on the patio,' Eliza said. 'Grab the hat, will you?' She pulled over, jerking to a stop, lodging her cigarette in the ashtray. A man in uniform was seated at one of the tables. As he stood up, Anna recognised the tall army officer with the chest full of medals she'd seen among the passengers in the airport's arrival hall. In the strong afternoon light he looked even paler than before.

Stepping towards the edge of the patio, the officer stooped down to see into the Jaguar.

'Catch!' Eliza called out, throwing the cap towards him. Her aim was good; the object spun through the air in a high smooth arc. He grabbed it and set it on his head. Then he flashed a broad smile, revealing white teeth that looked too big for his face. Eliza gave him a cheery wave, then swung the steering wheel and accelerated. As the Jaguar lunged forwards, a taxi veered out of her way. When the road ahead was clear, Eliza picked up her cigarette and drew in deeply, making the red tip glow. She blew out a long stream of smoke.

'I saw that officer at the airport,' Anna commented as the car cruised on. 'He must have been on my plane.'

'He flies in and out all the time,' Eliza said. 'He's an adviser to the Congolese National Army.'

Anna just nodded as if this made sense to her, even though she couldn't understand why America would be sending military advisers to the Congo. Africa was half a world away from the USA. But then, so was Vietnam, and she knew from Mr Williams that the Yanks, as he called them, were very concerned about political developments there. He'd tried to explain the issue to her – how there was the threat of Communism spreading across the world; the fall of one country leading to the next. Anna wished, now, that she'd pressed him for more detail. Sitting here beside Eliza, she felt very young and ill-informed, but she had no intention of asking questions about politics. It would only expose just how ignorant she was.

She tried steering the conversation to less confusing territory. 'Do you know the officer well?'

'I met Randall at the Embassy in Léopoldville a few years ago,' Eliza replied. 'We discovered we went to the same summer camp as kids. For some reason, that made us decide to become friends – as much as you can be, when you live in different countries.'

Anna noticed a faint blush colouring Eliza's cheeks as she spoke. Stealing a closer look at her, Anna saw that her lipstick was slightly smudged, and the smart hairstyle no longer perfect. Randall was more than just a friend, she realised. He was the one for whom Eliza had dressed up so carefully. Anna pictured her sitting in the back of the car with the officer – his long legs folded into the narrow space; her orange dress contrasting with the muted tones of his uniform.

Eliza remained silent as they drove on. When they reached the checkpoint she laughed and made jokes with the soldiers, but as soon as they were on their way again, she fell quiet. A frown marked her brow. Anna began to wonder if Eliza was annoyed with her. Perhaps she resented having to put up with this young woman who'd turned up at her door. Anna had met people before who volunteered to help, but soon tired of their role. Or it could be to do with Eliza's feelings about Karl. On the other hand, it was possible she was just one of those people who swung from one mood to another for no reason. Anna shifted uneasily in her seat, unsure whether to make conversation, or keep quiet.

At last they reached the grand entrance to the Lindenbaum property. As the car idled, Eliza honked the horn impatiently, even though the gatekeeper had already sprung into action. As soon as she could squeeze the car through the gap, she drove off fast. She barely slowed down as they approached a pair of zebras ambling along the driveway.

'Bloody things,' she cursed as they scrambled to safety. 'I should get rid of them.'

When they stopped outside the house, Magadi came to open Eliza's door, but she didn't move. She stubbed out her cigarette, then stared blankly at the mangled butt. After a long moment, she turned to Anna.

'I'll be going out again. Magadi will look after you.' She scanned Anna's face. 'You should have an early night. You look terrible.'

Anna was unable to think of a reply. Eliza's blunt remark reminded her of her mother. Marilyn was always upsetting people by being too frank. Her manners were elaborate, but at the same time, she was often quite rude. Even her clients – who paid for French lessons for their children – had to learn to take her as they found her. If she hadn't been such a good teacher, her business would have failed. Anna had always thought the trait was the legacy of Marilyn's difficult past. Now Anna wondered if this was simply the way wealthy women of the Congo behaved.

Anna followed Eliza and Magadi towards the front door, lagging a little behind. A light breeze had sprung up, but even with the cooler air, she found she had no energy. The exhaustion she'd been suppressing for hours was now rising to the surface, as if summoned by Eliza's words. She thought longingly of the guest room with its white-covered bed and ceiling fan; the little sink in the corner with pink soap and matching hand towel. It was like a desert mirage, shimmering ahead of her.

Inside, Eliza strode across the entrance hall, her feet drumming an urgent beat on the tiled floor. As she disappeared through a door at the far end, she called over her shoulder to the servant, speaking in Swahili. Magadi waited until she had gone from view, before turning his attention to Anna.

'You have had a long safari,' he said. 'You must be tired.' He avoided Anna's face as he spoke; she wondered if he, too, thought she looked a mess. 'Perhaps you would like to have a tray brought to your room?'

'Thank you,' Anna said gratefully. The last thing she felt like was sitting alone in a dining room eating a formal meal. 'I think I'll go up straight away.'

'Yes, Mademoiselle.'

As he turned to go, Anna headed for the stairs. Grasping the banister, she climbed steadily, passing beneath mounted animal heads whose vacant eyes appeared to follow her as she moved. Halfway up, she came to a sudden halt. She had an odd feeling that she'd been here, ascending these stairs before. She hadn't experienced the sensation when she'd been here earlier – she'd been too focused on following Eliza. But now, it all seemed deeply familiar to her – the sound of footsteps on thinly carpeted wooden treads; the smell of beeswax polish blended with the thick perfume of

African lilies that came from the floral arrangement near the front door. She recognised the smooth touch of wood gliding under her hand. And the feeling that her feet were too heavy; the effort of climbing so great. She would never reach the top. She was puzzled for a moment – she'd not been in Eliza's house before today. Then she understood: it wasn't this staircase she was remembering. She was going back to when she was a child, in Leopard Hall. It made sense. She'd been small, then; the staircase would have seemed like a mountain. Anna smiled, prodding the memory for more. Who was downstairs? What had she been doing? Then the smile left her face, the memory of fear prickling up her spine. It was not tiredness that was causing the child to drag her feet. And it was not that she was being banished from the place where people talked and laughed, where there was music, light and colour. She didn't want to go upstairs on her own. There was something waiting up there that filled her child's heart with horror.

Anna stared up at the line of oil paintings on the landing. What could she have been so afraid of? But the memory was like a chink in a wall. The scope could not be widened. And as she tried to examine the memory, it quickly faded to a blur. She was just overtired, Anna realised. So much had happened today. She was in a strange house in a strange land. Her mind was playing tricks on her. She was probably remembering a scene in a film. She just needed to eat and wash, then have a good long sleep. That was all.

Her room was dim, heavy curtains having been drawn shut against the heat of the day. The ceiling fan whirred overhead; someone had already turned it on, in anticipation of her return. Anna went straight to the sink in the corner, rinsing her hands thoroughly. The hospital was well run and very clean, but there might still be a risk of picking up nasty germs. When her hands were dry she went to sit on the bed. She thought of lying down while she waited for her meal, but feared she might fall asleep. She crossed, instead, to look out of the window.

Pulling the curtains aside, she pushed open the leadlight windows. The cooling breeze blew in but she barely noticed it – she was staring in surprise at the silver gleam of a vast expanse of water. She hadn't realised she was so close to the lake. At ground level it was hidden from view by trees and the high fences of neighbouring houses, but from up here she could see it all spread out before her: the colourful fishing boats bobbing at their moorings; the white birds hovering above the gently rippling surface of the water; the elegant curves of palm trees lining the shore.

Anna leaned forward, the lake drawing her into its sphere like a giant magnet. In the softening light, as afternoon moved towards dusk, the setting was idyllic. It was hard to imagine this was a place where fierce storms brewed. As she lost herself in the peaceful beauty of the scene, she thought of Karl, lying in his hospital bed, not far from where she was. She pictured his face, relaxed in sleep; his chest rising and falling with each shallow breath. His hand waiting to be held. Every little image was a treasure held inside her. She smiled into the gathering dusk. She couldn't wait for the night to fall, so the journey towards tomorrow could begin.

EIGHT

Wood shavings were scattered around Dan's feet, speckling the gravel with delicate curves of dark ebony. He was sitting on an empty ammunition box at the edge of the parade ground. He'd chosen a spot as far away as possible from the barracks. Here he could escape the smells of the latrines and the fuel dump, and instead enjoy the moist green fragrance of the jungle that grew right up to the perimeter fence. Normally when he came here he could hear birdsong, but today it was drowned out by the droning wail of a pair of Scottish bagpipes. At the far side of the yard, Dan could see Corporal McAdam marching up and down in time to his music. Dressed in his family kilt, a tam-o'-shanter on his head, he was the self-appointed Regimental Piper. Dan wondered if the other men found his playing inspiring, or if the instrument would suffer a terrible accident one day.

Closer to the centre of the ground, a wrestling match was about to begin. Two men were stripped to the waist, wearing only their trousers and boots. Their hands rested on their thighs as the umpire paced around them, holding up a stopwatch. Dan knew both of the contestants. They'd flown to the Congo in the same aircraft as him. One was a Belgian who'd been working in South Africa as a butcher. He looked strong, with well-toned muscles. His opponent was lean and wiry. A tattoo of an eagle with outstretched wings looked out of place spread across his bony chest. This second man, a British ex-paratrooper, wore a twisted smile permanently on his face. There was a dangerous gleam in his eyes. It had taken Dan about a second to mark him out as trouble. Waiting for the umpire to set them fighting, the two men were like volcanoes ready to erupt. Dan wondered if the wrestling would turn into a real fight, with real injuries, as it had the day before.

All the men were restless. There were about three hundred of them here at Lemba Base. They were undertaking training, but what they really wanted to do was go into action. And this wasn't going to be happening at all soon. There were no contracts for them to sign, and only a scant supply of uniforms or weapons. There was talk of an extended delay. No one – including Major Blair – knew if this was due to some logistical problem, or if the mission was being stalled at a political level. Whatever the real reason might be, it was no way to start a campaign. Fighting men need to keep moving – mercenary soldiers in particular. They were assault troops, by definition; garrison life did not suit them.

Some spent their free time swaggering around the base wearing bandanas tied over their heads; bullet belts slung across their chests; or shorts that barely covered their thighs. They carried personal weapons – pistols and knives – in plain view. Blair didn't like what he called 'fancy dress', but until he could issue uniforms he could hardly insist they be worn. Dan could see the frustration in the Major's face as he inspected his men. For his part, as an officer, Dan tried to set a good example.

Dan looked up as the umpire's voice rang across the grounds. 'One, two, three – go!'

The circle of onlookers crept in closer. The wrestlers raised their hands, then almost simultaneously lunged forwards, grabbing each other's heads. Cheers and taunts erupted as the men rolled together in slow motion, coating themselves in gravel dust.

Dan noticed a figure watching on from a distance. He recognised the man immediately. He was unusually tall and thin, and his skin and hair were so fair he might almost have been an albino. He had been at Lemba Base on and off ever since the mercenaries had begun arriving. Dressed always in battle fatigues, his rank was unclear, but he was an American military attaché of some sort. He spent most of his days talking with Blair or with the high-ranking officers of the Congolese National Army who made regular visits here. But sometimes – like now – he just stood around observing the recruits.

Shifting his attention back to his carving, Dan lifted up the hunk of ebony, turning it slowly to examine his work. It was going to be an elephant, but was only crudely formed as yet. When it was finished, he knew, the animal would look almost alive. Dan understood his subject intimately. He'd spent decades observing wildlife in the bush, learning the meaning of every tensed muscle, swivelling ear, waving tail. And he'd spent almost as long practising the art of carving.

Resting the elephant back on his knee, he angled his knife against the wood. With a deft movement of fingers, hand and wrist, he peeled off a long deep sliver, following the grain, cutting through the brown outer layer to find the deep black heart of the timber.

Dan watched himself as if from a distance, sitting there on the sturdy crate, in the patchy shade of a small tree. Part of him was still amazed to find himself here. So far away from the Mara – so far from his old life. He looked across to the barracks and other buildings. At first glance Lemba Base was impressive. It had been built in the colonial era by the Belgians – everything was solid and square. But now, the unit cooks were working outside, relying on traditional African charcoal burners, because the stoves in the kitchens weren't functioning. Pit latrines were in use, temporarily, while plumbers tried to unblock the toilets. Running water was intermittent. It was extraordinary how the facilities had deteriorated in the four years since Independence. If this was how the Congolese National Army ran its affairs, Dan reflected, it was no wonder they'd needed to call in outside help to win a war.

The wrestling match was now reaching its climax. Dan glanced up, seeing the two fighters staggering, punch drunk. He decided to go and watch the final round. Carefully he wrapped the carving in a cloth. It was the Maasai blanket that he usually spread over his bed. He hadn't done this in the barracks. It was against the rules, but more importantly, he feared it could disappear. It was his most precious possession.

The blanket had been a gift from an old Maasai chief whose little granddaughter Dan had once rescued and taken to hospital. She was only two years old when he'd come across her being carried on a cowhide stretcher by her uncles. They were headed for the Catholic mission, several days' walk from where they were. The child was moaning in pain, barely conscious, with a film of sweat on her face. Dan felt sure she would die if he didn't offer to help. His clients were unimpressed by the three-hour detour that ensued. They weren't too happy either about sharing the Land Rover with people who smelled of rancid butter and cows. They feared the child was carrying some infectious disease and kept a good distance from her, bunching up at one side of the vehicle.

As soon as Dan had handed the girl into the care of the nuns, he'd gone on his way, eager to get his guests to their campsite. When he next returned to the area he'd called in at the Maasai *boma* to see how she had fared. The old chief told him the white doctor had cut open her belly and removed something evil. Now she was well again. He showed Dan a shrivelled morsel wrapped in leather.

'Now she will be able to grow up and become a woman,' the chief said. 'Because you saved her.'

'The nuns and the doctor saved her,' Dan explained. But he knew the part he'd played had been crucial. It seemed the most useful thing he'd done in years.

He'd been about to return to his Land Rover and drive off, when the mother appeared, carrying the child in her arms, sound asleep.

Dan smiled at the sight of her, one arm flopping down, head nodding. Skin as smooth and dark as polished ebony. Somehow he found himself holding her, the mother standing back, laughing at the sight of a white man pretending to be a mother. Dan stiffened, irrationally afraid of dropping her. He wanted to hand her back. But as he moved to unload her, she murmured a protest in her sleep. He let her rest against his chest, her head warm, hard. Little fingers curled around his thumb. He looked down at her long eyelashes resting against her plump cheeks, her perfect bow lips.

'She's beautiful,' he said. As he spoke he felt the lump in his throat. Then there were tears burning behind his eyes.

Now, as he finished wrapping the blanket around his carving, he remembered parting with her. Giving her back to her mother. One moment, there was a weight in his arms. The next, nothing. He remembered his empty hands hanging limp at his sides.

Dan wiped the blade of his knife on his trousers, cleaning off wood dust. Then he tested the edge against the side of his thumb to see if it needed sharpening yet.

'The way you handle that thing would frighten any sensible man.'

Recognising the voice of the Major, Dan put down his wrapped carving, jumped to his feet and saluted.

'Stand easy, Sergeant.' The Major looked bright and energised. 'I have good news. You are to prepare for immediate deployment.'

Dan eyed him steadily. 'What's going on, sir?'

'I've received a directive from General Mobutu. The Simbas have taken the town of Uvira. It's in the north of Kivu Province. He didn't say this straight out, but I get the sense that the National Army barely put up a fight. I don't know what's wrong with them. Anyway, do you know the place?'

'Yes, sir. Uvira is close to the border with Burundi, at the top of Lake Tanganyika.'

'I don't suppose you've ever been there?'

Dan swallowed, his throat contracting. 'Many times. I lived in the south of Kivu, but I did some prospecting up there. I was a miner, back then.'

The Major went suddenly still. Dan had seen him do this before, to avoid showing emotion, whether annoyance or excitement. He liked to keep a cool demeanour. 'I'm delighted to hear that, Sergeant,' he said calmly. 'Local knowledge is pure gold in this place and almost none of us have it.'

Dan looked down at the ground, focusing on his boots. They'd been polished this morning and were gleaming in the sun. Now it was his turn to hide his emotions. When he signed up to fight in the Congo, he knew he'd most likely end up in Kivu. The area had been mentioned in that newspaper article he'd read back in Dar es Salaam. But now that the reality of going there was imminent, he felt uneasy. For a moment, if he could have turned back time, he'd have been in the Mara, far away from all this.

'Burundi is where the Simbas get their supplies, including guns, ammunition. All paid for by their Communist friends. Now that they have Uvira, they've got an open supply chain. And we can't allow that.'

'No, sir.' Dan welcomed Blair's businesslike tone. It was a reminder that they were here to do a job. An important job. Private fears, hopes and dreams were irrelevant.

'We're sending in a unit to retake the town. This is a covert action, coming from behind the front line. We've got to take them by surprise. I'm putting you in charge. You'll have thirty men and a good supply of vehicles, munitions. Everything you need. You will be supported by a unit of the National Army. They are to hold the town, when you've seen off the rebels.

'This is a dangerous mission – make no mistake,' Blair continued. 'You will be quite literally walking into the lion's den.' He paused, as if to allow Dan to express his reservations. When nothing was said, he gave a small smile. 'You're the perfect man for the job. Congratulations, Lieutenant Miller.'

Dan stood to attention again. It seemed the appropriate response for a man who'd just been promoted. The new title was not a surprise. He already knew that when a man was deployed as a mercenary he was given a rank one level higher than any he had held before. And he got an upgrade each time he signed a new contract. At face value the policy sounded unworkable – you could end up with several men entitled to the same very senior rank. The only reason the system could operate, Dan understood, was due to one simple fact: not too many men kept coming back to this job. Either it was so terrible that they didn't want to, or they were no longer alive.

Standing there, in front of the Major, Dan again searched his feelings for any hint of fear or regret. But there was none. He felt only relief. He was going to do something that mattered. He was going to fight for a good cause. And he would most probably not make it through. There would be no need to decide what kind of life to have next.

'From now on your dog tag is not to be taken off for any reason,' Blair instructed. 'I think we can scrape together thirty uniforms.' He smiled grimly. 'We might have to choose the men to match the shirt sizes.'

'Can I have a say in who I take, sir?' Dan asked.

Blair nodded. 'Meet me in my office in one hour and we'll go through the list. I'll have to send your contract after you. But the one thing I need right now is your will.'

'My will?' Dan almost laughed. 'I haven't got one. I don't own anything.'

'There's your life insurance. Twenty thousand dollars. Payable by order of the Congolese government, by a cheque from the Swiss Banking Corporation, Geneva. You have to say who should get it if you die.'

He met Dan's gaze, unflinching. Dan remembered the speech Blair had made to the men a few nights ago, outlining all the ways they might die, or lose their limbs – or other body parts that a man might value even more. Six volunteers had resigned on the spot.

Dan shook his head. 'There's no one.'

He could see Blair recalling that in the recruitment interview Dan had hesitated over the question about whether he had children. The Major touched him lightly on the shoulder. The tiny gesture was laden with sympathy, but when the Major spoke, his manner was brisk.

'It can be a dog's home. The church. I don't care, I just need to have something written down.'

'Yes, sir.'

'See you in an hour.'

As Blair strode away, Dan sat down again on the wooden box. He picked up his carving, resting it on his knee. For a long moment he just stared blankly down at the shrouded form. He could hear the men cheering as the last round of the wrestling match got underway. He told himself to get up – to go and watch the action. Or unwrap the carving and begin working again. But all he could do was bend his head, and bury his face in his hands.

NINE

Nurse Jansen walked ahead of Anna, retracing the path they'd taken the afternoon before. Her flat brown shoes squeaked faintly with each step, and her floral perfume floated back, blending with the smell of disinfectant. As they passed an open doorway, Anna glanced into a large ward lined with two rows of beds. The patients were lying straight and still under neatly tucked sheets. Each of them had a little cabinet at their side, on which stood a single glass and flask of water. Any personal possessions must have been stowed out of sight. There was nothing to jar the atmosphere of peace and rest. White curtains billowed gently as ceiling fans stirred the air. It felt like a safe haven from the world. Anna was glad that Karl was here, even though she knew that there was no hope of him being healed. Murphy had made that very clear. But at least in the Hôpital Européen there were drugs to hold his pain at bay. There were nurses on duty around the clock. And now Anna was here, too. She pictured herself tucking in his sheets, wiping his brow and murmuring words of comfort.

Soon they reached the corridor that led to Karl's private ward. With rising excitement, Anna quickened her step. As they neared the door, an African nurse emerged from the room. She stood still, shutting her eyes and puffing out a long sigh.

Anna frowned in alarm. 'What's wrong?'

'Nothing's wrong,' Jansen said quickly. Catching the nurse's eye, she gestured to Anna. 'This is Mademoiselle Emerson.'

The African woman stared, eyes wide with interest, then smiled politely and walked on along the corridor.

Jansen opened the door just a little way, leaning round it, keeping her body outside the room. 'Good morning, Monsieur Emerson. Your guest is here.' She stood back, ushering Anna past her. 'When you're ready to leave, Mademoiselle, just return to reception.'

Anna hesitated on the threshold, suddenly anxious now this moment had finally come. Glancing behind her, she looked at Jansen. The nurse gave a faint smile of encouragement. The gesture softened her face, making her appear younger. Anna nodded in reply, then stepped into Karl's room.

Morning sun spilled from the open doorway, gleaming on the polished lino floor. First the end of the iron bed came into view, and the mattress with its sheets folded into hospital corners; then she saw a pair of feet, making two small peaks beneath the bedclothes.

Karl Emerson was sitting up, his back supported by a pile of pillows; hands clasped on his lap. The mosquito net had been tied up, out of the way; sunlight fell over his face, making his eyes shine a clear bright blue.

As he met Anna's gaze his whole face lit up. 'My dear Anna.' His hands rose from the bed as if of their own accord, reaching towards her.

Anna smiled, unable to find any words. As she crossed to the bed she felt she was walking in a dream. Every movement seemed drawn out; every second loaded with meaning.

'Let me look at you.' Karl had a faint European accent, which made each word sound out of the ordinary. He took her hands in his, holding them tight. For just a second, Anna wanted to pull away. The hands, clamped onto hers, seemed claw-like, grasping. But she knew that was because they were so thin, the muscle wasted to the bone.

She held her breath as his eyes travelled over her body from head to toe. They were watery, their lids tinged with red, yet his look was piercing. She felt a twist of anxiety, as if – should she fail some test – her father might send her away. When he nodded approvingly, she exhaled with relief.

'Sit next to me.' Letting go of her hands, he patted the mattress beside him. The movement dislodged a newspaper that slid to the floor.

Anna sat there stiffly, her legs dangling over the side of the bed. Behind the citrus tang of aftershave or cologne, she detected a faint sour smell. The hard bones of Karl's leg pressed against her hip. She felt awkward, being close like this to a man of another generation. Mr Williams was the only older man she knew well, and he always kept a professional distance from her; sometimes, in the small space of the office or the lift, they circled one another like dancers following a complicated routine. But this man was her father. All the rules were different.

'How are you feeling?' Anna's voice sounded brighter than she'd planned. She eyed the drip line, still running into the back of Karl's wasted hand, and the array of medicine bottles on the bedside cupboard.

'So much better, now that you are here.' Karl smiled, the lines on his face deepening. 'I've waited so long for this moment.' Anna felt warmth running through her. His words seemed to come straight from his heart.

A comfortable silence settled between them. Anna studied him.

He was freshly shaved and wore new pyjamas, the same paisley pattern she'd seen yesterday, but in different colours. His greying hair had been combed and flattened with water or cream, the wisps banished. He looked younger and healthier than he had while sleeping. Anna felt the lure of his eyes, pulling her gaze into his. It occurred to her that he must have been very attractive in his youth. It wasn't just his physical presence; there was some deeper magnetism about him. When he looked away, Anna felt as if the sun had disappeared behind a cloud.

He shifted in the bed, trying to sit up straighter. Anna jumped to her feet, hurrying to reposition his pillows. She saw how weak he was; he looked like a fledgling struggling towards flight.

'Thank you, my dear.' When he was settled, he shook his head wonderingly. 'There is so much I want to tell you.'

Anna leaned towards him, forgetting her unease. There was so much she wanted to tell him, too – so many questions to ask. She didn't know where to begin.

'You'll want to know all about this dreadful illness that I have,' Karl said.

Anna nodded. It was as good a place to start as any.

'I'm going to die, you know. There's no escaping it. I'm well past hoping for a cure. But it doesn't matter now that you are here. I will leave this world a contented man.'

He fell quiet, then, just watching her. There was a look in his eyes that Anna couldn't read at first. Then the word came to her. Hungry. She felt a surge of joy – that he wanted her there so much. But it was mixed with confusion. If he had been missing her all these years, why had he not contacted her before now? She knew she couldn't ask him this, straight out. Instead she gestured towards the framed photographs. Discussing them could lead the conversation back to the past, where some answers might be found. 'I saw these last night. I came while you were asleep.'

'They've been such a comfort to me,' Karl said. 'Whenever some-one comes in here, I say – look, that's my beautiful daughter.'

Anna turned the phrase over in her head like a precious artifact. *Beautiful daughter.* She looked expectantly at her father, ready to hang on his next words. They would have to take turns to ask ques-tions; there was so much to cover – but she would let him begin. He must want to know how the journey from Australia had been. Whether she liked what she'd seen of Albertville so far. How she'd felt when Murphy got in touch . . .

But Karl was pointing towards his bedside cupboard. 'Look in there, Anna.' Reaching inside, she found a thick leather-bound folio tied with black ribbon. Karl motioned for her to lay it in his lap. 'There's no time to waste.'

Anna moved further up the mattress, eager to see what he had to show her. Embossed in gold on the front of the folio was an image of two leopards. She recognised them from the photograph. The stone guardians of Leopard Hall.

'You probably know all about this, from Marilyn.' Karl patted the folio. 'It's my obsession, I admit that.'

Anna shook her head, mystified. 'Mum's never said very much about you. She . . .'

'Hates me,' Karl finished for her. He shook his head. 'After all these years . . . But then, she was never one to let go and move on. Anyway – it doesn't matter.' He waved one hand, dismissing the memory of his ex-wife. Anna felt a quiver of trepidation, as if Marilyn might be able to feel the affront, far away in Australia, and would somehow hold her daughter accountable.

Karl fumbled with the ribbon ties, one hand tethered awkwardly to the drip line. His breathing, Anna noticed, was laboured. She hoped the excitement of her arrival was not too much for him. Finally, he pulled out a thick sheaf of papers. Anna glimpsed the top page, which was covered in short lines of type. It looked like some kind of list. A very long one, with lots of detail.

'This is the full catalogue of my collection.' Karl flipped through the pages. 'Well, technically, it's no longer mine. It now belongs to the Karl Emerson Trust. The most valuable pieces are already in London. There are the three Picassos.' He paused, as if absorbing his own words. 'Experts agree, they are the finest examples of his African period. And then, I have the actual masks that inspired them, along with some of the oldest *nkisi* figures on record. There are two hundred and thirty items altogether. It's the world's most complete collection of the art of the Congo.'

Anna looked at him in confusion. How could this be the most important thing for them to talk about, in this moment when they'd just met?

'I'm glad you haven't married, and lost your name,' Karl commented. 'It's much better that you are an Emerson. Everyone will know you are my daughter.'

'What do you mean, "everyone"?' Anna asked.

Karl just smiled, as if at a bright secret. 'It's not only the pieces themselves that are of such interest. It's the provenance. There's a whole archive of information about them. Village. Tribe. Even the name of the artist, in some cases.' He looked up, expectantly.

Anna managed to smile. 'That's very impressive.' She was beginning to wonder if Karl's illness was affecting his thinking. He was probably taking strong medicine for pain. Or maybe he just needed to get this business about his precious collection out of the way – then they'd get to know one another.

'About half of the works are still at Leopard Hall,' Karl contin-ued. 'My health let me down before I'd packed it all up.' He shook his head. 'I should have got out of the Congo four years ago, when the Belgians handed the place over – leaving it to be run by a pack of savages. But I didn't want to leave my home. Why should I? My father built that place from nothing.' His voice trembled with outrage. 'But now it's clear, even to me. There's no hope for this godforsaken place any more. They've got rebels running wild over half the country. The so-called Simbas.' He spat out the name. 'Animals in human form – though they've got a cheek, taking the name of a noble beast like a lion. The government can't control them. It's plain as day, Anna. The Congo is finished.'

Movement in the doorway caught Anna's eye. The African nurse was hovering there. Anna wondered if she'd overheard Karl's last words.

'Excuse me, Monsieur,' the nurse said tentatively.

Karl looked up. 'What do you want now?'

'I left my clipboard,' she said.

'Find it and get out.' Karl spoke carelessly, as if he didn't even notice he was being rude.

Anna looked away, unsure how to react. Her father was sick, but that was no excuse to treat someone like that. The nurse retrieved her clipboard from the top of the dresser and made a hasty departure.

Karl kept on talking. 'I want you to understand, Anna, how important this collection is. When Picasso first saw a Congolese mask at a Paris exhibition, he said it changed how he saw the world. He understood something new about painting. Work like this . . .' He patted the folio again. 'It shaped the course of modern art.'

Karl continued, but Anna scarcely heard what he said. She

stared down at a pair of slippers set beside the bed. She was surprised to see that they were leopard print. Not made of patterned fabric or even fake fur, but cut from the hide of a real animal. Leopardskin slippers for the master of Leopard Hall. It occurred to Anna that the real reason Marilyn despised leopard print quite possibly had nothing to do with it being 'common'. It just reminded her of her ex-husband and her old home.

Karl was now reading out the names of items from his list, explaining how significant they were. He didn't seem to notice whether Anna was interested. Or perhaps he didn't care. As Anna looked up, one of Marilyn's sayings came to mind. *A leopard doesn't change its spots.*

At last Karl returned the papers to the folio and began retying the ribbons. 'A lot of work has been done already. The university has a space ready, and a curator. You will be the figurehead – the face, and the name, to go with the endowment. Your title will be Executive Chair of the Trust. You'll need to be based in London, of course.'

Anna looked up, her lips parting in shock.

'I know,' Karl said. 'You can't believe it! But you must. Everything about your life is about to change.' He reached over to lay his hand on her arm. 'Anna, I'm handing over my life's work to you. This is why you are here.'

Anna shook her head slowly. She lowered her gaze, refusing to meet his eyes. Disappointment seeped through her, forming a lump in her throat. He hadn't invited her here because he'd discovered a long-buried love for his daughter. He just wanted to use her, for his own ends. She had a flash image of Marilyn's triumphant face.

'You don't need to thank me,' Karl said. 'You are my daughter. My only child. This is your birthright.'

Anna stood up, turning her back on him, and walked to the far end of the room. She folded her arms over her chest as if she could protect her heart. She knew Karl was waiting for a response, but didn't trust herself to speak. Behind her, she could hear the sound of his breathing, phlegm rattling in his throat. He began coughing, one round leading to a whole bout that went on and on. She felt an impulse to run out of the room – away from the gasping noises he was making, and away from the sight of him sitting there with his precious folio in his lap. She tried focusing on the sound of the ceiling fan, creaking away overhead. It took her a few moments to realise that Karl had fallen quiet. In sudden alarm she turned to find that he'd collapsed against his pillows, head tipped back, eyelids fluttering. A low moan escaped from his blue-tinged lips.

The next moments passed in a blur. Anna rushed into the corridor, calling for a nurse. The Matron must have been nearby; she strode into the ward and wheeled an oxygen cylinder from the corner of the room. When she'd clamped a clear plastic mask over Karl's face she took his wrist, her head bent over the watch pinned onto her chest.

'Is he okay?' The anger and disappointment Anna had felt were swept aside, replaced by an icy fear that Karl might die, right now, in front of her. There would be no time to move on past this unsatisfying start. The reunion with her father would be over, before it had even begun.

'Did you say something to upset him?' the Matron asked. There was an accusing look in her eye, as if she suspected Anna of deliberately causing trouble.

'No,' Anna answered. 'I've hardly said anything.'

'He's a very ill man, you know.' She smoothed the sheets, tucking them in tightly as if to make sure he stayed still.

'Do I have to go?'

The Matron pursed her lips. 'I suppose you can sit here, but don't disturb him. He needs to rest.'

Anna waited for the Matron to leave, before pulling over a chair. She sat down close to the bed. Karl lay there, eyes closed, his bony chest rising and falling as he strained to breathe. She wanted to let him know that she was here. Tentatively, she touched his hand. He gave no response. She stroked his mottled skin with her fingers.

Watching his face, half hidden by the mask, she tried to forget all that had been said this morning – imagining instead the conversations she'd dreamed they would have. She saw her father's blue eyes alight with interest as she talked about her beautiful apartment, her work and Mr Williams. How she still dreamed of taking up horse riding and planned to get a dog one day. She might even tell him about Gregory. Maybe Karl would understand her decision to end the engagement, even though Anna was confused herself. He would give wise advice. He would be loving and kind.

Lost in her thoughts, she barely noticed the passing of time. When she remembered to check her watch, she found she was almost due to meet Eliza out in the car park.

'Goodbye,' she said softly. Leaning over Karl, breathing in his smell, she felt an urge to rest her head on his chest and feel his beating heart. 'I'll come back in the morning.'

Anna pushed open the front doors of the hospital and stepped out into the midday heat. She felt the curious eyes of the nurses following her. They were ones she hadn't seen before but they obviously knew who she was. When she'd entered the foyer, silence had fallen as if she'd interrupted a conversation she was not meant to hear. She guessed the hospital staff didn't like her father. They thought he was rude and demanding and they probably felt sorry for Anna, being his daughter. As she'd passed under their gaze, she'd held her head high.

By the time she'd located the Jaguar, parked in a patch of shade, the optimism she'd felt back in the ward was already slipping away. She struggled to hide her feelings as she approached the car. When she climbed inside, she was able to give Eliza a bright smile, but she did not trust herself to speak.

They drove in silence for a time. Anna stared ahead. The luxurious folds of Eliza's skirt were a yellow blur in the corner of her eye. Eliza had dressed elaborately again this morning, presumably for Randall's benefit. But today there was no smell of cigar smoke lingering in the car. Anna distracted herself by wondering if the pair had spent their time together on the balcony of the Hôtel Albertville.

Eliza finally broke the quiet. 'So . . . how did it go?'

Anna prepared her words. *It was wonderful. Just to be together, after all these years . . .* But to her dismay, her eyes filled with tears. When she tried to speak, a sob broke from her lips. The tears overflowed, running down her cheeks.

Eliza nodded, as if able to guess how the visit had turned out. 'Don't say anything. Let's just get home. We could both do with a stiff drink.'

In the dim sitting room, Anna sat in a wing-backed armchair, the waxy leaves of a huge rubber plant brushing her shoulder. She had a cigarette in her hand. Eliza half lay on the couch, her high heels kicked off, bare feet tucked under her skirt.

Eliza picked up her drink, ice chinking against the glass, and took a long swallow. 'Do you want to talk about it? You don't have to.'

Tentatively Anna started to describe her encounter with her father. Once she'd begun, the words flowed out in a stream. She replayed all that he had said to her – and not said. Eliza listened without comment, just nodding her head now and then.

Finally, Anna fell quiet. She waited for Eliza to offer words of comfort, or perhaps to question her experience and offer another perspective.

Eliza seemed to be studying the carpet. Then she sighed. 'Perhaps I should have warned you, but I thought you needed to form your own opinion. The truth is, I don't like Karl much. If he was here at the house, I stayed away. I always found him . . .' She searched for the words. 'Let's just say he is not well-liked by people.'

'The Rousseaus are his friends.' Anna heard a defensive tone in her voice.

Eliza shook her head. 'They just feel sorry for him. Their parents were neighbours – I believe that's the connection.' She fished her slice of lemon from her drink and sucked it. 'From what I've seen of him, he's one of the most self-absorbed men I've ever met. Perhaps he's lived too long on his own, and learned to think only of himself. But then, what comes first, the cart or the horse? Maybe he's alone because he's . . . not a very nice person.'

Anna felt a knot of pain in her chest. Marilyn had been right. She should not have come here to Albertville. She gulped her drink, tasting a strong tang of gin. She thought of Mr Williams and his bottles of whisky, always ready to be brought out in an emergency. Following his example, she took another swig. She'd not eaten since breakfast and she could feel the alcohol going straight to her head.

'This is worse than having no father.' The statement came out blunt and shocking. Anna bit her lip.

'Lots of people wish they could have chosen the kind of father they got,' Eliza responded. Her words were businesslike but her expression was kind. 'Whatever Karl's like, you're still his daughter. Maybe you'll find a side of him that others haven't seen. Maybe . . .' Her voice trailed off, as if she'd lost faith in what she was saying. She drained her glass, crunching her ice, then stood up. 'Would you like to see my studio? I could show you my darkroom. I've got some printing to do.'

Anna understood Eliza was making an effort to distract her. The older woman sounded like a mother trying to divert her child's interest from something they could not have. 'I'd like that.'

'Just wait here,' Eliza said. 'I'll be back in a minute.'

When she was alone, Anna rested her head against the back of her armchair, letting the overhead fan play its breeze over her face. She felt suddenly exhausted, and was almost asleep when Eliza reappeared.

For a second, Anna didn't recognise her. She'd changed into a simple shift dress of blue linen. Her make-up had been scrubbed off, leaving her skin shiny and pink. Her hair was pulled back into a low ponytail. From a distance she looked childlike, as if she'd emerged, raw and vulnerable, from a cocoon of sophistication. As she came closer, the lines around her eyes and mouth could be seen. But it was not just age that shadowed her face, Anna realised. She looked worried, even upset.

Anna remembered the comment Eliza had made before driving off from the hospital: that they both needed a stiff drink. It occurred to Anna that maybe Randall was leaving town and Eliza was bracing herself for another separation. Perhaps Eliza needed a diversion as much as Anna did.

A red glow lit the small room, picking up rows of shelves, two benches and the bulky shape of an enlarger. There was a line of stainless-steel sinks over which hung strips of film negatives looking like washing pegged up to dry. The pungent smell of chemicals tainted the air.

Eliza leaned over a plastic tray, studying a sheet of photographic paper that floated in the bath of developer. She was wearing rubber gloves and a large apron. Using a pair of wooden tweezers, she moved the paper from side to side, swishing the chemicals over its surface.

'This is fast paper,' she commented. 'I'm after a grainy look, with high contrast.'

Peering over her shoulder, Anna waited for the ghost of an image to appear on the paper. Eliza had already exposed and printed half-a-dozen pictures since she'd brought Anna in here. They were all of exotic birds and flowers. Even in black and white they looked full of life and colour. Anna felt she could watch the developing process all day. What began as a hazy impression of shape and form grew steadily into a clear picture. It was like forgetting a dream, in reverse.

This next photograph was of an animal Anna had never seen before. It was like a delicately formed horse with a long neck and over-sized ears. What made the animal unusual were the black-and-white stripes that stood out on its haunches and upper legs. The rest of the body was a plain dark shade, except that below the knees the coat was pure white, looking like pairs of long socks. The overall impression was of a creature made up of parts that – while beautiful in themselves – didn't look quite right as a whole.

'It's a forest giraffe. An okapi,' Eliza said. 'I took this picture in the Ituri Forest. They're rare and very shy. I had to wait three weeks to get this shot.'

Anna wondered if there were lodges in the forest, where game hunters – like the ones she'd seen in the Hollywood films about safaris – stayed. She couldn't imagine Eliza going without her luxuries.

'I wouldn't have found her without the Bambuti,' Eliza continued. 'They're one of the pygmy tribes. They know everything about the forest. The old chief invited me to stay with them in their camp.' She smiled. 'It was so peaceful there.'

Eliza lifted the paper from the bath, holding it up. As she studied it critically, she stretched out one hand, feeling the air for something that was not there. 'Ah – wrong studio.' She shook her head. 'It drives me mad, I planned for them all to be the same but somehow that hasn't happened.'

'You have more than one studio?'

'There's one in each of the houses. I need to be able to work wherever I am.'

Anna thought of the framed pictures of animals, plants, trees and landscapes she'd seen out in the hallway. They were very striking with their unusual grainy look, and the content was extraordinary; Eliza obviously spent her time seeking out rare and interesting subjects. She took her photography seriously, as if it really were her 'work' – even though she didn't need to earn money. It occurred to Anna that Eliza could be a world-famous wildlife photographer whose reputation she should have heard of. She tried to think of a safe way to find out. 'Do you have lots of exhibitions?'

'I sell to people who approach me. Some really love the pictures.

Others just buy my work because of the Lindenbaum name.' There was no hint of wounded ego in Eliza's voice as she said this. She was so confident, Anna realised, that even in this creative arena she was not vulnerable. 'But that's not why I do it. I love the challenge of waiting for the perfect shot. When I look at it later I know it's something I've done myself.'

Anna nodded. It must be hard for Eliza, she understood, to find something she valued that money could not buy.

'And it gives me an excuse to roam all over the country without anyone asking questions.' Eliza laughed, as if she'd made a joke. Then she looked serious. 'Of course, it's not so easy now.'

'Because of the rebellion?'

'Yes. It's changed everything. I can usually get a travel permit from the government, as long as I'm not going anywhere near rebel-held territory. But it takes some arranging. And then, the soldiers on the ground don't necessarily accept it. There is room for all kinds of bother.'

Eliza slid another piece of paper into the developing bath and began moving it with her tweezers.

'Where did I put that timer?' she murmured, turning round to the bench.

As the chemicals swirled over the white rectangle, Anna stared in surprise at the image that began to form. Instead of an animal, bird or flower, there was a line of people. African men and one white woman . . .

Behind her, she heard Eliza catch her breath – then the picture was snatched from the bath. In the moment before it vanished in the red-tinted gloom, Anna registered that the men were in army camouflage uniforms, with metal helmets. And the woman in their midst was Eliza.

'I don't need that one.' Eliza turned to Anna, stripping off her gloves. 'That will do for today.'

Anna was woken from sleep by the sound of the windows rattling in their casements. A branch beat a staccato rhythm against the glass. She sat up, staring into the darkness. It sounded as if there were a wild animal outside, trying to break in. She reminded herself of what Eliza had said about the Avenue of Storms: that strong winds blew up over the lake. It was nothing unusual. Lying down again, she tried to fall back to sleep.

The noise of the wind was inescapable, even if she put her head under the pillow. Before long, she was wide awake. She found herself thinking about her visit to Karl – his obsession with his collection, and the plan he'd laid out for her. She tried to separate her disappointment about his priorities from the reality of what he was offering her. A new life in London. She pictured herself shopping in the King's Road – strolling into Bazaar to buy the latest Mary Quant fashions. Going to concerts and seeing The Beatles or The Rolling Stones live on stage. She'd spend her time visiting galleries and museums; dining in famous restaurants. Karl had made it sound as if people would be interested in her, because of the collection. She'd be invited to parties and openings. As she tried to picture it all, fear spiked up through her excitement. How would she make herself into the kind of person who would fit in with these Londoners? What would they expect of her? She was a secretary, and Melbourne was her home. Did she even want to change her life like that?

The fury of the winds outside mirrored the turmoil of her thoughts. She kicked off her sheets as if they were part of the future she was being offered. The change Karl was proposing for her was too huge for her even to imagine. But how could she just walk away? If she didn't take up the chance to be Karl Emerson's daughter, she might regret it forever. Lying there on the bed, she could feel tension invading her body. She wished Murphy had not been able to find her – that she'd never come to Africa. But then, she wasn't even sure of that, either.

She tried shifting her attention – thinking back to being in the darkroom this afternoon, and the photograph Eliza hadn't wanted her to see. Who were those soldiers? They looked as if they'd just come from the battlefield, in their camouflage fatigues and metal helmets. Why on earth was Eliza with them?

Anna sat up, swinging her feet to the floor. These thoughts weren't going to help send her back to sleep; there were no answers to any of the questions. She decided to try reading the novel she'd brought for the aeroplane trip. It was on the mantelpiece along with the large collection of medicines she'd lined up there this afternoon when she unpacked her suitcase. She'd put all her clothes, toiletries and shoes away in the empty wardrobe and chest of drawers. As she'd unfolded garments, draping them over coathangers or laying them in drawers fragrant with dried cloves and lavender, she wondered if it was worth making the effort. She wasn't sure she would be staying very long. If Karl kept focusing on his plans for her, without showing any interest in her life, or who she even was as a person, she didn't think she would be able to bear being around him. But she had kept on unpacking, steadily, carefully. It began to feel like a ritual, a bargain with some greater force. If Anna emptied her suitcase and put every last item away, the gesture of belief would help ensure that her encounter with Karl the next morning would take a new direction.

Fumbling for the switch to the lamp, she found her slippers and put them on. She didn't want to go barefoot, even just across to the mantelpiece. There were all sorts of dangerous insects in the Congo, she knew. Marilyn had told her about them. They came in from the forest, invading the houses. Spiders as big as your hand. Centipedes. Scorpions. There might even be snakes.

She was about to return to the bed with her book when an extra loud gust made the windows rattle even harder. She crossed to the window, drawn to find out what kind of madness was going on outside.

She stood back from the window, as if the wind might reach in through the glass and sweep her away. At first, the lake appeared as a vast black mass, like a hole in the landscape. But when she looked more closely she could see white-capped waves breaking over the surface. The trees and rooftops were only just discernible against the deeper darkness. She looked down at the garden below, where a light near the French windows cast a silver sheen over the lawn. Petals stripped from the garden beds hurtled past. The shrubs thrashed in a frenzy. The storm really was like a wild animal, its presence evident only in the havoc it created. She pictured it rushing up the Avenue of Storms, bending the palm trees. Dragging at the ships tied up at the wharf. It was hard to imagine that the wind would eventually die down; the lake would become calm again. In the same way, Anna told herself, the turmoil she felt would pass. A path ahead would become clear. She remembered the old nun she'd met on the aeroplane. Sister Emilia. She had seemed certain that Anna had made the right decision in coming to the Congo to see her father. As Anna stood there, gazing down from the window, she remembered the words the nun had said. They'd sounded wise and true. *Something good will come from all this. I am sure of it.*

Anna watched the hammock, slung between two trees, swinging violently from side to side. She saw a broken branch do cartwheels across the lawn. Then something else caught her eye. One of the French windows was opening. A figure dressed in white stepped out into the storm. Anna leaned forward, pressing her forehead to the glass. It took only a second for her to identify Eliza. She strode across the lawn to the shrubbery, her nightgown flowing out behind her, long hair streaming back from her face. In her hand she held what looked like an envelope.

As if drawn out of the shadows by Eliza's approach, a black shape emerged from the bushes, indistinct at first, then forming the outline of a man. His face and hands were as dark as his clothing. The lamplight glinted on the barrel of a gun slung over his shoulder.

Eliza clasped the envelope against her chest, then lifted it to her lips, planting a kiss. Anna watched, transfixed, as Eliza handed it to the armed man. The white shape disappeared from view. Then the man straightened up, giving Eliza a smart salute, before backing away into the shadows. Eliza stood still, looking at the place where he had been.

Anna hurried to turn off her lamp, in case Eliza noticed the glow from above. When she returned to the window, the garden was deserted, left to the chaos of the storm. The next moment the light by the downstairs entrance went out. Anna stayed at the window, clutching the sill, staring into the night.

TEN

Anna walked in slow circles around the hospital foyer. The reception desk was deserted and she was waiting for a nurse to appear so she could let them know she was here to visit her father. She liked the confident sound of her high heels on the terrazzo floor. She'd dressed up for this meeting in her smartest outfit, and spent extra time on her hair and make-up. She was hoping to distract Karl from his folio, drawing attention to herself instead.

As she passed the desk her eye was caught by a gleam of sunlight reflected on the gold lettering of the memorial plaque. The sight of the Lindenbaum name made her falter mid-step. She had been trying not to think about Eliza, but the questions she'd put aside flooded back. There was now a whole new set, on top of the ones prompted by the photograph in the darkroom. Why had Eliza been out in the storm last night, meeting a man in black who was carrying a gun? Why had he saluted her? And what was the secrecy surrounding the envelope she'd handed over? Whatever it contained was obviously personal, romantic: she'd kissed it before letting it go. But the American officer, Randall, was her boyfriend and she'd only just seen him. It made no sense. And Anna couldn't help thinking the nighttime meeting was connected in some way with the photograph. The speculations just went round and round in her head.

Eliza hadn't appeared for breakfast in the morning, so Anna had had no chance to talk to her – not that she'd have asked her any direct questions anyway. Marilyn had drummed into her daughter the importance of people knowing how to mind their own business. In some ways it had been easier for Anna to find herself alone at the dining table; she didn't have to struggle to keep her curiosity at bay.

As Magadi poured coffee from a silver pot, he explained that Eliza had gone out to take some photographs. She'd left early, as soon as the wind had died down. The telephones weren't working, apparently – the storm must have brought down a tree somewhere – but she had said she would arrange for a taxi driver to come to the house and take Anna to visit her father.

A car had appeared as promised – an old Renault with doors of different colours that looked out of place parked in the space usually occupied by the Jaguar. Anna had climbed in cautiously, sitting on a seat with the springs exposed. Black smoke trailed behind the car as it rattled along the road into the town. Struggling up the Avenue of Storms, the engine revved loudly as if the gears were not functioning properly. Even with the slow trip, Anna had arrived at the hospital ten minutes before visiting hours started. Now, as she paced steadily up and down, she checked the time on her watch. She'd been here over half an hour – and it had felt much longer than that. It came to her, suddenly, that Eliza would not be standing here meekly like this, just waiting. After hesitating for a second, she turned on her heels and set off up the corridor on her own.

Hurrying past the shared ward, she noticed one of the patients sitting up in bed. The young woman bent her head over a breakfast tray as she nibbled at a triangle of toast. The only clue as to why she was here was a bandage on her left arm. It looked so neat and white it was hard to imagine that a wound of some kind lay beneath.

Anna was just nearing the door to Karl's ward when she heard hasty footsteps behind her.

'Mademoiselle Emerson!'

Anna recognised Nurse Jansen's voice but didn't turn around.

'Please wait!' the nurse called out. 'You can't go in there.'

Anna opened the door. It was visiting time; she was entitled to be here, even if she had come without an escort. Two steps into the room, she stopped still, staring at the bed. The green sheet was pulled up, completely covering Karl's body – even his face was hidden. For a second, she made no sense of what she saw. Then shock flashed through her like an electric current.

Jansen came up behind her. 'I'm so sorry. We couldn't phone you. The lines are out of order.'

Anna walked over to the bed. Her legs were weak, her heart pounding. The shrouded figure was completely still, the chest no longer rising and falling. The drip line hung loose, draping the floor.

'We've just sent a driver with a message.'

Anna turned round, shaking her head in confusion. 'What happened?'

Jansen stood there, biting her lips, her hands clasped together. She seemed unsure how to respond to the young woman in front of her. In the end, she took a matter-of-fact tone. 'He passed away during the night. At two o'clock he appeared to be fine but when the changeover took place at six, he had gone.'

'But he seemed all right yesterday. He got overtired, but I didn't think he was in danger.'

'Neither did we,' Jansen said. 'He had that turn, but he recovered. He ate his dinner last night. I fed him myself.' Distress broke through her professional facade. 'You poor girl – seeing him like this, with no warning. They should have stopped you in reception. I'm just so sorry.'

Anna turned back to the bed. Karl was there, under the sheet, she told herself. He was dead. But it didn't feel real. She jumped at the touch of Jansen's hand coming to rest on her shoulder.

'I have seen this happen before. Sometimes a patient who is terminally ill chooses the time when they will depart.' The nurse's voice was gentle, but held an edge of certainty. 'Your father was waiting for you to arrive, and then you came. It brought him some peace. He was ready to go.'

Anna shook her head. How could he be ready to go? Their time together had only just begun.

'Do you want to sit with him?'

Instead of answering, Anna pulled the chair back to its place beside the bed and sat down.

'There's a nurse's call button over here, if you need anything.' Jansen pointed to a panel on the wall.

Anna nodded without looking away from the bed. She was aware of the nurse hovering as if reluctant to leave her alone.

'We didn't get the priest for your father,' Jansen added. 'He wrote "atheist" on his form. But we do have a chapel if you want to pray.'

'Pray?' Anna had the mad thought that there was still some way for Karl to be saved.

'For his soul,' Jansen said gently. 'Who knows, maybe he turned to God at the end.'

As the nurse left the room Anna bent her head, closing her eyes. She felt numb with shock. She could feel the deep stillness of the body in front of her. It seemed to spread into the room, making it hard for her to breathe.

Her hands clenched, futile. He was gone. It was all over. The long journey she had made ended here.

When the taxi reached the house, Magadi was waiting outside. Anna could tell by the look on his face that he already knew what had happened. He helped her climb out of the taxi, steadying her as she almost tripped.

While he paid the driver, Anna stood on the steps, hugging Karl's folio to her chest. She'd taken it from the cupboard before leaving the hospital. She had picked up the leopardskin slippers as well. She wasn't even sure why she'd done this. It just felt better than leaving them behind on the floor. Jansen had promised that the framed photographs and all Karl's other possessions would be sent to the Lindenbaum residence.

As the taxi drove away Magadi came to stand in front of her. 'I am sorry for your pain,' he said simply.

'Thank you.'

'Mademoiselle Eliza has not yet returned.' Magadi guided Anna inside, then led her upstairs. 'I will tell her the news as soon as she arrives.'

He lingered in the doorway to her room, looking unsure – as Jansen had been – whether to leave her alone. 'Can I do something for you?'

Anna had the feeling he was offering more than just the option of a drink or perhaps some clean handkerchiefs. She saw how the years had worn deep lines into his skin. Looking into his dark eyes she sensed a time-earned wisdom.

'I don't know . . .' Anna swallowed a lump in her throat. 'It's just that . . .' She gazed up at the ceiling. A spider was bundling up an insect in its web, rolling it over and over. 'I should be sad for him. But all I can think of is me. I came here to get to know him. And now I've got nothing to take away.'

She watched Magadi's face as he took in her callous words. He didn't seem shocked by her selfishness. Of course, he knew Karl Emerson: the man had often stayed here with the Rousseaus. No doubt Magadi had the same poor opinion of him as everyone else. Perhaps he understood, then, the true nature of Anna's loss. She would never be able to make sense of her history with Karl. She would never have the chance to find out if there was another side to him. Her dream of having a father to love and admire had been shattered.

Magadi's figure became blurred as tears filled her eyes. She bent her head, covering her face with her hands.

'Do not hide your tears.' The man's voice came to her as if from far away. 'A child has only one father.'

Anna sat on her bed, staring down at the insignia on the folio and then at the spotted slippers she'd placed on the floor at her feet. Her body felt frozen but her thoughts paced restlessly. She wondered what was going to happen now. Would she have to arrange a funeral? And what about the art collection? The Emerson Trust? Nurse Jansen, trying to be helpful, had told Anna as she was leaving that there was a lawyer who handled Monsieur Emerson's affairs. He paid the hospital bills and sent a bunch of flowers for the room each week. The hospital would contact him as soon as the phone lines were working again. Jansen gave Anna the lawyer's phone number, in case she had any questions to ask. Anna had eyed her in silence. She had lots of questions to ask, but she doubted this lawyer would be able to answer any of them.

Standing up, Anna crossed to the window. She undid the catch and swung it open. Hot air rushed in, carrying a muddy, leafy smell – the aftermath of the storm. She looked out over the lake, where fishing boats floated on water that was now smooth as glass. She let the image fill her mind, driving out thoughts of the hospital with its hushed corridors, the shrouded body on the bed . . . In the far distance, way across the lake, she could see the blurry shape of land. It was a completely different country, she knew. She'd seen it marked on a map in Eliza's sitting room. The name *Tanganyika* had been crossed out with blue ink, replaced with *Tanzania*. The territory stretched from the edge of the lake to the east coast of Africa.

And far away, across the vast Indian Ocean, was Australia. Melbourne.

Anna thought of her flat, empty and quiet; a layer of dust gathering on the furniture. She pictured her desk in the office, with a temporary secretary sitting at her typewriter. She hoped Mr Williams was being looked after properly, although not so well that he wasn't looking forward to her return. She thought of the secretaries meeting for their last-Friday-of-the-month drink after work. Had she been missed, she wondered? Or had the space she'd once filled just closed up behind her? The questions seemed so simple, and her daily life predictable and stable, compared with what surrounded her here.

She turned away from the window, glancing at her possessions spread around the room. Suddenly she wanted nothing more than to put everything back in her suitcase and return to her own world as soon as possible.

*

A zebra tore at a rose bush, pulling back rubbery lips to avoid the thorns before it plucked a pink flower with its teeth. Anna wondered if she should shoo it away, but then decided to let it be. She was sitting on the front steps of the house, and the effort of getting to her feet felt too much: the knowledge of Karl's death seemed to have settled in her body like lead. She gazed along the driveway with bleary eyes, willing the Jaguar to appear. She longed for Eliza to be here. The urgency she felt reminded her of how, as a little girl, she would run to find her mother when something had gone wrong. It made no difference how Marilyn responded; just the act of sharing her emotions brought relief. Even though Eliza didn't like Karl, Anna felt sure she'd be sympathetic, as she had been the day before. It was still only mid-morning, but Anna wouldn't be surprised if she ordered strong cocktails for them both.

At last, the Jaguar appeared, a white shape gliding along the driveway. As the car came to a halt at the bottom of the steps, the sun glinted on the emblem mounted on the bonnet – the sleek shape of the big cat poised, ready to pounce. Eliza emerged from the driver's side, holding a gift-wrapped box in her hand.

As she approached Anna, she took off her sunglasses and raised her eyebrows questioningly.

'Karl's dead,' Anna said. 'I'm going home.'

Her voice was steady, but as soon as the words were out, tears welled in her eyes. All the optimism she'd felt about going home, putting the whole episode in the Congo behind her, evaporated. She was left stranded in a wasteland of pain and disappointment.

Eliza hurried up to her, dropping the gift onto the steps, then pushing it aside with the pointed toe of her shoe. She spread her arms, bangles jingling as they gathered at her wrists. 'Come here.'

As Eliza drew her into an embrace, Anna buried her face against the older woman's chest, breathing in a musky perfume and the aroma of cigar smoke. She wrapped her arms around Eliza's back, holding her slender form close. Eliza hugged her more tightly. Even in the midst of her distress Anna felt a flicker of surprise. As she clasped Eliza, she had the sense that Eliza was clinging to her as well.

When Anna's tears finally eased, she pulled back. Eliza wiped her face with a clean linen handkerchief. When it was soaked, she produced another from her handbag, as if to signal that there was no need to stem the tears. Her own eyes were wet, mascara smudging her cheeks.

Leaving the gift behind on the ground, Eliza walked Anna inside, leading her to the sitting room. She called Magadi and requested he serve whisky and ice.

'And bring one of the cats,' she said. 'Whoever you can find.'

Within a few minutes Magadi delivered a large Siamese, creamy white with dark legs, tail and face. He held it out like an offering that could have been served on a tray. Anna had seen the cat before, prowling in the garden, looking half-wild. Now the creature was drowsy with sleep.

'This is Zelda.' Eliza placed her in Anna's lap. The cat settled there, closing her blue eyes, resting her chin on her paws.

Anna thought Eliza was going to leave her now – with the cat a replacement for her comforting presence. She probably had work to do in her darkroom: films to develop or pictures to print. Instead, Eliza just sat there, ice clinking as she sipped from her glass. The steady rhythm of Zelda's purring seemed to wrap itself around the two women, drawing them together. The soft tick of a carriage clock on the mantelpiece only added to the atmosphere of peace and closeness. It was hard for Anna to believe that she and Eliza had only known one another for a few days – and that very soon, they would say their last goodbyes.

ELEVEN

In the outdoor kitchen at Lemba Base an old woman, her back bent with age, poked sticks of firewood under a sooty cauldron. The traditional cloth she wore wrapped around her body was black, matching the colour of her skin. When the fire was burning high she picked up a wooden paddle and stirred the bubbling stew, releasing tendrils of steam into the air.

Several younger women were sitting on low stools just out of reach of the drifting smoke. They were peeling potatoes and onions. In contrast to the cook, they wore brightly printed cloths. One had a baby tied onto her back; its head bobbed when she moved. As they worked, there was a constant flow of conversation, broken by intermittent bursts of laughter.

Dan approached the group from the direction of the Quartermaster's store. He'd just been issued his uniform and the stiff new cloth of his shirt and trousers rubbed against his skin. The garments were not so different to his hunting clothes, but now he had a dark-red beret instead of a brimmed hat.

'You'll need your regimental badge,' Blair had advised him. He had pointed to his own beret where two silver emblems indicated his past service. There was the Maltese Cross worn by the Royal Green Jackets; the other one Dan didn't recognise.

'I lost mine years ago,' Dan had responded.

Blair produced a box from his desk drawer, tipping out a pile of tarnished badges. 'King's African Rifles, wasn't it?' Before long he found what he was looking for. Dan stared at the brass emblem. How many times had he rubbed metal polish into the familiar contours of the bugle horn topped by the King's crown?

'It's best if people know your credentials up front,' Blair had said, and Dan had to agree – though he didn't like the idea of wearing the badge of an unknown soldier, possibly collected from the battlefield.

As he reached the kitchen, Dan greeted the women. *'Habari ya kazi?'* How is your work?

They all stopped what they were doing, staring at him in surprise. Dan didn't know if it was because an officer in a smart uniform had bothered to greet them, or if it was that he spoke in Swahili.

The cook replied for them all, a delighted grin on her face. *'Nzuri sana, Bwana. Na wewe?'*

'Very good, also,' Dan replied, returning the smile.

He stopped by the stove – his body arranging itself automatically, hands behind his back in the stand easy position. As he stared into the fire, he was aware of the old woman at work beside him. Her movements had the ease and economy of someone who'd been doing the same tasks for a lifetime. He wondered if she could see past his steady demeanour, detecting his anxiety. He couldn't remember when he'd last felt as pressured as he did now. In his hand he held a provisional list of the men he'd chosen for his unit. They were just typed names at the moment, with file notes to go with them. But over the days and weeks ahead, Dan knew how real the men would become to him. He'd find out all their strengths and failings. He'd hold their lives in his hands. As a professional hunter, this responsibility wasn't foreign to him. Wrong advice or inadequate supervision could result in the death of a client. But Dan had always felt confident leading his parties. On a hunting safari he knew exactly what he was taking on – whether the target was a lion, elephant, crocodile; whether the game was moving in open country, thicket or swamp. But this situation was very different. There were so many unknowns. The maps Blair had shown him contained large blank zones. There was no information about the state of the road to Uvira. The locations of rebel strongholds were unclear. The whole idea of a front line didn't appear to apply.

'It's not going to be easy,' Blair had admitted during their first briefing meeting. 'That's why I've chosen you.'

Dan guessed the Major wanted to encourage him with praise, but it had the opposite effect. He was looking forward to meeting his second-in-command, and sharing the heavy load.

Second Lieutenant Hardy was due to arrive from Johannesburg tomorrow, along with a bunch of new recruits to replace the men Dan was taking to Uvira. Hardy was the one person, aside from Dan, whom Blair had appointed to the commando force. The Major said he wanted to know he could trust the man he was going to be dealing with if Dan dropped out of the picture. Blair and Hardy had fought together in the south of the Congo just a few years ago, during the Katanga uprising. Ironically, their enemy back then had been the Congolese National Army; the mercenaries were on the side of the insurgents. But now the ground had shifted.

Hardy had been an officer in the British Special Forces. He was younger than Dan – in his early forties – and was most likely stronger and fitter. His training was certainly more recent and rigorous. He'd also seen combat here in central Africa. Compared to him, Dan had only one point in his favour: local knowledge. Yet the truth was, he'd not been in Kivu Province for decades. And as for Uvira, Dan's memories of the lakeside town only seemed to become more elusive the more he tried to pin them down. Dan wouldn't blame Hardy if he felt he was superior to him, in fact if not in official rank. If so, Dan hoped the man would be professional enough not to display his feelings. For his part, Dan intended to do everything in his power to make it easy for Hardy to form a good partnership with him. He just hoped Hardy had the same plan.

One of the younger women appeared at Dan's side, offering a plate of peanuts. She was very pretty, with elaborately plaited hair. Her rounded breasts, covered only by a thin cloth, brushed against his arm. As he took a handful of nuts Dan eyed her uneasily. These village women shouldn't be here on a military base. There should be army cooks, men in uniform – just like there should be function-ing stoves and reliable showers. When the young woman had gone back to her stool, he turned to the cook, speaking in an undertone.

'My mother, listen to my warning,' he said. 'You must make sure these young ones are safe. Some of these soldiers are bad men. Do not trust them.'

'I hear you,' she said, her expression serious. 'When we come in here each morning, and when we go home, they search us. "Do you have weapons?" they ask. And we always say no.' She leaned towards Dan, pulling aside her robe. A long sharp knife was tucked into her woven belt. The hand-beaten blade had a thin, sharp edge and a savage point. 'I am the cook. I must have a good knife. Even they understand that.' She paused to give Dan a grim smile. There was a glint of steel in her eyes. 'If there is any trouble, I am prepared.'

'You are a tough old lady.' Dan's tone was humorous. 'Perhaps I should take you with me, into the fighting.'

The cook laughed. 'Indeed, I could defend you with ease.'

As Dan smiled at her, he wondered how much she and her companions knew about what was going on in their country – why these white soldiers were even here. Probably not much. They were preoccupied with feeding their families, getting the ground ready for the rains, falling in love, surviving disease, giving birth and burying their dead. He hoped for their sake the parameters of their world would not change – that this conflict would start and end without them being personally involved.

The cook turned back to her work. As Dan crunched the peanuts, still warm from the roasting pan, he ran through what he'd achieved so far today. Amazingly, he'd managed to secure most of the supplies he needed for the mission. They were already being moved to an empty hangar ready for transport. The Quartermaster had agreed to the requisition with a grudging air. If he had his way, Dan suspected, everything would remain on the shelves, labelled and boxed, neat and tidy. Blair had noted that the Belgian man had been raised in an orphanage – that was why he felt so at home in the regimented world of the army. Having been deprived of free access to food, clothing and other possessions in his early years, he relished being Quartermaster. He viewed the stores as his personal possessions, and waste was his worst enemy. This made him an excellent storeman – a point Dan appreciated. He knew his men wouldn't find themselves out in the field saddled with the wrong gear and missing things they needed. Some mistakes were annoying – like ending up with boxes of cutlery containing only teaspoons – but others could cost lives. It wasn't as if Dan could send home for new supplies.

The men were to be flown to a base in Kivu, closer to Uvira, where they'd collect their vehicles and heavy artillery. The Major promised there would be a fleet of jeeps and covered trucks, all brand-new. Dan didn't like the idea that he wouldn't see the vehicles until the unit was scheduled to start driving. He'd raised his concerns with Blair as soon as he was informed of the plan.

'I know what African roads are like,' he'd stated. 'If the vehicles are not in good order, I won't be moving.'

'Yes, you will,' Blair had said.

Dan looked him in the eye, saying nothing. He had to leave Blair room to stay in charge.

'Fair enough,' the Major said finally. 'I'll get some confirmation.'

They'd sat in Blair's office together, hour after hour, going over plans, assessing all the options. This morning they'd discussed the final selection of men.

'It's like baking a pudding,' Blair had said.

Dan wondered if the Major had ever actually baked anything, but he got the point: a commando force needed the right mix of ingredients. Young men were better at taking risks, since they still believed themselves to be immortal. War veterans were mostly older, but had the advantage not just of training, but firsthand experience. They knew what the chaos of conflict was like – how to pick out a shouted order above the screams of the wounded. They were familiar with seeing men die, and being the one to pull the trigger. Then there was personality to consider. The Force needed a few cheerful characters who would lift the mood of the group. Adventurers played a different role: they made everyone feel they were part of an enviable lifestyle.

Dan's force of thirty would be made up of five units, each with an experienced senior officer. Across the whole team there had to be a number of key specialists, such as the Chief Mechanic, Explosives Engineer and Signaller. And there had to be enough backup from men who could do a bit of everything. Most of all, though, Dan knew he needed tough, hard men in his commando force – the kind who would not flinch in the face of whatever came their way. People who qualified for this last group were the trickiest to assess. There was often a thin line between bravery and madness.

'*Unataka chakula?*' Would you like some food? The cook's voice cut into Dan's musing. He turned around to see her pointing at the pot of stew.

The rich red sauce was dotted with kidney beans and green pepper. In the mess they served Heinz baked beans, which were a poor comparison with the smoky, slow-cooked stew the Africans ate. He was tempted to accept the cook's offer – to sit down and join in the easy banter with these women, leaving his worries behind. But the military didn't view time the way these people did: as a luxury to enjoy, with plenty of room for meandering here and there. Dan had to stay on schedule.

'No, thank you, my mother. I must get back to work.' He gestured towards the main yard where the Sergeant Major could be heard shouting curses and threats at the volunteers.

The cook snorted dismissively. 'That is not work. Those men are wasting their strength. They could be digging in the gardens, growing food.'

All the women laughed at this suggestion. Dan joined in. He guessed that in their villages, gardening was considered suitable work for wives or daughters or young boys. The thought of these tough soldiers digging in the ground was comic to say the least.

'*Kwaheri,*' he said. '*Tutaonana.*' Goodbye. We will meet again.

Dan headed for the parade ground. Rounding the corner of a building, he paused, taking in the impressive sight of a hundred men formed into dead straight rows, doing push-ups with heavy rucksacks on their backs. Stripped to the waist, their bodies shone with sweat.

The volunteers were a mismatched bunch. Most looked to be in good shape, fit and strong. A few were underweight and scrawny; several had the overblown physiques of weightlifters. Too many wore the marks of middle age: muscles turning to fat, paunches at the waist.

Dan's gaze settled on the skinny man with the eagle tattoo on his chest – he'd been one of the contenders in the wrestling match a few days ago. He was now doing one-armed push-ups with apparent ease. Bailey was his name. His background in the British Special Forces meant he was as highly trained as a racehorse; an obvious pick for a commando force. But the man was dangerously volatile. At the end of the wrestling match he'd turned on the umpire and it had taken three men to peel him away. All the while, he'd worn that twisted smile on his lips. Dan knew Bailey would cause trouble, but he had a feeling the young volunteer would more than earn his keep. His name was on the list.

Dan ran his eyes along the lines, seeking another volunteer he'd chosen with even deeper reservations. Henning was Foreign Legion trained. Many of the men had a military bearing – their movements, whether standing at ease or on parade, had a formality born of years of training. But in Henning the manner was extreme. Everything he said sounded like a response to an order. His mouth snapped shut after each utterance. He even ate his meals with precision, putting down his cutlery as he chewed with a steady rhythm. His almost robotic behaviour was offset by a disconcertingly beautiful face. Henning kept his fair hair so closely shaven he looked naturally bald, like a baby. He appeared to have no eyebrows. When Dan had interviewed him, he'd explained that he had been born Scandinavian but now claimed a different citizenship.

'I am French,' he'd said. Then he'd used a French phrase,

immediately translating it. '*Par le sang versé*. By spilled blood.'

Pulling open his shirt, he'd revealed a scar that ran from his sternum across to the side of his abdomen. The edges were ragged, suggesting it had only been roughly stitched. It looked like the work of a bayonet.

'Why did you leave the Foreign Legion?' Dan had enquired.

'Once you are a legionnaire you are one for life. It is a state of mind.' The man stared him down, offering nothing more.

There was an unrelenting coldness in his eyes that made Dan cringe. A big part of him wanted never to see this man again. But at the same time, he understood that a truly tough soldier was standing in front of him. He would be an asset to the team. The man would also provide an opposing force to set against Bailey. It was something Dan had learned firsthand, in the Second World War: if you put men who were alike together, they held up a mirror to each other. Their vital qualities became more pronounced. It was an odd dynamic he could not explain – but the upshot of it was that Bailey and Henning would be a terrifying duo.

Dan's eyes ranged on across the parade ground, settling on De Groote, the ex-butcher from South Africa. He was doing slow steady push-ups; his huge hands, with fingers like sausages, were splayed on the ground. Dan had assessed him as being solid and reliable. Beside him was the twenty-eight-year-old graduate from the Military Academy in Pretoria. A superbly trained soldier, Becker was also fluent in French and German and Afrikaans, along with Swahili, Lingala and several other African languages. In Recruitment he'd told Blair he wanted to join the fight to save Africa from Communism. Blair had taken him on, even though he explained to Dan that he normally rejected anyone with an ideological or political agenda. Beliefs can cloud judgement, spelling disaster in the thick of combat. But in this instance, Blair had made an exception. After all, he shared the young man's views. As the Major had put it to Dan back in Johannesburg: the future of the free world was at stake. Then, also, there was the fact that having a versatile translator was as vital as a good supply of ammunition. Becker had been in the first group of candidates chosen to join the mission.

As the men removed their packs and began sprinting on the spot, Dan scanned the list in his hand. He was a man short. He'd just had to cross out the name of a volunteer he'd initially selected. During first-aid training last night the soldier had looked confused about how to tie a simple sling. Dan had been surprised; he had shown excellent skills until now. When Dan went to see what the problem was, he'd noticed a line of red marks on the man's inner elbow.

'I'm clean, sir,' the volunteer had said, meeting his gaze. 'I haven't used in years.'

Dan saw the plea in his eyes. Every man in the place knew a special force was being assembled, though the mission was secret. They all wanted to be picked – to be first into action, and to escape from Lemba.

Dan had examined the needle marks. Some were still inflamed, either from chronic infection or recent use. He couldn't be sure. After only a moment's deliberation he'd walked away. He wasn't going to take risks with a junkie. Whoever had carried out this volunteer's medical should have seen the telltale signs and sent him straight home – assuming he had one to return to.

The clink of metal and the hush-hush sound of cloth polishing steel punctuated the quiet. Dan stood to one side watching on as the men dismantled their guns, cleaning and lightly oiling them, before putting them back together. As they worked, the Sergeant Major trod the rows with a heavy step, stopwatch in hand.

The positive side of the delay in deployment was that there had been extra time for training. The men were now familiar with a whole array of armaments. The mercenaries were equipped with Israeli guns, the same as the ones issued to United Nations troops. The soldiers needed to know them inside and out, eyes closed. But they also had to be able to use the Chinese and Russian weaponry that would be captured from the Simbas. They needed a working knowledge of the arms used by the Congolese National Army as well. Plenty of these had ended up in rebel hands. Apparently, the Congolese had an unfortunate habit of retreating wholesale to avoid confronting the Simbas, freely abandoning vehicles, guns, ammunition; even their own wounded men.

'The Simbas terrify the hell out of the government forces,' Blair had explained. 'A few weeks ago some rebels made a phone call to a government post and told them they were on their way. The army deserted in full force before the Simbas even arrived.

'They have a secret weapon,' Blair continued. 'Witchdoctors.' He paused, clearly expecting Dan to express surprise, but the Lieutenant just nodded. He'd lived his whole life in Africa. That witchdoctors should be a more powerful force than gunfire and grenades was no surprise to him.

'They give the soldiers "medicine" that is meant to make them immune to bullets,' Blair continued. 'How they dreamed that up, I cannot imagine.'

'The Simbas aren't the first Congolese to have this belief,' said Dan. 'It started with the Belgians. They used to fire blanks to disperse crowds. There was the loud bang but no one got hit, so the Africans assumed it was possible for some bullets to disappear in midair.'

'Well, wherever it comes from, it's very effective,' said Blair. 'They have no problems getting their people to step in front of guns.' He smiled. 'The clever bit is they've got a whole list of rules and rituals that are meant to defeat the enemy. It's impossible to follow them all, which gives the witchdoctors a handy escape clause if the bullets turn out to be real.'

Dan didn't respond. He felt alienated, suddenly, from Blair's world. As a white African he was used to treating witchdoctors with respect. Whatever one thought of their beliefs, and some of the misguided treatments they administered, he'd seen their real powers at work.

'Anyway,' Blair went on, 'the soldiers believe whatever they're told. They don't mind going into battle armed with nothing more than spears and cattle clubs. They've got modern weapons too, provided by their Communist friends. But they are primitive people. And we can use that, Miller. They are impressed by noise and gunfire. You go in fast and furious – that's the best tactic.

'But you don't want to get caught,' Blair stressed. 'Torture is par for the course. They named themselves after an animal and that's how they behave. Basically, victory is the only option.' He paused for a few seconds, to give his next words emphasis. 'I recommend a fierce fight, leaving no opponent standing. It avoids a lot of trouble.'

Dan knew what he meant. No one wanted to order, or allow, cold-blooded murder of enemy captives, whether they'd chosen to surrender or been caught. But when there was no regular army to hand prisoners over to, there were few other choices.

Blair had continued at length, sharing what he'd learned during his extensive career. Now that he'd assigned Dan his own unit, Blair had dropped some of his reserve. Dan was glad of the instruction, but began to wonder if the lecture was entirely for his benefit: at times Blair seemed to be indulging in reminiscence.

Now, as Dan watched the Sergeant Major prowling the ranks, using a cane to swipe at men whose pace had dropped, all the advice he'd heard washed back and forth in his mind. Apprehension built like a wave inside him. Lifting his gaze, he stared out past the end of the parade ground. In the distance, beyond the barbed-wire perimeter of Lemba Base, was the forest. The soldiers became a blur of moving flesh at the edges of Dan's vision as he focused on the tall trees that grew there. Some had been standing firm for a hundred years or more. And they'd be here still, he reminded himself, when the Simba rebel armies had had their day, and were no more.

The Major's desk looked stranded, all alone in the middle of the large room he'd made his office. There was virtually no other furniture; just an extra chair and a high stool, and one filing cabinet with a missing drawer. The wooden floor had faded sections where carpets had once been and the bank of windows overlooking the air strip had no curtains, just bare hooks hanging from the rails. The walls were painted the ugly green that managed to appear in hospitals, jails and schools the world over.

When Dan knocked, Blair called him in, scarcely looking up from the paperwork in front of him. Dan's boots made hollow thuds as he approached the desk, saluted and stood at attention.

'At ease, Lieutenant. Take a seat. Have some tea.' He signalled to his adjutant who placed another cup on a tray that had been set out. The teapot and sugar bowl were stainless steel, but the brown jug and cups with a daisy pattern would have looked at home in a cottage kitchen.

Blair dismissed his assistant, announcing that he would manage the tea himself. After pouring out two serves of a dark brown brew, he added some badly mixed powdered milk, emptying the jug. White lumps floated on the surface of the tea. Without asking Dan's preference, he stirred teaspoons of sugar into both drinks.

'We're calling it Operation Nightflower,' Blair stated as he handed one cup to Dan. 'We still need a name for the Force, though.' He looked thoughtfully at the ceiling. 'Doesn't have to mean anything. In fact, it's better if it doesn't.'

Dan tried to think of a suggestion, but it was surprisingly hard to find a word with no connection to the reality they were immersed in. He wondered if Blair had come up with Nightflower – and if so, did he know that the name had a clear link with the Congo? There were lilies in the forests here that flowered only at night, forming islands of stunning beauty in the moonlight.

Dan watched in silence as Blair picked up the milk jug, studying its base.

'Denby stoneware,' the man read out. 'That will do. Force Denby.'

Force Denby. Operation Nightflower. Dan turned the words over in his mind, tension gathering in his stomach. Hearing these names made the whole venture feel more real.

'How's the list going?' Blair asked.

'It's done.' To replace the junkie Dan had added an ex-game warden from Rhodesia, who wanted to earn money to buy a farm. Then he'd typed up the list himself, using two fingers, wanting to keep it secret until he had Blair's approval. He was about to hand the page over when the sound of an approaching jet cut into the quiet.

'Damn. That'll be the Captain.' Blair frowned, checking his watch. 'Almost two hours early.'

Through the window, Dan watched the aircraft approach and descend. He recognised the livery and the insignia of a U.S. Air

Force plane. One just like it had visited Lemba Base several times since he'd been here. The aircraft flew low along the runway before taking off again, as if aborting the manoeuvre. Dan guessed the pilot was making sure the ground was clear of hazards.

As the plane circled, Blair gulped down his tea. 'I'm not sure if I'm advising the Captain or if he's advising me.' He allowed himself a small smile. Then he consulted a file marked *Recruitment*, rifling through the pages inside. 'Get hold of Higgins, Lawler and Mathieson. And Lieutenant Willis. Confine them to barracks until he's gone.'

'Yes, sir,' Dan said. 'May I ask why, sir?'

'They're Americans. If they are identified, they'll have their passports revoked.'

Dan frowned in confusion. Most countries disapproved of their citizens taking part in foreign conflicts; service in a mercenary army became a blank space on a man's professional record. But from what Dan had heard, most authorities just turned a blind eye. So why would the United States take such a tough line? After all, they had their own military advisers here in the Congo. One of them had just arrived right here at Lemba Base.

'I thought the Americans, of all people, were keen to fight Communism,' Dan said. 'Especially after the Cuban Missile Crisis.'

He remembered the fraught conversations he'd heard around safari camp fires following that emergency. It was just a couple of years ago. Clients told how they'd hidden in their homes, keeping their children out of school, terrified their cities were about to be destroyed. Fidel Castro. The Cubans. The Reds. Commos. The words were spoken in hushed tones, as though these fearful enemies might be haunting the African night, like demons.

Blair began putting documents away in a drawer. After a few

moments, he looked up. 'Miller, you need to be very clear on this. The Americans are not involved here. The Captain is on a social call. And the US bombers that will provide you with air support are not in Africa either.' He smiled, as if at a clever joke. 'They are on a maintenance break at a remote air base in the American desert. There's even paperwork to prove it.'

Dan swallowed hard as he absorbed Blair's words. The Major gave him a sharp look, as if guessing his thoughts.

'Look at it this way. I don't care where the aircraft come from, or who pays the bills. And neither do you, Lieutenant. We know why we're here. We just have to get on with the job.' He took off his beret and smoothed his hair. 'We'll get back to this briefing after lunch. Let's say 1400 hours.'

'Yes, sir.' Dan stood to attention and saluted, just as the aircraft reappeared, dropping down towards the runway.

Standing on the path that led to the mess hall, Dan looked across to the air strip. The plane had landed, and Blair was waiting at the foot of a set of metal stairs that had been wheeled up to the plane. As Dan watched, the door opened to reveal a figure standing ready to disembark. Dan recognised the American military attaché – the one with the hair and skin so colourless they might have been dipped in bleach. So this was the man Blair was calling 'the Captain'. . . The officer must spend half his time in the air – Dan's most recent encounter with him had taken place only a couple of days ago.

Dan had been passing Blair's office just as the adjutant had emerged bearing an ashtray piled with cigar butts. Through the open door he'd glimpsed the attaché lounging against Blair's desk, talking. The man's words, framed in a slow, broad accent, were still lodged in Dan's head: 'Tell him we're sending our own animals in.'

It was all Dan heard before the door snapped shut. He didn't know the context of the comment, but there was only one meaning he could make of it: the attaché was referring to the mercenaries as animals. Dan wondered what Blair thought about the men being spoken of that way. He'd taken pains to make it clear that this force was not going to be like the gang of ruffians that had operated in the south of the Congo not long ago. The Europeans had named those men *Les Affreux*, The Fearful Ones, because of the atrocities they committed. But this time Blair was in charge. His new commando unit was to be well trained, uniformed and disciplined. But the attaché didn't seem to be aware of that.

Dan had paused outside the office, wondering if he'd hear Blair's reaction. But then the Major had walked up behind him, approaching from the hallway. The American was talking to someone else, or – more likely, Dan guessed – on the telephone.

Now, as Dan watched the Captain marching across the forecourt alongside Blair, he thought again about what he'd overheard that day. The mercenaries were not only referred to as 'animals', but as '*our* animals'. As if they'd been hired by the Americans, not the Congolese government. Dan remembered what Blair had just said to him about the bombers that would support Operation Nightflower being stationed in the Congo secretly. Was the US military deceiving its own government? Or was the government deceiving the public, either at home or abroad – perhaps both? Whatever was going on, it made Dan feel uneasy. The situation surrounding this conflict was clearly not as simple as it had appeared to be, back in Johannesburg.

*

The smell of fried steak and chips drifted from the mess hall. Aside from the handful of peanuts, Dan hadn't eaten since breakfast, which was a long time ago – but he had no appetite. He still felt disturbed by the presence of the Captain on the base and all the questions it raised in his mind. He decided to collect a cup of coffee and then head back to the officers' staffroom to check his requisition orders.

As he neared the entrance to the dining room a man sauntered out, wearing shorts that only came halfway down his thighs, and red socks pulled up to his knees. A long scarf was draped around his neck. If he'd noticed the uniformed officer approaching, he showed no sign of it. Dan felt a flash of annoyance at the man's casual attitude. He didn't seem to realise he was on a military training base. He might have been dressed up for a picnic.

Dan stepped into his path. 'Return to your barracks, soldier,' he said quietly. 'And get dressed.'

The volunteer just looked at him. Then he glanced down at his attire and shrugged. Dan was aware of faces at the windows; figures appearing in the doorway.

'Do I have to repeat myself?' Dan spoke slowly, hoping to indicate that he was not in the mood for a joke.

The volunteer stood to attention, a cheeky smile on his face. 'I am already dressed, *sir*!'

With one movement, Dan grabbed him by the shoulders and pinned him against the side of a nearby water tank. The man's feet dangled helplessly, a few inches above the ground. His eyes were wide with shock. Dan's arm pulled back, his hand crunched into a fist. Then he paused, scanning the volunteer's face. His skin was satin smooth. Fluffy hair like duck down sprouted on his unshaven chin. He should still be in school. Dan's annoyance turned to disgust that someone of this age had been passed by Recruitment. They must be getting desperate for numbers, but that was no excuse.

'When did you arrive, boy?' Dan asked.

'This morning, sir.'

'Well, here's a tip. When an officer gives you a command, don't answer back.'

'No, sir.'

Dan let him fall to the ground. The lad scrambled, crablike, to escape. Straightening his shirt and repositioning his beret, Dan turned towards the door to the dining hall. He looked straight ahead, but could feel the gaze of many eyes, like sunburn on his skin. There was no alternative now, he knew. He had to go inside, look hungry, and wolf down a hearty meal.

He chose a seat at an empty table in the far corner of the room. Blair encouraged the officers to eat with the volunteers; he believed listening to mealtime chat was one of the best ways a leader could get to know his men. But right now, Dan wanted to be on his own. He chewed his way slowly through a piece of tough steak that he suspected had not come from a cow. He ate chips loaded with salt. As he forced the food down he felt a sense of bewilderment. What on earth was he doing here? He could have been in the Mara, far away from all this stress and confusion. With his eyes half-closed, he conjured a vision of an open plain, the grass tawny yellow, trees a dusty green. He could almost hear the buzz of insects singing in the midday heat and smell the sun-dried leaves, crushed by his boots, as he trod his path over the land.

The touch of a hand on his shoulder made him jump to his feet. As he spun around, jolting the table, his fork fell to the floor with a clatter. A short, stocky man was backing away, holding up his hands.

'I'm sorry. Very sorry.' He had a thick Belgian accent. 'I did not mean to surprise you.'

Dan looked him up and down, doing a swift assessment. He was not one of the recruits – that was clear. They weren't in uniform yet, but the regimental hairdresser had been hard at work. The volunteers' hair had been shaved off at the back and sides, with free choice about what grew on top. This man's hair half-covered his ears. And his dated business suit and open-necked shirt fitted none of the style statements Dan recognised. But the most obvious clue was in the Belgian's eyes. The men who'd signed up to the regiment had either the focused look of soldiers preparing for action, or the relaxed manner of people who didn't yet know what it was like; this man had the haunted, exhausted expression of someone returning from the battlefield.

'Sit down.' Dan gestured towards the servery. 'Have you eaten?'

The man almost collapsed onto a chair. 'I can't eat.' He held out his hand. 'I am Hendrick Bergman.' The way he said his name made it sound like a confession.

'Lieutenant Miller.' As they shook hands Dan noticed the dirt ground into Bergman's skin, and his callused palms. He was obviously someone who worked hard for his living – a farmer, perhaps. Not the kind of man who usually wore a suit.

Bergman leaned forward, a shock of dark hair falling over his brow. 'You are going to Uvira.'

Dan's eyes widened. 'How do you know?'

'I have a friend working here. He was the one who let me in and told me to find you and ask for your help. My family . . .' he broke off, taking a deep breath. His hands, gripping the table edge, were rigid. 'I have to get back to my family. We have a farm near Uvira. I had to go to Léopoldville to see my lawyer, and the bank. While

I was away the Simbas took over the whole area. I can't find out if they are all right. The radio is down.'

Dan nodded. It wasn't hard to empathise with what he was hearing; it would be any family man's nightmare. 'What about the neighbours? Have you tried to contact them?'

He shook his head. 'The last Belgian family left our valley soon after Independence. They saw what happened in Léopoldville and Elizabethville.' He paused. 'Do you know all this?'

'Some of it,' Dan said. He'd heard accounts of atrocities committed by the Congolese against Europeans. Independence had come so suddenly that there were virtually no Africans left to fill positions of authority. The new government didn't even get to find its feet before chaos descended. The army and police went on the rampage, unleashing the fury bred up over generations of Belgian tyranny. Defenceless men, women and children were massacred. It was an ugly story, whichever side you took.

'I would have taken my family and escaped as well,' Bergman continued, 'but we had nowhere else to go. Apart from us, the only Europeans in the area are at the mission. I cannot contact them either. The Simbas confiscate radios if they find them.' He shook his head. 'They believe the things have magic powers. That they can call down bombs from the sky.

'Lieutenant, I have a beautiful young wife, Clara. My son Hugo is only six years old. My daughter Elise,' his voice cracked, 'is twelve years old.' He broke off, his lips trembling. 'I've heard stories about what the Simbas do to women, even little girls . . .'

'I understand,' Dan said. 'If you give me directions to the farm, I'll see if we can get there. We'll do what we can for them.' He looked into the man's red-rimmed eyes. They seemed to have sunk into his head. 'I will try my best. I promise.'

'No, no.' Bergman shook his head. 'I have to come with you.'

'That's not possible,' Dan said gently but firmly. 'We can't take passengers.' He was certain Bergman was too young to have taken part in the Second World War; any other combat experience was highly unlikely.

'I know how to use a gun,' Bergman said, as if reading Dan's mind. 'I shoot game to feed my family. I kill animals that prey on my stock. I can do lots of things . . .' His words petered out. He just gazed at Dan, his eyes burning with intent. 'You must help me. I have to get home, to rescue my family. Or at least bury their remains.'

Dan stared down at the table. A cluster of ants were carrying away half a chip, dragging it over the minefield of burns and gouges that patterned the surface. He knew he had to say no to this man. The fact was very clear: Bergman was a liability. Unskilled. Personally involved. And an emotional wreck, already.

'Please, I beg you.'

Without looking at Bergman, Dan could feel his desperation. It emanated from him like the heat of a blazing fire.

'Go to the Quartermaster,' Dan said finally. 'Give him your measurements. Shirt. Trousers. Boots.'

A light flared in the Belgian's eyes.

'Then report to the officers' staffroom. There's a bit of paperwork to do.'

Dan watched the man half-run from the hall. Then he pushed away his plate and stood up, ready to return to Blair's office and receive the final briefing.

TWELVE

The secretary leaned forward, peering at the typewriter as if she wasn't sure which key to pick next. At her side, a manila folder spilled its contents across the desk. A coffee cup had been put down on one of the documents and a dirty ashtray was nearby. Anna sat in an overstuffed chair, her handbag resting on her knee. Though she tried not to listen, the ragged rhythm of the typing grated on her nerves; she felt like taking over and doing the work herself. The quality of the secretary didn't reflect well on Francois Leclair & Associates, the legal firm that managed Karl's affairs. Even her dress was inappropriate – the neckline too low, the fabric too clingy. And her bleached blonde hair, piled into four stiff curls on top of her head, was dark at the roots.

Anna shifted restlessly. She wasn't used to wasting time. And she wanted to get this meeting behind her as soon as possible. She kept her eyes trained on the door that opened onto the street, waiting for Monsieur Leclair to arrive. Apparently he liked to stop for coffee on his way to work. Anna was surprised he hadn't chosen to give up his treat this morning; he'd been so keen to meet with her.

He'd phoned the Lindenbaum house yesterday afternoon, as soon as he'd heard of Karl's death.

'Mademoiselle Emerson. I offer you my sincere condolences.' He'd spoken English with a thick accent that might have been French, German, Dutch, Scandinavian – Anna could not tell. 'It is a great tragedy. At least you saw him before he passed away. That is something to be grateful for.'

'Yes, it is. Thank you.' Anna made sure she sounded crisp and businesslike; she wanted Leclair to take her seriously.

At the other end of the phone line, the lawyer cleared his throat. He seemed to be trying to decide what to say next.

Anna took the initiative. 'I would like to discuss the funeral arrangements. Can you tell me what I need to do?'

'Nothing, my dear. My client left clear instructions. I am afraid there will be no funeral, just a burial. The plot has been purchased.'

'I see.' Anna's tone was neutral, but she felt a wave of relief. She wouldn't have to appear at a public occasion parading as Karl Emerson's long-lost daughter.

'But there are so many other things for us to discuss,' Leclair added. 'We must arrange a meeting as soon as possible.'

He had offered to drive out to the Lindenbaum home, but Anna had suggested she come to his office – she knew she'd feel more comfortable in a professional setting. Also, she wanted to wait until the next day. She assumed part of the conversation would be about the role Karl had offered her in the Emerson Trust. She'd made the decision to return to Australia, but beyond that she wasn't sure. She needed more time and she didn't want to be unduly pressured by Leclair. The appointment had been set for first thing the next morning.

During the rest of the afternoon she'd pondered all the options, but by the time she joined Eliza in the sitting room for sundowners she still hadn't reached a decision. She waited for the right moment, then put down her cigarette and drink and asked for Eliza's advice.

'What do you think about Karl's art collection? What's your honest opinion?'

Eliza's answer was blunt. 'The *nkisi* should have remained in the villages where they were made. They don't belong in London – or anywhere else but the Congo. I had several big arguments with Emerson about it. In the end, we couldn't sit at a dinner table together. Did he tell you how he got hold of the carvings?'

'He said they were purchased from the villagers, either by him, or by other collectors.'

Eliza snorted. 'Some may have been bought – for a pittance, from people who were desperate for money. Most were simply stolen by colonial officials. They would just walk into the sacred huts and take whatever they wanted. The people were too afraid to stop them. Others were taken by plantation owners. They were just as bad.' Anger sparked in Eliza's eyes. As her voice rose, her words became stretched out, making her American accent stronger. 'If you knew the history of this country, Anna, you would understand why the collection should never have existed in the first place. The people deserved to be left with something. So much was taken from them.'

Eliza had stood up and was pacing as she talked, pausing now and then to take deep draws on her cigarette and to gulp down her drink.

'Conrad wrote that novel, *Heart of Darkness*. Have you heard of it?' Anna shook her head, but Eliza wasn't even looking. 'It was set here, in the Belgian Congo. Since the arrival of the first white men, some of the worst crimes you have ever imagined were carried out here. Millions of Congolese were killed under Leopold's rule – murdered or worked to death. Things improved when the Belgian government took over, but not nearly enough. This land has been drenched with blood. And who was to blame? The State, the corporations, the landowners – they were all as guilty as each other.'

Anna listened in confusion. She and Eliza were sitting together in one of the Lindenbaum mansions, surrounded by the trappings of wealth. Out in the hallway there were framed photographs of a man she took to be Eliza's father, or perhaps her grandfather. There were images of him dressed in a white suit, patrolling his rubber plantations surrounded by Africans who looked like slaves. The American family had made a fortune here in the Congo, and Eliza – with her expensive cameras, servants, Paris couture and luxury car – was still benefiting from it. Anna didn't understand how her outrage on behalf of the Africans could be squared away with the life she led. Anna would have liked to ask Eliza this, but it wasn't the kind of issue a guest could bring up, especially when she'd been treated with such generosity. Anna lowered her gaze, tracing the patterns on a fine silk carpet that should surely have been hung on the wall.

'I know what you're thinking.'

Anna looked up, her lips parting. For a few seconds she felt certain Eliza had read her mind.

Eliza waved her hand around the room. 'You are thinking that all this is stolen too. And you are right. But everything is going to change. There has been a delay, that's all.' Nearing the mantelpiece Eliza turned round, wobbling on her high heels. As she grasped the standard lamp for balance, her drink slopped from her glass onto a coffee table.

Anna stood up. 'Are you all right?' Counting back, Anna reckoned Eliza must have consumed at least four cocktails. Eliza had drunk them methodically, one after another, while Anna was still sipping her first. All Eliza had eaten was one small sandwich with the cucumber filling removed. No wonder she was not making sense.

'Everyone must make their own choices,' Eliza went on. 'And take the consequences. Sure, there is right and wrong.' She gave a short harsh laugh. 'But there's an awful lot of everything in between.'

She sat down, resting her head in her hands. Anna rescued her cigarette from where it was burning a hole in the rug. After a short time, Eliza looked up, pushing back her hair from her face. When she spoke again, she sounded more like her usual self.

'You must consider all the implications, Anna. Weigh everything up.' She smiled, then reached out to pat Anna's knee. 'You know, you might enjoy life in London, at least for a while.'

The next morning Anna had taken an early walk in the garden, before the zebras were let out of their stalls. Though she was not able to see the lake from the garden, she could sense the presence of the vast body of water. She tried to draw from its calmness, clearing her mind. In only a few hours from now she was due in Leclair's office. The time to reach a decision had come.

She turned back towards the house. As she neared the front steps a sudden flapping broke out above her. Her stomach clenched with instant alarm. She spun round. Craning her neck, she looked up. Pigeons were launching themselves from the eaves of the house. They swooped down towards her, at the last moment wheeling away in unison. The rhythmic noise of wings beating seemed to enter Anna's body, filling her with panic. A long-buried memory rose up like mud stirred from a riverbed.

It was dusk. Bats streamed from the high rooftops of Leopard Hall, the scallop-edged wings painting their sinister pattern against the darkening sky. The air was torn with high-pitched screeching. Anna crouched over, the hem of her cotton dress brushing the ground, her hands covering her head. She had plaits, but still, she was afraid – bats could get caught in your hair, their struggles tightening the snare. They carried diseases and they peed as they flew. The very air seemed poisoned by their presence. She had to hold her breath, lungs bursting, until the very last of them had disappeared into the forest, the flapping shapes lost in the mass of blackness . . .

Anna made herself walk slowly back inside Eliza's house. If she let herself hurry, she knew she would break into a run. Magadi would ask what was wrong, and she had no answer she wanted to give. In the hallway she sat on the bottom rung of the grand staircase, the gleaming banister rising up behind her. She stared blankly ahead. Gradually the memory receded and her breathing returned to normal. In place of the fear she'd felt was the certainty she was looking for. The birds had delivered a sign from her past. She knew what she was going to do.

The sense of darkness had lingered, even after Anna climbed into the Jaguar with Eliza and they drove off, leaving the house behind. It had followed her here, to the jaded offices of Karl's lawyer. She could feel it now, at the edge of her consciousness. It added to the anxiety she felt about this meeting with Leclair. Wanting a distraction, she crossed to the far wall, where three pictures hung from a railing. There was an old photograph of a bridge, which could have been taken anywhere. In the image beside it, she saw the Avenue of Storms; two men wearing pith helmets were walking past the Hôtel Albertville. She moved to the last in the row. Instantly she knew the striking face that gazed out of the frame. It was the actress Audrey Hepburn. She was dressed in the white veil and habit of a novice nun. The wimple, framing her serene face, exaggerated her beauty. In the background of the picture was a man holding a camera, an assistant at his side.

'It's from the filming of *The Nun's Story*.'

Anna spun round, recognising the voice and the accent of Monsieur Leclair. She hadn't heard the door open, or his footsteps, but he was right there – standing behind her. She caught an impression of a figure that was short and round. His grey hair was scraped back from his forehead; thick eyebrows looked like caterpillars crossing his face.

'I took that photograph myself,' he said. 'Up near Stanleyville. Have you seen the film?'

Anna shook her head. As she studied the famous face she was reminded of the young nun she'd seen at the airport with Sister Emilia. Anna wondered again who the woman was, and why she'd chosen a life in a religious order. With such perfect looks she could have married well, and enjoyed a world of ease and pleasure. She could have become an actress.

'Wonderful story,' Leclair mused. 'Young nun, working with a dedicated doctor in darkest Africa. But no happy ending, I'm afraid.' His eyes lingered on the picture for a moment, then seemed to remember why Anna was here. 'Mademoiselle . . .' He smiled sadly. 'It is a privilege to meet you.'

As they shook hands, Anna noted his expensive suit and silk tie. She caught a whiff of cologne blended with tobacco.

'Please, come this way.'

The office was crammed with ornate wood furniture – a desk with claw feet, several bookcases, a sideboard. There was a table covered in files. Someone had dusted the timber surfaces carelessly, leaving clear tracks amid a haze of grey.

Anna sat in a high-backed chair with a bare wooden seat.

'Cushion?' Leclair enquired.

'No, thank you.' Anna didn't want to look too comfortable; she hoped to indicate that the meeting would be brief.

Leclair put his hands together as if to pray, then perched his chin on his fingers. He eyed Anna thoughtfully. 'I don't know quite where to begin.'

Anna leaned forward in her seat. 'My father told me about the plans for his art collection.'

'Good!' Leclair said. 'So you already know about the Trust?' He reached for a file on the desk. 'I'm sure you have lots of questions.'

'No, I have already —'

Leclair held up a hand to cut off her words. 'Let me explain everything.' From the crinkle around his eyes, Anna sensed he was expecting to enjoy his next speech. 'The collection is already famous. And very valuable. You won't own the works yourself, but still, there will be benefits for you, Mademoiselle. Huge benefits.'

Anna looked at him in silence. She was trying to decide how to begin her side of the story.

'Do you know anything about African art?' Leclair rose to his feet and crossed to the corner of the room. Anna turned to see a large crate made of raw wood. Nails stuck up along the top, where the lid had been prised off. 'Let me show you something. This consignment has just arrived from Leopard Hall.'

Anna stood up, moving closer, as Leclair reached into the crate. She couldn't help being curious about the objects whose names and numbers Karl had read out from his list. A mask appeared first. It was life-sized, made of carved wood. The features were so stylised it was barely recognisable as a face. The surface of the wood had the rich patina that only came with time and use. There were scars and burns; part of the long narrow ridge that formed the nose was chipped off. The mask looked ancient and very modern, both at the same time.

'This piece is from the Teke tribe,' Leclair said. 'I do not need to read the label to identify the style.' He gave Anna an enthusiastic smile. 'I have become something of an expert myself.'

Anna smiled back politely as he reached further into the box. He pulled out a few handfuls of packaging made of wood shavings. 'And this,' he said, 'is a *nkisi* – a power figure.' He grunted with the effort of lifting it out.

Anna recoiled from a human shape so grotesque it was the stuff of a nightmare. The figure was pierced all over with vicious-looking nails, spikes and knife blades. Only the face and hands had been left alone. The head was skull-like; the open mouth was caught in the midst of a scream. One arm was raised, the hand gripping a broken spear.

'There must have been dozens of these at Leopard Hall,' Leclair said. 'A hundred even. Do you remember the collection?'

Anna shook her head dumbly. When Karl Emerson had talked about his obsession in the hospital, she had never imagined anything like this. She swallowed on a tight throat. No one could imagine this . . .

'This example is from the Kongo tribe.' Leclair came towards her, cradling the statue like a small child in his arms. 'Look more closely.'

The eyes, made of pearl-white china, had no pupils. As Anna met the blank gaze she felt a chilling sense of horror. The rank smell of poorly tanned leather rose to her nostrils; it was backed by dust, mould and a strange herbal fragrance. The blend of smells felt disturbingly familiar to her. She took a step back.

'He had the pieces locked away, I believe,' Leclair said. 'Very few people were allowed to see them. But that's all about to change . . .' He tilted the statue towards the sunlight that streamed in from the window behind his desk. 'This figure has been made by a true artist. You can tell by the fine carving of the face. Age alone does not make an object like this authentic. It has to have been used for ritual purposes.'

He pointed to drips and splash marks on the head and shoulders. Anna tried not to guess what the stains might be from. There were clusters of matted feathers too, and fragments of cloth, dark and oily with age. Looking down over the torso, she saw small leather bundles pushed in between the piercings. What was hidden inside them, she could not begin to imagine.

Anna walked back to her chair and sat down. The solid wood behind her was like a shield at her back. She couldn't understand why Karl wanted to collect such things, or why anyone would wish to come and see them in a museum. She couldn't fathom Eliza's attitude to them, either.

'The proof of authenticity lies in the details,' Leclair kept talking; he appeared oblivious to Anna's reaction. 'The nails and blades must be hand-forged, each of them unique. That is one clue. And the placement of the items must be random. In the best examples they have been added over a long period of time. Many lifetimes.'

Anna heard a rustling sound as Leclair lowered the artifacts back into the nest of wood shavings – first the statue, then the mask.

Leclair smiled as he returned to his desk. 'You know, if it was not for your father, this priceless heritage would be lost. Objects made of wood do not survive in the villages. They rot away or get eaten by white ants. All this precious work will now be protected forever, in glass cases. Did Karl tell you the collection is to be housed at the University of London? I believe the Trust will have its office there. That is where you will be based.'

'No.' Anna shook her head.

'What do you mean?'

'I'm not going to be the Chair of the Trust. I don't want to be involved with the collection.'

Leclair stared at her. 'But . . .'

'Let someone else do it.'

'That's impossible. It cannot be anyone else. It must be you, Mademoiselle Emerson. You are his daughter!'

'Not really.' Anna fixed Leclair with a steady gaze, but added nothing more. There was no need for him to know how she felt about the fact that Karl Emerson had forgotten her for nearly twenty years and then contacted her only when he had a use for her.

'Under law, you are,' Leclair insisted. 'It makes no difference. None at all.'

'What makes no difference?' Anna frowned as she tried to make sense of what he was saying.

He sighed. 'I understand that your father did not have much to do with you when you were growing up. But I am sure he loved you in his own way. He has left everything to you.'

'Wait,' Anna said. 'You said "it makes no difference". What are you talking about?'

'I am just saying that under law, in this country – and in all others, as far as I am aware – an adopted child has the same status as a direct descendant.'

Anna stared, frozen. The man's voice was running on, words following words. Finally, she managed to speak. 'What did you say?'

'I was explaining that my client's will is very clear. There are no close relatives to contest it. And even if there were, there is no threat to your position. Perhaps you are afraid that all this is too good to be true. You are afraid to grasp your good fortune in case it is taken from you.'

'I don't understand . . .' Anna's whisper was barely audible.

Leclair took in a sharp breath, then he closed his eyes as if in pain. 'My God! I thought you knew.'

'I didn't know.' Anna's hands gripped her chair. 'Are you sure?'

The lawyer let out a long sigh. 'I am sure. I arranged the adoption. I arranged your mother's divorce as well, so that she could remarry. I am sorry, this is a terrible shock for you.'

Anna's thoughts whirled like snowflakes in a glass dome. Marilyn had been through two divorces? Yet she had so often criticised people who resorted to breaking up their families! Questions jostled in Anna's head. But one rose above them all.

'Then . . . who was my real father?'

'Emerson was your real father,' Leclair said firmly.

'Who was my . . .' She hunted for the right word. 'My first father?'

Leclair looked up at the ceiling as if searching for wisdom. When he spoke, he sounded wary. 'He was your mother's first husband. That is all I can say. I cannot tell you who he was, or anything about him. It would be a breach of confidentiality.'

'But I'm over twenty-one. Surely I'm entitled to know!'

'Maybe you are, I am not sure.'

'Can you just tell me where he came from? Is he still here in the Congo?'

'I am sorry, Mademoiselle. I am a busy lawyer, with lots of clients. Whatever I might have known about him, I have forgotten. Monsieur Emerson and I have not spoken about this matter since the paperwork was completed all those years ago.' He raised one hand, as Anna turned around, gazing at the filing cabinet. 'I'm afraid the documents are no longer in my possession. They were stored at another office, which was burned down during the riots. So you see, even if I wanted to help you, I cannot.'

There was a brief quiet. Anna shook her head helplessly as

the implications of these words sank in. Then Leclair continued. 'Anna – if I may call you by your first name – both of your parents have chosen not to inform you about your . . . status. Perhaps there is a good reason for this. But now that you are an adult, I understand that you may want to know the truth, whatever it may be. I suggest you speak to your mother.'

'I will.' Anna planned to call Marilyn immediately; she didn't care what time it was in Australia. But she remembered the look of fear on Marilyn's face when she understood her daughter was going to meet Karl Emerson. Perhaps this was the very secret she was worried about. She might well refuse to speak.

'Isn't there someone here I could talk to?' Anna asked.

Leclair frowned doubtfully. 'Your father was a very private man – some would say secretive. And he didn't mix very much with Albertville people. Most of his friends seemed to come from other places.' He shook his head. 'There's nobody I can think of.'

'How else could I find out?' Anna persisted. 'There must be official records . . . somewhere.'

'This is the Congo,' said Leclair. 'It is not like France or Australia. And since Independence, a lot has changed. The Belgians left in a rush. There was no handover to the Congolese, no training for the people to step into the new roles. Government offices are chaotic. I fear you would not succeed in locating such information.'

'But I can try,' Anna said. 'Please. Karl's dead. My mother is on the other side of the world. I want to know the truth.' She looked Leclair in the eye. 'I know he might be dead. And I understand that even if he's alive, he probably doesn't want to know anything about me.' She listened to herself with a sense of surprise. In these last few seconds the whole landscape of her life had changed, yet she was being calm and logical. Her mind was processing everything at a rapid rate, fuelled by the adrenalin rising in her blood.

'But if I just knew who my real father was and why he gave me away, maybe then I could accept Karl as my stepfather.' She nodded towards the crate in the corner. 'Perhaps I could even reconsider my response to his proposal.'

Leclair met her gaze. 'You are blackmailing me.'

Anna lowered her eyes and waited. Something new had been born inside her; she could feel it there, like a second heart beating in her chest. She didn't care where this path led. She wasn't afraid of having her hopes dashed once more. She would do whatever it took to find out what she needed to know.

'I cannot remember the details of your case,' Leclair said finally, 'but I would have ensured your original surname was not recorded on your birth certificate. I always do that when couples adopt. That way, the child can't find out the truth by accident. But the certificate always says where you were born. That information cannot be withheld.'

Anna reeled off the facts that she knew so well. 'I was born in a village called Banya. In the Lutheran Hospital.'

'That would be the place to start,' said Leclair. 'You might be able to persuade someone to show you the records. A gift of money might be required. American dollars. If that doesn't work, there could be someone in the area who remembers your family and would be willing to tell you. But then, most Europeans have left. And . . . my God, what am I saying? It's not safe for someone like you to travel around the countryside.' He adopted a tough tone. 'Mademoiselle, I am not advising you to do this. In fact, I advise against it. I wish to make that clear.'

'I understand,' Anna said. 'You will not be held responsible.' She stood up, offering him her hand.

'No, no, sit down,' Leclair said. 'Be sensible about this.'

Anna turned at the door. 'Goodbye, Monsieur.'

She walked past the secretary in a daze, pushing open the door and stepping out into the harsh sun. There was a bench not far along the street. She headed towards it, her legs feeling weak as the shock set in.

Collapsing onto the seat, she gazed ahead, barely aware of the passing cars, the smell of fumes mixing with the weedy aroma of the lake. Half-formed thoughts ran through her mind. Karl Emerson – the man no one liked, and who had shown no real interest in Anna – was not her father. She and her mother had had another life before they became a part of his world. It came to Anna, now, that there were no baby pictures among the framed photographs in the hospital – nothing taken before the age of three or four.

In Marilyn's album, at home in Melbourne, there was just one picture of Anna as a newborn baby. She was swaddled in blankets, her tiny fist crammed into her mouth. It was Anna's favourite photograph. Marilyn appeared so happy and relaxed, a proud smile on her lips. She looked more natural than she did in other pictures; her clothes were almost scruffy and her hair hung loose. A third of the print had been cut off, in the manner Anna was so familiar with. She'd barely paid any attention to the remnants of the man who'd been in the photograph. Now she thought back to the dismembered arm wrapped around Marilyn; the hand cradling her shoulder. It was not Karl's slim-fingered hand, she now realised – it was stronger, tougher. Then, even the portion of the chest, clad in a pale shirt, hinted at a more solid frame. She gathered the pieces of evidence up like treasure in her hands. They were all that she knew of the man who was her true father – whose very existence had been a long and well-kept secret.

THIRTEEN

Dan leaned against the side of the Land Rover, chewing a stalk of dry grass as he gazed aimlessly into the distance. He didn't need to look at his watch to know it was almost mid-morning – the sun was already high in the sky. He shook his head in frustration. The convoy should be well on its way by now. All the vehicles were loaded and the men primed to get moving. There was only one problem: they couldn't leave until Lieutenant Hardy arrived.

Dan's second-in-command had been delayed in Johannesburg, so it had been arranged that he would fly straight here to Kivu Base. When Dan had arrived he'd expected to find Hardy waiting, ready to join the group. According to the Congolese duty officer, the Lieutenant had indeed flown in as planned the previous day, but had since disappeared. Runners were sent to nearby villages to try and locate him, but so far they'd had no success.

Shading his eyes with his hand, Dan looked along the line of vehicles. Immediately behind the Land Rover was a semi-armoured jeep with half-moon windscreens made of bulletproof glass. Next came the troop carrier with its camouflaged canvas cover. There were two jeeps, followed by the five-ton Bedford truck stocked with supplies, and the smaller radio truck. A third jeep took up the rear. It was an impressive sight: all the vehicles were loaded with artillery. Guns were mounted on the bonnets; heavy gauge barrels protruded from side doors and stuck out over back seats. Hidden from view were bazookas, grenades, rockets and a huge store of ammunition.

On the patchy grass beside the vehicles the men lounged in groups, smoking, talking or resting. A small crowd had gathered around Corporal McAdam. He had put his bagpipes away and was now showing off another skill. Soldiers looked on, eager as children, while he made coins, handkerchiefs – and even an egg – disappear up his sleeve, behind his ear or into his pocket, before turning up in a completely different place. Like the other men, McAdam wore a military shirt, red beret and webbing neck scarf – but in place of trousers he sported a tartan kilt and a pair of long socks with a plaid pattern. The outfit was completed by a huge pair of army boots. Dan hadn't noticed before quite how tall and solid the Scotsman was. With his long red beard – which had somehow survived the attentions of the barber – he looked like an exotic giant, towering over his audience.

Volunteer Bailey had thought of another way to pass the time. He'd stripped off his shirt, baring the eagle tattoo, and appeared to be hunting unsuccessfully for a wrestling partner. As he moved from one volunteer to the next, Henning, the Foreign Legionnaire, was watching on. It took Dan a few moments to name the expression on the man's vulnerable-looking baby face: it was the look of a predator fascinated by his prey. It would not be long, Dan knew, before the two came into conflict. They needed to fight it out, before they could work together. But this was not the time or the place. Dan did not want Operation Nightflower to begin with a brawl in the ranks. He hoped that, for now, the men would remain apart.

Volunteer Smith came round from the driver's side of the Land

Rover. He squatted down, peering under the wheel arch. The ex-game ranger had already checked the vehicle over several times, once with Dan at his side. Both knew Land Rovers inside out, but this open-topped version, inherited from the Belgian Army, had been made under licence by Minerva in Brussels. The two men had played a version of 'spot the difference' as they studied the dashboard, bodywork and engine. They'd tightened up a few bolts and replaced a valve. Now there was nothing else to check – nothing more to do.

'What's the plan, sir?' Smith's soft Rhodesian accent suited his courteous, almost diffident manner. At first glance he was an unlikely candidate for a commando force, but Dan had detected a tough streak beneath the gentle veneer. He was also a man who knew, like Dan, how to live and work in the African bush. 'Do we just keep waiting, sir?'

Dan scanned the entrance area, but there was no sign of anyone hurrying in past the checkpoint; the Congolese guards were passing their time playing draughts using bottle tops on a hand-drawn game board.

'We will have to leave without him,' Dan said. He didn't like the idea of having to report his decision to Blair, but he had a schedule to meet. The route had been plotted out, and the convoy was meant to cover nearly 200 miles today. 'Get the runner.'

'Yes, sir.'

Dan climbed into the front passenger's seat, resting his elbow on the armrest, looking ahead. He might have been preparing to set off on a hunting safari, except that a machine gun obscured part of his view, and a belt of ammunition trailed down over his thigh. He eyed the weapon, already operating it in his head. Blair had warned him that the weak point of this particular gun was the cover for one of the valves; it stuck up too high and would have to be protected when the vehicle drove under low-hanging branches, or it would soon be ripped off. Strapped to the bonnet in front of the gun were two jerry cans full of petrol. There were eight more tied to the sides or loaded into the rear. Dan didn't like having so much fuel on board – it didn't take much imagination to know what would happen if the Land Rover was hit by a grenade – but every vehicle in the unit had to be self-reliant.

From behind him, Dan could hear orders being relayed down the line. He could already identify the voices of the officers and quite a few of the volunteers. Some were easy – there were accents to help: American, Australian, British, Belgian. With others it was the tone of delivery, or the choice of words. Learning the names and characteristics of strangers was a skill Dan had honed over the years of making instant friends of his hunting clients. With Force Denby, the task was the same, though the scale was much bigger.

As a wave of activity spread through the convoy, Dan sat still and quiet. At the beginning of each safari, he always took a moment to reflect on the journey to come. It was a habit that came from his childhood, when his father would invariably pray before setting off on a long drive over African roads, bending his head over the steering wheel and using words like 'vouchsafe' and 'mercies'. Dan preferred to rely on his own skills to ensure safety and take his chances with everything else, but the ritual still held some power for him. He looked down at the floor, focusing on the familiar pattern of the rubber mat, the Land Rover insignia in the corner. He heard the driver's door open. There was the brush of cloth on vinyl, then the slight movement of the vehicle's suspension as it took the weight of a second occupant.

'I'll take over in a few hours.' Dan turned as he spoke. Then he froze. It wasn't Smith beside him, as he'd assumed. He was facing a stranger. In an instant, he took in the untrimmed beard and moustache; the shirt half-undone exposing a civilian singlet; the bloodshot eyes; the bottle opener hanging from a cord around the man's neck. Dan checked the beret. Pinned at an angle was a tarnished badge with the initials SS and a downward-pointing sword: the emblem of the British Special Forces.

'Sorry to hold you up. I'm afraid I got caught up in the village.' The sour smell of alcohol followed the man's words into the air. He made a half-salute, touching his forehead with his fingertips. 'Lieutenant Hardy. Looks like I got here just in time.'

Dan gave no reply. He just eyed the man, stony faced, while thoughts raced in his head. Hardy had the voice of an English gentleman, but very little else about him fitted the picture Blair had painted. Something must have changed since the two men fought together in Katanga. Dan wished Blair were here to help make sense of the situation. As he tried to think how to respond, he saw Smith approaching, a questioning expression on his face. Beyond him, other men were now looking in this direction as well. In seconds, Dan knew, every man in Force Denby would have learned that the missing officer had turned up, at last, looking drunk and scruffy. They'd be waiting to see how their Commanding Officer was going to respond.

Dan jumped out of the Land Rover and strode round to the driver's door. He looked into the man's bloodshot eyes.

'Get out,' he said under his breath.

Hardy hesitated, then slowly disembarked. Dan pulled himself up to his full height, standing at attention. He fixed his eyes on Hardy, willing him to follow suit. Then he raised his right hand slowly and deliberately, letting the Englishman see that he was going to salute. By the time the gesture was fully formed, the two men's hands were moving in unison.

Dan introduced Smith. A second round of salutes was exchanged. Then Dan waved Smith towards the driver's seat. Hardy slid into the back, behind him, slumping to one side.

'Let's move,' Dan said. He gave his driver a tight smile. '*Safari njema*.' May it be a good journey.

'Yes, sir!' Smith leaned to press the ignition button and the engine kicked into life.

The road was flat and dry, with the remains of a gravel surface holding firm under the wheels. Dan took a swig from his canteen, wiping his mouth with the back of his hand. He scanned the landscape to each side, leaving Smith to watch the road ahead. Dotted with spindly trees and outcrops of rock, the look of the place reminded him of large parts of Tanzania. They were yet to enter the dense forest that was more typical of the Congo.

As he screwed the lid back onto the bottle, the vehicle lurched into a pothole. Dan grabbed the dashboard to steady himself. There was a grunt from the back seat. Dan looked over his shoulder, past the slumped figure of Hardy, towards the armoured jeep that was following at 'dust distance' behind them. He could just make out the face of the driver, De Groote, and his large butcher's hands gripping the steering wheel. On this good road, the column was travelling at about 30 miles an hour. They'd been on the move for three hours and the journey had been uneventful. It would soon be time to stop for lunch.

Up ahead, the road entered a thicket of trees and bushes. Dan stood up, his legs braced against the seat, in order to see over them.

His binoculars swung from his neck, the familiar weight reminding him of years of scouting for game. According to the latest aerial surveillance report, there was no rebel activity in this area, but Dan still wanted to keep a good watch. He ducked as the Land Rover passed under a low-hanging branch.

'You want to look out for spears, old chap.' The words came from the direction of the back seat. 'Look for the points, sticking up.'

Dan turned around. Hardy was now sitting upright. He'd buttoned his shirt, but his beret was crooked.

'That's one of their tricks,' Hardy added. 'They hide on the side of the road, and jump out of the bushes.'

'Thanks for the warning,' Dan said. He still had no idea how to respond to Hardy – or what to expect of the man.

'And look out for elephant traps.' Hardy's tone was neutral; he might have been reading out the social pages in the *Sunday Times*. 'I was talking to one of the Congolese at the Base. He's been fighting the Simbas up in the north. They've taken to digging holes in the road. A truck dives in headfirst, writing off the engine. But a jeep gets swallowed whole. It doesn't turn out well.'

Dan leaned closer, listening carefully now. He knew what a traditional elephant trap was like: a crater disguised by a covering of earth, leaves and branches. There were murderous bamboo spikes in the bottom.

'Apparently they even roll a spare tyre over the surface, last thing, to leave tracks. Pretty clever, really.' Hardy chuckled to himself.

'What else did you learn?'

'That's about it, from the soldiers. Mostly, they wanted to talk about witchdoctors and magic medicine. But I went to the village – I thought I'd make good use of my time, waiting for you lot to turn up. Cost me a lot in beer, but I heard a few stories. There was a local man who'd just been in a village near Uvira.'

Dan exchanged a glance with Smith – a mutual acknowledgement that the officer had been misjudged. Hardy was late because he'd been gathering Intelligence. He'd got drunk in the line of duty. 'What did he tell you?'

Hardy grinned, showing a chipped front tooth. 'He saw a Belgian plantation owner bury his family heirlooms in a rose garden before running for his life. But he didn't get far – he was shot dead. The man who told me the story isn't planning to be up that way again, so he sold me the Intelligence for a bargain price.' He patted his shirt pocket. 'He even drew me a treasure map.'

Dan narrowed his eyes. His first impulse was to confiscate the piece of paper. Clearly, it constituted an intention to loot. Then he remembered what Major Blair had said to him about the mercenaries during his briefing at Lemba Base. It was at the end of a long talk about maintaining good standards of behaviour.

'Always remember, Miller, your men are not angels. There will be looting, whether you like it or not. I limit my men to what they can use up or carry away in their pockets. I make it clear I will court martial murderers and rapists and hand out the punishment there and then. When you take Uvira, put a guard on the bank straight away. I don't want to have to explain a blown-up safe to my Congolese colleagues.' He'd gone quiet, then. Dan had sensed that Blair was considering the gulf between the ideal and the actual, between plans and outcomes – as every soldier should.

'Village coming up, sir.'

At first, Dan couldn't see what had caught Smith's eye. Then he noticed the cattle-hairs caught in the bushes. And a fragment of a car tyre, peeled off from a homemade sandal. Looking ahead, he detected the faintest haze of smoke.

'It's not marked on the map,' Dan commented. 'But that's not saying much.' He squinted into the distance. They were still far from anything that could be called the front line. There was no need to conduct what Blair called 'reconnaissance by gunfire', but they would enter with caution, on full alert.

They reached the outlying gardens, passing a child herding goats. He waved cheerfully, showing no sign of being daunted by the convoy as it ground past him.

'Let's hope the rest of the family are as friendly,' Hardy commented.

'Get yourself armed and ready,' Dan instructed him.

Before long the thatched roofs of conical huts appeared, clustered around a single large tree. Smith drove steadily but slowly towards the clearing at the heart of the village. The people retreated to the huts, mothers ushering children before them and closing the doors; men standing outside. There was no sign of weapons – not even a spear was to be seen.

'Stop here,' Dan said. 'Don't cut the motor.' He could hear the rest of the column slowing down, the drivers taking their lead from the front. 'Get my back.' He threw the instruction to Smith as he opened the Land Rover door, even though the volunteer was already lifting his rifle to his shoulder. Every time an order was given and obeyed, Dan knew, trust between an officer and his men grew.

Drawing his pistol from his holster, he clicked off the safety catch and kept his finger near the trigger. Then he strode towards a middle-aged tribesman who was standing in front of the nearest hut. Just as Dan came close, the door behind the man opened. Dan jumped to one side, using the flimsy planks as a screen.

The African shouted something, waving his hands. Peering

through cracks in the door, Dan glimpsed pale skin and white clothing, the flash of spectacles catching the light.

A man emerged from the shadows, arms raised, hands outstretched. He might have been praying or calling down a blessing – except that he was staring at the barrel of the pistol.

'*Je suis le Père Michel.*' His words tumbled out. '*Ne tirez pas!*' He repeated himself urgently in English. 'I am Father Michel. Do not shoot me!'

The priest wore a full-length gown and a pith helmet on his head. Both had once been white but were now pink with dust. He looked as if he'd spent a lifetime here in the Congo – his face was burned dark by the sun, contrasting with a white beard, sparse but long.

'I'm Lieutenant Miller.' Dan lowered his gun.

The priest raised bushy eyebrows. He waved one hand, taking in the convoy. 'Who are you?'

'We're with the Congolese National Army,' Dan said. It was better than announcing they were a commando unit engaged in their own operation – the priest would guess they were mercenaries. With the track record of *Les Affreux* well known in the country, he would fear the worst. The introduction was also true. The person Blair reported to was General Mobutu, the Commander-in-Chief of the Congolese Army. The General was also the mercenaries' employer – although Dan wasn't certain any more who was actually paying the bills.

'Thank God you have come.' The man let out a long breath.

Dan felt a flash of alarm. 'Are there Simbas around here?'

'Not so far, but everyone is frightened of them.'

Smith came to stand nearby, cradling his rifle as he swept the surroundings with an intense gaze. The village men watched him, unmoving, eyes narrowed with fear. Father Michel called out to them in a language Dan didn't recognise. Then he turned back to the two soldiers.

'I have told them you have come to destroy the Simbas. That we will be safe now.'

Dan forced a smile. He just hoped it would turn out to be that simple. He scanned the faces of the men who stood protectively outside their huts. They looked far from reassured by the presence of the military convoy in their village. Dan wondered if this was because they didn't trust the white men to save them from the Simbas – or if they just didn't trust soldiers, whoever they were.

Glancing around, Dan saw no sign of Hardy. He instructed Smith to set up sentries and give orders for the men to cook up hot rations over hexamine fuel stoves set up by the roadside. They needed to eat – but also, Dan knew, the sight of food being prepared helped create ease between people.

Father Michel gestured for Dan to follow him into the generous shade of the fig tree, where a fallen log, the bark polished smooth from use, made a long bench. As the two men sat down together and the soldiers unpacked their rations, the atmosphere of tension began to lift. Before long, children were playing again; women returned to their duties, pounding corn or tending cooking fires. Outside one of the nearby huts, a chicken made its final squawk as a knife came down on its neck.

'What do you know about the Simbas?' Dan asked Father Michel.

'They are causing a lot of trouble. I am in radio contact with several other missions. They managed to keep their radios hidden from the Simbas. We pass on news to one another. In the villages, the rebel soldiers are stealing food, burning houses. They are beating the men.' He lowered his voice. 'Everyone is very afraid.'

Before Dan could respond, a small girl ran up, offering him a piece of sugar cane.

'Can you tell me how to say "thank you"?' Dan asked Father Michel.

When Dan repeated the priest's words, the girl smiled shyly. Biting into the sugar cane, Dan began chewing at the soft fibre. As the watery sweetness broke over his tongue, he closed his eyes to express his enjoyment. The child giggled in delight. She lingered there, watching him intently. Then she said something, and Father Michel translated.

'She says, "You are indeed a white giant".'

'What does she mean?' Dan asked.

The priest shrugged. 'I do not know.' He returned to the conversation that had been disrupted. 'I have heard that in some villages people have been held captive. There are reports of torture. Women have been raped.'

Dan glanced at the child. Even though he knew she couldn't understand, it seemed wrong to mention such horrors in front of her. He felt an impulse to seek out her parents and instruct them to take her inside their hut – to close the door and keep her safe from the world. He turned back to the priest.

'What about the missionaries? And the other Europeans? Are they being harmed?'

'Some stations have been taken over by Simbas, but the missionaries have been allowed to continue their work. A priest was beaten for trying to protect one of his parishioners. A church has been burned down. But so far, it is the local people who have suffered.'

Dan looked back along the convoy to where the Belgian farmer who'd joined the unit was helping prepare lunch. He kept a little distance from the other men. His face still wore a haunted frown.

'One of our men comes from near Uvira.' Dan chose his words carefully to make sure he didn't give away Force Denby's mission. 'He's worried about his wife and children who are on their own, out on the family farm. Their name is Bergman. Have you heard of them?'

'No, I am sorry. May God protect them.'

Dan saw the concern written on the man's sun-worn face. Clearly he thought the Simbas could begin harming Europeans at any time. Force Denby needed to reach Uvira as soon as possible. But that would take several days, at least – maybe much longer. It depended on the state of the roads and the extent of enemy resistance.

'Do you know how far the Simbas are from here?'

'The last I heard, they are in the village of Kabwanga – two-thirds of the way to Uvira, on the other side of the river. But that report is a week old now.'

'Good. Thank you,' Dan said.

'As to other areas, the south of the province seems to be quite safe. I know people in Ruka and they have seen no sign of the rebels. Down in Banya, it is the same story . . .'

'I don't need to know about that.' Dan held up his hand to stop the flow of information. For decades he'd avoided hearing news of the area he'd once called home. He didn't want to change that policy now. Operation Nightflower was his only concern.

He turned back towards the convoy. The faint fishy smell of burning hexamine drifted across to him. He should eat, while he had the chance, then have a meeting with Hardy – regardless of the rocky start to their relationship, the Lieutenant was his second-in-command. Then, he should sit down with his Intelligence Sergeant and see what he'd learned from the villagers.

The moment the convoy had stopped, Becker and his offsider Corporal Dupont had started interviewing the local people. Dan had seen them moving from one group of tribesmen to another. Making use of his military college training as a linguist, Becker was conversing fluently in whatever local language was spoken here. They were an intimidating pair, heavily armed and wearing bandoliers around their necks. Few words passed between them, yet they worked like two parts of one person. This was their first joint action, but it looked as if they'd been operating together for years.

The South African and the Belgian had been drawn to one another the minute they'd met at Lemba Base. After sitting next to them on the flight to Kivu and hearing their conversation, Dan understood why. It seemed they shared some similar beliefs about the world, only some of which had come up in the recruitment interviews. As well as being anti-Communist, Becker declared himself to be a staunch supporter of his country's apartheid system. He disdained black Africans and didn't pretend otherwise. Listening to him speak, Dan was reminded of the South African he'd encountered in Dar es Salaam – and felt the same outrage bubble up inside him. For his part, Dupont was a great admirer of what his countrymen had achieved in the Congo – the grand cities, the prospering plantations. He thought it had been a terrible mistake to grant Independence to the Congolese, but since it had happened, he wanted to make sure a pro-Western government was in charge. Protecting the interests of the foreign mining companies, Dupont believed, was vital if there was to be any hope at all for the Congo. The more Dan heard the men talk, the less he liked either of them. When Becker shared around a packet of gum, Dan declined the offer.

The two soldiers were now standing outside a hut, not far from where Dan and the priest were sitting on the tree trunk. They were talking to one of the women. She kept her eyes downcast, shy and respectful, but the interchange appeared to be lighthearted, with onlookers sharing smiles. When they were finished with her, the pair approached an old man sitting on a wooden chair adorned with a leopardskin. He had a cloth draped over his head, almost covering his eyes, as if to provide a shelter from the scene in front of him.

'That is the chief,' Father Michel said indignantly. 'What do they want with him?'

'They just need to ask a few questions.' Part of Dan wanted to call Becker and Dupont off, and leave the man in peace. But whatever Dan thought of Becker, he had to let the specialist do his work.

'These people do not know anything,' the priest said. 'I can speak for them.'

Dan didn't reply. He had no reason to suspect the priest was anything other than honest and candid. But that didn't mean there wasn't another set of facts to be uncovered.

From Becker's tone of voice, Dan concluded that a friendly talk was fast turning into a full-scale interrogation. He shifted uncomfortably on the bench. He didn't like invading a traditional village like this and allowing his men to behave like bullies. But if there had been any deceptions regarding the allegiances held in this place, Becker's approach had the best chance of unveiling them. And information gained today could save soldiers' lives tomorrow.

Dan glanced around at the faces of the villagers. They were tense again and silent. He tried to see them through Becker's eyes. Were they simply afraid of these menacing soldiers? Or did they have something to hide? This was his new life, Dan realised. Trusting people was a luxury he had to forego. He looked at the sugar cane in his hand. Becker would have thrown it on the ground before letting it touch his lips. Not just because it had been in the hands of an African child, but because it could so easily have been poisoned.

Becker's demeanour softened; he smiled at the chief. It could mean he'd won the upper hand and was preparing to exploit his position; alternatively, he was satisfied nothing had been hidden. Dan didn't know which it was. The priest seemed reassured; he began talking about the work he was doing here in the village – evidently there was a school and an infirmary.

'Perhaps you can spare me some medical supplies? Medicines? Bandages?'

'I'm sure we can find something.' Dan stood up, intending to take the priest to meet the Medical Officer. He'd only taken a few steps when he stopped. Straining his ears past the busy hum of village and army life, he picked up the sound of drumming.

He moved towards it, as if drawn by a heartbeat that matched his own. The rhythm was deeply familiar to him. Everywhere he'd travelled in Africa, the voices of the different kinds of drums were similar. What he could hear now – coming from further into the village – was not the flighty beat of the dancing drum, or the low throb of the ceremonial drum. He recognised the dual tones of the call drum, which was able to mimic the pitch of the human voice. While Becker and Dupont were engaged with the chief, someone else was at work. A message was being sent out across the land.

In an area of open ground between several large huts, a man dressed in a loincloth stood by a drum made from a hollowed log with a slit cut in its top. About three feet long, the instrument rested on a cradle formed from forked tree-limbs. The height allowed the man to keep an upright posture, while using a pair of curved sticks to strike the drum. As he beat out his message, he stared intently along the valley into the far distance. He seemed oblivious to Dan's presence, or that of the villagers who had gathered around him.

Dan was aware of Becker arriving beside him. 'What do you think they are saying?'

'Whatever it is,' Dan said, 'it's urgent. They usually send their drum-calls in the early morning or late at night.'

'At the time determined by the ancestors?' Becker's tone was cynical.

'No. When the air is cooler. The sound waves carry further.'

Becker eyed the drummer warily. 'Do you think they can actually relay detailed information?'

Dan nodded. 'I've seen proof of it.'

Some years back, while on a foot safari in the remote north of the Mara, he'd been able to arrange the air evacuation of a sick client. A village drummer had contacted another, who had passed the message on. Eventually the news reached a mission from where it was radioed to the Flying Doctor Service. Whether there was an actual language of drums, Dan wasn't so sure. The distance covered would have meant using three different tribal languages. An old missionary nurse who had spent her life in the bush told him she thought it was a matter of telepathy. The drums assisted the transmission of thoughts. She'd suggested it was something like prayer.

'Is that what Methodists believe?' Dan had asked.

She'd smiled. 'There's more going on in the world than we can understand.'

'Even missionaries?' he'd teased her gently. They were old friends.

'Especially us.'

Dan looked around for the priest. He was standing a little way off, looking both confused and worried. Dan sensed he had no idea what the intent of the drummer was, either.

Dan turned to Becker. 'Ask him what he's saying. I don't expect a straight answer, but we might get a clue.'

The Sergeant spoke to the drummer, but got no response. An old man standing nearby answered instead. Becker translated his words.

'He's calling to the people in the hills – telling them they should celebrate.'

'Why?'

'Because foreigners have come to save them.'

'I don't trust him,' Dan said. 'Tell him to stop.'

Becker spoke, but the drummer took no notice. He just kept on sending out his message. The Intelligence Sergeant repeated his command, his voice raised. The villagers watched on, wide-eyed, as the drummer continued to defy the soldier. The tribesman's bravery seemed to enhance his stature; he looked taller, stronger – as if he were the conduit of an immortal presence, eternal and indestructible.

Dupont marched up to stand next to his partner. He rested his hand on his holster.

'Take it easy, Corporal,' Dan warned.

Just then, the sequence of beats came to an end; the drummer held his sticks still, poised over the hole in the trunk. The villagers followed the direction of his gaze – their faces turning as one – towards the end of the valley. The quiet was punctuated by small noises: the hum of insects, the whispers of children. Somewhere a baby began to cry. Then from far away – muffled but still clear – came another drum-call. Even Dan could tell that the same rhythm and the same tones were being repeated. The drummer in the next village had picked up the message and was in turn passing it on.

Dan frowned, trying to think. If news of Force Denby reached the Simbas, the element of surprise that could be used to advantage would be lost. But information once shared could not be taken back. There was only one thing they could do, Dan realised – give the drummer a new story to tell. He turned to Smith, who stood at his side.

'Get McAdam,' he said quietly. 'Tell him to bring his pipes.'

The red-and-green kilt flapped around the bare knees of the Scotsman as he marched steadily towards the place where the drummer still stood beside his instrument. The villagers lingered around him as if unsure what they should do next. McAdam carried his bagpipes wedged under his left arm. He'd replaced his beret with the tam-o'-shanter and wore a sash over his shoulder made from the same plaid as his kilt. As he came near, the villagers stared in amazement. Whatever strange attire and behaviour they'd seen displayed by Europeans in the past, nothing could have prepared them for the sight of the Regimental Piper. He stood out among the other soldiers, dressed in their khaki uniforms, like an exotic creature from a tribe of colourful giants.

Reaching a spot not far from where the drum rested in its wooden cradle, McAdam turned, drawing himself up to his full height, and saluted Dan. Then he paused, a showman gathering in his audience. He put the blowpipe into his mouth and blew into the bag. It really looked as if he were filling a third lung with air – breathing life into an inanimate being.

As a high wail escaped the pipes, the people nearest to McAdam shrank back. The Corporal positioned the swollen bag under his left arm and began to play. He closed his eyes, a frown on his face as he concentrated on the music.

Gradually, the villagers moved in closer. Fear gave way to dawning admiration. Though they would never have heard anything like this before, they responded as if they recognised something deep, perhaps mystical, about the sounds that enveloped them.

Even to Dan, the performance appeared magical. There was no connection between the timing of McAdam's cheeks puffing out and deflating, and the sounds that were created. The bag moved under his arm like something alive. As the pace quickened, his fingers flew up and down the pipe. The music swelled, powerful and haunting, reaching out over the land.

Looking around at his men, Dan could tell that every one of them was caught up in the emotion stirred by McAdam's playing. He could almost see, written on the soldiers' faces, thoughts of people and places left behind or gone forever. Dan felt the pull of the music himself. The sounds seemed to work their way under his skin, touching nerves he'd thought were long dead. Since he'd become part of Blair's regiment, the grey cloud that had oppressed him for years had dispersed. He could breathe freely again. But there was a price to be paid for the new clarity: there was nothing to shield him from the power of the music. He was swept by a deep longing that he didn't want to name.

He turned away from McAdam, scanning the whole scene. He was pleased to see that the sentries had held their positions and were alert and focused. Girard, the Signaller, had joined the crowd of onlookers. He wasn't watching McAdam, though; his eyes were fixed on the drummer. There was a rare expression of interest on the young Frenchman's face. Like other radio operators Dan had known, Girard was reserved and sombre; he usually had a distant look in his eyes as if his real life were being played out somewhere else – perhaps the realm in which dots and dashes took the place of spoken words. Whether Girard had witnessed the call-drum in use just now, or only heard about the sending of the message, Dan didn't know; either way, the Signaller was clearly fascinated. If he and the drummer had a language in common, Dan suspected the Frenchman would suggest a sharing of skills. Perhaps he'd produce his blinker lights and put on a display of his own, flashing a message in Morse to an imaginary post at the end of the valley.

McAdam finished his first song and moved straight on to a second as though he feared he might lose the chance to extend his time in the limelight. The chief rose from his chair, as if drawn to his feet by the fresh energy of a faster, lighter tune. He pulled back the cloth on his head so there was nothing to obscure his view. The look on his face was impossible to read. However impressive the piping was, the man knew it was connected with these armed men and their convoy of vehicles invading the countryside. As with the women working in the kitchen at Lemba Base, Dan wondered how much the tribesman understood about the conflict that was sweeping the Congo. He would have heard stories, many a blend of truth and fiction. No doubt the elders had held long meetings, trying to make sense of it all.

Not far away from where he was, Dan could see the spirit hut where they would have assembled. He identified it by the painted masks that topped the lintels and the charms dangling from the rafters inside. Deep in the shadows, Dan knew, would be all the sacred treasures of the village, created over generations by the finest artists in the tribe and tended by the *waganga*, the healers. In pride of place, among sculptures representing ancestors and significant animals, would be the *nkisi*. It was likely, Dan thought, that in recent times, fresh blades or nails had been brought to the statue, licked by the healer on behalf of the people, and hammered into the carving – as the people petitioned the unseen powers for the provision of that most simple of necessities: safety.

When the pipes fell silent, no one moved. Even the children were motionless. The music still seemed present, lingering in the air. McAdam handed his pipes to Girard. Then he produced a small silk handkerchief from his pocket. He waved the cloth around to show that nothing was wrapped inside it. Then he cupped his other hand. While the people watched, he fed the handkerchief into his fist until it disappeared from view. He said something Dan took to be the Gaelic equivalent of 'abracadabra' – but this was no party performance; he was grave and stern. After waiting a few moments for the tension to build, he opened out his hand. An egg lay on his palm.

Several women screamed and ran away, dragging their children behind them. A tribesman close to McAdam raised the machete he held in his hand – but only a fraction; he looked frightened more than threatening. Dan knew that eggs, of all items, held spiritual significance in many parts of Africa; they represented fertility so powerfully that many people believed if girls ate them their bodies would be disturbed and they might never become pregnant. Dan wanted to call out to the villagers that it was just a trick. It was not real magic, even though that was exactly what it looked like. Instead he remained grim-faced and silent. The best path to safety for these people lay in a swift defeat of the rebellion. Where this deception was concerned, the end would justify the means. When news of this witchdoctor's powers spread over the land, passed by one drummer to the next, the Simbas would be afraid of the White Giants that were headed their way. Like the soldiers of the National Army, they might retreat before the enemy arrived. Many lives would be saved, on both sides.

McAdam was preparing for another trick, evidently involving two coins and a piece of paper. Catching his eye, Dan shook his head. 'It's time to move.' He gestured towards the line of vehicles. 'Come on, lads. Let's go.'

He could feel the energy of his men, almost tangible in the air, as they fell in behind him. The pipes had drawn them together. As they strode down to their vehicles, they were no longer a group of individuals, with different dreams and plans, different reasons to be here. They were a single fighting force, thinking and moving as one.

FOURTEEN

The midday heat was like a fog that had invaded the house, creeping in around the closed curtains and lowered blinds. Drops of sweat pooled on Anna's skin as she paced up and down the hallway. Her footsteps echoed on the wooden floor, then made a muffled beat as she crossed the thick Persian rug. She passed beneath a lion's head mounted on a wooden shield. It seemed to follow her with a baleful stare. Her own eyes were fixed on the telephone as if her gaze could rouse it to life. Magadi had booked an international call with the operator; now he and Anna were waiting to be rung back.

She went to stand under the ceiling fan, tilting her face to the moving air. Closing her eyes, she pictured her mother lying sound asleep, far away in Australia. It would be the middle of the night there – cold and dark. When she heard the phone, Marilyn would fear the worst. Shaking off sleep, she'd fumble for the bedside lamp, then grab her dressing-gown before rushing to the hallway. Anna felt guilty about putting Marilyn through such anxiety. But it was not Anna's fault she had to make this call.

When the telephone finally rang, both Anna and Magadi jumped in surprise. For a moment, neither moved. Then Magadi picked up the handset, listening and nodding, before offering it to Anna. 'You have been connected.'

'Hello? Mum? It's me.' Anna tried to sound calm and confident, though inside she was already cowering from the outrage she feared was coming.

'What's happened? Are you all right?'

'Yes, I'm fine.'

'For God's sake, Anna! Do you know what time it is?'

'I'm sorry. I need to ask you something.' Anna decided to get straight to the point of her call, not even mentioning Karl's death. She fought to keep control, but the anger boiled up. 'Why didn't you tell me Karl was my stepfather?'

'What are you talking about?' The telephone line was startlingly clear; Anna could hear a tremor in her mother's voice.

'You were married before!' Anna continued. 'I had another father. How could you keep that secret from me?'

A long silence followed. Anna sensed her mother's shock, then the rising panic – as if thoughts and emotions could travel along the undersea cables, all the way from Australia to Africa.

'You didn't need to know.' There was a steely edge to Marilyn's words, as though she'd guessed where the questions were leading and was galvanising her defence.

'Who is my real father?'

Marilyn sighed. 'I'm not going to tell you anything about him. You will only be hurt. It's not a story you need to hear.'

'I want to know.'

'I have to protect you.'

'No. You have to tell me.'

There was silence again, broken by a faint crackle in the line. 'He was a bad man, Anna. He abandoned us. I was a young mother alone with a child. In the middle of the Congo. That's why I had to marry Karl. I never loved him, but I had no choice. Anna, I was desperate. I had nothing.'

'What was his name?'

She heard Marilyn draw a long breath. 'Come home, Anna. You belong here. With me. Just the two of us. We don't need anyone else.'

'If you won't give me any information, I'll find it myself.'

A cynical laugh burst out. 'And how will you do that? You wouldn't know where to begin.'

'I'm going to Banya.'

Now Marilyn caught her breath sharply. 'You can't. It's not safe. You must listen to me!'

Anna gripped the handset. She could feel her mother's power over her, pulling like an undertow.

'Leave well alone, Annie.' The use of the childhood nickname touched Anna's heart for a second, then sparked a flash of anger. 'You must trust me on this.'

Anna closed her eyes, running back over what Marilyn had said. Her father was a bad man. He had abandoned his family, leaving them with nothing. But if this was the truth, why was it kept secret all these years? Why hadn't Marilyn denigrated her first husband for his crimes, like she had Karl? And why had she been so afraid of Anna coming to the Congo?

'Trust me,' Marilyn repeated.

Words rose to Anna's lips, but she could not bring herself to utter them. They remained as a thought, hovering in her head.

I don't trust you.

'I have to go,' she said instead. 'Goodbye.'

Anna found Eliza sitting on a swinging chair in the garden. Her head rested against the back of the cane seat and her eyes were closed, but her face looked tense and strained. A cigarette poised between her fingers had burned down halfway, the ash forming a fragile tower on its tip. From her bedroom window Anna had watched the Jaguar arrive back at the house nearly half an hour ago. She'd waited impatiently for Eliza to come inside – there was so much she needed to tell her. When Eliza had failed to appear, she'd gone in search of her.

As Anna approached the chair she deliberately crunched the gravel underfoot, to announce her presence – but Eliza didn't respond.

'I'm sorry to bother you.' Anna hovered at a distance.

Eliza opened her eyes, staring blankly for a second. Then she sat up straight, flicking the ash from her cigarette onto the ground. 'Anna . . . I didn't know you were back. How was the meeting?'

Anna recounted what she'd learned from Leclair, and then described her conversation with Marilyn. Eliza listened without interrupting, though she looked surprised when she heard that Karl was not Anna's real father.

'So, I have decided to go to Banya,' Anna finished.

Eliza raised her eyebrows, nodding slowly.

'I know it could easily be just a waste of time. I probably won't find out anything. And even if I do, it could lead to more disappointment and pain. I might wish I'd never known anything.' Anna realised she was arguing against objections Eliza hadn't even raised. She changed tack, cutting to the question she wanted to ask. 'I was wondering if you could help me arrange transport. I don't even know how far it is from here.'

'About two days' drive. Maybe much more if it rains – most of the way it's a gravel road.'

'Could I hire a car, and a driver?'

Eliza shook her head. She drew on her cigarette, then blew out a long stream of smoke. 'No one would take you all that way.'

'Then what can I do?' Anna's voice rose. 'I have to get there . . .'

'I'll take you if you like.' Eliza used the same casual tone as she'd adopted when offering a lift to the hospital.

Anna stared at her. 'Really?' Then she shook her head. 'I couldn't ask you to do that. You've already been so kind.'

'I'm not being kind,' Eliza said. 'I just . . . I really want to get out of Albertville.' She eyed her surroundings – the tended garden, the grand edifice of the house, even the peacock that strutted past trailing bright feathers over the lawn – as if they were no more appealing than a concrete prison yard. She jumped to her feet, leaving the chair swinging behind her. 'It's a beautiful drive to Banya. The road follows the lakeside most of the time. And I've got some friends who live on a mission up that way. We could visit them if we have time.' As she spoke, her eyes brightened, her chin lifted; she looked years younger.

'When can we go?' Anna asked.

'Tomorrow. First light.'

The dawn sky was a deep pink at the horizon, fading to pale green above. The air was cool and still. From the yard behind the house came the sound of a rooster crowing. Only moments later, answering calls began echoing around the neighbourhood. Anna stood on the front steps, yawning. She could feel in her stomach the weight of the huge breakfast Magadi had served up while it was still pitch-black outside.

As instructed by Eliza, she was dressed for the journey in a khaki shirt and trousers and her walking boots. She held her broad-brimmed Akubra in her hand. On the ground at her feet was the small red suitcase Eliza had lent her so that she could pack what she needed for the safari. By the time Anna had put in her medicine collection and some spare sets of clothes, it had been almost full. But she'd managed to find room for her precious koala. When Anna thought of the toy now, stowed away in one corner of the case, she felt a wave of emotion. The childhood treasure held even more meaning for her now. She'd had it nearly from birth – which meant it was part of the life she'd shared with her real father. Anna pictured a man – just a hazy, dreamlike figure – jiggling the koala in front of a baby, making it dance, perhaps even putting words into its black felt mouth. Back then, the koala was brand-new, covered in thick soft fur. Anna imagined herself smiling into its two glass eyes – then looking up to the man who held the toy. She saw his hand, big and strong, as it appeared in the baby photograph, draping Marilyn's shoulder. But she could not begin to construct his face. She didn't know if he was blond or dark, if his eyes were blue or brown. She didn't know how old he was. She knew nothing at all.

Anna kicked restlessly at the stonework with the toe of her boot. She could hardly contain her eagerness to get to Banya and begin her search for information. She watched Eliza striding back and forth between the house and the car, calling instructions to Magadi; Anna had offered to help with the packing, but they didn't seem to need her. All four doors of the Jaguar had been flung open, along with the boot. The car was being loaded with camping equipment. It was just a precaution, Eliza had explained; there was a hotel they would aim for, but she didn't know if it was still running. And anyway, it was never wise to drive into the countryside without being self-sufficient.

It was clear that Eliza had set off like this many times before – every item, from the torch to the washing basin to the spade for digging a latrine, had its designated spot in the car. Anna saw a tent and groundsheet, two kapok sleeping bags and lilos being packed away. An aluminium trunk full of food went in, along with a plastic water container and a jerry can of petrol. The last provision to be fitted into its place was a whole case of Johnnie Walker whisky.

When Eliza came out to the car for the last time, she carried a rifle slung over her shoulder. At the sight of it, Anna felt a shiver of fear.

'What's that for?' she asked. Last night, Eliza had reassured her that where they were going was safe; the fighting was well to the north.

'Sometimes I shoot guinea fowl or a gazelle. The villagers are always grateful for some meat.' She smiled. 'It's the best way to make friends.'

'So, it's not for protection?'

Eliza shrugged. 'Leopards pose a danger in some areas. However, the Africans say that the leopard who kills is the leopard no one has seen.' She laid the rifle flat on the floor behind the front seats, before slipping a cardboard container of bullets into the glove box. 'I think we're ready.'

Both women shook hands with Magadi, who solemnly wished them a successful safari. As Anna met his gaze, she remembered how he'd comforted her after Karl's death. So much had happened since then, it was hard to believe the time involved was so short. She wondered what else would take place in her life before she saw the servant again.

Eliza sat behind the wheel, immediately turning on the engine while Anna slid inside next to her. Magadi waved from the steps.

Dressed in his white tunic, arm raised, he looked like a priest blessing their departure. The car accelerated away. Soon they were speeding towards the front gate, leaving the Lindenbaum mansion behind.

The windows of the Jaguar were wound down, letting a stream of fresh air into the car. Anna tucked a loose strand of hair under the silk scarf that was tied over her head. Eliza wore one as well – hers was patterned with yellow-and-green swirls. Anna had glimpsed a label sewn into the corner: *Christian Dior. Paris.* Her own scarf was plain and cheap, but it would do the same job of protecting her hair.

'There will be lots of dust,' Eliza had warned her while they were packing. 'Unless it rains. Then there will be lots of mud.'

So far, there was neither dust nor mud. Since leaving Albertville behind – heading inland at first – they had been driving on a tarmac road that was in reasonable repair. The Jaguar glided along comfortably. Eliza drove with one hand, steering expertly to avoid the occasional pothole.

They passed through bushy countryside dotted with spindly trees. It was not that different to the landscape of country Victoria. Anna was reminded of going on bushwalks with the Girl Guides, feeling brave and practical in her neat uniform, her compass hanging from a cord around her neck. The recollection prompted her to think of Sally Jacobs, who used to go on the trips as well. Just before Anna had left for Africa the two friends had met up for a drink. Sally had been shocked by the suddenness of Anna's plan, and worried about her travelling to such a faraway place as the Congo. Anna wondered what she would think if she could see her now – driving off with a woman she'd only just met, to a place she knew nothing about, to find out about her real father. Anna tried to imagine Sally's reaction, but found she could only evoke a very hazy picture. Sally was part of a world that was already becoming distant.

To the left, beyond the woodlands, there was a range of hills. It stretched into the distance as far as the eye could see. The slopes were covered with the dense forest that Anna had seen from the air as she'd flown into Albertville. There was something oppressive about the thought of the unbroken tree cover extending for hundreds, perhaps thousands, of miles, penetrating deep into the heart of Africa. It made her want to shrink away, and she was glad that Eliza had assured her that their journey to Banya didn't take them into the interior. As they drove, Anna kept her gaze averted from the band of dark green. But she could still sense it there, a lurking presence in the distance.

The woodland thinned, giving way to grassland. Then they reached an area of taller trees with striking yellow bark. Set apart from one another they were a beautiful sight with their spreading limbs and canopies like umbrellas. Some grew close to the verge, casting their shade over the car as it passed.

'They're fever trees,' Eliza said. 'Quinine comes from the bark.'

Anna looked at the trees with interest. She was taking chloroquine as a precaution against malaria. The white tablets were extraordinarily bitter. Even swallowed with lots of water, you couldn't escape the taste – but it was a small price to pay to be safe.

'It was the discovery of quinine that turned around the fortunes of the white man in Africa,' Eliza commented. 'It allowed them to survive and take the place over.'

Anna listened for the anger with which Eliza had spoken about the colonial era when they were discussing Karl's collection – but today her tone was light and mocking. She was in a better mood, and she was sober.

'There's another thing,' Eliza continued. 'Without quinine we wouldn't be drinking gin and tonic. When the British Army was in India during the Raj era, they were told to take quinine to prevent malaria. They tried adding it to water flavoured with fruit and sugar to hide the bitterness. Then they improved the taste by adding gin.' She smiled, her eyes crinkling at the corners. 'And that was the origin of one of the world's great inventions.'

Anna forced herself to smile back. She felt guilty – as if she'd been caught out thinking about Eliza's love of alcohol. She wondered if there was a case of gin and some bottles of tonic somewhere in the car, along with the whisky. Anna enjoyed having sundowners with Eliza. She liked the daring pleasure of drinking cocktails during the daytime as well. It was part of being in Eliza's exotic world – so different to her own. But at the same time, Eliza's constant drinking made her uneasy. There were several clients of Mr Williams who always turned up for meetings smelling of liquor and asked for a drink as soon as they sat down. Mr Williams was very cautious about doing business with them. He said he couldn't trust their judgement.

'I can see the lake.' Anna seized on a change of topic. The road had veered back towards the shore and now, between the trees, there were glimpses of water.

Before long, they reached an area of farmland, soon followed by a village. It was the first of a whole line of settlements. They were made up of tin shanties and traditional mud huts, with the occasional cement brick structure, presumably built by the government or a mission. Whenever they reached the edge of a village Eliza slowed down. Now and then she stopped the car to hand money to someone who had caught her eye. Anna would find herself smiling politely at cripples as they dragged themselves along the ground.

She waved back to a man whose head was tilted sideways by a large lump in his neck, and tried not to stare at one whose trunk-like leg, clad in rough skin, looked like something that belonged on an elephant. She turned away from nightmare images of festering skin infections, open sores and unhealed wounds.

'These people should go to the hospital,' Anna commented.

'There aren't enough hospitals or doctors, or even just small clinics,' Eliza answered. 'Not for the ordinary Africans.' She shook her head. 'You'd never guess the Congo is one of the richest countries in the world.'

'The Congolese are in charge now. Why don't they make changes?'

Eliza gave a brief harsh laugh. 'Let's just say the power is still in the wrong hands. And that is why there is no peace in this land.'

Anna looked at her expectantly. It sounded like the beginning of a conversation – but Eliza leaned forward over the steering wheel, looking preoccupied with the driving.

Although Eliza didn't know the people who lived in the villages, she still seemed able to assess the mood of each community. As they passed through one, she drove almost at walking pace, the windows down, calling greetings to the children who lined the roadside. She gave money to everyone who looked sick or hungry. As they approached another, she told Anna to wind up her window. There were no children to be seen, and the adults turned their backs to the car. A pack of dogs bounded alongside the Jaguar, in a frenzy of barking. Anna shrank from her window as a large white dog jumped up, claws scrabbling at the door, its muzzle drawn back, baring dark gums and curved yellow teeth. When the Jaguar finally left the hounds behind, beyond the outskirts of the village, Anna stared at a smear of saliva trailing across the window.

In the last village before the tarmac road ended, they had to stop at a military checkpoint. Eliza gestured for Anna to pick up the shoulder bag that was stowed at her feet. After greeting the soldiers with a smile, she produced a document that Anna guessed was a travel permit. The paper was worn, marked with fold-lines, the corners bent. Eliza showed the soldiers her camera equipment to help endorse the purpose of her trip.

'You're my assistant,' she murmured to Anna.

The soldiers posed for photographs and gave Eliza their addresses so she could post them a print when she got back home. While they examined Anna's passport, Eliza went to the boot and returned with a bottle of whisky. After handing it over, she spent some time chatting to the men. Before long they were just as friendly as the ones at the checkpoint in the Avenue of Storms.

On the other side of the military post the road turned abruptly to gravel, as if someone in an office, far away, had once drawn a line on a map to mark the outer edge of civilisation. Eliza eased off the accelerator as the Jaguar slewed on the loose surface, raising a cloud of dust.

After rounding a long corner, the road emerged from an area of tall trees standing close together. Now, suddenly, the lake – which had been hovering largely out of sight, like a bright dream only half-remembered – was revealed.

Glittering in the morning sun, the water was like a vast open plain scattered with diamonds. Offshore, the black dots of fishing boats could be seen, white birds wheeling in the sky above them.

Anna turned to Eliza. 'It's so beautiful.'

'I never get used to it.' Eliza glanced across to Anna, her sun-glasses flashing in the sun. 'Whether it's rough or calm, in daylight or at night. I just love looking out over it. You know, it is the longest lake in the world. And the second deepest. The only one that's any deeper is in Siberia.'

Anna noticed the pride in Eliza's voice, and the sense of ownership. She sounded like a mother praising her own child. This country was as much home to her, Anna understood, as it was to the black Congolese.

The road now followed the lakeside, clinging close to the shore, with only a fringe of sand and a line of palm trees standing between the edge of the gravel and the lapping water. The woodland continued on the other side, holding the dark forest at bay. There were outcrops of rock, among the fever trees, and the occasional large anthill, looking like a miniature castle moulded from red earth.

'Wind up your window,' Eliza instructed. She flicked on the fan. 'I'll try the radio.'

The car slowed down a little as Eliza leaned forward, a loose strand of hair falling over her face. She reached for the radio that was set into the varnished walnut dashboard. As she turned the dial, there was only the hiss of static. Then came a male voice, gruff and argumentative, talking in a language Anna thought might be Russian. After only a couple of words, the crackling airwaves took over again. Then a new sound was picked up. Someone singing.

'That's more like it . . .' Eliza adjusted the tuning more finely. A woman's voice, rich and strong, floated into the air. 'Billie Holiday.'

Anna had listened to jazz before – Gregory had some records he liked to play late in the evening – but she didn't recognise this particular track. Eliza hummed along with the lyrics. Anna picked up something about a blue moon.

'This is a "Voice of America" broadcast,' Eliza explained. 'They often play jazz.' She gave a brief laugh. 'Black Americans singing to black Africans. I'm not sure what the government's agenda is there. But you can be sure there is one. Just not as blatant as some of their other propaganda. News broadcasts, for example.'

Anna pretended to be absorbed in the singing. Even though Eliza saw the Congo as home, she was presumably still an American, and it made Anna feel uncomfortable to hear someone criticising – or being cynical about – their own country. She couldn't imagine herself speaking out against Australia. But perhaps that was just because she was so ignorant about politics. She had nothing to say.

Eliza turned up the volume until the jazz drowned out the hum of the engine. The singer was backed by piano and the light beat of a drum. It was a strong, catchy rhythm. As Eliza drove, she tapped her fingers on the steering wheel; her nails were dancing splashes of scarlet.

Anna gazed out at the African landscape. At first, the jazz music felt foreign to the setting. But then, as she listened, the song seemed to inhabit the land, and the land the song – until the two became one. Resting her head back against her seat, she let the music flow around her. With Eliza beside her, nodding in time to the beat, she felt relaxed, though she also nursed a glow of excitement. The Jaguar was a capsule of comfort and safety, moving along the road towards the village where she was born.

A mosquito whined in Anna's ear. After slapping it away, she took a tube of insect repellant from her shirt pocket. She was carrying around some antiseptic cream as well, along with a couple of Band-Aids. Back in Melbourne, she'd borrowed a book about tropical diseases from the library. Prevention was the first priority, she'd learned – avoiding bites, accidents and people who might transmit disease. A close second was getting immediate treatment even for small cuts or blisters, to stop infection.

She was leaning against the bonnet of the Jaguar, staring down towards the shore. The road was a little distance from the water at this point, and palm trees obscured her view of the beach. Eliza was down there somewhere, searching for a nest. Somehow, while driving along, she'd spotted a rare species of water bird. If she could take a picture of its eggs or young, it would be the first in her collection. Anna had expected to accompany her down to the water's edge but Eliza said she should wait in the car. The area looked uninhabited, but that didn't mean there weren't people around. It would be risky to leave the Jaguar unattended with all the rest of the camera equipment on board.

'If anyone comes,' Eliza had advised, 'honk the horn.'

Anna checked her watch. Eliza had been gone for more than half an hour. Remembering what the photographer had said about having to wait hours to get the right shot, Anna sighed with impatience. She wanted to get back on the road.

Just by chance, she looked down at her feet. Dozens of big black ants were swarming over her boots. She stamped frantically until they all fell off. For a moment, she just stared wildly, waiting to feel the burning stings. She was lucky; there were none – but the experience was enough to drive her to take refuge inside the car.

For a time she just sat there, gazing at the road ahead. Then, to pass the time, she decided to have one of Eliza's cigarettes. Anna had never smoked very much back in Melbourne – not like many of the secretaries, who always had a cigarette burning in an ashtray beside their typewriters. But her habit was increasing, being around Eliza. She extracted a cigarette from the box resting on the top of the dashboard. But then she realised the lighter was in Eliza's pocket.

She was about to give up the idea when her eyes settled on

Eliza's snakeskin shoulder bag. It was lodged in the space beside Anna's feet, within easy reach if they had to produce their passports or the travel permit again. There would almost certainly be another lighter in there.

Anna opened the bag. As the now familiar smell of Eliza's perfume rose up to her, she felt guilty – but she reminded herself that she'd already been invited to look inside, to find the permit.

The luxury bag was lined with pink watered silk. As Anna felt around for a lighter, her fingers met a small bottle. Pulling it out, she read the label. *L'Interdit*. Forbidden. It seemed an apt name for the perfume Eliza chose to wear. Anna had the feeling that if the older woman thought something were not allowed, she'd instantly be determined to do it.

The next item Anna produced was a blood-red Chanel lipstick. There was a heavy keyring that looked as if it were made of real gold. Several handkerchiefs. A packet of cotton buds. A gold cigarette case with *EML* engraved in italics. Anna was wondering what the *M* stood for, when she came upon a small diary. All her upbringing and her professional training told her not to open it – looking through a bag was one thing; snooping in a diary was another. But before she could stop herself, she was flicking through the pages. She was disappointed to find very little was written there – just some shopping lists; a few phone numbers; an entry about a dental appointment. Half of Anna was relieved that she didn't have to resist the temptation to read Eliza's private notes. But the other half was just hungry for any small detail about Eliza's life.

She was so unlike anyone Anna had ever come across before. Unpredictable – erratic, even. You never knew what she was going to say or do. And she was full of contradictions. She'd been so kind and supportive to Anna during all that had happened in the short time since they'd met. Yet alongside being a tower of strength, there was something vulnerable about her. Anna had the sense that her own presence met some need in Eliza – which made her, in turn, feel stronger.

It was not just Eliza's personality that Anna found intriguing. Anna had never met a photographer before. All the women she knew back in Melbourne were nurses, teachers, secretaries, hairdressers. Eliza was independent, running her own life without the need, it seemed, for a husband; there had been no mention of children, either. Then, there was Eliza's extraordinary wealth. Anna couldn't help but be fascinated by the amazing house and its furnishings, the Jaguar and all the luxurious clothes. Eliza didn't need to follow the latest fashions; she had her own exotic style. Mrs Williams, back in Melbourne, seemed dull and ordinary by comparison, in spite of all the time she spent studying magazines and shopping in Collins Street. Yet Eliza didn't really seem to care about her possessions – which only made her all the more interesting.

Anna was about to close the diary and put it away when she noticed there was a sleeve inside the back cover. Just the corner of a piece of paper protruded. After glancing back to check that Eliza was still not in view, Anna carefully pulled it out.

She unfolded a small sheet of paper. Some kind of list was printed there, written in French, with each item numbered. The ink was thick and black, blurred in places as if it had been smudged before it was dry. Holding it up to look more closely, Anna took in the heading: *Simba Code of Conduct*.

Her eyes widened as she recognised the name of the Communist rebels. She read on haltingly, stumbling over the words as she translated them like a child learning to read.

Have respect for all men, even those who are bad.
Buy goods from the village people with honesty. Do not steal
from them.
Always return anything you have borrowed, in good time and
without problems.
Pay for anything that you have broken. Be happy to do so.
Do not injure or cause harm to anyone.
Do not walk roughly over other people's land. Do not destroy
anything.
Respect women. Do not use them for pleasure, even if you
want to.
Do not be cruel to prisoners of war.

Anna frowned in confusion. She thought back to what Karl had said about the rebels. What had he called them? Animals in human form. Bloodthirsty savages. And Eliza, Anna remembered, had said the Congolese soldiers at the checkpoint were terrified of having to fight them. This picture didn't match with what she'd just read. Idealism shone through every word on the page. She doubted if soldiers anywhere in the world lived up to such high standards of behaviour. It made no sense . . .

Anna looked up, staring blankly through the windscreen. Why was this Code of Conduct in Eliza's diary? Anna tried telling herself Eliza must have found it somewhere and kept it out of curiosity – maybe even as a joke. But that didn't ring true.

She remembered the photograph she'd glimpsed – just for those few seconds – in the darkroom: Eliza posing with a group of African soldiers. The camouflage uniforms gave no clue as to which army the men were in. But one thing was for sure – Eliza hadn't wanted Anna to see it. Then there was Eliza's rendezvous in the garden on the night of the storm – the letter she'd handed over to a figure in black, who was carrying a gun . . . Could it be that Eliza Lindenbaum was involved in some way with the Simbas? That she was a Communist sympathiser? Anna shook her head. It was impossible.

She jumped at the sound of a bird breaking from the bushes nearby, wings beating as it launched itself into the air. Turning round, she followed the path of its flight. Then a flash of colour caught her eye: Eliza's green-and-yellow headscarf, just visible between the palm trees. Next, the ends of a tripod appeared, poking up against the sky.

Quickly, Anna tried to push the document back into the sleeve. The sweat on her fingers had dampened the paper and the page crumpled rather than slid. She had to force herself to slow down. Using one hand, she pulled the sleeve open wider. As the paper disappeared from view, she breathed out with relief. Dropping the diary back into the shoulder bag, she closed the zip.

'Sorry, that took ages.' Eliza appeared at the driver's door, leaning in over the seat to put away her camera.

'Did you find anything?' There was a bright tone in Anna's voice – maybe too bright, she thought – but Eliza was concentrating on putting a roll of film into her shirt pocket, carefully buttoning the flap.

'I found an abandoned nest; that was all. But I took lots of shots, looking past it, over the lake. There might be something there . . .'

Eliza appeared happier and more relaxed than Anna had ever seen her. Taking photographs obviously brought her pleasure. There was no tension in her face or body. The languid drawl and flippant manner were both gone. She didn't look like someone with a complicated life, weighed down with secrets. She didn't look like a wealthy heiress. She could have been an ordinary person, without a care in the world.

'Let's get back on the road,' Eliza said, turning on the ignition. She drove off, tyres spinning on the gravel. Soon, she was tapping her fingers on the steering wheel again, humming the song that had been on the radio earlier. She turned to Anna, a smile on her face. 'We're not far from Kivu Province now. We should be able to reach the hotel well before dusk. We'll still have some daylight up our sleeves if we find it's closed down and we have to camp in the grounds. Either way, we'll be fine.'

Anna smiled back, caught up in Eliza's mood. Her cheerful energy seemed to fill the car, like a fragrance in the air. It made Anna want to put aside the questions that were building inside her – to think only of getting to Banya, finding the hospital, and beginning her search for answers. Her quest was like a fire, glowing inside her. For now, she wanted to stoke the flames and enjoy the warmth.

She would wait until this evening, she decided – and then, when they were settled for the night in the hotel or sitting by the fireside in their campsite, she'd choose the right moment and ask Eliza to explain what was really going on.

FIFTEEN

The figure of a man could barely be detected, pressed up against the trunk of a baobab tree. Only the long barrel of his gun gave him away. In the fading light, it was silhouetted against the blue-grey sky.

Dan approached on open ground, making sure he stayed well inside the camp perimeter. The sentries had been ordered to treat any activity outside the imaginary boundary as hostile. If this fellow were anything like the others Dan had just visited on his rounds, he'd be ready to jump at shadows.

True enough, when the soldier heard Dan's footsteps, rustling through the grass, he spun round, raising his rifle. Recognising Dan, he quickly lowered it. Another recruit might have stood to attention, but Volunteer Thompson just gave a nod.

'All okay?' Dan asked.

'Yeah, I'm going fine . . . sir.' The man's words were stretched into a drawl. He only added 'sir' as an afterthought. Dan didn't know if Thompson was having trouble catching on to military protocol or if he was ignoring the whole concept. The thirty-year-old had never served in any kind of army. Dan suspected he hadn't even been a boy scout. At least, however, he seemed to know the difference between 'standing easy' and 'standing to'. Though Thompson sounded relaxed, Dan could see from his posture that he remained on full alert.

Dan moved up and stood beside him. Neither man spoke. From behind them came the cheerful clamour of thirty men putting up tents, lighting fires and preparing their meals. But the domestic scene felt cut off from this place at the edge of the camp. The trees, bushes, reeds and grasses that grew beyond the perimeter were all that seemed real. The sounds of the natural world filled their ears. Birds were already preparing for night, calling to one another from the trees, their cries eerily human. Insects buzzed and whispered in the undergrowth. The air was dense with a thousand small noises. Even Dan found it disconcerting. He was accustomed to watching out for dangers – animals, snakes, insects, steep gullies, cliff edges, quicksand . . . But not since his time in the King's African Rifles had he needed to be on the lookout for a human enemy. It made him deeply uneasy. He had to remind himself that – at least for now – his unit was nowhere near rebel-held territory.

Radio reports on aerial surveillance had confirmed what Father Michel had said: at least 100 miles and a river lay between Force Denby and the closest Simba troops. By tomorrow night, Dan would be feeling more cautious. When they halted the vehicles they'd remain on the track and set up camp on the verges; there would be no fires and a total alcohol ban. But for now, it was good to see the men relaxing – talking freely, getting to know one another.

That didn't mean the sentries didn't need to be watchful, though. A rebel group like the Simbas could easily have supporters dotted around the country. And Dan was well aware that – after generations of brutal treatment at the hands of the Belgian colonial regime – there must be many Congolese with a deep hatred of anyone who was white. The situation was complex. A case in point was the village where Force Denby had encountered Father Michel. Even with Becker's interrogation skills, it had been impossible to be sure whether the drummer who'd passed on information was pro-Simba or just anti-European. With this in mind, Dan had not scrimped on the number of sentries he'd posted. Tonight was like a dress rehearsal for the real performance. And it was better to be safe than sorry.

Thompson stood rock-still, scanning the bushland with a steady gaze. Dan noticed how his eyes kept wandering to the distance, as if the far horizon were his natural reference point, and how he stood with his feet planted apart, like someone accustomed to balancing on a heaving deck. When the volunteer had answered Blair's newspaper advertisement, he had just finished sailing his yacht, singlehandedly, from his home in Sydney to Cape Town. He'd survived punishing storms and the isolation of a lone voyage – now he was in search of an even bigger challenge. Dan remembered the first time he saw the young Australian. Thompson had the sun-bleached, salt-ridden look of a creature washed in from the sea. His hair was like white straw. The skin of his nose, cheeks and forehead – burned too many times – had turned pink and shiny; the rest of him was tanned a deep brown. The new clothes he'd worn for the interview were out of place on such a weatherworn character. He looked uncomfortable in a pair of lace-up boots; Dan guessed he was more at home with bare feet.

Blair and Dan had both recognised in the yachtsman the quali-ties of ingenuity, self-reliance and competence, combined with a streak of sheer madness. Apart from his lack of a military back-ground, Thompson was perfect commando material.

'I'll leave you to it, then,' Dan said.

Thompson didn't appear to have heard; he just kept staring ahead, a frown on his face. Then he seemed to realise the officer was waiting for a response. 'Sorry, sir. It's just . . .' He broke off, chewing tensely at his lip. 'I was thinking about something.'

'What's up?' Dan asked. He searched the man's face.

'I've never been this far from the sea before.'

Dan took a moment to absorb these words, then he nodded. 'I was the opposite when I went to the coast. I felt like an ant, stuck on the edge of a plate.'

Thompson gave a faint smile.

'But I got used to it,' Dan said. 'You will too.'

He was about to turn away, leaving the sentry to his duty, when he noticed a small black shape in one of the nearby trees. Squinting into the diminishing light, he saw a furry animal.

'See that?' He pointed towards the branch. 'It's a bush baby. You can see its tail hanging down.'

Thompson narrowed his eyes, searching. 'Ah, yes! Look at that. It's a tiny little bugger . . .'

'He shouldn't be out and about yet. It's not dark.' Dan found himself slipping back into his role as a hired hunter. He always encouraged his clients to appreciate the whole palette of life in the African bush, not just to hunt for the Big Five. 'You see them in lots of parts of Africa.'

The bush baby walked along the branch, planting its feet with care. Even at this distance it was possible to see the two huge shiny eyes and equally over-sized ears.

'There are so many predators in the forest. This little creature is completely defenceless. He relies on his senses to stay safe.' Dan broke off – he realised he was starting to sound as if he were in a wildlife film. He sometimes worked for a cinematographer from the

BBC, who made the effort to bring a projector when he came for another shoot, so he could show Dan the results of the previous trip. The narrator's voice was always very calm and authoritative – he had to persuade complete strangers to believe every word he said. A bit like a hunter, Dan thought – or a Commanding Officer.

As the two men watched, the bush baby turned its head, looking right at them. Against the darkening sky, the animal with its bulging eyes was like a cartoon cut-out. Dan couldn't help smiling. When he glanced at Thompson, he was smiling too, his teeth showing up white against his deep-tanned skin.

Leaning over the fire, Dan used the tip of his hunting knife to stir the contents of a khaki green can that was lodged on a bed of coals. He hadn't bothered to read the label, but thought he could identify bits of chopped meat floating in tomato sauce.

At his side, Volunteer Smith was using a plastic spoon to chase slices of something named 'Turkey Loaf' around his mess tin. He had opened his ration pack carefully, laying out the contents at his feet – there were packages of chocolate, crackers and cheese, cake, sachets of sugar and salt, toilet paper, matches, even chewing gum and cigarettes. The Rhodesian, with his formal manners, had been determined to eat the entrée, then the main course, followed by dessert and cheese and crackers, all in the correct order.

The other man sharing their fire was a stocky Welshman called Fuller – he was the Chief Mechanic. He was perched on a piece of a fallen tree he'd made a big effort to drag in from the bush.

Dan gestured at the makeshift seat. 'It'll be a pity to leave that behind,' he joked, 'after all that work.'

'Perhaps I'll bring it along.' Fuller grinned as he tapped a cigarette from its box. Tobacco was the only item among the rations that came in its regular packaging, and the red-and-white Marlboro colours stood out beside all the khaki and green. The match flared brightly, throwing a glow over Fuller's face. As he drew on the cigarette, Dan noticed remnants of engine grease ground into the skin of his hand. Fuller said he had left school at fifteen and worked as a mechanic ever since. He was one of those men who loved his trade. Whether he was talking about the vehicles that were in the convoy, or about luxury cars he'd repaired in his time, his eyes lit up with interest. During his first meeting with Dan, he'd explained that he had joined Blair's regiment because he wanted the challenge of working under pressure.

'You'll get plenty of that,' Dan had promised. He'd liked the man instantly, attracted by his open, friendly face and his lilting accent.

Every man in the Force had a partner, and Dan had paired Fuller with Smith, knowing they'd work together well. They would eat, sleep and fight beside one another until the mission was over, or they were – as Blair put it – 'parted by death'. Dan's own partner was Hardy, though as senior officers they'd be functioning pretty autonomously – which was lucky, since Dan found it virtually impossible to work with his second-in-command. Hardy didn't follow general instructions, even to set a good example. He just did whatever he felt like. Right now, for instance, he was not here at the fireside.

'Has anyone seen Hardy?' Dan asked. He guessed the Second Lieutenant had attached himself to one of the other groups – he was probably sharing the use of his bottle opener and telling stories about his adventures with Major Blair in Katanga. Dan thought he should go and find the man, and bring him to where he was meant to be. On the other hand, it was much more relaxing here without him.

'I've not seen him since we disembarked, sir,' said Smith.

Fuller shrugged. 'Neither have I, sir.' He didn't hide the dismissive tone in his voice. He had the typical Welshman's disregard for status; he was unimpressed by Hardy and saw no need to hide it.

Settling back to enjoy his cigarette, Fuller reached into the top pocket of his shirt and took out a pale-blue envelope. The corners were bent, the stamp peeling off. He held it out for the others to see. 'It's a letter from my son. I don't know how many times I've read it . . .'

'I didn't know you had a family.' Dan tried to remember the details in his file.

A shadow crossed Fuller's face. 'I only have Nicholas. My wife Bronwyn died from cancer two years ago. I couldn't raise my lad on my own, so I put him in boarding school. It's a good place – but very expensive. At least I don't have to worry about that any more.' His cheerful demeanour returned. 'I'll be all right for a few years, now. My pay's going straight into the savings account.'

'Is that why you signed up?' Smith asked.

Fuller spread his hands. 'What we're getting in three months would take me years to earn any other way.'

Dan busied himself with his cooking, stirring the brew once more, then removing the can from the fire. Fuller's words made his heart sink. He was pretty sure these details hadn't been revealed earlier on. Dan certainly wouldn't have chosen the mechanic for this mission if he'd known the man was a widower with a child to care for. Dan only hoped there were some decent relatives around to step in, if the worst happened.

When he'd emptied the can into his mess tin, he walked off a little way towards the edge of the camp. He tried not to breathe the smell that rose to his nostrils. The US Army rations were similar to what had been issued to the King's African Rifles in the battlefields of Abyssinia. The nondescript savoury smell that came to him now was hauntingly familiar. It was paired in his mind with the taint of blood baking in the sun, the sweet-sick odour of gangrene, the stink of latrines used by men with dysentery.

Dan ate quickly, burning his tongue. When he'd forced the last mouthful down, he returned to the fire.

Fuller had unfolded a flimsy sheet of airmail paper. Dan could see the childish handwriting that filled the page: big round circles; straight lines pressed into the paper; huge full stops. He pictured a bright child with lots of energy and a happy nature like his dad. Fuller would be keeping his head down, Dan decided. Fortunately his main role did not involve fighting. And there was every reason to give him extra protection. If the vehicles didn't keep moving, the Force was going nowhere.

Smith reached out a hand to take Dan's mess tin.

'I'm going to find Hardy,' Dan announced.

He had already taken a walk down through the encampment, keeping his distance so as not to disrupt the men's brief time of leisure. He'd only had to speak to one group, who had apparently forgotten it was not up to them to decide if they could be bothered to heat up their food. Dan had made his rules clear on this. The mission to capture Uvira was only the beginning for these men; they might end up spending months on the road or camped out in villages. Morale had to be nurtured like a delicate plant. Hot meals, sound sleep and the comfort of a fire were like sunshine and air. Some of the men were too inexperienced to know that the time would come soon enough when sleeping sitting up and eating cold food straight from a can would be their only option.

Now, passing along the line again, Dan absorbed the easy hum of conversation, interrupted by bursts of laughter. Several of the men had broken into their supply of whisky. As they swigged from the bottles, the last of the daylight glowed golden through the amber brew. Dan could tell who the veterans were by their choice of Scotch. Johnnie Walker was fashionable, but the Ballantine's bottles with their square sides could be packed much more efficiently than any other brand.

He passed Bergman, hunched over the fire, staring grimly into the flames. Dan could almost see his fears for his family written on his face. McAdam was sitting nearby, his tall figure casting a long shadow. He was making some adjustment to his pipes. Dan hoped he remembered he'd been banned from playing. Even here, in territory that was expected to be safe, it was too dangerous. The distinctive sound would carry for many miles, and could be followed to its source.

He jerked to a halt, catching sight of Bailey and Henning sitting together. Dan had decided to pair the men with other soldiers, at least initially, but their partners were nowhere to be seen. Dan studied the two for a few moments but could detect no tension between them. If anything, the Legionnaire and the British SS wrestler were ignoring one another. Dan was just about to walk on when he saw Henning raise his whisky bottle.

'*Vive la mort, vive la guerre, vive la Légion Étrangère.*' He took a long gulp, a dribble of liquor running over his chin.

'What's that bullshit?' Bailey asked.

Henning raised the bottle again. 'Long live death, long live war, long live the Foreign Legion.'

Bailey spat in the fire. 'Fuck the Foreign Legion.'

Henning carefully screwed the lid back on his bottle and placed it on the ground. He fixed his wide blue eyes on Bailey. There was a brief pause. Then Henning launched himself at Bailey like a dog on the attack.

A crowd quickly gathered as the two men writhed on the ground, each seeking to hold the other down. There were no cheers or cat-calls like there were during wrestling matches – just a deathly hush, punctuated by guttural animal sounds coming from the fighters.

Bailey managed to pull an arm free. He slammed a fist into Henning's face, making a bloody mess of the man's nose. In response, Henning threw an uppercut, crunching Bailey's head back. Then Henning tore open the Englishman's shirt, revealing the blue blur of the eagle tattoo, already shiny with sweat.

The men were so evenly matched the fight seemed to take place in slow motion. But the strikes, when they came, were lethal. Bailey's lip was split open. Blood from Henning's nose sprayed in the air. Dan could see there was a chance one of the men might kill the other. Or they might both end up so wounded they were useless to the Force. He was aware that several men were turning to him, expecting him to intervene. His hand hovered near his holster as he considered firing a warning shot. But then he folded his arms over his chest. It would be a mistake to start something he wasn't prepared to finish. Not only that, he knew that unless the conflict was played out to the end, it would never be over.

Dan winced as Bailey brought his knee up between Henning's legs. The Legionnaire loosened his grip on his opponent's neck, but that was all. Bailey said something then, words forced through gritted teeth. Whatever he said had an immediate impact. Henning froze for a second. His sudden stillness seemed to create a vacuum in which no one looking on could breathe or move. Then Henning's lips twisted. It took a few seconds for Dan to realise the grimace was meant to be a smile. Bailey smiled, too, his teeth red with blood.

The two stood up, panting from open mouths. Henning spat a pink glob of saliva onto the ground. Bailey wiped his mouth with the sleeve of his shirt, smearing the mess across his face. Then the men walked back to the fire and sat down.

Henning picked up his whisky, removing the lid. Tipping back his head, he took a long swallow. Then, keeping his eyes fixed ahead, moving only his hand, he offered the bottle to Bailey. The second man kept his own gaze averted as he accepted the offer.

For several moments, none of the other soldiers moved. Then, one by one, they drifted back to their own fires and the buzz of conversation broke out again.

Glancing around, Dan confirmed that the ruckus had not brought Hardy to light. He was beginning to be alarmed. Perhaps the man had wandered into the bush to answer the call of nature and lost his way back. Dan started asking the men if anyone knew where the Second Lieutenant could be.

'In the truck, sir,' someone called out.

'Thanks.' Dan took two steps towards the line of vehicles, then spun round. He recognised that self-assured tone; the English public school accent. He stared in amazement at the young man he'd collared outside the mess hall at Lemba. The indecent shorts and long scarf had gone. The boy was in full uniform; he held a bottle of whisky in his slender hand. 'What the hell are you doing here?'

The lad jumped to his feet, standing to attention. 'Volunteer Mason, reporting for duty, sir.'

Dan could barely believe his own eyes. 'How did you get here?'

'I volunteered as a dresser. The doctor got me on the plane. I sat up the front with the pilot.' He sounded like a character in the *Boy's Own Annual*.

'Doc Malone smuggled you here?'

'Yes, sir.'

Dan felt a rush of fury. What the hell did the Medical Officer think he was doing, bringing a kid like this on a commando mission? It was insane. But there was no way to send him back now. They'd just have to make the best of the situation.

'What did you say your name was?'

'Billy, sir.'

'Surname.'

'Mason, sir.'

'How old are you?'

'Twenty-one, sir.'

Dan raised his eyebrows.

'Eighteen.'

'How did you even get to Lemba?'

'I lost my passport. They gave me new papers at Recruitment.'

Dan shook his head in disbelief. There was a long tradition of mercenary soldiers being issued false documents; sometimes they got a whole new identity. But he was still surprised someone in Johannesburg had been prepared to do this for Mason – surely they must have guessed he was underage? It just showed, Dan thought, how desperate they were to fill their quota: there were not enough adult men who were mad enough to sign up. He sighed, motioning for Mason to sit back down. 'As you were, soldier.'

'Thank you, sir.' A grin broke over the boy's face, making him look even younger. He tried a salute, but got it wrong.

Dan walked away, still shaking his head. He wondered if Mason had loving parents, somewhere, who were desperately worried about him. They couldn't have known he was enlisting. Were they even aware that he was in South Africa? Perhaps there were devastated sisters at home, as well. Frantic grandparents . . .

As he strode towards the line of vehicles, his hands formed fists at his side. He'd be demanding an explanation from Malone in the morning. The fact that there was a shortage of volunteers willing to shift their focus from fighting to first aid was not an acceptable excuse. The deception was staggeringly irresponsible. But then, Dan reminded himself, Malone was not renowned for being a model citizen. He hadn't tried to hide the reason he wanted to become a mercenary soldier. Back in England, he'd been struck off the medical register. It was a matter of professional misconduct, evidently, rather than a failure of skill.

'Beggars can't be choosers,' Blair had declared. 'We're lucky to have a doctor at all.'

Dan knew he was right. A commando force had no backup medical corps to call on. Men with serious injuries could not be sent back down the line, let alone evacuated. The doctor just had to do what he could on the run. It was no job for the faint-hearted.

Reaching the Bedford truck, Dan walked round to the back, peering inside the canvas covering. In the shadows he picked out the shape of a man squatting in one corner.

'Hardy?'

There was no answer. Dan wondered if the officer was drunk again. 'Hardy, you should be out here, having something to eat.'

'I'd rather stay where I am, old man.'

'Well, I'd rather you followed my orders, like the other men.' Dan adopted an icy tone. He was tired of Hardy's antics. Where did the man think he was – in a swanky London club, talking to one of his chums?

'I can't come out. I must stay here.' Hardy stared towards the open back of the truck. Dan could see the whites of his eyes.

'What's the problem, Hardy?' Dan tried a softer manner. 'Perhaps I can help.'

'I don't like the jungle.'

Dan stared in surprise – whatever answer he was expecting, it wasn't this. 'What jungle? This isn't jungle.'

Hardy nodded his head knowingly. 'This is how it starts. Just a few trees. Then a few more. And suddenly, you can't escape.' There was a note of hysteria in his voice. Sweat gleamed on his face.

'Okay,' Dan said calmly. 'Take it easy. You don't have to come out. Just stay here. I'll bring you some food.'

Hardy ignored him. 'I can hear them.' His voice rose with alarm. 'They're coming!' He shuffled further back into the corner. 'Oh my God!' He buried his face in his hands.

Dan was about to climb onto the truck but then thought better of it. Hardy was clearly reliving some traumatic experience from the past. It was more real to him than what was happening in the present. Dan had seen soldiers in this state before. They had to be handled with care.

'It's all right, Hardy,' he said firmly. 'You'll be fine. Just hold tight. I won't be a minute. I'm coming back.'

He jogged towards the place where he'd seen Mason: hopefully someone in his group knew where to find Doc Malone. It looked as if Dan would be chatting to the Medical Officer sooner rather than later. He just hoped there were some strong tranquillisers in the field packs.

As he picked his way in the half-light, Dan thought of Hardy's behaviour since he'd joined the unit. He'd been drinking way too much, possibly taking drugs as well, in an attempt to control his emotions. But that solution hadn't worked; it had probably made things worse. Now, as the convoy moved deeper into the bush,

Hardy was falling prey to a nightmare and losing his grip on reality. He had once been a fine officer. Something must have changed him, in the time since Blair knew him well. Or maybe it had been the legacy of the very mission the two men had shared. Often, damage to the soul was not seen straight away.

Tranquillisers would only be a temporary solution. Dan didn't know what he would do with Hardy when the effects wore off. Perhaps when they reached Uvira they could hand him over to the Congolese Army. But there was a lot of ground to cover before then.

Dan thought of the map rolled up in the front of the Land Rover. Almost the whole area between where they were now and the target of Operation Nightflower was shaded in one solid colour. Dark green.

'Congo jungle,' Blair had said – as if Dan wouldn't be able to guess. The Major had worn a grim smile on his face as he tapped the map with his ruler. 'Otherwise known as hell on earth.'

SIXTEEN

The sun was low in the sky. Long shadows, cast by trees and shrubs, stretched over the road. Eliza turned her head from side to side as she drove, searching the roadside for a potential campsite. A couple of hours earlier, a flat tyre had interrupted the journey. Then the Jaguar had skidded off the road at a corner and become bogged in soft sand. Precious time had been lost; now it seemed unlikely they'd make it to the hotel before nightfall.

Anna chewed at her thumbnail, struggling to quell her anxiety. Since they'd entered Kivu Province, the dense forest that cloaked the hills had been steadily creeping closer. Now, both sides of the road were closed in with trees; there were only occasional patches of scrub and grassland. According to Eliza, none of them, so far, had been suitable for pitching a tent. All Anna could think about was that the sun would soon be setting. She wasn't even sure what she found more daunting: the prospect of being on the road when it got dark, or spending the night under canvas out here in the bush. When she and Eliza had first discussed this trip, all she'd cared about was getting to Banya. Now she had to face the reality of what they'd taken on.

Suddenly, Eliza pointed ahead. 'Look! What's that?'

Anna peered into the fading light. On the side of the road

there was a sign nailed to the trunk of a dead tree. It was small and crooked; nothing like the government road sign that had marked their entry to Kivu Province.

As they came closer, Anna could just make out some decorative red lettering, faded almost to oblivion. *Hôtel Royal Kivu*. As she read the name she felt a flash of relief – but then the decrepit state of the sign sank in.

'Let's cross our fingers.' Eliza swung the steering wheel to the right. 'I'd rather sit down with a drink, right now, than have to put up the tent.'

They travelled along a narrow driveway lined with palm trees. Anna glimpsed monkeys clambering among the fronds. As the car passed beneath one of them, there was a loud clatter on the roof. Something hard and round bounced over the bonnet. Eliza just drove calmly on. Before long they reached two spiky-topped iron gates, propped wide open. Beyond them, lawns spread away to either side of the drive.

Anna gazed out at flowerbeds overgrown with weeds, and shrubs strangled with creepers. The lawn was short but had a ragged appearance as if it had been gnawed by animals rather than mown. Ahead were several trees so completely covered in bougainvillea they were just mounds of purple flowers. Beyond them rose the rooftop of a building.

Anna leaned forward eagerly as the rest of the hotel came into view. It was two storeys high; in the middle of a whitewashed facade was a columned portico. Near the blue front door stood a stone fountain with a cherub in the middle. It reminded Anna of the quaint country hotels she'd seen in Mrs Williams' magazines. Anna smiled with relief, anticipating the safety and comfort inside.

But as they came nearer, Anna saw patches of bare brickwork, where the rendering had fallen off. At ground-level the whitewash was stained red with dust. The fountain was dry. Scanning the two rows of windows, Anna found that all the curtains were drawn. It gave the building a closed-in feeling, as if it were looking in on itself, rejecting the world outside.

Eliza brought the Jaguar to a halt in a deserted parking area with spaces marked by painted stones. When she turned off the motor the pair sat in silence. A small animal that may have been a rat streaked past the closed front door.

'It looks as if it's been empty for years,' Anna said.

'It doesn't take long for things to deteriorate here. It's so warm and wet. When the rains come, they cause damage. And there are animals always ready to move in.' Eliza opened her door. 'Let's see who's around.'

Anna climbed out, stretching her cramped legs. Looking up over the facade of the hotel again, she noticed a broken window on the upper floor. A grey smear of droppings stained the ledge. As she watched, a pigeon flew out, navigating expertly through a jagged gap. Anna's heart quickened as she pictured bats lurking up there as well, preparing to descend on the garden as soon as darkness fell.

'*Hodi!*' Eliza's voice echoed in the stillness. Anna knew she was announcing her presence to whoever was in charge of the property. It was an African custom, she'd explained to Anna, left from when huts had no doors. If someone approaches in silence, ill intent is assumed. Dogs that may appear to be sound asleep in the sun will leap up and attack.

After only a few seconds, a man appeared at the far corner of the building. He wore a traditional cloth wrapped around his waist. As he hurried over, he pulled on a black dinner jacket, the long tails flapping behind him.

Eliza greeted him in Swahili. Anna recognised the phrases by now, and was able to parrot them almost perfectly. The man responded with a friendly smile, his teeth standing out white in the fading light. His hand went up to remove the knitted hat he wore pulled down over his ears – but then he seemed to think better of it. He shook hands with both of the women in turn. It was an elaborate gesture that involved shifting the position of the clasped hands twice. He laughed, but not unkindly, as Anna failed to follow the correct pattern.

When the greetings were over, Eliza talked to the man for several minutes. At one point, he turned to address Anna.

'Welcome to Hôtel Royal Kivu.'

'Thank you,' Anna responded.

Shifting his gaze back to Eliza, he continued talking. She listened with an intent look on her face. Soon the two were smiling, then laughing. They seemed to have found some interest in common, beyond the travellers' need for a place to stay. Anna watched in silence, feeling like a child left out of a playground conversation. Eventually, Eliza shook hands with the man again. He gave Anna another warm smile. As he turned to walk away, she caught sight of a long sheath knife hanging from a belt at his waist.

Eliza headed for the rear of the car, calling back over her shoulder. 'He's the manager. The Belgian owners left the country three years ago. They're supposed to be coming back, but he doesn't know when.'

Anna hurried up to her. 'He's got a knife! I saw it . . .'

'He probably has a bow and arrow, too,' Eliza replied calmly. 'He's guarding the place.'

Anna forced a smile. She didn't want to appear nervous, when Eliza was clearly at ease. 'So where are we going to spend the night?'

'Well, there's no food in the place, no liquor, no running water and no power,' Eliza said. 'But Ndovu says we can have a room if we like.' She shrugged. 'We might as well. It'll save us putting up the tent. Apparently there's a patio on the other side with a great view.' She opened the boot. 'Let's get what we need for the night.'

Anna reached inside the car and pulled out her red suitcase. Then she just stood there, holding it in her hand. She pictured long corridors, lacy with cobwebs, a coating of dust on the beds. She thought of the man who claimed to be the manager – his bizarre outfit, and the long knife at his waist. She wondered if it wouldn't be better just to sleep in the car.

Eliza removed a cooler box from the boot, placing it on the ground. Looking up, she gave a reassuring smile. 'Don't worry. We'll be safe here.'

Anna frowned at her. 'How do you know you can trust that man? You only just met him.' She half-regretted her words as soon as she'd spoken. She knew she sounded just like Marilyn.

'We discovered we have friends in common,' Eliza replied. 'In fact, one of Ndovu's relatives is a gardener who works at my house in Léopoldville. Another helped me once on a photography safari.' She smiled again. 'We are in good hands.'

Anna felt herself being swept up in Eliza's confidence. It didn't seem to matter where they went, Eliza managed to find old friends or contacts, or she forged new ones, instantly and effortlessly. Anna didn't know how Eliza achieved this – whether it was a matter of her deciding to trust people or somehow conveying to others that she was worthy of their trust. However it came about, it certainly appeared to work.

Anna pulled out a picnic basket loaded with provisions and added it to the collection of luggage. Eliza was just fetching her camera bag from the back seat when Ndovu reappeared. He hoisted the cooler box onto his head, then found a way to pick up the picnic basket and one of the suitcases.

He set off back towards the hotel, walking with a smooth gait, balancing his load. Eliza headed after him, her bag swinging at her hip. Before long, the two were talking again. It occurred to Anna that with her ability to communicate so easily, Eliza would have made a first-class secretary – except that it was hard to imagine her obeying orders.

Ndovu led the way down the side of the building, then disappeared from view, Eliza at his heels. Anna felt a moment of panic, as if the pair might have gone forever, leaving her alone. Hurrying after them, she rounded the corner, stepping onto a patio.

She caught her breath as she took in the vista in front of her: the vast expanse of water, stretching as far as the eye could see; the endless sky above; and, closer up, the beach made of big round pebbles in pastel shades of pink, grey and yellow. No matter how many times she encountered the lake, its impact took her by surprise. Now, with the sun about to set, rosy light spilling over the water, the scene was awe-inspiring.

Putting down her suitcase, Anna walked over to a low concrete balustrade that separated the hotel from the beach. It was painted white to match the wrought-iron tables and chairs that were dotted along the patio. As she gazed at the lake she could hear Eliza and Ndovu talking behind her, their words blending with the gentle lap of the water against the pebbles.

Not far away was a child's swing. It hung motionless, the sun glinting on the chain. The level of the lake must have risen; water washed around the feet of the rusty metal frame. Anna imagined the children who had once played here. Little girls like the ones she'd seen at Albertville airport, wearing cotton dresses with white socks and sandals. Little boys in shirts and shorts. She could almost hear their laughter and chatter, and the sound of adult voices drifting over from the tables. The clink of wine glasses. The popping of corks. Music from a record player floating from open windows.

It was so quiet now, so still. Anna had the sense that she was standing on an empty stage. The characters were gone, the curtain lowered. This old world had come to an end. One day, a new story would begin here. But for now, the place was in limbo, caught between the past and the future.

Eliza sat on a low stool at the far end of the patio, feeding sticks into a small fire. The flames were surrounded by four blackened stones that formed a makeshift hearth. Ndovu had explained to Eliza that since the gas cylinders in the kitchen ran out, this was where he cooked. He'd done his best to protect the surface of the patio by putting down a layer of earth. But the pavers had still cracked from the heat, and there was a circle of charcoal that would never be removed. Anna wondered what the owners of the hotel were going to say when they eventually returned.

Next to Eliza's feet was a china plate on which lay four long thin fish. Ndovu had presented them to his guests, explaining that he'd caught them that morning.

'Do you like fish?' he'd asked Anna.

Anna had nodded, hiding her dismay at the sight of heads, tails, fins – all still attached. She enjoyed fish and chips, but was used to eating boneless fillets of flake. Only once had she gone fishing herself. She'd been invited on a family outing with Sally. She'd watched on in horrified silence as Mr Jacobs grasped a slippery fish, wrenching a hook from its gasping mouth. When he proceeded to slit open the belly, scooping out the innards, Anna had had to walk away, holding her hand over her mouth. Sally had been surprised at this reaction, until Mrs Jacobs gave an explanation. Her tone was kind, but her words, overheard, had struck Anna to the core.

'She has no father, remember. She's missed out on things like this.'

Ndovu had offered to cook the fish for the guests but Eliza had said she was happy to do it herself. Now, as she prodded the fire, breaking the sticks down into coals, she looked like an old hand at outdoor cooking. She suggested Ndovu take Anna into the hotel to collect what they needed for preparing the meal. It would be getting dark soon and it would be wise to get everything ready while it was still easy to see.

Ndovu opened a French window, ushering Anna inside. She took a few steps then stood still, taking in the tarnished grandeur of a large dining room. Dusty chandeliers graced the high ceilings. The tables were still covered in cloths, splashed here and there with bird droppings. Mould had formed patterns on the red velvet chairs. Dust balls clustered on the parquet floor. Overlooking the room, from a commanding position on the far wall, was a framed portrait of a man with a long white beard and moustache. There were gold epaulettes on his shoulders, a scarlet sash across his chest. Walking closer, Anna saw a title inscribed beneath the painting.

Léopold II, Roi des Belges et Souverain du Congo.

'Leopold II, King of the Belgians and Sovereign of the Congo.' Anna read out the translation as she looked back up over the portrait. She scanned the embroidered emblems on his chest, the white beard, neatly parted in the middle, the waxed moustache. Then she stared, frozen. There were two holes in the canvas. The man's eyes had been pierced. There was something about the precision of the tiny crisscrossed slashes that was more violent than a bigger wound. Anna felt her stomach clench with horror.

When she turned around she saw Ndovu watching her, his face impassive.

Anna swallowed, her throat suddenly dry. 'I need plates,' she managed to say. 'And some knives and forks.'

Ndovu guided her to a line of cupboards, before going on to the kitchen to find a frying pan. Left alone, Anna took a deep breath, telling herself to calm down. It was just a picture that had been vandalised. Someone poking fun at a stuffy old man. This kind of thing happened when buildings were unoccupied. She focused on selecting crockery, cutlery and linen. Everything was spotless, though the cupboard smelled musty. When she'd loaded up her arms she headed for the patio, glad to escape from the dining room – to be back outside, breathing the clear air.

Ndovu handed the frying pan to Eliza. There was a brief discussion, after which he wished the women goodnight and disappeared down the side of the hotel. Eliza explained to Anna that, since she had assured him they'd be fine on their own for the evening, he was going to eat with his family in the nearby village.

While Eliza finished raking the coals, Anna shifted a wrought-iron table across to the fire. She spread a white cloth over the dusty paintwork with its bulging pockets of rust. Then she set two places, laying out silver knives and forks and white plates, all bearing the insignia of the hotel. She added a pair of crystal salt-and-pepper shakers, a silver breadbasket – even an ornate candlestick. Pushing the defaced portrait to the back of her mind, she let her love of decorating come to the fore.

When she was satisfied with the table, Anna sat down near

the fire. She watched Eliza add a knob of butter to the frying pan, pushing it around with the tip of her knife. Turning to the fish, Eliza cut several deep slashes, exposing pink flesh. Then she rubbed in some chopped herbs she'd picked in the garden. There was a hiss as she dropped the fish into the pan. When their skin met the hot butter, the bodies jerked, then began to curl, as if they were coming to life again. Anna flinched at the sight but refused to turn away – if she was going to spend time with someone like Eliza, she knew she had to become less squeamish.

As it grew darker, Eliza lit a kerosene lantern, setting it down near the fire, adding a yellow tint to the red glow of the coals. Anna took a second lantern over to the table. The candlestick threw a spindly shadow, forming the leggy shape of a dancer.

'Did you find the lemons?' Eliza asked Anna. She shook the pan to loosen the fish, then flipped them over, one by one, with her knife.

Anna produced two lemons from her trouser pockets, selected from the supply provided by Magadi. He probably thought they'd be used in sundowners, but Eliza had poured whisky tonight, since there was no cold tonic.

'Cut some wedges for the table. I'm nearly ready,' Eliza said. Even when issuing orders, Anna noticed, she didn't sound bossy, like Marilyn. Her manner suggested they were equal partners sharing a task.

As Anna cut the lemons, her mouth watered. She realised how hungry she was. She and Eliza had nibbled on roasted peanuts but it was a long time since they'd stopped to consume Magadi's packed lunch. The cucumber sandwiches and rolls with cheese and pickles were a distant memory.

Eliza brought the pan to the table, scooping two fish onto each of the dinner plates. Anna removed a container of tomato and lettuce from the cooler, along with some olives, bread and cheese. Eliza had warned her not to set out the food until they were ready to eat. Anna didn't like to ask why, but feared it might have something to do with insects or perhaps even swooping birds.

Eliza topped up the glasses with whisky. Anna eyed the tilted bottle with its red-and-gold Johnnie Walker label, so familiar from Mr Williams' office. She couldn't help wondering what her boss would think if he could see her now. He'd be shocked and worried, but she knew he'd also be glad she was doing her best to find out who her real father was. She remembered what he'd said, when he was encouraging her to come here to the Congo.

I never met my father. But I've missed him all my life.

Eliza lifted her glass towards Anna, as if making a silent toast, then tipped back her head and swallowed the amber liquid in three gulps. Anna sipped hers, feeling the warmth sliding down her throat. Ignoring the cutlery, Eliza began eating with her fingers, pulling chunks of flesh from the bones. Anna gazed down at her two fish for a moment. The glistening eyes had turned white. Blind. She quickly cut the heads off, sliding them onto a side plate and covering them with her napkin. Then she followed Eliza's example.

The roasted skin was crisp and the flesh beneath it succulent. The tang of lemon blended with the taste of the herbs. Anna licked her fingers, smiling across the table at Eliza. 'It's delicious.'

'This is one of the best fish you'll ever eat, anywhere in the world. Migebuka. It's only found in Lake Tanganyika.'

Again, Anna heard the pride in Eliza's voice, as if the lake and its bounty were the work of her own hands. Anna didn't feel the same way about her own home country, Australia. She wondered if that was because Marilyn kept making it clear they didn't really belong there. The thought evoked a sense of loss, for something she'd never had.

They ate their fish and salad, using hunks of bread to sop up the buttery juices. When her plate was empty, Anna leaned back in her chair. She couldn't think when she'd last enjoyed a meal this much.

'Let's move back to the fire,' Eliza suggested. 'The smoke will keep the mosquitoes away.'

With a flicker of surprise, Anna realised she'd forgotten all about the need for insect repellant. She found herself scratching automatically, as she stood to pick up her chair. Eliza returned to her low stool, sitting with her long legs angled out to each side. After handing a cigarette to Anna she lit one for herself, blowing smoke towards the fire. Then she pulled off her scarf, running her fingers back through her hair, smoothing out tangles. In the firelight, she looked younger and older, both at the same time: the lines around her mouth and between her brows were deepened by shadows, but the warm glow added softness to the tone of her skin. She could have been Anna's mother, or she could have been her friend.

The velvet darkness and the drifting smoke seemed to wrap themselves around the two women, drawing them close. Anna's fears about spending the night in the abandoned hotel dwindled away. As long as she was with Eliza, she knew she would be safe. She felt relaxed and at ease. But then, creeping in from the edges of her mind were the nagging questions she had promised herself she would address. This was the time. There was no escaping it. Getting some answers mattered even more now than it had before. The closer Anna felt to Eliza, the more crucial it was to discover the truth.

Anna stared down at her hands, resting on her knees. Her outspread fingers made pale stars against her khaki trousers. The white band where Gregory's diamond ring had been was still faintly visible. But soon, she knew, all trace of it would be gone. She opened her mouth, willing herself to speak. But the words that came to her were not the ones she'd planned.

'I was meant to get married at the end of this year.'

Anna kept her gaze fixed on her hands, but she sensed Eliza watching her.

'I broke off the engagement,' Anna added. 'I gave back the ring. We cancelled all the bookings.'

Glancing up, she saw Eliza raise her eyebrows, responding to the statements. Now that Anna had begun, the words came tumbling out. It was like a confession she needed to make. 'Gregory was so hurt and upset. And he didn't deserve to be treated that way. He's a really kind man. Funny. Handsome. He has a good job. Lots of friends. He was a perfect fiancé.'

'But you weren't sure you wanted to spend the rest of your life with him,' Eliza said.

Anna nodded slowly. Eliza made it sound so straightforward: if you weren't sure, you weren't sure – that was it. She wondered if Eliza had learned this from personal experience. She looked over at Eliza's hands, cradling her whisky glass. She had removed all her jewellery for the journey and the absence of a wedding or engagement ring on her left hand was now striking. Anna felt sure she wasn't a spinster; she was too beautiful and rich to have been left on the shelf. She couldn't be a widow, either; they went on wearing their rings. And they kept their husbands' surnames – whereas Eliza signed her photographs as *E Lindenbaum*. She must be a divorcée, Anna thought; there was a secretary at the office whose husband had abandoned her, and she'd reverted to her maiden name. Anna wondered if Eliza had ever had children. Maybe there was even an adult daughter or son, somewhere in the world. In the cosy circle cast by the fire, she felt brave enough to ask about Eliza's past.

'Have you ever been married?'

Eliza shook her head. 'No.'

'You never met anyone you wanted to stay with forever?'

'Yes. Yes, I have. But . . . life is not so straightforward. At least not for everyone.'

Anna could hear the pain in Eliza's voice, as if – behind her facade of independence – she were as vulnerable as anyone else.

'What I regret most,' Eliza added, 'is that I never had a child.'

Anna reached impulsively to touch her arm. 'You'd be such a great mother.'

Eliza smiled. 'Maybe not the textbook version, but still . . . thank you.' She was silent for a few seconds, then shook her head as if to break free of her thoughts. 'But we were talking about you, Anna. Why you couldn't go ahead with the marriage . . .'

'The problem was with me, not him – I knew that. I just wasn't sure if I loved Gregory enough. I used to lie awake for hours, trying to work out what was wrong.' Anna faltered – the emotions that rose up took her by surprise. She felt tears pricking her eyes. 'I was afraid I was making a terrible mistake. I couldn't commit myself to someone else, because . . .' She hunted for the right way to express what she felt. Then it came to her, simple and clear. 'I didn't know who I was.'

The words dropped into the night like pebbles in a pond, ripples spreading – the meaning growing bigger than the words.

'Perhaps, deep inside, you knew there were things you needed to find out about yourself.' Eliza leaned towards Anna. 'And that's exactly what you are going to do.'

Anna felt a wave of excitement, but it was followed quickly by doubt. The two went together, she realised: the more you wanted something, the more you feared not getting it. 'But what if it all goes wrong? I might get to Banya and find no one knows anything about my father. I might discover he's dead. What if he's alive but he doesn't want to know me? Or he's . . . like Karl?'

'Finding out about your past is only one part of knowing who you are,' Eliza said firmly. 'The journey itself will have meaning. That's what I've learned over the years.'

'But I'm not brave, like you.' Anna's voice was low, almost lost in the shadows.

Eliza threw her cigarette into the fire. It balanced on a stick for a second, then fell into the bed of coals. 'You don't know who you will become,' she said. 'Did you ever imagine you'd find yourself here, on the edge of Lake Tanganyika, drinking whisky in the dark?'

Anna shook her head. Eliza was right. If someone had described this scene, just a month ago, she'd have laughed. The biggest adventure she could have pictured back then was a holiday on the Gold Coast. And yet, here she was . . .

As if led by Eliza's words, Anna looked towards the lake. It was a blanket of darkness. But as her gaze ranged across the velvet plain, she saw – away to the left, in the direction of Ndovu's village – dozens of lights floating on the water, just pinpricks in the black. 'Look!'

'They're fishing boats,' Eliza said. 'The men light lamps to attract the fish. They sail way out. Others come over from the Tanzanian side. They meet in the middle where the best fishing grounds are. If there's a storm, they all sail back ahead of the wind. They might end up in the wrong country, but it doesn't matter. Borders don't count to sailors.' She shook her head slowly. 'If only everything could be that simple.'

The two sat quietly, watching the lights move slowly away from the shore. As the night deepened, a sprinkling of stars appeared, mirroring the bright dots on the lake. The boundary between water and sky was lost in a seamless black, as if heaven and earth were now one.

Anna felt exhaustion creep through her body. She was much too tired to ask Eliza the questions she'd planned, and anyway, she didn't want to risk destroying the intimacy that had grown between them. She rested her head on her hands, her eyelids drooping. She heard the sound of the plates and cutlery being collected up, water being poured on the fire. Then Eliza led her inside and up a grand staircase, to the room that Ndovu had prepared for them.

The little red suitcase stood by a bed made up with white sheets. A basin of water had been provided, along with some soap and towels. A vase of lavender from the garden freshened the air.

When she'd washed and changed into her nightdress, Anna collapsed gratefully onto the bed. She was dimly aware of Eliza untying the mosquito net, letting the gauze drape down. Her last memory of the day was of a figure moving around the bed, tucking the net in under the mattress – slowly and carefully, so that not a single insect could find its way inside.

SEVENTEEN

Anna rolled over, gazing up through the veil of netting at a ceiling half-covered in decorative plaster mouldings. It was like a wedding cake, with flowers and bows picked out in pink and gold. It took a few moments for her to remember where she was: in a luxury suite at the Hôtel Royal Kivu. She could smell mouse droppings, along with the lavender, and just the faintest whiff of Eliza's L'Interdit.

Peering across to the other bed, Anna saw that the sheets had been tossed back and the net tied up. Eliza was gone.

Anna dressed quickly, choosing the outfit she'd packed specially for her arrival in Banya – the smart frock she'd worn for her meeting with Monsieur Leclair and a pair of shoes with a low heel. It probably didn't matter greatly how she looked when she arrived at the Lutheran hospital, but who could say where she might end up going after that? If one piece of information led to another . . .

A small smile of excitement played on her lips as she crossed to the window. The surface of the lake was wind-brushed this morning, stippled with specks of white. There was no sign of the fishing fleet. A single canoe nosed its way over the water, a man standing at the bow paddling with a long oar.

Down on the patio Anna saw the fireplace and the table they'd used the evening before. From weekends spent in the bush with the Girl Guides she recognised the messy look of a campsite in the morning – ash, burned sticks, and abandoned utensils that had been overlooked in the dark. A cut crystal whisky glass gleamed in the early sun. A large black bird with shaggy feathers stalked beneath the table, jabbing its beak at scraps of food.

Anna was about to turn away when she noticed two people standing together further along the shore. Red hair and fair skin immediately identified one of them as Eliza. Next to her was an African man holding a bucket in one hand. He was taller than Ndovu, with broader shoulders. Both figures were facing away from Anna, but she could read tension in their gestures.

She was just trying to decide if she should go down and join them, or if she would be intruding, when Eliza suddenly turned around. Striding up the beach, she swung herself over the balustrade, before crossing the patio. A short while later, Anna heard footsteps on the stairs. Then Eliza appeared in the doorway. Her cheeks were flushed, her eyes bright.

'Good. You're up. We have to go.'

Anna glanced at her watch. It was only seven o'clock. 'Did I sleep in?'

'No, not at all. I'm sorry. It's just . . . we have to leave.'

'Okay.' Anna threw her nightdress into the suitcase and closed the lid. She was keen to get on the road as soon as possible also.

Eliza picked up her own possessions. 'I'm afraid there's been a change of plan.'

'What do you mean?'

'I've had some unexpected news.' From Eliza's tone, Anna couldn't guess if this was good or bad. 'We're not going to Banya today.'

Anna just stared at her. 'What do you mean? Where are we going?'

'I'll have to drop you off with my friends the Carlings, at the mission. I'll be going on – further north. It'll only be a few days, then I'll come back and get you.' She smiled, a little too brightly. 'Then we'll go to Banya.'

Anna's lips moved as she processed the information. Then she shook her head. 'No – I'll come with you.'

'You can't,' Eliza stated. 'It's not safe up there.'

'Then why are you going?'

There was a moment of quiet. Eliza seemed to be hunting for the right answer. 'There's someone I want to see.'

'Who?' Anna frowned in confusion. What kind of person could be so important to Eliza that she would deliberately head into danger? Then a thought came to her. 'The man you sent that letter to!'

Eliza's eyes widened a fraction.

'I saw you give it to a soldier on the night of the storm. It wasn't for Randall, was it? You love someone else.'

There was another silence. Eliza's face was torn with indecision. When she finally replied her voice was low but firm. 'Yes. I do.'

Anna stared at her. This was just one more mystery, building on the questions already in her mind. 'Is he something to do with that photograph you didn't want me to see?'

Eliza gave no response. Her silence spurred Anna on.

'I found that leaflet about the Simbas in your diary.'

'What?' Now Eliza looked shocked and angry.

'I shouldn't have looked. I know that. I wanted to find the cigarette lighter.'

'A diary is private,' Eliza said.

Anna ignored her 'Something's going on . . . to do with the rebels.' Another idea came to her, sudden and shocking. 'He's a Simba! The man you're in love with.'

Eliza covered her mouth with her hand. She offered no denial. Anna could see thoughts racing behind her eyes.

'You're involved with them,' Anna said. 'You're a part of it all.'

'You mustn't say that, Anna. Please. Don't ever say anything like that.'

'Why can't you just tell me? Don't you trust me?' Anna could hear the childlike note in her voice. After the closeness of their evening by the fire, she felt betrayed.

'Believe me, Anna, I'd explain it all, if I could.' Eliza's words had a raw edge. She wiped one hand over her face, as if to relieve tension. 'But this isn't a game. Lives are at stake. You have no idea.'

She moved closer and put her hands on Anna's shoulders, looking into her eyes. 'You must forget what you've seen. You don't know what it means, anyway. Whatever you're thinking, you've got it wrong.' Her fingers tightened, pressing into Anna's bones. 'Please say you understand.'

'Okay. I understand,' Anna said. But then she shook her head. 'Can't you at least tell me something?'

'No, I really can't,' Eliza said. 'I'm sorry.' Then she gave a brief smile. 'When I come back, I'll take you to Banya. We can stay there as long as we need to. If we have to go somewhere else after that, we will. But you have to promise me that you won't tell anyone about the photo, the leaflet. About me.'

There was a short silence, then Anna nodded, meeting Eliza's gaze. 'I promise.'

Eliza let out a long breath. 'Let's go.'

Eliza drove fast, gripping the wheel with both hands. The windows were wound down and her hair, untamed by a headscarf, whipped around her face. She took her eyes from the road, throwing Anna a bright smile.

'You'll like the Carlings, I promise,' she said.

There was an eager tone in her voice; she sounded like a mother trying to enthuse a reluctant child. Anna guessed she felt guilty about the change of plan.

'Harry has a great sense of humour,' Eliza added. 'And Rose is one of the kindest people I know. You'll love the children. Lily has just turned eight. She's very serious and grown-up already. Sam is five. And there's the baby, Molly.'

Anna felt a twist of nerves at the prospect of meeting them all. She repeated their names in her head, as if she were preparing for a business meeting.

'I first met them on a flight from Léopoldville to Albertville. It must have been six or seven years ago – well before Independence. I invited them home to stay with me. Now, they visit a couple of times a year. The children love the house. They play hide-and-seek. Magadi makes all their favourite food. I have apples flown in from Kenya.'

'How do you know it'll be convenient for them to have me?'

'It will be,' Eliza insisted. 'They'll just be working. That's all they do. You can give Rose a hand with the children. She'll love that. And I'll leave some supplies.'

Anna wondered what Eliza had in mind as a bribe for the missionaries – presumably not a bottle of Johnnie Walker. 'How far away is it?'

Eliza pointed towards a distinctive conical hill in the distance. 'The turn-off is just past there. Then, it's about half an hour's drive into the forest.'

Anna looked at her in surprise. She'd just assumed the mission was on the lake, the hospital serving the fishing communities strung out along the shore.

'The Carlings call it "the jungle".' Eliza smiled. 'I think Harry grew up reading too much Rudyard Kipling.'

Anna turned her gaze inland, to where the canopies of tall trees formed a lumpy blanket of dark green. She remembered again what the forest had looked like from the air, as she'd flown into Albertville – the endless expanse of it, stretching away for hundreds of miles. It was hard to imagine that anyone could live in an environment like that – let alone a missionary family. Picturing herself in such a place was even more impossible.

She wondered if it would help for her to think of it as 'the jungle'. It sounded like something from a children's book – a place of adventures that always had happy endings. She thought of the tattered copy of *The Jungle Book* that she'd kept from her own childhood. It was still in her bookshelf, even though its dull green spine looked out of place with her modern decor. She'd loved reading about Mowgli, the little boy who lived with a family of wolves. Kipling's stories were set in India but she'd imagined them taking place in Africa, the setting of her own early years. When she was older, she'd been disappointed to learn that there were no wolves or tigers in that continent. Marilyn said there were no panthers, either. But she was wrong. Browsing through a library book one day, Anna had discovered that panthers were leopards that just happened to be born black.

The turn-off to the mission was marked by a stumpy white pillar that looked like a milestone. It was painted with a simple red cross. Anna braced herself as Eliza swung the Jaguar off the road and onto a narrow dirt track. Almost immediately, they entered the forest. It was like diving underwater: the light faded, taking on a greenish tinge. Craning her neck, Anna looked up through layers of leaves that all but blotted out the sky. Then she stared into the shadows, where thick vines hung like ropes trailing from a ship.

Low-growing branches dragged along the sides of the car as if reluctant to let it pass. Anna realised it would be impossible to turn around if they wanted to go back. They had to wind up the windows, to keep the branches from reaching inside. But still, the smell of the forest crept in through the vents. Mushrooms. Wet leaves. A whiff of dense, cloying perfume.

Eliza leaned over the steering wheel, her whole body rigid with concentration as she tried to keep up a good speed. A tense frown tightened her brow, but her eyes shone with anticipation. Sitting beside her, Anna could almost feel the excitement emanating like heat from her body. It was very clear that Eliza was desperate to get this detour over so that she could continue on her way to whatever – whoever – awaited her to the north.

Every so often Eliza had to stamp on the brakes as obstacles appeared in her path – fallen branches, rocks, small streams and gullies. At one point, she had to bring the Jaguar almost to a standstill as she navigated a deep pothole.

Anna covered her nose with her hand as a rank smell – like rotten meat – invaded the car. She scanned the side of the track, looking for its source. Then she gasped. A dead baby lay in the undergrowth, arms and legs flung out, forming a pale star-shape against the bed of leaves. The white skin was speckled with flies. A red wound marked its belly. Anna stared in horror, unable to speak – but already she could see that it was just a fleshy flower with a pink centre. White petals were spread-eagled over the ground.

'A corpse plant,' Eliza said. '*Stapelia gigantea*. The smell attracts insects that feed on dead animals. They land on the flower and get trapped in a coating of hairs. They are held captive for a while – then released, covered in seeds. That's how the plant spreads its genes around.'

Anna managed to nod.

'When I come back,' Eliza said, 'I'll take you for a walk.' She smiled into the forest. 'There's so much to see . . .'

Anna gave no response. Before she could even begin to think about Eliza returning, she'd have to survive the next few days. It was a daunting prospect. Already she felt closed-in by the trees, longing for the openness of the woodland plains and the lake. Then, there was the challenge of being left with a family of strangers who didn't even know she was coming. She hated the idea of being an unwanted guest.

'You probably think it all looks the same.' Eliza waved her hand at the passing parade of tree trunks. They all had smooth bark, glistening with damp. 'But if you spend a bit of time out here, you'll soon see that isn't true.'

Anna said nothing. She had no intention of wandering among the trees. She planned to find some small space in the Carlings' house where she could hide away and read her novel, killing time until Eliza returned.

'It appears to be uninhabited,' Eliza added, 'when, in fact, it's dotted with small villages and camps used by hunter-gatherers. The mission is in a central location. People walk to it from every direction. There's a whole maze of paths.'

Scanning the trees and undergrowth, Anna could find no sign that any human had ever set foot in this wilderness. There seemed to be no room for them: every inch of ground was crammed with vegetation; trees stood trunk to trunk, jostling for space.

She ducked instinctively as the Jaguar pushed under a low

branch. As she looked up, a small animal streaked across the track. It was white, with a dark tail and ears. For a crazy moment, Anna thought it was a Siamese cat. She was about to ask Eliza if she'd seen the creature as well, when the track made a sharp turn to the right. Without warning, a building came into view. It was set in a small clearing of bare earth.

As Eliza brought the car to a halt, Anna looked across to a plain, squat structure, with walls made of stone and an iron roof. It took a few seconds for her to see that there was a verandah running along the front. The whole thing had been closed in with sturdy wire mesh. Anna glimpsed, in the shadows beyond the barrier, a line of washing hung up to dry. There was a girl's frock, pink and frilly; a small pair of shorts and a row of nappies.

'Is that where they live?' Anna turned to Eliza. 'It's . . . like a cage.'

Eliza seemed as taken aback by the look of the house as Anna was. 'It wasn't like this last time I was here.'

'When was that?'

'Must be a couple of years, now.'

Anna frowned in confusion. Eliza had spoken so casually of dropping her off at the Carlings' home: Anna had assumed she was a regular visitor. 'I thought you were good friends.'

'We are,' Eliza said. 'I've seen them in Albertville. I just haven't been able to make it out here. Life hasn't been normal. I've been tied up, in other places.'

Anna picked up a defensive note in her voice. She probably felt bad about neglecting the missionaries – after all, she found plenty of time to devote to her art. But then Anna remembered Eliza saying that the photographic trips gave her an excuse to move around the country. Perhaps that was even their main function. You never really knew, with Eliza, exactly what anything meant.

There was a moment of quiet as the two stared at the house.

'Rose is very safety conscious,' Eliza said eventually. 'She has to be – because of the children.' She shook her head faintly, as if to escape from her thoughts. 'I'll just turn the car around.'

She drove on a little way, to where the track ended in a turning circle. Pushed off to one side, its roof shrouded in overhanging branches, was a Land Rover. It had once been white, but squashed fruit made a leopard-print pattern on the bonnet and tyre guards. Painted on the vehicle's side were the words *Gift of the People of the United States of America.* As Eliza swung the Jaguar round, facing the way they had come, Anna noticed the Land Rover was missing one wheel, the axle resting on a pile of stones.

Parking in front of the house, Eliza turned off the engine and climbed out. As Anna opened her door, warm wet air folded around her. Insects whirred and buzzed; birds called to one another from far overhead; there was a sawing noise in the undergrowth that sounded like a rattling breath.

'There they are – Lily and Sam.' Eliza pointed to two small faces pressed up against the wire. Four sets of fingers reached into the outside world. An African woman appeared behind them, her tall figure framed by an inner doorway. She cradled a blond baby against her chest. A shawl draped her arms, the stark white contrasting with her black skin.

'That's Adina – the *ayah*.' Eliza lifted her hand to wave.

Anna trailed behind her as she crossed the clearing. When Eliza neared the verandah the little boy began jumping up and down in excitement. The girl, Lily, just gazed at the visitors with a slowly growing smile.

There was a creak of rusty hinges and a door opened. The *ayah* stared through the gap. No one stepped outside.

'Adina?' Eliza called to her. 'I'm Eliza Lindenbaum. Remember me?'

Adina leaned over the threshold. She was young, with smooth black skin marred only by a line of ritual scars – raised bumps like insect bites marching across her forehead. A baggy dress made of blue-and-white gingham hung from her shoulders. A look of recognition crossed her face.

'You have returned at last!' She made a beckoning gesture with both hands. 'Please. Come inside.'

Anna followed Eliza up onto the verandah. She noticed the smell of beeswax polish, backed by a musty hint of mould. As the door shut behind them, Eliza bent down, taking both children into her arms. Sam threw himself at her shoulder but soon wriggled free, running to pick up a toy aeroplane. Lily just buried her face against Eliza's chest. She wrapped a long strand of red hair around her fist.

After a time, Eliza pulled away, Lily reluctantly relinquishing her.

'This is my friend, Anna.' Eliza addressed Adina as well as the children.

The *ayah* smiled shyly as she and Anna shook hands. Sam studied the stranger with curious eyes.

'Hello,' Lily said cautiously. Then she turned to Eliza, grasping her hand. 'I want to show you my book. I've written four new stories.'

The girl had an American accent, which Anna presumed indicated the nationality of her parents. As she made this connection, she was struck by the fact that she knew almost nothing at all about her hosts.

'I'm sorry,' Eliza said. 'I can't look at it right now. I'm not staying.' As Lily's face dropped, she touched her under the chin. 'But I'm coming back in a few days. Then you can show me.'

Lily looked up, her eyes wide and trusting. 'Promise?'

'Promise.' Eliza held out her hands to take the baby from Adina. 'Hello, Molly.' She stroked the soft blonde hair, already forming curls, and then kissed a plump cheek.

'She is growing very well,' Adina said proudly.

'She is,' Eliza agreed.

As they admired the baby, Anna looked around her. They were in a long narrow living room with several doors opening into other parts of the house. The furniture was made of dark wood, the hard surfaces softened by a few cushions, some of which had clumsy crocheted covers that might have been made by a child. There was a bookcase with a row of serious-looking texts with gold writing on the spines and some smaller cloth-bound books that reminded Anna of ones she'd seen during her occasional visits to churches for weddings or at Christmas. At the far end of the room was a blackboard, wiped clean. A shelf with puzzles and games. A jar of paintbrushes. An abacus. By the biggest window was a terracotta pot containing a small rose bush. There was a single flower, with delicate pink petals.

'May I offer you some tea or coffee?' asked Adina. 'Mrs Carling is not here at this moment but she will return very soon.'

'I'm afraid I have to leave straight away.' Eliza switched to an African language and began talking quickly, an urgent tone in her voice. Adina nodded intermittently, turning her eyes from Eliza to Anna and back.

Watching on, Anna felt torn between wishing Eliza would wait here and explain the situation directly to Mrs Carling when she returned, and wanting her to hurry up and leave. The sooner Eliza continued on her way, the sooner she could return.

When Eliza finished speaking, she turned to the children. 'Come to the car. I've got some treats for you!'

They shook their heads in unison.

'We aren't allowed outside without Mommy or Daddy,' Lily explained.

'It's only to the car —' Eliza began, then stopped herself. 'Of course you're not. Just wait there.'

As Anna followed Eliza down the steps she glanced back at the house, fenced in with mesh. The gaps between the crisscross bars were large enough to allow in snakes, scorpions, even rats or bats. The metal itself was solid. The barrier was obviously intended to protect the inhabitants from something big and strong. And it had been put up in the last couple of years – yet the family had been here much longer. Some new threat must have emerged.

Anna hurried after Eliza, reaching for her arm. 'Is it because of the Simbas?'

Eliza shook her head. 'I remember now. Rose wrote to me that she was worried about chimpanzees. They'd just heard from a missionary family in another part of the Congo who had lost their five-year-old son. He was taken from their house.'

Anna looked at her in surprise. At Melbourne Zoo, chimps were a favourite with young and old alike; they entertained the biggest crowds of visitors, swinging from ropes or playing with old car tyres.

'The mature males hunt monkeys as prey. They've been known to take human children by mistake.'

Anna's eyes widened. 'You mean – they *eat* them?'

Eliza gave a shrug that could have meant yes or no. 'Look, you don't need to worry about it. It's only small children who are at risk. Or pygmies – but they know how to look after themselves.' She glanced back towards the verandah. 'Don't say anything to Lily and Sam. Just pretend it's normal, having to stay inside.'

Before Anna could respond, Eliza turned away, checking her watch. 'It's nearly eleven.' The realisation that the morning was almost over seemed to spark a fresh urgency. She strode back to the car, unloading the cooler and a box containing more food. She added a tin of toffees and a bag of fruit for the children.

Anna dragged her suitcase from the back seat. Feeling its familiar weight swinging from her hand, she was reminded of arriving at the Hôtel Royal Kivu. It was only yesterday, but felt much longer ago than that. Eliza pulled out the picnic basket, now dusted with ash from their fire on the hotel patio.

'Don't you need to keep anything for yourself?' Anna asked.

Eliza shook her head. 'I'll be looked after.'

The words were dropped into the air with such confidence. Anna felt a flash of envy as she absorbed their meaning: Eliza knew she would not be let down.

I'll be looked after.

Anna thought of the photograph she'd seen of Eliza and the soldiers. There was something about the expressions on their faces and the way their bodies fitted together – self-contained, yet close – that went with these words. Anna identified, in that moment, something rare and precious that she wished she could have for herself. But then, as she pictured the guns, the camouflage shirts and battle helmets, envy was replaced by a spike of fear. Anna had no idea where Eliza was going, or what she was intending to do. All Anna knew was that it was going to be dangerous.

She put her hand on Eliza's arm, stopping her in her tracks. 'Please be careful?' she pleaded. As she spoke, everything the two had shared in the time since Anna had arrived in the Congo flashed through her mind. 'Come back safely.'

Eliza rested her hands on Anna's shoulders, giving her a smile.

'Don't worry about me. I've got nine lives – like a cat.' She stepped towards the driver's door, as if ready to leave. Then suddenly, she was back beside Anna, pulling her into an embrace. As the women clung together Anna closed her eyes, breathing Eliza's perfume, feeling the softness of her hair against her cheek.

The moment seemed to stretch out, and yet be over in an instant. Eliza waved towards the house, her gesture mirrored by four little hands reaching out through the wire. Then she jumped into the driver's seat. The engine roared into life, and she drove off without a backward glance.

As the car disappeared from view, Anna took a step after it as if pulled by an invisible cord. Then she stood still, staring at the empty track, the tyre marks fresh in the soft red earth. Her hands tightened into fists and her breath caught in her chest. She was swept by an irrational belief that she would never see Eliza again.

The cards were bent at the corners, the edges soft with wear. Lily dealt them out into neat little piles, one for Anna, one for Sam and one for herself. The three were sitting on the floor, on a mat made from woven rushes. Anna's legs were folded to one side, her skirt pulled down over her knees. Sam was sprawled on his belly. Lily had been kneeling earlier but had now rearranged her posture to mimic Anna's.

'Do you know how to play "Happy Families"?'

'I think I remember,' Anna said.

'You have to collect four to make a family. Mr, Mrs, Master and Miss.'

'But don't get the frogs,' Sam said.

'They're his favourites,' Lily told Anna, 'but don't listen to him.'

Sam narrowed his gaze as he arranged his cards in his hand. 'I want to go first.' He turned to Anna. 'Have you got Miss Rabbit?'

'Sorry.' Anna shook her head. She eyed her cards. They all showed animals dressed as humans. One had a frog in a sailor's outfit, clearly bound for adventures far away. She guessed this might be a card that held a special appeal for Sam, cooped up here in the mission house. She wondered how she could make sure he ended up with it.

'You have to ask for what you want,' Lily said patiently.

Anna turned to Sam. 'Do you have Master Shrew?'

Each player took their turn and soon there were several complete families laid out on the mat. Mice. Badgers. Robins. Owls. Creatures of the English countryside. They all looked friendly and kind, with no hint that one family might, in real life, prey upon another.

As Anna listened to the children's requests and added her own, she kept thinking about Mr and Mrs Carling – wondering what they were doing. She knew almost nothing about missionaries. She had vague ideas that there must be a church nearby, perhaps a small school and a clinic as well. She pictured the couple hard at work, sparing no effort to help the Africans. Meanwhile their children were barricaded inside their house, being cared for by an *ayah*. It was hard to imagine a life more different to Eliza's with all her luxuries and adventures. Anna wondered how they'd all come to be such good friends.

At twenty past twelve, Lily pointed to the clock mounted above the bookcase. 'It's time for Mommy and Daddy to come home for lunch.' She and Sam went to stand near the front door.

Anna joined them, peering out through the wire mesh towards the turning circle. 'What have they been doing?' she asked.

Lily looked at her in surprise. 'Working at the hospital, of course. They were going to do an operation this morning. A boy has a bad pain in his tummy.'

Anna stared at the girl in disbelief. 'An operation? Out here?'

Lily nodded. 'Daddy is the doctor. Mommy helps him.'

'We don't go there,' Sam said solemnly, 'because there are lots of people with bad diseases.'

Anna suppressed a shudder as she recalled the scenes she'd encountered in the villages: people suffering from horrible medical conditions that had been left untreated for far too long. No doubt the situation was the same, out here in the forest – or even worse.

'Mommy checks our schoolwork when she comes back.' Lily's voice broke into Anna's thoughts.

With an effort, Anna focused on her. 'Have you finished what you were meant to do?'

Turning round, Anna saw Lily's exercise book lying open on the table. When she'd first walked back inside the house, trying not to think of the Jaguar speeding away, Sam had led her to a chair and begun showing off his toys. He had an aeroplane made from two bits of wood nailed together. A selection of Matchbox cars with chipped paintwork. A book about dogs. Lily had made a show of being more mature; she took out the exercise book and pretended to be busy with schoolwork. But she watched Anna constantly, peering from beneath lowered lashes. When Sam had produced the pack of cards she'd eagerly joined the game.

'I've only done half,' Lily confessed. 'But I don't care. I hate mathematics.' She tossed her head, her straight blonde hair fanning out around her face. The ends were ragged and one side was longer than the other. Someone – presumably her mother, or Adina – had snipped it off crudely, perhaps even using a basin as a guide.

A mission station was no place for vanity, Anna guessed. She wished she'd removed her red nail polish for the journey. Lily was fascinated by her manicure; during the card game she'd literally taken Anna's hand, in order to study the shiny varnish close up.

On the dot of twelve-thirty, a woman emerged from the trees, just beyond the turning circle. Skirting the Land Rover, she headed for the house. Anna took in a slender figure in a plain blue dress and solid lace-up shoes. Blonde curly hair was pulled back from her face into a bun. Loose strands, frizzy in the humidity, formed a halo around her head. Sun gleamed from a pair of gold-rimmed glasses.

'It's just Mommy,' Sam said, his voice low with disappointment.

'Daddy must be too busy,' said Lily.

As she neared the house, Mrs Carling waved at her children. Then she held her hands in the air like a soldier surrendering. Adina hurried to open the wire door.

'What a morning!' Mrs Carling stepped up onto the verandah. 'Daddy couldn't stop today.' When she saw Anna, she faltered in surprise, her hands still raised.

Anna smiled nervously. 'Hello.'

'How did you get here?' Mrs Carling glanced back towards the track, looking puzzled.

Before Anna had a chance to answer, Adina began a hasty exchange with Rose, in what sounded like Swahili. Anna picked up Eliza's name. The missionary's face brightened, then a frown creased her brow. She seemed to be asking questions the *ayah* was not able to answer.

Anna fidgeted nervously, then collected herself. This was the moment to try and take control. 'Let me introduce myself.' She stepped forward, ready to shake hands.

'No, no!' Mrs Carling waved her back. 'Don't touch me.'

Lily and Sam followed their mother to the end of the verandah, where she removed her shoes. A basin of water had been set out on a small table, along with some bright blue soap and a frayed towel. Rose washed carefully, fingers wrapping over fingers as she worked the soap into a foam. She rinsed her hands and dried them meticulously. Only then did Lily and Sam approach her.

Mrs Carling offered her hand to Anna. 'I'm Rose. Welcome to our home.'

Anna clasped it lightly. Even though she'd just seen Rose washing, she worried there might still be lingering germs. She didn't like to think what kinds of diseases might turn up in a jungle hospital.

Sam's voice piped up. 'She's called Anna. She's got the rabbit family, and the foxes. But I got all the frogs.'

'She brought some toffees for us,' Lily cut in. 'Adina's looking after them.'

'I see you've made friends with the children already,' Rose said. Like Lily and Sam, she had an American accent, but it was blended with something else.

'I'm really sorry to turn up like this, without any warning,' Anna said.

'Not at all,' Rose responded. 'You're an answer to our prayers! One of our nurses has gone home to his village for a wedding and the other one is sick. We could do with an extra pair of hands over at the hospital – even just for a few days. We're snowed under.'

Anna's polite smile froze on her face as she absorbed Rose's meaning. She shook her head. 'I'm sorry. I'd like to help, but I can't.' She knew she was being rude, but she felt certain the Carlings' hospital – out here in the forest – would be a far cry from the Hôpital Européen. She didn't even want to visit the place, let alone be put to work there.

Rose studied Anna's face, as if trying to read her thoughts. 'You don't need to worry,' she said kindly, 'I'll show you what to do.'

'It's not that,' Anna explained. 'I just can't cope being around people with diseases. I don't like blood . . . or anything like that.'

Lily's eyes were wide with interest, turning from the visitor to her mother and back. Anna guessed she didn't often hear anyone expressing unwillingness to do their duty. Anna felt guilty about not wanting to help; no doubt Eliza would have been happy to do it. But Anna was new to this country. It was true that she'd overcome lots of challenges in the short time she'd been here; as Eliza had pointed out during their conversation at the Hôtel Royal Kivu, she'd changed. But that didn't mean she could suddenly become someone she was not.

'I really can't be a nurse,' Anna said firmly. 'I'm very sorry.'

Rose's eyebrows lifted a fraction. Anna lowered her eyes, but could feel the woman's gaze travelling over her – taking in the smart dress, the shoes with a slight heel, the lipstick. She could almost feel Mrs Carling coming to the conclusion that Anna was self-indulgent, perhaps spoiled. She had some lessons to learn, and the mission hospital was the place for it to happen.

'You'll be surprised how quickly you get used to it,' Rose said briskly. 'You can come with me after lunch. I will lend you some clothes if you don't have anything more suitable.'

Anna looked at her in silence for a moment. 'Eliza said I could help with the children.' She gave Lily a quick smile, hoping to spark her support. It was her last hope.

'Please, Mommy, let her stay with us,' Lily said, picking up the cue.

'There will be time for her to do both.' Turning to the *ayah*, Rose took Molly into her arms, kissing the baby on the cheek. 'Now, let's eat, shall we?' She led the way to the dining table.

The provisions Anna had brought from the car had disappeared into the kitchen; the meal the *ayah* served consisted of bean stew piled onto thick slices of homemade bread. As she breathed the steam that rose from her plate, she felt rising nausea – her stomach was knotted with anxiety. She wondered when she would have to face going to the hospital. Perhaps she could explain that she was feeling unwell, or say she was too tired. She forced herself to begin eating. All the food tasted strange: the butter was faintly rancid, the bread over-ripe with yeast, the stew smoky. Under the watchful eyes of Lily and Sam, she struggled to empty her plate.

Rose talked about the work of the mission, and how it was originally supported by her husband's home church in Massachusetts. Several years ago the funds were diverted to another project and since then, Eliza had been covering the costs.

'She's a very generous person,' Rose said. 'I don't know where we'd be without her. Of course, there's plenty more work that could be done, if we had even more funds . . .'

Anna wondered if Rose thought her surprise visitor was another wealthy woman who might be looking for a cause to support. She started to explain why she'd come to the Congo – but Rose held up her hand.

'No, stop – please. Let's hear your story tonight when Harry's here. There's no point in you having to go through it all twice.'

'Of course,' Anna agreed. She already understood this remark was typical of Mrs Carling. Every word Rose said, every movement she made, signalled practicality and competence. No wonder she had no time for Anna's fear of blood and germs. She was kind as well, though – just as Eliza had promised. Rose hadn't hesitated to welcome the stranger she'd just found in her home. She was probably the perfect missionary wife. Anna looked over at the wire barricade, which kept the children safe from marauding chimpanzees. Another woman might have baulked at the ugliness of a home that had been made into a cage. But then, another woman wouldn't have been prepared to raise her family out here in the Congo jungle.

Rose turned to her son. 'What have you got to show me?'

Sam brought over a drawing of an aeroplane with a long line of windows. This afternoon, he declared, he was going to draw a picture of Eliza's zebras. Rose ruffled his hair affectionately. Now and then, Anna noticed, a twitch passed over her face: both eyes screwed up for a second. It made her look nervous, even though Anna knew that could not be the case.

Before shifting her attention to Lily's schoolwork, Rose directed Anna to the bathroom so that she could get changed. Opening up her suitcase on the torn lino floor, Anna located a khaki skirt and shirt. As she pulled them on she looked around the room. The bath was clean but stained with orange rust below the taps. A bar of the bright blue soap Rose had used sat in a chipped china dish. Though there was a faint smell of bleach suggesting recent scrubbing, mould grew in the grouting between the tiles, forming a pattern of pink and green. The towels were threadbare and faded. Apart from a small metal cabinet mounted above the sink, the walls were bare. The only bright spot in the place, aside from Anna's red suitcase, was a yellow plastic duck perched on the edge of the bath. There was a key element missing from the space; it took Anna a few seconds to work out what it was: there was no mirror. It made her feel strangely vulnerable to be denied the familiar sight of her own reflection – to be faced instead with blank spaces that gave nothing back.

When Anna reappeared in her bush clothes, her lipstick rubbed off and her hair in a neat ponytail, Rose nodded her approval. She closed the exercise book she'd been examining and headed for the front door, signalling for Anna to follow. The children stood at the wire barricade, watching the departure.

When they were well away from the house, Rose stopped. She turned to Anna, a faint frown on her face. 'Do you know where Eliza's gone? Or what she's doing?'

Anna's pulse quickened. 'She didn't really say.'

'It must have been a very sudden change of plan. I'm surprised she didn't come to the hospital and explain.' Rose's eyes flinched again. 'There's nothing wrong, is there?'

Anna took a few moments to reply. She didn't want to lie to Rose; she had the feeling the missionary might be able to tell. 'No . . . she just got a message about something she had to do. She seemed quite excited about it. She was happy.'

'Oh, that's good.' Rose looked relieved. She gave a tolerant smile. 'You never really know what's going on with Eliza. She dances to her own tune. She's been very kind to us, you know, over the years.'

'She's been very kind to me, too.' Anna's voice caught in her throat. Eliza had only just left, but already she longed to see her return safely. She pictured the rifle Eliza had loaded into the Jaguar back in Albertville; she was glad it was there, even though she hoped its presence would serve no purpose.

The pair walked on without talking until they reached the Land Rover. Then Rose stopped again, eyeing the bare axle. 'It's a pity we missed seeing Eliza. She might have been able to pick up our new wheel on her way back here. It's at the Catholic mission a bit further along the main road, towards Banya. We had one stolen right off the axle. The spare went missing, too.' Rose sounded sad rather than outraged.

'Why would someone do that?' Anna asked. The forest didn't

look like a place where the local people drove around in vehicles.

'They want the tyres. They use the rubber to make sandals, door hinges, mats – all kinds of things . . . It's an irony, really, that rubber is so sought after, when it comes from here in the first place.' She pointed into the forest. 'See the wild rubber vines?'

Anna peered at the thick ropes that hung from the trees, and others that seemed to rise up out of the ground. None of them looked familiar to her. She was disappointed; she kept hoping she would begin recognising things that she saw or heard or smelled, now that she was back in the area where she was born.

Rose walked past the Land Rover, disappearing down a narrow path into the forest. Anna hesitated, peering after her. Tangled branches met overhead, forming a tunnel. The light was dim, the air dense with the smell of rotting leaves and fungi. She thought there might be another corpse flower somewhere out there. She pictured running back to the house and resuming her place in the game of 'Happy Families' – swapping the buzzing and screeching of the forest for the sound of the children squabbling over their favourite cards, and Adina singing English nursery rhymes to Molly. But Anna knew she had to go on: if she didn't follow, she felt sure Rose would simply come back and get her.

Plunging into the forest, Anna walked quickly like someone crossing thin ice, fearful it might collapse beneath them. She kept her eyes on the ground ahead, the mud imprinted with the deep-treaded soles of Rose's sturdy shoes.

When they finally emerged from the forest, they stood in a clearing facing a long, low building with doors and windows all covered in wire mesh. Now that Anna had absorbed the image of the Carlings' home, the cage-like appearance seemed almost normal.

'This is the hospital,' Rose said, gesturing with one hand. 'The main ward is at one end, next is the maternity ward. And the theatre. Behind this building, out of sight, is the leper colony.'

Recoiling instinctively, Anna took a step back towards the path. An image came to her from a film she'd seen not long ago, set in medieval times: a leper with a face so disfigured he looked barely human, and limbs covered in filthy bandages. As he hobbled along on stunted feet he rang a bell and called out in an eerie voice, 'Unclean. Unclean.'

Anna swallowed. 'I thought leprosy was something from the past.'

'Not here in the Congo, I'm afraid.' Rose smiled. 'Don't look so alarmed, dear. It's really quite hard to catch. And anyway, it's not the disaster it once was. We have Dapsone now. A cheap and effective cure. We hope to wipe it out completely in this area.'

As she talked, Rose moved on towards the entrance to the building, Anna following behind her. On the other side of the wire mesh a large cat stood on its hind legs, stretching up, its body long and lean, claws hooking over the crossbars. Anna recognised the striking markings of a Siamese – a white body contrasting with dark ears, face, legs and tail. She remembered the fleeting glimpse she'd caught of a similar animal streaking through the forest.

Stepping inside, Anna was met by a strong smell of disinfectant blended with kerosene and something sweet and ripe, like rotting fruit. She was in a long narrow corridor with three doors. Above each was a hand-painted sign; they identified the two wards and the operating theatre that Rose had mentioned. As Anna took in her surroundings, a second Siamese cat appeared. It gazed at her with big blue eyes as it stalked close to the wall. A tiny kitten tottered along behind – a miniature version of the adult, but with paler markings.

Anna looked at Rose, frowning with confusion. An African

hospital didn't seem the place for keeping pets.

'We breed them for the leprosy patients,' Rose told her. 'They each take one home when they leave. As you probably know, people with leprosy very often lose sensation in their extremities. While they're asleep at night, rats can chew their fingers and toes right off, and they don't even wake up.' The woman's tone was matter-of-fact; she might have been reporting on the weather. 'We chose Siamese because they have the best reputation when it comes to hunting.'

Anna fixed her eyes on the kitten, trying not to let the images evoked by Rose's words settle in her mind. In the quiet she heard the distant rumble of a generator. Then, from behind one of the doors came the distinctive cry of a peacock. She recognised it straight away from the time she'd spent at Eliza's house in Albertville.

'What are the peacocks for?' Anna asked cautiously. She felt like Alice in Wonderland – she'd fallen into another world where the normal boundaries of reality could not be relied upon.

Rose looked bemused for a moment. 'Oh, that,' she said as the cry was heard again. 'That's not a peacock. It's a baby. Born last night. Six pounds, four ounces. A healthy little girl.'

She walked off along the corridor. Anna forced herself to follow, taking steady breaths, struggling for calm. She knew she should be able to control her emotions – she'd been trained to do so. But at the same time, she felt sure that when Miss Elliot was handing out her advice, she wasn't expecting that one of her secretaries would ever end up in a situation like this.

At least it was only for a few days, Anna reminded herself. Then Eliza would come back and rescue her. She tried to work out exactly what Eliza's words might have meant. Three days? Four? Surely five at the very most. Anna would just have to find a way to survive. The time would pass, and soon she would be gone.

EIGHTEEN

In the dying light, the river was a dark ribbon winding its way through the forest. Dan stood on the bank, watching the water slide by. Around his feet, the ground had been trampled into a quagmire patterned with footprints. Over the last couple of hours the soldiers of Force Denby had taken turns to wash here. While sentries kept a lookout for Simbas, Volunteer Smith had made use of his skills as a ranger, watching for cruising crocodiles. Some men had waded cautiously in the shallows; others had gone further out, duck diving and splashing like children. The rinsing away of sweat and dust had felt like a ritual preparation for the next stage of the mission. Once this river had been crossed, the convoy would be on a steady roll, heading for Uvira.

A mosquito whined as it hovered around Dan's ear. He waited for it to fall quiet, then slapped the side of his face in the spot where he estimated it would be. Checking his hand, he saw blood. He didn't know whether to hope it belonged to him or to some-one else – either way, he was glad he'd taken his weekly dose of Camoquin. Not far offshore, a fish broke the surface, flicking its tail with a splash. Ripples spread over the water. As he breathed the smell of marsh mint and mud, Dan could have been at home in the Mara, a fly fishing rod in his hand. But he knew that if he took two steps backwards, the river would disappear. The forest would be the only reality. Even with his gaze set firmly on the water, he could feel it there behind him, like a human presence breathing down his neck.

When the convoy had entered the forest the day before, Dan had felt a wave of recognition so strong he'd been unable to speak. It was more than twenty years since his work as a prospector had taken him into the rainforests of the Congo. Yet every plant, every flower, the song of every bird, seemed to reach out to him. He'd been able to ignore them by concentrating on the road ahead – looking out for mines or traps or any sign of human presence. But now, standing here alone, his mind was drawn back to the long treks he'd made into unmapped terrain, following creek beds and collecting samples of sand and gravel. He could almost hear the sound of his footsteps as he tramped the lonely paths, and feel the weight of his boots clumped with red mud and rotting leaves. He remembered the rhythm of his step, steady and slow. And how it would speed up near the end of the journey as his eyes turned towards the edge of the forest. He felt, again, the urgent longing to be back home where he belonged – with them. Sounds came to him – the murmur of a mother's song, a child's bright laughter . . .

Dan rubbed his hand over his face, shaking off the memories. He'd agreed to come to the Congo. Now he had to focus on the task at hand. If he let himself be drawn back to the past, he wouldn't be able to think or act clearly in the present. He'd be risking the safety of his men – letting down people who had good reasons for wanting to make it home in one piece.

Raising his binoculars, he scoured the opposite shore. There was still no sign of life over there – no hint of lamplight or fire. It looked as if the Intelligence radioed from headquarters was correct:

the Simbas were still some distance away. Most of the information came from Air Support, who carried out regular raids on Simba bases. The pilots – who were, confusingly, anti-Communist Cubans who'd fled Castro's regime in their homeland – could fly their U.S. Air Force bombers with virtually no risk: the Simbas didn't have a single aircraft, or even any anti-aircraft artillery. As far as could be ascertained from the air, the rebels hadn't moved much past Kabwanga in a whole week, and their forces had not been reinforced. They still seemed to have no idea what was coming their way.

Panning to the left, Dan focused on the dim outlines of a wooden bridge that spanned the river a few hundred yards away. He could see where the men had been at work adding planks and struts to strengthen the structure. There had been one trained sapper on the job – an American ex-marine who was listed as an Italian citizen on the paperwork – and a couple of unskilled volunteers. They'd laboured hard, and the bridge was now deemed safe for the convoy to cross.

While these men were at work, Bailey and Henning had carried out reconnaissance on the other side. They were now operating as partners, the wounds on their faces the only reminder of their fight. The pair had reported finding nothing of interest, except a snake the size of a fire hose. Bailey had brought back a trophy: a bleached jawbone that looked more human than ape.

Now, the Force was just waiting for night to fall. The sky was clear and when the moon rose there should be just enough light to see without torches or lamps. Another Commanding Officer might have pushed on during daylight, but Dan didn't like the idea. Intelligence and reconnaissance reports could both be wrong. On the bridge, the men would be exposed and trapped, with no room to move.

Dan pushed his way back through a stand of tree ferns, emerging near the edge of the road. Vehicles were parked to each side of him. The khaki and green tones of paintwork and canvas melted into the backdrop of the forest. There was a complete fire ban, and even cooking stoves were forbidden now that night was falling. He felt a burst of satisfaction. This was how a commando unit should look – almost invisible.

He made a quick tour of the convoy, checking on the men. Since the road was hemmed in by trees, many of them were eating their rations while sitting inside the vehicles. Dan was pleased to see that Hardy was with Bergman, playing cards. With the help of sedatives issued by Doc Malone and the removal of his supply of whisky, the Lieutenant had been much calmer; if he still had episodes of delusion he was keeping them to himself. He even made intermittent efforts to do his job. But as a precaution, Dan had assigned the Belgian farmer to be his constant companion.

Billy Mason was standing beside Fuller, the youth's weedy frame contrasting with the compact but sturdy build of the Welsh mechanic. The two were leaning over the bonnet of the armoured jeep, deep in conversation. Fuller looked up as Dan passed. Dan lifted his hand in a gesture of approval. This was another babysitting arrangement – one that he'd had to put in place, following the events of the day before.

During the lunch break, Dan had noticed Billy in the company of a volunteer called Nilsen. While the other men had been unpacking their ration boxes, the pair had decided to go sightseeing in the forest. Dan had watched them kicking toadstools at each other, fragments of bright yellow, orange and red flying through the air. It was harmless fun, but when they disappeared from view, Dan began to feel uneasy. Nilsen had extensive military experience, but it was mostly in desert locations. There was a chance he could get disorientated in the forest. Dan was just about to send Smith after them when he heard Nilsen whooping and laughing, and Billy's thin high voice chiming in. Looking up from his ration tin, he saw some of the treetops shaking. Then came a sound Dan recognised: the alarm-cry of a large primate, perhaps a chimpanzee, ringing through the forest. Before long, fearful screeches filled the air.

As Dan rose to his feet, he exchanged a look with Smith. The next moment, a chimpanzee rushed onto the road – a young female with a tiny baby clutched to her chest. She stared wildly around her, gibbering in fear.

'Bloody idiots.' Smith spat with disgust.

Dan moved towards the chimpanzee, calmly but quickly. He waved his arm to signal that everyone else should stay away. Even a small female like this was stronger than a man; and a mother defending her child could draw on almost supernatural power. He kept his gaze averted as he approached, so as not to look aggressive. Skirting her, he strode in among the trees.

'Nilsen!' he called out. 'That's enough!'

Searching his surroundings for signs of other chimpanzees, he ploughed into the undergrowth, his steps driven by rising anger. Then he heard pistol fire. Two shots. He launched himself in the direction of the sound. Emerging from a tangle of ferns, he found the soldiers in a small clearing. Nilsen stood over a black shape sprawled on the ground. He still held his firing stance, his pistol gripped by two hands.

'Damned thing went for me, sir.'

The chimpanzee was a mature male. He was writhing in agony, pink froth bubbling from between his wrinkled lips.

'Hand me your weapon, soldier,' Dan said coldly.

Nilsen turned in surprise. After eyeing his Commanding Officer for a few seconds, he relinquished the pistol. Dan passed it to Billy.

'Finish him off.'

'What?'

'He's in pain. Kill him.'

The boy stared in horror from the gun to the chimpanzee. The animal's breath rattled in his barrel chest, his eyes rolling back in his head. One furry hand reached towards the sky, bare dark fingers clutching at the air.

'Go on.' Dan fixed Billy with a hard glare.

'I can't.' He swallowed, his hand covering his mouth.

'Just leave it, sir,' suggested Nilsen. 'It won't last long.'

Dan's grip on the pistol tightened. An urge to strike the man's face with the barrel rose inside him. He knew this feeling – how it fed on deeper anger, breeding up a monster that could run out of control. He took a breath, then used the gun to gesture towards the road. 'Get back where you're meant to be, both of you.'

As the two stalked away, Dan raised the pistol and racked the slider to load the chamber. He was not new to the task of dispatching an animal that had been wounded by someone else. However carefully he tried to manage them, hunting clients were sometimes too enthralled by the chase to listen to his instructions. An injured animal would often run off at speed, fear overcoming crippling pain. It was a golden rule among hunters that no game should ever be left to a slow death. It wasn't fair on the animal, or on any human who might wander into its path. Dan was lucky this chimpanzee was immobile. Once, he'd had to follow a trail of blood for a whole day before he found a lion – whimpering in agony, yet still lethal – and was able to bring the ill-fated hunt to an end.

He aimed the pistol, bracing for the recoil. Then he hesitated.

The chimpanzee looked so human. He could see a whole life story held in its eyes, still so clear and bright. Birth. Childhood. Maturity. Fatherhood.

He squeezed the trigger, the shot ringing out through the trees. The body jerked as it was hit, then went still. Blood welled from the wound, trickling onto the forest floor. A spray of white orchids turned red. Dan stared at it for a moment before heading for the road.

Dan shepherded the female and her baby back into the forest. Then he signalled to his men that it was time for the convoy to move on. The dead chimpanzee was soon left far behind. But for the rest of the day and the night that followed, Dan's thoughts kept returning to those bright eyes and the dark-skinned hand clutching at the air. Now, just the experience of seeing Billy Mason again brought it all back. As Dan set off for his Land Rover to prepare for the river crossing, his ears echoed with the cries the female had made when she encountered the lifeless body of her mate.

Rounding the boxy mass of the Bedford truck, he paused, squinting into the gathering gloom. He could see two soldiers standing with their backs to him at a sentry post. He frowned. Only one was meant to be there; as far as Dan was concerned, loneliness was a prerequisite for vigilance.

He walked towards them, staying in clear view so they could identify him if they turned round, but moving silently – the habit of a hunter.

'Look at this, man.'

Dan recognised Dupont's voice. He edged sideways until he could see the soldiers better. The Corporal was feeling inside his shirt pocket.

'What have you got?' The other man was the Intelligence

Sergeant, Becker.

'You can't tell anyone. It's a secret.'

Becker laughed. 'I'm an expert on secrets.'

'No, I really mean it.'

Dan slid into the shadows, taking cover. He didn't like being an eavesdropper, but he had an instinctive distrust of this pair. Whatever secret Dupont intended to share, Dan wanted to know what it was.

In the half-light he could just see the soldier holding a little black bag. It reminded him of the velvet pouches ladies brought on safari to keep their jewellery in. As Dupont tipped it up, Dan narrowed his eyes. Something small and white fell onto the man's open palm.

'What is it?' Becker bent closer. Then he answered his own question. 'A human molar. What have you done – robbed the tooth fairy?'

His joke did nothing to dispel the sense that something dark was about to be revealed.

'Who do you think it belonged to?' Dupont asked.

Becker didn't answer. His face was rapt with interest as he waited for the other man to speak.

'Lumumba.' Dupont lingered over the name. It sounded gentle, like something one might murmur to a child. Yet it sent a chill down Dan's spine. Patrice Lumumba had been the first Congolese Prime Minister, elected at Independence. His time in the limelight didn't last long. Within twelve weeks he was removed from power in a military coup. Not long after, he was assassinated. Dan stared at the molar resting on Dupont's hand. He didn't even want to think how the ex-Belgian Army officer had come by such a gruesome relic.

Becker whistled softly. 'I heard his body was dissolved in acid . . .'

'It was,' Dupont confirmed. 'The trouble is, bones and teeth are much harder to get rid of than you might think.'

There was a short silence. The cries of river birds seemed suddenly loud. Becker leaned closer. Dan could only just hear him speak. 'Were you there?'

Dupont nodded, his thin lips curled into a smile. When he spoke his tone was hushed at first, but pride soon drove up the volume. 'Two of us, and a few blacks, were sent to dig up his body. He'd been dead a few days. The smell was bad and he didn't look too good either. We cut him up with knives. There was a hacksaw as well. We wore masks at first, but then we didn't bother. We just drank whisky to hide the smell. We threw all the bits into the barrel of sulfuric. It ate up the flesh, all right. But it left bits of the bones, and most of the skull. It didn't touch the teeth. We scattered the remains in the bush. I think I was the only one who kept a souvenir.' He held up the tooth so that it caught the last of the daylight. 'We spent another day there, just drinking whisky. One of the boys had an acid burn on his foot, but he didn't even feel it, he was too drunk.' A strange, high laugh broke from Dupont's lips. 'It was crazy, man. Just crazy.'

'They didn't want a hero's grave for him.' Becker nodded thoughtfully. He looked unaffected by the horror of the story. He lit a cigarette, turning his back to the river to hide the flare of his match. 'Who put you up for the job?' he asked curiously.

Dupont seemed unsure whether to reply. Eventually, he shook his head. 'I can't say.' A sly smile teased his lips. 'Some people know how to keep secrets from you, my friend.'

Becker shrugged. 'The Belgians were involved in the assassination, and the coup. The CIA played their part as well. Where I come from, everyone believes that. The details don't really matter. Poor old Lumumba. He should have asked for the toothpaste – better than being tortured for days, then put in front of the firing squad.'

'Toothpaste?' There was a puzzled frown on Dupont's face as he eyed the molar.

'Eisenhower said he wanted him eliminated. Someone took him at his word. A scientist at the CIA created a special tube of toothpaste flavoured with snake venom. He brought it to the Congo himself, in his briefcase. Someone was to squeeze some onto the Prime Minister's toothbrush. That was the plan for getting rid of Lumumba.'

'You are not serious?' Dupont gave a twisted grin.

Becker blew smoke through his teeth. 'I'm deadly serious.'

As the two men laughed quietly together, Dan backed away, making sure he wasn't heard. He wished now that he hadn't stayed to listen. He didn't care how foolhardy and dangerous this man Lumumba was – according to Blair, he had virtually offered the Congo to the Soviets on a plate, free of charge – what he'd just heard was sickening. When he was at a safe distance he picked up his pace, keen to leave the grim account behind him, a dark blot in the night.

'Everything all right, sir?' Smith asked as Dan reached the Land Rover.

'All fine,' Dan responded as he opened the driver's door.

Smith was sitting on the passenger's side, cleaning the barrel of his rifle. Dan knew that some of the men – given half a chance – would carry out this task by firing off rounds of ammunition. But the game ranger wouldn't have contemplated such a wasteful practice. He was drawing a piece of cloth through the barrel.

As Dan watched him at work, he was aware of a general buzz of activity in the convoy. Like Smith, all the men were now preparing for the crossing: stripping down their guns, testing trigger actions and reload mechanisms, checking ammunition belts. They knew that their lives – and those of their mates – depended on the state of their equipment. Before going into action the soldiers would also look over their personal items: love letters, Bibles, photographs, crosses, lucky cigarette lighters. Blair might scoff at the Simbas with their belief in magic, but the commandos had plenty of their own talismans.

Turning to the vehicle behind him, Dan saw that Bailey was helping Henning transform his face with camouflage paint. The Legionnaire's baby blue eyes now looked even bigger; the overall effect was deeply sinister. Dan wondered if Thompson was going to get a make-up job. With his bleached-blond features he should have been the first in line.

Dan swung himself up into his seat, then reached around to get his own rifle, resting it over his knee. He needed to prepare too. He'd issued instructions for the soldiers to be battle-ready when the convoy crossed the bridge. No action was expected tonight – or tomorrow, for that matter. But it was never too soon to have a proper dress rehearsal.

Rain beat down on Dan's helmet, streaming over the peaked rim and onto his face. He strode the length of the convoy, calling out orders to the men. The water swallowed his words, so he ended up waving and pointing as well.

Half the vehicles were bogged to their axles. Men who were not at work digging around the tyres were cutting branches to shove in front of them. McAdam was lying on the ground with only his legs and a length of tartan kilt sticking out from under one of the jeeps.

Fuller was in the cabin of the Bedford, leaning out of the window, watching the rear wheel spinning. Bailey and Henning were setting up a winch, running a cable around a tree trunk and back to the armoured jeep; they worked together like a single machine, with no need for communication. They'd stripped off their shirts – Bailey showing off his tattoo and Henning revealing the jagged scar. As they strained to attach the winch line, Dan could see the outlines of every muscle in their arms.

The rain had started almost as soon as they'd crossed the bridge. During the morning the road had softened steadily and it was now just a channel of mud. The convoy was barely making any progress.

Scanning the scene, Dan spied Billy sheltering under a plant with leaves as big as umbrellas. His arms were wrapped around his chest; he looked cold, in spite of the steamy air. Dan wondered if he might be coming down with malaria.

'Get to work, soldier,' Dan called out to him. He knew that if the lad didn't keep moving, he'd sink into a miasma more cloying than the mud and more dangerous than disease.

A closer look at the chaos revealed that the situation was slowly being brought under control. The radio truck slid to one side as it was winched onto firmer ground. The Bedford was close to being freed. The other vehicles were ready to move on. Only the armoured jeep was still bogged.

Smith appeared at Dan's side. They swapped grim smiles.

'At least we know we're safe from the Simbas,' Smith commented.

Dan nodded. Becker had held an information session about the rebels back at Lemba Base. He'd given a humorous talk about their beliefs, which included the idea that their witchdoctors' medicine had the power to make bullets turn into water. For some reason this meant they couldn't fight in the rain.

'Let's hope they're sticking to the rules,' Dan replied. He met Smith's gaze. Their exchange may have been lighthearted, but they'd both lived in Africa long enough to know the Simbas' beliefs were no laughing matter.

Dan was about to make a visit to the radio truck to see if any new messages had come in, when a cheer went up from the front of the convoy. The armoured jeep was on the move again. Dan hurried over to it, his boots sliding in the mud. As he came close, he saw what looked like pieces of red concrete under the rear wheels. De Groote was standing next to the vehicle, rubbing his huge hands with delight.

'Bits of a termite mound, sir,' he said to Dan. 'I saw my *oupa* do that once. Works like magic.'

'Well done,' Dan said. Taking a second look, he glimpsed dozens of termites, rushing madly to escape the ruins of their castle. 'Let's go.'

The sentries ran in from their posts, jumping into moving vehicles.

While Dan steered the Land Rover, Smith turned on the wipers. After a couple of sweeps both blades began juddering over the windscreen.

'The rain's stopped,' Smith said.

Dan looked up at the sky. Sun was breaking through the clouds, shafts of light streaming towards the earth. All around them the wet forest gleamed like a table set with silverware.

The convoy moved slowly, vehicles slewing over the road. But they made steady progress, inching their way across the countryside. Around noon they reached a marshy area where tall reeds bordered one side of their path. Dan consulted his map, referring to the compass mounted on the dashboard as he checked their location.

Glancing up to look for a landmark, he saw a tiny movement in the branches of a bush.

There was the crack of a rifle shot. Dan dropped the map, his hand already reaching for his weapon. Then a hail of gunfire opened up, coming from the thicket of reeds. Bullets sang in the air, ricocheting off metal, cracking glass.

'Off the trucks and take cover!' Dan yelled.

Men leapt from their seats, taking up positions behind their vehicles, spraying the undergrowth with gunfire. Urgent voices cut through the loud stutter of machine guns.

The attack was coming only from their left. Dan narrowed his eyes as he tried to work out the strategy at play. There should at least be some snipers firing from another direction. It made no sense – however, it made defence and counterattack much easier.

Dust rose from the road where enemy bullets hit; but the return fire, from Dan's men, was heavier and more constant even though they were shooting blindly at hidden targets. The reeds swayed as bullets tore through the stalks, opening up the vegetation. Dan saw Bailey and Henning elbowing their way over the ground towards the source of the gunfire.

Hardy was standing up in the turret of the armoured jeep, swinging the machine gun in a slow arc, pounding the enemy. From his vantage point, Dan speculated, he might be able to see the other soldiers: there was something deliberate about the way he aimed and fired. It looked effective, but he was very exposed up there – just waiting to be picked off.

'Get down off there, Hardy!' Dan called out.

Whether he heard or not, the Lieutenant didn't respond. There was a look of grim pleasure on his face. Suddenly, Dan saw Billy standing by one of the jeeps, too far out in the open. He was trying to reload his rifle, but his hands just fumbled uselessly. Before Dan could even call out to him, Fuller was running over, tackling the boy, throwing him to the ground and lying on top of him.

Time seemed to stand still, the whole place echoing with gunfire. Bailey and Henning disappeared into the reeds. Moments later Dan saw two grenades sail through the air; then twin explosions threw a body up, like a rag doll, against the sky.

Enemy fire slowed and then began to peter out. Crouching figures, just heads and shoulders in view, could be seen moving through the bushes that grew beyond the reeds. They were aiming for the forest. Hardy followed them with his machine gun, picking them off one by one.

'Cease firing!' Dan shouted.

The command was repeated down the line, with new words, new accents.

'Hold your fire.'

'All right, hold it!'

Then it was all over. Quiet descended, a strange hollow stillness.

'Secure the area!' Dan commanded.

Soldiers ran into the bushes, ducking between the reeds. Looking behind him, Dan saw Hardy still standing up in the turret, like a jack-in-the-box waiting for a new game. There was no point in telling him to be more careful: that there could still be snipers out there. The Lieutenant had already made it clear that he was prepared to court danger. Anyway, Dan thought the risk of a sniper attack was slim. The way the rebels had fled, it looked like a full retreat.

'Cover me,' he said to Smith, then he ran to where Fuller and Billy lay, dropping to the ground beside them. A patch of earth nearby was splashed with red. 'Fuller – are you hit?'

The man rolled over, exposing Billy. The boy's shirt was soaked with blood.

'Doc! Over here!' Dan shouted.

Billy sat up, staring in horror as he ran his hands over his body, searching for his injury. He looked confused when he found he was unharmed. At his side, Fuller still lay outstretched. As Dan looked on, a dark stain began spreading across the Welshman's chest.

Fuller stared up at Dan, his eyes widening in shock. 'They got me.'

'Doesn't look like much,' Dan lied. 'Doc's on his way. He'll fix you up.'

Fuller clutched at his shirt pocket with a shaking hand. Dan could see the outline of the folded letter; he pictured the blood already seeping into the soft blue paper.

Doc appeared, throwing down his medical kit and kneeling beside the injured man. Within seconds he was at work, ripping open the soldier's shirt, cramming wadding into a wound in the side of his chest.

'More wadding, Dresser,' Doc said to Billy.

The boy seemed not to hear. 'It's my fault,' he said. 'I was in the wrong place.'

Doc held out one hand. 'I'm still waiting.' He spoke calmly. 'Do what you're told. There's a good lad.'

Billy remained immobile for a second, then jolted into action, pulling a bandage from the bag, opening the packet with his teeth.

'I'm going to die.' Fuller's voice was raw with panic.

Dan put his hand on the man's shoulder. 'Volunteer Fuller – that is not going to happen. Do you hear me? You do not have permission to die.'

Fuller just stared at him.

'I said, do you hear me?' Dan pushed him to respond.

'Yes.'

'Yes, *what?*'

'Yes, sir.'

Dan glanced at Doc, who gave the faintest lift of one eyebrow. Dan forced a smile as he turned back to Fuller. 'You are going to be fine. That's what Doc says.'

Thompson appeared at Dan's side, breathless, sweating, his white hair sticking out from under his helmet. He pointed towards the rear of the troop carrier. 'De Groote's been hit. It looks bad. Very bad – sir.' He ran one hand over his face, smearing blood.

Dan turned round to make sure Doc had picked up the information, then jogged after Thompson, hunched over, behind the cover of the vehicles.

From six feet away, Dan could see that De Groote was dead. There was a gaping hole in his head, right near his temple. His beret, lying on the ground beside him, glistened with blood. His eyes had an absent stare.

'Thompson, get back to Doc and tell him to stay where he is,' Dan said. 'Just quietly.'

Dan looked down at the butcher's hands splayed on the ground, the skin still orange from breaking up the termite mound. Dan had a flash image of a little boy on safari with his grandfather, their car stuck in the black mud of the *veldt*.

The moment of reflection was cut short by two gunshots, fired from a pistol, just a few seconds apart. Dan stiffened, waiting for more – but there was nothing; just the voices of the soldiers calling to one another as they scouted the area.

'What should I do with him, sir?' It was De Groote's partner.

'Wrap him in a blanket and put him in the truck,' Dan said, As

285

men began drifting across, he planted himself in their way. There would be time for them to pay their respects later on.

'Check your vehicles,' he instructed. 'As soon as we get Fuller stabilised, we're moving on.'

He was heading back up to where he'd left Fuller, Billy and Doc Malone when Bailey and Henning stepped onto the road in front of him. They each carried at least half-a-dozen guns. Layers of ammunition belts crisscrossed their chests, which were still bare after their efforts with the bogged vehicles. They were a daunting sight, laden with weapons and bullets, their faces streaked with grease paint. Henning was stern-faced and upright, in line with his trademark military bearing. Bailey's triumphant smile made him look half-mad. Dan was glad Blair wasn't here to see the pair. They were more than worthy of the nickname *Les Affreux*.

'Plenty of spare banana guns here,' Bailey said. He was referring to the Kalashnikovs with their curved magazines. The hand-rolled cigarette lodged in the corner of his mouth waggled as he talked.

'Look at this!' Henning held out an old rifle, grimy with oil and dust. 'It's a Mauser. World War One. German.'

Dan recognised the distinctive bolt action – the first of its kind that really worked well; the guns had once been used all over German East Africa. With a small corner of his consciousness he wondered how the Simba owner had kept up a supply of ammunition. He must have been refilling old cases with black powder and lead.

Dan gestured towards the radio truck that doubled as a store. 'Put it all in there.'

Henning tucked his trophy under his arm, in a gesture of ownership. Dan looked deliberately away. He didn't want to endorse the robbing of corpses. On the other hand, the Mauser was a beautiful piece. It would be a shame to see it rust away in the bush.

'You might want to look at this, sir.' McAdam's voice came from a little further along the road. He beckoned for Dan to follow him, then disappeared into the reeds. The stalks were almost as tall as the Scotsman, but the ground rose steeply, creating a hidden vantage point with the road in view below. This was a perfect spot for an ambush. Dan frowned as he put the facts together. Someone had known Force Denby was coming. The front line was still a day's drive away, assuming the pilots hadn't misread what they observed. This was a hunting party sent out especially to greet the White Giants.

His mind elsewhere, Dan almost stepped on the first of the bodies. For a moment, what he saw and what he knew didn't match. A khaki uniform and the scattering of bullet cases told him it was a soldier lying there. Yet, at Dan's feet, there was a child.

He lay as if sleeping – eyes closed, thick lashes resting on smooth black skin, lips slightly parted showing small pearly teeth. His pink-palmed hands were like flowers half unfurled. Where his neck met his collarbone, on one side, a bullet had entered, tearing a neat hole.

'They're not much more than bairns, the lot of them,' said McAdam, his voice rough with outrage.

There were dozens of bodies. Most lay where they'd been hit, but a few looked as if they'd tried to crawl away. They were all teen-aged boys dressed in over-sized uniforms, shirtsleeves and trouser legs hacked off or rolled up. They wore bits of palm frond around their necks, and their green berets were adorned with scraps of animal fur and feathers. Some had *pangas*, spears and catapults at their sides. Squashed into the ground were the remains of hand-rolled cigarettes along with red-and-blue wrappers from Bazooka chewing gum.

Dan stared around him in silence. When Blair had talked about the youth arm of the rebellion, the *Jeunesse,* Dan imagined them sprinkled through ranks of adults, or acting as camp helpers. But in this fighting force – all dead, but for the few who may have escaped – he could not see a single adult. That was why they'd only fired from one side of the road, Dan realised. They had no idea what they were doing.

McAdam pointed at one youth whose mouth was half-open, revealing a wad of bright green *khat* leaves. He shook his head. 'All part of the magic, I suppose.' He bent to point at the forehead. There was a tiny white scar in the shape of a cross. 'They've all got this, too.'

Dan studied the scar, then checked the other faces he could see. The Scotsman was right. This must be the mark of the Simbas – a piece of information that Becker had missed. Some of the boys were new recruits to the cause; their scars were barely healed over.

'Why didn't they send a proper unit?' Dan frowned, puzzled. It was common enough for youths to be sacrificed in war – but in this instance, it made no sense. If the Simbas were worried about the arrival of foreign fighters, surely they'd send a force that had some chance of success.

'Maybe they're overstretched. Tied up back in Uvira,' McAdam suggested.

'Let's hope so,' said Dan. Perhaps the bombing raids were seriously eroding the Simbas' capacity. If this were the case, it boded well for the conflict to come.

Walking along the line of rebels, Dan did a rough count. He felt sick. It was sheer carnage. Lots of the bodies had more than one wound; a few had even more. Dan was surprised there were no survivors – until he remembered the two shots he'd heard. He busied himself with the counting. Twenty-nine, thirty . . . There was something odd about the scene that nagged at him, though. Then he realised, there was not enough blood. Perhaps the young soldiers had been given marijuana as well as *khat*. He recalled a story told by one of the other hunters at East African Safaris who'd fought against the Mau Mau rebels in Kenya. He said the wounded Africans didn't bleed as much as they should and it was put down to being high on weed. The drug made blood coagulate more quickly.

A blowfly buzzed down, settling on the face of a dead soldier sprawled backwards over a bush. Dan watched it walk across the young man's chin, through the straggly hairs of a half-grown beard. Another fly landed on one of the wide, staring eyes. Dan's own eyes blinked as he turned away.

He was about to head back to the road when he saw another Kalashnikov on the ground nearby – one that Bailey and Henning must have overlooked. Bending to pick it up, he heard a rustling sound close to his foot. Then a hand clutched his boot. Dan jumped away, grabbing a knife from his belt. He stood still, staring into the reeds. A young Simba, dirty and bleeding, began hauling himself forward, dragging one leg. He looked up at Dan, eyes wide with terror.

'*Rehema. Rehema,*' he pleaded. Mercy. Mercy.

The soldier looked about the same age as Billy – or even younger. He was virtually a child. His lips were trembling. Dan gazed down at him, shaking his head in disbelief.

'*Una umri gani?*' Dan asked. How old are you? He didn't plan the question – it just came out, driven by rising outrage. Surprise and hope flitted over the Simba's face as he heard the Swahili words.

'*Mimi nasoma darasa la sita.*' I am in class six. Dan had to bend down to hear the reply. The boy's voice was faint. His breathing was shallow. He was falling into shock.

Dan looked at him helplessly. There had been clear instructions in the briefing about what to do in a situation like this. They'd been delivered in a firm tone by a mercenary paratrooper with years of experience who'd been standing in for Blair. A commando force takes no prisoners. It's not possible when there's no backup transport, no garrison down the line and no option of an air evacuation. Forget the Hague Convention, the officer had advised, and Queensberry Rules, for that matter. Mercenaries have their own code.

'We ask no quarter. We give no quarter,' he'd said. 'It's as simple as that.'

Dan's hand jerked to his pistol, then flinched away. He looked up at the sky, staring into the blank, clear blue. From the road came the subdued hum of voices. There was the sound of falling glass – someone knocking out a shattered window.

When he moved, his limbs seemed to be acting ahead of his thoughts. He found himself crouching beside the boy. There was a gasp of agony as he slung the slender body over his back, manoeuvring him until the weight was settled evenly. Dan clasped one narrow thigh and one arm. As he set off for the road, he felt the head, encased in its helmet, lolling behind him. The legs with their big boots stuck out to the side.

When Dan emerged from the reeds, stepping onto the road, the first soldier he encountered was Becker. A smile spread over the Sergeant's face as he walked over to examine the Simba.

'Ah! You've brought me a live one!'

Dan shook his head. 'He's just a kid.'

Becker's eyes narrowed as he picked up the meaning of Dan's response: the soldier had been rescued, not captured. 'Give me half an hour with him, sir.'

'He's injured.'

A harsh laugh burst from Becker's lips. 'So is Fuller. And De Groote's not feeling too good either. We're not on a picnic here.'

Dan eyed the man in silence. Becker was right. The rebel could be a mine of information. If he died, crucial Intelligence would be lost. 'I'll talk to him myself.'

Becker shook his head in disgust. 'It's my job. Let me do it. Sir.'

'I think you heard me, Sergeant.'

As Dan turned to keep walking, he heard the man spitting on the ground.

Up ahead he could see Fuller laid out on a stretcher in the middle of the road, Billy and Doc at his side. He'd been wrapped in a blanket. With a surge of relief Dan seized on the fact that his head was uncovered. Fuller was still alive, at least for now. His young son was not an orphan.

Dan focused on this thought as he strode steadily on. He pictured a boy in far-away England, perhaps at this very moment writing another letter to his father. He tried not to think about this other boy, whose limp body draped his shoulders. At some point – he wasn't sure exactly when – he'd made the decision to save the life of a Simba. Whether he was doing the right or the wrong thing, Dan was not at all sure. He wondered if it was possible to do both at the same time.

NINETEEN

Anna cradled a kitten against her chest. It purred with a steady rhythm, its whole body vibrating under her hand. As she stroked the soft fur she gazed down the length of the ward. It was divided by a curtain halfway down, separating males from females. The narrow beds were shrouded with green mosquito nets. The patients were barely visible, but Anna could picture each of them in her mind. There was the young boy recovering from surgery to remove a ruptured spleen. There was a woman who had almost died from pneumonia complicated by an underlying disease that Dr Carling had yet to diagnose. Then there was the bored young man, fit and strong, with a bandage on his leg. Her gaze skimmed past his bed – the dressing looked innocent enough, but she knew what lay beneath. She focused instead on an old man – a pygmy, no bigger than a child – who'd had a tumour removed from his neck.

The kitten squirmed in Anna's arms, then began mewing loudly. Without noticing, she'd tightened her grip – now she was clinging to the animal as if it were a lifeline. With its picture-book markings and cartoon antics, it felt like her only link with the everyday world. Nine days had passed since she'd been left behind at the mission, and Eliza had still not returned. Anna could see why prisoners started marking the walls of their cells, afraid to lose track of time.

As the first week bled into the next, she felt as if she'd been here for a whole month, or even longer.

She didn't know what to make of Eliza's continuing absence. Sometimes she felt angry and betrayed – imagining Eliza enjoying the company of her boyfriend and his companions, deciding to extend her visit. More often, Anna felt sick with worry that something bad might have happened. She couldn't discuss her concerns with the Carlings without breaking her promise that she would say nothing to anyone about Eliza's links with the rebels. And anyway, there would be no action the missionaries could take. Anna had no idea of where Eliza had actually gone, or exactly whom she was going to see. All Anna knew was that it was a secret. She just had to hope Eliza was safe. When the Carlings prayed each morning at the breakfast table, she had taken to adding her own silent plea – to any power that might be out there in the universe – for her friend's protection.

Anna tried to keep her focus on the work she did each day. She had settled into a regular schedule of moving back and forth between the hospital and the house. It was surprising how quickly she'd adapted to the experience of being in the wards. Her initial reactions of panic interspersed with disgust and pity already seemed distant to her. In the main ward, as well as the maternity ward, she calmly assisted Rose in her nursing tasks and accompanied Dr Carling on his rounds. It was rare, now, for her to have to turn away or run outside to get some fresh air. She could even cope with helping to care for the lepers – though this was still her biggest challenge.

It had been only Anna's second day at the mission when Rose had insisted on taking her Australian guest on a visit to the colony.

'Treatment and rehabilitation of people with leprosy is a major part of the work we do here,' she'd explained. 'Most of the patients are burnt-out cases. The disease is no longer active, but the residual nerve damage causes lots of problems. We run a daily clinic for them.'

She'd led the way down a line of wooden huts, introducing Anna to the residents as they sat outside in the sun. One by one the lepers reached out to her with fingerless hands that looked like mangled paws.

'What do they want?' Anna asked Rose, shrinking away. She could smell the fluids that seeped, rosy yellow, through the patients' clothes and bandages.

'A greeting. A smile.'

Anna waved, her lips frozen into a thin line. A face knotted with lumps swam into view; where the nose should have been was a gaping hole. There was a man with no foot. It was like a journey through a nightmare: every face, every body, was maimed in a different way.

When Rose stepped into one of the huts to talk to a bedridden patient, Anna took the chance to escape. Back in the yard of the main hospital she ran behind a tree, bending over to vomit into the grass. Rose soon appeared, approaching with a questioning look. Anna was unable to speak. She shook her head, indicating that she couldn't face going back. But Rose just touched her arm in a soothing gesture.

'You'll get used to it, my dear. I find it helpful to look into their eyes. I try to see the real person that is there, inside that damaged body. Picture them as a perfect little child, loved by their family.'

The advice sounded too simplistic to be meaningful. Yet every time Anna went back to the leprosy clinic and took her place at Dr Carling's side, she found she was more able to do as Rose had suggested. One morning, as she was changing the bandages of a young woman – breathing in the sweet-sick smell that came from dying flesh – she began trying out some simple Swahili words she was learning. Soon, she was laughing with the patient. When the job was done, Anna had looked up to see Rose nodding her approval. The satisfaction she felt had stayed with her all day.

Outside her shifts at the hospital Anna's life followed a set pattern. She spent the afternoons supervising Lily and Sam's lessons and reading stories to them. When Dr Carling came home from work, she joined him in playing with the older children, while Rose stayed with Molly and Adina. There were games of badminton on a makeshift court in the clearing behind the house. Sometimes they kicked a football around or started a game of tag. Harry Carling was a big man, with long limbs, but he moved with great energy. As he sweated in the heat he ran his hands back through his short sandy hair, leaving it standing up in damp spikes. If he was worried about the threat of marauding chimpanzees, he showed no sign of it. He looked relaxed and happy – quite unlike the harried person Anna saw at the hospital. Playing with his children seemed to help him leave behind all his concerns.

Anna had hung back at first, feeling self-conscious joining in games with Harry; he was off-duty but she still saw him as the doctor whose every word she must carefully obey. But it proved impossible to deny Lily's demands that she take part. Soon Anna was as much involved in the outdoor games as the Carlings were. While chasing Sam or fighting for possession of the football, she often found herself noticing the interactions between Harry and Lily. The casual affection between father and daughter was clear. Watching on, Anna felt an irrational sense of loss, as if she had been left out of a performance in which she should have been given a part.

When the light began to fade, and the shadows between the trees turned dark, it was time to go inside. Adina went home to her village after preparing the food, leaving Rose to serve the evening meal. The Carlings ate by the light of kerosene lanterns. Normally, the generator was kept running until bedtime, but the diesel supply had to be conserved until the new Land Rover wheel arrived from the Catholic mission. Since the radio had suddenly stopped working – Harry had dismantled it but not yet discovered the source of the problem – there was no way to find out when this would occur.

The lanterns cast a yellow glow over the circle of faces around the dining table, adding a magical feel to the setting. As Harry told stories to make everyone laugh, played tricks on the children and teased his wife, Anna watched on with a wistful eye. This was what a real family was like: there was laughter, warmth, companionship. And at its heart there was a father, strong and loving and kind.

When it was the children's bedtime, Lily and Sam kissed Anna goodnight, hugging her close as if she were already an intimate part of their world. She smiled into their hair as they pressed against her, and breathed in their smell of toothpaste and soap.

Harry and Rose spent their evenings reading textbooks on medicine and theology, or writing letters to friends and colleagues back in America. Sometimes they just sat with their cups of tea, talking about their work. At first, as Anna joined them, she missed having a cigarette or one of the sundowners she'd got used to sharing with Eliza, but the impulse soon disappeared. There were more important things to think about. The list of challenges the missionaries faced seemed endless. In addition to running the hospital, they headed up a church; beyond the leper colony was a third building where people from nearby villages met for mid-week Bible studies and literacy classes as well as Sunday worship. Harry and Rose included Anna in their discussions, asking for her reflections on her own experiences. Sometimes they smiled at what she said, but they were always sympathetic and encouraging. When the couple retired, Anna remained in the sitting room. She slept there on a kapok mattress, the bright moonlight shining in through the wire mesh and casting a crisscross pattern on her pillow. She felt safe, cocooned inside the house, listening to the blend of two voices – one high, one low – filtering through the wall.

Anna could have been lulled into complacency if there was no urgency about bringing this interlude to an end. But she was plagued by her fears for Eliza. Every time she emerged from the path near the turning circle, she looked for the Jaguar, hoping to find it parked beside the stranded Land Rover. At work in the hospital, she would picture Eliza walking through the door, striding between the beds, the scent of L'Interdit floating on the air. Eliza would give her an explanation for the delay – one that involved nothing too serious, but nothing too inconsequential, either. Then they'd be on their way.

Anna still clung to the vision of reaching Banya and beginning the search for her father's identity. One good thing to come out of this detour to the mission was that she would now be able to arrive at the Lutheran hospital with a letter of introduction. The Carlings knew the medical superintendent there, Dr Bonhoeffer. They were sure he'd offer his help. Anna had been encouraged by the Carlings' support for her quest. When she'd explained the purpose of driving up here from Albertville, they'd understood immediately why she needed to find out the truth about who she was. Rose had talked about her own father – a Scotsman by birth, who'd spent most of his life, and had raised his family, in India. He was a missionary doctor, like Harry.

'A father means so much,' Rose had said, 'especially to a girl . . .' She'd stroked Anna's shoulder, offering a kind smile. 'We will pray that you succeed in your mission. But always remember, Anna, whatever happens, you have your Father in heaven, watching over you.'

Anna had nodded politely. The words were spoken with conviction but they meant nothing to her. She dreamed of meeting a flesh-and-blood father who lived and breathed, who could wrap her in his arms and look into her eyes . . .

A rasping cough, coming from the patient with pneumonia, drew Anna's attention back to her duties. Bending down, she placed the kitten on the floor. As soon as it was free, it bounded away as though afraid of being held captive again. Anna crossed to the hand basin to wash her hands. She didn't want to end up with ringworm or toxoplasmosis, or any of the other animal-borne infections Rose had warned her about. The Carlings took hygiene very seriously and had made sure Anna knew all the rules. At the mission, drinking water was boiled for a full three minutes to kill germs. The family only ate well-cooked food or raw fruit and vegetables that had been soaked in a solution of potassium permanganate. Even the smallest cut was daubed with disinfectant. They couldn't afford to get ill, Rose explained. Apart from anything else, there was too much work to do.

Anna dipped a small bar of soap in the mud-tainted water, then rubbed it over her hands. Her skin was getting raw from the constant scrubbing. She'd had to cut her nails short so that germs couldn't hide under them. The varnish was chipped, and her attempts to remove it with methylated spirits had failed. By the time she reached Banya she would be ashamed to let anyone see her hands.

As she worked the lather between her fingers, she looked out through the window, past the wire mesh, towards the leper colony. There were often patients to be seen loitering at the boundary. They kept to their own area to avoid upsetting the other Africans. The lepers might be cured of their disease but that didn't mean they were free of the stigma it carried. That would remain with them for life.

Today, the only person Anna could see was Mboko, one of the gardeners employed at the mission. He was sitting not far away, on a bench in the hospital compound. From his moving lips Anna could tell that he was singing. He held a bunch of carrots, still crusted with red earth, dangling from one hand. Where his other hand should have been was only a stump. He used his forearm to clutch a chicken to his chest. The first time Anna had encountered him she'd taken him for a leprosy patient as well. But when she asked the Carlings why the gardener had lost his whole hand to the disease and not just his fingers, Harry had a very different story to tell.

It was only her third night at the mission. She had been sitting with the couple at the dining table, sipping her second cup of tea. The children were already in bed, their nets tucked carefully in. The shadows cast by a moth dancing madly inside the glass funnel of the lantern added to the nightmare quality of what Harry had revealed.

He'd painted the backdrop first. Mboko was born in the era when the Congo belonged to King Leopold of Belgium. The colony was almost as big as the whole of Western Europe. The King used it as his personal piggy bank, plundering its resources.

He forced the Congolese to harvest rubber for him. It was before plantations had been established so they had to leave their villages and go deep into the jungle. Wild rubber comes from vines that can't be tapped like trees; the Africans had to smear the sticky sap onto their skin as they worked, building up a thick layer. Then they had to tear it off when it was dry, ripping away hair and skin at the same time.

The officers of King Leopold's *Force Publique* travelled the land collecting the rubber. A certain quantity was required from each village. If the quota wasn't reached – often because the villagers had had to spend time growing food for their families – the police handed out brutal punishments. Rape, torture and murder were the order of the day.

King Leopold's men became suspicious that the officers they sent into the villages might be wasting time and precious bullets hunting game instead of punishing Africans. To address this problem they worked out a system whereby for each bullet used, there had to be some proof that a man had been executed. The best way to show this was to cut a hand off the corpse and bring it back. So it was that after each tour of the villages, the King's men returned with whole baskets of severed hands. Often they had been smoked over fires to preserve them for the journey.

Sometimes, though, it wasn't possible to kill enough men. Time ran out, or the officers were too lazy, or they were, indeed, spending their time hunting game. They took to cutting hands from the living. The easiest of prey were the women and children.

This wasn't happening in the Dark Ages, Harry pointed out. It was the early 1900s. In America, Henry Ford had opened a factory for making automobiles. The electric washing machine had just been invented. People were riding the subway in New York. Einstein was expounding his theory of relativity. It was hard to believe Leopold's barbaric regime could be part of this modern world.

Mboko had been one of the innocent victims. His little sister suffered a similar fate, and so did his aunt. Nearly sixty years had passed since the day the men of the *Force Publique* came to his village looking for hands to match the tally of bullets. Mboko still remembered the pain and terror he'd felt. But he was barely able to speak about it, even now.

When Harry finished giving his account, he fell quiet for a while, staring down at the table. The ticking of the clock above the bookcase competed with the staccato sounds of insects coming from outside. Anna's thoughts turned to the painting she'd seen in the Hôtel Royal Kivu – the King's eyes spiked through with a knife.

'Violence breeds violence,' Harry said eventually. When he looked up at Anna, his eyes burned with passion. 'Make no mistake – what is happening in the Congo now is part of what happened then.'

'You mean the rebellion?' Anna was eager to hear what he thought about the Simbas. But as Harry took a breath, Rose put her hand on his arm.

'We don't discuss it,' she said firmly. 'We're just missionaries, here to do our work.'

Harry let out a long sigh, then nodded his agreement. 'You are right, my dear.'

A dense silence filled the room. The air felt heavy with the dark weight of Mboko's history. Rose pushed back her chair, scraping the floor. Anna thought she was going to suggest they all go to bed, but instead she brought a game of Snakes and Ladders over to the table. She made Harry and Anna each choose a counter to place on the board. The rattle of the dice broke the quiet, followed by the light tapping of counters. Gradually the game captured their attention. Harry smiled when he landed on a ladder and shot up the board. Rose groaned when she found herself sliding down a snake. Anna leaned eagerly over the board as her counter moved into the lead. By the time the game was over, the bleak mood had lifted. The three were laughing and chatting as if the world were a carefree place. This was how the missionaries survived, Anna realised: they found ways to retreat from the pain and hardship that surrounded them every day. They replenished their reserves of strength so they could go back into battle again.

She thought of that process, now, as she gazed out at Mboko, still resting on the bench in the shade. She suspected it wasn't only the foreigners who had to live this way. The Africans were always laughing, she'd noticed, as if practising cheerfulness were a vital skill. She watched the gardener put down the chicken, which staggered for a moment, before strutting away. As he got to his feet, he looked across to the window. Seeing Anna, he smiled and waved his stump. She returned the gesture, soapy water dripping from her fingers.

She was just reaching for the hand towel when she heard footsteps approaching along the corridor. She knew it was Rose; her businesslike step was completely different to Harry's heavy tread. Hurrying to the nearest bed, Anna bent over to tuck the net more neatly under the mattress. She'd finished all the tasks she'd been given, but she still wanted to be found looking useful.

Rose was writing notes on a clipboard as she entered the ward. Like Anna, she wore a green pinafore sewn from a worn-out sheet. It was tied tightly around her body, showing off her slim waist and upright posture.

'I've checked all the nets and mended one hole,' Anna said, 'and I've fed the little girl.'

'Her relatives didn't come?' Rose frowned. 'I'll have to send someone to speak to them. We're not running a hotel.'

She walked over to the bed of the young man with the bandaged leg, and swept the net aside. After exchanging Swahili greetings with him, she beckoned Anna over. 'Let's see if we can get another inch today.'

Anna braced herself as she moved to stand at Rose's side. She'd helped with this task twice before and her revulsion had waned, but she still didn't want to look at what was about to be revealed.

Rose unrolled the bandage and gave it to Anna. Then she peeled back a square of gauze. Anna grimaced at the sight of a thin white worm emerging from a weeping red hole. Part of the creature had been wound around a matchstick, its head tethered by a piece of silk thread. Each day Rose had been turning the stick, gently pulling the worm from the body of its host. The goal was to remove the whole thing without damaging it. The job would take weeks, since the worm might be as much as three feet long. If it died in the process, the body was much harder to remove. If it broke off, the rest of it would remain in the man's leg and serious infection could result.

Rose prodded the worm's head with a cotton bud. 'Good. She's still alive.'

Anna found it hard to think of the disgusting creature having a gender, but Rose had explained that the guinea worms found inside humans were all female. They entered a person's body as larvae, swallowed in drinking water. When they grew to maturity, they pushed their way out through the skin in order to discharge their own larvae. Anna knew all this, because Rose always gave her assistant a mini-lecture about the case in hand; Harry did the same. Anna had the uncomfortable feeling that the Carlings believed it was only a matter of time before she decided to give up the idea of being a secretary and turn instead to nursing.

'Ready?' Rose raised her eyebrows.

'Ready,' Anna confirmed as she grasped the patient's leg firmly to make sure he made no sudden movements. Rose began twisting the stick, her face bent close, lips pursed with concentration. After the first turn, Anna looked away; she didn't want to watch, in case the worm was going to break. She focused instead on her apron. It had been sewn by hand, perhaps by Adina. There was an old bloodstain near the hem. It was the shape of a heart, the red turned to rust.

When Rose was satisfied with the length of worm that had been extracted, she told Anna to release her grip. Then she began replacing the dressings, covering the wound as well as the matchstick with its string-like wrapping. Now that the crucial part of the task was over, Rose seemed to lose her concentration. She rolled the bandage too tightly and had to take it off and try again. Anna waited for her to start giving the usual detailed background to the next patient's case, but Rose was unusually quiet.

When she eventually straightened up, Anna hovered at her side, waiting to be led to the next bed. But she didn't move.

'I'd like to talk to you, Anna.' Rose sounded even more serious than usual.

Anna chewed her lip anxiously as she ran back over the events of the day, wondering what kind of mistake she could have made.

'You mustn't mention it to Harry.' Rose glanced over her shoulder as if to check that her husband wasn't around.

Anna hid her surprise that there might be any secrets between the Carlings. 'I understand,' she said. Maintaining confidentiality was a skill she practised daily in the office.

'Did Eliza talk to you about the Simbas? Did she say anything about them?'

Anna's mouth dropped open. 'What?'

'The rebels. You asked Harry about them. You must know who they are.'

'Yes . . .' Anna tried to sound vague. 'A little.'

'Does she think they're going to keep on moving south?' A spasm tightened Rose's face for an instant. 'It's just that with no transport we're trapped here. And now the radio's broken we don't even know what's happening.'

'Are you very worried?'

Rose forced out a laugh; it sounded like air being expelled from a balloon. 'Of course not. Not really . . .'

Anna noticed Rose's hands were clasped together, her knuckles blanched. She wasn't as strong and calm as she appeared, Anna realised.

'I can tell you for certain that it's safe in this area.' Anna gave a reassuring smile. 'Otherwise Eliza wouldn't have offered to drive me to Banya.'

'She'd know, wouldn't she?' Rose didn't sound very sure.

'Yes, she would,' Anna said firmly. 'She's got contacts everywhere. She knows everything.'

'But the situation could change, in time,' Rose said. 'I'm just concerned because of the children . . .'

Anna felt a rush of sympathy for her. She thought of all the effort Rose made to keep Lily, Sam and Molly safe – making them stay inside, where they were protected by wire screens; washing her hands so carefully when she came home; removing her shoes . . . 'Why don't you and Harry go back to Albertville with Eliza?' Anna suggested. 'Just for a while – until the rebellion is over.'

As she spoke, Anna realised she had very little idea what she was talking about. She didn't know what it would actually mean, for the rebels to win or be defeated. But she did know that she wanted to comfort Rose. And she refused to consider the possibility that Eliza might not ever come back here.

'Everyone could fit into the Jaguar,' she added. 'It's huge.'

A look of raw longing flashed across Rose's face. 'Maybe we could go over to my sister. She's a nurse at a leprosy mission on an island on the Tanzanian side of the lake. I've been wanting to take the children there ever since they were born. I'd like to see the hospital – they've got all the latest medicines and equipment. But most of all, I'd love to see Lydia. I really miss her.' Rose's voice trembled, then she fell quiet. After a moment she shook her head. 'But we could never leave the hospital without someone to take over from us. What would happen to all these people?' She waved a hand at the rows of beds. 'Four years ago we were evacuated. We went to stay with Eliza in Albertville. It seemed the right thing to do. When we returned, the patients had disappeared. Lots of them probably died. Only the people in the leper colony were still here, and they had suffered too.'

'What made you leave?' Anna asked.

'It was right after Independence. All the senior officers in the *Force Publique* had been Belgians, and when they pulled out – all at once – there was chaos. Africans began raping and killing Europeans, looting their homes. They targeted the Belgians mainly, but as a precaution missionaries all over the country were evacuated. But, as it turned out, the ones who trusted God for protection and stayed at their stations were quite safe. No one lifted a finger against them. We regretted our decision to abandon the mission. We don't want to make that mistake again.' Rose sounded as though she were having an argument, even though there was no one offering an opposing view.

'Harry's quite sure the Simbas wouldn't harm us,' she continued. 'We've met one of their leaders. Philippe was his first name – I've forgotten the rest. He was in the first government formed after Independence. Harry wrote to him about the need for a school in this area. He came all the way out here, and had *chai* with us in the house. He promised to help. But then Lumumba was killed and he lost his position. He's a rebel officer now, high up in the Simbas. Harry can't believe he'd let his men attack civilians.'

Anna picked at the hem of her apron, where a loose thread hung down. She thought of the soldiers she'd seen in the photograph – Eliza's friends – imagining them arriving at the mission house, parking their trucks in the turning circle. She remembered the Code of Conduct she'd seen in Eliza's bag. Surely Harry was right – they wouldn't harm an innocent missionary family . . . But there seemed to be another side to the rebels. The soldiers at the checkpoint in Albertville were afraid to fight them. They feared the powers of their witchdoctors. Karl had described the Simbas as animals in human form.

Anna looked over Rose's shoulder towards the window covered in wire mesh. If the barricade could keep out a chimpanzee, would it withstand an attack by soldiers? It might delay their entry to the house for a while, Anna thought, but no more. She hated the thought of Lily, Sam and Molly being hurt, or even just frightened.

'Perhaps you should at least send the children away to Albertville?' she suggested. 'Magadi would help look after them.'

Rose didn't seem to have heard; she began pacing up and down beside the bed. 'We have to remember this conflict has nothing to do with us. We just have to stay right out of politics. I keep reminding Harry about that. We need to make sure we're seen as completely neutral.'

'Talk to Eliza when she comes back,' Anna insisted. 'Ask her what she thinks.'

Anna's voice seemed to break Rose's train of thought. She looked blank for an instant – then she made an obvious effort to regain her composure. She loosened her hands and smoothed back her hair. 'That's a good idea, Anna.' She gave a brave smile. 'I wonder what's happened to our friend. She must have been badly delayed. But then, time means nothing to Eliza. Perhaps she's caught up taking photographs. I know what she's like. She'll wait forever to get that perfect shot.'

Anna looked towards the door of the ward, trying to think of an excuse to get away; she was afraid that everything she knew about Eliza must be written on her face. One of the adult cats prowled into view. Anna recognised the mother of the kittens by the kink in her dark tail. She carried something in her mouth. As she came closer, Anna saw it was a rat. The limp body draped from the feline's jaws, its tiny feet hanging down.

The cat padded silently towards the two women, gazing up with big round eyes, the clear blue of the Congo sky. Right in front of Rose's feet, she dropped her prey. Blood oozed from the rat's mouth, dripping onto the floor.

Rose stared at the small corpse for a moment. Then the spasm crossed her face again. She clasped her hands together in front of her chest.

'I can't stand it,' she whispered. She spun on her heels and half-ran from the ward. When she reached the corridor, Anna saw her jerk to a standstill. Bending her head, she hid her face in her hands.

TWENTY

Dan ran his hand along the waxy surface of an antique dining table, looking at the grain. English oak, he guessed. The width of the boards said it was from a tree at least a hundred years old. Someone had taken good care of the table over the years, but there were recent scratches in the polish along with several small burns that looked as if they'd been made with a cigar. At the head of the table, a chair lay on its side – whoever had been sitting there had stood up in a hurry.

Dan assumed it was the Congolese man who was now slumped on the floor near the French windows. His heart was no longer beating, but blood still seeped from his body, staining the Persian carpet. From his shoulder tags Dan knew he was a senior officer of the rebel army. He must have avoided the initial assault on his troops, staying here at the command post instead of joining them in the lines – but he'd not survived the clean-up.

At the other end of the table was a typewriter surrounded by neat stacks of manila folders. A sheet of paper was wound into the carriage. Dan pulled it out, glancing over a half-written memo. It was badly typed with missing letters and lots of errors – the work of a soldier, not a secretary. Dan knew enough French to see that it was a routine report; nothing of great interest. He left it there for Becker to check.

A field radio had been set up on a sideboard, the receiver dangling on its wire. As he picked it up, listening to static, Dan imagined one of the Simbas sending a frantic report to his headquarters as the convoy of foreign soldiers approached. Unless the man had escaped to the forest, his body would now be lying outside in the main street.

Dan scanned the rest of the room, taking in a bundle of *khat* resting on a silver platter along with a banana, its yellow skin speckled with fruit flies. There was the usual array of military paraphernalia – notebooks, sheets of carbon paper, rubber stamps and inkpads. A map had been mounted on the wall, crudely nailed over the red-and-cream flocked wallpaper. Crossing to stand in front of it, Dan's eye travelled from Kabwanga, the village where he was now, east towards the pale blue mass of Lake Tanganyika. There he saw the name of the key rebel stronghold, circled in red pencil. Uvira. Dan felt a stirring of excitement. The goal of Operation Nightflower was not far away.

Intermittent bursts of gunfire could be heard in the distance. Dan's men were still securing the perimeter. Whether they were actually exchanging shots with Simbas or just using gunfire as a precaution when searching buildings, Dan did not know. The soldiers were now well practised at this scenario: clearing out pockets of resistance, handing over survivors to Becker for questioning, searching for Europeans in need of rescue, collecting up weapons. It had taken five days to reach Kabwanga from the river crossing, the journey slowed by a range of obstacles – sections of road washed away, downpours of rain, fallen trees blocking their path. Along the way the commandos had fought the Simbas in a whole string of villages. In each location the rebels had put up a fight that was fierce at the start, then petered out as they melted into the forests.

Dan suspected many of the rebels had already lost heart by the time the confrontation began. The drums, now backed up by radio reports, would have passed on sobering accounts of the actions of the White Giants. Bailey and Henning may well have acquired folklore status to rival that of the conjuring witch doctor. They had rigged up body harnesses so they could blast away with two banana guns at a time. Watching them at work was an unforgettable sight. Then, there was the terrible massacre of the teenage soldiers, the *Jeunesse* – something Dan tried to avoid remembering. More than all of this, though, the news of the bombing raids would have struck fear into the rebels. The White Giants, it seemed, were able to summon aircraft at will and call down balls of fire from the sky.

Several times a day, Air Support would fly over the convoy, the pilots dipping their wings to acknowledge Force Denby below, before roaring on to locate their targets. The commandos would arrive at the next settlement to find that all the buildings that had been commandeered by the rebel army had been reduced to ruins. Military posts and makeshift barracks were strewn with the dead and injured. It was a brutal, one-sided battle, but it produced a swift outcome – and, as Blair was always quick to point out, if a conflict becomes protracted, everyone suffers.

The commandos had escaped, so far, with only a few casualties. Nilsen was the most seriously injured – a spear had lodged in his thigh – but Doc Malone had done a good job stitching him up. If the antibiotics prevented infection, he'd be fine. Fuller was now deemed to be out of danger, though he might need surgery to repair his shoulder when they reached Uvira. The young Simba whom Dan had rescued was almost completely recovered.

De Groote was still the only fatality. The South African had been buried at a Catholic mission, where the nuns promised to pray for his soul. Dan had carved the soldier's name into a piece of wood so that one day his relatives might be able to find where he lay. During the wake, the man's possessions were auctioned to raise funds for his wife. Dan had paid a vast amount for a bottle of Ballantine's and a cheap penknife that he didn't want. It seemed the least he could do.

A heavy toll on civilians was avoided because most of the villagers would flee into the forests as the convoy approached. A few were caught in the exchange of fire, though, and some fell victim to the bombing campaign. The pilots relied on Intelligence combined with visual surveillance to choose their targets, but mistakes were inevitable. Dan wasn't aware of any Europeans who had been killed or injured so far. It was his job to try and make sure this didn't happen. It distressed the men and caused negative publicity for the mission. Their lives didn't matter any more than those of the Congolese, but the emotions surrounding them were different. Apart from anything else, they were outsiders in the Congo – like pet animals let loose in the jungle, they were ill-equipped to survive. He wished they'd all had the sense to escape before they found themselves in the thick of a war. The missionaries – including nuns and priests – were the most vulnerable. Most didn't even have a basic rifle to defend themselves with. And they refused to run away from danger. Their belief in heaven made them too brave for their own good.

Dan had encountered evidence of brave Simbas as well, their actions presumably inspired by their own doctrines. He was still haunted by the memory of entering the remains of a bombed mission hospital. A dead rebel soldier, still dressed in battle fatigues, was on an operating table. There was a gaping slit in his abdomen; an oxygen mask covered his nose and mouth. Another Simba lay on the floor below him. A piece of metal, turned into a missile by the blast, had pierced his chest. Blood bloomed like a full-blown rose across his green surgeon's gown. There was a coating of plaster on his black skin. Dan had stood beside the dead man, wondering who he was and where he had learned his medical skills. He'd insisted that his men move the two bodies to a shallow grave.

That night, the commandos had camped in a hotel run by a Greek man and his wife. They'd insisted the place was still open for business, even though a bomb had taken out one wall, exposing the bar with its rows of bottles to the outside world. Bailey was soon to be seen dancing on the bar, his boots leaving footprints on the long white towel, a bottle of ouzo in his hand. Dan had drunk more whisky than he should have that evening, trying to drive the grim memory of the slain surgeon from his mind. But as his focus on his surroundings grew fuzzy, the vision in his head became only more real.

It was in the same village that McAdam had rescued two Italian priests who'd been locked in the mission dispensary for weeks and given minimal food and water. They were hungry and afraid; one had a black eye and the other a swollen lip. McAdam escorted them to the Bedford truck, one arm around each of their scrawny waists, holding them up. But when the convoy was ready to move on, the pair had insisted on being left behind.

'We have forgiven our captors,' one of them claimed. 'And we have work to do here.'

Dan tried to persuade them to change their minds. The goal of Force Denby was to reach Uvira. They weren't in a position to secure the villages along the way. The Simbas who'd retreated to the forest would soon re-emerge.

'We're not leaving holding forces,' Dan warned. 'I can't say when the National Army will arrive.'

One of the old priests had smiled. 'We don't trust them, any more than the Simbas. We only trust God.'

It was a fair point. The government forces had a reputation for abusing civilians. Some villagers feared them as much as the rebels. Dan was not surprised that this should be the case: it was the story of armies the world over. Power and corruption went hand in hand. Troops that were not kept firmly in check often fell prey to pack behaviour that individual soldiers would have been ashamed of, in their normal world. Once the slide began, shadows soon turned to darkness.

Dan gazed blankly at an ashtray overflowing with butts – a filigree of smoke rose from one that was still smouldering. He knew he should go and find out what had delayed Becker. There were Intelligence issues to be addressed: the command post needed to be searched. And then, Dan had to tour the perimeter they'd set up around Kabwanga, to assess security. But the effort of being on full alert for days – always ready to face the acute stress of combat, and with all the key decisions in his hands – had taken its toll. He had to seize this chance to have a few moments to himself.

He crossed to a small writing desk set beside the empty fire-place. On the table stood a whisky glass, the bottom stained gold with the last drops of liquor. There was a book lying open beside it. Dan flipped it shut, checking the cover. His eyes widened in surprise. It was a Shakespeare play. *Hamlet*. Nearby lay a postcard showing a picture of Lake Tanganyika at sunset. On the back were just a few words penned in loopy cursive.

Ma chère petite fille . . . My dear little daughter . . .

Dan stared at the card. In his exhausted state, he felt for a moment as if it had been left here for him to read. The phrase was so simple, the blue ink so clear and bold. It seemed to taunt him – reminding him that he was a man who'd never been free to write these words, even once, to his daughter. Who didn't even know where she was living. What kind of woman she'd become.

The sound of heavy boots crossing the hallway made Dan turn around. Becker strode into the room, wiping his hands on his trousers. A spray of blood darkened the front of his shirt. A leopardskin cap was perched on his head. Dan wondered if he'd taken it from a dead Simba, or one who could still talk.

'Good hat, ay?' Becker said, after making the briefest of salutes. 'One for my collection.' He swept it off, turning it over in his hands. 'Don't ask me why men who call themselves lions love to wear leopardskin.'

Dan eyed him with distaste. When Becker derided the rebels he felt a perverse desire to defend them, as if he'd become confused about whose side he was on. 'The leopard is a symbol of strength,' he said curtly. 'They are the supreme hunter.'

Dan was, himself, fascinated by the solitary animals. Leopards were not prey to emotional bonds. Even breeding pairs didn't stay together once the mating was done. They didn't hunt in packs, like lions or soldiers. They managed just fine on their own.

'That's what I mean. The Simbas couldn't hunt for their own arses.' Becker prowled the room as he talked, opening folders, flicking through documents. He glanced at the typed memo and tossed it aside. When he reached the small table he picked up the copy of *Hamlet*.

'It seems we have an intellectual here,' he said with a sarcastic smile. 'Though you'd think a rebel would be reading Marx or Chairman Mao.'

He began rifling through the contents of an army rucksack he found in the corner, tossing items onto the floor. A white T-shirt, stained under the arms. Some spectacles. Binoculars. A pair of sandals. When he was ready to move on, he kicked them all from his path.

'By the way,' Becker said, 'we are to look out for the Okapi. If we find him, we have to make sure he stays alive.'

Dan looked at his Sergeant with interest. 'Okapi' was the code name for one of the most senior Simba officers. Named after the rare, elusive forest-dwelling animal – nearly impossible to track and even harder to successfully stalk – he held almost mythical status among the rebels. He would appear in one place, meeting with officers, inspecting troops – then disappear before turning up somewhere else. Hardy had dubbed him the Scarlet Pimpernel. Most of the men had no idea what the Lieutenant was talking about – Dan had only vague memories of a novel of that title that he'd read at school. But Hardy's rendition of a quote from the book, performed at the fireside, drew laughter. His upper-class accent made the character sound even more theatrical than would have been conveyed on paper.

'"They seek him here, they seek him there, those Frenchies seek him everywhere."' Hardy had prowled the circle of men as he talked, his hands making flourishes in the air. '"Is he in heaven, or is he in hell? That damned elusive Pimpernel."'

'Well, we haven't seen him around here,' Bailey had commented. 'So he must be in heaven.'

A smile came to Hardy's lips. 'Ah, but have you seen a little red flower?'

Dan had swapped a look with Doc Malone – the two were always on the lookout for signs that Hardy was slipping into unbalanced thinking again. But then Dan remembered that the character in the book signed his letters with a drawing of the red flower after which he was named.

Watching Becker now, Dan narrowed his gaze. 'They think he's here? In Kivu?' This was news to him. The rebel leader had last been seen much further north – which made sense. Like Blair, he probably spent most of his time directing action from well behind the lines. 'When did you hear this?'

'Some Intelligence came through yesterday.' As Becker spoke he was checking the pockets of a coat hanging on the back of a chair.

Dan felt a flare of annoyance. The Signaller knew he was meant to deliver radio messages to the Commanding Officer first, and only then to the Sergeant. 'What did Girard tell you?'

Becker shrugged. 'Not much. Our man was seen south of Uvira a couple of weeks ago, maybe less – the dates are hazy. But now he's disappeared. So I guess he could pop up here, or he could be in Uvira. Or . . .' He broke off to smirk at Dan. 'He could have crossed the lake and joined up with his Commo buddies. He could be in your territory by now.'

Becker liked to remind Dan that his homeland, Tanzania, was run by a left-wing President who actively supported the rebellion in the Congo. Dan never responded to the taunts. Obviously it was a bad idea for a newly independent African country to be leaning towards China and Russia. But, on the other hand, Dan had heard the President – known by his people as *Mwalimu*, or Teacher – declaring his vision for the republic. One of Nyerere's remarks had stuck in Dan's mind: that Africans should dream of everyone having a bicycle, not a few having a Mercedes. When he thought of the people he so often saw out in the bush – walking the dusty roads for days at a time, carrying on their backs a few items for sale at a market, or a sick child in need of medical care – the goal made good sense to him.

There was also the fact that under Nyerere's leadership the

country had seen a peaceful transition to Independence. The government was stable and there had been no bloody backlash against Europeans. There were some obvious explanations for this. The British had never exploited their colony ruthlessly, like the Belgians had across the lake – not that there were the vast resources to plunder in the first place. And they'd deliberately fostered the skills of Africans to prepare them to take over the reins. There were no doubt other reasons as well why the two countries had fared so differently these last few years, but Dan thought Nyerere had also played a key role in the way things had turned out. He was not about to enter a debate with Becker about the President, though. There was no point. To Becker, everything in life seemed to be black or white, whereas Dan encountered plenty of grey.

Becker continued his search of the command post, wrenching open drawers, emptying the contents onto the floor. The pilots had overlooked this house as a target so, for once, there was an undamaged site to inspect. He reminded Dan of a hungry ferret, led by his nose.

Dan crossed to the French windows, standing over the body of the dead officer. He considered dragging him outside, where he should have been all along – keeping his comrades company. The soldier's beret had fallen off. Dan bent down, peering at his forehead. There was the ritual scar of the Simbas: the tiny cross, etched in white on his black skin. Around the man's neck was a leather cord. The top of his shirt was undone and Dan could see a small leather bundle – a witchdoctor's charm – lying against his chest.

Dan was used to observing how Africans lived with one foot in the modern Western world and one in their traditional past. But he'd never seen the contrast stand out as sharply as it did in this conflict in the Congo. Passing through rebel-held territory, the commandos regularly encountered evidence of the witchdoctors' presence: bridges, road signs and milestones were draped with palm fronds. The Simbas' bayonets, gun barrels, helmets and bumper bars were decked out in the same way. It was surprising how ordinary foliage could look so menacing, even to white men who had no belief in spells. As the rebels confronted the commandos, they screamed out war cries, evoking the power of the magic *dawa* that would turn bullets to water. The regimental witchdoctor led the charge, dancing at the front of the ranks, adorned with feathers, leopardskin, lion tails, dried fetishes, all flapping as he moved. Dan had never seen one fall – once the shooting began, the soldiers closed in around their witchdoctor, keeping him safe.

It was hard to see how the beliefs of the Simba rebels fitted with their array of modern weaponry – the automatic firearms, armoured vehicles, grenades and rockets that their Soviet friends provided. It was even harder to see how the military role of a witchdoctor made sense to someone like this dead officer, with his Shakespeare play lying half-read on the table, and the postcard written in French. Smith believed the rebel leaders might be manipulating the witchdoctors to control the ordinary soldiers and bind them to the cause. Maybe *khat* and cannabis were distributed among the ranks for the same purpose; an altered mental state was conducive to mystical experiences. Dan thought Smith could be right. On the other hand, perhaps the men at the top truly believed in the powers of the witchdoctors. Or they were determined to show respect for the ancient traditions of their people. It was impossible to know which idea was true. Maybe they all were.

At the sound of voices Dan looked up. Through a window he saw Thompson and McAdam approaching the grand front door. Next he heard footsteps on the parquet hallway. There was an odd, mismatched beat – the yachtsman was limping slightly; he'd taken a bullet in his calf, but the wound was shallow and as soon as it had been bandaged he'd been eager to be 'back on deck', as he'd put it.

The two soldiers entered the room. As they saluted, Dan wrinkled up his nose. 'You still stink, Thompson.'

The man grinned. 'Sorry, sir.'

'He'll be walking to Uvira,' McAdam said, a hint of humour in his voice.

Thompson had insisted on removing a tooth from the dead body of an elephant that had stopped the convoy, half-blocking the road. The carcass was a hulking mass of maggots, rotting in the sun. Thompson claimed he'd collected teeth from stranded whales over the years while surfing the remote beaches of Western Australia. He'd used a tyre lever to dig a molar from the elephant's jawbone, slipping his souvenir into an old ration tin. The smell had clung to him ever since. It was still there now, almost masking the raw tang of adrenalin-fuelled sweat.

'The eastern sector is under control, sir,' McAdam reported. 'Bailey and Henning are with Smith and Bergman, closing up on the other side.'

'What have you found?'

'The same as usual. The locals are starting to come out of hiding. Some look okay, lots don't. Smith found a shed with some women locked inside. You don't need to ask what their contribution to the rebellion was.'

Dan said nothing. He just hoped that when the government troops arrived, the women wouldn't have to suffer again. 'What about the Europeans?'

'Again, same as before. Lots of theft, some beatings. Most people had run out of decent food. Nothing really bad reported though.'

Dan smiled with relief. Kabwanga had been held by the rebels for some time and he'd feared a heavier toll on the small European population that had been caught up in the occupation. McAdam's report boded well for Bergman's family; his farm was not far from here.

'Did you find the orphanage?' Dan asked. Girard had relayed instructions from headquarters to check on a Baptist orphanage. There had been no word of the missionaries for months.

'Turned into a barracks.' McAdam's mouth twitched. 'Short beds. Not very comfortable, I'd say. Locals reckon the missionaries got the bairns out before the Simbas took over. No idea where they went, though.'

Dan nodded. 'Get Girard to send a report.'

'We've got an English family in the truck,' Thompson volunteered. 'Three kids and their parents. All down with malaria. Doc's looking after them.'

'What's next, sir?' McAdam asked.

Dan picked up his rifle. 'I was just going to take a look upstairs in case there's a stockpile up there.'

He was hoping for a few more minutes of solitude, but as he set off up the stairs the two men fell in behind him. The first room they came to was locked. McAdam didn't hesitate to shoulder open the door; the panels splintered like matchwood under his weight. There was a single bed below a window, still made up with lace-edged linen. The rest of the room was filled with crates of liquor. Dan picked up a bottle of Red Heart Jamaica Rum. The label, cut in the shape of a heart and printed with red ink, looked exotic and romantic.

'That's good stuff.' Thompson grabbed one for himself. 'I always drink rum at sea.'

'Pirate,' muttered McAdam. He opened another two boxes, frowning at the bottles inside, before locating some single malt whisky.

Dan led the way back out to the landing. The next door hung slightly ajar, a key in the lock. He pushed it open. The room was softly lit, sunshine filtering in through lace curtains that covered the windows, hanging in gathered tiers. Dan took two steps inside before he jerked to a halt. His vision seemed jumbled – made up of dislocated fragments. Ivory-pale skin, slender limbs. Long dark hair fanning out from the face of an angel. Bow lips, soft and red. Eyebrows like tiny raven's wings.

A young woman lay on her back, one arm flung out across the pillow – the gesture of a child abandoned to sleep. Her eyes were closed, edged with black lashes like slivers of a dark moon. Her white breasts were full and firm, rising up from her chest. Her nipples a soft pink. At the top of her parted thighs was a triangle of hair. And there, below one collarbone, almost over her heart, was a vivid circle of red.

Dan's hand rose to cover his mouth as he stared at the bullet wound. Torn skin puckered round the edges of a weeping hole. The blood was the same red as the label on the empty bottle of rum that lay at the woman's side. Spilt liquor spread a sweet acid tang into the air.

Dan was dimly aware of McAdam crossing the room, bending down. 'Look at this.'

He held up a long white robe, his big hands dwarfing the narrow shoulders. At first glance, Dan thought it was a nightdress; then he realised he was looking at the habit of a novice nun.

'For Christ's sake . . .' Thompson turned away, then spun back, as if believing that the second time around, the scene would have changed into something he could comprehend. 'He's executed her. That fucking bastard downstairs. He's had her up here, locked in this room.'

Dan thought Thompson was right. This was the reason the officer wasn't out with his men. He'd come back to make sure his prisoner would not be able to speak to her liberators. He must have been caught just as he was leaving the command post. He'd lost his life, but that didn't seem a big enough price for him to pay.

Dan stared at the delicate hands, resting against the sheets. Her ring finger was bare: she was engaged to God, but had not yet become his bride.

'She's only young,' McAdam said. 'Maybe early twenties.'

Dan nodded. She'd lost the soft, half-fledged look of a teenager but her face was still unlined.

'I've got a sister that age,' Thompson responded.

They looked at Dan as if waiting for him to speak. He was their Commanding Officer. He should have something to say.

I have a daughter that age.

'Let's cover her up.'

He eyed the sheet, creased and tangled beneath the motionless body. Wherever he looked it was marked with stains – stiff patches of dried semen, some tinged pink with blood. His stomach clenched with fury. Crossing to the window, he yanked down the lace curtains, shedding dust into the air. He laid the cloth out on the bed like a shroud.

Dan straightened the woman's body, bringing her thighs together and her arms down to her sides. There was no hint of rigor mortis setting in; she'd probably died in the past couple of hours. Her eyes were closed, as if she'd used the last of her energy to shut out the sight of her prison.

With the help of the other men Dan lifted her onto the curtain. She was surprisingly heavy, as though the horror she'd endured had been stored in her body, turning it to lead. Running his hand through her hair, he smoothed the silky lengths over her shoulders. His breath snagged in his chest and came out like a small sob. Gently, he wrapped the fine lace over the woman, swaddling her like a baby.

He stood looking down at her for a moment, his beret in his hand. Then, sliding his arms under her shoulders and knees, he lifted her up. As he carried her towards the door her head fell back, exposing her milk-soft neck. Her hair was a dark cascade reaching almost to the floor.

Dan's step was slow and cautious on the stairs. He staggered once, as his boot caught on the edge of the carpet. Entering the dining room, he walked straight past Becker and on towards the front door. He had no idea where he was headed – he just wanted to take the young nun away from this house where she had suffered so terribly.

As he stepped out into the garden, he felt the sun on his face and smelled the sweet perfume of a frangipani. Four commandos were approaching the house – Hardy, Bailey, Henning and young Billy. They carried their guns at their hips, the barrels swaying as they moved. Seeing Dan standing there, they stopped. Hardy took off his beret, his gesture mirrored by the others. Dan eyed them in silence. He felt frozen deep inside, as if the darkness of one evil man held his own soul in a fist.

A sound, coming from behind, made him turn round. It was Thompson, kicking the dead officer, his boots thudding like dull blows of a sledgehammer into the lifeless flesh.

TWENTY-ONE

Bergman led the way, pushing through the undergrowth, bent over at the waist. Dan followed, keeping his head down, with Henning and Bailey at his heels. A screen of bushy trees hid the farm from view but fence lines were visible tracking up the cleared hillsides of a small valley.

Reaching an area of long grass, Bergman threw himself down, gesturing for the others to do the same. The four soldiers crawled low to the ground. Bergman parted the grass, leaning forward. There was a look of mixed fear and anticipation on his face – they were just a stone's throw away from the rear of the simple wooden farmhouse that was his home.

Smoke curled in a thin plume from the brick chimney. Sheets and towels hung on a clothesline, stirring in the light breeze. Parked near the open back door was an army jeep. Dried mud caked the wheels and the panels were rusty and dented. The driver's door was missing. Dan's gaze was caught by a palm frond lashed to the bumper bar. It shared space with a human skull, the eye sockets forming two black holes.

Dan glanced sideways at Bergman. The man was staring at the jeep, his lips moving as if forming silent words. His fears had been confirmed; the Simbas had taken over his house.

Scanning the rest of the farmyard, Dan saw a child's tricycle tipped onto its side. He tried to make some meaning of its presence there. But it could have been abandoned this morning, or six weeks ago.

He placed his hand on Bergman's shoulder, feeling tension in the knotted muscles. He considered ordering the man to wait here – his judgement would be badly clouded by emotion. But Dan knew nothing would stop Bergman from joining the others in their search of the house. Whatever awaited them there, he had to see it too.

'You stick with Henning, every step of the way,' Dan reminded him.

The Legionnaire was going to lead the action; he and Bailey had compared their experiences with carrying out a silent kill and decided who had the best credentials. The plan was to avoid using firearms for as long as possible. If Bergman's wife and children were inside the house, an attack would put them at risk: the rebels might turn their prisoners into hostages. Or shoot them, as the officer in Kabwanga had done.

'Where's the chicken coop?' Dan asked Bergman.

'Over there.' He pointed to the right of the jeep.

Dan nodded. The location gave him his bearings. Before leaving Kabwanga, he'd studied Bergman's drawing of the layout of the farmyard and the house. The map was imprinted in his mind. He turned to Henning. The soldier's eyes conveyed an icy calm. He looked like a cat, ready to pounce, every nerve in his body switched on. He had his knife in his hand. Slung over his shoulder was his rifle – the one that he always carried. It had been given to him when he joined the Foreign Legion. It went with him into every battlefield; the day it was left behind somewhere would be the day that Henning died.

Dan checked on Bailey. He was stripped to the waist, prepared for a fight. 'Ready?'

'Ready as hell, sir.' The soldier's face was stony, his eyes narrowed with fury. Dan knew he was thinking about what had happened to the young nun. Anyone wearing the uniform of the Simbas, or even connected with them in any way, was in line to pay for the crimes that had been committed against her.

Henning moved first, disappearing into the bushes. Dan followed, ducking his head as branches flicked into his face. They slunk along the side of the chicken coop. The ground under their boots was speckled with white down; the mushroom aroma of poultry droppings floated in the air. The hens crooned softly as if it were any ordinary morning. Dan almost stumbled over something buried in a pile of compost. Pushing some straw aside with his boot, he uncovered a brown Bakelite box with the back smashed off, and a broken plastic dial with red printed numbers – the remains of a UHF radio receiver. No wonder Bergman had lost touch with his homestead. The Simbas had decommissioned the radio to ensure that no one used it to call down bombs from the sky.

Dan waited with Bailey and Bergman, hovering by the shed while Henning crossed the yard. He was a wraith, melting into shadows, emerging closer and closer to the house. The back door was propped open by a brick. Six empty beer bottles, sunshine gleaming from the brown glass, were lined up on the sandstone step.

Henning froze as a dog lunged from an old water tank lying on its side, jangling a chain that was tied to its collar. A low growl gave way to a full-scale alert bark, the big black-and-white hound straining against its tether. Dan turned to Bergman. The man hadn't mentioned there'd be a dog. Dan toyed with the thought that the animal might not belong on the farm, but the look of recognition on Bergman's face – a fleeting glimmer of warmth – confirmed that it did.

After a few seconds, a figure appeared in the doorway: an African man wearing a torn khaki singlet and army trousers that hung low on his hips. As he scanned the area, frowning, he scratched his belly. Then he picked up one of the bottles and hurled it towards the dog. It connected with the animal's chest, before smashing on a slab of stone at its feet.

Henning was flattened against the back wall of the house, edging towards the doorway. When he was close, he kicked over one of the remaining bottles. As the Simba looked down, Henning grabbed him, covering his mouth. He slammed his knife into the base of the man's skull, thrusting upwards. The body shuddered for a few seconds, then Henning lowered it to the ground.

Dan pushed Bergman in the back. 'Go.'

The farmer ran to join Henning, who was wiping his knife on his trousers. The Simba's body lay twisted at their feet.

The dog stopped barking. Lifting its head, it sniffed the air. Then it started whining, dancing on the end of the chain, tail thrashing in the air.

Dan and Bailey ran across the yard, zigzagging from one bit of cover to the next until they made it to the other side of the door. There was a moment of stillness as the men regrouped. Small gestures – a crook of a finger, a flick of the eyes – stood in for words.

Henning led the way inside, moving silently on his toes. They were standing in a kitchen with a table and chairs set in front of a wood stove. Dan scanned the room, taking in a half-gnawed corncob on a china plate, alongside a wad of *khat*. There were muddy footprints on the lino floor. The gingham tablecloth was splashed with food stains. A bullet belt draped the back of a chair.

His eyes latched onto a children's picture book that lay open on a rag mat.

'*Ni wewe?*' a male voice called from another room. Is that you?

Henning was already following the sound to its source. As he pushed open a door, Dan glimpsed a piano and a glass-fronted cabinet. There was a cry of surprise, cut short – then a heavy thud. In the brief silence that followed, a pistol shot rang out. Bergman pushed past Dan.

A man in battle fatigues sat on the couch. His eyes were wide with surprise. Blood streamed from a wound in the back of his skull. Bergman lunged across to him.

'*Yuko wapi familia yangu?*' Where is my family? Bergman shook the man by the shoulder.

'He can't hear you,' stated Henning. 'His medulla oblongata has been scrambled.'

Bergman turned to a second man who was sprawled on the floor, a bullet hole in his chest – clearly as dead as his companion.

'Why did you kill them both?' Bergman demanded. 'You should have left one alive.'

Henning's eyes widened, a cloud of anger gathering in the blue. Before he had time to respond, Bailey pulled him away. 'Let's go.'

The men moved through the rest of the house. Dan, Bailey and Bergman had pistols drawn. Henning held his rifle, the butt resting on his shoulder; the tip of the barrel seemed tied to his sweeping gaze with an invisible cord.

Dan paused in the children's bedroom. He searched the room, taking in a framed piece of embroidery – a scene from a nursery rhyme. There was a homemade doll's house and a wooden train set. The innocence of the scene was turned strangely sinister by the proximity of the three dead men. Dan stared at one of the single beds. A table had been pushed up to the end, extending its length. An army shirt, folded neatly, lay on the pillow.

Back in the hallway, Dan met Bergman emerging from the main bedroom. A woman's cotton nightdress draped from his hand, the fine cloth at odds with his work-worn skin. Dan got the sense that he'd picked the garment up and didn't even know he was still clutching it.

'The children have been sleeping there with Clara. I saw their clothes. And Elise's slippers. Hugo's teddy.' Bergman's voice sounded half-strangled. 'But they're not there now.'

From outside came the sound of a semi-automatic pistol being fired. Through the sitting-room window Dan could see Bailey standing in the yard, shooting into the air. The convoy had stopped back down the road, well out of sight of the farm. The moment gunfire was heard the vehicles would speed towards the house – all except the Bedford truck, which was now loaded down with refugees, mainly desperate women and children from Kabwanga, as well as the injured soldiers.

Bailey began striding around the yard, kicking open doors to outhouses. Chickens ran from his path, squawking and beating the air with their wings. He approached the dog, holding out his hand. The dog lowered its head, hackles rising along its back. It lunged towards Bailey, pulling the chain taut. As Bailey lashed out with his boot, the dog snapped at his leg. Bailey slid his knife from its sheath.

Dan strode to the window, smashing his pistol through the glass; then he leaned to call through the hole. 'Bailey!'

The soldier turned around. He had the same hungry look on his face as he did when he was about to begin a wrestling match.

'Leave the dog alone. That's an order.' As Dan gave his urgent command, two thoughts were tangled in his head: the hound might be able to find a scent, and help pick up a lead; and a man whose family was missing didn't need to have his dog slaughtered as well.

When he turned back to Bergman, Dan saw the man's chest was heaving. His eyes were wide with panic. 'They might be locked up somewhere. They could be hiding.'

'They might be in Uvira,' Dan pointed out. 'Or on another farm. They could be anywhere.' He gazed out of the window, beyond the farmyard to the distant fields. He'd made it clear to Bergman that if the rescue mission was going to turn into a search, it would have to wait until after Uvira had been captured. The momentum of Operation Nightflower couldn't be allowed to stall, and there were people in the Bedford truck who needed to get to the hospital.

'I know you have to keep moving.' Bergman's voice cracked as he spoke; his eyes held a sheen of tears. 'But please . . .'

Dan looked down at the floor where his mud-crusted boots rested on threadbare carpet. He knew this was a situation where a Commanding Officer had to stand firm and not waver from the plan. He could feel Bergman's desperate stare like the heat of a camp fire burning his skin.

'We'll search for one hour,' Dan said finally. 'With all the men, we should be able to cover the property.'

Bergman swallowed, his throat tightening. 'Thank you.'

As the vehicles pulled into the yard, filling the space, Dan sent the commandos out in their pairs. Within minutes the farm was dotted with khaki figures, fanning out across the yard and the fields. The hound proved useless; when it was released from the chain, it just stuck to Bergman's heels as the farmer jogged towards a cowshed at the far end of the yard.

'Clara!' he called out. 'Clara!' His voice was sharp with panic.

'Elise! Hugo!' Dan could hear the names being repeated like a travelling echo, by the other men.

McAdam was one of the last to emerge from his vehicle. He was dressed for combat, wearing a battle jacket along with his kilt. As he walked towards the house, a thought came to Dan.

'Get the pipes, McAdam. Play something.' He almost said 'as loudly as you can' but he knew by now that the bagpipes had only one volume – high.

The Scotsman looked confused – but nevertheless he reached into the rear seat of his jeep. Soon, he was filling the tartan-covered bag, his cheeks puffing. Powerful strains of 'Amazing Grace' flooded the air.

Thompson threw Dan an odd look. 'What's that for? Bergman doesn't even like the bagpipes.'

'I'm not trying to cheer him up.' Dan pointed into the distance, past the boundary fences, towards the forest. 'For all we know, they're up there, hiding. I want to let them know we're not Simbas.'

'Amazing Grace' was followed by 'Balmoral Castle' and 'Mull of Kintyre'. Dan knew McAdam's repertoire by now. He sometimes wished that one of the men had a violin or even a ukulele. There was a mournful tone to the pipes that pervaded every tune, even the wedding marches. Here at Bergman's farm the pathos felt like an admission of defeat.

When the hour was up, Dan blew the Land Rover horn to call the men back to the convoy. Then he busied himself with the vehicle, checking the oil. He didn't want to meet Bergman's gaze when he returned.

Slamming down the heavy bonnet, he looked up, his attention caught by an egret soaring overhead. He followed its path towards the forest. A patch of red caught his eye. He narrowed his eyes, focusing carefully. There were more fragments of colour – blue, green. He swung round, leaning into the Land Rover to grab his binoculars.

Three figures were running down the hillside. A girl with long blonde hair streaming out behind her. A woman wearing a straw sunhat, holding a little boy by the hand. Dan shifted his gaze to each side of them, searching for anyone else who might be there – someone less obvious, wearing khaki clothes. But the three figures were alone.

'Bergman!' he yelled. 'I can see them!'

His words were relayed from one commando to another. Soon every man was standing still, staring at the hill.

The figures grew nearer, clearer, larger. Bergman was pelting over the fields towards them. Dan handed his binoculars to Smith.

'Keep your eyes on them. Look out for company.'

His stomach was knotted with tension: he felt a chilling dread that something could still go wrong. A miracle was unfolding, and he feared it was too good to be true.

He watched Bergman take his wife into his arms, holding her close. The children hugged him too. The four individuals melted into one.

They started walking again, down the hill towards the commandos. Dan could see them talking, laughing, crying. As he watched, Bergman stopped. He knelt in front of his daughter, stroking her face and running his hands over her hair as if he needed to touch her to make sure she was really there. Dan looked away for a moment, a twist of pain in his heart.

As the family approached, one of the soldiers started clapping. The others joined in, creating a ragged applause. Smiles spread over dust-streaked faces; shadows of exhaustion lifted from bloodshot eyes. The men fed on the scene, taking it into themselves: bright images to lay over all the darkness they'd had to absorb.

When the little family reached the yard, Hugo broke away from his father's sheltering arm and went to retrieve his tricycle. Dan was standing nearby. The boy looked accusingly at him as if he suspected he might have pushed it over.

'That's a nice bike,' Dan said, drawing on his rusty French.

The boy ignored him. He turned to look back up towards the forest. Reaching into his pocket, he pulled out a mushroom, bruised and broken.

He started talking, too fast for Dan to follow. Seeing the intensity in the boy's eyes, Dan summoned Becker to translate. He watched the child's face as he listened to the high, thin voice, followed by the Sergeant's deep tones.

'We found lots of good mushrooms,' Becker said. 'But Mummy dropped them. Then we started running. We had to leave Kiboko behind.'

'Who's Kiboko?' Dan asked. The word meant 'hippo' in Swahili. The animal was lethally dangerous, yet most people still saw it as a tubby comic creature; its name was sometimes used for a pet. Dan wondered if there was a second dog in the family.

Becker's eyes widened as he translated what came next: 'He's a Simba. He's our friend.'

'Where is he now?' Dan asked, concealing his own surprise.

'He ran away. You won't find him. He's going home.' Hugo's lip quivered as he gazed at the damaged mushroom. 'We won't see him any more.'

Dan looked across to where Bergman stood, embracing his wife. She was staring over his shoulder towards the forest, an anguished expression on her face. Dan turned away, gazing blankly at the clothesline. As a gust of wind billowed the sheets, more washing was revealed. Some children's clothes. A tea towel. Pillowcases. Then, set away by themselves, there was a camouflage army shirt and a blue dress patterned with red flowers. The two garments seemed to be dancing a duet in the breeze.

Dan turned to Becker. 'We're going.'

Becker was staring at Clara, his eyes narrowed. 'I need to talk to her.'

'No, you don't,' Dan said. 'You can't.'

'Something's gone on here.'

'If it has, it's nothing to do with us.' He grasped Becker's elbow, pulling him aside. He leaned close to the man's face, speaking into his ear. 'Stay away from the Bergmans – all of them. Or you'll be on the first plane out of Uvira. You will be discharged for failing to obey orders. I mean that. I hope you believe me.' He paused to let the words sink in.

He turned to Smith. 'Tell Bergman he's got time to grab a few things, but don't let the kids near the house. Get them all into the radio truck. We're pulling out in fifteen minutes.'

'What about the dog, sir? We can't leave him here.'

'Bring the dog too.' Dan shook his head, giving a grim smile. 'And anyone else you happen to meet.'

Smith smiled back. 'I'll try and avoid that, sir. I think we have enough company already.'

Dan walked over to the Land Rover, climbing into his seat. He rested his head on the steering wheel. He recalled the instant when he'd first identified the three figures on the hillside – the upwelling of pure joy he had felt. Now reality was seeping in, unclear and messy.

He hoped this man, Kiboko, had protected the family out of

common decency. But it was quite possible Clara had had to pay a price for his kindness. Maybe she'd even offered herself freely? During the war Dan had heard accounts of people believing themselves to be in love with their captors. The boundaries between fear and the instinct to survive became blurred, giving birth to a twisted bonding. And when a mother's love was at play, the potency would be even greater.

He looked up, seeing Bergman's face still lit with joy. If there were secrets, he just hoped they would remain hidden. Bergman deserved to enjoy his future with his family. Dan didn't want to picture him having to face that awful moment when the ground begins to shift. When the cracks open up, then widen into a chasm. When a man loses his footing and finds himself swallowed alive.

Dan closed his eyes. He could feel himself being drawn back to the day when his own life was changed forever – when the dream of a joyous reunion turned into a nightmare. Normally he could fight off the grip of the past, but right now he was too tired, his emotions too raw. And this setting – a simple farmhouse in a Congolese valley – was too familiar. It had been nearly two decades ago, but the memory returned to him clear and vivid, the details barely touched by time.

It was late in the dry season. The forest trees, drawing up water through deep roots, were flourishing in the heat, but the woodland that bordered the lake was scorched dry. The grass around Dan's ankles was sparse and brittle. He could feel every stick and stone through the worn-out soles of his boots. A kitbag, frayed at the openings, swung from his shoulder. It thumped his back with each step, beating an urgent rhythm that matched his gait. He was sleep-deprived and hungry; a bullet graze on his thigh throbbed. But he barely felt the discomfort. He was going home.

The Second World War had been over for months. Since being demobbed in Nairobi he'd crossed half of East Africa, travelling by train and ferry, hitching rides on trucks and motorbikes. Finally reaching Kigoma on the western border of Tanganyika, he'd gazed over the lake to the distant hills of the Congo. A fisherman had agreed to take him across. They'd sailed by night when the fish were biting. The moon shone down on them, the satin-smooth water parting gently at the prow of the boat, then closing behind them, seamless.

From the stony shore on the other side Dan had walked all the way to Banya, sleeping the first night under an upturned canoe, then paying a few coins to stay in the homes of Africans. During the many hours spent alone, one thought dominated his consciousness. He would soon be home – holding his wife and daughter in his arms. It was the same vision that had kept him going – kept him alive – during his five long years of service in the King's African Rifles.

Now, as he began to recognise well-known landmarks, a voice of fear began whispering in his head, familiar and insistent. It reminded him that nearly three years had passed since he'd last had a letter from Marilyn. In the remote part of Abyssinia where he'd been fighting, mail could not be sent or received. Even though Banya was far from the battlelines of the war, there could have been accidents, illnesses. Anything could have happened. But Dan silenced his trepidation. As he headed back to his world he refused to entertain anything but hope.

When he finally reached his home valley, a new energy fuelled his steps. He looked around him as he strode along, tracing the shapes of hills and rocky outcrops; he took in the tangled green of the forest and the upright grey trunks of the rubber plantations.

As his own plot of land came into view, he stopped for a few moments, savouring the sight of his home. At a distance the cottage was like a toy, small and perfect. Smoke rose from the chimney, rising straight up into the breathless air.

Walking on down the hillside, he pictured his arrival. He'd creep up on them; make it a surprise. Marilyn would turn from the stove, or perhaps look up from her sewing, and just see him standing there. He imagined how a smile would spread across her face. The joy erupting in her eyes – those grey-blue irises that he'd seen reflected in so many skies, in so many places, for so long.

The image of her, naked, flooded his body. He could feel her slender legs wrapping around his. The touch of soft skin furred with tiny hairs that glowed gold in the sunshine. The smell of her, drawn deep into his lungs. The taste of her on his tongue. Her wetness on his fingers. He wanted to be inside her, filling her, making her his own again.

Soon he was running down the hillside, stumbling over the rough ground. He kept his eyes fixed on the cottage, searching for them: the tall figure that would be instantly familiar to him, and the other, smaller one that would not.

When he'd left home his daughter had been just a toddler – bright-eyed, with clinging hands, stocky legs and a sticky face. She had Dan's dark hair and eyes, and her mother's high forehead. She talked constantly, though often only Marilyn knew what she was saying. The world belonged to her and she wanted to examine every corner of it. She knew how to put on a tantrum when her plans were thwarted, but mostly she was happy and loving. Her face was like a mirror to her heart, every emotion painted there, then wiped away. When she slept she had the peaceful face of an angel. Every time Dan caught sight of her, in the first light of morning or when he returned from the mine office at night, his own heart brimmed with emotion. The Africans used to tease him, calling him *Mama Toto* – mother of the child – because he adored his daughter and didn't try to hide it.

During the first two years he'd been away, Dan had received several letters from Marilyn; when they reached him in some desert outpost, the envelope stained and worn through on the edges, it felt like a miracle. Marilyn wrote about the concerns of daily life – how she managed to survive on Dan's pay by growing food and trading any surplus with neighbours. She described her loneliness without her husband. But mostly she devoted her letters to sharing news about Anna. Dan had been given accounts of new vocabulary and advancing skills. He'd heard about minor accidents and a bout of malaria; there had been a description of a three-year-old birthday celebration and a rare chance to have a pony ride. Anna's height was measured, her changing features were described. But the Box Brownie was broken, and there was no spare money to buy film anyway. Dan had received no photographs. Even if he had, they'd have been out of date by now. All he could do was imagine the child his daughter had become.

He pictured her as graceful and good-natured, taking on the qualities that went with her name. 'Anna' had been chosen from a book Marilyn had found in the small library at the Lutheran mission. A name for a boy had been chosen easily – William, after Dan's father. A girl was more difficult. Dan had taken his turn to study the pink pages of the book, one letter a night. He read in bed, by the light of a small lamp, while Marilyn dozed beside him. Now and then he would reach out to touch her, causing her to smile.

'Are you touching me because you love me,' she'd asked one night, 'or because you love the baby?'

'I love you both.' Dan had traced the outline of her body with his eyes: the mound that was their unborn child. In that moment, everything was in the future – the birth, the baby, their new life as a family. Part of him wanted to keep it that way: untouchable and safe.

When Dan reached the end of the book he turned back to the beginning – to the name that had first caught his eye. Having gone from A to Z he was now certain he'd found the right name for a daughter. *Anna*. He liked its lyrical sound, but the meaning was what decided him. Bringer of good things.

When the baby was born, a beautiful little girl, he'd known the name was perfect.

Drawing close to the cottage now, Dan began to notice its faults. He saw the rust in the secondhand roofing iron that had been there from the beginning. And the cracks in the concrete, caused by a lack of reinforcing steel. He saw how the bare timbers – cut by his own hand – had twisted and split as they dried. With his discharge pay, he'd at last be able to buy some new materials. He was going to fix it all. Start again. Get everything right, this time.

Nearing the woven fence, he stopped. He felt suddenly nervous, like a young man meeting his new girlfriend. What would Marilyn see when she looked at him? He'd just had his thirty-seventh birthday – celebrated on the road with a warm beer and a burned chapati purchased from a wayside stall. The first signs of age were visible on his face, accentuated by long-term exhaustion, stress, the effort of overcoming fear, and the constant work of forgetting what had to be forgotten. The few grey hairs starting to show at his temples didn't concern him. He just hoped that the things he'd seen, the things he'd done, were not reflected in his eyes. He didn't want to carry the darkness, like a contagion, back to his home.

He ran his fingers through hair stiff with dust. Sweat seemed welded to his skin. His clothes were impregnated with it, backed by the sour smell of rancid butter that lingered from Abyssinian food. He yearned for a long bath in the tin tub, and the comfort of clean clothes that were any colour but khaki.

The dry season garden looked plain and tired. Running his gaze across the bare vegetable plot and the patch of sun-scorched lawn, he searched for a child's sunhat, a tennis ball, perhaps even a doll. On the verandah he looked for one of Marilyn's novels, being re-read for the tenth time. Instead he saw two empty kerosene tins converted to buckets with wire loops for handles. A blackened cooking pot lay on its side near the water tank. An old rooster strutted the yard, his tail feathers thin and ragged. Nothing else moved.

The back door creaked open. Dan held his breath. An old man stepped out, slowly, feeling his way with his feet. His eyes were milky with cataracts.

'Musa!' Dan recognised his neighbour. The Makanda family worked a plot of land on the other side of the hill. Dan and Marilyn had met them at the market and become casual friends. Dan was surprised that the ageing patriarch would be visiting Marilyn – it was a long walk here for someone who was nearly blind.

As the men shook hands – three times, as custom demanded – Musa's clouded eyes searched Dan's face.

'*Umerudi!*' he said. You have come back!

Dan looked at him in confusion. Where was the smile, revealing teeth worn down to stumps? Where was the welcoming laughter? He felt a chill of misgiving.

'*Yuko wapi familia yangu?*' he asked. Where is my family?

'They have gone,' Musa said. 'Others are living here now. I am living here.' There was a note of defiance in the man's voice that matched his jutting chin.

Looking past Musa's shoulder into the main room of the cottage, Dan saw Marilyn's willow pattern crockery stacked on the kitchen shelf. The Royal Doulton had been a wedding present from the family she'd worked for in Kenya – it had been a generous gift for a lowly governess. The set was depleted, now – there were not enough plates in the pile – and a cup had a missing handle. He couldn't imagine Marilyn being careless with her crockery. He certainly couldn't imagine her leaving it behind. Something must have happened to make her move away in a hurry. Dan tried to think what it could be, but he had no clue.

'*Nini kimetokea?*' he demanded. What has occurred? Without meaning to, he grabbed Musa's shoulder, squeezing it until he winced.

'They moved away,' Musa answered. 'Three harvests have passed. It is a long time. This is our place now.'

Dan swallowed. All that time he'd pictured them here, when they were somewhere else. 'Where have they gone?'

Musa pointed towards the rubber plantations. 'Your wife and your child, they no longer walk on their feet. They ride in cars. They eat meat, not beans. They have new clothes. They have everything.'

'What are you saying?' Dan rubbed his hands over his eyes as if he, like the old man, was unable to see clearly. 'Where are they living?'

'*Nyumba ya Chui,*' Musa said. In the House of the Leopard.

Dan shook his head, frowning. Had Emerson's wife befriended Marilyn? It didn't seem likely; the Miller family was in that unfortunate category known as 'poor whites': above the Africans, but only just; and without the exotic appeal of the natives. But the war had changed so many things, cutting down some barriers and erecting others. Dan remembered, now, that Marilyn had mentioned the master of Leopard Hall in one of her letters, reporting that he hadn't signed up for military service. He claimed he had to manage his plantations. Armies need vehicles and vehicles need tyres, so growing rubber was an essential service. The fact that Emerson didn't even visit his plantation office, instead leaving all the work to his overseer, was irrelevant. Presumably he had just continued his life of leisure while other men were on the battlefields. He'd not had to be parted from his wife.

Dan turned in the direction of the plantation, his eyes trained into the distance. The rubber trees were like a silent army swarming over the land. Concealed from view in the middle of the plantation, like a treasure in the heart of darkness, was a huge old mansion that had been built during King Leopold's rule. Dan had never seen the place, but like everyone in Banya he'd heard the rumours. There was supposed to be a whole wall covered in leopardskin. A fountain in the foyer. In the sitting room there were strange paintings of distorted figures that looked barely human, including one in which a white woman was wearing an African mask. The biggest source of conjecture was the private museum at the Hall, containing artifacts gathered from all over the Congo. There were said to be hundreds of masks and *nkisi* – though the exact nature of the collection was a mystery since it was rare for anyone, even Emerson's guests, to be allowed to view it. African staff never stayed long at Leopard Hall because the presence of the museum made them uneasy. No one believed anything good could come of forcing so many sacred objects – each possessing their own power – to share space together.

Leopard Hall was famous, also, for parties. The guests would fly to Albertville from all over the Congo and overseas as well. They'd drive up to Banya in a cavalcade of Jaguars, Daimlers and Rolls Royces, stopping en route at the lakeside hotels. There was a story that the butler met the arrivals at the front door offering French champagne and cocaine. During their stay at the Hall, Emerson's guests would wear at least four different outfits per day. At night the women would emerge from their rooms in glittering evening gowns they'd bought in Paris. Ten-course meals were served by Africans dressed in velvet suits, sweating in the heat.

Dan had seen Emerson and his young French wife in Banya on a few occasions, but that was all. He was happy to keep his distance from people like them. He despised their wealth, accumulated over generations of exploiting the Congolese. While travelling across the country prospecting, Dan had heard many terrible stories about the colonial regime firsthand from the victims. He'd listened to accounts of whole communities being executed by the *Force Publique* so that a rubber plantation could be established on the site of their village. He'd met people who'd had their hands cut off, as little children, under the supervision of Belgian officers. There were stories of rape and even cannibalism. The atrocities were at their worst under King Leopold, but even after he'd been pushed to hand over his personal colony to the Belgian government, the forced labour had continued, merciless and unrelenting. The State, the corporations and individual landowners were all in it together. As far as Dan was concerned, the Emersons had a lot of blood on their hands.

He turned back to the cottage, taking in the dilapidated state of the building and the grounds. He hated to think of his wife and child being any part of the Emersons' world, but he understood how hard it must have been for Marilyn surviving without him for five years. Her friends would have been as hard-pressed as she was, with their own men away. Dan had no relatives Marilyn could call upon for help, and her family was on the other side of the world. She would have had only the Lutherans to offer her support. If she'd found a way to get help from the plantation owner, who could blame her? It occurred to Dan that the Emersons probably had children by now. Perhaps they needed a governess. In Kenya, Marilyn had taught French and piano along with all the usual school subjects.

'Is Marilyn working for Madame Emerson?' he asked Musa.

The old man looked around him as if hunting for words. He scratched his chin, horny nails scraping a thin grey beard. Then he shook his head slowly. 'The first wife of Bwana Emerson is no longer at Leopard Hall.' He gave a faint shrug as if to convey the hopelessness of protest at the hand of fate. '*Pole sana,*' he added. I am very sorry.

A wave of nausea swept through Dan's body. His arms stiffened at his sides, his hands balled into fists. Part of him clung to the thought that there was some misunderstanding, but in his heart he knew the meaning of what Musa was telling him. Bending down, he picked up his kitbag, the webbing matching his grip, the familiar weight settling onto his shoulder. The bag, containing his meagre possessions, felt like his only anchor to reality.

As he turned to walk away he saw relief on Musa's face: the owner of the cottage had not tried to repossess his property. The look was blended with curiosity. What does a white man do when he learns news like this? What does any man do . . .?

Briefly, Dan wished he still had his machine gun or his sniper's rifle. But shooting Emerson would be too easy – the act too remote, too clean. He didn't need a gun, just as he didn't need the help of any comrades. He would hunt down his prey on his own, like a leopard. He'd take Emerson apart with his two bare hands.

The anger had felt right; the next move obvious. Dan had set off towards the Hall, his exhaustion replaced by a new strength powered by sheer fury. Slipping back into combat procedure, he formed a plan of action: he'd carry out reconnaissance first, then design the attack. He would subdue his emotions as only a seasoned soldier could do. And he'd think only of the current mission, not asking questions about what would follow.

He had counted each step that brought him closer to his target. He thought he knew what he was doing. But he could never have guessed, at that moment, the true nature of the challenge that faced him – that it would ask much more of him than he could have ever imagined.

Within the walled compound of a monastery half-a-dozen fires burned, making bright circles in the gathering dark. People sat around them perched on little wooden chairs that had been brought over from the schoolroom. There were the commandos, blending into the background in their camouflage fatigues, and the various Europeans who'd joined the convoy, along with a few local people. Then, there were the twenty-odd priests who lived and worked here. Until a few hours ago they'd been prisoners of the Simbas, locked up inside their church. Now they were sharing the fireside with the soldiers who had rescued them. In the failing light the stains of blood and dirt were barely visible on their white robes. But the men's faces showed the marks of beatings and the pallor of exhaustion.

Dan walked between the groups, searching for Hardy. Now that Bergman was busy with his family, Dan wanted to keep an eye on the Englishman himself. He found his second-in-command by one of the smaller fires, sitting on his own. He was using a stick to reposition his ration tin over the coals.

'You didn't like the menu tonight?' queried Dan, as he squatted next to him. The two priests who normally cooked for the community of White Fathers had made a cauldron of stew from supplies of meat and vegetables left behind by the Simbas. Dan had enjoyed the meal, which had been flavoured liberally with fresh herbs from the kitchen garden.

Hardy shook his head. 'I'm a great admirer of tinned beef and potatoes. It reminds me of boarding school. Happiest years of my life.' As he leaned over the fire he grimaced against the heat, showing his chipped tooth. The bottle opener hanging from his neck swung from side to side.

The two men sat quietly together. All the experiences they'd shared during Operation Nightflower had begun to forge a bond of companionship. They could hear the conversation drifting across from the neighbouring fire. Some of the priests were recounting their experiences. Most of them spoke simple English, though with thick Italian accents. Dan stared into the fire as he listened to their accounts of cruel humiliation and random torture. Dan was impressed by their resilience. When Bailey and Henning had forced open the church doors they'd stumbled into the sunshine barely able to walk, yet they were waving and cheering. Only a few hours had passed since then and already the men seemed calm and reflective. One was already talking about the need to reopen the clinic.

Hearing Bailey's voice, Dan turned to look for him, hoping there was no trouble brewing. The soldier was sitting between Thompson and an old priest with a thick black beard. Bailey had turned his chair around; he straddled the seat, leaning his elbows over the back. Like the other men, he had to angle his bent knees to each side, looking like a gangly spider, in order to sit so low to the ground.

'We suffered night and day,' the old priest was saying. 'But we sang hymns and we prayed. God heard our cries and delivered us from our enemies.'

'Oh, really?' Bailey responded. 'It was God?' He narrowed his eyes as he talked past his cigarette. 'I thought we were the ones who shot the Simbas.'

'You were the instrument of God's divine will,' another priest said.

A heated discussion ensued, hinging on the question of whether God could use Bailey to act on His behalf, when Bailey was an atheist. It was dominated by the youngest-looking of the priests, a man with smooth skin and only a fluff of hair on his chin. He waved pale hands with long fingers as he elaborated on his argument.

Suddenly Bailey jumped to his feet, tipping over the chair. 'You're talking bullshit. You know that?' He strode round the fire and confronted the priest. 'I mean, answer me this: Why did God let the Simbas capture you in the first place? He could have saved us all this trouble. That's what He should have done. He should have fucking done something.'

Dan stood up. Catching Bailey's eye, he gestured for him to back down. Dan understood that after what had happened to the young nun at Kabwanga, it was impossible for Bailey – as it would be for any of the men – to have a calm debate about God's power to protect. It would be best if the topic were changed. Dan didn't want to witness a wrestling match between a soldier and a half-grown priest.

Bailey grabbed the chair and moved it out of the circle. Sitting on his own, he brought out a bottle of Scotch whisky he'd confiscated from somewhere and began drinking. Dan turned away, hoping the liquor would help Bailey wind down, not up.

'He's got a point, you know,' Hardy commented. 'But it's not the kind of thing to argue about. No one's going to change their mind. It's a waste of time.'

Dan was about to respond when he sensed movement behind him. He spun round, his hand on his holster. Recognising Bergman standing there, he relaxed. 'Don't creep up like that. Someone will shoot you.'

'Sorry.' Bergman pulled up a spare chair.

'How are they – Clara and the children?' Dan asked him.

'Tucked up in bed. Henning's over there. I know it is safe here, but still . . .'

Dan nodded. He understood it would take a long time before Bergman felt at ease about the security of his family.

'I wanted to thank you, again,' Bergman said. 'You did not want to let me come with you and who could blame you for that? But you agreed. And now, because of you, Clara, Elise and Hugo are safe.'

Dan smiled, accepting the man's gratitude. Whatever complexities might lie ahead for the Belgian couple, they were together, along with their children. They were alive and safe. At least one good thing had emerged out of the inevitable trail of horrors that was called a war.

'I admit I wasn't too pleased when you turned up at the mess hall that day,' Dan said to Bergman. 'But you've been an asset to the Force. What are you going to do when we get to Uvira?'

Bergman shook his head. 'I do not know. We cannot go back to the farm. But we have nowhere else to live. Maybe we could move to the south. I might be able to get a job in Albertville.'

Hardy shook his head. 'You've got to get out of the Congo.

Getting rid of the Simbas won't be the end of the trouble here. There'll be no peace in this country. It's too wealthy for its own good. And there are too many snouts in the trough. I was in Katanga, you know. I saw what was going on. You've got the Americans, the Belgians, the British, just to name a few . . .' He started counting on his fingers. 'Then you've got the mining companies and the rubber barons. Everyone's playing their own game. And now the Chinese and the Soviets have jumped in too. The Congolese never had a hope in hell of being left alone to run the place. But they still dream of having the use of their own resources. It's a recipe for instability. Ongoing disaster. You don't want to be here, Bergman. Trust me.'

Dan eyed Hardy curiously. This was the first time he'd heard the Englishman express any political views, yet he sounded well informed and vehement. His words made Dan think back to his own recruitment interview. How unquestioningly he'd accepted Blair's claim that fighting the Communist rebels was the most important thing Dan would ever do in his life. That the future of the free world was at stake. Dan had simply assumed that victory would bring peace to the Congo. The interests of the newly independent country would be protected. Looking back, it seemed very naïve.

'Why did you say yes to Blair?' he asked Hardy.

'I got his letter. I needed something to do. Somewhere to go.' Hardy broke off, a grimace of pain tightening his face. 'I was a mess, you see. Off the show. I thought if I got back into a commando force, I might be able to find my feet again.'

Dan nodded slowly. He'd come to the conclusion that Hardy had been traumatised by his work as a soldier here in the Congo – probably in the Katanga mission where he'd fought alongside Blair. Dan had sometimes wondered how much insight Hardy had into his predicament. Now Dan knew the soldier had been aware all along of the toll that combat had taken on him. It was sadly ironic that Hardy had believed jumping back into the fire offered the only chance of survival.

As Dan processed this thought he felt a creeping sense of recognition. Maybe his own decision to join up had been prompted by a similar desperation. For quite different reasons to Hardy, he'd felt lost. He had no home, no family, no purpose. He'd fallen for Blair's proposition unquestioningly – because he'd needed to be rescued.

Bending his head, Dan rubbed his face with his hands. If this were true, where did that leave him now? What would he try next, to make some meaning of his life? He looked up, concentrating on the fire. He knew he couldn't afford to follow this train of thought. He was the Commanding Officer of Operation Nightflower. Thirty-odd men had been entrusted to his care – and now he'd collected half a truckload of civilians as well. The only way ahead was forwards. To Uvira.

Hardy had turned his attention back to Bergman. 'So, you must move to Belgium as soon as possible. Or somewhere else in Europe.' Bergman opened his mouth to speak, but Hardy held up his hand. 'I know. For that, you need money. But never fear. I have a plan.' Giving a conspiratorial wink he beckoned his two companions to join him on the other side of the fire. 'Shhh, shhh. It is a secret. No one must know.'

Dan swapped a wary look with Bergman. Hardy had slipped into a theatrical manner reminiscent of his impersonation of the Scarlet Pimpernel. Clearly, he'd been lucid and focused just now, but some of his shifts in mood and behaviour were very abrupt. To humour him, they moved their chairs.

Hardy unbuttoned the chest pocket of his shirt. The cloth was greasy with fingerprints as if he checked the contents often. Dan wondered if, like Fuller, he kept a precious letter there. He felt a flicker of curiosity at the thought of gaining an insight into the Englishman's personal life – though how this might be of any help to Bergman he had no idea.

Hardy drew out a piece of folded paper. As he spread it over his knee, Dan saw it was a map. He recognised the rough drawing from the morning his second-in-command had first turned up for duty, drunk and unkempt after his all-night visit to the village. The ink had run in the humid conditions but the markings were still discernible.

'This is your ticket out of here,' Hardy informed Bergman, 'to a new life.'

He explained what Dan knew already: that the map showed the location of some family heirlooms that had been buried by a man who was no longer alive.

'All you have to do, my dear fellow, is go and dig a hole – right there.' He pointed at a spot on the map marked by a small cross. Lit from below, the paper was translucent like old parchment. 'The owners were known to be wealthy. You're going to find valuable pieces – diamonds, gold, rubies. I'll find out the name of an auction house in Brussels.'

Bergman shook his head. 'I could not do that . . .'

'If you don't find the treasure, it'll stay there forever. No one else knows the secret.' Hardy held the map over the flames. 'I could burn this now . . .'

Dan exchanged another look with Bergman. Hardy didn't sound mad – everything he said made sense. But still, the whole scene was like something from a boy's adventure story. Buried treasure.

A secret map. With his chipped tooth and bottle opener, Hardy looked the part as well.

Bergman let out a long sigh, burying his face in his hands. In the quiet, gravy bubbled over the side of the ration tin, hissing as it landed on the coals. When he looked up, Bergman turned to Dan.

'What do you think, Lieutenant?'

Dan knew that Bergman had used the officer's title deliberately: he was looking to Dan as his superior. Since the farmer had joined Force Denby he'd started thinking like a soldier. Dan eyed him in silence. How could he explain that he was not the person to ask? Just because he was the Commanding Officer didn't mean he knew how a man should look after his family. He'd lost his own daughter. He'd handed her over to be raised by another man. He'd walked out of her life . . . The recriminations erupted from his subconscious, as familiar as the contours of his own face. Then came the trail of counterarguments. Giving her up didn't mean he had let her down. She had gained all the benefits of being part of an affluent family. She hadn't been made to deal with complexities she was too young to understand. Her life had not been turned upside down. Dan had lost, but she – surely – had won . . .

Dan rubbed his hands over his face, wanting to escape from the interminable debate. He shook his head. 'I don't know, Bergman.'

The three men sat in silence. Hardy's hand, grasping the map, still hovered over the flames. From the other fireside, Bailey's voice could be heard again. The tone was belligerent and angry, but Dan didn't listen to what was being said.

'Get them out of here.' Dan was almost surprised by his own words; they just came out of his mouth, unplanned. 'Move to Europe. Do whatever you have to do. Just keep them safe. You don't want to look back and regret the decision you made.' He met

Bergman's gaze. 'You wouldn't want to live with that.'

The confusion cleared from Bergman's eyes. He grasped the map, laying it carefully in his lap.

'Good man,' Hardy said. 'Now put it away. Someone could kill you for that.'

Bergman folded the paper and slipped it into his shirt pocket, buttoning it up carefully. Excitement dawned slowly over his face. 'Thank you, Hardy. I owe you my deepest gratitude.' He sniffed, and wiped his nose with his free hand. 'You must give me your address in London. I will write to you and let you know how everything turns out.'

Hardy smiled, his lips curling in at each corner. Then he looked away, staring into the heart of the fire. 'There'll be no need for that, my friend. I won't be going back there.'

Dan watched him uncertainly, wondering exactly what he meant. When Operation Nightflower was over the men would have the choice of taking on a new assignment or signing off and going home – returning to whatever passed, for each of them, as normal life. Hardy had proved to be one of the most valuable members of Force Denby, but his mental state was still fragile. In all conscience, Dan would not be able to recommend him for redeployment.

Hardy must have been blissfully unaware of his senior officer's reservations about him. Sitting there, he seemed more relaxed than Dan had ever seen him before. He looked, in fact, deeply relieved. It didn't make any sense. The biggest battle of the mission was imminent; by midday tomorrow the convoy would reach Uvira. Yet Hardy had the look of a man who had already faced his final battle and tasted victory.

Dan stood up, stretching shoulders cramped from the long hours of driving while on full alert, looking out for an ambush. 'I'm going to find Doc and get an update on Fuller.'

'I saw him with one of the priests, over at the stores truck,' Bergman said. 'He was giving out some supplies.'

Dan nodded. 'I'll head over there, then.'

As he walked through the compound, he picked up fragments of conversation, glimpses of faces. He saw Becker deep in conversation with a Congolese man wearing a long black gown, probably a trainee priest of some sort. Dupont, sitting with them, was pulling something out of his pocket. Dan hoped it wasn't his souvenir of Lumumba, or some other grisly relic. He moved on towards the truck, pausing to check on Billy. The young man had an impressive black eye. Henning had been schooling him in the art of shooting a .375 magnum but Billy had not managed the recoil very well; the telescopic sight had slammed into his eye socket.

'You should stick to a sensible firearm,' Dan told him. 'We're not out here hunting game.'

Billy smiled, wincing. He was clearly proud of his injury, though Dan couldn't see quite why.

Reaching the truck, Dan walked round to the back. He could hear no voices, but there was the sound of movement inside.

'You there, Doc?'

The noise ceased abruptly. Dan edged closer, peering in through a tear in the canvas covering. A figure was crouched on the floor of the truck. There was a bulging rucksack next to it and some ration boxes. Dan recognised the young rebel soldier he'd rescued, by his distinctive woollen hat. It had been given to him so he could hide the scar on his forehead. Having his identity as a Simba on show would raise questions that couldn't easily be answered – by Dan, or by anyone else. Was he a prisoner? A deserter? A spy? The truth was, he was none of those things. He was just a boy who'd found himself stranded a long way from home.

Dan thought back to the night when the injured captive had been interrogated by Becker. Dan had insisted on being present; fortunately the Simba spoke Swahili to the South African, so Dan was able to listen in. The soldier had given his first name as Pierre. Lots of Congolese born before Independence was on the horizon were given French first names. It offered them a better chance at finding a place in the colonial hierarchy. They might even be able to become an *évolué*: a member of the official category created by the Belgians for Africans who'd managed to adopt European ways. Aside from meeting educational standards, candidates had to pass home inspections to show that they had – as the name suggested – evolved. Particular criteria were assessed, such as: Do the children wear pyjamas? Does the family eat with a knife and fork? Is there an inside toilet? Proper furniture? *Évolués* enjoyed many privileges, including being able to send their children to better schools or join European social clubs. Perhaps this was the future that Pierre's parents had dreamed of for their son. Instead he'd ended up joining a rebellion.

The Simba's family name was Mahele. This had been of no interest to Becker; it wasn't linked with anyone in his files. But he'd wanted to know every detail of the soldier's involvement with the rebel army. He didn't address his subject as Pierre; he preferred 'Prisoner' or 'Soldier' along with a range of derogatory names. He'd frightened the teenager with threats and promised punishments. He'd been tough on his subject, but Dan knew it was necessary. As a member of the *Jeunesse*, Pierre could easily have been – even unknowingly – a mine of information about the situation in Uvira, and about the rebels' broader plans, their resources and networks. But it had soon become clear, even to Becker, that Pierre knew nothing at all. He was not a rebel. He didn't know the political goals of the Simbas. He'd never even heard of China or Russia. He'd run away to join the army, lured by the promise of new boots and a uniform. When Becker pushed him to give more details on his motivation, Pierre had explained that he'd wanted to escape from his home. His father made him work too hard. His mother nagged him. His brothers were mean to him and his sisters annoyed him. He wanted to see more of life. Listening in, Dan couldn't help smiling. The story was so mundane – and so universal. It could have been Billy sitting here, squirming under Becker's harsh gaze as he explained his dissatisfaction with a life that he knew too well.

Dan stayed where he was for a few moments, peering through the canvas. Pierre seemed frozen with indecision – unsure whether to stay still and quiet, or try to get away. Dan moved round to the open back of the truck.

'Pierre!' he called out. '*Unafanya fujo?*' Are you making trouble?

The boy's eyes were wide circles in the shadows. He tried to lunge past Dan, but had no hope of succeeding. It cost Dan almost no effort to grab and hold the slight figure. Peering past him into the truck, Dan looked at the contents of the open rucksack. He identified ration tins, bandages, an enamel cup, a water canteen, the corner of a blanket. '*Unkwenda safari?*' Are you going somewhere?

Pierre went limp in Dan's arms. He knew he'd been caught; there was no room for anything but cooperation.

'*Nataroka tu.*' I am running away to another place.

He jerked his head towards the forest that bordered the monastery fields. It looked like a wilderness, as always, but Dan knew there were paths there for Pierre to find.

'Where are you going?' Dan asked.

'I want to go home.' Pierre's voice caught in his throat. 'Please. I miss my family.'

Dan's grip softened. The boy didn't know his precise age, but he couldn't be older than fourteen. Yet he'd already suffered more – and seen more suffering – than any man should, in a lifetime. Dan hadn't had much time to spend thinking about what to do with his captured Simba, but the problem had been nagging at the edges of his consciousness. If Pierre ended up in Uvira when the National Army arrived, he'd be shot on sight, and Dan couldn't take the boy along with him on another mission. Now Pierre had found a solution for himself. Dan felt a wave of relief. The teenager belonged at home in his village, back in the classroom with his friends – not here in a commando unit that was about to take on the task of storming a town.

'Is it very far to your home?' Dan asked.

Pierre shook his head. 'I can walk there. That is why I have chosen this moment to run away.'

Releasing his hold on the boy, Dan gestured towards the rucksack. 'Do you have enough food?'

'Yes, but I need a gun.'

'No, you don't,' Dan said firmly. 'It will only make you a target. Just keep away from people. Go straight to your village. And stay there.'

Pierre seemed torn between wanting to argue for a rifle and being relieved he was going to be allowed to carry out his plan. Taking a step back, Dan looked him up and down. In place of the uniform he'd been given – matching the ones worn by the commandos – was a set of civilian clothes. There was something about the long red socks and the above-the-knee shorts that looked oddly familiar. Dan remembered the first time he'd seen Billy – parading outside the mess at Lemba Base; being insolent when commanded to go and get changed. Dan saw himself throwing Billy up against the water tank, infuriated by his attitude. If someone had told Dan back then that the brat would end up in his commando unit he'd never have believed them.

'Billy gave me some clothes.' Pierre answered Dan's unspoken question. 'I gave him a gift in return.'

Dan looked at him for a few seconds, wondering what the trade had been; he decided not to ask. 'Are you ready to go now?'

Pierre nodded. 'I am ready, sir.' He gave a brisk salute. Dan felt a sense of regret that he was leaving. Malone would miss his help. Smith had become quite fond of the kid. Creeping away like this, Pierre was denying everyone the chance of a farewell. But it was safer this way. There could easily be Simba sympathisers in the area. If his story became known, someone might go after him. It was best if it looked as if he'd made a lucky escape from captivity.

Pierre retrieved the rucksack, swinging it onto his back. Dan accompanied him to the perimeter to clear his presence with the guard. The commando on watch was Lawler, the American who'd been rebranded as an Italian. Since he would have found himself surrounded by real Italians over in the compound, he'd been selected for sentry duty. He stood to attention as Dan approached.

'Evening, sir.'

'Evening, Lawler. Stand easy.' Dan gestured to Pierre. 'He's leaving us.'

The volunteer was chewing gum. His jaw kept moving. 'Sure. I won't shoot him.'

'Thank you,' Dan said. Lawler came from the 'don't ask questions, don't give anything away' school of soldiering. His partner was Girard, who spent his time receiving classified radio messages. The men stuck together but rarely seemed to speak. They made a perfect pair.

Dan gave Pierre a smile. '*Bahati njema.*' Good luck.

Pierre eyed him solemnly. 'I give thanks to you, my father, from deep inside my heart.'

After delivering these words he strode away without a backward glance. As Dan and Lawler watched on, he ducked between the corn plants, veered round pawpaw trees, jumped over ditches. The knitted hat bobbed up and down; Billy's socks were streaks of bright red.

Beyond the fields he reached open bushland. There he broke into a run, the rucksack bouncing on his back. He pulled off his hat and held out his arms as if breathing deeply, embracing his freedom.

Nearing the edge of the forest, he stopped and turned back. He was barely visible in the dusk light. Dan thought he lifted his hand, waving or saluting, but wasn't sure. Then he was gone.

TWENTY-TWO

A road sign came into view; large black letters marching across a cream background. *Bienvenue à Uvira.* The writing was blurred by bullet holes and a palm frond was tied to each of the posts. As the Land Rover rolled past it, Dan rested his hand on the machine gun, his eyes raking the surroundings. The convoy might have been entering the fringe of any Congolese town: there were the usual collections of huts, stalls and garden plots. But there were no people. Dan guessed they'd have fled from the area at the first sound of the bombers approaching, just over an hour ago. The only sign of life here now was a brown goat that skittered along the side of the road, bleating loudly.

Dan leaned over to Smith, who was sitting upright in the driver's seat, tense and alert. 'There should be a roadblock about a mile from here.'

'I'll be ready,' Smith responded.

As they drove on, both men looked ahead to where columns of dark smoke rose into the air. The nearest one was not far away.

Dan turned round to check the convoy. Hardy was already standing in the turret of the armoured jeep, head and shoulders visible above the hatch. He was like a performer waiting at the edge of the stage, poised and focused. Dan was familiar with his routine by now. It was a memorable sight. Hardy entered into a dance with his weapon, moving with fluid grace as he adjusted his aim. The soldier's own body seemed part of the feedback loop that made the machine gun function – the power of each recoil drove the next explosion, in a constant cycle, with Hardy at its heart. His goal was to make sure the enemy was too paralysed with fear and confusion to counterattack. Suppressive fire, it was called. The work of the turret gunner looked easy – as if it were just a matter of having plenty of ammunition at hand. But it took great skill as well as bravery to be as lethal as Hardy.

'We must be getting close,' Smith said.

'It'll be just round this next bend,' Dan agreed, 'then along a bit so they can see us coming.'

He raised his hand – a signal that would be passed down the line. It was time to release safety catches, move fingers close to triggers. Brace legs, arms, backs. Focus eyes. Send last thoughts to people far away. Say a prayer.

The lead vehicles of the convoy moved slowly towards the road-block, blasting with all the weaponry they could wield. Hardy's turret gun was higher than the Land Rover; together they forged a two-level attack. A smaller jeep, with Bailey at the wheel, dodged from left to right, keeping access to a clear firing line. Commandos from other vehicles that had stopped further back ran along the verges, ducking behind huts and trees.

The enemy was shooting from behind 44-gallon drums lined up to block the road. Sandbags provided extra cover and troop carriers were parked behind the defence line, offering more shelter. It took Dan only seconds to assess the work of Air Support: a crater in the road, a destroyed building, a jeep on its side. Whatever toll this had taken on the troops, some level of order had been restored. There was an impression of purpose in the arrangement of men and hardware. This wasn't a repeat of the usual chaotic charge, led by a witchdoctor. The officers in control here knew what they were doing; and the ordinary soldiers understood how to follow orders.

Dan closed his ears to the sounds of battle – gunfire, grenades exploding, shouts and cries. He concentrated only on aiming and firing. The other commandos needed no instruction from him. At the edges of his vision Dan saw them working in their pairs, pushing relentlessly forwards.

The battle seemed brief and protracted, both at once. There were specks of time in which a body fell; a spent ammunition belt was hurled away; a window shattered, releasing a cascade of shards. Then there were long stretches of madness in which all detail was lost. There was a blur of noise and movement, with only one point of focus: down the barrel of a gun.

Dan knew when the tide began to turn. Return fire dwindled. There were no commands; only shouting. A troop carrier drove away, careering over the battlefield. Before long the rebel army disintegrated into a pack of individuals. Each man was now fighting for his life, one eye on the enemy, the other hunting for a way to escape.

Soon the only movement was that of the soldiers fleeing – frantic figures disappearing among the buildings. Then a strange stillness settled over the scene.

The convoy moved on, entering the suburbs of Uvira. Substantial homes lined the streets now, fronted by fenced gardens bright with blooming flowers. There were parks with swings and picnic tables.

The next checkpoint the commandos reached was abandoned. The roadside stoves where local women should have been cooking corn to sell to the soldiers were just pots of dead ash. The guard box was unoccupied, its palm frond decorations dangling over empty space. Smith drove the Land Rover up to a timber pole resting between two drums that formed the barrier. It had been crudely painted with stripes of red and white. Selecting low ratio, he pushed the pole onto the ground and drove over it.

Dan scanned the area to each side of the road. There was not a Simba to be seen. He guessed the troops had been moved out from here to help defend the perimeter. That meant the Simba Command was in real trouble. It fitted with what Dan knew from reports passed on by Girard. Air Support had bombed the main barracks in Uvira, along with the weapons depot and the command post. The rebels had been crippled. Now it was up to Force Denby to clean up, before moving in and taking control.

As the convoy headed on towards the town centre, there were intermittent engagements with enclaves of soldiers. In the midst of one exchange of fire, Dan caught sight of a pram abandoned outside a café. Picturing a baby left inside he was about to tell Smith to drive closer, but then he saw it was stacked with charcoal, the upholstery blackened and torn.

A dog shot past, running full pelt. Its white coat was splashed with blood.

An arrow hit the spare tyre mounted on the Land Rover bonnet, the iron tip lodging in the rubber.

A bullet chipped the steering wheel. Smith ducked instinctively, his metal helmet sinking to his shoulders, but he kept driving. Another bullet glanced off the tyre guard. Dan swung his gaze from side to side until he found the culprit: a sniper installed on a second-storey balcony above a nearby shop.

Jumping from the vehicle, Dan dived into a side street. With his back to a brick wall he looked up. A rebel soldier stood at the wrought-iron railings, a rifle at his shoulder. Dan took a breath. This was a moment to use up an extra few seconds and make sure of the aim. Stepping forward, he squeezed the trigger. As the bullet struck, the figure slumped forwards over the railings. His helmet fell to the street below, striking the tarmac and rolling away, disappearing between the wheels of the armoured jeep.

Dan scanned the streetscape, searching for more snipers. Seeing movement from the corner of his eye, he jumped aside just as a vehicle reversed at speed out of a laneway. As he flattened himself against the wall again, he stared in surprise. The rear window of the car was gone. Through the open space, edged with the remains of shattered glass, he saw the driver's face. A woman, looking back over her shoulder, straight at him. He caught an impression of fair skin, long red hair. Lips parted. Eyes wide. Then the driver rammed the car into first gear, revving hard, lurching away.

Dan stood still, gazing after it, taking in the distinctive curved boot and wide chrome bumper bar of a Jaguar. The luxury car had seen better days. The white paintwork was spattered with mud, the shine lost beneath a coating of dust. A line of bullet holes marched across the boot – the results of a spray of machine-gun fire, from close range. Before Dan had a chance to react, the car turned down another side street and was gone.

The Land Rover had moved on a short distance. As Dan jogged after it, he revisited the bizarre image in his mind. Swinging himself back on board, he turned to Smith.

'I just saw a Jaguar,' he said, 'with a beautiful woman at the wheel.'

Smith grinned. 'Wishful thinking, sir.'

Dan turned back, wanting to get another glimpse of the car and its occupant – an irrational impulse, since the Jaguar had headed away from the main road. All he saw was the rest of the convoy straggling along the route.

'Did you take down her number plate?' Smith joked. He reloaded as he drove, steering with his knees.

Dan smiled grimly. 'Didn't have time.'

'Well, she shouldn't be out shopping in this,' Smith said.

A burst of gunfire cut off his words.

'Take cover!' Dan yelled the command as he leapt from his seat. Smith joined him on the side of the road. They lay on their bellies in the gutter, firing across the street. A contingent of rebels were making a last stand there, using a postal van as a shield.

Dan looked up to see the armoured jeep rolling steadily towards the rebel position. McAdam was safe, in the driver's seat, ensconced deep inside a metal cave; but Hardy looked even more exposed than usual. He was standing tall, his helmet missing from his head. The barrel of the turret gun swung in its slow arc, dispensing bullets.

Dan ducked as another spurt of gunfire raked the ground nearby, raising puffs of concrete dust. He felt the sting of a bullet graze on his arm. Pain sparking anger, he rose to his knees. Leaning back a little, he gave himself over to the familiar pattern: hunt, aim, shoot, reload . . .

Time passed, short or long, he could not tell. Eventually there was no movement – no return fire – from the area around the van. The last rebel fighter had met his end.

Spitting dust from his mouth, Dan got to his feet and ran towards the Land Rover. Glancing back over his shoulder, scanning the scene, his step faltered. The turret of the armoured jeep was empty. Hardy was gone.

Spinning round, he moved into a sprint. Alarm spiked inside him, even though he knew that with the action now over, Hardy had probably retreated to the cabin. He'd be talking to McAdam; lighting up a cigarette.

Dan passed the driver's window but McAdam was turned away, looking down. Without breaking his stride, Dan launched himself up the side of the turret, shrugged off his gun, then swung himself down through the hatch. His feet landed just to one side of the place where Hardy lay, curled up like a child. McAdam held the man's wrist, his fingers seeking a pulse.

In the dim light and cramped space it was hard to see, but Dan counted at least four entry wounds, two exits.

'He's gone.' McAdam's voice was gruff with distress. 'I saw when he got hit, but he wouldn't get down. He just kept shooting. Then he copped it again. It was as if . . .' He broke off, shaking his head.

'He'd had enough.' Dan gazed bleakly around him. In the interior of the modified jeep all the running gear was exposed – the suspension, the steering mechanism, the bolted sheets of metal plate. The overall effect was brutal and hard, like the work it was built for. Turning to McAdam, Dan waved his hand, taking in the setting. 'He was finished with all this.'

As he looked back at Hardy, his eye was drawn to the man's shirt pocket – it lay flat, the flap unbuttoned. Giving the precious map away had been the soldier's last act of kindness; a legacy for a friend. Getting the convoy into Uvira was his final achievement.

Dan bent to see Hardy's face. The eyes were closed, his brow relaxed. A quirk in the corner of his mouth conveyed a hint of his trademark irony. Dan found himself smiling in response, the image blurring behind a film of tears.

Hauling himself back up and out of the hatch, Dan grabbed

his gun, half-falling down the side of the turret. As he headed for the Land Rover, his boots pounding the road seemed to match the heavy beat of his heart.

The lake was calm and flat, the blue water mirroring the clear sky overhead. The warbling song of waterbirds floated on the still air. Dan leaned back against the side of the Land Rover, looking across to the opposite shore – to the outline of the Burundi hills. This narrow neck of the lake was the conduit for the Simbas' supplies. But from today, the line to this neighbouring country would be cut off. Force Denby had taken Uvira; Operation Nightflower was a success. It was a moment for celebration. But all Dan felt was an aching tiredness that seemed to come from deep inside him. Resting his head on the side window, he closed his eyes. But he could not relax. Adrenalin still pumped through his body, jangling his nerves. His ears hummed with the dull echo of gunfire. He tried to focus on a drop of blood that was running down his forearm; he felt a fly settle there, its light footsteps crossing his skin.

Pictures flashed through his head like scenes from a film. There was a pair of boots linked by nothing but flattened trouser legs to a mess of flesh and bone. The barrel of a rifle – flung like a javelin by a man on the run – nosing the dirt. A goat sprawling on its side, its tongue framed against the oil-slick surface of the road. And a little girl dressed in a torn party dress of pink lace, standing on the side of the road clutching a naked doll almost the same size as she was. The pair both had the same white skin and big brown eyes, snapped open.

This last image captured Dan's attention. He turned it over in his head like evidence from the scene of a crime. Was there a dark shadow in the child's eyes? Had something terrible happened to her? Or was she just staring in awe at the sight of the battle-stained commandos driving into her town?

She was with two adults whom Dan took to be her parents. They looked tired and shabby but joyous in their relief. They had joined the other residents of Uvira, who had filtered slowly and cautiously out into the streets, eventually lining the town square to welcome their liberators. Everyone had been waving and cheering. There was a surprising number of Europeans here. Most of them had the frugal look of missionaries or simple farming people like the Bergmans. But there were some who reminded Dan of the wealthy clients he took on safari; though exhausted and dishevelled, they still managed, somehow, to look pampered. He wondered what had made these wealthy people stay here. Did they not want to relinquish their privileged way of life? Or was the Congo the only home they knew and loved?

As Dan lifted his hand in greeting, smiling and nodding, he kept his finger poised near the trigger. There were lots of Africans out in the streets as well, adding vibrant song and dance to the mood of celebration. No doubt most of them were genuinely pleased to see the commandos. But among the people who had suffered under the rebel occupation, there would be collaborators. There might even be Simbas in disguise, blended into the crowd. Dan recalled Becker's comments about the leader they called the Okapi. Perhaps even he was here, hiding in plain sight.

As the Land Rover ground slowly along, Dan kept scanning the rows of faces. It only dawned on him gradually that he was looking out for someone in particular. The woman in the Jaguar. His encounter with her had been fleeting, yet the glimpse of her face, her hair, her eyes, seemed burned in his memory. With the skill of a hunter, he searched for her, his whole body poised to latch onto any clue. But there had been no sign of her, no glimpse of the Jaguar. By the time the convoy reached the harbour, Dan had given up. In fact, he had begun to wonder if he'd even seen her – or the white car – at all.

TWENTY-THREE

A beetle lay on its back, rows of stick-legs waving in the air. Anna used the tip of her pencil to roll it onto its feet. It scurried away, disappearing under a petal that had fallen from the potted rose plant. Anna poked the pink husk, causing the beetle to rush to another refuge. Something about the frantic movement made her want to pick up the dictionary that lay nearby and squash the beetle flat. Instead, she rested her head on her hand, staring at the pot plant. Most of the flowers had now bloomed and died. The gradual loss of petals, one by one, marked the steady progress of time. Nearly three weeks had passed since Eliza's departure. Anna was haunted by the deepening fear that something terrible must have happened to prevent her return. When she let her thoughts dwell on what this could be, a cold lump formed in her chest, making it difficult to breathe. She longed to confide in Harry and Rose – but so far, she'd resisted the temptation. Now and then, one of the Carlings commented on the delay in Eliza's reappearance, but they didn't think it was out of character for her to change her plans. With the radio broken, they pointed out, she had no way of getting a message to them. They reassured Anna that Eliza knew how to look after herself – she was completely at home in the Congo. They felt sorry for Anna being stuck here for so long, having no choice but to put her trip to Banya on hold, but they were not concerned about Eliza.

Anna knew they'd think very differently if they realised their friend had driven north, deliberately heading into danger. But Anna had promised she would keep Eliza's secret. She might have considered speaking privately to Rose, in view of the exchange they'd had at the hospital, except that only minutes after Rose had run from the ward that day, she had returned to work, tying on a fresh apron, her facade of strength firmly back in place. Anna guessed she regretted having revealed her emotions; ever since, she'd been a little distant with Anna, and studiously calm.

The fact was, there was no action the Carlings could take, anyway. The mission was cut off from the outside world. The Land Rover was still stranded, and the radio was dismantled, all the parts spread out on a pillowcase so that nothing could be mislaid. And even if there had been a way to make contact with someone, who would it be? Anna had tried to think of any friend or connection of Eliza's who might be able to find out where she'd gone. She wondered if Magadi was aware of the secret life of his mistress; the relationship between the two was longstanding and seemed to go beyond what was merely professional. Anna even considered whether the American officer, Randall, could be of some use. But there was no way to raise the alarm about Eliza's disappearance without exposing her connection with the Simbas. Whenever Anna considered the implications of this, she remembered what Eliza had said to her in the bedroom of the Hôtel Royal Kivu.

This isn't a game. Lives are at stake.

This memory led her inevitably back to the evening at the fireside – the intimacy that the two women had shared. This only evoked in Anna an even deeper urgency. She wanted to do something, anything, to help Eliza. But there was nothing she could do. Her thoughts just went round in circles.

When she stopped agonising about Eliza, Anna shifted her focus to her plan of going to Banya. She'd given up all hope of getting there any time soon. But that didn't mean she'd stopped thinking about her father – who he was, why he had disappeared from her life, where he was now . . . Watching Harry with the children was a constant reminder of what she had never experienced; every interaction she observed – a kiss or a hug, the casual teasing and playing of games, even reprimands over misbehaviour – made her more determined to get to the Lutheran hospital and see what she could learn about her own father. In the meantime, though, she sometimes felt as if she might end up staying at the mission forever – trapped like a princess in a fairy story, in a house in the middle of the forest. The only antidote to her fears and frustration was to try and keep herself occupied.

Anna turned her attention back to the morning's work. She wound a new piece of paper into the carriage of Rose's old-fashioned typewriter that had been installed at the end of the dining table like an honoured guest. Fixing her eyes on a pile of handwritten notes to her right, she began to type. The fluid movements brought her some calm – but before long, her fingers were jarred by two keys that collided and stuck. As she disengaged them, she thought of the new IBM 'Selectric' that Mr Williams had bought for the office. The golf-ball head had put an end to keys that malfunctioned. Not only that, it had allowed Anna to choose different fonts – even to swap styles within a single document.

She wondered who was sitting at her desk now. Was the new girl remembering to brush the dust from the carriage? Did she always use a coaster under her water glass? Anna waited to feel a shaft of jealousy at the thought of another secretary presiding over her domain. But though she prodded her emotions, she felt nothing. Her life in Melbourne seemed so distant. The wide straight streets, lined with pruned trees set in concrete-bound squares of earth, were like something from a dream. She could hardly picture the small neat park where she ate her lunch. And the idea of spending her day typing letters to people she didn't know, about things she didn't understand, no longer seemed to make much sense.

She looked at the thick pile of pages she'd already completed. She was working on the manuscript for Harry's latest book, which was going to be published by the Mission to Lepers Press. He welcomed her corrections to grammar and spelling and had even accepted some suggestions of rewriting. The manual would be used by doctors all over Africa and in places like India and the Pacific Islands as well. Rose was looking forward to sending a copy to her sister in Tanzania. The job was worth doing well.

Leaning over one of the handwritten pages, Anna struggled to decipher a phrase. When Harry scrawled long words like 'rehabilitation' or 'prevention', the individual letters blurred into a wavy line, their meaning only evident from the context. He was writing about techniques to prevent leprosy patients injuring themselves. He'd explained to Anna that, contrary to what most people thought, the disease itself didn't cause fingers and toes to fall off. Rather, the bacteria damaged the nerves, resulting in numbness. Mutilation was the outcome of repeated accidents and infections.

'Pain is not a curse,' Harry had stressed to Anna. 'It is one of God's greatest gifts.'

Without pain to sound an alert, he elaborated, a tiny stone in a shoe could wear a hole through the skin, causing an ulcer; a hot metal cup could sear the palm of a hand. A foot, placed too close to the cooking fire, could be burned. In the course of an ordinary day there were dozens of ways that people who could not feel pain might injure themselves. Dapsone, the miracle drug, could eradicate the bacteria that caused leprosy, curing the disease. But the nerves didn't regenerate, so the damaging effects of leprosy continued for life. Strategies had to be adopted to help preserve the patient's body. Harry had described some of them in the chapter Anna was typing now: 'Protecting Anaesthetic Hands'. To go with the text, Rose had produced drawings showing simple devices that helped prevent burns: a wooden tray for a hot plate; an insulated holder for an enamel mug; a bamboo sheath for the handle of a metal spoon. The book was a joint project, drawing on the abilities of both husband and wife. And now Anna had been brought in, to add her contribution. When she had started the task, she'd assumed she would be leaving it half-completed – she'd still been expecting, each day, that Eliza would return. Instead she was approaching the final chapter.

Anna thought back to the first session of typing. The whole family, including Adina, had gathered to watch. For once, Anna had the chance to show off a useful skill that no one else possessed. She'd typed with perfect accuracy without even glancing at the machine. They'd all watched in awe as her fingers flew over the keys.

'Will you teach me?' Rose had asked. 'I have to do the newsletters and mission reports. Typing properly would be so much quicker than using one finger!'

Anna had avoided a direct answer. She didn't want to be discouraging, but she knew it took months of practice to reach a useful standard. You needed a book and a teacher, and many hours of spare time. Anna had learned to type at secretarial school. The classes had begun with single letter exercises; then combinations of two letters, then three. Everything had to be repeated again and again. A wooden cover was placed over the typewriter and the student's hands, to make sure she could not even peep at the keys. After the simpler exercises were mastered came words and sentences. Eventually it was time for the big test: the sentence that contained every letter of the alphabet. *The quick brown fox jumps over the lazy dog.*

How many times had Anna typed that line? Hundreds, surely. Yet it only occurred to her now – sitting at the Carlings' dining table – that the words made so little sense. Surely any dog, no matter how lazy, would leap to its feet at the first smell of a fox? And why would a fox not engage with another carnivore? A picture came to her of a fox and a dog tearing one another apart. Ripped skin, loose fur, flashes of teeth. A fight to a bloody death. Anna closed her eyes. Living here with the Carlings, she realised, was affecting the way she thought. The wire screens were a constant reminder of the danger of wild animals. The trees that surrounded the house looked as if they were locked in a violent combat with the wild rubber vines that strangled their branches. The very air, here in the forest, felt dense with conflicting energies – living, dying; birth and decay. The hospital mirrored the same themes. Sometimes she thought she was going mad; but then she felt as if she were just living in the real world for the very first time. The sense of being tossed relentlessly between different perspectives was exhausting.

Forcing herself to focus again, Anna turned to the next page. Almost immediately she was distracted by sweat running down her left temple – a slow trickle cooling her skin. She wiped it away, then dried her hand on her skirt. From the kitchen came the sound of laughter. Lily and Sam were in there, helping Adina make biscuits. Anna could imagine the creations that were in process; the children used the dough to make people, animals, cars and planes. The biscuits always changed shape during the baking so that Anna had to work hard at pretending she knew when she was biting off a leg and when it was the wheel of a car.

She was about to resume typing when a distant hum, like the sound of an aircraft, eased into her consciousness. Turning her head to escape the noise from the kitchen, she strained to listen more closely. The hum was overlaid by outside sounds as well – birdcalls and the rhythmic buzz of insects. For a time, Anna thought it had disappeared. But then it returned – louder and closer. Her hands froze, poised over the typewriter. There was no mistaking what she could hear: it was a car, approaching along the track.

Scraping her chair back over the floorboards, she jumped to her feet. The wire screen snagged but she shook it free and burst outside. Then she stood still, staring at the bare earth of the narrow road. She pictured the white car coming into view: the curved tyre guards set to the side of each headlamp; the sloping bonnet with its gleaming jaguar mascot.

At last, between the branches and vines, she saw glimpses of white. Barely remembering to secure the screen behind her, she ran down the steps. She stumbled on an exposed root, and slipped on a patch of mud. Moments seemed to stretch into minutes – then, at last, the vehicle came into view.

A jolt of shock ran through Anna's body, her arms stiffening at her sides. She was staring at one of the smallest cars she'd ever seen. It looked barely roadworthy. The white paint was blotched with rust and the bumper bar hung down at one side. The front part of the roof was made of canvas, with a tear down the middle. It had headlamps that stuck up like bugs' eyes. Nothing could have looked less like Eliza's Jaguar.

The car came to a halt, then the door swung open. A walking stick appeared first, followed by a white helmet-shaped sunhat. Then a figure emerged: a frail-looking man, who used the roof of the car to pull himself to his feet. Anna surveyed him in silence as the joy and relief that had swept through her dissolved into disappointment.

The visitor walked towards her. His face was deeply lined and a white moustache drooped to his chin. He wore a cream linen shirt with short sleeves, along with a pair of khaki trousers. The casual look was offset by a black bow tie. Combined with the pith helmet, the overall effect was eccentric.

He approached Anna with outstretched arms. 'I hardly recognised you! What a beautiful young woman you have become!' He spoke in English, with a cultured accent.

Anna took a step back. 'I . . . don't think we've met.'

'Oh, you probably don't remember me,' the visitor said. 'You were only a little girl when I last saw you. No taller than this.' He held one hand at hip height.

Anna swallowed. For one mad instant the idea came to her. *Could this be him?* But it made no sense. Her father wasn't looking for her. And this man was so old. At close quarters, she could see red veins patterning his wrinkled skin. His eyes were watery. The hand gripping the stick was knobbly with arthritis.

'Are you home from boarding school?' he asked.

Anna frowned in surprise, then she realised that to someone as old as him, anyone would look young. She shook her head. 'I'm not who you think I am.'

The man's gaze faltered. 'You are Frank and Deborah's daughter. Rosemary? Or was it Helen?'

'No, I'm Anna Emerson. I'm staying with the Carlings.'

'Who are they?'

'They live here.'

'Oh . . .' A look of confusion crossed the old man's face. For a moment he appeared completely lost. Then he recovered himself, removing his helmet. White hair was swept back from his face.

'Let me introduce myself. I am Dr Richard Kendall.'

'Pleased to meet you.' Anna gave a fleeting smile; all her attention was now focused on the car. It was a flimsy, ramshackle vehicle – but it was mobile. This was what the Carlings had been praying for! That God would send someone to them – someone who could drive to the Catholic mission and find out what had happened to their new wheel. She wondered if she should invite the doctor inside for a cup of tea, then run to get one of the Carlings, or if she should just ask for his help herself.

'Are you telling me the Maitlands don't live here any more?'

'That's right. They must have left years ago. The Carlings have been here for a long time.'

Kendall closed his eyes. He seemed to be making a conscious effort to absorb the news. Anna sensed his intellect, slowed with age, struggling to adjust to this fresh information.

'What a pity,' he said finally. 'I was looking forward to seeing them. The Maitlands are dear friends of mine. We haven't been in touch for years, but I thought they'd still be here.' He pointed towards the house. 'I stayed in this place not long after it was built, you know.'

Anna was barely listening. She was planning the letter she was going to write to the Catholic mission, and ask Kendall to deliver. She didn't want to disrupt Harry or Rose's work unnecessarily; this was a chance for her to act on her own initiative. But she had to make sure she didn't let this opportunity slip through her fingers.

The letter had to be clear and strongly worded, demanding serious attention.

'What's all that wire mesh for?' Kendall now swung the stick to take in the whole facade. 'It wasn't here before.'

'There are chimpanzees in the area. It's a safety precaution.'

'Safety?' He snorted dismissively. 'Missionaries are too soft these days. In my time we took danger for granted.'

'The Carlings have three young children to think of,' Anna said curtly. She felt defensive of the family – as if she were one of them.

'At my first hospital a lion came right into the ward. It walked between the beds. We just left it alone and it wandered out again.' Kendall's gaze was distant. 'That was more than sixty years ago. I came out to Africa as a young man. And look at me now.'

'Did you work near here? Is that how you met these people you came to see?' Anna moved closer to Kendall, suddenly interested. If he had been around this area for that long, he might know something about the family at Leopard Hall. He might have heard rumours of the divorce, and who was involved. Perhaps he'd even worked at the Lutheran hospital . . .

But Kendall shook his head. 'I knew Frank and Deborah in Uganda. We all served with the Church Missionary Society. When they moved down here, I came to visit them. I've always had a love of travelling. Now I'm retired I have plenty of free time. I'm looking up all of my old friends. Saying hello again, and goodbye. Before it's too late.' His words trailed off, as if he were becoming lost in his memories. Then he roused himself, checking his watch. 'I hope you'll forgive me if I don't come inside. It would be too sad, being in the Maitlands' home without them. I think I'd rather just keep driving. If I set off now, I'll be at my next destination by lunchtime. There's a school, just a little way further up the lake, past Banya.

I know the principal. He's expecting me. He answered my letter.'

Kendall lifted his hat, ready to take his leave.

'Wait! I need to ask you to do something,' Anna said.

The man paused, half-turned away. 'Of course. I'd be happy to help – if I can.' A wistful tone entered his voice. 'I'm not as useful to people as I once was.'

'We have to get a message to the Catholic mission, and our radio is broken down.'

'You know, we never had radios,' Kendall responded. 'We managed without them. People have become too reliant on equipment.'

Anna swallowed her exasperation. 'The new wheel for the Carlings' Land Rover is at the mission. Someone was meant to bring it back but they haven't turned up. It's the only vehicle here.'

'No radio and no car?' A faint smile touched Kendall's lips. 'It is like the old days, after all.'

'Please. This is serious.' Anna grasped the man's forearm. She felt the wasted muscle cloaked by loose skin. 'We wouldn't even know if the Simbas were coming. And we wouldn't be able to get away.'

'What are you talking about? Do you mean *simbas* – Swahili for "lions"?' Kendall looked confused again. 'You said chimpanzees before.'

It took Anna a few seconds to make sense of this remark, then her eyes widened in surprise. 'The Simbas are the rebels. Don't you know about them?'

Kendall scratched his chin, fingernails scraping white bristles. 'I did hear there was some kind of uprising – up in the north, I believe. But the government seems to be in control. Everything was quite calm down in Albertville. You know, I was in Tanganyika during the Maji Maji Rebellion. It was German East Africa back then – before the British took over.'

'You have to go to the Catholic mission,' Anna broke in. 'It's between here and Banya. You'll be able to find it – there's only one in this area. I'll give you a letter to deliver.'

'Yes, write everything down,' Kendall said. 'My memory is not what it used to be.'

'I'll just go and type it out. Would you like to come in and sit down?' As she spoke, Anna felt optimism rising inside her, like a warmth in her blood. Making contact with the Catholic mission would surely result in someone driving out to the Carlings' place. They'd bring the latest news of the Simbas, along with the Land Rover wheel. Having transport again would change everything. Harry could arrange for the radio to be mended, which would mean Eliza would have a way of getting in touch. And Anna could ask Harry to take her to Banya. He could introduce her in person to the Bonhoeffers. She'd worked hard here at the mission. Surely, by now, she'd earned a few favours in return?

'I'm happy to wait here,' Kendall said. 'I've been sitting down for hours, driving.'

'It won't take long,' Anna promised.

She took two steps back towards the house, then stopped. A vision came to her of Kendall being reunited with his old friend – being distracted by the excitement, then getting caught up in his stories. She pictured her letter lying abandoned, crumpled and muddy, on the floor of the car. The fact was, someone needed to go along with the old man and make sure this vital message was delivered. She thought, again, of running to the hospital to get the Carlings. But she feared Harry might choose to trust Kendall rather than interrupt his work at the hospital. After all, he wasn't afraid of the Simbas. And Rose would have to comply with whatever view her husband took.

It was obvious what needed to happen. Anna had to go with Kendall. She could get a ride back from the Catholic mission with whoever delivered the wheel. She chewed tensely at one of her fingernails, stripping away part of the cuticle, but barely noticing the sharp pain. She had no idea if it was still safe in this area – it was possible the fighting could have spread south since she'd been here. Kendall hadn't seen anything that concerned him on his journey here, but she didn't know how vigilant he'd been.

As she turned over the quandary in her mind, she looked up towards the house. Lily and Sam must have heard the unusual sound of voices outside; they were now standing at the door, gazing out. Anna remembered the day she'd first seen them there, when she'd arrived in the car with Eliza. She knew them so well, now – all their individual traits. Lily's love of stories. Sam's obsession with skyscrapers and his fear of being sucked down the plughole in the bath. As she watched the children they began waving – their hands like white birds flapping behind the wire. They looked so small, standing there; so vulnerable. A strange energy hatched inside Anna's body. It was like numbness spreading in reverse. She felt strong, brave. She knew she would do anything in her power to make sure that the Carlings were safe.

She turned back towards the car. 'I am coming with you.'

Kendall stared at her in surprise. 'Oh, I thought I was going to take a letter. I miss things, sometimes.' Confusion blended with embarrassment on the time-worn face. He gestured towards the vehicle. 'I must warn you, I have only two horsepower. That's where this car gets its name. *Deux Chevaux*. The journey will be noisy and slow.'

Anna took a breath, caught between excitement and trepidation. 'I don't care. Let's go.'

TWENTY-FOUR

Kendall sat forward, hunched over the wheel, as he drove. The engine had a tinny whine; it reminded Anna of a lawn mower. She couldn't imagine how she'd ever mistaken the noise for the low purr of the Jaguar. She averted her gaze as Kendall fought to change gear using a primitive-looking mechanism mounted on the dashboard.

'This car is on its last legs!' He raised his voice over the flapping of the torn canvas roof and the loud rattle that came from somewhere under the chassis. Glancing at Anna, he gave a rueful smile. 'But then, so am I.'

She smiled back at him. His candour was disarming, and she was impressed by his sense of adventure. At his age, many old people rarely left their sitting rooms but the retired doctor seemed determined to make the most of whatever time he had left. Anna sensed he was a man who had led a life of his own choosing; he'd enjoyed the journey and didn't want it to end. The noise of the car had prevented him from launching into any more stories. He'd have some interesting tales to tell, but Anna was grateful for the lack of conversation. If they were talking, he'd eventually want to know about her life as well – and that would bring up complexities she didn't feel like trying to explain.

She shifted restlessly on the thinly padded upholstery. Then she tried leaning against the door, but the interior panel had been removed on this side and her arm pressed up against bare metal. In the end she gave up trying to be comfortable and just stared ahead, willing the journey to pass as quickly as possible.

There were no landmarks that Anna recognised – just the unending parade of trees and tangled vines. She knew more about the forest, now, than when she'd first come here. Harry had taught her the names of some of the trees and plants. He'd shown her the poisonous toadstools decked out in candy colours that grew right near the house. He'd pointed into the undergrowth identifying carnivorous plants and describing the various means they used to snare a meal: pitfall traps, flypaper traps and snap traps. Anna could see that breaking down the forest into its component parts was his approach to living at close quarters with such a dominating presence. She had started calling the place 'the jungle' like the Carlings did, but she didn't think the word – with its soft sound, and the link with exotic stories – matched what she experienced: the shadows that moved; the noises, muffled and secret or piercingly loud; the pungent smells. During her weeks at the mission she'd never strayed from the path that led to the hospital or taken even a step beyond the perimeter of the clearings that surrounded the hospital and the house. She would be glad when they entered the open woodlands that bordered the main road. When she could see the horizon – hidden from her for weeks – she'd be able to breathe more freely again.

At the end of a long straight section of the track there was a sharp turn to the left. As the car swung round, Anna's suitcase slid along the back seat. Now she could see it from the corner of her eye – a red blur. The image led her thoughts back to the scene at the mission house, when she'd run inside to get changed and collect some things to take with her. Lily had watched on as she removed the suitcase from the cupboard where it was kept. There was no need to spend time packing; Anna had been using the case like a wardrobe, keeping all her clothes folded away inside. Setting it down on the floor, she had hurried to the bathroom to grab her toothbrush. While she was there she'd stripped off an old skirt and blouse Rose had given her, and had a quick wash. Then she'd pulled on the smart red-and-white spotted dress she'd had on the day she arrived here: the one that she'd planned to wear when she went to Banya. As she smoothed the skirt over her hips she'd felt a flutter of excitement. Who could say where she might end up today? Who she might talk to?

When she'd returned to her suitcase, Lily had been sitting on the floor next to it. Tears were running down her face.

'What's wrong?' Anna asked.

'You're going away.' The girl's lower lip quivered. 'Everyone just goes away.'

'It's only for a few days. I'll be back.'

'That's what Eliza said. She promised she'd come back and she never did. She doesn't like us any more.'

Anna knelt down beside Lily. 'That's not true. She wants to be here. I know she does. She will come back. And so will I – very soon.'

'Are you sure?'

'Yes. Nothing will stop me. I promise.' Looking down into Lily's face – the child's wide clear eyes like watery ponds – Anna felt a shiver of fear. Uttering such bold words felt like tempting fate.

'I'll be really lonely.' Lily bent her head, letting her tears drop onto the floor.

Anna smoothed a strand of hair from the child's wet cheek. 'I've got an idea.' Opening her case, she took out her toy koala. In the dimly lit hallway, its one eye gleamed brightly. 'I'm going to leave Koala with you, to keep you company.'

Lily took the toy, smoothing its sparse fur. 'He sleeps with you,' she stated. 'I saw you cuddling him that time – remember?'

Anna smiled, nodding. Lily had come into the sitting room late one evening, when Anna was lying on her makeshift bed. It had been the end of a difficult day in the hospital; one of the babies had died. Anna couldn't get the image of its tiny face, wizened with dehydration, out of her mind. She'd found comfort in hugging the soft toy against her chest. When Lily had appeared, looking for the book she was reading, she'd asked to see what Anna was holding. She'd examined the koala with interest.

'Where is the other eye?' she'd asked.

'It was lost long ago,' Anna had explained. 'I've had him since I was a baby.'

'Are you going to keep him forever?'

'Yes. I hope so.'

Now, as Anna closed up her suitcase, Lily was rubbing the koala against her cheek. A wisp of loose fur drifted to the ground. She kissed its nose, then handed the toy back to Anna.

'You won't be able to sleep without him.' She made the statement an unarguable fact. 'But now I believe you. You're coming back.'

Anna hugged Lily close, stroking her hair for a few moments. For reasons she couldn't name, there was a mist of tears in her own eyes. 'I have to go now.'

'When will I see you?' Lily asked.

'Quite soon, Mr Baboon.' Anna adopted one of Sam's rhymes, trying to lighten Lily's mood.

'In a while, Crocodile,' Lily responded, smiling through her tears. 'See you later, Alligator.'

When Anna had tucked the koala back into the suitcase, Lily took her hand and held it tightly as they walked out to the sitting room.

Instead of typing the letter she'd planned – addressed to the Catholic mission and beginning 'To whom it may concern' – Anna had written a quick note to Rose and Harry explaining what she was doing. She'd shown it to Adina, and then put it on the table beside the manuscript. The *ayah* had agreed it was important for the Land Rover to be mobile again, and she could see the visitor hovering impatiently at his car. However, she was uneasy about Anna leaving without the Carlings knowing. She'd followed Anna to the door, a frown knitting her brow, bunching the neat line of her tribal scars. Sam had already seen his sister's tears; now he picked up on Adina's ambivalence as well. As Anna was about to step outside, he'd clung to her leg. She'd had to peel off his arms and push him away.

Thinking of the scene now, with the mission house slipping further and further behind her, Anna felt a lump in her throat. She was touched by the children's reaction to her departure. It made her conscious of the fact that for the last three weeks she'd been a part of a real family. She'd grown to love the way the Carlings all held hands when they said grace before meals. She enjoyed the comforting sound of Harry and Rose talking together while she read her novel before bedtime. The couple were probably only ten years older than her, yet in their presence she felt, sometimes, more like one of the children than their peer. When she lay on her mattress, breathing the smell of wax crayons and pencil shavings that wafted from the school corner, she felt safe and at home in the mission house, cocooned from the jungle by the sturdy wire mesh.

But the sense of belonging was an illusion, Anna knew. She

wasn't really a part of the Carling family; she was just a visitor passing through – and an uninvited one, at that. She thought of her own home: the flat in Melbourne where she lived by herself. It would feel so quiet and empty compared with the busy Carling household. Just the thought of returning there made her feel lonely.

She pictured the suburban bungalow where she'd grown up – in some ways it still felt like her real home. But the idea of being back there was even less appealing. She didn't want to see her mother. Regardless of Marilyn's motivation, Anna couldn't forgive her for concealing the very existence of her real father. Anna had been entitled to know the truth, especially once she became an adult. Yet even now, Marilyn was refusing to divulge any information about him. A deep gulf had formed between mother and daughter. Eventually, their relationship would have to be rebuilt, but for now, Anna didn't want even to think about Marilyn. It only made her feel more isolated.

This time last year, thoughts about what kind of place she would call 'home' would have led Anna naturally to Gregory and the life they were planning together. They'd talked about moving to the outskirts of the city to create a family home with a big garden, ready for the children they would have. But that dream was gone. There was no point in Anna speculating about how her fiancé would have reacted to her going to the Congo. It wasn't worth pondering whether he would have encouraged her or not. Whether he might even have come with her, and how that scenario would have played out . . .

As Anna stared out at the wall of greenery that draped each side of the track like a densely embroidered curtain, she wondered where Gregory was now. She pictured him walking along the esplanade in St Kilda, hand in hand with a new girlfriend. Or was he in London on business? Shopping in Harrods, perhaps; buying a gift to take home for someone special . . . Jealousy reared inside her, even though – after the conversation with Eliza at the Hôtel Royal Kivu – she was now more certain than before that ending the engagement had been the right decision. She couldn't commit to spending her life with Gregory. But imagining him with another woman was a stark reminder of where her choice had left her. There was no one at her side.

Anna had plenty of friends – some were from secretarial school; others she'd met at Williams, Gordon & Sons – but her one longtime companion was Sally. The girls had met in primary school. Marilyn had always encouraged Anna's link with the Jacobs family because she admired Sally's father, who was an alderman. The friendship had survived years spent apart while Sally studied in Canberra and Anna stayed in Melbourne. Only last year, they'd been planning to travel to Queensland together. But then Michael had entered the picture, capturing all of Sally's attention. Since the engagement the two friends had barely seen one another, except at events surrounding the wedding

Anna thought back to when the private investigator, Murphy, had first contacted her to deliver the message from Karl Emerson. She didn't remember having been discontented with her life at the time – lonely or unhappy. Now, she understood that she must have been; why else had she been drawn to the Carling family, and to Eliza, so quickly and so deeply? This would explain why she couldn't picture her old world in Australia with much clarity. Why her images of the place were fuzzy and vague. And why she had a sense that if she returned, it might all disappear like a mirage as she walked towards it. The truth was, her life back there had been lacking in substance.

In contrast, memories of recent events seemed vibrant and full of colour. Pictures paraded through Anna's head: the mission house, the hospital, the clearing where the children played. Then she thought back to the journey from Albertville. The lakeside hotel. A meal for two cooked over an open fire.

Anna's ribs seemed to tighten around her lungs as an image of Eliza came into her mind, clear and detailed. It was not the glamorous, perfectly made-up face that Anna saw – the one Eliza wore when she was going to meet Randall. Anna remembered her in the garden, the day the decision to take the journey to Banya had been made. Sitting alone on the swinging chair Eliza had looked so tense and worried. There had been something fragile about her as well.

Anna closed her eyes, swept by a wave of despair. But she knew she could not give in to it. She had to keep hoping for the best: that Eliza was safe and well. Wherever she was right now, whatever she was doing – she was with her Simba friends. And her secret lover. Anna replayed what Eliza had said, just before they parted: *I'll be looked after.* She'd sounded so confident and sure. Whatever was happening, she would know exactly what to do.

Anna thought about what Eliza would say if she could see her now – setting off on her own like this, with Kendall. She felt a flash of pride at the knowledge that Eliza would approve. She'd understood from the beginning that it was vital for Anna to find out about her father. And Anna knew she'd made the right decision as well: she had to pursue her plan to reach Banya, and getting the Land Rover back on the road was the next step. Now, even more than before, there was no room for failure. Because when she considered the path she'd been on – where she'd come from and where she was now – she knew that the stakes had grown. She didn't just want to learn information about her father. Even meeting him, getting to know him, would not be enough any more. She wanted him to lead her into a whole new world – his world. She didn't want to go back to the life she had known.

It was crazy to have such a fantasy, she warned herself. She was doomed to disappointment. But a new dream had been born, and it was growing only stronger – bigger – with the passing of time. She could feel it there right now, living and breathing inside her . . .

Kendall braked as the car hit a pothole. Anna was thrown forwards, almost hitting her head on the dashboard.

'Sorry – I didn't see that!' Kendall called out. 'My eyes aren't so good any more. Are you all right?'

'Yes. I'm fine,' Anna assured him. She sat up straight, bringing her thoughts back to the present, and keeping a watch on the track. It would be a disaster if they crashed into a fallen tree or had some other accident out here. There was no one to come to the rescue. And they were so vulnerable in this flimsy car. She couldn't wait to be back on the main road.

The change seemed to come suddenly. One moment the track was enveloped by forest; the next, the canopy was thinning, letting in the sunlight. Soon, patches of sky became visible between the branches. At ground level the undergrowth retreated from the verges. Then at last, the junction came into view.

Kendall brought the car to a halt, pushing in the clutch and keeping the engine revved to avoid stalling. Anna searched the road. Part of her expected to see some military presence in the area: a convoy of dark green vehicles like the ones that clustered around the checkpoints back in Albertville; or even lines of marching soldiers. But the road was empty. The only sign of life was a crow, pecking at a long black snake that had been squashed into the gravel.

Kendall turned to the left, slowly accelerating. The noise inside the vehicle had diminished; whatever had been rattling underneath was now still – whether this was due to the smoother road, or if some part of the car had finally fallen off, Anna could not guess.

They passed a young boy herding a few goats. He smiled at the travellers while he used his stick to prod the animals out of their path. As Anna waved at him she felt a wash of relief. He looked completely at ease. He was even chewing on a piece of sugarcane. She let her muscles relax – neck, shoulders, back, hands. Then she flexed her fingers, before resting them in her lap. Only then did she realise how tense she had been.

Kendall began asking about Dr Carling's work at the hospital. Anna was pleased with the amount of information she was able to give him. She described the clinic at the leper colony and explained how Harry and Rose were working on a book about the management of burnt-out cases.

'In my day there was no cure, you know,' Kendall told Anna. 'The best we could do was give daily injections of chaulmoogra oil – subcutaneously or into the muscle. It was very painful and not very effective. The worst thing was that we had to remove all the babies who were born in the colony. Leprosy isn't particularly infectious where adults are concerned – most people are more or less immune – but the young are much more susceptible.' Kendall shook his head. 'There were terrible scenes. Sometimes people hid their children and only brought them out when there were signs they'd been infected. A pale patch on the skin is usually the first thing you see. I can tell you, every time I saw one – especially on a young, perfect body – it used to make my blood run cold.'

Kendall slowed down as another figure appeared on the road

ahead. It was a tribesman, marching along with a steady gait, a spear resting over his shoulder, angled to the sky. As the car approached he moved languidly to the side of the road.

'I'll ask him for directions to the Catholic mission,' Kendall said, winding down his window. 'To make sure we don't miss it.'

Anna watched the two men as they talked in what she assumed was Swahili. The retired missionary sounded fluent – he must have used the language in Uganda; Eliza had explained that it was spoken, usually as a second tongue, throughout most of East Africa. The conversation seemed to take ages, but Anna knew by now that the greetings alone were lengthy. As the words flowed back and forth, she searched the African's face for any sign of concern, but like the goatherd he looked perfectly relaxed.

Eventually, Kendall waved at the tribesman and drove on. 'It's just over this next hill. We look for a signpost to a big house owned by a European. *Nyumba ya Chui*, the fellow called it. House of the Leopard. Anyway, we take the next turn to the right.'

Anna spun around to him. 'What did you say? Did he mean Leopard Hall?'

'That sounds right – the Swahili translation isn't always precise. Do you know the place?'

'I lived there.' Anna's voice was faint. 'When I was little.'

Kendall craned his neck, looking over at her. 'It's your family home?'

'It was once.'

'Ah, so you come from this area. I wondered where you fitted in. You don't look like a missionary.' He glanced at Anna's hands with their red nails. Since she couldn't remove the polish she'd been painting over the chips. The coating of lacquer was now thick, the colour even stronger. 'Are they still living there, your parents? So many Europeans have left the Congo, now. Not the missionaries, of course . . .'

Anna shook her head. 'There's just a caretaker and some servants.' She remembered Karl explaining that the local staff had been kept on after he left for Albertville, to watch over the house as well as the rest of his precious collection. The plantation had been leased to another landowner.

'How long since you saw the place?'

'I left when I was seven.'

Kendall's eyes fixed on Anna, briefly but intently. She could see that his interest was piqued: he was not only a teller of stories; he collected them as well.

'Is that why you've come back here?' he asked. 'Taking a trip down memory lane?' When Anna gave no reply, he continued. 'There's nothing like visiting the house where you lived as a child – seeing all the special places, the secret corners, cubby houses . . .'

'I don't remember much about it.' Anna's hands twisted in her lap. She recalled the sudden fear that had come over her as she'd climbed the staircase in Eliza's mansion – the chilling sense that something horrible awaited her upstairs. Then there was that time when she was walking towards the front steps of Eliza's house: the pigeons flying down from the eaves had been transformed, in her mind, into a stream of bats.

Kendall smiled knowingly. 'Memories will come flooding back to you. That always happens to me.'

Anna just shook her head. She didn't want to know what visions of her childhood years, spent in that house, might rise up next.

'But you could meet people who knew you! Some of the staff – or the local villagers. The Africans love it when Europeans make the effort to come back and say hello.' Kendall spoke with growing excitement. He glanced at his watch. 'We've got time to drop in – as long as it's not too far off the main road.'

As he spoke, Anna turned to him, her eyes widening. She hadn't thought of this . . . If people remembered her, they might remember other things as well. How Anna came to be living at Leopard Hall. Why Karl Emerson had adopted her as his daughter. All the things that Marilyn would not say.

'We don't have to go there, though,' Kendall said. 'I always like to revisit the past – but not everyone's like me. We can just head straight to the mission. You decide.'

Anna didn't answer straight away. Part of her didn't want to go anywhere near Leopard Hall – but a stronger part couldn't give up this chance of finding some clues to her past. What if the Lutherans were unable to help her – or unwilling?

When she finally spoke, she kept her tone casual. 'We might as well drop in – since we're here.'

'Exactly,' Kendall agreed. 'What have we got to lose?'

TWENTY-FIVE

The turn-off was marked by an elaborate sign: a cut-out shape of a leopard made from solid metal with holes for the spots. The animal's legs were outstretched, head held low, as if it were on the run, keen to reach its destination. It was mounted above the words *LEOPARD HALL* formed from wrought iron. An arrow pointing inland hung below.

Kendall turned the car onto a road that was almost as wide as the one they were leaving. As they passed under the sign, Anna looked up. Sunlight glanced from lots of little dents in the metalwork, clustered around the leopard's head. Before she had time to wonder what had caused the damage, the sign disappeared behind her.

After just a short distance, the open woodland ended, and they entered the plantation. Nothing could have been less like the tangled chaos of the jungle. Here, the trees grew tall and straight, in long lines. Between the leaf canopy and the carpet of green at ground level, the trunks and branches were bare and grey. In the alleys between the rows, the daylight quickly faded to black.

'These are rubber trees,' Kendall commented. 'But you know that, of course.'

Anna gave no response. The setting felt familiar to her, but indirectly – it might have been a scene from a film or even a dream.

Peering more closely, she could see wide cuts in the trunks where the bark had been stripped away. She knew the purpose of this from geography classes at school. It was to release the sap. But the wounds had all healed over; there were no cups to catch the drips. Anna noticed that vines were just beginning to creep up from the forest floor. The plantation had clearly been neglected by whoever was leasing it. There was a deep stillness to the place. The trees, standing in rows, were like soldiers who had been called to attention and then forgotten.

Anna looked along the road. The sun was high in the sky, the shadows short and dark. The trunks were pale slashes at the periphery of her vision. Whereas the wild forest had pressed in around the car, the plantation was kept at bay by the width of the road. But the trees seemed to be watching, waiting, planning their advance. Something stirred in Anna's head, roused by the sight of them there. She could feel the memory creeping back to her like one of the Siamese cats approaching its prey.

She was in a huge car – even bigger than Eliza's Jaguar – crouched behind the back seat, folded up like a puppet with no strength in its limbs, trying to be smaller than she was. Vanilla-tinged perfume and cigarette smoke drifted from the front. Marilyn sat in the passenger's seat. She was talking to the driver, laughing with him. Her arm reached across, her hand resting on the man's shoulder. It was Karl. Anna didn't know how she knew, but she did. The little girl wasn't focused on the adults. Looking up from her place on the floor, she had her eyes fixed on the far window. The trees slid steadily by. She held her breath, watching them. If she looked away, even for an instant, she knew the car would never make it out of the plantation. They'd be driving through the trees forever . . .

'Here we are!' Kendall's voice called her back to the present.

Lifting one finger from the steering wheel, he pointed at two tall gates that spanned the road up ahead. One was closed but the other hung carelessly ajar. A spiky-topped fence stretched away to each side of them. The rows of rubber trees ended at this boundary, clear sunshine falling onto the open ground beyond.

'That's a fine example of Art Deco style,' Kendall said. 'The place was probably built in the twenties. I can't wait to see the house.' He smiled, eyes wide with enthusiasm. 'Architecture is another interest of mine.'

Anna looked at the lines of upright bars interlaced with curly leaf motifs – all forged from solid metal like the road sign. The combination of strength and decoration gave the impression of prison gates in disguise. She didn't remember having ever seen them before, but couldn't be sure.

As the car came to a halt, Anna noticed that there was something tied onto one of the gates. It was dusty green and had the shape of a giant feather. It looked like a branch from a palm tree. She pointed it out to Kendall.

'Oh, that'll be from Palm Sunday,' he said. 'Africans love to put up decorations for a special occasion. No one bothers to take them down afterwards.'

Anna tried to remember what Palm Sunday was all about. She hadn't been raised going to church, but Marilyn had sent her along to Sunday School – it was a part of being properly educated, like taking piano and tennis lessons. Anna vaguely recalled an activity that involved cutting out paper palm leaves, sticking them onto a picture of people waving with outstretched arms, their hands empty.

'It's a big thing in Uganda – no doubt it's the same here,' Kendall added. 'The Africans fill the churches with palm branches and carry them around in the streets.' He interrupted his story to point at the gate that hung open. 'I reckon I can squeeze past there.'

As he steered through the gap, Anna saw the palm branch close-up. It looked freshly cut; the frond was still green. She wasn't sure when Palm Sunday was, except it was in the lead-up to Easter – the day was linked, in her memories, with looking forward to chocolate eggs. Easter was nearly two months ago – before she'd even come to the Congo.

Kendall gave a wry smile as he continued talking. 'They like the idea of the Son of God riding into town on a donkey and all the people welcoming him by waving palm leaves and laying down their garments for him to ride over. The Jews were thumbing their noses at the Romans. You can see why the Africans identify with the story.'

Anna was no longer listening. She was looking out over what must once have been parkland with expansive lawns and gardens. Now, hump-backed cattle grazed here, their meandering tracks crisscrossing the flattened grass. Floppy-eared goats chewed at the bare stalks that stuck up from the garden beds. Anna was reminded of the setting of the Hôtel Royal Kivu – but these grounds looked even more neglected.

They drove on, flanked by hedges that were sprouting into trees. The road swept to the left in a long curve. As the car rounded the corner, Kendall whistled through his teeth.

Even at a distance, Leopard Hall was impressive. The three-storey mansion dominated the land around it, standing out against the skyline. Kendall peered ahead eagerly as he drove towards it.

When they were nearer, Anna scanned the sweeping facade, taking in all the details. The four tall columns were topped with deco-rative scrolls. Extensive wings ran off to left and right with rows of fan-topped windows. There were several balconies with metalwork that matched the gates. The place looked familiar to her, to a degree that she thought went beyond what she'd seen in photographs. Like its surroundings, the house had become very run-down. The walls had once been rendered white, but they were now blotched with dark mould. It crept from the ground up, colonising the window ledges and the flutes of the pillars, and seeping down from the eaves.

The road divided into two, forming a loop that ran past the front of the house. Kendall drove right up to a set of steps and stopped. Anna leaned forward to see past him. Her eyes fixed on the stone leopards that sat to each side of the huge front door. She glanced over the windows, shrouded by lace curtains. There was no movement or sign of life.

In the quiet, something ticked inside the dashboard. Anna could hear Kendall's breath, slightly wheezy in his chest.

Turning from the house, Anna saw a concrete fountain – waterless, like the one at the Hôtel Royal Kivu. She prodded her memory for any further hint of recognition. Feeling nothing, she turned to the formal garden overtaken by weeds. A flash of colour caught her eye. An African woman was sitting in the shade of a frangipani tree. A brightly patterned cloth draped her shoulders, but it was the shape on her lap that drew Anna's attention. There was something familiar about the shimmering turquoise, the sweep of intense colour. It was the limp body of a peacock. The woman's hands jabbed steadily as she plucked out its feathers, letting them fall. Her head was bent over her work.

'*Hujambo, Mama.*' Kendall called out a greeting as he opened his car door.

The woman lifted her head, staring at the visitors. At first, she seemed undecided about how to respond. Then she threw down the bird, and began making shooing motions with both hands. Feathers flew into the air.

'She's telling us to go away.' Kendall's voice expressed mixed surprise and dismay. 'It seems we're not welcome.'

Anna's eyes narrowed. There was a sense of urgency in the woman's gestures – she seemed more alarmed than hostile. Anna looked back towards the house. The front door was still closed. There were no faces at the windows. She didn't know what to make of the woman's reaction. Then she noticed a dark green shape over by a hedge. Her stomach lurched with fear. It was an army jeep, almost concealed by the camouflage tones bleeding into the background. The battered vehicle was missing a door; the paintwork was splashed with mud. A line of dents along the side panel matched the ones Anna had seen on the road sign.

'Let's go,' Anna said to Kendall. 'Quick!'

'What?'

'There are soldiers here.'

'Are there?' Kendall raised his eyebrows. 'Where? I'd better talk to them – explain who we are . . .'

'No. They might be Simbas.' Anna's voice rose sharply. 'Get us out of here. Now!'

Kendall's features stiffened as he registered her fear. Shutting his door, he tried to restart the car, but the ignition failed.

'Hurry,' Anna pleaded. 'Please!'

A figure appeared from behind an outbuilding: an African man in combat fatigues, a machine gun swinging lazily from his shoulder. He was doing up the flies of his trousers. Anna fixed her gaze on his beret. It was not red, like the ones worn by the government soldiers in Albertville – it was green. Catching sight of the visitors, he straightened up in surprise.

Kendall's hands shook as he pressed the ignition again and again. The soldier ran towards them, waving and shouting out something Anna couldn't understand. Then he raised his gun to his shoulder. At that moment the engine finally kicked in. Kendall accelerated, the tyres spinning on the gravel. Anna gripped the seat with her hands, bracing herself as they lunged forwards.

As the car pulled away from the house, distance lengthening behind them, she gasped out a ragged breath.

'That was close,' Kendall said. 'That fellow didn't look very friendly. Was he one of the rebels, do you think?'

Gunfire cut off his words – a long stream of shots, ripping through the air. A scream tore from Anna's throat as she ducked, her hands rising instinctively to cover her face. Kendall's head fell forward onto the steering wheel, his body crumpling. The car stalled, then slowed, veering to one side before coming to a standstill.

Anna sat motionless, stunned for a few seconds, then she turned to Kendall, dragging at his shoulder. As he fell towards her, his hands clutched at his head.

'I've got you,' Anna said. She repeated the phrase over and over, as if it had some meaning. Blood oozed from a hole in the doctor's scalp, staining his white hair. She felt its sticky warmth bathing her hands. Kendall's eyes were wide with shock. They fastened onto hers and stayed there. She saw the life in them fade to glass.

Anna's chest heaved. Craning her neck, she looked behind her. The soldier was shouting, the gun still aimed at the car. Anna thought of trying to move Kendall's body and take his place behind the wheel. Before she had time to even try, another round of shots hit the vehicle, shattering the windscreen. In the dense quiet that followed the outburst, Anna sat frozen with terror. Blood dripped onto her lap. Torn fragments of the canvas roof drifted slowly down.

The soldier yelled again, his voice closer now.

Anna pushed open her door and half-fell from the car. Scrabbling to her feet, she held both hands in the air.

He was jogging towards her – a big man with a rounded belly that bounced with each step. When he came to a halt by Anna, he stared at her as if barely able to believe she was real. He was chewing gun, his jaw moving up and down, lips flaccid.

Anna swallowed, trying to still her panic. Words started tumbling from her mouth. *'Je m'appelle Anna Emerson.'* My name is Anna Emerson. 'I am Australian. I am just visiting here . . .' Her voice petered out and she was quiet for a second. Then a burst of anger surprised her. 'You shot that old man. You killed him. He was a doctor. He did nothing wrong!'

The man stepped back, as if surprised by her attack. His bloodshot eyes turned to slits. *'Ferme-la!'* Shut up.

He swung the barrel of his gun to indicate that Anna should move away from the vehicle. She stared at the weapon. It looked too small to be responsible for the damage that had been done. The soldier grunted impatiently, then raised the gun, aiming at Anna's head. A sly smile stretched his lips as he lowered the barrel to the level of her breasts, pointing first at one, then switching to the other.

Anna walked a short distance, then stood still. Her heart was pounding; every nerve in her body was taut. She had an impulse to run towards a nearby hedge, plunge into the scratchy depths and disappear from sight. But she knew she had no chance. He'd mow her down before she took her second step.

The man circled her, eyeing her from all angles as if she were a beast in a sale yard. He reached out to touch her hair, pulling a long strand through his fingers. She jerked her face to one side as he stroked her cheek, then her neck. His clammy fingers moved on to touch her arm, then her dress. His skin against hers felt numbingly cold, yet burning. Her stomach heaved as she breathed the stink of stale alcohol, only faintly cloaked with mint. She longed to bring her arms down and cover her breasts, but was afraid to move them. She wanted him to know she was surrendering.

'*Allez, bouge!*' he said. Move! He pointed towards the house.

On shaking legs Anna set off along the driveway. It seemed to take a long time, step following step. Twice, she glanced over her shoulder towards the car. She felt she should not be leaving Kendall even though she knew there was nothing to be done for the old man. He was gone.

When she reached the formal garden she searched for the figure seated under the frangipani – her eyes fastening again on the coloured cloth and the turquoise flash of the peacock. Anna stared at the woman with desperation. Their eyes locked together for a moment, then the African looked down at the ground.

As her step faltered, Anna gasped at a sharp pain in her back – the barrel jabbing into her spine. She staggered on.

A group of soldiers had gathered, milling around the front of the house. As she walked towards them, random images caught her attention, breaking through the haze of shock. Most of the men were in army uniforms – green shirts and trousers with matching berets. But one wore a mauve velvet dressing-gown, another a white linen jacket and a ladies hat. There was a man with a bandage on his head, seeping blood. Another leaned on a crutch made from a broomstick. Anna caught the glint of a long knife like the one carried by the caretaker at the lakeside hotel. She saw the ivory butt of a pistol lodged in the waistband of a pair of checked trousers. A fragment of a palm frond, adorning a metal helmet, trapped her gaze. It looked chillingly sinister now; nothing to do with a celebration.

The soldier walking behind Anna, herding her along, called out to the ones on the steps. An interchange ensued, conducted in Swahili or some other African language. The man wearing the checked trousers pointed back towards the car, talking vehemently. He seemed to be voicing disapproval. One or two of his companions clearly agreed with him, but others shook their heads. Anna deduced there was an argument going on about the death of the old man. She had an irrational feeling that if everyone could agree the shooting was wrong, time could be turned back and the innocent doctor saved.

As the words flew back and forth, Anna eyed the soldiers. She was pretty sure they were Simbas. The berets weren't the only clue; the government soldiers she'd encountered had been, on the whole, friendly and polite – nothing like these men. She searched the uniforms she could see, looking for a mark of rank. Even if these people were rebels, she might still be able to appeal to someone in charge. Ordinary troops were probably uneducated; an officer would be different. But the soldiers all looked the same: dirty and untidy. She turned from one face to another, forgetting rank and hunting instead for some hint of sympathy. But the smiles she saw were snide and calculating. And only one man, older than the others with greying hair, looked uneasy or even ashamed; he avoided meeting her gaze.

The argument ended and the gun barrel prodded her on. As she climbed the steps, the soldiers moved aside. She felt their eyes travelling up and down her body. She wished she'd chosen to wear trousers; she could feel the skirt brushing her thighs.

The man closest to the door bowed with mock courtesy, waving both arms towards the interior. He grinned, revealing a front tooth broken off at the root.

'*Entrez, Mademoiselle.*'

Anna walked between the two stone leopards and stepped inside.

Black-and-white marble tiles passed under her feet as she crossed the foyer. The light tap of her heels was followed by the thud of the soldier's boots. Catching her shoe on the edge of a Persian rug, she stumbled. The gun barrel jabbed into her back again, pushing her to keep moving.

Adrenalin pounded through her body, sharpening her senses. Her eyes latched onto the details of her surroundings: the murky paintings on the wall, the heavy antique sideboard, a vase with no flowers. She picked up the smell of food being cooked somewhere and heard the voices of the men who had followed her inside — murmurs of surprise; a burst of laughter.

She walked past a wine bottle lying on its side, the contents dribbling out onto the rug. Through an open doorway she glimpsed a large room with a whole wall that appeared to be covered in leopardskin; the furniture was draped in dust-cloths. A silver candelabra stood on an oval table next to a pineapple hacked in half and an oily-black machine gun.

A staircase rose up ahead. The banister was made of dark wood, rounded and thick like a giant snake, sweeping away in a long curve. The Simba steered her towards it. At the bottom step Anna hesitated. The other soldiers had remained by the door; she would be relieved to get away from them, but she didn't want to be alone with this man who had murdered Kendall. She remembered the feel of his hand on her face and how he'd aimed at her breasts with his gun. For a moment she felt lost in panic. Her head felt light. But somewhere inside her, an instinct for survival stirred. She knew she had to act now — to take back some control. She'd seen

Mr Williams do it plenty of times. You begin with one small act of assertion, then look for a chance to build on it.

She turned to face the soldier. The sudden movement made him aim his gun at her, but she didn't flinch. When she spoke, she struggled to keep her voice strong.

'*Je veux voir votre chef. Votre commandant.*' I want to see your leader. The man in charge. The soldier jerked up his head, taken aback by her tone. She made herself hold his gaze.

'*Tu le verras quand il reviendra,*' he responded. You will see him as soon as he returns.

There was a more respectful note in his voice. Anna took the chance to press her advantage. 'Where is he?' she demanded.

'He is searching for our enemy, the government army. When we find their camp, we can attack them.' A smiled crossed his face at the thought. Then he pointed his gun towards the landing. 'You will wait for the Lieutenant up there.'

Anna felt a flicker of relief at hearing the rebel leader referred to by the military term: it meant the Simbas did have a proper chain of command. Perhaps her situation wasn't as bad as she'd thought. The Lieutenant would surely be outraged when he learned that an innocent old man had been slaughtered. He would understand straight away that this young Australian woman had nothing to do with the conflict in the Congo. Anna would explain to him that she was a missionary. A nurse, working in the hospital. He wouldn't allow her to be harmed. He might even deliver her back to the Carlings.

As she climbed the stairs, Anna's legs felt weak and shaky. She clung to the banister. Looking down, she saw the ornate posts that supported it, slipping steadily past. A flash of recognition pushed up through her fear. She remembered the feel of these posts – rounded, smooth – in her child-sized hands. And how she used to touch each one of them as she moved from step to step, delaying the time when she would reach the landing.

Now, as she forced herself on, Anna felt a mad impulse to repeat the gesture. Instead, she just kept her eyes fixed ahead, looking up at the stuffed leopard that waited for her at the top of the stairs, watching her with its green glass eyes.

On the landing she stood still, staring towards the end of a long hallway. Sunlight poured in through open doorways to the left and right – but it was the closed door at the end that drew her gaze. It was painted black, with a big gold handle. She remembered how she used to try and avoid looking at it, as she ran for the sanctuary of her bedroom. The door was always kept shut. Locked. But that didn't mean the darkness couldn't escape, creeping out through the crack at the floor . . .

The soldier barked at Anna to keep walking. He was beside her now, his shoulder bumping hers. When they reached the first doorway, Anna took in a space containing two single beds. One had an army rucksack on it, a dark bulky shape that looked like a crouched animal. On the other bed lay an injured man, a bandage around his waist leaking yellow fluid. Anna had never been in here before. The little girl wasn't meant to even look inside the guest rooms. They were kept clean and tidy, the beds made up at all times – ready for the crowds of visitors. They seemed to arrive without warning, the big cars sweeping up the drive. Leopard Hall would be quiet and empty for weeks, then suddenly the place would fill with people. The big rooms downstairs would ring with the sound of laughter and music. Anna remembered how the new energy would pervade the house. Marilyn would smile. Karl would emerge from his black mood and become charming;

nothing was too much trouble for him, nothing could go wrong. Anna would creep around, trying not to get in anyone's way. She loved peeping into the dining room to see all the guests eating and talking. She spied on the ladies dancing, long skirts swirling, and the musicians with their shiny instruments. From the landing she watched champagne corks flying up the stairs, bouncing off the leopard's head . . .

The Simba pushed her on along the hall. He checked each room but they were all dotted with soldiers' possessions. Then they reached a small room squashed between a bathroom and a toilet.

'In here,' the soldier said, nudging her inside.

Anna stared around her, recognising the buttercup-yellow walls and the frieze with its pictures of rabbits that bordered the ceiling. This was the room that had once been hers. The narrow bed was still there, covered by the familiar counterpane printed with pink ballerinas. A dressing table stood near the window. Anna kept her eyes away from the mirror. She didn't want to see her face, blanched with fear, or her dress marked with the doctor's blood.

The Simba followed her in, a bulky presence in the small space. As he closed the door, Anna's stomach twisted with alarm. She crossed to the window, getting as far away from him as possible.

'How long will it be before the Lieutenant arrives?' she asked.

'He will return soon.' The Simba smiled. 'But we have time to play together first.'

The man's hands went to his belt. Eager fingers slid the leather strap through the buckle. Anna stared in horror as he came towards her.

She pressed herself against the window. Glancing behind her, she looked down to the ground below. If she managed to open the window and jump out, she might just survive the fall. But she'd land in a bed of tall sisal plants and become impaled on the sharp thorns that topped the woody leaves.

The soldier undid his buckle and let the belt hang open. His fingers moved to the top button of his trousers.

Anna was frozen with terror. She tried to think, but her mind seemed blank. Then a thought came to her, rising like a bubble in a pond, breaking the surface.

'I know Eliza Lindenbaum.' She threw out the name like a talisman.

The man's face stiffened. 'What did you say?'

'Eliza Lindenbaum is my friend. She would not want you to hurt me. Her boyfriend is one of you. He would be very angry.' She hoped the Simba understood the grammatical structure of her sentences. Eliza's boyfriend *would* be angry. Not *will* be. Anna's fate was not set.

The Simba spat on the carpet, a glob of mucous forming strings over the pile. 'The Okapi . . . He is no longer a Simba. His woman has no power. They are both finished.'

Anna stared at him, shocked into silence.

The man shook his head impatiently. 'Why are we talking about others? In this room, there are only two people. Me. And you . . .'

He reached a hand towards Anna's face. She lifted her chin and turned away.

'You will see that a black man is a good lover.' He grasped his genitals through his trousers and thrust his hips towards her. 'Compared to the white man, we are very big.'

Anna shook her head. 'No! Leave me alone!'

His face contorted with anger. He grabbed Anna by her hair, pulling her face round towards his. She saw hatred in his eyes. 'Why should I leave you alone? White men do what they like with our women. They take whatever they want from us. Now it is our turn.'

He dragged Anna across to the dressing table. Standing behind her, he made her bend over it. The top of her head was pressed against the mirror; her cheek rested on a lace doily, its pattern pushing into her skin.

'Wait.' Anna forced the word from her throat. 'You are stronger than me. I won't fight you. But I —' She swallowed on a wave of revulsion. 'I prefer to lie down. Let's do it properly. I will be nice to you.'

The soldier let her stand up and turn around. He eyed her suspiciously for a moment, his lips pursed – but then he nodded. With clumsy fingers, Anna unzipped her dress and let it fall to the floor. At the edge of her gaze, the pool of red looked like fresh blood. Her hands wanted to wrap themselves over her chest, but she made them reach behind her back as if to undo her bra. Then she paused. 'It is your turn.'

The man nodded. A smile stretched his lips.

Anna tried to return the gesture but her mouth just trembled.

As the soldier lowered his trousers to his hips, he exposed stained khaki underpants. His erection pushed against the thread-bare cloth, the dark skin showing through. Anna waited until his trousers were nearly at his knees – then she lunged at him, pushing him in the chest. Driven by sheer terror, her movements were precise and fast. He toppled to the floor, his legs trapped. Cursing loudly, he grabbed at her foot. For a second he had her ankle in his hand, but she jerked free and wrenched open the door.

Out in the corridor she turned towards the stairs – but another soldier came into view. Spinning round, she ran the other way. She had no plan; there was nowhere to go. Suddenly she was at the end of the hallway, facing the closed door. She could now see that the area around the gold handle was peppered with bullet holes and the wood of the frame was splintered. As she launched herself against it, the door opened. She tumbled inside.

A rank smell closed in around her: dead animals, mould, a musky fragrance like dried herbs. Anna was sprawled on the floor in her bra and underpants. Her knees were stinging and pain came from where her cheek had met something sharp. Lifting her head, she found herself staring into the blind white eyes of a carved statue. A gaping mouth breathed hundreds of nails, sticking out at all angles. The body was a cage made of woven strips of metal. It was full of small leather bags that looked like tumours crammed into its innards. The legs and arms were spiked with rusty knife blades. In one hand there was a metal-tipped spear, aimed towards the doorway. Dimly, Anna recognised that it was similar to the statue Leclair had shown her – the one he'd called a power figure: a *nkisi*. Only this version was the size of a grown man. Towering over her, it was like a material image of the terror she felt.

Turning to the doorway, she saw the soldier arrive at the threshold. Instead of launching himself at her, he just stood there, his boots planted apart, hands hanging at his sides. The other Simba joined him. The two men were rock-still, wide-eyed.

Anna stood up. She moved back against the statue as if seeking the protection of a living person. The nails pricked the bare skin of her back. Looking around her, she saw that there were fifty or more of these power figures – all in different shapes and sizes. Most were human, but she saw one in the form of a dog, its body bristling with nails. Another was a snake. They were grouped together at this end of the room, massed behind her like a silent army.

The soldier from the bedroom pulled on a cord around his neck, producing a leather pouch from inside his shirt. He clutched it tightly in his hand. The second man muttered something. Then the pair crept backwards, keeping their eyes fixed on Anna until the door swung closed.

As their footsteps died away into silence, Anna remained immobile. She expected the soldiers to return, their courage galvanised, anger taking over from fear. She tried not to picture what they might do to her then.

But minutes passed and the door stayed shut. Gradually her terror faded; her pulse slowed. Her legs were still shaky, so she sat on the floor by a stack of tea chests that were piled against the wall. Blood trickled from her scratched cheek and her shins were bruised. But for the moment at least, she was unharmed.

She stared at the statues gathered around her. Their animal smell seemed to fill the air, invading her lungs. Dozens of pairs of blank white eyes were fixed on her. She felt like a mouse trapped in the open with nowhere to run. She knew the presence of the *nkisi* had protected her; it was only because of them that the Simbas had been afraid to pursue her in here. But her fear of the soldiers was now merging with an even deeper dread. A cold sweat broke over her skin.

She pulled up her knees, clutching them against her chest. She told herself the statues were just artifacts – objects of curiosity that people might examine in a museum. But the sense of horror only grew stronger. Anna could feel it being fed from somewhere deep inside her. Then a memory rose up, erupting into her consciousness. It was vivid and detailed – building on all the other pictures that had come back to her since she'd returned to Africa.

She had just had her sixth birthday. She should have known better, at that age, than to trespass in a forbidden place – but she was not strong enough to withstand the lure of a special secret. It must have been a servant who had left the door open; her father would never have been so careless. Anna had been returning to her bedroom, breathless from skipping up the stairs, when she'd made the discovery. She had edged along the hallway, looking back over her shoulder, keeping a guilty eye on the landing. She knew she wasn't allowed in her father's private room. She just wanted to take a quick look, to see what he kept in there.

Cautiously, she wrapped her small fingers around the gold handle. Then she pushed open the door.

The faces came to her first, rushing out of the dark. The blank white eyes. Gasping mouths, swallowing blackness. Blades glinting, their tips aimed at her heart. Then she saw the ghostly bodies, floating towards her . . .

Her screams brought Karl running into the room. He flicked on the overhead lights, sapping the scene of its power. The statues were still frightening, but they were no longer alive. Whimpering in terror, Anna threw herself at her father, clinging to his chest. But he grabbed her, pushing her away. Then he slapped her hard on the face with his hand.

As a punishment for disobedience, she was locked in her bedroom. She waited for her mother to come and rescue her, but Marilyn must have been too busy. The day had turned into night. Anna's *ayah* was sent to escort her to the bathroom. The African brought water, but explained that she'd been forbidden to offer food. The Bwana had made it clear: the girl had to learn her lesson. Rules are there to be followed.

Anna had lain on her bed, wide awake, for what felt like hours. She was afraid to close her eyes. She clasped her toy koala against her chest, her fingers digging into the hard body beneath the fur. She couldn't stop thinking about the ghastly creatures she'd seen.

They were still there, not far away. She'd broken into their secret world. One day, she knew, the door would be left unlocked again. Then they would come and find her . . .

As the memories of that long ago night flooded back, Anna sat still, as if her body were frozen in time. She closed her eyes, reliving her horror of the *nkisi*. Her fear of Karl's white-faced fury. The dawning realisation that Marilyn was not going to come to her. That she was completely alone.

Now – nearly twenty years later – Anna was back in this room where the nightmare had begun. She felt strangely calm. It was as if the collision of past and present terror had led to one force absorbing the other. The power of both had been diminished. Her mind was clear.

She understood that the fear she'd experienced while she was so young had settled deep inside her. That it had guided her ever since, like a close companion always at her side. Sometimes she'd been aware of its presence – making choices for her, giving her advice. But she hadn't known where the caution and anxiety had come from. She just felt a need to be safe, which always foiled her attempts to be brave and free.

Opening her eyes, Anna scanned the faces of the *nkisi* that were closest to her. If she focused on them one by one, she could see their individual characters. Many of them were fierce, but some were more sombre and proud; others, like the dog, were almost comical. As she began to breathe more easily, her body relaxing, she looked further, taking in the whole space she was in.

Karl Emerson's private museum was a huge gallery, occupying most of this wing of the house. A cathedral ceiling reached up into the third storey. She looked at the rows of spotlights mounted on the walls, their moon-shaped faces now blank and dull. And the empty shelves and vacant plinths, all covered in black velvet. Then she returned her gaze to the artifacts collected together on the floor – waiting to be packed up in the tea chests and sent on their way to London.

No museum curator would want them, now. Whoever had been charged with the task of keeping the air-conditioning running had failed in their duty. The *nkisi* had begun to merge with the moist air of the jungle. Mould had grown over their skin – they looked as if they'd been dusted with snow. Anna remembered Leclair saying the *nkisi* would not survive in the village spirit huts; a museum was the only place where they could be preserved. But like people, they were not meant to last forever, Anna realised. Left behind here at Leopard Hall, they'd been saved from an unnatural destiny.

Anna crossed to the nearest window, weaving a path between the statues. Turning the latch, she pushed it open. The outside air flowed in – still hot, but fresh and dry. Red velvet drapes hung at each side of the window. She grabbed one of them, yanking it down. As she gathered the curtain around her body, her sweat stuck to the fabric – it was too heavy and thick. But she didn't want to be dressed only in underwear when the soldiers reappeared.

This side of the room overlooked the rear of the house. Anna peered down into the garden. A large tan dog lay stretched out on the overgrown lawn. Birds fluttered in the branches of a tree dotted with red flowers. The scene was peaceful and calm. You would never know that something terrible had happened, just close by. Anna had a flash vision of Kendall's body falling forwards onto the steering wheel. His blood leaking, sticky, onto her hands. To banish the memory, she thought of the old man as he had been when he was alive. She remembered the way he'd talked so passionately about his love of travel and architecture. And how he was apologetic about his car and his body both showing the ravages of time. She saw, again, his shamefaced look when he realised he'd become confused. And recognised his ready kindness to a young woman he'd only just met. Tears came to her eyes, softening the flowering tree to a blur. With every part of her being she wished she could turn back time. She would tell the doctor she didn't want to see her old home; that they should drive straight on to their destination. She couldn't bear the thought that she was even partly responsible for Kendall's death. She wondered what the Simbas had done with his body – whether it was still in the car, or had been moved. It didn't matter, she told herself. He was no longer here. He was on a new journey, now.

Lifting her gaze, she stared into the distance where the rubber trees pressed in at the boundaries of the parkland. She thought of the drive to Leopard Hall, through the plantation. It dawned on her then that Kendall had been the only person who knew that she'd come here. Her letter to Rose and Harry said she was going to the Catholic mission. If she disappeared, no one would ever know what had happened. She thought, suddenly, of Eliza. No one knew where she was, either.

Anna remembered what the Simba had said when she mentioned Eliza's name.

They are finished.

She bit her lip, almost drawing blood. Was he saying that Eliza and her boyfriend were both dead? The thought was too awful to contemplate. But the man's French was far from perfect. He might just have meant that they could serve no purpose for Anna. That they no longer had any power.

Anna gripped the windowsill with her hands. She clung to shreds of optimism. Eliza was a survivor; she would find her way out of any trouble she was in. And when Kendall failed to arrive at the school, his friend would send out a search party. They might meet the tribesman who'd told the two foreigners about the turn-off to the House of the Leopard. The Lieutenant might return here soon and offer Anna his protection . . .

But these hopes were like bits of small change, of scant value. As she tried to grasp them they kept slipping between her fingers. She was left with only one cold fact: she was on her own, at the mercy of the Simbas. No one was going to come to her rescue.

TWENTY-SIX

Time stretched out – two hours passed, maybe three. The soldiers did not reappear, although Anna could hear their voices outside the closed door. The terror she'd experienced slowly faded. But she could still feel it there inside her – like a crouching animal, ready to rear up again. She sat back on the floor by the tea chests, then moved again to the window, staring down into the garden. The tan dog was now chewing hungrily on a large bone. Nearby, there was a broken wine bottle, the dark glass gleaming in the sun.

When the door finally opened, Anna was taken by surprise. She spun around, her hands instinctively poised, ready to strike out. Her heart pounded. Then she took a deep breath. She knew that showing fear would make her more vulnerable. She had to pretend to be strong.

The first soldier to come into view was one of the Simbas she'd seen at the front door; he was still wearing the mauve dressing-gown. He was followed by an older man with grey-speckled hair and a wrinkled face. She noticed that his uniform had been washed recently; it was still creased from where it had been wrung out by hand, then dried quickly in the sun. This observation was meaningless but she felt an impulse to hunt for even the smallest tidbits of information, as if it might give her some shred of power.

'*Vous êtes autorisée à utiliser la salle de bain,*' this older man announced. You have permission to use the bathroom. 'We will go with you.'

'Thank you,' Anna responded. But she didn't move from the window. She was reluctant to leave the museum, even though she did want to go to the toilet. She realised that the gallery was like a spirit hut, of the kind she'd seen in one of the villages during her journey – but on an enormous scale. Anna was under the protection of the resident ancestors. A whole crowd of them. She didn't know what might happen if she stepped outside the sanctuary. On the other hand, she didn't want to have to ask for something to use as a potty – and then present the vessel and its contents to one of the men to be emptied. She sensed that it was vital she preserve her dignity, not for its own sake, but to maintain her stature in the minds of the soldiers. As she gazed around her, weighing up what to do, her eyes came to rest on the *nkisi* crafted in the shape of a dog. If she took it with her, she'd maintain her link with the others. She picked up the statue – casually, as if the gesture were simply what anyone would expect of her. She cradled the dog against her chest, the clusters of nails and blades digging into her velvet wrap. Close up, the mouldy herb smell tickled her nose.

As she approached the doorway, the men fixed their eyes on the *nkisi*. She laid her hand protectively over its back. Her shiny red nails contrasted with the dull metal of the rusted spikes. The effect was striking, even to her. The Simbas looked torn between being impressed and repelled.

The bathroom was halfway along the corridor. Anna walked between the two soldiers, her light step interspersed with the heavy thud of their boots. From downstairs came the sound of laughter and the rhythmic banging of someone cutting wood.

'Here.' The man in the dressing-gown pushed open the door.

Anna stepped into a small light bathroom with floral wallpaper and pink porcelain tiles. It had once been a pretty room, but now it stank of urine and the basin was grimy. Anna lifted up her makeshift cloak to avoid wet patches on the floor. At least there was some toilet paper. She used a few sheets to wipe off the seat so she could sit down. The Simbas had made her leave the door open a crack; she couldn't tell if they were peering in, but she hardly cared. Bending her head, she rested her face in her hands, closing her eyes. She tried to pretend she was back in the Carlings' house in their toilet that was dingy but clean. She saw the little wooden step painted with rainbow spots that had been built for Sam to stand on, and the crayon scribble on the back of the door. The image evoked a flood of despair. It was hard to believe that only hours had passed since she'd left the mission house. Rose would have returned for lunch by now and heard of Anna's departure. She'd be picturing her safely at the Catholic mission, or with the friends of the old doctor, when the truth was so different. Kendall was dead; Anna was a prisoner of the Simbas. It felt like a nightmare that had to come to an end. Except that it was real.

When she was finished, Anna crossed to the basin. She picked up a sliver of creamy yellow soap, breathing the familiar fragrance of Imperial Leather. Water trickled from the tap. The sight of it made Anna realise how thirsty she was. She longed to put her mouth under the spout. But she knew how strict Rose was about drinking only boiled water. Anna couldn't risk becoming ill. If she appeared weak and useless, the authority she drew from her connection with the *nkisi* would be undermined; the men's fear of her would evaporate. She allowed herself to moisten her lips, but that was all.

Avoiding the dirty hand towel hanging on a hook, she checked a cupboard and was relieved to find a clean one. She dampened the cloth and used it to wash herself. The curtain, draping her shoulders, formed a screen from watching eyes. She scrubbed all her bare skin, long and hard. She began with her belly, marked with Kendall's blood. Then she moved on to her arms, her neck, her chest. She felt as if the Simba, touching her in the bedroom, had left indelible fingerprints. Even parts of her body that the man had not touched seemed dirtied by him. As she rinsed her face, tears pricked her eyes – but she didn't let them flow. Once she began to cry, she knew shock and terror would take over. She might not be able to bring her emotions back under control. She bent over the basin, scooping water onto her hair, smoothing the locks between her fingers. Then she stood still, water dripping from her skin, gazing at herself in the mirror. The silvering had failed in some areas, causing smudging and dark spots. The glass was dusty. In the bleary, fractured reflection the cut on her face was barely visible. She looked almost normal.

When she emerged from the room, the soldiers led her back towards the end of the corridor. But when they reached the entrance to the little bedroom they stopped. One of them pushed open the door. The red-and-white dress, stained with Kendall's blood, was still lying where she'd dropped it on the floor. Anna stiffened, panic shooting through her like an electric shock.

'You may sleep here.' The older man pointed to the bed. Anna searched his face. She could see no sinister glint in his eye, but that didn't mean she was safe.

'No. Not here.' She tried to sound firm. As she spoke she lifted the *nkisi* towards the soldiers, her hands tightening their grip, sharp nails pressing into her skin. The men inched away from it, letting her go past them.

Anna headed back towards the gallery. She made herself move slowly, even though she wanted to bolt. It was as if she were following the steps to a complicated dance. If she kept up the rhythm and control, she'd make it to the end. If she faltered, everything would be lost.

The soldiers watched from the doorway as she walked back in among the *nkisi*. From the look in their eyes they might have been witnessing someone entering a cage full of lethal snakes.

After a few steps she stopped and turned around. 'I need my suitcase,' she stated. 'It was in the car.' She waited for the older man to acknowledge that he understood her, then she continued. 'And I would like a cup of tea, if you would be so kind. With sugar and milk.' She remembered how Eliza spoke to her servants: she wasn't blunt, as Anna knew Marilyn would have been. She made her courtesy into a gift, so that the response was not an obligation but a choice. Anna had seen how well this worked – the staff tried extra hard to please. The more tasks they carried out, it seemed, the more they admired their mistress. 'I need some water, as well. It should be boiled for at least three minutes.' She held up her fingers, counting off the numbers.

There was an interchange between the two men, then the younger one disappeared, leaving his companion to guard the door.

Anna smiled at him. She wanted the Simba to see her as a person, not just a prisoner. 'I am Anna. What is your name?'

The man hesitated, but then replied. 'Luka.'

'You speak good French.'

'I went to school.'

'Do lots of the Simbas speak French?'

Luka shook his head. 'The ones who guard you have been chosen because of their skill. But most of the men are uneducated. They cannot read. They cannot even count their money. There are not enough schools in our country. Independence has not changed anything. We are still poor.' He lifted his head. 'That is why we are fighting the government. We supported Lumumba. He was going to bring change.' His voice rose vehemently. 'He is our hero.'

Anna avoided his passionate gaze. She'd picked up from Eliza that interference by European powers had played a big part in bringing down the first Congolese Prime Minister. Anna thought there was even a suggestion they were involved in his assassination – but she wasn't sure. Her understanding of Congolese politics was very inadequate. Eliza was her main source of information and much of what she'd told Anna was piecemeal and confusing. Sometimes Eliza had expressed points of view that were in direct conflict with one another. Now, Anna understood the reason for this: Eliza had been playing two different roles – she pretended to be a friend of the American officer, Randall, and his colleagues; but all the time she was in league with the Simbas.

Thinking about Eliza brought a sinking fear to Anna's stomach. She considered asking this rebel soldier if he knew what had happened to her – what exactly had been meant by the man who'd said Eliza Lindenbaum and the Okapi were 'finished'. But Anna was afraid she might learn that Eliza was dead. She would not be able to bear it.

She decided to change the subject completely. Ranging over possible topics, she settled on asking about the man's family. She remembered how eagerly the soldiers at the checkpoint in Albertville had handled Eliza's gift of baby clothes – the gentle expressions that came over their faces.

'Do you have children?' she asked.

'Of course.' Luka gave a proud smile. 'I have two sons and a daughter. There is a fourth child also, but he is still waiting to be named.'

Anna nodded. The Carlings had told her that in this country of high infant mortality, people avoided becoming attached to their babies until they were weaned. The ones who made it through the transition had a reasonable chance of surviving. It was only then that they were given names.

'How many children do you have?' Luka asked curiously.

Anna shook her head. 'I am not married.'

The man's eyebrows rose, then the corners of his lips turned down as he frowned. 'I am sorry for you. You are already old and no one has chosen you.'

Anna didn't respond. She hadn't intended the conversation to become as personal as this. She moved over to the window, standing in a pool of sunlight, her back to the door.

Before long the soldier in the dressing-gown returned, carrying the red suitcase. He put it down on the threshold, pushing it into the room with his boot. Then he produced a glass bottle of water from his pocket.

'It was boiled for tea this morning,' he said. 'That is all I can bring you.'

Anna met his gaze. Her requests had only been partially fulfilled, but she wasn't sure enough of her position to complain. Instead she smiled graciously as she accepted the water. 'Thank you very much.'

When the guards pushed the door shut again, forcing it into the damaged frame, Anna opened the suitcase. She was relieved to find no sign that anyone had been looking through her possessions. As she lifted out her clothes, eager to abandon the heavy velvet drape, the smell of insect repellant rose up. It reminded her of a time when getting malaria was the worst disaster she could imagine.

She selected a khaki bush shirt and trousers, thinking it would be wise to appear as unfeminine as possible. But then she realised she didn't want to look like a soldier, either. And it might be better to look smart. In the end she put on her best frock. It was an unusual design, with a mix of stripes and plaid – not a Mary Quant original, but one inspired by her style. As Anna slipped the dress over her head, reaching behind her to pull up the zip, she thought back to the day when she'd gone shopping for this outfit. The woman she'd been then – strolling the aisles of Georges – could not have begun to comprehend the situation in which Anna now found herself. She wouldn't be negotiating with the rebel soldiers, and finding a way to survive as a prisoner in this room. Anna had changed so much in the time she'd been here in Africa. She could feel the strength that had grown in her, like a taut muscle ready to be used.

The burst of confidence lasted only briefly, though. As she sat down on one of the museum plinths, crossing her legs and folding her hands, the stillness of the room pressed in on her. The statues, standing in random groups – some looking her way but most of them facing one another – seemed to be cutting her out of a secret conversation. She thought of the Carlings' house with the lively chatter of adults and children. The cheerful singing of grace before each meal, the whole family holding hands . . .

Anna bent her head as a new wave of fear washed over her. She'd avoided thinking about the threat to the Carlings; her own situation was enough for her to face. But she knew the family could be in real danger. Rebel soldiers might already be heading their way – Leopard Hall wasn't likely to be the only place overrun with Simbas. Harry's belief that missionaries would not be harmed had proved to be unfounded. The man who'd killed Kendall had no idea who the doctor was, and clearly didn't care. Whatever the Lieutenant might think about the shooting was irrelevant; the officer was absent. If this band of Simbas was anything to go by, the rebels were erratic and out of control. Anna shuddered at the thought of the Carlings falling into their hands.

Lifting her face, she gazed bleakly across the gallery. She pictured the last time she'd spoken to Lily, standing in the corridor, packing her suitcase for this journey. She remembered how she'd offered the girl her toy koala as a kind of ransom, and how Lily had so trustingly refused. Then they'd said their goodbyes.

See you later, Alligator.

Quite soon, Mr Baboon . . .

A chill fell over Anna as she replayed the childish exchange. It was so innocent and carefree – it felt like a magnet for evil. She reminded herself of how Harry and Rose prayed each morning for the family to be protected from danger. They laid out all their concerns about diseases, wild animals, snakes and insects. They mentioned the threat of witchcraft alongside the ordinary accidents of daily life. They always sounded so confident that their prayers would make them safe. But then, Kendall had probably prayed every day too, and he hadn't been saved. Perhaps the old man's life didn't matter so much, Anna thought; he was already nearing the end of his days. Maybe there were other factors at play that she knew nothing about. Whatever the truth was, she hoped desperately that Harry and Rose's prayers did have some real power. She tried to send them her thoughts, warning them to be prepared. She imagined the couple sitting down to an urgent prayer time, turning to the Bible for strength. Words and phrases flowed into her mind – fragments of quotes she'd picked up from Harry's daily readings.

'The Lord is my strength and my shield . . . my rock and my

fortress . . .' Anna's voice sounded loud in the quiet room. She eyed the *nkisi*, wondering if the spirits they represented could hear her – and if they could, what they would make of the things she said. 'Though I walk through the valley of the shadow of death, I will fear no evil . . . I will never leave you nor forsake you . . . Until the end of time . . .'

When Anna's supply of quotes ran out, silence returned to the room. The words were a comfort to her, but she wanted something more tangible to cling to. Reaching into the suitcase, she felt among her clothes until her fingers settled on the familiar shape of the toy koala. She carried it over to the window – she found herself drawn constantly back to the view of the outside world. Leaning against the frame she stroked the soft fur. As she absorbed the rhythmic movements, she was aware of her breath becoming deeper and slower. She felt the warmth of the sun shining in through the glass, touching her face. She tuned her ears to the sounds she could hear. The distant clatter of pans from the kitchen. The hum of voices. A door slamming. She tried to imagine they were the sounds of an ordinary household. She tried to believe that everything was going to be all right, in the end.

The next time a guard peered cautiously into the room, making his inspection, Anna was still standing there, cradling the koala in her hands. As she turned around, he fixed his eyes on the toy.

'What have you got there?' he demanded.

She carried it across to him. He stared in surprise, then looked over at the *nkisi* as if wondering which of them had spawned this strange creature. Seeing the object through his eyes, Anna understood that with its animal fur – patchy with age – and the single glass eye, it looked at home here in the museum.

'It belongs to me,' she told the man. 'It was given to me when I was born. It's a koala bear, but it's made from kangaroo skin.'

The man looked at her blankly. She guessed he'd never heard of these animals. And he was probably puzzled as to why someone would use the skin of one animal to make a replica of another. She wondered if it was possible to convey the fact that there were many more kangaroos in Australia than koalas – therefore their lives were less precious. But it was too complicated even to begin to explain.

When the guard left her alone again, Anne returned once more to the window. As she gazed towards the distant rubber trees an image of her mother's face came to mind, evoked by the talk of her childhood toy. A spasm of pain gripped her heart as she pictured how horrified Marilyn would be if she knew what was happening to her daughter. Quickly Anna pushed the thought away. Contemplating Marilyn's anguish only added to the burden of her own emotions, which were already nearly too much to bear.

As the day wore on, and the Lieutenant had still not arrived, the guards brought Anna some food – bean stew and an unripe banana. She made herself eat, even though she felt nauseous. She wanted to preserve her strength for whatever was coming next.

But nothing happened. She made another visit to the toilet. She drank more water. She moved from standing at the window to perching on the plinth to sitting on the floor, and then repeated the cycle again. As the sun sank low in the sky and the daylight began to fade, she knew she would be spending the night in here. She shifted a grand sofa upholstered with gold brocade from the far corner of the room, dragging it over to the window. She tried lying down, covering herself with the curtain. The makeshift bed was comfortable enough, but she felt exposed in the open space of such a large room. Selecting some of the larger *nkisi*, she moved them across to the window as well, wrapping the bodies in the curtain to protect her hands from the spikes. She placed the statues in a circle, facing inwards – forming the boundary of an inner area, the sofa at its heart. She felt safer, then, as if the *nkisi* were her sentries, keeping watch over her. The koala rested on the cushion she was using as a pillow; the dog statue was at her feet.

When night fell, she lay awake gazing into the moonlight – longing for sleep yet afraid that the nightmare she was living would haunt her dreams. Eventually, exhaustion dragged her into unconsciousness.

The next morning Anna was woken by the sound of the door scraping open. She jerked up her head, eyes widening with shock as she remembered where she was. She had to take a few slow breaths before she was ready to stand up.

The young guard in the dressing-gown was waiting for her in the doorway. One sleeve of the mauve garment had been torn off and his left eye was puffy. Anna guessed he'd been in a fight. As he took her to the bathroom, he asked her how she'd slept, as if she were a guest in his hotel. She found herself responding to his friendly manner.

'What happened to your eye?' she asked.

'I drank too much whisky. I insulted another man. He was bigger than me.' The man looked shamefaced, like a schoolboy confessing to bad behaviour.

'You should put some ice on that bruise,' Anna suggested.

The guard appeared mystified, then laughed out loud as if she'd made a joke.

When they returned to the gallery, he produced a banana and a hunk of bread from his pocket. As he handed it over, Anna noticed a patch of pale skin on his forearm. She leaned across the threshold to look more closely.

'How long has that mark been there?'

'A long time,' he answered. 'Since the last harvest.'

'Does it hurt?'

He looked embarrassed by her interest. 'No.'

'Is it itchy?'

As he shook his head, Anna glanced back into the gallery. She scanned the floor, looking for the loose nail that had fallen from one of the *nkisi* when she'd dragged it over to the window. She couldn't see it, so she crossed to the nearest statue and tried tugging the nails until she found another that was loose. She indicated that the Simba should hold out his arm.

The man complied, watching her with wide eyes, a look of fearful fascination on his face. Anna touched the skin patch with the sharp end of the nail. It was a delicate task; you had to take care to touch lightly, all over. A nail wasn't as good as a pin, but it would do the job. She could tell by the man's lack of reaction that the whole area was completely numb. She could hear Harry's words in her head: *Hypopigmented. Asymmetrical. Hairless and dry. Raised surface. Defined edges . . .*

When she was finished she looked the guard in the eye. 'Listen to me. I have something important to tell you. You have tubercular leprosy.'

As he heard the word *lèpre*, the man stared at her in horror. 'No! I am sorry for what we have done.' He wrung his hands in desperation. 'It was not my decision to kill the old man. Do not punish me. I beg you.'

Anna looked at him in confusion. 'It's got nothing to do with me. What I want to tell you is that there is medicine for this disease.

A cure. You must go to a hospital. Take your family as well.'

'Please. Do not curse my family. They are innocent.'

The man backed away from her, half-running along the corridor. When he didn't return, Anna tried to raise the topic of leprosy with the other guards, pointing out that it was contagious, especially to children. But they claimed not to understand what she was saying.

After this incident the Simba guards treated her with even greater respect. They brought her cups of tea and pieces of fruit, leaving the offerings on the threshold. They patiently responded to her constant questions about the Lieutenant, explaining that he must have been delayed. They had lost radio contact with him. Anna had the impression the soldiers were as keen as she was to see the officer back here. No doubt they wanted advice about what to do with their captive.

She spent hours standing at the window, looking beyond the garden and the plantation to the distant jungle. She fantasised about running into the trees, disappearing into the undergrowth. Finding a way through the plantation to the main road . . . But she knew she had almost no chance of getting out of this room and along the corridor. If she did, she'd never make it down the stairs, let alone out of the front door and through the grounds. She kept coming back to the Lieutenant. She imagined how he would greet her with a friendly smile. How he'd be so sorry about what had happened. How he would set her free and deliver her back to the mission. She warned herself that it was a fragile dream. The officer might be no different to the monster who had killed Kendall – but there was no other source of optimism. And without some hope to cling to, she knew she would never survive.

TWENTY-SEVEN

Dan searched the ransacked office of the bank manager, looking for something to write with. Eventually he found a sheaf of paper – thick and soft, embossed with the insignia of the *Banque du Congo Belge*. A silver-plated fountain pen was located at the back of a drawer. Pulling up a padded leather chair, Dan sat down to write.

He pushed his pen along the page, forming words that seemed too bland for what they meant. *Casualty. Deceased. Enemy combatants.* After only a few lines he dropped the pen and sat back in the chair, stretching out his legs and letting his arms hang at his sides. He felt restless, sitting here at a desk. He wished he could have been out in the streets with the other men; they were touring the town, sector by sector, double-checking there were no remaining enclaves of rebels.

Glancing back over what he'd written, he sighed with impatience. Blair had asked for the report to be sent to him, stressing that it was to be Dan's top priority, even though there were much more important matters calling for his attention. Dan wasn't sure who it was for, but presumed someone at a higher level was demanding information – perhaps they wanted to know exactly how their money had been spent.

Dan had already debriefed with the Major by radio. He'd confirmed that Force Denby had taken control of Uvira. Only three days after their arrival in the town, elements of normal life were beginning to return to the community.

The task of defeating the Simbas had not been as difficult as Dan had expected. Earlier this morning, he'd learned the reason for this. He and Becker had interviewed the local police chief, Inspector Tabati. He was a Congolese man, only recently promoted to replace his Belgian predecessor. They'd sat in here together, their conversation punctuated by birdsong coming from the tree outside.

Inspector Tabati had given an account of what it had been like for the townspeople, living under Simba occupation. Early on, it was not too bad. Property was stolen; people were subject to ritual humiliation and beatings. Over time, though, the situation had deteriorated. There were reports of executions, rape and torture. The Congolese bore the worst of it, but there were European victims as well. Tabati had spent lots of time in the company of the Simbas, playing a tense game of cat-and-mouse with them, trying to appeal to the officers who disapproved of the behaviour of some of their colleagues. He had been able to negotiate the release of captive nuns, and the wife of one of the missionaries. But in many cases, there had been nothing he could do.

It was during one of his endless meetings at the Simba headquarters that Tabati had heard soldiers discussing radio reports that had come in from an outlying command post. They talked about the White Giants who were able to communicate with one another without needing to use words, and about their witchdoctor with a red beard who had the power to call down fire from the sky. The men were very afraid of having to fight the foreigners. When Air Support began bombing Uvira the Simbas started to talk of retreating before they arrived. A mutiny broke out. For a time, the Simbas had been shooting at one another. In the ensuing disorder four policemen were executed. One of them, Tabati explained, was his brother; the others were close friends.

He'd sat in silence for a time. He appeared to be still in shock. His voice was flat, his eyes dead.

A grim smile had appeared on Becker's face. 'A mutiny . . . Animals turning on animals.'

Tabati continued his account. 'The next morning, I saw trucks and jeeps loaded with Simbas, driving out of town. That was two days before you arrived.'

Becker had leaned towards Tabati, looking him in the eye. 'Filthy cowards. We'll get after them, don't you worry.'

Dan had made no comment on this promise. Force Denby's task was to stay and hold Uvira until the government forces arrived. The latest reports from headquarters said the Simbas were gaining momentum in some other areas of the Congo. There was plenty more work to be done. But Dan had not yet received word from Blair on what the next commando mission might be. He hadn't begun the task of deciding which men should be recommended for a new contract, or ascertaining who would be likely to accept. He didn't even know what he intended for himself. He just felt drained and hollow inside. This was quite normal at the end of a deployment, he knew – even a successful one. The action was over. The goal had been reached. But behind the relief and euphoria, a soldier soon began to count the cost. What had been gained, and at what price? Did the ends justify the means? They had to spend time looking back, before they thought about what might come next.

Dan rubbed his hand over his face, wiping away sweat. There was a ceiling fan but the electricity had failed again. Looking around the room, he took in the mess of papers, manila folders and stationery supplies that had been pushed into a pile in the corner. The wastepaper bins were overflowing with empty beer bottles, banana peels and pineapple husks: the aftermath of a Simba supper party. With Billy's help, Dan had collected up the rubbish, and someone now needed to remove it. But none of the men wanted to be stuck inside, doing mundane jobs, any more than Dan did. Billy – standing on guard duty on the front steps – had a sullen look on his face. Dan knew the young man wanted to be out parading the streets looking for girls to impress – which was exactly why Dan had kept him here.

It had not taken long for the Congolese prostitutes – elegant, long-limbed women with faces like ebony sculptures – to seek out the commandos. While the men were still erecting their tents on the cricket pitch, the ladies had appeared, dressed for the evening, their faces painted, though it was still mid-afternoon. No doubt they'd entertained the Simbas when they were in town; now they were eager to provide their services to these foreign soldiers. A couple of European women had turned up as well: Dan suspected they had the same agenda but they took a more subtle approach. A teenager like Billy would be easy prey to anyone who set her sights on him. Before the lad was let loose in town Dan wanted to make sure Doc Malone had a chat with him about the dangers of venereal disease, and handed over some French letters.

As the Commanding Officer, Dan was the big prize as far as prostitutes were concerned. They assumed he had higher pay to go with his status. The women targeted him any chance they got; one had even turned up here at the bank. Dan made it clear he wasn't interested. In the past, he'd sometimes paid for sex. Since he was always on the move, as a hunter, he wasn't in a position to offer anyone a long-term relationship. A business arrangement seemed the fairest option. But right now, when he thought of being with a woman, what came to mind was not a seductive vision of a firm body enfolding his. Or the weight of a breast, cradled in his hand. Instead he saw, in harsh clarity, a sheet marked with bloodstained semen; a body that was too still, the skin too pallid. And a bullet hole in a young nun's chest – a savage wound in perfect flesh.

Cutting off his thoughts, Dan looked up at a framed photograph above the door. It was of Monsieur La Plante, the bank manager. Someone had thrown a wad of chewed *khat* at his face – remnants still clung to his cheek. Dan wondered where the man was now. The process of accounting for all the residents of Uvira had only just begun, and La Plante had not yet come forward. It was quite possible that he was dead. On the other hand, he might be about to walk in the door at any moment. If he did, he would be dismayed. The rebels had used explosives to blow open the door of the safe. Whatever cash and valuables had been in there were gone. The whole place was a mess. But the building itself had not been damaged. The sturdy doors still hung in their frames. Window glass was broken but the bars remained a barrier. This was why Dan had chosen the premises for his command post. Security was vital. There was still the possibility that, hidden among the civilians of Uvira, there were Simbas in disguise.

Dan looked out through the open door of the office, towards the public area of the bank. When he'd walked in here two days ago he'd recognised the distinctive walls made of pressed tin decorated with leaves and flowers, painted green, and the terrazzo floor with the inset slabs of marble. He'd been in this bank once before, many years ago, when he was on a prospecting trip. He was newly married at that time – keen to finish his work and get back to his wife and his half-built home. He'd had to brush off his clothes and stamp the mud from his boots before entering. The tellers were hard at work handing over bundles of money to well-dressed customers. Expensive perfume mingled with the smell of beeswax polish. People spoke in muted tones. High heels tapped over the spotless floor. But the ambience of wealth and sophistication was jarred by the stark presence of wire mesh and bars. The tellers sat in caged enclosures – but whether they were being kept in or the customers were being kept out wasn't obvious. The scene could be read both ways. Dan had felt uncomfortable in the place, and as soon as he'd taken his turn at the counter, depositing a small amount of cash, he'd escaped outside.

Looking back to that time now, Dan wondered what he would have thought if he'd known that one day he would be sitting in the manager's office. Not a client doing business, but a mercenary soldier. A gun for hire. He would have been shocked to the core. But then, what would he have thought if he'd known he was going to be swept up in a world war? That he would learn to become a fighter, and find he was good at what he did? That he would leave his family as a husband and a father, and come back home to find he was nothing at all . . .

Dan looked up at the sound of footsteps, his hand moving automatically to his pistol. It would be easy to feel safe, enclosed in a building like this one – but he knew better than to relax. Maintaining vigilance when the crisis was over was not easy. It was for this reason that he'd ordered the men to set up a camp, even though they were keen to take rooms in one of the hotels. Dan wanted them to remain battle-ready. Once the sense of discipline and focus had dissipated, it was hard to rebuild.

As the footsteps came closer Dan recognised the brisk gait of the Signaller, Girard. The Frenchman walked up to the desk and saluted. A bystander would never guess the volunteer was still living under canvas; he looked as neat and tidy as a soldier in a garrison with a laundry at his disposal. His fastidious ways matched his work: he was very accurate. If he sent a message, he got it right. No detail was lost in transmission.

'At ease, Signaller.' Dan motioned him to approach the desk.

Girard handed over a written message, while also giving his verbal report.

'The arrival of the government forces has been delayed,' he said. 'They are in transit from Albertville. However, they are confronting rebel activity.'

'In the south?' Dan frowned. 'That could be the soldiers who retreated from here. But you'd think they would have run north, into Simba territory.'

'The road north from Uvira has been cut off.'

'What do you mean?' Dan asked impatiently. He could see the Signaller was savouring his role as the one who knew all the answers. He was keen to share his information, but liked to control the flow.

'A commando unit of twenty-five men is positioned about 60 miles from here. Paratroopers. Dropped in four days ago.'

Dan's jaw fell open in surprise. 'Paratroopers? Why didn't we know about this?'

Girard's face gave no response; it was not his job to speculate on the motives of his superiors. Dan guessed Blair had his reasons for keeping his secret, but he couldn't think what they might be.

After a short silence, the Signaller continued dealing out his information. 'The paratroopers are coming here to Uvira.'

'How are they travelling?'

'I have no information on that, sir.'

Dan answered his question for himself. They'd be commandeering vehicles from the Simbas, and maybe from civilians as well. He looked out of the window, the patch of blue sky fractured by wire mesh. He wondered what kind of outfit they were. It could be just a bunch of ordinary volunteers who'd been taught to jump out of aeroplanes. On the other hand, it could be a proper Special Forces unit. He turned back to Girard, his eyes adjusting to the shift from harsh to muted light. 'Are you in radio contact with them?'

Girard shook his head. 'Force Villeroy are not responding.'

'Villeroy?' Dan raised his eyebrows. 'Where did Blair get that from?'

A gleam of enthusiasm broke through Girard's impassive mask. 'My mother used to collect porcelain plates. One of her favourites was made by a German company called Villeroy & Boch. When Major Blair gave me the name, that's what I thought of . . .'

Dan nodded, a smile touching his lips. 'So he's picked up another piece of crockery.' It seemed a whole lifetime ago that Blair had found the name Denby on the bottom of a jug.

'That's all I have, sir,' Girard said.

'Thank you.' Dan dismissed the Signaller with a wave, his thoughts already turning to the meaning of what he'd just learned. He was soon to be joined by another unit. With more men to manage security, the soldiers could turn to helping with some of the other issues the town faced. On the other hand, the arrival of newcomers would upset the dynamics of his own force. And he didn't like the feeling that Blair had sprung this on him, perhaps deliberately. He could see the reasoning in forcing retreating Simbas towards the south, into the arms of the government forces. Cut off from the Simba heartland they'd be vulnerable. And they wouldn't be adding to the strength of the northern frontier. It made sense.

Except for one problem. Dan didn't like to think what was going to happen, down south, to the civilians caught in the middle. Gangs of Simbas on the run, driven by fear and heady with the freedom of being mutineers, would be more dangerous than ever.

Dan began to think of all the people he'd known, in and around Banya. His daughter came to mind first, of course – but he felt sure that as she grew up she'd have moved away. She'd have completed her education in Europe, and was now probably living somewhere like Paris or Brussels. He couldn't imagine Marilyn and Karl were still at Leopard Hall either. After Independence, as the supply chains broke down and infrastructure began to fail, their luxurious lifestyle would have become impossible to sustain. They would have felt insecure in such an isolated spot. No doubt they'd moved to one of the cities, or left the Congo altogether. Maybe they were in South Africa – it was a popular refuge for Europeans wanting to escape from countries that had gained their Independence; down there, the whites were still firmly in charge. Dan's reasoning only went so far, though. The fact was that he couldn't be certain Anna was not still at Leopard Hall, or living somewhere else in the Congo. He regretted his longstanding policy of avoiding any circumstance where he might hear news – even by accident – of the Emerson family. But there was nothing he could do about that now. He just had to believe his assumptions were correct: Anna was safe and happy in another part of the world.

Dan turned his mind to other people. The Bonhoeffers at the Lutheran mission. The Carters, who ran the general store in Banya. Bill McFarlane, who was the supervisor of the mine. The Makandas, who had taken over Dan's farm. All the other African neighbours. A dozen names and faces came to him. He'd left the country nearly twenty years ago. Many of the people he'd known could have moved away, or even died of sickness or old age. But some would still be there. They might already be caught up in the conflict. Or still be going about their normal activities, unaware that the decisions of a man called Blair, far away from where they were, had suddenly changed their fortunes.

As he thought, Dan's gaze ranged aimlessly over his desk. Then something caught his eye: a rubber stamp lying on its side. The raised letters stained with red ink spelled the word *URGENT*. His stomach tensed. He felt he was being called to take some action. But there was nothing he could do, beyond raising his concerns with Blair during the next scheduled radio communication. He was not in charge. He was just a pawn playing his part in a game being run by someone else. An image of the American Captain came to his mind: the tall figure with white skin and hair, who looked smart even in his fatigues. What had he said about the mercenaries? *We're sending our own animals in.* The words of ownership had stuck in Dan's mind. And then, Blair had hinted that the CIA was paying the mercenaries' bills. The fact was, Dan didn't even know what game he was caught up in. Now, the surprise appearance of Force Villeroy added to his unease. He could feel the ground under his feet shifting, his balance threatened.

He reminded himself of the expressions on the faces of the people of Uvira as they cheered the arrival of their liberators. Whatever else was going on, the relief and joy of these civilians was something real and true that he could hold onto. There had been that little girl, with the big dark eyes. The mother holding a tiny baby wrapped in a bloodstained towel, sitting on the pavement as if too exhausted to stand – but smiling . . .

Another image came to Dan, then. A glimpse of a face, seen through a shattered window. Wide eyes. A piercing look. He saw the bullet-riddled Jaguar speeding away. Since his arrival in Uvira, Dan had seen no sign of the distinctive car. But he hadn't been able to forget the encounter in the side street – the driver's face was fixed in his head. He had looked out for her at the meeting of European residents held at the Uvira Club. He'd toured the dining room, searching the crowd. Several beautiful women took the chance to meet his gaze. But he knew none of them was her.

Retreating to the bar, he'd asked the African cocktail waiter if he was aware of anyone who drove a Jaguar and had long red hair; in a place like Uvira the staff of the club were the richest mine of local knowledge. Kefa had shaken his head. He claimed he had a good memory and knew all the Europeans in the town – therefore the woman must be a stranger, newly arrived, or just passing through. But that made no sense, Dan had argued. Uvira had been occupied by the rebels for weeks, and under threat for much longer. It was hardly a popular destination for tourists.

The waiter had agreed. 'Perhaps you dreamed of her,' he suggested. 'You should have a drink, and forget about her.'

'You are right,' Dan had responded. 'I should.' But as he looked back towards the dining room, he had felt an odd sense of loss, as if he were giving up something precious. It was completely irrational. Even assuming the woman was real – and there was some reason why Kefa didn't know of her – there was nothing to say Dan would like her if they got the chance to meet. She was quite likely the spoiled wife of a rich plantation owner – the kind of person Dan had to tolerate in his safari work, but whom he would never want to know as a friend. It made sense to put her out of his mind.

'You look sad,' Kefa had said. 'Let me help you.'

He had prepared a cocktail that he called an Uvira Sunset. When he offered it on a silver tray, Dan had eyed the drink doubtfully;

shots of green, red and yellow liqueur had blended to form a muddy brown brew that looked like river water. It tasted mainly of sugar, but the fire on Dan's tongue promised to dull the edges of the emptiness he felt. He had swallowed it in two gulps, and ordered another.

The hospital corridor smelled of stale vomit and urine, only faintly tinged with disinfectant. The walls were stained and the floors muddy with footprints left by army boots. Dan passed an African man in an orderly's uniform wielding a mop, working ineffectually to combat the chaos.

'*Habari ya kazi?*' How is your work?

'*Nzuri sana, Bwana.*' Very good. The words were delivered with a bright smile.

Dan smiled back, struck by the optimism he so often encountered in Africa. He wondered if there were any level of disorder that would have forced the man to admit that circumstances were bad.

'You are here to see your friends?' the orderly asked.

'Yes, I am.'

The response came easily to Dan, yet it took him by surprise. At the beginning of Operation Nightflower he'd had no intention of making any of the soldiers into his friends. But now he felt a real bond with several of them, including Fuller. The unit had almost become like his family – or, at least, the closest thing to a family that he was ever going to have. The feeling was reciprocal, Dan knew. Lots of the men had been solitary figures, like him, when they'd signed up. That was why they were here. They might have taken on the idea of fighting against the Communists, to protect the free world – but really, they were just fighting their own isolation and loneliness.

Reaching the entrance to the European men's ward, Dan squeezed past a stretcher that had been abandoned in the doorway. A middle-aged nurse was bending over a bed, lifting the end of a mattress and folding the sheet into a hospital corner. As Dan walked towards her, she looked up.

'Good morning, Lieutenant,' she said, smiling brightly. One lens of her spectacles had been cracked and she had a bandage on her arm, but her uniform was neatly pressed, her shoes gleaming. She might have been on duty in an ordinary hospital, where everything was clean and functional – not one that had been overtaken by war.

Dan smiled back at her. 'How are my men getting along?'

'The Norwegian is full of complaints, except he's sedated at the moment. The Welshman is bored. I'm thinking of giving him the same medicine.'

'Sounds like they're doing well.'

Dan walked on towards the far end of the ward. He passed half-a-dozen empty beds, then came to an old man with grey hair who appeared to be unconscious. Dan couldn't help pausing, waiting to see the man's chest, shrouded in a white sheet, rise and fall before he moved on. Next he saw a young boy, curled up on his side. Wisps of blond hair protruded from a bandage that covered his head like a turban. Apart from Nilsen and Fuller, there were only six more patients in the room.

It had been a very different scene in here on the first morning after the commandos arrived. When Dan came to check that his men had been admitted, he found the place packed with Europeans. Some were sick, others were suffering from injuries. Many were traumatised; quite a few were just hungry. They flowed into the ward from the outpatients section. The Matron had only allowed the most serious cases to be admitted. Everyone else was sent over to the Catholic church where the nuns had set up a clinic for bandaging and basic medical care. Matron had to keep all the resources she could to manage the load on the main wards, which catered for the Congolese.

In these wards, every bed was occupied, with extra bodies placed on mattresses on the floor. A large number of the patients were rebel soldiers – in some cases lying right next to civilian victims of Simba torture. Now that the commandos were no longer on the move and had the backup of police officers, Dan had issued orders that any rebel who surrendered must be given care and protection. If they needed medical attention, they were to be brought to the hospital.

So far, Dupont was the only one of the commandos who'd been caught violating the new code. He'd been seen turning his back on an injured rebel who was begging for help, intending to leave him to die. Henning had been outraged by his actions, to a degree that had surprised Dan at first; then he realised the Legionnaire simply couldn't tolerate orders being ignored. As far as he was concerned, rules were rules: a firearm is never abandoned in the field; a song is never left half sung or a ration box only partially consumed; and an order to care for prisoners must be followed. Henning had threatened to break several of Dupont's bones. If Dan hadn't intervened, there could easily have been another patient in the European men's ward.

Dan had posted McAdam to guard the Simba prisoners. He was armed with his bagpipes as well as a banana gun. Even if the men had been capable of moving from their beds, Dan doubted they'd risk a confrontation with the White Giants' witchdoctor. He'd seen their faces when McAdam played his first tune, wanting to impress a Scottish nurse.

Dressed in hospital gowns, the Simbas didn't look like soldiers any more. They seemed lonely and confused, as if they weren't sure how they came to be here, so far away from their homes. And behind these emotions was fear. They were well aware that they were prisoners not of these Europeans but of the Congolese National Army. Allegiances in this conflict were strongly influenced by tribal loyalties. When the government troops turned up, the prisoners would find themselves in the hands of men who were not just military foes, but traditional enemies. They were being treated well for now, but their future was not bright.

As Dan approached the two beds occupied by his own soldiers, he saw Nilsen asleep, propped on one side to keep pressure off his wounded thigh. Fuller was reading his letter. Luckily the Welshman knew the words by heart: much of the writing had been obliterated by a dark patch of dried blood. As Dan stood by the bed, Fuller raised his hand in a salute.

'Good morning, sir.'

Dan pulled over a chair and sat down. 'I've got some good news. I received clearance for a medical evacuation. You and Nilsen will be taking a trip to Jo'burg. You're going home.'

Fuller smiled. 'Home . . .' He repeated the word, savouring its feel on his tongue.

Dan smiled back. 'Lucky you.'

'I've made a decision,' Fuller said. 'I'm going to take Nicholas away from that boarding school. He means the world to me and I want to see him every day. When Bronwyn died, people told me I couldn't look after him. They said a little boy needs a mother. And without a woman in the house he was better off in boarding school. But he doesn't like it there. He gets bullied because he's Welsh. He's homesick. So when I go back, I'm going to stand up to them. I don't care what anyone says.' Fuller's hands clenched as he spoke. 'I'll fight and I'll win. I'll have him home. What do you think, sir?'

It was a few moments before Dan could speak. When he did, his voice was husky. 'I think you are right. A man and his child can be a family.' He took a breath. 'I wish I'd known that a long time ago.'

Fuller met his gaze. Dan waved one hand. 'But the past is the past. You don't get a second chance.' He looked down at the floor. 'Just . . . don't change your mind. Stick to the plan.'

'I will,' Fuller said.

Dan stood up to go. 'I'll see you tomorrow, out at the air strip.'

As he walked away, he felt a lightness in his step. Fuller's boy was coming home. No more lonely dormitory, no more bullying. Tea every night with his dad. Football games in the local park. Dan thought of all the suffering that had filled the last weeks – the half-grown bodies of the *Jeunesse* sprawled in the tall grasses; the murdered nun; Hardy bleeding on the floor of the armoured jeep; all the dead Simbas with their useless charms hanging around their necks, blood pooling in their veins. Something good was going to happen now. It felt like one small, clear victory, the meaning of which would survive the test of time.

Dan stood at the edge of the cricket grounds looking across the rows of tents. Here and there a soldier had hung up some laundry to dry; there were a few civilian garments, the colours and patterns seeming frivolous beside the even tones of the uniforms. Otherwise the camp was neat and tidy. The unit vehicles were parked a little distance from the tents. One of the volunteers, trained by Fuller to be Second Mechanic, had made sure they were all cleaned, repaired and refuelled. The man had now turned his attention to a motley collection of jeeps and trucks that had belonged to the Simbas. These vehicles would be handed over to the government forces in due course, along with the cache of rebel weaponry that was stored in a locked room at the bank, but for now the items didn't really belong to anyone. Dan had already given a Land Rover and two jeeps away to a group of missionaries who ran an orphanage and a school. He recalled the gratitude on their faces at the prospect of becoming mobile again; their vehicles had been seized by the rebels and never returned. Lots of other residents of Uvira had approached Dan with various requests for help too. He had a long list in the notebook tucked in his pocket.

As he gazed across to the central pitch with its rectangle of smoother green, he tried to decide which issue to address next. His mind wouldn't settle, though. His thoughts kept drifting back to Fuller, lying in his hospital bed. When Dan had endorsed the decision to bring Nicholas home, and hinted that he had a personal connection to the issues Fuller had faced, a look had passed between the two men. Dan had almost opened up and told his own story. He imagined the relief of laying it all out, to someone who might truly be able to understand the agony of the decision he had made, all those years ago. But there was no point in doing that now. History could not be rewritten. You could go back through events again and again. You could examine the facts over and over, looking at them from every angle. But you couldn't create a different ending.

He took out his notebook and flicked through the pages. But the words were meaningless. The ink blurred in front of his eyes. When he lifted his gaze he didn't see the camp, or the wide swathe of patchy grass. His thoughts carried him back nineteen long years.

He was a young man again, dressed in a war-worn uniform, the smell of motorbike oil on his hands, the taste of dust in his mouth.

The garden at Leopard Hall was a mosaic of colour. The roses were in full bloom, their vibrant tones upstaged only by the iridescent turquoise of the peacocks that trailed their feathers over the lush lawns. Dan climbed off the old motorbike he'd borrowed to come out here, lifting it onto its stand. During the ride, he had begun to calm down. He'd told himself there might be some mistake. Marilyn and Anna had left their home – that was obvious. But exactly why and how this had happened was not certain. Musa, the African who had usurped the cottage, was not necessarily the most reliable source of information. As he'd turned over all the possible scenarios in his mind, Dan had given up planning ways to deal with Emerson; his focus had shifted to Marilyn. He clung to the hope that – assuming she was, in fact, living at Leopard Hall – she would be able to say something or do something that would mean the situation was not as he'd been led to believe.

The sight of the grand house, though, aroused his emotions again – his disappointment and shock; the sense of betrayal. On the front doorstep, he ignored the heavy knocker, formed in the shape of a leopard's head, and pounded on the wood with his fist. The door was opened by an African butler dressed in a long white tunic, with a leopardskin cap on his head. Dan didn't wait to be invited inside; he pushed past the servant, striding into the foyer. The air was unnaturally cold and faintly perfumed. Vases full of flowers coloured the edges of his vision.

'Where are they?' he demanded.

'The Bwana is not here,' the butler said. 'You must not enter.'

He eyed the intruder nervously, no doubt guessing the soldier might be armed.

'I want to see Marilyn.' Dan walked from room to room, the butler hurrying after him. He checked a library, with walls full of leatherbound books. He scanned a huge dining room, where silver gleamed on the sideboard. Then he opened a third door, entering a sunny space decorated in pastel tones.

Marilyn was sitting at a desk, her head bent over a pile of white cards.

'Is that you, Karl?' As she turned around, shock flashed across her face. She jumped up, dropping a gold pen. It rolled across the parquet floor until it met Dan's boot.

For a long moment, the two just stared at one another. Dan hardly recognised his wife. The long wispy hair was gone; so was the pink flush to her cheeks. Her skin was matte, smooth, with no hint of sunburn. Her eyes were lined with black, the lids a powdery green. Her mouth looked bigger, painted red. She wore high-heeled shoes and a silky dress. She was like someone from a magazine. A film star. Or royalty. The Queen of Leopard Hall.

Dan took a breath, trying to keep control of his reactions. 'I heard you were here. I went to the house.'

Marilyn nodded slowly. She gestured for the butler to depart. When they were alone, she covered her face with her hands. 'I'm sorry. I'm sorry . . .'

As she repeated the words, Dan looked at her in silence. He understood exactly what they meant. Musa had not misled him. He felt harsh accusations coming to his lips. He wanted to tell Marilyn that she was a shameless adulterer. She was greedy and weak. She'd ditched her husband for a rich man, while Dan was doing his duty as a soldier. But when he thought of the rough cottage on the hillside, and compared it with this place where Marilyn was now, he couldn't blame her for what she'd done. He knew her too well. She had always been attracted to wealth. That was why she'd chosen to become a governess, so that at least she could stand on the fringes of a world that was glamorous and sophisticated. When she'd married Dan she'd been content with a simple life for a while, because she loved him. But then he'd gone away. She'd spent too much time left on her own with Anna. No wonder she'd been tempted by a man like Emerson.

He gave her a steady look. 'I understand how difficult it must have been for you.' That was all he said.

Marilyn's eyes filled with tears. 'It was too hard. I couldn't manage.' She pressed her lips together, shaking her head helplessly.

Dan took a step towards her. The tears stirred up a thread of hope that finding her here, in another man's house, was just a nightmare that could be brought to an end. 'Marilyn, we can change all this. You can leave Karl. Come back to me.'

'I can't.' The tears spilled over, carrying a streak of mascara down Marilyn's cheek.

Dan wanted to put his arms around her, to comfort her. He searched her face for some hint of the love they'd shared. 'Yes, you can,' he insisted. 'We can get away from here. We could move back to Kenya. Start again.'

Marilyn shook her head. Her gaze travelled around the room. Dan saw her eyes resting on the pretty cushions and drapes, the porcelain ornaments, the fine silk rug. This was Marilyn's study, he guessed. She may have decorated it herself.

'I'm happy here,' she said.

Dan watched her resolve harden, the softness evaporate.

'I want a divorce,' she added. 'I'm going to marry Karl.'

Dan's lips moved as he struggled to take in the meaning of her words. 'I thought he already had a wife.' His tone was sarcastic and bitter.

'She went away. They are divorced now.' Marilyn looked down at the floor. After a short silence she continued. 'They didn't love each other any more.'

A sound came from Dan's mouth – a gasping laugh that was a cry as well. 'And now you don't love me any more.'

Marilyn lifted her gaze. 'I love Karl.'

Dan looked into her eyes again, wanting to know if she was speaking the truth – or if she was really just attracted by the man's wealth. But she was a stranger to Dan now; he could not tell. Jumbled thoughts flooded his head. He kept coming back to the cold hard truth: Marilyn was going to remain here with Emerson. His marriage was over.

'What about Anna?' he asked. He couldn't imagine how he could be a father to her, when she lived in a place like Leopard Hall.

Marilyn didn't answer; she just bit her lip, white teeth pressing into the red lipstick.

Dan felt a rush of fear. 'Where is she? Is she all right?'

'Yes, she's fine. She's . . . well. She's happy here, too.'

'Where is she?' Dan repeated.

'She's not at home.' Marilyn spoke quickly, then paused for a second before continuing. 'Her governess has taken her to Banya for a riding lesson. We're getting her a pony of her own. She loves horses. And dogs, too.' She was almost gabbling now, as if mundane talk could hold back what was coming. Dan noticed that her voice had changed, along with her face – the English accent she'd adopted in Kenya was now overlaid with a touch of something European.

'When will she be back?' he asked. 'I need to see her.'

'Dan . . .'

He flinched at the sound of his name on her lips.

'Anna doesn't remember you. She was so little when you left. And we've been here three years, now. She thinks Karl is her father.'

Dan stared at Marilyn, his blood turning cold. 'Didn't you talk to her about me?' He thought of the scenes he'd imagined taking place over the years: Marilyn showing Anna photographs of her father, adding new information, bit by bit, as the little girl became old enough to understand why her daddy had gone away.

'I didn't know if you were ever coming home,' Marilyn responded. 'We came here to live with Karl. She needed a father.'

She made it all sound like a simple equation, the ending obvious.

Dan was struck silent. He felt as if he'd fallen into a dark pit of pain, jealousy, despair. When he finally spoke his voice was thin and hoarse. 'So . . . what's going to happen now?'

'If you love her, you'll do what's best for her,' Marilyn said. 'You will let her be who she thinks she is. An Emerson.'

Dan's shock turned to fury. He grabbed a flimsy chair and sent it smashing into the wall. A picture fell, glass breaking. Marilyn recoiled from him, her eyes wide with fear. Dan could see that she was about to scream for help. He forced himself to stand still, to bring his hands to his sides.

In the tense stillness a clock ticked loudly. Suddenly Dan couldn't bear to be in Marilyn's presence any longer. He spun round and half-ran from the room. As he crossed the foyer his boots echoed on the tiles. The black-and-white squares passed beneath his feet in a blur.

Outside, he took a deep breath, but he still felt as if he were struggling for air. Though the sun warmed his skin, he was cold inside. He walked towards the motorbike in a haze of confusion.

He was about to throw his leg over the seat when movement in the shrubbery caught his eye. The leafy branches shook; then they parted. A small face peered out. Dan froze, his fingers gripping the handlebars. At first glance the little girl was a stranger. But then a shiver ran through him as he recognised vestiges of the baby face he knew so well. He murmured her name. 'Anna . . .'

'Hello,' she called across to him. She waved her hand. Dan felt his heart leap as he searched the open face and the dark, bright eyes.

'Would you like a cup of tea?' The words were fluent, with no hint of a baby lisp.

Dan's heart throbbed as he shook his head. 'I don't think so.'

'Please,' she insisted. 'I'm having a picnic.' She pointed back through the bushes.

Dan looked away towards the house. He felt a surge of anger that Marilyn had lied to him about Anna being in Banya. He wondered if she'd watched his departure through a window and was now about to run out and send him away. It wasn't a scene he'd want a child to witness. He let a few seconds pass. The door remained shut.

'Come on,' Anna pleaded, her head tilted to the side. 'It won't take long.'

Dan shook his head again. But he couldn't make himself walk away. Why should he? Anna showed no sign that she knew who he was. He wouldn't betray his identity – he wasn't going to reach into his daughter's life, on impulse, and turn it upside down. But he could sit with her, talk to her, just for a little while. What harm could that do? He pushed his way through a gap between two hibiscus plants, the red flowers brushing his face.

A blue-and-white checked cloth was spread over the freshly mown grass. A child's plastic tea set had been laid out. There were miniature pink-and-white plates and matching cups and saucers.

In the middle of the cloth were some lids that belonged to jars. They were piled with flower buds and torn leaves. There was a tiny bowl of gravel. A milk jug full of water.

'You can sit beside Koala.' Anna pointed towards the toy, which had been placed opposite her. The animal leaned to one side, tilted by the grass beneath it.

Dan was swept by a wave of recognition. He knew the contours of that furry head and body so well. He remembered the rounded ears, the quirky black line of the mouth. Hiding his emotions, he made himself take his assigned place, crossing his legs.

'He's lost an eye, poor thing,' Dan commented. He was amazed that he sounded so normal – inside, he felt as if his heart were being torn into pieces.

'It came loose,' Anna explained. 'My *ayah* sewed it back on, but she didn't do it very well.' She glanced around her. 'She'll be back in a minute. She's gone to get my sunhat. You have to tell her that I'm not bothering you. I'm not, am I?'

Dan shook his head. He couldn't take his eyes off her. She looked less like Marilyn than she had as a toddler. Did that mean she was more like him? Or just more her own self . . .

Anna leaned forward, looked at him intently. 'Why are you staring at me?'

'Because . . . you remind me of someone. But she was younger than you. Not even two . . .' Dan's voice faded to a whisper. He wondered if at some deep level – beyond memory – the cells of his daughter's body, mirroring his genes, might speak to her.

Anna cocked her head, curiously. 'Where is she now?'

'I haven't seen her for a long time,' he said. 'I went away to fight in the war. I didn't want to, but I had no choice. I only just got back.' If some part of Anna knew who Dan was, he wanted to explain the reason why he'd abandoned her for all these years.

'My daddy didn't go to the war,' Anna said. 'He was too busy.'

Dan caught his breath. *My daddy.* The phrase had dropped casually from the child's lips. Marilyn may have lied just now about Anna being in Banya, but she'd been telling the truth when she said Anna believed she was Emerson's child.

'Would you like some peanuts?' Anna offered the bowl of gravel. With clumsy fingers, Dan filled his plate.

Anna lifted a teapot next, raising her eyebrows and nodding towards her visitor's cup. Dan couldn't help remembering all the times – hundreds, maybe thousands – that he'd seen Marilyn enact this exact sequence of gestures.

Anna filled Dan's cup with water. She poured too much, and it overflowed onto his hand.

'Sorry.' She giggled. Her parted lips showed half-grown front teeth, their edges still ridged. Baby teeth clustered behind.

'I got money from the tooth fairy,' Anna said, as if reading his mind. 'I don't know how she got in. Mummy wouldn't leave the window open because of the air-conditioning.'

'Fairies are clever, and very small,' Dan said.

'I suppose so.'

There was a brief quiet as Anna served rosebuds to the koala. Dan stared into his cup, where strands of what looked like water weed floated in green swirls. He guessed there was probably an ornamental pond in the grounds, perhaps even a lake. He wanted to ask Anna where she'd collected the water. Had there been an adult around in case she fell in? Could she swim? Could she read? Did she still love nursery rhymes . . .

Using his thumb and one finger, he lifted the cup and pretended to drink. 'Very nice.'

Anna sighed. 'It's tepid, I'm afraid.'

Dan smiled, the cup poised against his lips. She sounded so grown-up, mimicking her mother again. But her rounded face, her milk-soft hands, still held echoes of her younger self. He longed to pull her to him and bury his face in her hair, breathing her smell.

'Are you going to come back another day?' she asked.

He couldn't answer. He felt tears burning his eyes. When she looked at him quizzically he just shook his head. 'I have to go now.' He placed his cup back on its saucer and got to his feet. 'Goodbye.'

Anna held up the koala, jiggling it in the air. 'Goodbye! Goodbye!' She threw him a smile, innocent and sunny.

Dan turned and walked away, pushing back through the hibiscus. He tried to fix the image of her in his mind so that it would always be there for him to see. But as he stepped onto the driveway and headed for the bike, he could feel it fading already.

He kicked the motor into life, then let out the clutch. Gunning the accelerator, he roared away from Leopard Hall. As he sped through the parkland, he lifted his face into the wind, the air blasting his skin. In his chest, his heart hammered with pain so deep that it felt like fear. In the plantation the rubber trees flashed past him, a grey blur behind his tears.

There had been another meeting with Marilyn a few days later, conducted in a private room in the Banya Hotel. Emerson had been at her side, his arm hovering protectively around her shoulders. He did most of the talking – adopting the assured tone of a rich and influential man who knew he would get what he wanted.

Dan had to listen to him laying out the facts of the situation. It was not complicated, Emerson explained. The returned soldier had no job, no house, no extended family. He had no home to offer a child. Whereas Emerson was in a position to offer Anna everything she might need or want, both now and in the future. There was a description of some of the luxuries Anna currently enjoyed. The governess. The *ayah*. The toys and clothes. She was six years old, Emerson reminded Dan. And she knew no other way of living.

She knew no other father.

Dan struggled to remain calm, to think clearly. It was like holding firm under gunfire, only there was nothing he could do to protect himself. While he let Emerson speak he watched Marilyn's face. When she'd walked in, he'd barely recognised her. She was wearing even more make-up than when he'd last seen her, as if she wanted to hide behind a mask. It was impossible to tell what she was thinking or feeling. Dan was torn between wishing he could be alone with her, and fearing it would be too much for him to bear.

When it was his turn, finally, to express his views, he made sure his tone was firm. He said that money was not everything. He didn't want his daughter to grow up in a place like Leopard Hall, surrounded by wealthy people, most of whom probably didn't even work hard for their living. He stated that he intended to fight for his daughter – he wanted to have shared custody. But Emerson pointed out that Dan had no money to pay a lawyer. And even if he did, the legal bid would fail. What judge would order a child who was used to living in a place like Leopard Hall to spend time with a man she didn't even know, who lived in an ex-army tent? How would she come to terms with the idea that Dan Miller was her father, when she believed that title belonged to someone else?

Everyone Dan spoke to – friends in Banya who were sympathetic to his predicament – endorsed Emerson's argument. And the truth was, Dan couldn't disagree with it himself. He spent long sleepless nights making up different future scenarios, but in the morning none of them looked sound.

In the end he accepted the proposal put forward by Emerson's lawyer. Dan would divorce his wife on the grounds of her infidelity. And he would permit her new husband-to-be to adopt his daughter. This legal framework would ensure the security and stability that a child needed to have. The documents were drawn up in Albertville and brought to Banya for Dan to sign.

When the day came for the transaction to take place, Dan had taken time off from the job he'd managed to get as a farmhand. He'd scrubbed the soil from his hands and changed into clean clothes. Arriving early at the hotel, he'd waited outside in the shade. As he watched the people who passed by, he wondered if any of them could imagine how he felt – a man who was about to sign away his fatherhood; a soldier who had found out there was no way for him to fight. The law was not on his side. Neither was popular opinion. And the most powerful weapon in his possession – his love for his child – was working against him. He remembered how Anna had looked when he'd seen her in the garden at Leopard Hall. Happy. Well fed. Healthy. Innocent and carefree. He knew he couldn't jeopardise all that. He loved her too much to dismantle her world when he wasn't sure what he could offer in its place.

Emerson's lawyer had greeted him on the landing – alone, as had been agreed. The man was dressed in a jacket and tie in spite of the heat.

'Monsieur Leclair,' he introduced himself, holding out a hand.

Dan gripped it briefly, then he was ushered into the meeting room.

'Let us get straight to work,' Leclair suggested. He spoke slowly, as if to make sure Dan could follow his accented English. 'You know the intent of the documents. They are all standard.' He gave Dan a steady look. 'I am led to believe you have made a number of verbal commitments to your wife as well. You have agreed not to make any contact with your daughter. You are going to leave the area. And so on.'

'That's right.' Dan's voice was barely audible.

'It is the best thing in a situation like this. It is kinder to everyone.'

Dan's gaze narrowed. He got the feeling the lawyer was speaking from experience. Was this something that had happened to other men? Other soldiers who had come home to their families, full of hope for the future, and just longing to be held, comforted, healed . . .

A waiter appeared at the door. 'Can I bring you some refreshments?'

Leclair waved him away. 'Monsieur Miller is not staying.' He gave Dan a sympathetic look. 'It is best to get this over with as quickly as possible.'

'In case I change my mind,' Dan suggested. He could feel his swallowed anger like a lump in his guts.

'I am sure you have thought this through very carefully. And you have come to the right decision.' The phrases fell easily from the man's tongue as if he'd said them many times before.

Dan ignored the chair that was pulled out for him, preferring to stand. The lawyer handed him a fountain pen, then turned the pages for him, pointing with his finger, the nails neatly trimmed.

'Sign here. And here. And here again . . .' Leclair said. 'I will be the witness. I can deal with all that later. Your . . . wife . . . has already signed, as you can see.'

Dan's gaze lingered on Marilyn's name. Even her handwriting had changed. He remembered how, in the days after their wedding, she'd practised her new signature – *Mrs Marilyn Miller*. She'd looked so proud and happy . . . Dan brought his hand to his mouth as pain sliced through him. He felt the devastation that lay behind his outrage at her betrayal. On top of the agony of losing his child, these other emotions were too much to bear. He stuffed them down inside him, like clothes into a kitbag – love and hurt bundled together, buried deep.

When the last dotted line had been filled, Dan stood still, staring down at the ink, the shiny black turning dull as it dried on the paper. The lawyer gathered up the pages, slipping them into his briefcase without delay, snapping the clasp shut. He held out his hand, but Dan just walked away.

In the lobby downstairs there was a stuffed leopard on display beside an ornate hat stand. Dan stopped to look at it, his mind searching for a new place to rest. He wondered if the trophy was a cast-off from Leopard Hall – the ears looked chewed, the coat patchy. There was a cowed look in its glassy eyes. The animal was like a vision of how Dan felt. All the power was gone from its once-lethal body. There was now wire in place of bones, straw standing in for muscle, and just a hollow space where its warm heart had once been.

TWENTY-EIGHT

Anna lay on the gold brocade sofa, a matching cushion propped behind her head. She stared up at the high ceiling where a family of geckoes stalked the rafters. Through the open window she could hear songbirds calling to one another and the gentle cooing of pigeons. She tried to draw the calm sounds inside her, imagining them travelling through her body, easing the tension that made her exhausted and alert, both at the same time.

Turning onto her side, she looked at the *nkisi* that were grouped around her. Something about the angle of the early sunlight reaching in through the window made them look even more sinister than usual. The eyes and chin lines were deeply shadowed, and the clusters of nails and blades thrown into sharp contrast. Anna had to remind herself of what Eliza had told her: that the *nkisi* took the place of written records in a community, and that the tokens hammered into the wood signified stories, dreams and promises just as often as threats or curses. Thinking of them this way, Anna wished she could add a symbol of her own – a tangible sign of her desperate hope to be freed.

Three nights and nearly four days had passed since her arrival at Leopard Hall – though it felt much longer. She thought all the time about the Lieutenant, wondering when he would finally return. Her anxiety made her restless. To pass the empty hours she took regular walks around the gallery. She set off, stretching her legs with each step. She always took a different pathway from one part of the room to another. Sometimes she skirted all of the *nkisi*, sticking close to the walls. Sometimes she passed to the left of the cabinets, sometimes to the right. It was part of the dance. It wasn't about trying to be safe, like her childhood counting of trees and banister posts. It was a matter of staying calm. And it helped keep away the creeping fear that four days would turn into five, then a week, or longer. And she'd still be here.

Returning to the window, she stared down at the garden. She was holding her koala, picking at a loose thread where a seam was coming apart. The tan dog she'd seen the first few times she'd stood here had disappeared and not returned. Now in its place there was a peacock, its tail feathers hacked short. The bird seemed confused by the loss of its colourful train. It wandered in aimless circles, stopping now and then to look backwards. Suddenly it flapped its small wings in panic, scooting across the grass and disappearing into the shrubbery. Anna leaned closer to the glass, trying to see the cause of its fright.

Two men appeared on the stone patio below. They were bent over a heavy load. Anna's stomach lurched with horror as she saw what they were dragging between them: the limp body of an African man. He wore army trousers but his torso was bare. He was being carried face down, his head lolling between his shoulders. A trail of blood smeared the flagstones behind him. The men pulled him on, across the lawn, his boots scoring lines in the grass.

As the soldiers disappeared behind a tree, Anna's head fell forward against the glass. She felt its smooth hardness against her forehead. Her mind wanted to put the ravaged peacock together with the dead man, as if the two violations were related. She knew it made no sense. It was just an attempt to find the reassurance of logic, connection, where there was none.

She'd only been standing there for a short time when she heard footsteps in the corridor and the sound of the guard outside the door scrambling to attention, picking up his gun. She turned round, tightening her grip on the koala. At moments like this she didn't know whether to feel hope or terror or something in between. The Lieutenant might be coming at last. Or it could be one of the Simbas bringing food. Or the worst might be about to happen.

The door swung open, revealing a man holding out a silver tray loaded with bowls and what looked like small tins of food. Anna recognised the face of the soldier, but he wasn't one of the regular guards. As she walked over to him she studied the tray with growing surprise. Until now, she'd only eaten simple food – fruit, vegetables, eggs – that she assumed had been plundered from the local people. It sometimes didn't even come on a plate, let alone a silver tray. Now her gaze travelled from a tin of *foie gras* to a jar of black caviar set on fine china crockery. There was a hunk of Christmas pudding, rich with plums. Someone must have been searching through the Leopard Hall pantry.

Anna raised her eyebrows questioningly. 'Why have you brought all this?' She had a panicked, crazy thought that this was her last meal.

'The Lieutenant has told us to take special care of you,' the man explained.

'He's here?' Anna looked over the man's shoulder towards the stairs.

The soldier shook his head. 'We have spoken to him on the radio. He has asked us to make sure you are safe and comfortable.'

Anna smiled. Hope burst up inside her. 'That is kind of him.'

'We are to treat you like a princess.'

Anna screwed up her eyes cautiously. His remarks were starting to sound extreme, but there was no hint of sarcasm in his manner.

'He has told us to make sure that no man touches you. Not even one bit.'

'Is he going to let me go?'

He shook his head. 'The Lieutenant admires white women.'

He was silent for a moment, just standing still holding the tray. The fishy smell of caviar suddenly made Anna feel ill.

'So, now you will have children.' He smiled, showing all his teeth. Anna saw what looked like a wad of chewed leaves, wedged against his purple gums. His spit was green.

'What do you mean?' Anna asked, her voice just a whisper.

'You are going to be his wife.'

When the guard had gone Anna retreated to the corner of the room, sitting on the floor, hugging her knees to her chest. The solid walls behind her back seemed to offer some sense of safety. Tormented by visions of exactly what her new role was going to be, she clung to the hope that there had been some misunderstanding, perhaps an error in the translation. But at the same time she knew the grim truth: she'd seen it written in the eyes of the guard, in his knowing smile.

She must have sat there for hours, her body frozen with shock and fear. She was surprised when the guard reappeared holding the silver tray, announcing that it was time for lunch. She left the food untouched, only drinking the tea, her trembling hand bumping the bone china cup against her teeth. The scenario was repeated in the evening. She kept her gaze lowered when the guard opened the door and set down the tray, as if she were already ashamed of the person she was going to become.

When it got dark she went to lie on the couch as usual. She huddled under the velvet curtain, sweating in the heat but feeling the need to be covered up. It was impossible to relax; her heartbeat felt too strong, her breathing too fast. Crossing to the window, she looked blankly into the night. She remained there until she was ready to collapse with exhaustion. She lay down again, but barely slept at all. When the morning dawned, light flooding into the room, she was almost too tired to be afraid any more.

It was still early when the guard appeared at the door with the breakfast tray. When he didn't put it down straight away, Anna eyed him in silence. It took her a few seconds to realise he had a look of brimming excitement on his face.

'*Vous allez en voyage,*' he informed her. You are going on a journey.

Anna felt a prickle of tension travel through her body. She couldn't tell if she was being given good news, or bad.

'Where to?'

'You are being taken to the Lieutenant. He is no longer intending to return to the House of the Leopard. We are bringing you to his new place of residence.'

'Where is that?' Anna dreaded hearing the answer to her question. She imagined another big house overrun with soldiers – this time, though, there would be no *nkisi* to shelter her.

'Somewhere north of here. That is all I know.'

'But there's fighting up there!' Even as she spoke Anna wasn't sure why she was protesting about danger when she was about to be forced to become the 'wife' of a Simba Lieutenant.

The soldier shook his head wearily as he responded to her

exclamation. 'There is fighting everywhere.'

He set down the tray, but Anna just stared at it. When it became clear that, once again, she was not going to eat anything, he took her to the bathroom. He told her to wash carefully, but not to take too long. When he led her back to the gallery, he stayed close to her as if afraid she might disappear.

'You must put on your best dress,' he advised. 'You want to please your husband.'

He retreated to allow Anna to get changed. She put on the plain-est clothes she could find – a simple cream shift and flat shoes. Then she packed up her suitcase, and stood ready to be taken away.

When the guard returned he looked puzzled by her outfit, but he was clearly in a hurry. Joined by another soldier, he escorted her downstairs, carrying her suitcase. Anna's gaze darted from side to side as she walked. She had the idea that there might be a chance to escape – to run off and hide in another part of the house. Glimpses of her surroundings seemed fractured, yet detailed. There was the tan dog, sprawled on the floor, its pink tongue draping onto the black-and-white tiles. Flies danced in the air, surrounded by dust motes. A boot caked with mud lay under a sideboard. She tried to pause, but she was marched straight to the front door, flanked by the soldiers. She barely had time to take in a view of the garden before she was being told to climb into the back of a covered truck.

'*Bon voyage*,' one of the guards said, polite and cheery, as if she were setting off on a holiday. She collapsed onto a bench seat. Several soldiers climbed in after her. The engine fired up, emitting a burst of fumes, then the truck rumbled slowly away. Before long, Leopard Hall was disappearing out of sight.

*

An ammunition box slid on the oil-stained floor as the truck bounced along the road. Anna grabbed her seat with both hands, trying to avoid bumping shoulders with the Simba who sat beside her. Diesel fumes blended with the smell of alcohol that wafted from his mouth, turning her stomach. A machine gun rested across his knees. He played with the safety catch, flicking it on and off. The soldier opposite her – an older man with a half-healed burn on his cheek – stared down at the floor. There were two other men. They kept their faces aimed towards the open end of the canvas awning, where the orange ribbon of the road stretched away into the distance.

Anna bent her head, staring down at her hands. Her skin looked sallow – the light inside the truck was tinted brown as if the colour of the canvas had leaked into the air. Wedged between her feet was her suitcase. With each bump it hit the seat but she didn't bother to move it. She felt paralysed – trapped like a fly in a web. What she did or said or thought had no meaning. She estimated the truck had been on the road for over two hours now. For most of that time it had been followed by an open-backed Land Rover carrying more soldiers. But just a short while ago the second vehicle had drawn to a halt without warning. The truck had stopped as well. During a shouted conversation Anna had learned that the Land Rover had a flat tyre. It was agreed that the truck would drive on. The Land Rover, which could be driven faster, would catch up when it had the new tyre in place. The Simbas were obviously keen to get to their destination as soon as possible.

Anna looked out through the back of the truck, scanning the empty road. It was narrow and rutted; the forest grew in close to the verges. She measured the distance to the canvas opening, picturing herself lunging towards it, throwing herself onto the road, escaping into the trees. But even if she made it out of the truck, she knew that by the time she got to her feet she'd be cut down by a bullet.

As she was gazing helplessly at the patch of blue sky, a low rumble – like distant thunder – penetrated the noise of the truck. The soldier beside her sat up straight and alert. The sound grew louder. Then a black shape appeared in the sky: a small black cross, growing bigger, nearer.

'It's a plane!' Anna announced. There was a note of triumph in her voice – she had the irrational idea that its appearance meant she was going to be rescued. She watched the aircraft drawing closer and closer, the twin propellers now visible. The way it travelled, dipping and weaving, reminded her of a toy. Leaning forwards, she trained her eyes on the sky. It soon became clear that the plane was following the line of the road as if it were, like the truck, confined to the narrow pathway.

Urgent words passed between the Simbas. Their eyes rolled with fear, the whites standing out in the muted light. Anna felt a chill of terror as she understood what was happening: the plane was tailing the Simba vehicle.

The truck engine revved, then the brakes were slammed on, as if the driver couldn't decide how to respond. A powerful roar filled the air. The vast hulk of the aircraft was now so close it seemed as if it were going to land on the truck. Suddenly, flashes burst from the middle of each wing. The road erupted into a thick cloud of dust. Anna screamed as the canvas tore apart. Beside her, the soldier's body was flung to the floor. She felt a blow, like a fist punching into her body. The next instant she was rolling over and over like a tumbleweed – out through the remains of the canvas, hurtling through the air, thudding into the ground. She saw the truck accelerating away, but then it was hit by another explosion.

A limp figure flew out of the driver's door. The vehicle veered into a tree and stopped, the door hanging open.

The roar died down as quickly as it had built up. Anna was engulfed in silence, her ears deafened. Her heart pounded as if it were trying to break out of her chest. The air felt as though it had been sucked away beyond the reach of her mouth. She was frozen with shock, unable to think. A burning pain came from her leg.

Only moments later the scenario was replayed – the plane circling round and swooping back down. Anna covered her head as more shells pounded the earth, shrapnel flying into tree trunks, snapping branches, ripping bark. As she looked up through a curtain of dust, the truck was hit again. It transformed into a ball of fire and black smoke.

The plane pulled away, climbing against the sky. Anna saw a Simba thrashing on the ground not far away – a silent pantomime. The movement lasted only seconds, then the body became still.

Anna spat dust from her mouth and blinked to clear her eyes. A burned sulfur smell caught in her throat. Yellow-brown smoke hung in the air. From where she lay she could see dead soldiers on the road. Some were missing limbs, the severed pieces scattered at a distance from the bodies like discarded clothes. Flames licked the cabin of the truck. Shreds of burning canvas hung like bunting from the metal frame of the canopy. Dotted around the scene were ammunition boxes, kitbags, rifles and other items. As far as Anna could tell, she was the only survivor – when the shell hit its target she must have been sheltered from the impact by the bodies of her guards.

Raising herself onto her elbows, she looked down towards the source of the pain. The cream dress was pulled up around her waist, exposing her legs and underpants. Her gaze skimmed past dozens of small wounds – cuts, grazes, scratches – fixing on a deep gash in her left thigh that was bleeding badly. As adrenalin kicked in, her thoughts raced. She remembered the Girl Guide first-aid course she'd done years ago: there had been instructions about how to apply a tourniquet. Searching the ground nearby, she saw a piece of khaki cloth that looked like the remains of a jacket. She clawed her way over to it, dragging the injured leg. Her shoes had come off, and she dug the toes of her right foot into the road, gaining purchase on the loose surface. When she had the cloth in her hands she managed to tie it around her thigh, gasping in agony as she pulled the ends together and tightened a half-knot.

She turned to look down the road. Heat shimmered in the air; the only movement came from a lizard that waddled across the track, detouring around a pothole. In the distance she could see a simple bridge made from fallen logs – apart from that, there was just the narrow ribbon of orange gravel, hemmed in on both sides by the forest. She wondered if the Land Rover had been attacked like the truck: it was a much smaller target, harder to see from above. She tried to estimate how soon it would arrive, assuming it was still on its way here – but she had no idea of the time needed to change a tyre. Shifting her attention, she eyed the edge of the forest. The closest trees were only a short distance from where she lay. This was her chance to escape – but she had to get off the road and out of sight before it was too late.

Dragging her wounded leg, she forced herself to crawl towards the verge. The pain deepened with every movement she made. Only her fear of being recaptured kept her struggling on. She fixed her eyes on the tree trunks, the bushes, the velvety gloom of the forest floor. Ferns parted, brushing her face as she finally entered the undergrowth. It was cooler in the shadows, the air clear of smoke and dust. Though she wanted to stop there, she pushed herself on, edging deeper into the thicket.

She didn't rest until she could no longer see the road when she looked over her shoulder. If the Simbas arrived, she hoped they'd assume her body was part of the charred wreckage of the truck. A thorough search might uncover clues that this was not the case – in spite of the khaki bandage, Anna was still bleeding; there would be a telltale trail of red. Also, she didn't know whether her shoes had been burned in the truck or were lying on the road somewhere. But she was counting on the soldiers being keen to move on in case they met a similar fate to that of their comrades.

Finally, she collapsed onto the ground. Her heart hammered in her chest and her breath came in gasps. As her hearing slowly returned she strained her ears into the distance, listening for the sound of the Land Rover. The throbbing pain radiating from her thigh was now spreading through her body. At first she fought against it, clenching her fists, gritting her teeth. But as shock turned to exhaustion, she gave in, letting it sweep through her in waves – wrapping her in its grip, dragging her down into blackness.

A trail of ants crossed the leaf-layered ground, antennae probing the air. Anna watched them approach her fingers, but she barely had the strength to move her hand. It had taken all her energy to sit up and then drag herself across to a tree, resting her back against the trunk. When she'd first regained consciousness and found herself lying on the ground, all she'd been able to think of was the pain that pounded through her. She didn't even know where she was. Now her fear had crowded back in, raising her heart rate again.

She had no way of knowing how long she'd been hiding in the

forest. It felt like hours, yet visions of what had taken place out on the road kept flashing through her head, as stark and detailed as if they had only just occurred. The memories came in fragments. She saw a helmet flying through the air. Red earth spurting up like a fountain from the road. The silver tray borrowed from Leopard Hall rolling over the ground. A severed arm, still encased in a shirt sleeve, dangling from a branch of a tree.

Anna shook her head to clear this last image from her mind. She moved her hand to her lap, resting it on her knee, and watched the ants continue on their way – an army marching neatly in unison, ten abreast. Then she examined her thigh, checking that the bleeding had stopped. To her dismay, fresh blood was pushing up again, through the cloth that covered the hole; the pressure was not sufficient to staunch the flow. She undid the knot and tried to pull the bandage tighter, but her fingers were shaking and weak.

Exhausted by the effort, she let her head fall back against the trunk. She ran her tongue over her lips, then swallowed saliva, trying to soothe her thirst. She'd had nothing to drink since leaving Leopard Hall, and had lost a lot of blood. Dehydration was making her light-headed: her thoughts were hard to string together. She couldn't decide what to do. She wanted to get back to the road – there might be a water canteen somewhere among the debris. But she couldn't risk being caught out in the open. Even if the Land Rover never appeared, other Simbas might arrive at the scene – the Lieutenant was expecting the delivery of his wife; he could have sent out troops to see why she'd been delayed. On the other hand, she couldn't just stay here in the forest. She needed urgent medical care. She had to get to a hospital. She imagined Harry examining her, his hands steady, his voice calm. He'd pack the wound to stop the bleeding. If a donor could be found, he'd order a transfusion. Or he'd set up a saline drip. The wound would be cleaned. Maybe surgery was required. A course of antibiotics would be started straight away. Infection bloomed in the tropical heat – everyone knew that. Gangrene was a risk. The leg could be lost. But none of these considerations would matter, Anna knew, if she kept on bleeding. Exsanguination would occur. She wondered how many hours she had left, before she would die.

Closing her eyes, she let the haze cloud back into her mind. The noises of the forest seemed to grow louder as if her other senses were compensating for the loss of vision. She heard insects buzzing and clicking, and the bell-like call of a bird. There was a distant sound like a rushing stream, taunting her with the dream of cool water – but it might have been the product of her thirst. There was a peeping noise, too, that could have been a frog, except it came from the leafy canopy above. Perhaps it was a climbing frog. Anna felt an impulse to laugh at the idea – a tree frog. It was the kind of thing Sam would make up as a joke. She could feel hysteria building inside her; she knew that if she did start laughing, she would not be able to stop. She tried to focus on where she was – on the smell of toadstools and damp leaves, on the salt tang of blood on her lips.

It took a few moments for her to notice when the sounds ceased – first the birds abandoned their songs, then the insects fell silent as well. Her body stiffened, a shiver travelling up her spine. She picked up a shift in the atmosphere, like a change of pressure in her ears. The sensation was impossible to describe. She just had a feeling that she was being watched.

Slowly she lifted her face. She found herself looking straight into two yellow-green eyes – wide and shiny, with dark pupils, the lids outlined starkly in black. She took in the tawny coat speckled with brown spots. Thick white whiskers fanning out from a black triangle nose. The jaw hanging open, lower incisors standing up like sharpened pillars. She caught a glimpse of a pink tongue.

Anna gasped, pressing herself back against the tree.

The leopard stood motionless. It was only a few yards away from her, at the edge of the small clearing. Breath rasped in and out of its mouth, making a soft purr. Anna whimpered with fear. As if in response to the sound, the animal's top lip curled back, skin wrinkling behind its nose. The upper teeth were revealed – even longer and sharper than their lower counterparts.

Anna braced herself for the attack. She knew from watching the Siamese cats at the hospital how the claws, curved and sharp, would be unsheathed from the silent padding feet. She imagined the teeth closing over her throat.

As the huge cat took a step closer, she screamed. The cry reached out through the trees, but Anna knew there was no one to hear – no one to come to her rescue. The green eyes widened; the shoulder muscles bunched. For a long moment the leopard was poised on the brink of action – rocking forward; flinching back. Then it lifted its head, tilting it a fraction to one side. The movement was infinitesimal, but hinted at a change of mood. The animal took a step backwards, followed by another, the actions so fluid that it seemed ethereal.

As silently as it had arrived, the leopard retreated into the bushes, the mottled coat merging with the leaf-patterned light, twigs and leaves left waving in its wake.

Anna stared wildly after it, searching the trees. Though the animal was out of sight, she knew it was still there, watching her. She kept scanning the bushes. She had the idea that if she looked away, the leopard would attack; if she could just keep her gaze constant and unwavering, the predator would be held at bay. The idea had no grounding in logic – it was as senseless as counting tree trunks and banister posts. But it was all she could think of to do.

Time seemed frozen, the air breathless. Anna scoured the shadows constantly, seeking any sign of tawny fur, dark spots, the gleam of an eye. But there was nothing. Seconds turned into minutes, then time stretched out further. She pressed her hand against her thigh, feeling the seeping wetness. Her throat was raw, as if it had been scoured by the screaming. She let her head drop forward, her chin resting on her chest. Her eyelids lowered, then closed. There was no point in fighting. Whether the leopard came back for her, or she bled to death – she knew that this was the end.

TWENTY-NINE

The blast of a car horn, embedded in the raw engine noise of a vehicle with no muffler, brought Dan to the front windows of the bank. Billy was standing on the steps staring in disbelief at the car that had just drawn up. It was an ordinary Buick sedan, but there was a dead bushbuck strapped onto the roof. The animal's head with its pointed horns hung down over the side windows. A human skull and two crossed bones were mounted on the bumper bar. A white bra hung like a flag from the radio aerial. In the company of these bizarre adornments the radiator grille had the look of a set of chrome teeth.

A fair-skinned man wearing a paisley shirt climbed out of the back seat. He yawned, stretching his arms above his head. The shirt fell open, revealing two ammunition belts slung across a bare chest. Three more European men emerged, all carrying automatic rifles. Only one of them wore a uniform – a green paratrooper's jumpsuit – but in place of a beret he had a bandana made from what looked like a piece of curtain material. A young chimp rode his hip like a baby. As Dan watched, the man took a long swig from a beer bottle.

Dan strode outside, just as a second vehicle arrived. This one was a jeep, fairly new, but filthy. The driver and passenger wore straw sunhats along with army trousers. They'd torn the sleeves from their shirts, revealing suntanned biceps patterned with tattoos.

Billy turned to Dan, wide-eyed. He gripped his gun, but kept the barrel pointing down.

'Looks like our paratroopers have arrived,' Dan said dryly. 'They haven't had a chance to tidy themselves up.'

In the seconds it took for him to scan the men and their vehicles, Dan pieced together the story behind what he could see. The soldiers of Force Villeroy had not limited themselves to commandeering vehicles. They'd been looting civilian property, hunting game, desecrating a body – and who knew what else. He wondered what had happened to whoever was meant to be in charge.

'Lieutenant?' The man in the paisley shirt walked up to Dan. He gave a lazy salute. 'Pleased to meet you.' He spoke with a slow drawl, reminiscent of an American accent but mixed with something else. 'I'm Captain Swain.'

Dan's hand froze, his salute half-formed. This man, wearing what Blair would call 'fancy dress', was Villeroy's Commanding Officer – and a captain.

'The rest of my boys are settling in at the hotel,' Swain continued. 'But I thought we'd call in here first.'

Dan forced himself to gather his composure. 'I'm pleased to meet you. Sir.' Looking behind him, he gestured towards the interior of the bank. 'This is the command post. Come inside and I'll show you around.'

Dan did a mental tour of the premises. The place was looking more presentable now. The rubbish had been removed and the rooms tidied. Becker had taken over the Assistant Manager's office, but there was still more space for the newcomers to occupy.

'I don't need to see it,' Swain said. 'We're moving over to the hotel. Much more comfortable than a bank.'

'It's less secure,' Dan stated. 'The situation here is —'

'The hotel looks fine to me.' Swain cut off Dan's words. 'Plenty of room, food, drinks . . .' He squinted up at the sun as he talked. Deep wrinkles around his eyes showed his age – pushing sixty, at least. Long in the tooth for a paratrooper. Dan guessed he was another of Blair's old colleagues from Katanga, perhaps employed without an interview like Hardy had been. Dan glanced over the other men. Most of them were of a similar vintage. They might have fought with the bands of mercenaries who had earned the nickname *Les Affreux*. Whatever their story was, they were old hands at their trade; they hadn't become such dissolute characters in the five short days since they were dropped into Kivu.

'Come and see me,' Swain instructed Dan. 'I'll be in the bar.'

Dan eyed the man in silence. Swain was a captain. His rank was senior to that of a lieutenant. But Dan was still the Commanding Officer of Force Denby. He didn't have to take orders from the man who was in charge of this rabble. And if the two units were going to be working together, Dan needed to make sure his status was respected. This was the moment to take some initiative.

'Let's just get started in here,' he suggested. 'There's a lot of work to do. I'm keen to fill you in.'

Swain didn't move. He planted his legs a little apart as if braced for a round of sparring. The silky shirt gleamed in the sunshine. 'I might as well make things clear,' he said. 'Your men are to be brought into Villeroy. You'll be reporting to me.' He grinned. 'I feel sure we'll get along fine. As long as you can loosen up, man. Take it easy.' He looked past Dan's shoulder towards the entrance to the bank. 'How did you go with the safe?'

Dan gave no answer. He looked along the street towards the

Hotel Uvira. Its grand entrance was flanked by potted palm trees, now stripped of all their fronds, just the trunks sticking up. The green-and-white striped awning was in tatters; during the Simba occupation it had apparently been slashed by soldiers playing with knives. He wondered how the owners, Monsieur and Madame Dormier, were going to react to the arrival of this new group of mercenaries; the Belgian couple had only just become free of the rebels and now another lot of undisciplined soldiers was about to descend.

Taking a deep breath, Dan looked back at Swain. He forced himself to salute, then turned and walked away. Billy followed him inside.

'What did that all mean?' the young man asked. 'Is he the new boss?'

Dan turned to face him, looking him up and down. 'Get your face clean, soldier. And find your beret.'

'Yes, sir.'

'Then go and get Girard,' Dan instructed. 'Tell him to come straight here.'

On the pavement outside the hotel, a group of the paratroopers was playing cards. They sat on ammunition boxes drawn up around an antique table they'd dragged from the foyer, ignoring the protesta-tions of Madame Dormier. As they slapped down cards and called out their bets, they swigged from bottles of beer. The man with the pet chimpanzee was amusing himself burning a thick wad of Congolese bank notes, one by one, in an ashtray. The ground at his feet was strewn with banana peels.

Dan was standing nearby, trying to have a conversation with

Swain. Several hours had passed since the arrival of the paratroopers. It was now late afternoon. The Captain had exchanged
his patterned shirt for a jumpsuit. It was cinched in at the waist
with a belt made of leopardskin, obviously taken from a Simba,
dead or alive. He wore a beret, but there were no badges to indicate
his past service.

'Just go over that again, Lieutenant,' Swain said. He swatted a
fly from his neck, then studied the remains smeared on his palm.

Dan was explaining what he'd learned from Tabati about the
mutiny and the retreat to the south. The importance of the subject
warranted a formal briefing, but Swain had insisted on standing
outside in the sun. Dan had been unable to reach Major Blair by
radio, so there was no third party to mediate. Dan had no choice
but to try and find a way to work with the Captain. There were
issues that required urgent attention. Girard had picked up a radio
transmission from a Methodist mission station. The person speaking
was safe right now, but had heard of other Europeans being taken
hostage. The situation was quickly turning into a crisis.

'My proposal is that I take my men and go south,' Dan said.
'There are missionary families out on their own in the bush. And
other Europeans as well, on the plantations, and around the mines.
I'm very concerned about their safety.'

'The government army has men down there.'

'They'll be sticking to the main road and the towns along the
way. We can't rely on them.'

'That's true,' Swain agreed. 'And they're bloody useless anyway.
I've been involved in plenty of conflicts in my time. I've never seen
such a hopeless bunch of amateurs.'

Dan bit back a response. He wondered if Swain had any insight
at all into the soldiers of the National Army. They were mostly

reluctant fighters who'd signed up to earn a meagre wage and now just wanted to go home. They were tribal people, on the whole, who didn't embrace the idea of the Congo as a nation, independent or otherwise. They didn't even know the difference between Communism and Capitalism. The power brokers in the cities meant nothing to them. Regardless of who won this conflict, they didn't expect that their lives were going to improve.

'I'll get onto the people in Albertville and see about stirring the Congolese along,' Swain said. 'Meanwhile, I'm sending you north. There's unfinished business up there. You'll get a full briefing.' He nodded towards a bundle of papers that he'd dumped on the edge of one of the concrete urns. 'I've got new contracts for your people to sign. And one for you, of course.'

'I request that you reconsider, sir,' Dan began. 'The situation is urgent. We could end up with civilians being used as human shields by the Simbas.'

'Where would they get that idea?'

Dan's jaw clenched. 'Well, it's not new, is it?'

Swain looked interested. 'Have you seen it done?'

'I met someone, once, who was present at the Vinkt massacre.'

Swain nodded vaguely. 'Remind me.'

'The Wehrmacht captured more than a hundred refugees who were trying to escape from a town in Belgium, and used them to form a human shield so they could cross a bridge under fire. About eighty of the hostages died.'

'All right, I get your point. I'll seek further Intelligence,' Swain said. 'Let's put that fellow Becker of yours onto it. I've just had a drink with him. He knows his stuff . . .'

Dan pressed his lips together, saying nothing. He wasn't surprised the Captain had already formed a connection with the

Sergeant. They made a good pair. Dan didn't trust either of the men to make a priority of rescuing isolated families. They had bigger fish to fry.

'Meanwhile,' Swain added, 'I suggest you and your men get used to the idea of looking that way.' He swung his arm, pointing past the denuded tops of the palms, towards the north.

It was at this moment that Henning and Bailey rounded the corner. They'd just returned from touring the perimeter and were due a couple of hours off. Henning was dressed impeccably, as always. Bailey looked quite presentable as well. Since arriving in Uvira, he had started wearing a full uniform. Dan didn't know if he was being influenced by the presence of the matrons of the town, who perhaps reminded him of his mother, or by a desire to impress the younger women. Regardless of the reason, the smarter dress suited him. He looked not only cleaner but healthier, somehow. Now, at the end of the shift, his shirt was half-unbuttoned – revealing the head and shoulders of the eagle tattoo – but it was still neatly tucked in.

As the two men caught sight of the newcomers, Dan watched their faces freeze and their postures transform. He was reminded of cats responding to an alien presence, fur lifting, limbs growing long and tense. Muscles coiled, ready to spring. He guessed this was a territorial response rather than anything personal – it was unlikely that Henning and Bailey both had past history with any of these men.

One of the paratroopers stood up. He took off his shirt, showing his chest, which was emblazoned with a tattoo of a tiger. As he watched Bailey approach, there was a tilt to his jaw, a faint sneer on his lips. Dan could see a contest of will and ego looming that was going to end in bloodshed.

Dan had no choice but to end his conversation. 'If you would just excuse me, sir.'

Swain waved him away, looking quite happy to join the group around the table. Dan marched along the street to accost his men. He handed Henning the keys to the Land Rover. 'You're driving,' he said. 'Let's go.'

For a few seconds, the pair looked torn. But as Dan met their gaze, they snapped to attention.

Once they were inside Dan's vehicle, he explained who the troops were. Then he broke the news that Swain was now in charge.

'You're fucking kidding,' Bailey said. 'He doesn't even look like an officer. And as for the pack of animals he's got with him . . .' He spat out through the window.

Dan quelled a desire to smile. The man sounded as outraged and judgemental as a reformed smoker being asked for a light.

'I haven't been able to get onto Major Blair yet,' Dan said. 'So let's just wait and see. There might be a misunderstanding.' He tried to sound reassuring, but the fact was that Blair had made the decision to send the Captain and his men to Uvira. It was a reasonable plan for the two units to be merged, but why hadn't a lower-level officer been selected for Villeroy, so that Dan could be in charge? He felt hurt and betrayed, on behalf of his men as much as himself. It felt as though the success of Nightflower had not been recognised. Then, there was the puzzle of why Blair hadn't sent men of a better calibre. Perhaps there weren't many recruits for him to choose from. He may have had no room to move. Maybe the decisions were even coming from someone else. Dan knew he would probably never know the answers to these questions.

They set off in the direction of Sector Seven, the next area due to be checked. Dan didn't expect to see anything suspicious there;

he was really giving Henning and Bailey the chance to absorb the information they'd just learned. And if he was honest, he needed some time out to try and adjust to the new situation as well. He sat in the passenger's seat, his arm draped over the machine gun. Henning drove with his usual mechanical precision, while staring through the windscreen from under a lowered brow. Behind him sat Bailey. He kept kicking the seat with his boot, creating a restless staccato beat that Dan knew would soon start to annoy Henning. None of the men spoke; a moody quiet enveloped them.

After driving for some time they reached the narrow streets of the sector. Dan's gaze trailed over the lines of small huts. This was a poor part of town, where only Africans lived. The air smelled of charcoal, kerosene and open drains. There was a large square of common ground worn bare by foot traffic. Women dressed in bright clothes sat there in groups, on mats spread over the earth. In front of them were piles of peanuts and small pyramids of tomatoes and yams.

A little boy rode a scooter between the mats, raising dust and squashing a bunch of greens. A woman shouted at him, but the kid just grinned and kept going. Dan smiled at the scene. It was so ordinary. Only days had passed since this place would have been silent and empty, the people driven inside by fear of what might happen during the showdown between the Simbas and the White Giants. It was extraordinary how the natural life of a place asserted itself after a crisis. The same scenario was being played out all over Uvira, among the Europeans just as much as here.

When they neared the boundary of the sector, the scene began to change. The streets became wider, the houses more solid.

'Do you want to keep going, sir?' Henning enquired. 'Or head back to base?'

'Back to base,' Dan replied. 'It'll be dusk soon.' He sighed, mentally preparing himself for another encounter with Swain. When Henning reached the next corner, he took a turn to the right. The lake was visible in the distance. Lit by the late sun, it was like a swathe of pink satin.

Dan looked idly out at the passing buildings. Henning had to stop while a dog with a lame leg hopped slowly across the road. They were beside a large old factory that looked abandoned. Several of the ground-floor windows were broken and the vehicle entrance was boarded up. Dan stared at the sign that hung above the doorway. It showed a picture of a girl holding up a bottle. Her teeth were white and her smiling lips bright red. Her hair was a mass of golden curls. The image brought a twist to Dan's stomach. It was instantly – painfully – familiar. Marilyn used to buy *Vinaigre à la Fille Souriante*. There was always a bottle, with this colourful illustration on the label, in the kitchen of the cottage in Banya.

Henning must have noticed the sign too. He read out the name with a sneer in his voice. 'Smiling Girl Vinegar. I'm not surprised the business has failed. It is a stupid name.'

'I guess it is.' As he spoke, Dan glanced across the upper floor of the building, noticing how the windows reflected the sun's glow, mirroring the pink of the lake.

Henning slapped the steering wheel impatiently. 'Come on, dog. Get moving.'

Dan swept his gaze back, focusing on one of the windows. He'd seen something there – just for an instant. A woman's face. It was like a fragment of a dream, half-remembered. An oval of pale skin. Dark eyes, just smudges. An impression of lips; nothing more. Before he'd had time to see the face properly, the figure must have stepped away, the glass becoming a blank sheet of pink once again.

As Henning let out the clutch, the Land Rover edging forwards, Dan put his hand on the driver's arm. 'Stop. Stop here.'

The soldier looked at him in surprise. 'Right here, sir?'

Dan stared up at the window. He wondered if he could have imagined what he'd seen – the vision evoked by some strange combination of the face on the factory sign and the haunting memory of the woman in the Jaguar. But Dan was a game hunter and bushman as well as a soldier; picking up the details of a scene, capturing them in his head, was second nature to him. He didn't make mistakes.

He turned to Henning and Bailey. 'We're going inside.'

As Dan climbed out of the Land Rover, he was aware of the two men swapping looks. Then they snapped into combat mode, falling in behind him, covering his back, pistols drawn.

Reaching the doorway, Dan paused. In other circumstances he might have hammered loudly on the door and waited for someone to answer it – then the soldiers could see if any help was needed. But this scenario was not that straightforward. Why had the woman ducked away from the window when she realised she'd been seen? Why was she even here, sheltering in an abandoned factory, days after the town had been liberated? Who was she? And what was she doing?

Where there were unanswered questions like this, Dan preferred a cautious approach. Bailey had made the same assessment. He took a drag of his cigarette, then extinguished it so that tobacco smoke would not betray their presence when they entered the building.

Dan turned the handle of the door and pushed. It didn't budge.

'Let me have a go,' Bailey said in a low voice. He had his shoulder flexed, his body poised to throw his weight against the panel.

Dan shook his head. He gestured towards a spot near the handle.

Splintered wood showed where the door had been levered open. Dan turned the handle again, pushing harder. The door moved a fraction. 'There's something behind it.'

There was a scraping sound as Dan forced open a gap. As soon as it was wide enough he pushed his way inside. The air smelled of dust and mould overlaid by the acid tang of vinegar. He scanned a large space, taking in the huge wooden vats and the barrels lined up on their cradles.

The three moved through the shadowy factory, eyeing hundreds of dusty bottles lined up in rows, some empty, others full of liquid. There had been no Simbas on the rampage in here; the place looked as if it had been left untouched since the day it was closed up. A broom stood by the main door, a pile of dirt beside it. Dan pictured the last person to leave the factory, taking the time to sweep the floor. Perhaps they thought it was a temporary closure, just until the economy improved.

Dan headed towards a staircase in the far corner. As he stepped on a loose floorboard, bottles clinked together, making a soft musical sound. He froze, letting the movement settle.

At the bottom step, he turned to Henning and Bailey. With a hand gesture, he ordered responsive fire only. He peered up the stairs, squinting in the fading daylight. The banister was made of metal, polished by decades of use. Dan ran his free hand along it as he climbed. There was no dust; this was the access that was in use by whoever was above him.

At the top of the stairs he entered a short corridor with open doorways to left and right. Peering past a stack of old packing crates, he saw a bicycle wheel and the hose of a vacuum cleaner. With a flick of his finger he told the others he was going to search the first room.

'Stop there!'

A voice came from somewhere nearby but Dan couldn't find its source. Then a figure appeared in the furthest doorway, a tall, slim woman. Long red hair draped her shoulders. Dan remembered the mysterious driver of the white car. This person wore civilian clothes – trousers and shirt – but had army boots on her feet. Light glanced from the barrel of a Kalashnikov, raised and aimed. From her grip Dan could tell she knew how to use the weapon.

'I'll shoot you if you come any closer,' the woman called out.

She was American. Not young, Dan estimated, but not old either. Her tone was clear and matter-of-fact. Dan heard the faint click of the safety catch being turned off. He exchanged glances with Henning and Bailey. She meant what she'd said.

'We're not here to cause any problems,' Dan responded. 'I saw your face at the window and came in to make sure you were okay.'

'Then you can go.'

In the quiet Dan could hear the woman's jerky breath. Behind her bravado she was afraid.

'I'm Lieutenant Miller.' He spoke calmly. 'These are two of my men, volunteers Henning and Bailey.'

'I know who you are,' the woman said. 'You're mercenaries.' She made the single word sound like an indictment.

Bailey looked at her with disgust. 'We're fighting the Simbas. Rescuing people.'

She seemed about to respond when a sharp cry suddenly pierced the stillness. It reminded Dan of the sound made by an animal caught in a gin trap. The woman looked behind her into the room. Her face was taut with distress.

'Who's in there?' Dan asked. He took a step closer.

The barrel of the Kalashnikov jabbed towards him. 'Don't move.'

'Okay. Okay.' Dan raised his hands, his pistol pointing to the ceiling.

The cry died away into a moan.

'We can help,' Dan said, 'if you tell us what's going on.'

The woman was silent for a moment, her face torn with indecision. Then she shook her head helplessly. 'My friend needs morphine. He's in terrible pain.' There was a raw edge in her voice.

'What happened?'

'He was shot in the abdomen. I thought he was getting better, then he got a fever.'

'We can take him to hospital.'

'No. He . . . can't go there.'

Dan narrowed his eyes. A man was in agony in that room. There must be a real reason why his companion wasn't seizing the offer of help. Were the pair criminals, on the run from the law, who'd been caught up in the fighting by mistake? It didn't seem likely, but it was the best explanation Dan could come up with.

'We've got a field pack in the Land Rover,' he told her. 'It's got morphine in it. But you'll have to let us see him.'

'No.'

'Well, that's the deal,' Dan said firmly. He sensed Henning and Bailey moving in closer to him, ready for action.

The woman stepped forward into the hallway. As his eyes adjusted to the changed light, Dan saw that the front of her shirt and trousers were stained dark red.

'Are you hurt too?' Dan asked.

'It's not my blood.'

Dan studied her face, shiny with sweat. There was a smear of dirt on her cheek. The long hair was matted into stiff strands. She looked different to the person he'd glimpsed in the rear-vision mirror of the Jaguar – but he felt sure it was her.

'What's your name?' he asked.

She looked as if she were considering how to answer him. When she finally spoke, she seemed to be addressing herself, as much as him. 'It doesn't matter who I am, any more. It's over now.' She looked him in the eye. 'My name is Eliza. Eliza Lindenbaum.'

Dan stared at her. Anyone who'd ever lived in the Congo knew that name. The Jaguar was probably just her everyday car; she'd have a Rolls Royce or two at home as well. He could think of nothing that would explain her presence here in an abandoned vinegar factory in Uvira.

Eliza lowered her rifle, but Dan noted that she left the safety catch turned off. In response he returned his pistol to the holster on his belt. When he gestured for his men to do the same, they complied. They looked unarmed, now, but Dan knew Bailey had a second pistol in a special pocket he'd added to the back of his trousers. The moment Eliza looked away from him, he'd slip it out. He'd keep it hidden from view, but ready for use in a flash.

The woman backed away from them, disappearing into the room. Dan went after her. As he stepped over the threshold, he breathed the familiar battlefield smell of blood and damaged flesh. It was lighter in here, with a bank of windows running along the wall. His eyes went straight to a stainless-steel bench, topped with a make-shift mattress made from pieces of carpet. He stared in surprise. An African man lay there. A soldier, still wearing the remains of a uniform. His shirt was unbuttoned, revealing a wide bandage made from cloth around his upper abdomen. He wore army trousers, the waistband soaked in blood. His head turned from side to side like a newborn baby searching for milk. Dan's eyes focused on his forehead. There was a small white cross. The mark of the Simbas.

'He's thirsty all the time,' Eliza said. 'His lips are dry.' She put down her rifle and picked up a bottle. She lifted his head gently, pouring water into his mouth. Most of it dribbled straight out, running down his neck.

'Exsanguination results in dehydration,' Henning said. He stepped forward, looking more closely at the man. 'You can see, his eyes are sunk in.'

Eliza turned to him. 'Are you a medical officer?'

Henning shook his head.

'He's from the Foreign Legion,' Bailey said. 'He knows everything.' There was no hint of sarcasm in his tone. 'Let him look.'

Eliza lifted the bandage away. A dark hole made a blot on the black skin. Plasma leaked from the wound, glistening like fresh tears.

'The bleeding stopped,' Eliza said. 'He seemed better. But then he started shaking. He's had a fever for two days. He says things that don't make sense.' A shudder crossed her face. 'He sees things that aren't here.'

Henning nodded. 'Hypovolemic shock. There's not enough blood in his body for his heart to work properly. The brain is starved of oxygen.' Very gently he felt the area around the wound, then moved his probing fingers up towards the ribs. 'It is rock hard. His abdominal cavity must be full of blood. Infection has set in. How long ago was he shot?'

'Six days ago.'

Henning raised his eyebrows – just ridges of skin, the white hair almost invisible. Dan knew what he was thinking. This soldier wasn't a casualty of Force Denby's entry into Uvira. He was shot before they arrived. Perhaps he was a victim of the mutiny Inspector Tabati had talked about.

'He will go into organ failure unless he gets a blood transfusion,' Henning said. The way he spoke English, carefully delivering each syllable, made his words sound brutally blunt.

'Simbas are being treated in the hospital,' Dan said. 'It's better to be captured than dead.'

Eliza shook her head slowly. 'The National Army will interrogate him, sooner or later. He'll be tortured. In the end he'll be executed.'

Dan was quiet as he absorbed her words. 'I might be able to protect him, at least for now. My unit is controlling the town. I am the Commanding Officer.' Even as he was speaking, he remembered his words were no longer true; but surely even Swain would stick to the basic rules of war in a public setting like Uvira.

'No one can protect him,' Eliza said. 'He's too important.'

In the quiet that followed, the man started mumbling. His words were unintelligible but Dan thought he was speaking Swahili. The Simba had a distinctive face – finely formed, handsome, with high cheekbones. Dan felt he'd seen it somewhere before. Perhaps it was in the deck of photographs Becker kept in his shirt pocket: his collection of 'wanted' Simbas. Many were so blurred they were almost meaningless; some were years out of date. But the Intelligence Sergeant loved to show them around. As Dan searched the injured man's face, noting the sweat beading on his skin, an image flashed into his mind. It was of Hardy reciting his quote about the Scarlet Pimpernel.

He turned to Eliza. When he spoke, his voice was low as if he were delivering a secret. 'He's the Okapi.'

Pride lit Eliza's eyes fleetingly. Then she shook her head. 'Not any more. He left the Simbas. He had to.' Her eyes screwed up as though she were remembering events she did not want to revisit. 'His dreams are gone. His life is over. It's all over.'

Suddenly she covered her face with her hands. They were shaking. She was on the brink of collapse, Dan realised. He guessed she'd had very little sleep over the four days, and probably no proper food.

Dan turned to Bailey. 'Get the field pack. There should be some ration boxes somewhere too.'

As Bailey set off at a jog, Dan looked around the room. It appeared to have been used as some kind of laboratory – perhaps it was where the vinegar was tested. There was a sink in one corner and a second stainless-steel bench. A desk stood near the door. Dan saw some car keys attached to a leather tag decorated with the Jaguar badge. There were two empty whisky bottles – not Ballantine's, but Johnnie Walker. Hanging from the back of a chair was a snakeskin shoulder bag and a silk scarf. Dan could have been on safari, looking at the possessions of one of his wealthy clients. They were bizarrely out of place in this setting.

When he turned back to the bed, the man had opened his eyes. He was staring blankly at the ceiling. His lips were drawn back from his teeth in a grimace of agony. Eliza moved into his line of vision.

'I'm here, Philippe,' she said softly. 'Just hold on. These men have morphine. You'll get it very soon.'

She picked up one of the man's hands and held it in both of hers. Her pale fingers stood out against his dark skin. Dan watched her face. A look of tenderness softened the distress that gripped her features. He could tell that the two were more than comrades or friends: they were lovers. A chill spread inside him. The man, Philippe, was almost certainly going to die. Eliza was going to be left alone. He could already see the cloud of grief hanging over her, waiting to descend.

The three stood around the bed, watching Philippe in silence. Dan felt helpless, seeing him writhing in pain. If it had been an animal lying here, anyone with a gun would be putting the creature out of its misery. From down in the street came the sound of the Land Rover door being slammed. Then there were footsteps thumping over the floorboards and moving on up the stairs.

Bailey dropped a ration box onto the desk and brought the field pack over to the bed. Henning rifled through the box, finding the morphine and unwrapping a syringe. He held up a glass ampoule, flicking it with his finger to make any bubbles rise; then he snapped off the top. Dan undid the man's trousers, pulling down one side to expose a hip. As the needle went in, and Henning pushed on the plunger, a look of relief came over Eliza's face.

The next few minutes passed slowly. The morphine didn't seem to be taking effect. Philippe's jaw was still clenched with agony.

'The circulatory system has collapsed,' Henning explained. 'The drug is just sitting there under the skin, not being carried away . . .'

'Give him some more,' Eliza said. 'Please.'

'It is dangerous,' Henning warned. 'When it eventually disperses, he will have a double dose. It could kill him.'

Eliza drew in a long breath. She leaned towards Henning, her blue eyes dark with despair. 'Is he going to die, anyway? Tell me what you really believe.'

Henning lowered his gaze. In his face, Dan glimpsed the softer man the Legionnaire might once have been. 'He is not going to live.'

Eliza looked at Philippe, her eyes filling with tears. She pressed her trembling lips together, then she turned to Henning. When she spoke her voice came out in a whisper. 'Take away the pain.' She repeated her words, finding strength and clarity. 'Please. Take away the pain.'

Henning looked at Dan, his brow knotted with uncertainty. Dan met his gaze. He knew he was being asked to give a soldier permission to kill, outside a field of combat. It was not a difficult decision to reach; and all he had to do was nod. Yet his head refused to move. He looked, again, at Philippe. The man was gasping for air. He turned towards Dan, as if aware that this white man held in his hands the power to release him. The pleading in his eyes was intense, yet the emotion seemed to come from far away, as if Philippe had already begun his journey to another place.

'Do it,' Dan murmured to Henning. 'Let him go.'

When the second ampoule had been emptied, and then a third – this time directly into a vein – Henning rubbed the area around the injections.

Gradually the pain faded from Philippe's face. He turned towards Eliza, his eyes seeking hers. His lips moved. No sound came out but Dan recognised the words that were formed.

'*Nakupenda sana.*'

Eliza brought Philippe's hand to her face and held it there. Tears ran down her face. 'I love you too. I love you with all my heart.'

Dan pulled over the chair so that Eliza could sit down beside the bed. She lowered herself to the seat while still holding Philippe's hand. She bent her head over him, her hair falling forward, hiding her face. The natural red colour was darkened with crusted blood, Dan saw. He could smell the sweat on her skin, blending with traces of stale perfume.

Dan watched Philippe's chest rising and falling, slow and steady. Eliza's teardrops fell, forming glistening spots on the black man's skin. After a few moments, Dan moved away, standing over by the desk. As if by unspoken agreement, Henning and Bailey joined him, leaving the two alone. In the light that pooled by the window they were like actors abandoned onstage, just waiting for the curtain to come down.

Philippe's breathing became shallow and uneven. Dan saw that his eyes were closed. Eliza kept hold of his hand. Her knuckles whitened, her grip tightening – as if she could, even now, prevent him from leaving. Dan's own eyes ached with tears. This woman was a complete stranger but her pain touched him. Like a husband or a father, he wanted to be able to come to her rescue – to save her from what she had to face.

Eventually, the figure on the bed became still. There was no sound of breath passing between the parched lips, no movement of the ribcage. Eliza let out a long moan that rose into a wail. Then she laid her head on his chest. Her shoulders heaved as she broke down and sobbed like a child.

THIRTY

The shadows deepened as the last of the daylight dwindled quickly away. Philippe's body, laid out on the bed, was just a black shape, his features no longer visible. Eliza sat on a chair at his side staring down at him. Her shoulders were hunched and her hands were clasped in her lap.

The three soldiers were a little distance away, perched on wooden packing crates. Henning sat bolt upright. He was motionless, like a carnivore preserving energy between bouts of action. Bailey lounged beside him. He was rolling a cigarette, the paper hanging from his lip as he selected tobacco from a pouch. His foot tapped an impatient beat against the floor. Dan rested his back against the wall, his legs stretched out in front of him. His eyes ranged around the room, but always returned to Eliza. She'd tied back her blood-matted hair, exposing her face. The shadows emphasised her cheekbones and the curve of her forehead. Her eyes were dark hollows against the pallor of her skin.

Almost an hour had passed since Philippe's death. After the initial outpouring of grief, Eliza had been calm and quiet. She had replaced the bandage to cover Philippe's wound and then buttoned his shirt, smoothing the cloth over his chest. She'd dipped a piece of torn towel in water and washed his face. Then she'd used the same cloth to wipe away her tears. Now she was cloaked in stillness, as if her thoughts were turned deep inside. Dan recognised that she was consciously adapting to what had just happened, and preparing for what was coming next. It was a process familiar to any soldier. Like an artist reworking a painting, strengthening tone and form, she was rebuilding her armour.

Dan's own emotions were shifting as well. He was still touched by Eliza's pain; if anything, her bravery made it all the more poignant. And he felt the tragedy of Philippe's death – he'd never become inured to the experience of seeing a strong, healthy man die from his wounds. But now he began to think about the meaning of Eliza being here with the Okapi. She must be a supporter of the Simbas – or even an actual member of their army. A surge of outrage ran through him as he remembered the scene at the ambush: the slaughter of the *Jeunesse*. That was just one of the atrocities for which Simba Command was responsible. Philippe had been one of their leaders. Who knew what role Eliza might have played? The couple may have distanced themselves from the Simbas recently, but that didn't change the past.

Leaving aside the actions of the Simbas – and Dan knew well enough that in an armed conflict virtually no one ended up with clean hands – there was also the puzzle of why someone like Eliza would even consider supporting the rebellion. The Lindenbaums owned assets in the Congo; they were the sort of people who had the most to lose from Communism taking root here. And although the family had a long association with this place, they were still Americans – and their country was supporting the current government. It didn't make any sense.

He began to wonder if Eliza could have been drawn to the rebel cause solely through a love affair with Philippe. Perhaps her emotions had blinded her to any other reality. But that didn't fit with what he'd already seen of her. She had confronted the soldiers so boldly – even after all she'd gone through during these last few days. Dan had never encountered a woman who displayed such resilience. She just didn't come across as someone who would be led helplessly by her feelings.

As he watched her from his seat on the wooden crate, he remembered how she had captured his attention the time he first caught sight of her. Now, he was only more intrigued. He had to keep reminding himself that Eliza was guilty – at the very least – of supporting the enemy. The fact was, Dan shouldn't be sitting here with her in this abandoned factory; he should be taking her into custody.

Dan wondered what Henning and Bailey were thinking about the situation they'd all found themselves in. He suspected they were as uneasy about Eliza's allegiances as he was. Yet he could see in their eyes the same respect for her that he felt.

Standing up, he crossed to the windows. The top of a tree was visible across the street; birds were already roosting in its branches. It would be dark very soon. Philippe's body needed to be removed from here and buried. It wouldn't last long in the heat. Dan couldn't imagine just walking off and leaving Eliza alone here to deal with the situation. Nor was he intending to take her – or the body – to Swain. Regardless of who Eliza was, or what she may have done, he was going to help her.

He considered his next step; there weren't many options to choose from. Philippe's grave had to be in a secret location. Otherwise there was a good chance his body would be dug up and desecrated – by the ordinary people of Uvira who had suffered at the hands of the Simbas; or Tabati's policemen; or even members of the commando force, now that Swain was in charge. Dan remembered the scene at the riverside when Dupont had shown off his grisly souvenir. Whoever the Okapi had been – whatever he was responsible for – he deserved for his remains to be treated with basic respect.

Dan went to crouch beside Eliza. 'We can't stay here any longer,' he told her. 'We need to move Philippe's body.'

Eliza turned to face him. Her eyes were red and swollen. 'Where are you taking him?'

'We're going to bury him for you. Now.'

Her eyes narrowed as she processed his words. 'Why would you do that?'

'I want to help you.'

The answer was so simple she seemed to accept it at face value. 'I'm coming too.'

'Of course.'

Eliza met his gaze. 'Am I a prisoner?'

Dan shook his head. 'As far as I can tell, you are a civilian.' He glanced over her tailor-made bush clothes, avoiding looking at her army boots.

'I am,' she confirmed. Dan didn't know if that meant she had left the rebel army, or had never signed up.

'There are some empty graves at the cemetery,' he continued. 'A whole row of them was prepared for unclaimed bodies brought in by the police. Nobody will notice if one gets filled in overnight.' He searched Eliza's face as he talked, reading her reaction. 'We'd have to be quick. There won't be a priest or anything like that.'

Eliza kept her eyes on the bed as she responded. 'Philippe wouldn't care where he was buried, or how it was done – as long as he was laid to rest on Congolese soil. He believed in the future of the Congo. That was his religion. This country meant everything to him.'

Dan heard the pain behind her words. He guessed she was not only mourning the loss of her future with Philippe, but all the losses of the past as well. It couldn't have been easy for her, being in love with a rebel leader who constantly moved around the country. The cause would always have come first.

When Dan straightened up, Bailey and Henning jumped to their feet, eager for action. At a sign from him, they moved over to the bed. Bailey took hold of the dead man's shoulders; Henning gripped him by the knees.

Crossing to the desk, Dan gathered up Eliza's possessions for her. When he dropped the car keys into the shoulder bag, he saw a fat wad of American dollars, nestled alongside a hairbrush and a few rolls of Kodak film. There was a novel, too, but he couldn't read the title in the dim light. He pushed the silk scarf in on top, the fabric snagging on the rough skin of his hands.

As he handed the bag to Eliza, she stood up, nodding her thanks. She watched Philippe's body disappearing through the doorway. She took a few steps after him, but then turned around, going back to her place by the bed. She stood there, running her hands over the pieces of carpet where he had lain. The simple gesture seemed to express the pain of parting more strongly even than tears. Dan watched her helplessly. She needed someone to hold her, comfort her – but he was a complete stranger, not a friend.

After a few moments, Eliza lifted her head, wiping her eyes with the back of her hand. Then she turned and walked out of the room, pausing only to pick up her rifle, slinging it over her shoulder.

*

A near-full moon shone down over the cemetery, casting a cold light over the graves. The headstones marking the older burials, closest to the church, were tilted at odd angles; the newer ones were straight and level. Over by the far boundary the fresh graves stood side by side in a long row. Amid the piles of earth were several gaping holes. Dan chose the one closest to where the Land Rover was parked under a tree. Eliza's Jaguar was there, too; she'd collected it from a street near the factory and driven here, tailing the Land Rover.

When Bailey and Henning had removed Philippe's body from the back seat, Eliza helped wrap it in an African cloth she'd produced from her car boot. Then the men carried the shrouded figure to the grave. They moved as quickly as they could. Dan wasn't keen to linger in the cemetery any longer than was necessary. There was a main road nearby, with sporadic traffic. He didn't want to attract unwanted attention.

Dan helped Henning and Bailey lower the body into the hole. Then they stepped back, allowing Eliza to throw in the first handfuls of earth. She watched on as the soldiers took turns to shovel in soil, using the spade that was kept in the Land Rover for when the vehicle got bogged. They worked fast, their sleeves rolled up, their faces shining with sweat. Now and then they froze as a car drove along the road, headlights beaming into the night.

When the burial was finished, the four figures stood in silence around the heaped earth. A nightjar flitted past, chasing a moth. Eliza was the first to turn away. She walked over to where her car was parked. The men followed her. Lifting the boot, she brought out two bottles of whisky.

She passed one to Bailey and then opened the other. She took two long gulps, closing her eyes as she drank. In the moonlight the shadows of exhaustion under her eyes looked blue. Her fingers, wrapped around the bottle, were dusted with red dirt.

'Here.' She offered her whisky to Dan. He swallowed a mouthful, feeling its fire in his throat. As he handed the bottle back, his thoughts turned to the question of where Eliza would go now. If she had any friends here in Uvira, she'd not sought their help in the last few days, so he presumed she wouldn't now. She could hardly turn up at a guesthouse in the state she was in. The hotel, with its new occupants, was out of the question, regardless of her appearance. Someone might recognise her – for all Dan knew, Becker had Intelligence on the Okapi's girlfriend and had circulated a description of her. The Sergeant didn't always communicate fully with his Commanding Officer; it was part of a power game he played. Dan couldn't even take Eliza back with him to the cricket ground and pitch her a tent. She'd be no safer there, from Becker, than at the hotel.

'Where are you going to spend the night?' he asked.

'I've got a tent in the car,' Eliza replied. 'I'll get food from somewhere.' She glanced in the direction of the lake. 'I'll find a spot to camp.'

Dan felt sure she was capable of taking care of herself, but tonight was not just any ordinary occasion. 'Will you be all right on your own?'

Eliza sighed softly. 'I've lived for years with the idea of losing Philippe. I was often in danger myself, but not as much as he was. I think I knew, deep down, that I'd end up alone. Now, it's finally happened.' She looked across at the grave for a moment, her eyes shiny with fresh tears. Then she put the lid back on the bottle, and turned to Dan. 'Thank you for everything you've done – all of you . . .' She waved her hand towards the other men, who were still standing nearby. 'I won't be staying around here, so I'll say goodbye.'

'Where are you heading to?' Dan couldn't stop himself from asking. He felt responsible for her, but it was more complicated than that – after the experiences they'd just shared, he found it hard to accept that she was just going to drive away and he'd never see her again.

'Back down south,' she replied.

Dan looked at her in alarm. 'You can't do that. It's not safe.'

'What do you mean?'

'There are Simbas down there now. That's where they retreated to.'

Eliza frowned at him in surprise.

'They were cut off from the north by another commando unit. The government forces have come up from Albertville. The whole area is turning into a battlefield.'

She shook her head, as if she were struggling to keep up with what he was saying.

'Air Support is dropping bombs all over the place,' Dan continued. 'There are reports of the rebels taking civilians hostage. It's a nightmare.'

Eliza leaned closer to him, horror dawning over her face. 'My friends live on a mission near Banya.'

'They could be in serious trouble,' Dan said, swapping looks with Henning and Bailey. 'Apparently it all happened very quickly. There was no time for anyone to be evacuated. I don't know all the details, though. Information is still coming in. Are your friends in radio contact?'

'I only tried them once, from the place where I met up with Philippe. I wanted to let them know I was changing my plans. But I couldn't raise them.' Eliza looked stricken by remorse. 'I didn't keep trying. We came up here to Uvira. There was so much going on.'

'Tell me exactly where they are. I'll get the Signaller onto it.'

Eliza chewed tensely at her lip. 'They've got three children there. And I left someone with them. An Australian girl who was staying with me in Albertville.' She shook her head. 'Poor Anna, she's only been in the Congo a few weeks. If soldiers turn up – whoever they are – she'll be terrified.'

Dan was no longer listening. The name, Anna, was reverberating through his mind. So was the fact that Marilyn was Australian, even though it was irrelevant.

'I'll have to take the risk and drive down there,' Eliza said. 'If you can try the radio first —'

Dan broke in, cutting her off. 'Who is she? Anna . . .'

'Anna?' Eliza looked puzzled by the change of focus. 'It's a strange story. She came to Albertville to see her father. Only he turned out not to be her real father. She discovered he adopted her after he married her mother. So she wanted to go to Banya where she was born, to search for information.'

A tingle travelled through Dan's body, lifting the hairs on his skin. 'Who was he? The man she came to see?'

'Karl Emerson. He owns a rubber plantation near Banya. He was married to her mother. But there was a divorce and Anna was taken back to Australia. She grew up there.'

Dan stared at her, motionless. His heart pounded; the air seemed to have been crushed from his lungs. 'It's her.'

Eliza eyed him in confusion. 'Do you know them – the Emersons?'

Dan shook his head. It was impossible to believe – but what Eliza had just told him could only mean one thing. His daughter was here, in Africa. Anna was searching for him. He pushed himself away from the car, walking in a daze. He felt as if one of his daydreams had invaded the real world. Yet this was truly happening.

He looked back at Eliza. 'I'm her father.'

The words seemed to fill the air, leaving no room for anything else to be said or even thought. Eliza's lips parted in amazement.

Dan turned towards the south where clusters of stars patterned the night sky. He scoured the horizon, as if he might be able to see beyond it. But there was only darkness. Sudden urgency penetrated his other emotions. Anna might be safe in the company of Eliza's missionary friends. But she might be in danger. She could already be in the hands of the Simbas.

'Come on,' he said to Eliza. 'Let's go.'

He spun on his heels, beckoning Henning and Bailey. Then he headed for the Land Rover at a run.

THIRTY-ONE

The tents were a row of dark-green peaks dotting the grass plain of the cricket ground. The faces of the men gathered around their camp fires glowed red from the flames while their backs and shoulders were painted silver by the moon. As Dan approached, he scanned the seated figures. Lots of the soldiers were missing. It was evening now, but not yet time for bed – he guessed they must have decided to take advantage of his absence to join the paratroopers at the hotel. The ones who remained were those he would have expected to stick to their orders. He could see McAdam sitting on an empty ammunition crate, his bagpipes resting on his lap. Thompson was squatting on his haunches nearby, tying an elaborate knot in a piece of cord. Girard sat a little way off, tending a small fire on his own. Lawler and Willis, two of the rebranded Americans, were deep in conversation, their heads close together. Malone was there, too – though there was no sign of Billy. Among the other faces, Dan picked out the Second Mechanic, along with his combat partner. Sharing their fire was Smith; he was reading a book, the pages angled to catch light from the flames. At his feet lay Bergman's dog, his chin resting on the man's boots. Smith had offered to find a new home for Remi after the Belgian family had departed for Albertville en route to Brussels. There hadn't been any luck yet – lots of unwanted dogs were roaming the streets of Uvira, and Remi was a rough-haired mongrel. But Smith hadn't given up; he kept on making enquiries. Meanwhile, the man and the hound were rarely seen apart.

Bailey and Henning were walking on either side of Dan, escorting him like a personal guard. Dan knew they'd heard his exchange with Eliza at the cemetery, but the implications of what he'd discovered had not been discussed, either there or on the drive back to base – Dan was too caught up in the turmoil of his emotions to want to talk, and the two men had respected his silence. When they'd reached the cricket grounds Eliza had remained in her car, parked at the entrance. Dan felt reluctant to leave her there, even briefly, while he spoke to the men. He was afraid she might just disappear again – but he knew that was an irrational thought. They both had the same goal and they needed one another's help to reach it.

As Dan came to a halt, the men got to their feet. Their eyes passed from the Lieutenant to his companions and back. Dan could see they were trying to read the telltale marks of blood and dirt on the soldiers' uniforms. There had been no new action for days and there were questions in their eyes.

'Get everyone together,' Dan instructed Henning and Bailey.

As the two strode off in different directions, he headed for the area that was used as a parade ground. He tried to focus his thoughts on what he was about to say to his men, but the extraordinary news Eliza had just conveyed to him kept replaying in his mind. He turned over the facts like tangible objects in his hands. Anna had grown up on the other side of the world, in Australia. She'd only just discovered the truth about her relationship with Emerson. Now she was here in the Congo – searching for her real father, a man she knew nothing about but wanted desperately to meet.

And she was in danger.

Dan stared blankly across the cricket pitch. On one hand he was brimming with hope, excitement and joy; on the other he felt a cold weight of dread – the two extremes were almost impossible to contain.

The sixteen men assembled quickly, leaving their fires to burn down unattended. They stood to attention in straight rows, until Dan told them to stand easy. Willis asked for permission to smoke, which led to a hurried sharing of cigarettes and matches. Then silence fell. The men watched Dan's face, clearly eager to learn why they were having an urgent briefing late at night.

Dan got straight to the point. 'I have to let you know that I am leaving the unit. I will not be taking up a new contract.' He paused while a murmur of shock spread through the group. The dog, sitting at Smith's feet, lifted his ears, sensing rising tension. 'I have already filed positive reports on all of you,' he continued. 'Blair has approved your reappointment. Swain has got contracts ready for you to sign. As you know, the next mission will be taking you to the north.' He took a breath. 'I'm heading south.'

In the dense quiet, night birds called to one another from across the field.

'Can you tell us what's going on, sir?' asked McAdam. There was a sharp edge to his Scottish accent, which Dan understood. Since Hardy's death, the Corporal had been promoted unofficially to second-in-command. It wasn't fair of Dan to make an announcement like this without a prior conversation, but he'd had no choice. He wanted to be on the road within the hour and he had to make every minute count.

'I have just found out that my daughter is near Banya,' Dan

stated. 'I've got to make sure she's safe.'

'I didn't know you had family here in the Congo, sir,' said McAdam.

'Neither did I,' Dan said. As he spoke he turned to Smith, meeting his puzzled gaze. He wished he'd had time to talk to him in advance, too. The Rhodesian was Dan's closest confidant. The two had spent many hours chatting together about what they would do when they left Blair's regiment – about Dan's lack of interest in returning to work with East African Safaris; and Smith's dream of buying a farm somewhere in Africa. Dan had never mentioned Anna. There had been no point, until now.

Girard stepped forward. 'I'm afraid the news from Banya is bad, sir. I just received an update from the National Army. They killed off a bunch of Simbas at a Catholic mission not far from there. Twenty priests are reported missing. Abducted or executed. No one knows.'

Dan's arms stiffened at his sides. He addressed the listening men. 'So you understand. I have to get down there. Straight away.'

'You mean you're just going off on your own?' asked Smith.

'There's a woman, too,' Dan said. 'She's a friend of my daughter.' He looked across the field as he spoke. The Jaguar was a white shape in the distance.

When he turned back he saw that Smith had followed his gaze. His eyebrows lifted a fraction.

'It's not much of a team. One man, one woman,' commented Willis. His drawl made everything he said sound ironic but there was a worried frown on his face.

'It doesn't sound like a great plan,' Thompson contributed. He spat a toothpick onto the ground.

There was a brief quiet. Then Henning stood to attention. He gave a slow and accurate salute. 'I wish to volunteer, sir.'

Bailey took a step forward. 'Me, too. Sir.'

Dan felt a rush of relief at the thought of the two men joining him – but he banished the emotion quickly. He shook his head. 'It's not a proper mission. I've got no support. In fact, Swain's not even going to know what I'm doing. I'm just leaving.'

Bailey grinned. 'I'm sorry I won't be there to see his face.'

'It's going to be very dangerous,' Dan pressed on. 'Air Support is bombing the place. The National Army is attacking the Simbas. We could get caught in the crossfire.'

Henning acknowledged the information with a curt nod. Bailey shrugged.

Dan's eyes narrowed. He could see that the pair were deadly serious, and undeterred. 'You need to know there's no money in this. And I have no idea where we will end up . . .'

His voice trailed off as Smith moved to stand beside Henning, the dog at his heels. 'I'm coming too.'

Three more men stood to attention. Thompson. McAdam. Doc Malone.

'I'm in, too,' Lawler said. 'I'd rather fight for free than work for Swain. He's a fucking cowboy.' Dan had to smile; the man sounded exactly like a cowboy himself.

Dan stood in silence, scanning the faces of the volunteers. He could see them thinking fast; they'd spoken impulsively and now the reality of the situation was catching up with them. But none of them withdrew.

'Thank you,' he said simply; a thousand words couldn't express how grateful he was.

The mechanic spoke up then. 'I can't come with you. I need the paid work. But I'll help you get organised with transport.'

'I'll only take rebel vehicles,' Dan said. He wanted to avoid committing actual crimes, like theft – especially now that others were involved. 'We'll be using their weaponry as well.' The cache of munitions was still at the bank, and Dan had the key in his pocket.

The mechanic gestured towards the area where he'd been working on the Simba jeeps and trucks. 'Take your pick.' He gave a wry smile. 'If you want to disguise yourselves, you'll be off to a fine start. It's probably best to take along a National Army flag too.'

'Tell us how we can help,' said another of the men. There was a wistful note in his voice as if he wished he were able to join the volunteers. Dan knew he had elderly parents back in Greece who relied on his income.

'We'll need petrol,' Dan responded. 'Water. Ration boxes. Two field radios. Backup batteries. I want you to estimate the dollar value of what we take. I'll pay before we leave.' In his pocket was a bundle of bank notes. Eliza had handed it to him as he was climbing out of the Land Rover. She didn't suggest what it was for; he had the impression she was accustomed to using cash to remove barriers, whatever they might be. He turned to Malone. 'We need medical supplies as well.'

The doctor nodded. 'I'll bring them along.'

Dan eyed him for a moment. Malone had been working tirelessly at the hospital since arriving in Uvira. He didn't care whether his patients were soldiers, civilians or prisoners – he was kind to them all. Whatever the words 'of good character' meant, they clearly applied to him, even though he'd come to Force Denby with a murky record. Dan had taken pleasure in writing him a glowing reference.

'Coming with me won't be good for your reputation, Doc,' he warned.

Malone gave a small smile, just a quirk of his lips, and said nothing.

The Signaller put up his hand like a schoolboy asking to speak. 'I have to stay here. But I can get in touch with the National Army and let them know that Major Blair has sent a commando unit to the south.'

Dan's eyebrows rose. 'You know you'd be up for conspiracy if you were caught transmitting false information?' His tone was serious. In a mercenary army a drumhead court-martial was often little more than an informal meeting. With someone like Swain in charge, it could end with a bullet.

'If the Captain questions me, I will tell him I informed my Congolese colleagues that you are illegal combatants. But you know what radio messages are like. There can be interference; translations can be wrong. There is room for misunderstanding.'

'Thank you, Girard.' Dan was touched by the man's proposal – he'd probably never been responsible for a less than accurate communication in his entire career. 'And one more thing – look out for Billy. See if you can get him sent home.'

Dan addressed the whole group again. 'All of you who are staying here – you don't know anything about this. When we've gone, retire to your tents. I'll leave a note for Swain with the cash. You aren't involved in any way.'

Before dismissing the men, Dan paused, letting his gaze pass over their faces – silently thanking the ones who were joining him, and saying goodbye to the rest.

The road was narrow and deeply rutted. Dan drove as fast as he could, the jeep bouncing over the corrugations. He was missing his Land Rover – his hand reached for the gear stick without the instant familiarity he was used to; the seat felt wrong and the canopy flapped overhead. But the engine was well tuned and the brakes sound.

In the clear moonlight it was possible to drive without using the headlamps, and Dan preferred to keep as low a profile as possible. He looked out at a landscape formed of velvet shadows edged with silver. Smith was in the passenger's seat, studying a map by the glow of a torch. The convoy was following a minor road that was little more than a track. The aim was to avoid meeting up with the government army. In the best-case scenario an encounter would slow the commandos down; in the worst case there could be an exchange of gunfire – even assuming Girard had succeeded in informing the National Army Command about the new mission to the south, the troops on the ground might not get the message.

When the way ahead was smooth enough to allow Dan to take his eyes off the road, he checked his rear-vision mirror. Light rain had dampened the dust. He could see Smith's dog lying on the back seat, its black-and-white markings standing out against a khaki army blanket. Looking further, he saw the convoy stretched out along the track: there were two more jeeps and an open-tray Dodge truck. Sheltered in the midst of the military vehicles was the Jaguar. Eliza was at the wheel, handling the car with skill, negotiating mounds and ditches. Dan picked out the pale shape of her face behind the windscreen. A strand of her hair was blowing out through the open window, whipping back and forth in the moving air. Lawler was sitting next to her, the barrel of his gun resting on the dashboard. Dan wondered if the two Americans were talking to one another, or if the volunteer had preserved his usual reticence.

Dan had to be at the head of the convoy, otherwise he would have ridden in the car with Eliza himself. He'd not yet had the chance to ask her any of the questions that were on his mind.

He was hungry for more details about her contact with Anna, but more importantly, right now, he wanted to know the truth about her relationship with the Simbas. Eliza was part of his team. He'd provided her with ammunition and a second firearm. But he wasn't sure how much he could trust her. She was deeply concerned about her friends at the mission, and about Anna – that was clear. But was she really prepared to go into battle against the rebels she had once supported?

There was so much Dan did not know about Eliza and Philippe. What had caused the Okapi to resign from his role? Had Eliza been directly involved with the decision, or was she just following Philippe's lead? And how had the Simbas reacted to the departure of one of their leaders? It had occurred to Dan that the shooting could have been Philippe's punishment for abandoning the cause. Then, there was the whole background to Eliza's story. Dan wondered how long she and Philippe had been lovers – and how their paths had crossed in the first place. He recalled Becker saying the Okapi was educated in America: could the two have met over there, drawn together by their shared ties to the Congo? Had Eliza Lindenbaum been a covert supporter of the Independence movement for years? If so, she'd done a good job of keeping it secret. If such a story had ever come out, it would have made front-page news across East Africa, if not Europe and America as well.

It went against all Dan's military training to have such an unknown quantity in his ranks. But if he were honest, this wasn't the only reason he wanted to spend time talking to Eliza. He was instinctively drawn to what he'd seen of her in the short time since they'd met. She'd shown such bravery, even in the face of her distress over Philippe. She was competent, too. He remembered how ably she'd handled her Kalashnikov. And the snippets of what he did know of her story intrigued him. Alongside all this, Dan was well aware that Eliza was a very attractive woman. And he'd shared some potent experiences with her. He knew he couldn't fully trust his judgement where she was concerned. He sensed Henning and Bailey might have fallen under her spell too. He warned himself to be careful – to keep a professional distance from her. He couldn't afford for anything to go wrong. He had to focus all his attention on getting to the mission and finding his daughter. Nothing else mattered.

As he steered the jeep around potholes and anthills, he imagined his arrival at the mission. He told himself that Anna would be alive and well – he couldn't afford to entertain any other scenario. He pictured the moment when he would take her in his arms, holding her close and letting her know that she was safe. Feeling the touch of her skin, her hair; breathing her smell, drawing it into his lungs . . .

At this point in the fantasy, Dan's thoughts petered out, dwindling to nothing, like a forest track choked with vines. He had no pictures for what might come next. How life would unfold for him and Anna – beyond the point of their meeting – he could not even begin to imagine.

THIRTY-TWO

Anna lay on a bed made of leaves and bark covered by an old piece of cloth. Whenever she moved, the makeshift mattress rustled like a voice whispering in her ear. She gazed up at the thatch of dried reeds that formed a roof above her, idly tracing the patterns made by tiny pinpricks of daylight. From outside by the fire came the sound of people talking – a low hum broken by the high voice of a child.

Lifting her arms, she studied the array of cuts, scratches and burns that marked her skin. Jagged red lines showed the paths of bits of flying debris. There were deep purple bruises as well. The injuries were like a map of the explosion left behind on her body. Shifting onto her side, she looked down at the more serious wound on her thigh. It was now covered with a wad of dry moss, tied in place by a string made from vines. She picked up the astringent smell of the sticky brew that had been smeared over the tear in her flesh. Whatever the medicine was made from, it seemed to be working: her leg was still very painful – she could hardly bear to move – but the throbbing had died away.

She had been lying in this hut for several days, now – perhaps it was even as much as a week; she'd lost track of time. The slice of the world that was visible through the doorway had become familiar to her. She recognised the people who walked past, along with all the different sounds and smells that were part of their daily life. Yet every time she awoke – whether from a deep sleep or a nap – it would take her several seconds to recall where she was, and how she came to be here. The memories returned to her in dislocated pieces; she had to grasp them one by one, laying them out like tiles in a mosaic until finally the whole picture was revealed. She would spend a few moments taking in all the details, absorbing their meaning – going back over all that had happened, again and again. It felt like the only way to keep a grasp on reality.

Long after the leopard had disappeared into the trees, Anna had waited in terror for it to return. As time passed, with no sign of the animal, her fear had given way to despair. She was still losing blood, slowly but steadily. She was dehydrated, and too weak to stand up. There seemed only one likely outcome to her plight – she was going to die here, at the foot of the tree, alone.

But just when she was certain that this would be her fate, the sound of distant voices came to her, filtering through the trees. At first she thought they were part of a vision evoked by her longing for human company. But as they grew louder, nearer, she lifted her head, listening intently. The murmuring evolved into words, though they had no meaning. There was the pad of footsteps. Snapping twigs. Rustling leaves.

She stared in the direction of the sounds. Perhaps the Simbas in the Land Rover had finally arrived at the scene of the attack. She couldn't decide whether to call out or remain quiet. In that moment, she didn't know which ending she preferred: staying here to die, or being recaptured.

Suddenly the noises were close at hand. Then two figures pushed their way out through the undergrowth, straightening up as they entered the small clearing. They were draped in dark cloths – covered from head to toe, their faces hidden. Anna gazed at them, rigid with shock and fear. They looked sinister and unworldly, like creatures from another realm.

As they approached Anna, their heads turned from side to side. Long spears topped with pointed shards of metal swung towards the place where the leopard had disappeared. One of them bent down, studying the ground as if seeking hidden clues. There was the flash of a knife blade, held at the ready. Anna's breath came in gasps. She tried to push herself up onto her knees – to at least face the intruders from a more equal height. But there was no strength in her limbs. She collapsed back against the trunk.

More people emerged from the trees, entering the clearing. Soon there were nearly a dozen of them. They all wore the same dark cloth veils as if they were members of some secret society that required their identity to be concealed. Anna didn't think they were Simbas – she could see no reason why the rebels would want to put on a disguise; and even though the clearing was now crowded with bodies, she picked up none of the smells she associated with soldiers: petrol, alcohol, tobacco or the oil they used on their guns.

The taller of the first two figures to arrive came and stood in front of Anna. He spoke to her in a low voice, forming words that she didn't understand.

Anna looked up at him, shaking her head. '*Parlez-vous français?*' Her own voice was thin and hoarse. When there was no response, she tried addressing him in English. 'Who are you?'

The man ignored her. He turned to one of his companions, firing off a stream of words. As she listened to the reply, delivered in a softer tone, Anna clutched at her leg. The attempt to move had sharpened the pain – the wound was like a fire, burning her alive. The agony made her feel light-headed: her body began slipping sideways. Just as her head neared the ground the tall man reached down to catch her. As he lifted her up, holding her against his chest, Anna felt the swell of powerful muscles through the veil. She closed her eyes, taking in the smell of dried sweat, untanned leather, and a strange sweet odour that was familiar to her but which she could not name.

She was lowered onto a cloth that had been spread over the ground. Staring up, she tried to peer in past the veils to see the faces that hovered over her, but the leaf-filtered light in the forest was too dim. She was offered a drink from a vessel made from a hollow gourd with a decorative pattern burned into its yellow skin. It had a musty taste but she gulped it down gratefully. She could almost feel the liquid entering the parched cells of her body.

The tall man crouched beside her leg. Anna couldn't see clearly, but she felt him tying something tightly over her wound. After initially increasing the pain, the pressure seemed to ease its potency. The other figures watched on, talking in low voices. After a time, several of them came to stand around the place were Anna lay. At a signal from the leader, they bent down, grasping the sides of the cloth and raising her up.

They manoeuvred their burden between the trees, lifting Anna over fallen trunks, down into gullies and up the other sides. The task was difficult; several times she was almost dropped. The bearers paused now and then to swap places with others of the group who were following behind.

Progress was slow. Anna gazed up into the treetops, watching rainbow-feathered birds and monkeys with long tails looking down on her as she lurched past. She listened to muted conversations that seemed to merge with the soft warbling of birds. She had no idea where she was being taken, or who these people were – or why they were covered from head to toe as if they were afraid of the sunlight. From their spears and knives she guessed they were hunting in the forest; perhaps they lived here as well. Harry and Rose had talked about ancient tribes who moved between camps built among the trees. Many were pygmies – like the ones Eliza had stayed with when she photographed the okapi. Some of these veiled people were short, but most were of average height. They didn't speak French or English; the simple questions Anna asked them went unanswered. The few Swahili words she'd picked up were useless. If they talked to her, she could only shake her head. She didn't know if she should be afraid of them or not – whether they had some purpose in rescuing her, or were just showing compassion. She clung to the knowledge that, whatever happened to her next, at least she would not be alone.

After what felt like at least an hour the bearers came to a halt. The man at the head of the party called out, his voice penetrating the forest. After a few moments a response bounced back like an echo. Then the group moved on again, winding between the trees.

Anna saw no change in her surroundings until the succession of trunks and vines was suddenly interrupted. She looked up into open sky. Peering around her, she took in a wide, long clearing, lit by shafts of golden light. The rays streamed down over a collection of small huts, little more than mounds of dried leaves, each with a hole for an entrance. Smoke drifted from a central fire encircled by blackened stones. The carcass of an animal – red-skinned, still raw – was roasting on a spit.

As Anna was carried into the settlement, more figures appeared, coming out of the huts or walking across from garden plots carrying hoes and baskets. Like the hunting party, they were all wearing cloth shrouds – though some people were hastily arranging the veils to cover their faces as they approached.

Bodies pressed in around the stretcher. There was a clamour of competing voices, strident with surprise and alarm. Anna was carried across to a larger hut with a wide entrance. The ground inside was layered with huge leaves, overlapping to make a carpet of green. The bearers lowered her onto it, then filed back outside, ducking their heads as they reached the doorway.

Left by herself, Anna stared around at walls that were made of leaves, matching the floor. She was strangely calm, considering her circumstances. The complete powerlessness that she felt was liberating; she knew she had no choice but to trust these people – whoever they were.

It was not long before another veiled figure entered the shelter, squatting next to the bed. A stream of soothing words flowed beneath the chatter that came from onlookers who had crowded the doorway. From the timbre of the voice, Anna thought it was a woman speaking. Her cloth was a faded blue, with remnants of indigo in the folds of the hem; it carried a musky perfume reminiscent of the white trumpet flowers that bloomed along the path between the mission house and the hospital.

Before Anna had a chance to greet the woman, a little girl arrived, wriggling in to kneel beside her. The child's face was bare, her features thrown into contrast by light from the doorway. In this setting where everyone else was veiled, she looked very exposed – as if she'd been unmasked. She was arrestingly beautiful. Her eyes were bright, edged with long lashes; her skin was like black velvet. As she stared at Anna, her mouth dropped open in frank amazement. Looking at each of Anna's features in turn she touched the matching part of her own face as though she wanted to see if they were the same.

The woman produced some green leaves from under her cloth. She said something to the child, who instantly abandoned her game and, instead, began pointing at Anna's mouth, miming the act of chewing.

Anna parted her lips to accept the leaves. When she bit into them, a sharp sweet flavour was released. As she held the sap in her mouth, her tongue turned numb. Anna assumed it was some kind of medicine – and that she was in the care of one of the traditional healers Rose had told her about.

The woman moved around to let the light from the doorway fall over Anna's leg. Carefully she removed the vines that had been bound over the wound back in the forest. Then she untied the strip of khaki cloth that lay underneath. As she began peeling it away, Anna lifted her head in alarm. She pictured the hole in her flesh gaping wide open again, blood gushing out. But the healer's movements seemed measured and assured; she made more soothing sounds with her tongue. Anna lay back again, trying to relax. She looked at the child, who was still gazing at her with fascination as if she were a rare species of wildlife whose habits were yet to be discovered.

The medicine worked quickly; by the time the last section of the cloth was pulled free, the pain was already dulled. As the wound was revealed, the healer let out a hiss of dismay. With one hand she pressed a wad of cloth over the fresh flow of blood; with the other she probed the hole, her finger digging under the skin. She lifted her veiled face, as if by cutting off her vision – half-obscured as it was – she would be able to feel more keenly. After a time she gestured to the child, who passed over a knife; it had a hand-forged blade like the ones that pierced the bodies of the *nkisi*. Anna looked quickly away as she felt the pressure of its point invading her body.

Blood ran freely over her skin, warm and wet.

Her awareness of what happened next was vague. Her mind turned hazy, the small details of her surroundings swimming into a blur. She was conscious of liquid being poured over her skin in a long stream. Then there was more pressure on her leg. As she drifted into sleep she felt another bandage being wrapped round and round and round . . .

When she awoke from her drugged sleep, she lay still for a while, gazing out through the entrance to the hut. She didn't know how much time had passed. By moving her head, she was able to see the central fireplace. Flames leapt high, standing out against the green wall of the forest behind. The skinned creature was gone, the spit bare.

The little girl crept over from the far corner of the hut. The simple cloth that she wore tied over one shoulder parted as she moved, revealing her bare legs and trunk. She had the fluid movements of a cat. When she saw that Anna's eyes were open, she turned towards the doorway and called out, her voice loud and clear.

The healer returned. This time she remained outside the hut, peering in. She pointed at Anna's leg and then held up what looked like a large coin. When Anna raised herself onto her elbows, she could see the piece of metal quite clearly, lit up by the late sun. It was stained with dried blood. The edges were curled over as if they'd been melted in a furnace.

Anna studied the object in silence. She knew it had been dug out of her leg – with neither a surgeon nor an anaesthetist in attendance. She wished she had a way of expressing her gratitude for the skilful operation. She was about to shift her gaze to the healer's face, to at least offer a smile, when something caught her attention. Ignoring the pain from her leg, she sat upright, leaning forward, studying the healer's hand. The fingers that held up the fragment of metal were bent at an unnatural angle. So was the thumb. On the back of the hand the tendons stood out like ropes. Anna's eyes widened as she took in the meaning of what she could see: the image before her was one that could have come straight from Harry's copy of *A Guide to the Management of Leprosy*. She could picture the caption under the photograph: *nerve palsy contracture*.

Anna stared at the veiled face of the healer, picking up the faint gleam of her eyes. 'You have leprosy.'

The woman was motionless for a few seconds – then she nodded slowly. Perhaps she'd heard the word 'leprosy' before, or she knew the French word for the disease – *lèpre*. The remark acted like a magnet, drawing the other people back towards the hut. Anna studied the veiled figures as they gathered around. Now that she was looking for clues, she glimpsed evidence of misshapen feet and hands, and profiles that were abnormal.

Anna pointed towards the healer's hidden face, indicating that she should remove the covering. After a brief hesitation the woman raised one hand, grasping the blue cloth with her bent fingers. Anna braced herself to hide her reactions. After her shifts at the hospital she was accustomed to seeing people with leprosy, but each sufferer was ravaged in a different way. The worst cases, to whom treatment had come very late, were almost impossible to confront without flinching.

As the veil was lifted back Anna imagined her own face was made of marble. When the healer's features were revealed she didn't allow even a flicker of a muscle. She pretended to be Harry – breaking down what she could see into its separate components.

Lumps covering most of the face. *Lepromatous nodules*.

No eyebrows or eyelashes. *Damage to the structure of the skin*.

Flattened nose. *Cartilage absorbed into the body.*

One eye milky. *Inflammation of the cornea.*

She let her eyes settle on the forehead; the skin was like the surface of an unmade road – there were deep corrugations, the edges crumbling like dried clay.

As if encouraged by her equanimity, others in the group began removing their veils. Some of the people were not very badly affected – a few looked almost healthy. Their black skin helped camouflage scars and swellings. But many had only remnants of fingers and toes. The hunting party must have been made up of the fittest people – plenty of those gathered here were leaning on sticks. An old man's face was just a mass of tumours. A woman appeared to be blind, both corneas covered with a milky film. The young man next to her had handsome features with striking deep-set eyes, but where his nose should have been there was a gaping hole, glistening with mucous. Everywhere Anna looked she saw bandages – strips of cloth, or wads of moss tied on with vines – leaking pus and blood. As a slight breeze stirred she picked up the sweet rotten smell she recognised from her work with the Carlings.

As her gaze travelled from one face to another, Anna's thoughts turned to the clinic Harry held in the leper colony. He'd be able to cure these people of their leprosy and offer treatments for their damaged bodies. She told herself she would have to find some way of letting them know about the mission. Perhaps there was a means by which they could get there. But then the realisation came over her, in a flood of cold dread, that she had no knowledge of what events had taken place while she was away – and what might have happened to the Carling family.

She sat still, staring at the people gathered in the doorway. Her fears about the missionaries, and Eliza as well, crowded in on top of the distress she felt at the pitiful condition of these lepers. She was overwhelmed by emotion. Tears filled her eyes, the ruined faces becoming a blur. At a gesture from the healer, the crowd melted away. The woman sat down next to the bed, the child beside her. A comforting quiet seemed to flow out from the healer, filling the hut. Anna closed her eyes, letting herself drift away, again, on the tide of pain.

When she awoke for a second time, the day was nearly over. She watched the shadows lengthening, the patches of sunlight slowly shrinking. As dusk approached, all the insects and birds and the small scurrying animals fell quiet. A hush fell over the forest. It was as if, between day and night, the land was taking in a deep breath.

Into the lull came the sound of a drum. Anna lifted her head, turning towards its source. Through the doorway she could see an old man over by the fire in the centre of the clearing, pounding on a double-ended drum that he held between his knees. His hands were like paws, yet he made the curved stick dance like a wild creature over the wood. He was talking through the drum, Anna knew. Rose and Eliza had both described this phenomenon to her, though in quite different terms – the missionary was uneasy about it, whereas Eliza was intrigued. As Anna listened to the low throbbing beat, overlaid with a flutter as light as the movements of a butterfly, she imagined the sound travelling up into the treetops, then spreading out over the land. A puzzled frown crossed her face. The veils the people wore, and the warning call the hunters had made as they reached the secluded settlement, suggested secrecy. Yet the drummer was drawing attention to the camp. She wondered if the drumming was a daily event, or if this occasion was unusual. It even occurred to her that the message could be about her. She wished she knew what was being communicated, and to who. But like the voices of the people who had brought her into their camp, the language of the drum was a mystery.

The beat slowed, but grew louder. The message now sounded urgent, insistent – mirroring the thoughts in Anna's head. In the shadows the sound loomed large, filling the air. It seemed to enter her bloodstream, joining with the beat of her heart.

After that first day, the veils were not worn again. As Anna lay on her bed, filling the empty hours by looking out through the doorway of the hut, she was soon able to distinguish between the various characters that moved around the camp. She estimated there were about thirty individuals, all Africans. They ranged in age from old folk with grey hair to young men and women in the prime of life. There were a couple of teenagers too; but the little girl was the only child. Many of the people wore almost no clothing – just a loincloth or grass skirt. Their bared bodies were evidence of how leprosy functioned as a disease, causing most damage to the extremities: the trunks, breasts and shoulders looked surprisingly normal. Even among the lepers who were most disfigured, Anna discovered, vanity persisted. Everyone she saw wore some form of adornment – a necklace made from cowrie shells or bone beads; leather anklets and bracelets decorated with feathers; even fur hats, in spite of the heat.

As the people went about their daily tasks, Anna took the opportunity to study them. They worked very slowly, with many setbacks. She saw how easily they injured themselves. Quotes from Harry's manuscript often ran through her head. The key words were 'prevention' and 'protection' – and there were many failings in both of these areas. At the same time, though, she was struck by the way individuals adapted to their limitations. A hand with no fingers was somehow able to tie a knot or pluck a bird. A homemade crutch replaced a woodcutter's need for a foot. The blind woman managed to feel her way around the cooking fire in spite of her toughened skin.

Each morning Anna saw the hunting party set off, armed with spears and accompanied by a pointy-eared dog that communicated through a strange blend of singing and howling instead of barking. Some of the men carried bulky nets made from thick string knotted together. They had their dark cloths tied over their shoulders; Anna presumed this was so that if they encountered anyone on their journey, they could cover themselves up. She was now sure the existence of the camp was not a secret – after her first evening here, the drummer had been at work again. Nobody paid him any special attention, so it couldn't have been out of the ordinary. The purpose of the shrouds must be to spare strangers the experience of looking at deformities – to avoid reminding people of what it meant to be a leper. Anna remembered Harry saying that in Africa nearly everyone was terrified of catching the disease. It didn't matter how often he explained that transmission between adults was rare – and that there was, anyway, a cure – the other patients at the hospital refused to go anywhere near the leper colony. Sometimes they insisted on seeing the doctor wash his hands before they would let him touch them. Anna realised that this deep-seated fear could mean that other communities would not like having lepers living in their area. The forest settlement might be tolerated only as long as its residents kept to themselves.

She wondered how long they'd been living here in the camp. The garden plots she'd glimpsed appeared to be well established, but she knew plants grew quickly in the rainforest. Peering out through the doorway she could see very few items that had come from elsewhere. Everything from cooking utensils to clothes to weapons were made of clay, leather, homespun fabric or hand-forged metal. The natural tones blended in with the forest. The few exceptions – some factory-woven printed cloths; sandals made from bits of car tyre; enamel bowls – looked old and worn. Any articles of European clothing that Anna saw were in tatters. She guessed they might be the same garments their owners had been wearing when the first symptoms of leprosy were noticed and they were forced to leave home. She understood that the community had no choice but to be self-sufficient. No one would engage in trade with lepers – they wouldn't even want to touch goods that they had handled. The fact that there was very little contact with the outside world fitted with the astonished reaction of the little girl when she first saw the visitor. Anna could well have been the only white-skinned foreigner, and the only completely healthy person, the child had ever encountered.

The isolation may have kept these people safe – especially during these dangerous times – but they'd paid a high price. They probably had no idea that their disease could now be cured, and the spread of infection stopped. Even if they were aware of the existence of Dapsone, they were almost certainly not receiving treatment – the drug had to be taken under a doctor's supervision, over a period of time. Judging by the evidence of fresh injuries, the lepers had never received any teaching about how to protect their nerve-damaged bodies. They were living trapped in the past.

Ignorant of what they were missing out on, the residents of the forest camp seemed content. Harmonious singing could often be heard, interrupted now and then with bursts of laughter. There was constant conversation. Anna wished she could join in. She wanted to get to know her companions here, and discover their stories. How had the healer learned her skills? Which of the adults – if any – was related to the little girl? Where were all the other children that the women, with their drooping withered breasts, must have birthed?

Anna knew the people were curious about her, too. She could see it in their eyes. She imagined learning their language, piecing it together word by word. Some things would be simple. *Leaf. Beetle. Sun. Rain. Smile.* Others would be more difficult to convey.

Aeroplane. Secretary. Australia.

Simbas. Prisoner. Wife.

A heart hammering with fear . . .

Anna tried to keep her focus on what was happening around her, but nightmarish memories hovered constantly at the edge of her mind. So did the sickening fear that something terrible had happened to Eliza and the Carlings. Then, there was the knowledge that she might never, now, be able to find out about her father: the world beyond the forest was too dangerous for her to return to – and she had no way of knowing when this situation would change. She had to accept that she might never discover the truth about her past. There would be no answers to the questions that plagued her most. Why had her father abandoned her? Why had he cut off all contact with her just because he and Marilyn divorced? Didn't he love her at all?

Anna was left alone with her emotions, unable to share them with anyone, and unable to act. Stranded on the bed, she would clench her fists, feeling impotent and frustrated. Because of her injury she couldn't do anything or go anywhere – she wasn't even able to drag herself outside to go to the toilet in the forest; she had to use a gourd-bowl and rely on others to empty it. She had to wait for food and water to be brought to her. For all practical purposes, she was as much a prisoner here as she had been in the room at Leopard Hall.

Once these dark thoughts took over, she saw the forest camp in a harsher light. While life here might not seem to be too bad – there was plenty of food, and fresh water from a nearby stream; it was safe; there was no sign of conflict in the community – the fact was that every ordinary daily activity was hard work for the lepers. Hunting, gardening and foraging were all a trial. Keeping bandages clean and dry was impossible; no wonder infections and injuries had taken such a toll. And Anna felt sure the people must yearn for their relatives, and the old life they'd been forced to leave behind. Perhaps they felt as trapped here as she did. She felt the weight of their predicament pressing down on her.

The brightest moments in her days were when the little girl came to the hut – her presence offered a welcome diversion. Anna found out that she was called Bela, via a lengthy process that had involved lots of pointing, and repeating of her own name. Bela liked to bring things for the visitor to see: a stick insect as long as her forearm; a chameleon, blanched with fear; a sweet potato, its purple skin still clumped with earth. She also liked to examine Anna's hands, touching the remains of the red nail polish; or to play with her hair, running the long strands through her fingers.

One afternoon as Anna lay on her side, gazing out towards the fire, Bela brought something extra special to show her. She arrived with it hidden behind her back. After waiting a short while to let Anna's curiosity build, she brought out a wooden mask.

At first glance Anna assumed the artifact was like the ones she'd seen in the gallery at Leopard Hall – but she soon discovered this mask was quite different. The nose was split in two. Round bumps marked the cheeks and forehead. The mouth was just a hole, with pointed teeth and no lips. It was a face formed by leprosy. The overall effect was strange, but not frightening – it had the look of a friendly monster from a child's storybook.

Anna smiled and nodded to show that she was impressed. Bela sat down beside the bed, leaning over the mask. She traced the wooden features with her fingers, circling the bumps, stroking the damaged nose. There was an expression of reverence on her face – this was obviously a very precious object. Anna wondered where it was kept. Perhaps there was a spirit hut somewhere in the camp, where the mask was housed along with the community's *nkisi*. She promised herself that as soon as she was able to walk she would seek the place out. She wanted the chance to see a power figure in its natural setting. Then she'd be able to imagine how the *nkisi* in the gallery – the spiky-backed dog, and all the other statues – might have looked in the places where they belonged.

When Anna had finished examining the mask, Bela put it carefully aside. She pulled a leaf from the wall – it was huge; the size of her torso. She began tearing holes in it, making a mask of her own. She hummed to herself as she worked. Anna watched the child's nimble fingers sculpting holes for eyes, nose, mouth.

Suddenly, she felt a sharp pain in her toe. She yelped in alarm. Swinging round, she saw a small furry animal scurry across the floor.

'A rat!' She shrank away from the place where it had disappeared into the leafy wall.

Bela looked mystified by Anna's reaction – then she laughed, showing a half-grown front tooth. Anna forced a weak smile in response. As she examined a tiny puncture mark in her skin she remembered what Harry had told her about numb fingers and toes being gnawed away while their owners were asleep.

'Do you have cats here?' she asked Bela. The words were

unintelligible, she knew – but it was hard to always remain silent. She meowed, to show what she meant.

Bela was delighted by this new game. She mimicked the sound, making it louder, stretching the syllables out. After several renditions she collapsed into giggles. Anna's heart sank. It was clear that Bela didn't recognise the noise made by a cat. Nor was she surprised to see a rat running around inside a hut.

Anna turned away from her. She found she couldn't bear to look at the child's perfect face, her graceful hands. For all she knew, Bela might already have leprosy; it took about five years for the first symptoms to show. If this were the case, urgent treatment was needed before irreversible damage occurred. If Bela was still free of the disease, she needed to be protected from catching it in the future. It was vital that she – along with all the other residents of the camp – have access to a supply of Dapsone. But there was a shortage of hospitals in the Congo, even in peacetime. And now the country was locked in a civil war. It was a hopeless situation. A sense of outrage stirred inside her. She felt as if she were watching a crime being carried out in slow motion, right before her eyes; and she was unable to intervene.

Pretending she was tired, Anna lay back down. After a while Bela got to her feet and crept outside. Anna watched her skip away towards the fringe of garden plots, calling to one of the people working there. Bela would reappear before long, Anna knew, chewing on some kind of treat – nuts or fruit, or even a piece of honeycomb. She was the centre of attention here. The only precious child. But all the love that was poured out would not be able to save her.

I will save her.

The words came into Anna's mind, bold and clear. For a moment she embraced their meaning. She imagined a journey out of the forest, to some place where help could – miraculously – be found. Then she shook her head. What was she thinking of? She was bedridden, trapped in the jungle, unable even to communicate with the people around her. She was weak, and beset by nightmares. Why should Anna imagine she could rescue Bela? She could not even save herself.

But the thought would not go away. Instead it settled in Anna's head like something that was alive, with a will of its own. It brought her a surprising sense of calm. She didn't know what her own future held. Maybe she had no future. So much was beyond her control. The idea that she might be able to help Bela and the other people here – even in some small way – felt like one sure thing that she could hold onto.

THIRTY-THREE

Dan stretched out his arms as he drove, pressing his back against the seat. His muscles were cramped, his eyes ached from studying the road and hunger gnawed his stomach. But a fierce energy filled his body. Since leaving Uvira the convoy had moved steadily without a break until dawn lightened the sky. After a quick meal the vehicles had set off again. They'd now been driving for half of this new day. Good progress had been made. It had been possible to remain on the minor road; so far there had been no sign of other soldiers – Simbas or government troops. The commandos were more than halfway to Banya. Their route was now following the path of a river: a grey-brown ribbon of water could be seen meandering through the forest to the right.

Smith was studying the map, his finger moving over the folded paper. 'There should be a turn-off somewhere around here.'

Dan raised his eyebrows. 'Where to?'

'A mission hospital, by the look of it. There's a red cross and the symbol for a church.'

Dan made no comment. He didn't like the idea of driving past the settlement without checking on the people there, but if the commandos took detours, it could take days to complete their journey. He had no way of knowing how much time, if any at all, could be spared.

The signpost appeared only a short distance along the road. It was hand-painted in bold letters.

'Presbyterian Mission,' Smith read out. 'Two miles.' He leaned forward, peering past Dan. 'It must be just beyond those trees.'

Dan looked in the direction Smith indicated. A white cross, mounted on a rooftop, rose out of the forest. It stood up against the sky like a beacon. Almost without making the decision, Dan found himself slowing down. Then he stuck out his right hand, signalling to the convoy that he was turning.

He glanced across at Smith. 'Let's take a quick look. We're not getting mixed up in anything. We'll just clean out the rebels if they're there, and keep going.'

As the jeep rattled along an even narrower track, Smith turned round to the back seat, ordering Remi to drop to the floor. Then he stood up, gripping the machine gun that was mounted beside him, his eyes raking their surroundings. Dan drove with one hand, his rifle aimed over the side of the jeep. Nearing a bend, he slowed to walking pace. As the jeep nosed around the corner a collection of buildings came into view. There was a house, a hospital and a church – all freshly painted in matching tones of green and white. They looked so new and neat that they reminded Dan of something from a toy box, set out ready for play. His grip on his gun relaxed as he saw that there were no military vehicles here. In the parking area was a Volkswagen Beetle and a white van that looked as if it might serve as an ambulance.

Bringing the jeep to a halt, he scanned the buildings, beginning with the house. Red-and-white checked curtains were drawn back, exposing shiny clean windows. He waited for a face to appear at one of the panes, or the front door to swing open – but everything remained quiet and still.

Dan shifted his attention to the hospital, identified by a red cross painted on the white facade. There was no sign of life there either – apart from a scrawny chicken that strutted across the front steps.

He looked around the grounds, seeing a decorative garden bed with succulents laid out to form the words *Praise the Lord*. An object caught his eye, lying on the path not far away. Focusing his gaze, he saw a blue plastic baby's rattle.

'Let's take a recce,' he said to Smith. He swung himself over the side of the jeep, his rifle lodged under his arm. Using hand signals, he directed four men to search the house and two others to come over to the hospital. He gestured for Eliza and Lawler to remain in the car.

Dan ran across a small quadrangle, keeping his head down. Smith, Malone and Thompson were on his heels. He jumped over a low concrete wall that edged the verandah, then he burst inside the building, the barrel of his gun following the sweep of his gaze. He took in a small ward with six beds – all empty. There were sheets trailing across the floor; one of the mattresses was askew. A half-full drip hung from a stand, its line dangling loose.

Dan ran on, entering an operating theatre with rows of instruments laid out on a tray. Used swabs were piled into a kidney dish. A facemask lay on the operating table, alongside a scalpel with a smeared blade.

'Looks like everyone left in a hurry.' Dan's voice bounced off the walls of the small room.

Smith met his gaze, grim-faced. 'Even the patient?'

Dan stared at the soiled wads of gauze. A sense of foreboding gathered in the pit of his stomach. 'Let's move on.'

After checking a storeroom and an office, they returned to the quadrangle. The other men had finished searching the house. Dan raised his eyebrows questioningly.

Bailey took a drag from his cigarette, holding it with his lips, not his hand. As he blew out smoke, he shook his head. 'Nobody around. Remains of a meal on the table. Looks like three adults. Four kids. There's a high chair as well.'

'I found a second parking area,' Henning contributed. 'A truck has been there – a Russian ZIS-5. Original tyres. I know the tread marks. And there are prints of army boots. Chinese Army issue.' He waited for Dan to nod before continuing. 'A palm tree has been cut down. Only the bottom part of the trunk is left.'

Dan's shoulders slumped as he bent his head. The rebels had come and gone, and now the place was deserted. It was impossible to be sure what that meant. The Simbas were unpredictable. For every account of atrocities being committed there were other reports of only minor theft or verbal abuse. There were acts of inexplicable mercy in the midst of violence. But the emptiness of this place was ominous. Dan remembered Girard's report about hostages, and the risk that they might be used as human shields. Could the Simbas have taken everyone with them? Surely sick people and young children were more trouble than they were worth? He stared towards the forest that bordered the clearing. Maybe at least some of the people here had had time to escape. They could be in hiding. He decided it would be worth getting McAdam to play his pipes to let them know that help had arrived. He hoped they'd hurry towards the sound – the commandos couldn't wait here long. Half an hour; no more.

As Dan turned around to locate the Scotsman, he noticed a footpath edged with painted stones at the far end of the parking area. It led in the direction of the river. Nearby there was a white bench and a picnic table arranged beneath a tree. In the eerie quiet of the abandoned mission the picturesque setting had a sinister feel. Dan strode towards it, his gun ready at his hip.

Only a short way along the path, he came to a wooden landing stage jutting into the river. His step faltered. The sun-bleached planks were caked with blood. It sat in pools, thick and dark, flies buzzing in the air above.

Drawing closer, he saw crisscross patterns of red footprints – army boots interspersed with bare feet. His eyes came to rest on one pair of prints set apart on its own. Clear and perfect. Made by the feet of a small child. Dan swallowed on a wave of nausea. A weight settled heavy and hard like a stone inside him.

When he turned back, he found the other men had followed him. Thompson was leaning into the bushes that lined the shore near the landing stage – he was retrieving items of clothing, throwing them onto the path. A man's linen shirt. A plaid skirt. A boy's T-shirt. A shoe with a scuffed toe. A little dress, pink with a pattern of yellow butterflies. Malone joined Thompson, reaching into the undergrowth, extracting more garments. Smith watched on, his face a mask of disbelief. He walked away, bending over, his shoulders heaving.

Dan picked up a small blue shirt. At the collar was a name tag of the kind mothers sew on their children's clothes when they pack for boarding school. *Timothy Winston* was woven in blue thread. Dan tightened his fist around the soft-worn fabric as he pieced the evidence together. A nightmare scene unfolded. He saw the Simbas marching their captives out of the house and the hospital, then herding them down to the landing stage. Judging by the amount of blood that had been shed, the soldiers must have used machetes, not bullets, to dispatch their prey. The terrified people must have been forced to take their final walk to the end of the platform before they were killed and their bodies flung into the river. The number and nationality of the victims could not be known, but from the clothes it was clear that the missionaries – including their children – had been among them. They had been made to strip before being slaughtered. The Simbas had not kept the garments; they just wanted to humiliate their victims. Dan could not imagine the torture that had been endured here – adults and children alike watching one another meet a terrible end. Even the baby. He thought of the urgent prayers giving way to screams; the figures crumpling and falling one by one. Then the bodies bobbing in the muddy water, leaking eddies of blood, as the current swept them away.

He looked downriver. Everything was peaceful and calm, with no hint of the horror that had played out here. A stork sailed down, skimming the surface of the water with its feet. Dan stared at the ripples spreading towards the banks.

When he turned around, Eliza was standing behind him. Her hand was pressed against her mouth, her fingers shaking. He saw the shock and horror burning like a fire in her eyes. When she spoke, her voice was just a whisper.

'How did this happen?'

The words, though barely audible, seemed to echo in the air. Dan looked at her in silence. He knew each of the war veterans standing here had heard that same question before – asked in different languages, in different countries – muttered in private or screamed out to the world. He was aware that for Eliza the agony went beyond this immediate tragedy to the whole disaster of the rebellion. As he searched her stricken face, the outrage he'd felt over her involvement with the Simbas and his suspicions about her loyalties evaporated. Sympathy rose up in its place. He wanted to tell her that he understood how dreams and reality could take different paths – how something that had started out looking clear and good became twisted. And how darkness, once let loose, could grow to blot out the light. But he found he could not speak. Instead he just laid the boy's shirt back down – adding it to the small pile of clothes that represented the rest of the family. Then he took a last look at the river. A fluttering movement at the far end of the platform caught his eye. A palm frond lodged between two planks was waving in the slight breeze. The telltale hallmark of the Simbas. Nearby was a patch of white. Dan walked towards it, avoiding the pools of red, his boots making a hollow sound on the wood. He saw that a piece of folded paper had been pinned to the decking with a handmade nail. Picking it up he read a note written in a thick lead pencil of the kind children use in school.

Il n'y a pas de Dieu. Il n'y a plus de dimanche. There is no God. There are no more Sundays.

He stared at the paper, smeared at the edges with blood. He presumed it was a message left by the Simbas, aimed at whoever discovered this gruesome scene. The way the letters were pressed into the paper he could almost feel the animosity behind the words. He knew the emotions were not directly connected to the missionaries who'd been killed here – the soldiers who'd arrived in their trucks were strangers to the area. From what had been written, it seemed their actions had been fuelled by resentment of Christian teachings. It was not hard to understand why the rebels felt this way. The troops were led by witchdoctors; the men were loyal to their traditional beliefs. Few Europeans understood or respected the spiritual practices of Africans. It was generally agreed that in an ideal world all the Congolese would convert to Christianity. Villagers who did make that choice were often required to burn down their sacred huts, throw away their drums and destroy their *nkisi*. Dan understood how traumatic this would be, even to some of the converts – let alone other Africans looking on. But were experiences like these enough to drive men to slaughter innocent children?

As Dan re-read the chilling words on the note, his thoughts turned to some of the conversations he'd held these last weeks – with civilians and soldiers, Africans and Europeans. He was aware that the true motivations of the Simbas who'd been at this mission were likely to be more complicated. From the years he'd spent living in this country he already knew how badly the Congolese people had suffered under colonial rule. Now their hopes for a new life after Independence had been shattered. Foreign powers were still running the country from behind the scenes. Some of the people Dan talked to believed that the Belgians, the Americans and the British had all been involved in plans to have Lumumba assassinated – which fitted with what Dan had picked up himself from listening to Becker and Dupont. The leaders who stood in Lumumba's place catered too much to the interests of outsiders. Among the ordinary Congolese, disappointment had turned to despair. It was not surprising that anger had boiled over.

It was against this backdrop that the terrible scene here on the landing stage had been enacted. The victims may have paid the price for their desire to convert Africans to their religion – but there were other issues at play. The missionaries had been punished for what other foreigners had done to the Congolese in the past, and what they were still doing, right now. Foreign governments, along with their armies and Intelligence agencies, private companies, the powerbrokers of the church, even the United Nations – they'd all helped create this nightmare.

Dan stood alone on the wooden platform, breathing the smell of blood baking in the sun. All the misgivings and uncertainties that he'd ignored while he focused on the urgent tasks in hand now gathered around him. The stark reality came into focus. He should never have signed up for this war. If every last Simba were killed, there would still be no peace in this land – not until the wrongs of the past were put right, and the Congo was granted real freedom. And this was as likely to happen as a snowstorm in a tropical rainforest. He thought back to Blair's inspiring words about fighting for the future of the free world. Did the Major know the true agendas of the people he served, Dan wondered – or was he ignorant and naïve? Perhaps he was just blinded by his desire to be a soldier with a job to do. Regardless of his intentions, the Major had played his part in deepening the chaos in the Congo. So had all the mercenaries he'd recruited – including Dan.

The scrap of bloodied paper was still clutched in Dan's hand. He knew the note should be kept; it was evidence of a crime and should be handed to someone in authority. But he also knew the real reasons for the massacre would never be acknowledged; the backroom partners in this atrocity would go unnamed. Feeling sick to his stomach, his heart tight with anger, Dan screwed the paper into a ball. Then he bent to pick up the palm frond. He hurled both objects into the river. They floated side by side for a while, like two little boats. Then the paper sank into the water and the Simba talisman sailed on alone.

He strode back to the riverbank, where the other soldiers stood in a group, awaiting his instructions. Eliza was a little further along the path. As Dan met her gaze he could see that her thoughts, like his, were already turning from this place. She was thinking of the mission where they were headed. He nodded faintly. Her eyes mirrored his own unspeakable fear: that the same terrible violence might have been inflicted on her friends the Carlings. And Anna.

'Let's get out of here.' He gestured for the others to follow him as he headed back up the narrow path. As he broke into a jog, he heard the thud of their boots behind him and the rustle of bushes parting as gun barrels brushed by. Reaching the parking area, he scanned the scene. Everything was as quiet and still as when the soldiers had first arrived. From the direction of the jeep came the sound of Smith's dog whining to be set free.

THIRTY-FOUR

Dan drove in grim silence, his eyes fixed on the road. Beside him, Smith was equally quiet. Barely a word had passed between them since they'd driven away from the mission station. The horror of what they'd discovered there was a haunting presence in the air. Smith had brought the dog over from the back seat to sit in the footwell. He stroked the hound's head, his hand moving mechanically. Remi watched him with an intent gaze. His ears were pointing forwards and his brow was wrinkled as if he were picking up on the emotions that surrounded him.

The sun was halfway down the sky, casting slanting shadows across the road. Dan kept up the pressure on the accelerator. If he could maintain this pace, the convoy should be able to reach first Banya, then the Carlings' mission, before night fell. Dan tried not to imagine what might be awaiting him there. He tried not to picture the scene he'd left behind, either. That just left the landscape – trees, rocks, earth, jolting past him – as a focus for his thoughts.

The first clue to what lay ahead was a series of small craters in the road. Dan looked up instinctively – as if he might still catch sight of the aircraft that had flown overhead, strafing the ground. But the sky was empty and there was no sound of a prop engine. A puzzled frown came onto his face. Why had Air Support targeted this inland road? Dan had found no sign that rebel troops had been along here. In fact, this section of the route seemed seldom used by anyone. Vines were creeping in from the verges. The last village the convoy had passed was miles back. He glanced across to Smith, eyebrows raised.

As they came round the next corner, Dan slammed on the brakes. The road was blocked with the wreck of a burnt-out truck. He checked his rear-vision mirror, seeing the vehicles behind him slowing to a halt. Turning back to the truck, he took in the scene ahead. There were two dead bodies in army uniforms lying on the ground. The men's faces were bloated, tongues protruding. Their black skin had taken on the bluish tinge that Dan knew too well. It was hard to say how long the soldiers had been here. The humid conditions sped up the process of decay. Items that must have been blown from the truck before it caught fire were spread across the ground. Among the debris Dan noticed a helmet decorated with a strip of leopardskin. His gaze came to rest on a green beret. He turned back to Smith.

'Simbas . . .'

Smith frowned. 'Heading back up north to regroup?'

Dan shrugged. 'Who knows? I don't think anyone's in charge down here.'

He scanned a wider area, looking further along the road, where he noticed a simple bridge made of logs felled over a stream. The only sign of life came from birds scavenging along the banks. He breathed the smell of burned oil and spent explosives, backed by the cloying stink of decomposing flesh. Remi was sniffing the air, too. Hackles stood up along his back and his neck. Smith tied the hound to the door handle with a rope.

Grabbing their guns, the two men jumped out of the jeep. Dan glanced back along the convoy. The other soldiers were already following suit. They'd been in this situation many times before – they all knew that before detouring around the truck they had to make sure there were no survivors. Even badly injured soldiers could aim a gun and squeeze a trigger. Men in better shape might have retreated into the bushes that lined the road.

The stillness of the place was accentuated by a chorus of noises – buzzing flies hovering over the corpses, the distant sound of rushing water, the usual chirping and screeching coming from the forest.

Dan's boots crunched over the ground as he walked. Many of the objects he saw scattered on the road were in pieces; some were burned beyond recognition. The undamaged items stood out in contrast: a ration box, a rifle, a kitbag. There was a woman's shoe lying on its side. Dan eyed it for a moment, thinking of its owner – some innocent army camp follower who had hitched her last ride on the ill-fated truck.

As he approached the destroyed vehicle, with Smith at his back, he reconstructed the events that had taken place here – the attack from above, the explosion, the fire. Some of the soldiers had been thrown clear of the wreck, but others had been incinerated.

At the rear of the truck Dan discovered a third unburned corpse – another African, clad in an army uniform. As it came into full view, he jerked to a halt, staring at the grisly sight. The head was missing. So was one of the legs. Where the abdomen had been was just a bloodstained hole.

'Holy hell . . .' Smith murmured.

Dan swapped a look with him. As a game ranger, Smith would know as well as he did that this was not the result of the explosion. It was the work of an animal. The hole in the body had been chewed.

The absence of the head, with its hidden prize inside the skull, was further evidence. Crouching down, Dan studied the ground. A paw print was visible in an area of sandy gravel. He took in the four toes and the distinctive shape of the pad; there was no mark left by the claws.

'Leopard.'

Smith nodded. 'A large male.' He pointed to a line of tracks leading towards the edge of the road. 'Looks like a normal gait. Uninjured.'

Dan shook his head in surprise. A healthy carnivore usually preferred to kill its own prey. And man-eaters were a much rarer phenomenon than their almost mythological status suggested.

'He's picked up a taste for human flesh,' Smith said. 'And probably not just from here.'

Dan looked at the gory remains in silence. He thought of all the corpses that were strewn across the battlefields of the Congo – in villages and fields, and on the sides of roads. Many victims of this conflict, whether soldiers or civilians, didn't get a proper burial. The survivors were traumatised and overwhelmed; often the best they could manage was to drag the bodies away from their homes. There wasn't always a river handy, like there had been at the mission station where Dan had just been.

'I've seen how it works,' Smith said. 'A couple of years ago I was asked to help get rid of a man-eater. It was following an outbreak of typhoid fever.' Dan had the feeling the man was talking just to break the silence. 'There weren't enough healthy people to dig graves so the dead were just dragged into the bush. The local leopard started to expect a daily feed. When the epidemic was over, the free meat delivery stopped. He had a liking for human flesh by then so he began hunting for himself.'

As Smith spoke, Dan eyed the lower branches of the trees and the dark spaces between the bushes. He wondered how recently the leopard had been here. From the sun-baked remains it was impossible to guess. The animal could be far away by now – the solitary cats liked plenty of space; some had a range of 50 square miles. On the other hand, there was still a lot of food left to be consumed. The leopard might be close by, waiting to return to its meal. It would be wise to be cautious.

He looked along the road, intending to shout out a warning about this added danger – but the soldiers were already heading back towards their vehicles. Eliza was among them, armed with her banana gun. Her head turned from side to side as she walked, her eyes trained on the bushes. If she was unnerved by the situation, she showed no sign of it.

Dan looked up at the sky, checking the position of the sun. Not only had this disruption caused a delay, but the convoy would now have to proceed with extra caution. He tightened his jaw, feeling deepening concern. He didn't want to let another night go by before they reached the Carlings' mission. Spinning on his heels, he strode back towards the jeep. He was nearly there when a gleam of metal caught his eye – a round, flat object protruding from a clump of ferns. At first he thought it was a hubcap, but it was too big. When he looked more closely he saw it was a silver serving tray. It was large and ornate, with a crest engraved in the middle – the heirloom had obviously been pilfered from a grand home somewhere. That it should end up here, in this scene of carnage, seemed to symbolise the bizarre nature of this conflict that Dan was a part of. The Simbas wanted their fair share of the wealth of the Congo. All these men had acquired was a useless souvenir. And then they'd been killed.

Reaching the jeep, Dan jumped into his seat. The other soldiers were now climbing into their own vehicles, looking as eager to get moving as he was. With a jolt of alarm, he saw that Eliza was no longer with her partner. Dan located her a short distance away. She was standing rock-still, peering into the bushes. Lawler was already running back to get her. Henning was hard on his heels. Dan raised his gun, looking down the sights, ready to shoot at whatever – whoever – had caught her eye.

He watched as she reached down, picking something out of the foliage. When she straightened up, she had the remains of a small red suitcase in her hand. The lid was half blown off. There was nothing inside. But from the look on her face, Dan knew that the object held some special significance.

As he arrived at her side, Eliza looked up. Her eyes were wide with alarm. 'I lent this to Anna. It was at the mission.'

It took a moment for Dan to take in the meaning of her words. Then his heart turned cold.

Eliza dropped the case. 'We have to get there.'

They'd only taken a few steps back towards the vehicles when Dan saw Henning freeze. The next moment he was raising his rifle – aiming into the trees. There was the faint click of the safety catch being turned off. Following the direction of the gun barrel, Dan stared into the undergrowth. He could see no hint of the dark-spotted coat of a forest leopard, or the telltale gleam of bared teeth. He felt a spike of admiration for Henning; the man had eyes like a hawk.

Dan waited for the shot. Instead of firing, though, Henning raised his hand. Beckoning. The gesture was very clear: he might have been a policeman directing traffic. Some fern fronds moved and a figure emerged, crawling on hands and knees. It was an

African soldier wearing battle fatigues. Using a sapling to pull himself to his feet, the man limped into the road, holding his hands in the air. His bloodied uniform hung from his body in shreds. Dan saw the small scar on his forehead: the shape of a cross.

The Simba took two more steps, then collapsed onto the ground. While Henning dropped down beside him, Bailey plunged into the bushes, pistol drawn. He crashed around, looking for anyone else who might be hidden there. Lawler moved up to stand with Eliza; he was on full alert, ready to spring into action.

Henning extracted a knife and a pistol from the rebel soldier's pockets, tossing them behind him. Then Malone began applying his medical skills – pushing back the man's eyelids to check his pupils, and taking his pulse.

Dan pulled a water canteen from his belt and handed it to Henning. 'Keep him conscious,' he instructed. 'I want to talk to him.'

As water was splashed over his face, the Simba moved his lips. Dan squatted down beside him.

'*Umewatendea nini wamisionari?*' he demanded. What have you done to the missionaries?

There was no response. Dan got Henning to ask the same question in French. In the silence that ensued Dan shook the Simba's shoulder, making him wince. He felt an urge to shout into the prisoner's impassive face.

What have you done to my daughter?

The words rose up inside him, unspoken, yet roaring in his head. He had a flash image of Becker at work – and for just an instant, he wished the ruthless Intelligence Sergeant were here at his side.

Eliza knelt down beside Dan. Her arm brushed against his. The moment of contact steadied him, like a calming word. He reminded himself that this man and his companions might just be simple thieves. Or they might be completely innocent of any wrongdoing.

'Let me try,' Eliza offered.

She began speaking a different African tongue to Swahili. Dan recognised it as Lingala – he used to have a basic grasp of the language when he was prospecting up in Orientale Province. But that had been back before Anna was born; he'd forgotten most of it now.

Eliza spoke slowly but insistently. Still, there was no reply. 'I will try Tshiluba,' she said. 'But I'm not fluent.'

When she spoke again the soldier opened his eyes. He looked at Eliza in amazement, as if she were a ghost come to life. He whispered something to her. She gave him a faint smile.

'What's he saying?' Dan asked.

'He is naming the Okapi.'

Eliza exchanged some more words with the Simba. She spoke haltingly, stopping to hunt for vocabulary; there were pauses while she struggled to understand what she was hearing. Eventually she turned to Dan.

'He says he has not seen any missionaries. He has not been to any place where such people live.' Her eyebrows lifted in surprise as she translated the man's next remark. 'When he began the journey that brought him here, he was at the House of the Leopard.'

'Leopard Hall?' Dan stared at her in confusion. 'Show him the suitcase. Ask him where it came from.'

Eliza sounded patient and calm as she phrased the question but Dan could tell she felt the same urgency that he did. As she listened to the Simba's response, Dan searched her expression for clues to what she was learning. Her face became a mask of shock and distress. When it was her turn to speak, her voice quavered with emotion.

'He says it belonged to a white woman who was in the truck. I asked him what she looked like.' She broke off, her words catching in her throat. 'He said she was young. Beautiful.'

Dan looked back towards the burnt-out vehicle, recoiling from the memory of the charred remains still resting on the blackened seats. He hardly noticed when the Simba spoke again. But as Eliza relayed his words the tone of her voice brought him back.

'She didn't die in the fire. She was on the road. He saw her!'

Dan shook his head, struggling to absorb the new information. Then he leaned over the Simba, looking into his bloodshot eyes. 'Where is she? Where did she go?'

Eliza touched Dan's hand. 'He does not know. He was looking after himself. She just disappeared.' She turned towards the headless corpse nearby, but didn't name the obvious fear.

'When did all this happen?' Dan felt torn between hope and despair.

'It has been several nights and days,' Eliza reported. 'He's not sure. At first he salvaged food and water that had been in the truck. Then he didn't have the strength to move.'

Dan stared into the forest. Had Anna been carried away by the leopard? Or had she taken refuge in the bushes, like this Simba had done? Perhaps she, too, had managed to collect some supplies. It was hard to imagine anyone surviving an aerial assault – being blown from a truck – without being hurt. She could be lying among the trees, injured and in desperate need of rescue. But surely she would have shouted out for help? She'd have heard the sound of English voices, and the noise of the convoy arriving. Perhaps she was too weak to make herself heard. Or she might have wandered too far away. Or . . . He refused to let any other option lodge in his mind.

Stepping onto the verge, Dan cupped his hands, shouting, 'Anna! Anna . . .' His cries seemed to be swallowed by the forest; muffled by moss, tangled up in the vines. There was no reply.

He swung around to face Smith, who was standing guard behind him. 'Start looking for tracks. Get Bailey to cover you.'

Soon all the soldiers were taking part in the search, but with the dense undergrowth, the task was time-consuming and fruitless. After a while, Dan returned to the road and summoned McAdam.

'The convoy will have to keep moving on to the mission,' Dan said. 'But I'm staying here.'

McAdam nodded slowly. Dan knew he was thinking the situation through for himself. The Commanding Officer was too emotionally involved for his decision-making to be relied upon. Also, in this unofficial band of commandos, the men were on more equal terms.

'Keep Henning and Bailey with you,' the Corporal suggested, 'and Smith, of course. I'll take the others. That's an even split.'

Dan was silent for a moment. When the numbers were halved, so were their chances of surviving an encounter with the enemy. But there was more hope of finding Anna if he had help. He signalled his agreement. 'Leave us one of the radios. Try making contact when you get there.'

'Yes, sir,' McAdam responded. 'We'll listen out for something from you, too.'

'Take the Simba with you,' Dan added. 'He can be admitted to the hospital at the mission – all being well.' The two men exchanged looks, the euphemistic words hovering between them.

All being well . . .

'And Miss Lindenbaum?' queried McAdam.

Before Dan could reply, Eliza appeared at his side. He heard her take a breath – then she spoke in a tone that was clear and firm. 'I'm staying too.'

Dan shook his head. More than anything, he wished she could stay here with him – if they found Anna, she would want to see a familiar face. But the image of the chewed carcass was fresh in his mind. 'It's too dangerous here.'

Eliza ignored him. She addressed McAdam. 'When you get to Banya, pick up a local resident to be your guide. Everyone knows where the Carlings live. Take my car with you, so you've got room for them all. Get them out of Kivu. Down to Albertville. Make sure they're safe.'

There was a tremor in her voice as she spoke about her friends. Dan saw that she was torn. She wanted to stay and help find Anna, but the Carlings were precious to her too. And she'd known them for years. He wondered if he should take the decision out of her hands and simply order her to go with McAdam.

As if she'd heard his thoughts, Eliza turned to look at him. Her eyes were dark with distress. 'I drove Anna up from Albertville. Then I left her behind at the mission. I didn't look after her.' She pressed her lips together for a second, before going on. 'Whatever has happened to her – it's my fault. My fault.'

Dan could feel her anguish as she repeated these last words. He had the sense that – once again – she was referring not just to Anna's fate but to a wider guilt she felt about other choices she'd made. He knew what it was like to be weighed down with regret and remorse; and to be confronted by a reality that wasn't what you'd planned. You couldn't go back and change the past. All that you had left was the future.

As he nodded his agreement, he felt a sense of relief. Eliza was Anna's friend. They'd been together only a short time ago. He thought of them talking, laughing, swapping stories. It made his daughter seem more real – and more likely to be found.

*

Dan walked slowly along, scouring the surface of the road. This was the area where the Simba said he'd seen the white woman lying on the ground. There was no sign, yet, that anyone had been here – no footprints or other impressions in the sandy gravel. No blood. Dan had continued to call out Anna's name, his voice turning hoarse with desperation. But there had still been no response.

His eyes settled on the shoe that he'd seen before. It had held little meaning for him then, but now that he looked at it more closely, he saw it was well made, expensive. He felt a twist in his stomach. It belonged to Anna. Part of him wanted to pick it up – to feel inside for the imprint in the soft leather left by her foot. But that would be a distraction. He kept moving steadily on, his eyes sweeping the ground. Smith was doing the same, not far away. Eliza was covering a sector as well; as a photographer, she'd said, her eyes were trained to notice fine details. Henning and Bailey were on guard duty – watching out for the return of the leopard, or the arrival of more Simbas.

As he walked further on, beyond the area that had been identified, Dan thought back over the interchange with the soldier, trying to work out if there could have been any misunderstanding. He almost regretted sending the man off with McAdam. There was no chance, now, to interview him again. Dan had given up the idea of trying to find any other source of information. If somebody had heard the explosion or seen the black smoke rising from the truck, they'd have come to investigate. And if that had occurred, the ration box and rifle wouldn't still be there. Nor would the silver tray. Aside from the wounded Simba, it seemed almost certain there had been no witnesses to what had taken place here, even after the fact.

Near a piece of aluminium melted to a shiny puddle, Dan came to a standstill. Then he bent to peer at the ground more closely. At his feet was an oily-looking patch of brown. Ants clustered around it, their bodies fanning out like a fringe of black hairs. As he stared down at it, Dan felt a sinking dismay. It took a lot of blood, from a serious wound, to form a stain like that.

Nearby, there were marks on the road – scrapes and scuffs, some blurred footprints. There was a long smear of blood. A couple of dark red spots.

'Over here!' he called out to Smith and Eliza. 'I've found something . . .'

As he followed the trail towards the edge of the road, he assessed what he could see. He tried to view the task with a dispassionate eye. The injured person had been unable to walk. They had pulled themselves along, trailing one leg. That meant they were hurt, but not too weak to move.

He knew it might not have been Anna who'd been here on the road, bleeding, before then struggling towards the forest. It could have been one of the three soldiers who were now corpses. There might have been another survivor who was no longer around. But as a bushman and a soldier, Dan had learned to listen to his instincts. A gut feeling could disrupt logic and lead a person astray – but more often, the impulse was one to follow.

He gazed into the forest, at the tangled mass of trees and shrubs, sewn together by creepers and vines.

'Anna,' he whispered. 'Where are you?'

Reaching the grassy verge, he searched for some sign that she had pushed her way through the foliage in front of him. In the drier country where he took his hunting clients, the trees and bushes were brittle and spiky; a sharp eye might pick out a snagged fragment of cloth, or a hair, or notice a broken twig. But these rainforest plants had leaves that were smooth-edged and supple; their stems would bend, not snap. If a local tracker were here, he might detect something that was out of place. But Dan could find no clues. He plunged into the undergrowth, searching under bushes, ferns, low trees.

Cupping his hands around his mouth, he shouted into the trees once more. 'Anna!'

He strained his ears to hear a reply – but as before, there was nothing. All he could pick up was the incessant background noise from the forest, punctuated by the thud of heavy boots as Henning and Bailey paced the road, sticking to their tasks. Remi was whining again. With a burst of irritation, Dan spun around towards the jeep. He could see the dog clearly through a gap in the bushes. He was pulling at his rope, panting, his tongue hanging out. The hound could smell the leopard, Dan knew – even if the predator was long gone, its scent would have lingered on the bodies where it had fed. But Remi didn't appear to be afraid. He looked more like a wild animal himself, preparing to attack.

Dan's feet seemed to move ahead of his thoughts – as he picked his path back to the road, then on towards the jeep, he was still making connections in his mind. Remi was no lapdog; his coat, streaked with bald scars, told the tale of too many injuries. And Bergman would have spent plenty of time hunting – every farmer in Africa shot game for the table and culled animals that were a threat to the livestock. A hound worth his keep would know how to track a wounded animal; his own dinner depended on making sure the game was found and brought home . . .

Smith must have read Dan's intention. He reached the jeep first, and untied Remi's rope. The dog bounded from the seat, immediately putting his nose to the ground, pulling against his master's grip on the leash. His sturdy shoulders were bunched; his body was low slung. The tail, with the kink at the end, waved like a pennant.

Smith hauled Remi over to the pool of dried blood. The dog sniffed at it, but then looked up distractedly. He kept turning towards the body that had been savaged by the leopard.

'There's too much going on here,' Dan said.

'Give him time,' Smith responded. He knelt by the dog, pointing at the blood. 'Here. Look. Come on, Remi!'

The commands were clearly meaningless, even when Henning gave them in French. Bergman must have had his own special form of communication – words, gestures, the rituals of the hunt. Dan struggled to contain his impatience. He was acutely aware of the steady sinking of the sun in the sky.

Smith kept on drawing the hound's attention back to the blood. Suddenly, without warning, Remi seemed to make a decision. He stood still for a few seconds, blowing air out of his nose like a horse. Then he put down his head, latching onto the trail, taking the same path Dan had already followed.

Dan went after the dog alone. He didn't want extra people in here who might foul the trail, and he knew he could trust Remi to let him know if there was a fresh smell of leopard in the air. Pushing through dense foliage, he emerged in an area of more open ground lying between tall mahogany trees. Remi nosed his way along confidently and quickly. Dan knew that scents lingered longest in shady, protected places where the air was still; the conditions in the forest were perfect. He slung his rifle over his shoulder to free his hands as he ducked under branches and dodged tall ferns.

In a small clearing Remi came to a halt, standing at the foot of a tall African oak. Moss-clad roots reached out from its wide base, bulging from the earth like giant snakes. The dog explored the area in front of it, sniffing avidly. Dan could see nothing there apart from layers of dead leaves.

After a few moments Remi began jogging around the open space, his nose fixed to the earth. But then he returned to the foot of the oak. Dread formed a lump in Dan's throat as he peered up into the spreading limbs above him. He expected to see a limp body hanging there – the abandoned prey of the leopard. But the branches were bare, apart from a green coating of fairy ferns. There were no claw marks in the bark. And Remi was not looking up, or sniffing the trunk; he was focused only on the ground at the base of the tree.

Straining his eyes in the gloomy light, Dan studied the area more closely. He saw a large toadstool nearby, its cap forming a mauve disc. There was a brown smear of blood on one side. Dropping down beside Remi, he grabbed a handful of damp leaves. Holding them to his nose, he breathed in. He picked up a familiar metallic smell. When he rubbed the leaves with his fingers a brown stain printed onto his skin.

Dan knelt there, motionless, gazing down at the ground. His heart thumped in his chest.

Anna had been right here. Her blood had seeped into the earth.

But now she was gone.

The five figures stood in the middle of the road. Nobody spoke. Remi sat at Smith's feet – head up, ears pricked. He was waiting for his next command. But there was nothing more that could be done tonight – the light was fading; in the forest it was already difficult to see.

Dan knew he should make a decision about what they would

do next. The safest option was to drive on to another area and return at dawn to carry out a search. But Dan didn't want to leave. This was the last place where Anna had been. Whether she was dead or still alive somewhere, he was not prepared to abandon her. Not again. When he looked around at the faces of his companions, he knew they felt the same way. They all kept staring into the forest as if they expected Anna to appear. Dan considered the option of setting up the tents that had been stowed in each of the vehicles. Leopards normally had a nervous temperament and would stay well away from an unfamiliar structure made of canvas – however, an animal whose behaviour had been corrupted by contact with humans was an unknown quantity. It might be wiser for the group to assemble in the two vehicles that had solid cabins and try to sleep with the windows wound up – but then, with everyone squashed in together it would be unbearably hot. The best plan, Dan decided, was to gather around a roaring fire – a source of fear to most wildlife – and take turns to keep watch. Remi was their best protection; the dog would remain alert even while sleeping.

Once Dan announced his decision, everyone sprang into action. Henning dragged the dead Simbas into a pile on the far side of the truck. He poured petrol over the corpses and set them alight. The smell of rotting flesh was replaced by one that was disconcertingly similar to roasting meat, but the smoke rising in the still air carried most of it away. Henning watched on with a look of grim satisfaction. Dan knew the man didn't like to see a body left unburied, regardless of the risk of attracting carnivores. In Henning's book it was bad form for a soldier not to do what he could – when he had the chance – to preserve the dignity of the enemy.

Bailey, meanwhile, got to work packing a hollow log with explosives, then blowing it to pieces. He couldn't hide his enjoyment of the task, or his sense of accomplishment at creating instant fuel. Eliza helped him drag the splintered portions of deep red hardwood across to the camp fire. Remi had been let off his leash, but Smith was keeping a close watch on him. Dan found himself following the movements of the dog as well. It was like having a child in their midst – a welcome distraction from the thoughts that haunted him.

It was after sunset when Henning picked up the sound of a radio transmission. As he ran to his jeep, Eliza dropped a stick she was using to prod the fire and went after him. Dan followed her, his eyes fixed on Henning's face as he lifted the receiver to his ear. The man's pale features stood out in the dusk light. He nodded briskly, then he gave a 'thumbs up' sign.

'The Carling family, they are all safe.'

Eliza's eyes filled with tears of relief.

Henning continued the communication. He relayed each piece of information as he received it. 'The Simbas raided the hospital but they did not stay. There was a lot of damage but no one was hurt. McAdam says they will all leave for Albertville tomorrow.'

'Thank God for that,' Dan said. At least one nightmare was coming to an end. He tried to smile but his face felt wooden, as if it belonged to someone else. His emotions were like a tangled string. Some part of him that he despised was unable to fully grasp the good news – the fact that Anna was still missing obscured the joy he wanted to feel. He walked away by himself, afraid that this darkness inside him might be visible in his eyes.

Looking up, he saw the shaggy silhouette of a fishing owl perched on a branch that overhung the road. It was not far away; Dan could almost see the featherless legs and talons, designed to plunge into water. Soon, it would begin its night's work, hunting fish and frogs in the nearby stream. Dan grasped this train of thought to escape his turmoil. He imagined the bird swooping silently, barely ruffling the water as it carried off its prey.

He heard a light footstep behind him. Then Eliza was standing at his side. In spite of the tainted smoke that clouded the air, he could smell just a hint of the distinctive perfume that she wore. She said nothing. She just put her hand on his shoulder.

The small gesture shattered his composure. Before he could measure his words, they poured out. 'I'm afraid we won't find her. It will all be finished. Before it's even begun.' His voice was raw with despair. 'I'll never see her. I'll never hold her in my arms.'

He knew that he should be able to be strong. Eliza cared about Anna too. And she was grief-stricken – she'd just lost the man she loved; the rescue of the Carlings didn't change that. But when Dan reached inside himself he found no weapon he could use to combat his weakness. At this minute he had nothing to offer – to Eliza or anyone else. He could see no light ahead. He focused on the touch of the woman's hand, the faint warmth that reached through the cloth of his shirt. Only the presence of another human – circling like a planet through the same dark space that he occupied – held any comfort.

The owl called out, a low note followed by a series of short high-pitched hoots. From longstanding habit Dan waited to see if another owl would reply, or if this was a solitary bird. As he listened in the dying light he noticed that a hush had fallen over the forest. These were the last minutes before the brief tropical dusk turned to blackness. All the insects and birds that had buzzed and screeched during the day were now at rest. The night shift was yet to take over.

Into the lull came a new sound, travelling on the breathless air. At first there were just a few isolated beats, but then a rhythm developed. Dan stiffened in surprise, recognising the voice of a talking drum. He turned his head towards the source. The throbbing pulse was coming from the forest. His lips parted as the realisation came to him that somewhere – hidden among the trees – was a village. He turned to Eliza, watching the same understanding dawn across her face.

At that moment the owl called out again, its resonant cry riding over the drumbeat. Dan looked around just in time to see the bird spread its huge wings, dropping from the branch. Catching the updraft, it soared into the air like a plane.

The owl flew above the road in the direction of the bridge. There it dipped one wing, slicing the air. Wheeling round, it headed upstream, as if answering the call of the drum.

THIRTY-FIVE

Smoke drifted in the still morning air, forming soft wisps of blue. Anna leaned towards the fire, using a stick to retrieve a sweet potato. There were still another half-dozen of them roasting in the embers. They had to be turned over regularly so they didn't burn. It was hot work – the fire added to the steamy warmth of the air. But Anna was glad to be doing something useful. In the last few days she'd been able to make her way slowly across to the fireside using a borrowed crutch. No longer trapped in the hut, she had a better picture of what was going on in the camp, and she felt more a part of it all.

The hunters were out in the forest; they'd left at the first glimmer of dawn carrying their loads of nets, their bodies adorned with weapons, the dog with its nose to the ground leading the way. While they were gone, the other people worked in the gardens. From where Anna sat – perched on a log with her legs stretched out in front of her – she could see a woman digging in a vegetable plot with a stick. A man stood nearby with a gourd he'd filled from the stream. He poured water over each of the plants in turn. Bela was picking tiny snails off their leaves, squashing them between her fingers.

When the potato had cooled a little, Anna broke it open, picking out chunks of sweet white flesh. Her hands were smudged with charcoal from the blackened skin; she knew her face was dirty, too. Her hair had been plaited by Bela – not in cornrows, the way the Africans did theirs, but one behind each ear. When Anna had run her hands over the braids, she'd known straight away that they were of unequal thickness. The parting was off-centre. Once, Anna would have unravelled them as quickly as possible, but she didn't want to dishearten Bela. And anyway, no one in the camp cared what their visitor looked like. It didn't matter that her cream dress was stained, or that the hem was torn. Anna looked down at her roughened hands. Her nails had grown; the half-moons of white below the chipped red varnish were a clear marker of how much time had passed since she'd left Albertville. She wasn't sure exactly how many weeks it had been – but it felt like a whole portion of her life. Anna knew she would be unrecognisable to people back in Melbourne. Mr Williams would be unable to believe his eyes. The detective, Murphy, would no longer be able to match the young woman with her profile. What Marilyn would have to say about the state she was in, Anna didn't like to imagine . . .

As an image of her mother's face came into her mind, Anna stared blankly down at the steaming potato. She didn't know if Marilyn was aware of what was happening in the Congo – whether she could have discovered, somehow, that her daughter was missing. When Anna pictured Marilyn, frantic with worry, she felt guilty, but underneath, she was still angry that she'd been refused any information about her father. If Marilyn had responded differently in the phone call Anna had made back at Eliza's house, Anna would not have had to come to Banya. And she would not be where she was now.

Anna shook her head, clearing her thoughts. She couldn't think about Marilyn. Just like she couldn't think about the Carlings, or

Eliza, or the search for her father. It was pointless to let herself worry about how long she had already been here, or what would happen next. She had to keep her mind in the present. She tuned her ears to the forest, picking out different birds and insects. She didn't know what species any of them were, but during the days she'd spent lying on the bed she'd learned to recognise many of the sounds. While she was listening, she focused on what she could feel. The trickle of sweat edging down her back. The hard timber of the log on which she sat. The dull pain in her leg. To occupy her eyes she studied the wooden crutch that was on the ground at her feet. She could see how it had been made, using a forked stick. The crossbar had been lashed in place with lengths of sinew, then padded with a wrapping of monkey fur. The wood had a smooth patina formed from many years of use. Marks burned in the surface made a decorative pattern of crisscrossed lines and spots.

Anna was about to pick up the crutch, to look at the motifs more closely, when a distant sound caught her attention, standing out from the usual array of noises. She cocked her ear in the direction from which it came. When it grew louder, closer, she recognised the song-howl of the hunting dog. She frowned in surprise – the hunters didn't usually return so quickly. They must have been successful very early in their expedition.

Leaning towards the fire, Anna used a stick to remove the remaining potatoes so they'd be cool enough to eat when the hunters appeared. She looked across to where the forest path opened onto the clearing. Very soon, the men would come into view, proudly showing off their prey. If they had a large animal, it would be tied by its legs to a pole and carried between two people. Birds and other small prey were usually stuffed into leather rucksacks. Yesterday, one of the hunters had walked into camp with a dead monkey tied to his body by its arms and legs, giving the impression of a macabre game of piggyback.

While Anna was still waiting for the men to emerge, another unexpected sound captured her attention: it was the warning call that she remembered from the day she'd first arrived here, carried on the makeshift stretcher. One of the gardeners gave the echoed response. All around the camp, people began pulling on their cloths, concealing their faces and hands. Anna watched on, trying to decide if she should feel alarmed. Perhaps she should hide in the hut. She was struck by a longing to be able to talk to someone – to ask questions and receive an answer. Grasping the crutch, she managed to haul herself to her feet.

She'd hardly moved any distance from the fire when the first two hunters entered the clearing, draped in their veils. Anna checked for evidence of their success – but the rucksacks hidden under the shrouds looked flat and empty; there was no large carcass to be seen. And when the dog came into sight, there was no swagger to its walk. It kept looking back over its shoulder. The chief hunter had to urge the animal to keep moving. As it came closer, Anna saw that the white blaze on its chest was stained with blood as if the dog had been in a fight. She barely had time to absorb this detail when the bushes that screened the entrance to the path moved again. The patchy tones of leaves and plants consolidated into a pattern that was ominously familiar: the camouflage print of military clothing. Anna felt a stab of panic. But in the same moment, she saw that the soldier had fair hair and pale skin. Even in the midst of her shock she felt how powerfully this fact spoke to her. Her fear was swept away by a surge of relief. Where the Simbas had been terrifying, and the government soldiers daunting, she knew this man was her saviour. He was one of her own kind.

She saw two more soldiers coming behind him. The guns in their hands and the spiky outlines of ammunition belts didn't spark the acrid fear she'd come to know so well. The heavy boots, the wide belts, berets – they all spelled the same thing.

Safety.

As the soldiers moved further into the clearing, Bela ran up behind Anna, clutching her uninjured leg. The child whimpered with terror.

'Don't be frightened,' Anna said. She put her hand on Bela's head, smoothing the tight curls. 'They won't hurt you. They are —'

Her voice died in her throat. She saw a flash of red hair. A woman's face. She stared in disbelief. 'Eliza . . .'

A moment later she was wrapped in her friend's arms. Anna clung to the khaki-clad figure, closing her eyes. 'I thought something had happened to you up there – where you went . . .' She spoke into the softness of the woman's chest, her face still buried. Eliza responded by saying nothing, just hugging her more tightly.

After a little while Anna pulled away. She searched Eliza's face, taking in the grey shadows under her eyes. She looked exhausted. There was something haunted – sad – about her expression. Anna felt a shiver of dread. 'What's wrong? What's happened to the Carlings?'

'It's all right.' A faint smile came to Eliza's lips. 'They are safe. They've been rescued.' She looked down at Anna's bandaged leg. 'You're hurt!'

'I was wounded. But there's a healer here. She took care of me.' Anna stared over Eliza's shoulder as she talked. Four soldiers now stood in the clearing. They had muddy boots and the bottoms of their trousers were wet – they must have been wading through water. They held their guns behind them as if pretending they weren't armed. One had a black-and-white dog on a leash. It was pulling in the direction of the hunters' hound, showing its teeth. The song-howl had transformed into a throaty growl. No one was paying any attention to the dogs. The men just stood still, gazing at Anna as though they couldn't believe she was real.

Anna felt the same way about them – their presence here was a miracle. She turned back to Eliza, shaking her head in confusion. 'How did you find me?'

'We stopped because of the truck,' Eliza replied. 'I saw the suitcase. There was a Simba who told us about you . . .' Her words petered out. She seemed distracted – as she spoke she kept looking across to one of the soldiers. 'We heard the drum, so we followed the stream. The hunters found us and brought us here. But we were already looking for you. That's why we were on the road —'

Eliza broke off. She turned around, staring straight at the man who was the focus of her attention. A potent look passed between the two. The dark-haired soldier was standing a little apart from the others. His gun was slung over his shoulder and his arms hung free at his sides. His hands were spread open as if showing that he had nothing to hide. In spite of his strong stance, his broad shoulders, there was an air of vulnerability about him. His eyes met Anna's with a burning gaze.

Handing his gun to one of the other soldiers, he moved towards her. Bela's arms tightened around Anna's thigh. The man didn't watch where he was walking; he almost stumbled on an exposed tree root. His eyes were trained on Anna's face.

He stopped an arm's length away from her. Looking down, he murmured gently to Bela in a language she obviously understood. Her fingers loosened their grip, just a fraction.

Then he lifted his gaze again. 'Anna . . .' His tone was soft, questioning.

Anna's heartbeat quickened. Her lips parted as she caught her breath.

He spoke again. 'You were a little girl, the last time I saw you.' His voice cracked. 'Six years old.'

As his meaning sank in, Anna felt a shiver travel up her spine. This man had known her as a child.

'Who are you?' She already knew the answer to her question. She could feel it in her heart – in every cell of her body. But she wanted to hear him say the words.

'I'm your father.' He spoke with reverence, as if the phrase were sacred. He smiled. 'Dan.'

Anna looked at him in silence. She could feel the questions gathering inside her, lining up to take their turn. But for now, she just wanted to absorb the truth of this moment. Her father had come to find her. He was right here – standing in front of her . . .

Her eyes fastened onto the details of his face: the crinkled skin at the corners of his eyes; the deep tan; a scratch on his left cheek, still healing. She saw the sheen of sweat on his skin; the stubble shading his chin. She didn't recognise anything about his features. He could have been a complete stranger. Yet some deep part of herself – more connected with animal instinct than thought or even emotion – was drawn to him.

She took a step nearer, resting her weight on the crutch, dragging the injured leg after her. The end of the stick sank into a patch of moss, tipping her off balance. Dan reached out to steady her, closing the space between them. His hand on her skin was like an electric charge. As if driven by its power she let herself fall against him. In the same instant he was reaching for her. As he held her against his chest, she clung to him, feeling the power of his hardened muscles, the warmth of his flesh. She breathed the smell of canvas and gun oil, the marshy aroma of the stream, the tang of fresh sweat. She drank it all in – the proof that he was real. The moment was so like the ones she'd lived out in her daydreams, over so many years. She felt small again, like Bela. Her father was big and strong. He would protect her from every kind of danger.

He was here.

As Dan and Anna embraced, something changed in the air. There was a sense of release, like the coming of rain after the tension of a brewing storm. The leader of the hunters began to sing. He chanted out a line, and then his companions repeated it, following different harmonies. The chorus swelled as the other residents of the camp assembled. They moved their bodies in time with their voices, hips swaying and heads bobbing beneath the dark cloths.

Lifting her face, Anna saw Dan smile at what he could hear. The song of the hunter rang out, bold and clear – like the voice of the talking drum traversing the land.

'What is he saying?' she asked.

Dan translated as another round of chanting began. 'A father and a daughter have met here today. Their journeys took them far apart, but now they have been brought back home again.' Tears ran down his face as he talked but he didn't pause to wipe them away. 'Now we are celebrating. There will be a feast. We are all happy. Even the angry dogs will become friends. Because something good has happened.'

Anna felt a smile rising to her lips as she tasted the salt of her own tears.

It was so simple and so huge.

Something good had happened.

THIRTY-SIX

Pebbles crunched under Dan's boots as he strode along the shore of the lake. It was close to dusk and the light was dwindling. Already the racks of drying fish were just silhouettes against a blue-grey sky; the brightly painted hulls of the wooden fishing boats had faded to swathes of pastel. He stopped in the middle of the line of vessels. There were seven boats, side by side – their prows grounded on the stones, the sterns afloat.

Dan reached out to catch the end of a rope that was being thrown his way by a fisherman. There were shouted instructions for him to tie it onto a hand-carved rowlock. As he did so, he scanned the scene around him. There was movement everywhere – people hurrying back and forth. Dan's men were working with Africans from the nearby village, loading up the boats with a mismatched collection of cargo – alongside suitcases and military kitbags there were clay cooking pots, chickens in woven cages, baskets of all sizes, and bundles tied up with cloth.

Dan picked out Eliza's tall figure, standing in an area of bare earth between a row of mud huts and the beach. She was translating for Doc Malone, who was putting drops in an African child's eyes – tilting back her head, lifting her lids. At the same time Eliza was watching to see who else needed her assistance. She had her bag slung over her shoulder; the end of her silk scarf trailed out, looking incongruous with her dirty khaki clothing. She'd already paid the fishermen, in advance of the voyage – peeling notes from her wads of American dollars. But Dan knew she would be quick to reach into the bag and produce more money if required.

The fishermen were erecting the masts. Thompson was helping with the task – he was crouched inside one of the hulls, grasping the end of a pole. Dan saw a smile of sheer pleasure on his face. The yachtsman may have come to terms with spending time deep inland, surrounded by forest, but now he was back in his element. He had taken off his boots and rolled up his trousers. His eyes, reflecting the gleam of the water, seemed even bluer than before.

The masts were made from long slender tree trunks, the upright lines interrupted by bends and kinks. The stays that held them in place were not straight either; everything was handmade and individual. Some of the boats were very old. In spite of Thompson's enthusiasm, Dan surveyed the open craft with apprehension. Lake Tanganyika was wide and very deep. Storms blew up here that would have been impressive in the open sea. But the fishermen knew how to handle their vessels. They often went out as far as the middle of the lake to fish. If the weather turned bad, they thought nothing of proceeding to the far shore, if that was safer than returning home. Lifting his gaze, Dan stared across the water to the faint outline of land on the other side. It hovered there like a vision – at once daunting and enticing.

Turning back to the beach, he looked over to where the people from the forest camp were sitting on the stony shore. Their most precious possessions were still there, in their midst; they would take them on board themselves. There were two large baskets that contained the village drums, statues and masks. A third held the *nkisi* – in the dim light it was just a mass of dark spikes. There were a few moss-wrapped plants as well, hastily dug up from the gardens. The hunters prowled protectively around the group, spears in their hands. The veils, covering their faces and flowing down to their toes, flapped softly in the light breeze that blew in off the water.

The occupants of the mud huts were gathered on the beach as well. Those who were not helping with preparations watched on with keen interest – though they eyed the strangers warily; mothers kept calling curious children back to their sides. The Carlings stood with the village chief, an old man with a crooked back and grizzled grey hair. Harry was deep in conversation with him, gesticulating with both hands. Rose was next to him, her head tilted as she listened in. Little Sam hovered close to her, his eyes wide and solemn. He was clutching something draped around his neck. Peering closer, Dan realised it was a Siamese cat. A family pet, he guessed, that could not be left behind. He made a mental note to make sure Remi and the Carlings didn't end up in the same boat.

Adina, the *ayah*, was holding the Carlings' baby. She'd been rescued from the mission along with the Europeans. One of Harry and Rose's patients was here, too. The young man lay on a blanket not far from them; a drip line ran down into his arm. Harry had told Dan how all the patients had fled the hospital when the Simbas turned up and began ransacking the place, stealing drugs and other medical supplies. But this man, recovering from surgery, was unable to walk. The Carlings couldn't leave him behind. The couple was distressed at having to abandon all the Africans who depended on their hospital. They took some comfort, though, from the fact that the rebels had been afraid to enter the leper colony, so that part of the mission had not been disturbed. The supplies of Dapsone were kept in the hut that served as a clinic, right in the heart of the place. Harry's assistant would be able to continue with the treatments, at least until the tablets ran out.

The smell of kerosene floated on the air. The fishermen were lighting the lamps and setting them in place on the boats. Dan had initially thought it would be safer for the fleet to make the crossing purely by moonlight in case the boats loaded with people attracted attention. But the lamps would normally be lit – at least two per vessel – to attract the fish. And once it became dark, bright spots in the blackness would be all that was visible. The flotilla would look like an ordinary fishing fleet setting out for a night's work.

At the sound of footsteps behind him, Dan spun around, his hand moving automatically to his gun. It was Smith. The soldier stood briefly to attention, his rifle slung over his shoulder.

'Nearly ready, sir,' he said. 'They're just getting some more kerosene for the lamps. And the hunters' dog has gone missing.'

Dan almost smiled. There was always an extra problem that came up. 'Tell them to hurry up and find it. We can't wait for a dog.'

'No, of course not.' Smith sounded unconvinced.

'Make sure Bela goes with the Carlings. I want all the children together. And put Bailey in charge.'

As Smith walked off, Dan's gaze shifted to Anna, who was sitting on a cloth spread out under a small fig tree. It must have been the tenth time he'd checked on her in the last hour. He had to keep reassuring himself that she was really here. That she hadn't disappeared. Her sudden presence in his life seemed too amazing to be true . . .

Bela and Lily were kneeling beside her, building piles of pebbles. Lily sat very close to Anna. Seeing them together – a young woman and a little girl – brought a lump to Dan's throat. It reminded him of all the years that had passed while he and Anna were apart. All the time that had been lost and could never be regained.

Last night, while they were camped on the roadside near the burnt-out truck, waiting for dawn when the search for the source of the drumming could begin, Eliza had told Dan what she knew of Anna's story. But there was so much more that he wanted to find out about his daughter. So much that he had to tell her. Almost every moment since they'd met, Dan and Anna had been surrounded by people. When they'd finally found themselves alone – back in the forest camp, sitting at the fireside – he had been aware that the interlude of privacy would be short. Dan's group, along with Anna, would have to leave the place as soon as possible. He was worried that the jeep and truck they'd left behind could be stolen or damaged. It would be a disaster to end up stranded in this area. Then, there was McAdam and the others to consider: the group had to be reunited as soon as possible. Dan had seized his opportunity with Anna, going straight to what he needed to say most.

'I never wanted to leave you, Anna.' His voice had been halting, and husky with emotion. He was reaching into a part of himself that had been cut off for a long time. 'I believed it was the right thing to do – for you. I loved you more than anything. All these years I've tried to forget what I felt. But it never went away.'

In the quiet that followed he'd watched Anna absorb his words. When she smiled, her eyes swimming with tears, joy had stirred deep inside him, so potent that it hurt.

Now, as he watched her face, he felt another wash of emotion – warmth, backed by an edge of concern. The daylong journey out of the forest and across to the lake had been difficult for Anna. Henning had given her some strong painkillers before they set off. She'd been able to negotiate sections of the path, using the crutch. Dan had carried her over the roughest parts. He still held onto the memory of her resting against his back – the warm weight of her body, the tickle of her hair against his cheek. The physical closeness had been awkward at first, but eventually it felt as natural as if she were a little girl again, a bundle in his arms.

In the jeep they'd sat squashed together, with Eliza on the other side of Anna, pressed up against the passenger door. As he drove Dan had done his best to steer around bumps and potholes, trying to avoid jolting Anna's leg. But the condition of the road was bad, and he had to keep looking ahead for signs of danger, while keeping a check on the loaded truck coming behind. The three-hour journey had felt interminable. When they'd finally reached the fishing village and been reunited with the other party, Anna had almost collapsed on the beach from exhaustion. But now, after a rest, she was bright and alert again. Dan watched her gaze shifting from the children at her side to the various groups of onlookers, then to the soldiers and fishermen – taking in all the action around her. She looked tense, perhaps even a little overwhelmed; but at the same time, excitement lit her face.

This was her dream, unfolding before her eyes . . .

The way it had all come to pass still felt unreal to Dan. The plan had been born and set in motion almost in the same breath. It had begun back in the forest camp, with a radio message from McAdam. The crackling of the set had drawn Henning away from the fireside where he'd been giving Bailey a lecture about leprosy. Ever since the residents of the camp had removed their veils the English soldier had been keeping his distance. The man who'd never flinched in the firing line had been afraid to come near them. Henning was explaining everything he knew about the disease, tropical medicine having been part of the Legionnaire's exhaustive training. His words were being endorsed by Anna. Leaving Bailey to absorb all the information, Henning had hurried over to receive the transmission. Dan had followed him.

McAdam's voice came on air. The Corporal reported that his group had been unable to get through to Albertville. Large numbers of well-organised Simbas were on the move in southern Kivu – more than could possibly have retreated from the north.

'Someone's pouring in new money,' McAdam said.

Dan nodded. 'The Soviets, I'm guessing,' he responded.

'We were lucky to see the first of them before they saw us,' McAdam added. 'After that, we couldn't risk going on. Not with the children on board.'

He went on to say that he'd led his small convoy back out of danger, heading instead towards the lake. The party was now sheltering in a fishing village. The Carlings were friends with the chief there – not long ago, Harry had saved the life of his only son. The small settlement, on a headland jutting into the lake, had been largely bypassed by the war. It was a haven of safety. At least for now.

'Stay where you are,' Dan instructed McAdam. 'We'll join you there.'

'What are we going to do then, sir? I don't think we can risk going back out on the road.'

Dan was silent for a moment, staring into the forest, the radio receiver resting in his hand. He could feel the sun, hot on his back. While he was still thinking – weighing the options – words came to his lips.

'We have to get out of the Congo. Across the lake. To Tanzania.'

Through the static he sensed the Scotsman's surprise. It was mirrored in Henning's face as well.

'We'll hire some fishing boats,' Dan stated. 'We'll need two or three.'

'What time frame are we working on?' McAdam's manner was calm. As always he was quick to take on new information.

Dan hesitated. He didn't want to rush Anna too much. She had to say goodbye to these people who had saved her life, including the little girl who was obviously her friend. But if the Simba presence was increasing, it was only going to get more dangerous to move around – and more difficult to escape.

'We'll get to you as soon as we can,' he said finally. 'We will aim to sail tonight.'

Dan left Henning to take over the communication, collecting details about how to find the location of the village. When he returned to the fireside his mind was already racing. He looked blankly at the people gathered there. Bailey and Anna had been joined by Smith and Eliza; the latter pair had just finished their tour of the huts and gardens. Bela was playing with Remi close by, watched avidly by the hunters' dog, which was tied to a tree.

Dan relayed the information McAdam had given him. He shared his proposal to join the Carlings and the other soldiers at the lakeside village – and to escape across the water to Tanzania.

'It's safe there,' he said. 'Peaceful.' He looked at Anna. 'It's my home.'

Eliza was nodding her agreement. The other soldiers exchanged looks of surprise, but then mirrored her response. Dan waited for Anna's reaction.

She eyed him with a steady gaze. 'We have to take everyone.' She swung her hand to take in the whole camp.

Dan stared at her, stunned into silence.

'These people can't stay here,' Anna added. 'They need treatment. They have to be cured. But if the Carlings have left their hospital, other missionaries must be doing the same thing.' Her voice rose, driven by emotion. 'There won't be anywhere for them to go.'

Dan knew she was right. As news of civilian massacres filtered out to the world, more and more foreigners would be evacuated from the Congo. Convents, monasteries and mission stations would soon be empty of Europeans. And the doctors, nurses and teachers wouldn't be coming back any time in the near future. They would have to wait until it was safe again. And it was hard to see how that day would ever come. Foreign powers with vested interests simply wouldn't allow the Communists to win – they'd throw more weight behind the Congolese government; there would be more mercenaries brought in. Opposing powers would be equally determined to make sure the rebels succeeded. Even if the Simbas were finally defeated, another group would rise up. The people who dreamed of true freedom for the Congo would never relinquish their hopes.

Dan looked over at the crowd that was now gathered around the hunters, standing a short distance from the fireplace. He estimated there were around thirty people there. It was not impossible to imagine getting them all out of the forest – the able-bodied ones could help the others. Piling everyone onto the Dodge wasn't out of the question, either. There was a long tradition of overloading trucks in Africa; Dan had seen over sixty people board a vehicle of a similar size. It might be difficult finding enough boats to carry so many passengers. For the right payment, though, Dan thought it could be done. But crossing the water was only the beginning of the saga. Dan frowned, shaking his head.

'Where would we take them?'

He addressed the question to Anna even though he knew she could not have an answer. There was a tense quiet. Dan tried to imagine arriving in Tanzania with a cargo of thirty-odd Congolese.

Even if they landed well away from the port town of Kigoma, news would soon travel. Who could say how the government would react to refugees arriving by boat? Especially ones infected with leprosy. Glancing across to Eliza, he guessed she was thinking along the same lines.

'I know!' Anna said suddenly.

Dan turned to her. She was leaning forwards, her eyes burning with belief. 'Rose has a sister who lives on a leprosy mission. It's on an island, somewhere on the Tanzanian side of the lake.' Anna turned to Eliza. 'Have you heard of it?'

'Yes, I have,' Eliza confirmed. 'The Carlings have talked about visiting her for years. The island is almost directly across from where we stayed at the Hôtel Royal Kivu. The fishermen will know it, for sure.'

'We could settle them there, at least for a start,' Dan said.

'Then I could go and speak to people in the government. I have contacts,' Eliza said.

Dan nodded. He remembered the other conversation he'd had with Eliza last night, when all that she knew about Anna had already been shared. She had talked about Philippe, explaining that she'd first met him when they were both at university. Eliza had been secretly involved with the Independence movement in Africa ever since. Over the years she and Philippe had formed links with many of the key players. There was Lumumba, of course, here in the Congo; Mandela in South Africa; Kenyatta in Kenya – and the man who was now President of Tanzania, Julius Nyerere.

Watching Eliza now, Dan could see that she was already making plans. There was a glow of optimism on her face, banishing the despair that had held her in its grip. Her face was alive, her eyes bright.

Though no one had translated the conversation, the people of the camp were drawing close, picking up on the excitement. Eliza began explaining the proposal to them in Swahili, mixed in with bits of another language. She looked back towards Anna often, including her in the conversation even though she could not understand it. Words flew between Eliza and the Africans. Their faces showed confusion and doubt, then dawning amazement and relief.

'They want to come,' Eliza announced. 'They want to get cured. They want Bela to be safe.'

The response was so simple, but the implications so huge. Dan took a deep breath. One thing was for sure – he wasn't going to let Anna down. And he could see the plight of the people, the vulnerability of little Bela. He had to find a way to make the plan work. He told himself it was just another mission. You took it step by step. You relied on your men. He looked across to Henning, Bailey and Smith. He could see they were already inspired by the prospect of a new mission. Set against the scale of suffering in this country, rescuing thirty people was nothing. But if there was no answer to the big questions, no cure for the illness of war, then a small victory only mattered more.

Anna stared over the lake at the thin dark smudge on the horizon. It was strange to think that it was another country. Tanzania. When she'd first seen the name written down it made her think of the island that was just across Bass Strait from Melbourne. Tasmania. The pronunciation of the two names was different, though. And Australia was a whole world away from here. She could hardly believe that her old home even still existed.

She turned her eyes to the right, imagining where the island might be. She pictured the photograph on the wall of the Carlings' house. Whoever had taken it didn't have Eliza's expertise; you had to look closely at the washed-out print to see all the details. There was a collection of buildings set around a cove – the hospital, the church, a few houses and the little dwellings that made up the leper colony. There were two other American families living at the mission, according to Rose, as well as her sister. It would be a different life there, for Lily and Sam. There would be other children to play with, a school to attend. No bars on the windows. The village was surrounded by forest and farmland. You could even see the cows dotted over the grass. Rose had told Anna the mission was self-sufficient as far as food was concerned. And of course the lake supplied endless fresh water. And lots of fish. The place sounded almost idyllic. Anna could hardly wait to see it for herself.

Resting back on her hands, she stretched out her injured leg. It was throbbing again, after all the activity of the day. She was impatient for it to heal. Watching Eliza stride along the shore, relaying instructions from the soldiers to the Africans, she wished she could be more useful herself. She turned her gaze to Dan, who was standing by one of the boats, talking to a group of fishermen. There was a tense frown on his face as if he were feeling the weight of the responsibility he'd taken on. Anna felt a surge of pride when she saw how the other men looked to him for instructions. He was their leader. It was obvious how much they respected him. She sensed that they liked him as well.

What she saw in Dan didn't fit with what Marilyn had said about her first husband. But it matched with the facts Anna knew for herself: that he had come to find her. He'd risked his life to rescue her. When he'd told her that he had always loved her, she believed it was true. At the right time, they would go back over all that had happened, and make sense of the whole story. But for now, the focus was on the present. They had a big task on their hands – other people's destinies were at stake. The past could wait. Thinking about the future wasn't important now, either. It was like a land hidden beyond the horizon. When they reached it, they'd see the next part of the terrain – but not yet.

As Anna looked on, Dan left the fishermen and began walking towards her, a look of anticipation on his face. The breeze, stronger now, blew his hair back from his face. He called out as he approached.

'It's time to go.'

The sun had set; the lake was bathed in the afterglow. Watching the colours of water and sky change was like seeing a painting being formed. There were brush marks of pink overhead; the water was turning deep blue. The boats were just black shapes, their masts rising up against a purple sky.

It didn't take long for all the passengers to be lifted on board and settled into their places on the narrow wooden seats. When everyone was ready, the village men heaved the vessels off the pebbles, then the fishermen used long oars to push their way out into deeper water.

In the leading boat, Anna and Dan sat together, gazing forward over the prow. As the hull parted the water, small waves peeled away to each side. White foam danced on the surface. Behind them the fishermen were at work, hauling the sail up the mast. The canvas flapped for a few moments, then billowed into a smooth curve. Sewn from many small pieces, and patterned with mends and patches, it was like a map that told the story of a whole lifetime of voyages.

The boats moved away from the shore, masts tilting in the freshening breeze. Soon, the last of the daylight was gone. For a time, the flotilla was engulfed in darkness, broken only by the glow of the lamps. Then, as the forests of the Congo were left far behind, the moon appeared, peeping above the eastern horizon. It rose in the sky, round and full. A silver sheen spread over the water, lighting the path ahead.

POSTSCRIPT

Over the next months the civil war in the Congo continued to escalate. As the West gave added support to the Congolese government, Eastern powers increased their backing of the Simbas. The rebels gained ground, taking over key towns and cities, including Albertville. Their success did not inspire a return to the original values of the cause – the Simbas carried out terrible massacres of Europeans and Congolese alike. Foreign mercenaries helped stop the bloody rampage and push back the rebels. By the end of the year, only pockets of Simba resistance remained.

In early 1965 the Communist revolutionary hero Che Guevara arrived in Tanzania. With his Cuban troops he crossed the lake to the Congo to try and rejuvenate the rebellion. His efforts failed and he retreated in despair.

Later that year the Simbas were finally defeated. But as Dan had predicted, this did not bring an end to the conflict. More than fifty years later, there is still no peace in the Congo.

AUTHOR'S NOTE

Congo Dawn is a work of fiction inspired by real events. Operation Nightflower did not actually take place, but was partly modelled on missions that were carried out by mercenary commando units in the Congo during the 1960s. None of the soldiers are real people. Information was drawn from a range of sources including memoirs by ex-commandos, media reports, archival films and photographs.

Similarly, parts of the story dealing with the capture and massacre of civilians, many of them missionaries, reflect the kinds of events that took place during the Simba rebellion, but are imaginary.

The historical and political background to the story is based on research but seen through the eyes of fictional characters whose points of view are of their place and time.

Among the many books that provided valuable source material were: *Missing – Believed Killed* by Margaret Hayes; *Out of the Jaws of the Lion* by Homer E Dowdy; *Congo Mercenary* and *Congo Warriors* by Mike Hoare; *King Leopold's Ghost* by Adam Hochschild; and *The Congo from Leopold to Kabila* by Georges Nzongola-Ntalaja.

ACKNOWLEDGEMENTS

Congo Dawn is the first of my African novels to be set outside Tanzania, where I was born. The decision to enter new territory was made while I was on a visit to Lake Tanganyika in the company of my parents and my husband. We were at Jane Goodall's chimpanzee research station on the eastern shore of the lake. Standing on the pebbly beach, I saw the hills of the Congo faintly visible in the distance. My eyes kept returning there. Gradually it came to me that this was the place where my next literary journey would take me. It proved to be a daunting undertaking – a step into the unknown. But as always, there were many people standing behind me.

Roger Scholes read every chapter of the novel as it was written, and helped me deal with material that was new and complex. This is the twelfth book we've worked on together and I'm deeply grateful for his contribution to all of them.

My sister Hilary Smith also read *Congo Dawn* as it was being created, offering welcome encouragement. I was constantly in touch with my parents, Robin and Elizabeth Smith, asking questions on topics ranging from where spare fuel drums are stored in a Land Rover to Swahili translations, and a hundred other things. They, too, read the work along the way.

I also relied on responses to the story from other members of my family – Andrew and Vanessa Smith and Clare Maxwell-Stewart. As well as being some of my first readers, each of them drew on their own areas of expertise, including military history, East African literature, and medicine. Their input was invaluable.

I am grateful for the huge support given by my sons, Jonny and Linden Scholes, along with Freya Sonderegger and Emily Martin. Their company made a long journey feel shorter. Thank you also to the broader family, the 'curry girls', the Devon Walk crew, members of my book group and other good friends.

Very special thanks go to my wonderful publisher Ali Watts, who was a key part of the writing process, and to Lou Ryan, who was behind the book from the very beginning. Thank you to Saskia Adams for her insightful editing and also to Clementine Edwards and Amanda Martin. I greatly appreciate the support given by Julie Burland and Nikki Christer, and the amazing work of the whole team at Penguin Random House, including Deb McGowan in Tasmania. Thank you to Nikki Townsend for the beautiful cover.

As always, I am grateful to Fiona Inglis, Kate Cooper and others at Curtis Brown literary agency, and to all my overseas agents, publishers and translators. I would especially like to acknowledge my French publisher, Belfond, who has supported me over so many years. Thank you to Françoise Triffaux and Valérie Maréchal and also to my translators Françoise Rose and Laurence Videloup.

Finally, I want to thank all my readers, from nearby and far away, especially the ones who make the effort to contact me. The shared reflections on my stories become part of my writer's journey.

BOOK GROUP NOTES

1. What did you make of Anna's decision to head to the Congo, and then deeper into the jungle? Did she really have any choice?

2. At the lakeside hotel Eliza tells Anna that 'the journey itself will have meaning'. How is this proven true in the story?

3. When Dan joins the Commando unit he is told, 'It will be the most important thing you will do in your life.' Do you agree?

4. Anna comes to understand that some of her feelings stem from 'the part of a girl's heart that belongs to her father'. Discuss the significance of the father–daughter relationship in the novel.

5. Dan forgives Marilyn for leaving him. Can you?

6. When Dan saves the life of a Simba rebel, he briefly questions his own actions. Do you think it is possible to do the right thing and the wrong thing, both at the same time?

7. If violence breeds violence, can love do the same? In what ways is this idea played out in Congo Dawn?

8. There are many different battles in the book – people fight physical foes, but also fear, disease, ignorance, guilt, deception. Can you identify other forms of conflict in the novel?

9. The mercenary soldiers are all fictitious, but were partly inspired by real people who fought in the Congo. Can you understand someone making this choice?

10. The Congo jungle is experienced very differently by the various characters in the book. Describe the contrasting relationships with reference to the local people, the missionaries, the mercenary soldiers, the Simbas, Anna, Dan and Eliza.

11. Discuss the symbolism of the leopard.

12. By the end of the book, which characters have come to gain more than they lose?

Katherine Scholes
The
Rain Queen

'A big, sensuous, splendid novel'
OVERLAND

THE RAIN QUEEN

*Two women, bound by a shocking event, drawn to a vast
and beautiful country they cannot forget.*

Kate Carrington has cut all ties with Africa, the land of her birth. Her past
is buried alongside her missionary parents, the last reminders locked safely
away in the attic. But when a mysterious woman moves in next door,
Kate's carefully constructed world is torn apart.

Annah Mason has led an extraordinary life – one that has taken her
from a hospital in Langali to the company of rainmakers deep in the
Tanzanian bush. Her connection with the Waganga people has brought her
the great love of her life, and freedom beyond her dreams. Yet she carries
with her a painful secret. Now, the time has come for her to tell
her story – to finally set Kate free.

The international bestseller that has captured hearts the world over.

'This most moving book, whose every breath is a love-song for Africa and her
people, is a faultlessly woven cloth.' *Le Monde* (France)

'One to keep you reading late into the night.' *West Australian*